EBULON
Book One of
The Keepers of the Truths Series

A Novel by
E.F. Winters

2025 Kenspeckle Production LLC

Published in the United States by Kenspeckle Productions LLC
Distributed by IngramSpark and
Lightning Source as Print on Demand

Library of Congress Cataloging-in-Publications Data E.F.Winters &
Kenspeckle Productions
ISBN 978-1-940531-05-2

Printed in the United States of America

Book design by E.F.Winters & J.L.Winters
Art work by E.F. Winters
Cover design by E.F.Winters & J.L. Winters

Also by E.F. Winters:

MEMELOOSE: The Island of the Dead
First in category winner
Somerset Awards
Chanticleer Writing Competition

SHARKS AND MINNOWS
Book One of the
Jolie Chronicles

GHOSTS in the GRAVEYARD
Book Two of the
Jolie Chronicles

CATCH the DRAGON'S TAIL
Book Three of the
Jolie Chronicles

THE PEOPLE'S GIFT

SIGNEY'S BEAR

FOX IN the FOOTLIGHTS

EBULON

Book One

The Keepers of the Truths

A Novel by

E.F. Winters

Kenspeckle
Productions, LLC

CHAPTER ONE

"For each world saved, there is a cost. For each world lost, there is a reckoning." (The Matriarch's Journal; The Book of the Rhune.)

Like the fingers of a god's hand, bolts of flame striped the sky reaching toward the Brittlegrass Plains below.

At each strike point spheres of dense energy crackled and sparked reaching out like cold, blue, skeletal arms desperate to be released from their chemical prison. Pulled back and wrapped into the sphere's center, the pressure grew until no element could be what it had been, and the spheres exploded, freeing the altered elements in unnatural flame. Snaking through the dry grass, the hot, blue fires sought each other out, connecting into one wall stretching across the Brittlegrass, bearing down on the mud hut village of the Cumin Ra.

"No!" Gutte sat up, his breath stuttering in hissing gasps, the leathery hide beneath the scant fur on his chest expanding and contracting. The cave's darkness smelled of ash, herbs, and stale air. He heard his quick breaths, his racing heartbeat, a whimper developing in the convulsion of his gut.

Then he remembered. His gray, fur shoulders slumped, and his chin sagged to his chest.

He had made offerings to the gods. He had cast the bones of his ancestors, begging for help, but no answer had come.

Gutte rolled off the furs that had been his bed for the last four days and crawled across the stone floor toward the cave's mouth. Flesh and bone felt heavy after the days of ritual fasting. As he pushed past the hide-covered opening, crossing the invisible boundary that separated the worlds, light assailed his eyes. He collapsed onto the stone ledge.

Lying on his belly, Gutte blinked against the sun and looked out over the Brittlegrass Plains. The white sky stretched above like a taut drum skin.

It was only a dream, the Spirit Speaker tried to calm himself.

But what if it wasn't?

Seven days ago, the gods had shaken the Black Mountains that marked the Brittlegrass' western boundary as if they would flatten the world.

It was the wet season on Ra when everything should have been green. The small creeks that crisscrossed the Brittlegrass should have been feeding shady copses and ravine oases. But something was wrong. None of that had happened.

Instead, in the afternoons, when the sky thundered life promising rain, not a cloud appeared in the wide, white sky. Day after day, the hard, baked ground thirsted for water that did not come, and Ra's children suffered.

Gutte rolled onto his back and stared up at the color-drained sky.

"Mother Ra, have pity on us," he begged. "Tell me what I should do, not because I am worthy, but for the sake of your children, the Cumin."

The sky rumbled.

Was it a sign? Gutte wondered. *It must be.* Thunder without rain was unnatural, and how else was a Spirit Speaker to recognize an omen except by how it stood out against the normal pattern of life? But if there was a message here, Gutte could not interpret it. Boors had taught his reluctant apprentice the common rites and practices a Spirit Speaker needed to facilitate the cycles of Cumin life, but Gutte had never understood the higher mysteries. Might his dream have been a warning--something a true Spirit Speaker would have understood?

No, he thought harshly. A true Speaker would understand dreams of portent, but his own were foolish imaginings, born of his fears and inadequacies.

Gutte propped himself on his elbow and viewed the tranquil landscape below. The sea of Brittlegrass was a golden wash all the way to the Black Mountains. Twisted belts of sun-bleached ochre marked low spots where, in years past, creek beds had supported copses that sheltered travelers. But no Cumin journeyed across Ra's belly now. Every soul worked the fields with one eye on the sky, praying for rain. Angry gods or not, the land must be tended. It was more than a routine amid uncertainty for the Cumin of Ra: It was survival.

Gutte shaded his eyes against the sun, his gaze touching a brown female.

*Umma...*his lover's name was like the soft murmurings Cumin mothers chanted to their cubs as they nursed.

Spilling measured amounts of water from her gourd, Umma worked her way down the row, wetting the base of each fragile shoot emerging from the dirt. Stopping to arch her back against the weight of her pregnant belly, her eyes rose to the cliff ledge, lighting up when they met Gutte's. He could almost hear his secret lover whisper, "*Welcome back, my beloved.*" The warmth of Umma's affection drew the Spirit Speaker back into the world as neither hunger nor thirst had.

Umma Ra would be a fine mother with her broad back and soft fur, smelling of Brittlegrass and cook fires. She was strong, and tender, and had a wide flat nose--good for smelling danger. She would keep their cub safe.

Gutte felt a raw pang of regret that he would never be able to claim their offspring. A Spirit Speaker belonged equally to all clans and none. Jealousy or perceived favoritism could not be allowed to create a rift in the community. Another male would stand beside Umma and her cub before the elders: a brother, a friend. Another would weave his clan's colors with Umma's into the cub's first braids on its name day, declaring the cub's parentage. Even if everyone knew it was a lie.

Tossing her long brown clan braids over her shoulders, Umma lifted her empty water gourd and headed back to refill it at the spring, her milk-full breasts and grass skirt swaying in gentle rhythm with her hips. Gutte's worries melted away in the face of her simple abundance.

The piercing squeal of a ring-reed flute pulled his attention to the South. His nephew, Grub, clambered to the top of one of the clay mounds that freckled the plains at the base of the cliff sheltering the village's east side. With more fervor than artistry, he blew a shrill blast into his new name-day gift. Poised between cub and adult, Grub took himself very seriously, but it would be weeks before he could play anything resembling a tune on the instrument. Still, if the cub practiced, in time, the village would have a new wind singer to help with their ceremonies. The youngling leaped off the mound, followed by a quick flash of silver.

Bibi. Gutte felt a flood of affection for the pindling, albino outcast who shadowed his nephew so tenaciously.

"*These two are the Cumin's future,*" a flinty voice spoke in the Spirit Speaker's head.

CHAPTER ONE

A god. Gutte was all attention.

"Spirit?" He closed his eyes, trying to hold the tenuous connection. "Tell me your will. I will follow your wisdom." The image of a green, bald-faced being with a bird's, black eyes and long, white, unbraided hair formed in his mind. Strange symbols glowed faintly beneath the spirit image's green skin.

"My will is of no importance," the spirit declared.

"But it is. Of course, it is," Gutte protested. *"I am a Spirit Speaker. I listen for the wisdom of the gods."*

"There are no gods here, Spirit Speaker. Beware of those who claim that title. Their goal is to take your reason and replace it with their own, but there is malice and greed, and it is come to Ra. When a boulder falls, the grass below will be crushed," the apparition cautioned. *"Tell your friends to run."*

"What do you mean? Who are you?" Gutte asked. *"What is happening?"*

"I am Hagriva Rhune, a Keeper of the Truths. There is no time to say more. Tell the Cumin what I have said."

"No, please, you cannot go. The Elders will not leave the fields if I cannot explain," Gutte remained as the spirit's exited. He was not the only one in his village who lacked faith in his abilities. Gutte was not gifted. At the time of Boors' disappearance, he had not been fully trained. He had only become the village's Spirit Speaker because Boors had gone. *"Tell me why the sky talks but gives no rain? Tell me what we have done to make the gods angry and how to appease them to save my village."*

"Stop," The Rhune's voice thundered. *"If your village wishes to live, they must go now. Tell them to hide in the caves at the foot of the cliff,"* the being showed her impatience.

"They will not go," Gutte protested.

"Then they will die." The Rhune's image abruptly vanished.

Gutte opened his eyes.

No bird called.

No blade of grass whispered.

The insects stilled their wings, suspended in the unnatural stillness pressing down on Ra like a choking hand.

Dark clouds appeared in the stark, white sky roiling angrily toward the flat plain. From beyond the sky came a mammoth roar.

It is coming.

Gutte felt the hot edge of his dream leering at him on the far side of his next breath. He held the air in, desperate to stop the world's forward tumble, held it until his lungs burned, refusing to let go of the fragile thread holding the Cumin on the edge of annihilation.

Far out on the plain, the white-haired spirit stepped from the nothing. Planting one end of her staff on Ra's surface, the Rhune's black, bird's eyes scoured the land. Furless and shriveled like the last wrinkled grape on a winter vine, her hair and robes flapped in a wind for which she was both the source and center.

Her face turned toward Gutte, her fierce, black eyes shrinking the distance between them.

"Something has shifted in the many planes of the living. The Balance has been tilted and chaotic forces turn their attention to the small, peaceful worlds they once ignored, deeming them insignificant. I fear that Ra cannot survive their malicious attention."

Gutte wondered if she spoke to him or other beings, unseen. Her words made no sense. He only knew to do as he had been taught, begging for interference on the Cumin's behalf.

"Take my life for theirs," anguish bled from Gutte's soul.

"There is nothing you could give that they do not already plan on taking," the spirit said, sadly.

Gutte blinked in confusion. *"But all we have is theirs. We deny the gods nothing."*

"Did you not hear what I said to you? This human plague has nothing to do with gods," she scoffed in disgust. *"Those who attack you are beings of flesh and blood who have come for your world, and they will take it. We are too few to stop them.*

"I know what is in your heart, Gutte Ra, but let it go," the spirit told him kindly. *"No matter how much we wish it, one moment cannot become forever."*

Gutte leaped to his feet. "Run, Umma! Run!" he shrieked.

As one, the villagers' heads turned to look up at the ledge.

The white sky split, the thunderous crack reverberating across the Brittlegrass Plains as fingers of fire streaked across the white sky. The villagers' attention turned to the plain.

Bolts of fire speared the dry grass, flaming into huge balls that rolled over the ground, consuming everything as they traveled. The balls grew, colliding and combining, until they made one, long, snaking wall of fire that moved forward across the width of the plain.

"Run to the caves!" Gutte waved his arms frantically, trying to regain the attention of the Cumin below.

The Rhune stood in the firewall's path. Pushing the winds, she worked to change its direction.

It changed.

Then changed again, continuing its race toward the Cumin village.

Lit up like a star by the symbols streaming beneath her skin, her presence glowed amid the stinking, black smoke. Disappearing and reappearing a dozen times in different locations within a heartbeat, she placed herself between the wall of flame and the Cumin in the field, working to turn the flames away.

As Gutte watched, she stopped. Holding to one spot, she placed her hands on the ground.

Slowly rising back to stand, the Rhune spread her arms wide and slowly brought them in to her chest. Jumping high into the air, she landed hard against Ra's surface sending energy deep into Ra's core.

Cracks began to break the surface of the Brittlegrass blocking the firewall's progress and it faltered.

We are saved! Gutte rejoiced, believing the old one had achieved her goal.

Then, like a determined predator, the fire leaped the chasm, first in one place, then in many.

Cyclones of wind, dust, and torrents of water flew off the Rhune's staff, twirling toward the fire. And still, it came on.

The ancient spirit's glow faded amid the moil to a slowly pulsing glimmer.

She looked up at Gutte, her black eyes hollow with regret.

"I am sorry." She disappeared as the fire stampeded over where she had taken her stand.

Roaring like a wounded animal, black smoke and blue flame bore down on the Cumin who stood staring at its onslaught, stunned beyond action.

"Run!" someone cried, breaking the Cumin's silence into chaos.

Umma looked up to where Gutte stood on the cliff ledge and put her hand on her swollen belly.

"Run, Umma," Gutte whispered. "Run for us and our unborn cub."

Umma glanced over her shoulder at the galloping fire. When she turned back, Gutte knew she would not run. She had accepted her death and would meet it with grace, her eyes on her lover, her unborn cub cradled in her arms.

"We will *wait for you in the next world, Gutte Ra,*" she mouthed words that Gutte heard with his heart before the flames took her.

"No!" Gutte fell to his knees, his cry burning from the air as the villagers' bodies flamed to ash that blew away on the wind.

The heat pushed in front of the firewall rushed the cliff tossing Gutte like a twig against the hard, rock face.

He lay on the ledge, red flames licking over its edge, blistering the leathery soles of his feet. The stone beneath the Spirit Speaker grew hot, the fierce fire scorching all sweetness from the air.

He could hear the downy hairs in his ears sizzle as they curled and crumbled.

Even the movement of his breath across his arm felt as if it seared the fur from his hide.

A pernicious stench rose from Ra's wounded body as dark gases billowed from the gaping clefts gouged into it. Molten rock bubbled up from the gaps, exploding into the air.

The Spirit Speaker lay where he had been thrown, making no effort to save himself. In every way that mattered, he was already dead.

It is over now, he thought, gratefully, staring up at the sky now darkened like a bruise. Slowly he drifted into unconsciousness.

A furless figure stepped out of the smoke, its hide as colorless as sand, its drab eyes hard and unforgiving.

"*Not gods,*" the old Rhune had said. Not gods; something else. Another of the pale beings joined the first.

"*What have you done?*" Gutte accused them, silently. "*They were mothers and fathers, cubs and elders. You could have saved them. What kind of beings are you that you did not even try?*" He wanted to scream at their pale faces, but bile clogged his throat. He could not even cry for the dead; his body had no water left.

Furless hands lifted the Spirit Speaker. Placing him on a litter, they carried him to a silver egg the size of a large boulder. A third pale being stood in a hole cut into one side of the egg. He looked down at Gutte and grunted, disgustedly.

"Was the other shuttle able to save any others?" the first being asked.

"There was nothing worth saving." The pale being went back inside the silver egg.

The first being looked down at Gutte. *I am sorry. I could not save the others; only you two.*

These two are the Cumin's future, Hagriva Rhune had said.

Grub and Bibi. Gutte tried to raise his head, searching for his nephew and the little albino. Two of the pale-skinned beings passed by, carrying a stretcher with a single furry Cumin lying on it. Gutte strained to see who it was but fell back, dizzy, and spent.

"Lie quietly now. You are both safe," the pale man assured him.

No, not me. It must be Grub and Bibi. Gutte grabbed at the stranger. "Not me! I am not the one. I don't want to live!" he screamed. Then everything went black.

CHAPTER TWO

"**F**or those who must see to believe, how do you define the invisible?"
(Anonymous; The Book of the Rhune).

The glow of Ebulon's midnight moons shone through the slatted shutters, glimmering on the stone floor like iridescent fish in a dark pool. The room was a masterpiece of comfort the master's touch subtly played out in color and texture, blurring the line between nature and design.

A gnarled tree appeared to grow from the green stone floor. Carved from a single, prodigious burl, its branches formed a bed, four posts twisting and twining to support a canopy. A silken mist of sheer, glittering curtains concealed the bed's inner sanctuary.

A young woman moved in and out of the fragmented moonlight. The long sleeves of her robe fluttered as her bare feet marked an invisible circle on the floor. Arms outstretched, her fingers formed a gesture of warding and warning. With a sudden spin, she disappeared, then reappeared, moving in the opposite direction.

Something is wrong.

Eropa felt it in the planet's vibration, heard it on the breeze coming through the lattice, and smelled it exhaling from the leaves outside her window.

Focused by her practice, the Rhune shifted her awareness from Iredipa palace to the city below, seeing through inner sight what her physical eyes could not.

Neat rows of sandstone houses in the city fell away from terrace to rooftop, ending at the white sand shores of the Silver Sea.

Whatever this trespass is, it is not centered here.

She stopped circling. Expanding her awareness, she drew energy up through the soles of her feet, through the core of her body, releasing it as she released her breath out into the multiverse. With no more effort than another might slip off a robe, the Rhune left her body.

CHAPATER TWO

As much an element as the wind or the stars, Eropa touched each of Ebulon's five moons: Rampal, Teagra, Hylosch, Tunis, and Tye-aire. Two days before the Festival of Lights, mining facilities on the moons were deserted--shut down for the holidays. The first four moons had no new tales to tell but on the fifth...

Something is out of place here.

A solitary Taiban watchman stood on the far side of Tye-Aire. He stank of fear.

Eropa projected her spirit to the watchman's side and froze.

The vast, metal, belly plate of a monstrous spaceship blocked the stars above them, a navigational star chart etched on its underside.

It was not the Taiban system.

Resembling the head of a spear, the starship's lines fanned back to a body textured in geometric patterns, both inset and outcropping, low-profile doors large enough to accommodate smaller vessels, and turrets.

"How did the Taiban warlords build such a ship without the Free Men knowing?"

"Calm yourself," Eropa spoke directly into the Taiban's mind, but the man refused to take comfort.

"We've poked the hornet's nest one too many times, and now even here we will suffer for it, just like we did on the Taiban worlds. Everything we have tried to build for ourselves, they will destroy. There is no safe place left. There is no place left to hide. The Warlords will hunt everyone who has tried to rebel against them and crush us all."

"You are wrong!" The Taiban winced in pain at the force of the Rhune's disagreement. "I am the Pira Eropa Rhune, and I tell you that we have yet to begin to fight the Warlord's tyranny. As long as we hold to The Truths, fear will not drive Ebulon to collapse."

A small Taiban reconnaissance vessel flew out from behind the alien starship and fired on the behemoth.

The watchman gasped as the monstrous starship returned fire, obliterating the tiny ship.

The Pira and the Taiban stared at the empty space where the returning Taiban vessel had just been, stunned at the absolute finality of the sudden violence.

How could we have been found without even one of the Sisterhood giving warning? The young Pira felt as if she were sliding slowly, inexorably, down a steep decline toward a hole of infinite depth.

"Find your bed and remain there," rallying, she commanded the watchman. Wrapping strands of energy around the old Taiban's mind, she bound him to silence. "When you wake, you will remember only that you drank too much buvo." The man's face went blank, then he turned and dutifully shuffled off to his bed.

Eropa refocused, reaching out to her teacher. "Hagriva, I need you."

Her mentor did not answer.

Wherever Ebulon's Matriarch's spirit traveled this night, it was far from Ebulon.

Eropa tried her connection to another familiar path.

"Father, wake the Council of Elders immediately and call them together. Ebulon is hidden no longer. We have been discovered and may come under attack at any moment." She severed the link, blocking further contact. As Mahal and the Voice of the Ebulonian people on the Council of Elders, her father would have questions, but Eropa had no answers for him.

Eropa focused on the alien starship.

Who are you, and why have you come? She asked, not expecting a reply.

A piercing scream of intense anguish nearly split her mind in two, and she pulled herself back, compressing her energy to a small, shielded kernel.

Nothing more followed the first assault, the silence ripe with radiating waves of pain and angst.

The Rhune studied the vessel, unable to separate the feelings of despair from the ship itself. Who were these intruders, and why had they come?

Curiosity and intention moved her awareness closer.

Suddenly, she found herself skidding across the floor of her bedroom in the palace. Slamming into the far wall, she sat gasping for breath, struggling to re-orient herself to being forced back into her body.

CHAPATER TWO

"Grasp not for answers, but for the peace that brings acceptance, whatever those answers may prove to be," a woman's gentle contralto cautioned.

The quote was a familiar one, known to every school child since it was scrawled on the wall of a cave by an ancient Rhune in the First Age and despite their philosophic differences over the practices of high magic versus the smaller, natural magic of healing, the Truths united both orders, Keesch and Rhune alike.

Dakmira Keesch stepped forward. The holographic map concealing the corridor between Eropa's and her father's rooms healed behind her.

The Keesch healer was a handsome woman--past the prettiness of youth. Her sky-blue robe matched clear, honest eyes, the spring green trim picking up the pale green tone of her skin. Strands of silver glinted in the brown braid draped over her shoulder.

"Are you injured?" she asked, her concern as a healer taking precedence over other concerns.

"Only my pride," Eropa answered, chagrined.

"Good. The Council of Elder's Voices are gathering in the Library." Dakmira fetched Eropa an outer robe of heavier fabric. "When will Hagriva arrive?"

"I do not know." The younger woman walked to her desk. Taking out pen and paper, she began to write a message.

The Keesch woman frowned. "But she knows what is happening?"

"I find it best to generally assume that Hagriva knows everything," Eropa replied curtly.

"And what exactly do you mean by everything?" Dakmira asked.

"The intruder's force field repelled my spirit, Dakmira--my spirit!" Eropa blurted. "Consider the ramifications of that." The Keesch woman's habitually passive expression registered dismay. "The vessels' presence surprised one of the Taiban Free Man pod-pullers hauling back returnees from the Cluster," Eropa added. "The Taibans fired on the alien ship, and it fired back. There was nothing left. Not even debris."

Dakmira's breath caught. "Blessed Mother, the Matriarch's absence is ill-timed. There are dangerous undercurrents at court right now and Hagriva's seat at Council has been vacant far too often."

"There are always undercurrents at court," Eropa dismissed the consort's concerns. "The clan Voices squabble like spoiled children."

"There are those who would turn the Matriarch's absence to their advantage. This new development could strengthen their cause," Dakmira persisted. "Miratha Dum'Laiere…"

"An alien starship orbits our world, Dakmira-Keesch. I think we have more pressing concerns than Miratha Dum'Laiere's misguided ambitions."

Dakmira paled. "You are saying that the intruders are not from the Taiban Cluster?"

Eropa shook her head. "No. They are from much farther away."

"Hagriva must attend this council meeting, Eropa!" Dakmira's musky scent changed as fear enlivened the mix.

"And she will come," Eropa tried to reassure the Keesch woman. "When she is able. Our Matriarch is responsible for the beings on many worlds, not only ours," Eropa pointed out. She neatly folded the note she had written and went to the door. A page popped to attention outside. "Do you know the compound of the Taiban, Captain Bobalo in the District?" she asked the boy.

"Yes, Pira."

"Can you take this to him for me?"

"Yes, Pira."

She held the note back. "You are not afraid to go alone to Little Taiba after dark?"

The boy blinked several times before answering. "No, Pira." Eropa waited. "Well, maybe a little bit afraid," he admitted.

"Good. Courage does not require us to act without fear. It requires us to act despite it. I would not ask you to do this if it was not urgent, but I can easily summon another page for the task. It is not important who delivers the message, but it must be delivered. I do not want you to agree to go if you cannot finish the job. This message must get to Captain Bobalo within the hour, even if you have to scale the walls of his compound or shout him out of his bed."

"I will deliver it, Pira," the page told her. "I promise."

"Into Bobalo's own hands, you understand? No matter how much anyone tries to frighten you into giving it to them. Just keep repeating my name and Bobalo's."

The page nodded. "I am a very fast runner, Pira. Very fast."

CHAPATER TWO

"Good, and tricky, too, I hope?"

"A little tricky, I think." The boy's eyes crinkled in a smile.

"Then you will do well. Pirates like tricky boys."

"Pira?" the boy stopped her before she turned away.

"Yes?"

"Is Captain Bobalo really a pirate?"

Eropa smiled. "Some say so, but he is also a good friend. Now go." The page scurried off, slipping across the stone floor as he took the corner at a run.

"Be careful, Eropa," Dakmira called after the young Rhune as she moved out into the hallway. "Putting yourself at risk now will not change the past."

Eropa paused. "You speak with my father's voice."

The consort lifted her chin. "He is a good man and a good father."

But is he a good leader--a warrior if necessary? Eropa wondered silently. She pushed the thought away. A general without a trained army or advanced weapons taking on these intruders would find only suicide to reward his courage. The culture of war that once ruled Ebulon's clans had long been relegated to a footnote in history, leaving only the Mir temple brothers of Aum Lung Shilat.

"I am a Rhune, Dakmira;" Eropa replied. "I will do what the Truths require of me."

Dakmira's mouth tightened. "You are young and untried, and some lines are difficult to see until after they have been crossed."

Anger flashed in the Rhune's eyes. "I am not my mother," she said firmly.

"No, but when facing a certain threat, a person might be tempted to seek an uncertain solution. Experience would be required to know whether or not this was a good choice."

Eropa's jaw tightened. "You think me overconfident?"

"I think the magics you have been taught to rely on are dangerous," Dakmira answered.

"Spoken like a true Keesch." The Rhune's smile, though bearing a hint of apology, contained a Rhune's mockery of the more timid Keesch. "But this situation, however--it proves out--cannot be met with a poultice from your healer's bag, Dakmira. This is not a healer's mission or even a diplomatic one." Eropa's eyes glowed like the coals of a banked fire. "A Rhune adept's skills are primary among the resources that we have, and we must use them. I understand your concerns about my youth and inexperience, but I am the Pira, tutored in The Truths by those in the Inner Circle of the Mir Temples and by Hagriva Rhune herself. I have been trained for this, or something like it, for most of my life." The young Rhune's power was so intrinsic to her self-concept that she did not know herself apart from it.

Dakmira Keesch swallowed hard. "You have spoken to Master Pranseas?"

"The temple monks do not concern themselves with politics."

"This is different," Dakmira argued.

"No, it is not," Eropa insisted. "I cannot ask the temple Mirs to get involved when I do not even know what I should be asking for." The Pira took in a slow breath. "I appreciate your concern, Dakmira, but there is too much at stake for any of us not to try everything we can to protect our world. I believe that I can do this. It is my duty to try."

Eropa headed for the Council of Elders's Library. There were expectations, the weight of which she was just beginning to feel.

CHAPTER THREE

"Knowledge is more water than stone; it runs in a continuous flow and cannot be witnessed in its entirety by any single person." (The Truths as spoken by Theasylla; Third Matriarch, from the History of the Rhunes; compiled in the First Age).

A forest of stone columns stood like sentinels in the Mir's Library, their feet planted on the ivory marble floors, their heads supporting a dome in the shadowed expanse above. The light from dozens of floating orbs warmed the stone and polished wood surfaces, seemingly paused in a golden gloaming between day and night. But it was night, and Aless Mc'Larick knew it. She had seen Ebulon's late moons receding toward the horizon from her palanquin window.

Ebulon's Voices had gathered around the carved, ebony tables on the ground floor of the library--mezzanines of shelved books stacked story upon story above them.

The Mahal's summons had pulled many of the Voices from their beds, but Lady Aless Mc'Larick had not been among them. Sleep came hard to a widow within sight of her century mark.

We all knew this day would come.

The head of the Mc'Larick clan sat hunched in her hoverchair, squinting at the library's dome high overhead, its stained-glass glory now cloaked in darkness.

When the sun again hits the dome, what changes will have come to our world? she pondered.

The oldest section of the library had been built by early members of the Mir order, even its most recent additions predating Iredipa's status as the new seat of government. The library's scale and grandeur were a monument to Ebulon's warrior-scholar tradition, which had valued education as well as skill with sword and staff, but Aless' great-grandfather, Feross Mc'Larick, had been the last to earn his position as clan chief by the strength of his sword arm.

"Would that he was alive today." Aless made a sour face. "Ebulon could use a few men of courage right now."

"Did you say something, Lady?" Aless' page, Loury, asked sleepily.

CHAPTER THREE

"The mutterings of an old woman, Loury. Pay no attention. Your friends, Stanton and Clovis, are against the far wall." Aless indicated with her head where several other pages sat. "You should join them since you must be up at this late hour." The girl padded off, grateful to be released to the company of her peers.

Aless settled her shawl about her shoulders. Were her colleagues' fears the source of her chills?

Perhaps. Six hundred years of peace left Ebulon ill-prepared to resist an invasion. *Will the clans vote to resist? Will they reach out to the Brohars of the Mir temples, or will they simply cave to a future they see as inevitable?* Aless wondered.

"These Taiban pirates have betrayed us." Lord Lector's sleeves swept the air like flags waved by the dogmatic. Unlike most of his peers, Harscham Lector had arrived perfectly groomed, his robe unwrinkled, his silver-blond hair coiffed. "Ebulon could not possibly be discovered 'by accident'," he railed. "We are not on the way to, or from, anywhere. If Taiba's warlords have found us, where else should we look but to those who beat their sticks against the warlord's gates, then race back here with their tails between their legs to claim refuge?" Known for his elitist views, Lector exposed prejudices that smoldered beneath the surface of Ebulon's fragile acceptance of the Taiban Free Men and Women granted refugee status some twenty-five years ago when one of their vehicles crashed on one of Ebulon's moons.

"Lector is right," another Voice spoke up. "If not for the Free Men, the warlords would not have turned their attention our way."

"The Taiban's stake in Ebulon's remaining secret is as great as our own," Nikodamus Mir disagreed.

Lector grunted. "Everyone knows a pirate cannot keep a secret after a second drink. I say that we have been betrayed!"

Lady Aless had no special affection for the Taiban revolutionaries living as refugees on Ebulon but her early training as a Rhune had given her an egalitarian view of humanity and their responsibilities toward each other. Mostly, she just disliked Lector and his less-than-secret lover, Miratha Dum'Laiere, and all their grubby ambitions and opposed them on almost any pretense.

"And who would listen?" A young diplomat stood.

Frevin Mir, the pumped-up peacock and pet project of his uncle, Wallish Ner'anset: yet another clan acting on delusions of their own importance.

Murmurs rippled through the room at this newly pledged member having the audacity to voice his opinion on such an important issue--one he could not possibly understand, but no one spoke out officially. The young Mir was known to be a rising star, his appointment based on his long friendship with the Pira, Eropa Rhune.

Aless studied the young Mir, then grunted in disgust. Except for his blatant ambition, Frevin Mir was bland in every way.

I would have credited the Pira with having better taste in men and friends.

"Ebulon is a child's bedtime story on the Taiban worlds," the young Mir continued. "Any warlord who openly claimed to believe that our world actually exists would be a laughingstock." He added what he must have believed to be a "politic" smile to soften his words.

Too calculated, young Mir, Aless thought. *Too calculated by far.* Her attention drawn by movement on her right.

Eropa Rhune had entered, her arrival concealed by columns and shadow.

Nikodamus Mir's daughter had the fresh attraction of youth, her strong resemblance to the ancient woodlands race, the Spinney, unquestionable. Small-boned and short of stature, the young Pira's bright, auburn curls fell unbound to her waist.

Aless knew of no one outside of Eropa's father, Nikodamus Mir, and this Frevin who could claim to know the girl. As the only child of the notoriously flawed Dupira Rhune and Ebulon's gentle Mahal, the girl had spent most of her life at the old capital, Alden Baierd, the sole student of the aged Matriarch.

With Hagriva in the midnight years of a life unnaturally lengthened into a third century, Eropa undoubtedly knew more about Rhune esoteric practices than any other living being on the planet, except Hagriva herself, but she would never have experienced the life most girls had: trading secrets with a friend, imagining different possible futures, flirting, or experimenting with sex. Who would have dared?

Certainly not Frevin Mir. Aless snorted.

Her education--declared complete, Eropa returned to Iredipa, but she did not participate in court life. Quiet at council meetings, she kept to herself and did not socialize.

Quite like her mother.

Aless could understand the young Rhune's justification for this lack of interest in social collateral. One day soon, she would become Ebulon's

Matriarch, whereupon pseudo friends and ex-lovers could quickly become a liability. But as a senior Voice, Aless recognized the inherent hubris of the Pira's choice.

Even the most powerful woman on the planet could benefit from support.

Unlike the practiced deception of Iredipa's courtiers, rumor had it that the Pira's lithe grace was earned through years of training by Mir monks in the traditional martial practices of Ebulon's past. If the stories were true, this quiet girl was also a formidable opponent.

And this will be our new Matriarch, Aless mused.

Eropa turned and caught the older woman's eye.

"In my grandfather's day, someone would just have cut Lector's heart from his chest and been done with it," the older woman addressed the Pira privately mind-to-mind, shielding her thoughts from her colleagues in the room.

"Hagriva often expresses a similar sentiment." Aless thought she caught the hint of a smile at the corners of the young woman's lips.

"The matriarch is not fond of the new court fashion?" Aless asked.

"The matriarch is not fond of the new court," Eropa clarified bluntly.

Aless pressed her lips together. *"Then we have something in common."*

A page scurried to Nikodamus' side.

"Forgive me, Mahal, but there is a Taiban outside," the boy stammered, his eyes as round as buttons. "Captain Bobalo."

"A Taiban?" Lector scowled. "What is he doing here?"

Eropa stepped forward into the light from the glow globes. "He is here at my invitation." The Rhune's deep scarlet hair flowed like liquid flame down her back.

"An inspired entrance, Pira." Aless chuckled.

If she had not seen Eropa, Aless would have thought the Rhune had magically appeared among them. Judging by the faces of her colleagues, that was exactly what they thought. It did nothing to soothe their rattled nerves.

"Let Captain Bobalo in," the Rhune told the page.

"You cannot bring a traitor into our council!" Lector screeched, the pitch of his voice imitating that of a scolding fishwife.

Eropa fixed the Voice in a cold gaze.

"I am not. I am asking an ally to join us: I have not yet begun to search for traitors."

The Voices shrank into a chilled silence.

A burly man dressed in fire-bright colors entered the library. Strong, sculpted cheekbones and bushy, black eyebrows balanced a hawkish nose. His pants were barely visible between thigh-high red boots and a striped leather vest. The shirt beneath it was patterned in a different set of red and gold lines. He wore his thick, wiry, black hair in hundreds of tiny braids, each secured with gold thread knotted with a tiny, silver bell. A rope of the braids was twisted together at the nape of the Taiban's thick, muscled neck. The leader of the Free Men movement had the nut-brown, sun-kissed complexion common to Taibans with eyes the color of spicy mustard. A full, lower lip cut the mat of his thick, black beard. A powerful presence with the build to match, Bobalo stood out among the gray-robed clan Voices like a live ember among gray ashes.

"Traitor!" Lector pointed a shaky finger at the new arrival. "How dare you come here? We took you in. We gave you sanctuary, and this is how you repay us?"

Other Voices followed his lead, shouting their accusations and insults.

"Silence!" Nikodamus raised his hand, commanding order. "Let Captain Bobalo speak."

"This is not our doing." Bobalo's words came out in moist gusts, heaving each syllable past the dense thicket of his beard. "Ebulon is our home, too. Most of our children know no other."

A middle-aged woman, clad not in traditional robes but in the purple and orange of the Dum'Laiere clan rose.

Aless smirked. *"Give her an opportunity, and Miratha will jump in"* she commented wryly.

Miratha Dum'Laiere was the chosen representative of a powerful clan, one experiencing a resurgence of influence since she had become their Voice. Suing for decades to be officially recognized as Hagriva Rhune's descendant, Miratha had been slowly gathering support within the Council for years, and Aless suspected fomenting dissatisfaction with the current balance of power along the way.

"We have harbored your people for two decades, Captain Bobalo," the Dum'Laiere woman's voice was a tiger's purr, the death rattle, and claws hidden behind soft, glistening fur. "Surely, you do not claim--that in all that time--not one of you has had an unguarded moment, whispered an unfortunate secret during pillow talk, or bragged when their tongues were loose with drink?" The purr became a snarl. "Or perhaps they betrayed Ebulon just to save their own skins."

"The first blood spilled here was Taiban blood," Bobalo rounded on her. "The blood of Free Men!" That set off another eruption of dissension among the Voices.

"Enough," Eropa raised her voice above the noise. "Your fears and prejudices serve no purpose in this council." She stared the Voices down like naughty children, waiting for them to become quiet again before turning back to her guest. "I apologize for my colleagues, Captain Bobalo. Thank you for coming at this late hour, and please convey our condolences to the families of the men lost in the intruders' attack."

She had everyone's attention now.

The Taiban nodded. "Thank you, Pira, I will. The Free Men offer their support—whatever you need."

"We will need it," she assured him.

Aless noted the look of understanding that passed between the Pira and the Taiban revolutionary.

This is not the first time these two have met. Despite the enigma that the Pira represented to the court, this Taiban pirate *knew* her. Aless was intrigued. What mysterious events had drawn these two together in a society designed to keep them apart?

"Captain Bobalo," Aless addressed him. "What did you mean when you said that blood had been spilled?"

"One of our vessels was returning from a mission in the Taiban Cluster when it came upon the alien starship. The Free Men, probably believing the intruders were Taiban warlords who had discovered us, fired. The intruder's ship fired back. The Taiban ship was obliterated. None of our people survived," Bobalo finished.

Mila Juna, the Voice of a minor house, jumped to her feet. "If the Taibans fired on the intruders, we are already dead. These off-worlders will not know that the Taibans acted alone--without our authority. They will believe that we have attacked them."

"It is possible," Bobalo agreed reluctantly.

"If the intruders are not from Taiba, then who are they, Pira? Where do they come from?" Frevin Mir asked.

"They are not from the Taiban System," Eropa declared. She walked to the center of the room and began to draw glowing lines in the air with the tip of her finger, re-creating the star chart from the belly of the alien vessel. "The underside of the starship bears this chart. Judging by the position of the blue sun, I believe that this planet is the one we call Stabos." She pointed, then moved her finger. "This is their planet of origin."

Bobalo sucked in his breath. "Great Mother, what are they using for fuel?"

"A question I hope the Mirs will be able to answer once we are able to gain access to the ship," Eropa replied.

Miratha Dum'Laiere jumped to her feet. "Where is the Matriarch? Why is this child addressing the Elder's Council? She is not even an elected Voice."

"I am the Matriarch's Voice in her absence and therefore, the Voice of the Rhunes," Eropa countered calmly.

"Bravo!" Aless silently cheered. For anyone paying attention, Miratha Dum'Laiere's move to discredit the Pira was not unexpected; she had coveted Eropa's position since the child was thrust into it at five upon her mother's death. The ambitious woman had been content to ignore Eropa as long as the girl Pira remained a silent observer at council meetings, but to claim the Matriarch's authority made her an obstacle that had to be dealt with. Her belief that she should be Hagriva's heir--due to kinship with the Matriarch--was not taken seriously by anyone outside her circle, but with the council drowning in uncertainty, Hagriva's absence had created an opportunity she could not resist trying to exploit.

She had not considered the opposition of a woman as formidable as Aless Mc'Larick.

Aless increased the air pressure to her hover chair, raising herself above her colleagues' heads. "The Voice of the Rhunes is, and always has been, the Matriarch's," she declared in a clear voice. "Hagriva Rhune holds and defines that title. These facts are uncontested." The years had shrunk Aless' body and given her a halo of winter-white hair, but they had also given her seniority in the Council of Elders. "The Pira Eropa Rhune attends our Council at the request of the Matriarch, as her heir, chosen to receive The Gift on the Matriarch's passing. Council protocols state that in Hagriva's absence, the Pira Eropa will be recognized as the Matriarch's representative, holding all powers as if she spoke with the Matriarch's voice."

Miratha's mouth puckered as if she had sucked on a lemon.

Eropa gave an imperceptible nod to Aless, acknowledging her support. "The Taiban fighter's attack was unfortunate and the results tragic," Eropa declared. "But we cannot allow it to remain a boundary between us. We must reach out to the intruders from a position of strength. Every moment we delay encourages them to believe that this attack came from us and that we are merely waiting for them to strike because we cannot defend ourselves."

"If what you say is true, we cannot defend ourselves," Lector argued.

"Losing is just a word as long as you survive." Bobalo turned to Eropa. "My people will fight however we can."

"And who would you be fighting for us or yourselves?" Mila Juna demanded. "Why would Taibans fight for Ebulonians?"

"Certainly not because we've been treated equally," Bobalo shot back.

"We are all in this together, Mila," Nikodamus intervened, ever the peacemaker. "There is no benefit in divisions between 'us' and 'them'. And what about the Temple Mirs and the Trove Discoveries? Surely there must be something of use?"

Eropa frowned at him. "That is for another discussion." She turned away. "Because I do not plan to fight."

"If you suggest that we try and meditate them out of orbit, I am going to vomit," Miratha complained. "We cannot 'wish' these intruders away."

Eropa surprised them with her declaration. "If we are forced to fight this starship, Lady Miratha, we will lose."

Miratha frowned. "You discount your own people's courage? My grandmother, Hagriva Rhune, would not give up so easily."

"I do not discount Ebulon's courage, nor their resolve, nor even what may be hidden away in the Trove of Discoveries, but none of these things addresses our lack of preparedness now."

"Call in the Temple Mirs to back up the palace guard," Miratha argued.

Eropa's chin went up. "Tell me, Lady Dum'Laire, how did Mila Juna's nephews come to join the palace guard?" Eropa asked. Miratha and Mila Juna exchanged glances.

"He is from a good family, educated, and trained in the ancient skills of the Glister Sword."

"And your second cousin's son, who also joined a few months past. What were his qualifications?" Eropa demanded. "What are the criteria for any of our young recruits?"

"Growing out of your page uniform," Aless muttered under her breath. "And having connections at court."

"Fighting cannot be our first option," Eropa did not wait for Miratha to answer, her point made. "Fighting requires training and resources that we do not have because we have chosen not to support that path on our world. There are no more than a few hundred Mir monks left in the mountain temples. The palace guards' ranks are filled with boys with inadequate skill or experience."

"You have the free men and women you have given refuge to," Bobalo declared. "We are trained and experienced."

"In thievery and thuggery," Lector quipped.

Eropa shot him another look. "I appreciate your offer, Captain Bobalo, and we will most certainly need your help, but your numbers are small, and your technology insufficient for an open assault. We need to buy ourselves time to look into the Mirs' Trove. We need a plan that maximizes the strengths we have."

"Meaning what?" Miratha frowned.

"While it is true that we cannot match the alien intruders in technology or fighting power, we have other skills, skills they are unlikely to know about or recognize."

Lector threw up his hands. "Magic again; it is the Rhunes' answer to everything. That is how we got into this mess. You Rhunes told us that we should put aside our weapons, that we did not need them, and like fools, our ancestors believed you. *You* did this. You are responsible. You promised to protect us!" Agreement and dissent filled the chamber. There had not been a war in their lifetimes or the lifetimes of their ancestors back too many generations to remember. Peace was the cornerstone on which the Rhunes had taught them to build.

"The man has a point, Pira," Aless spoke privately. *"How can you expect to best a starship like this with spells and incantations?"*

"I do not need to," Eropa replied. *"I only need to best the men who control it."*

"By the Mother, where is Hagriva? This child will kill us all," Miratha complained.

Eropa ignored her. "Do not fall prey to the false belief that technology is a greater asset than the power of the human mind. 'Fear is its own defeat'," Eropa quoted a Rhune Truth. "These aliens will see our lack of technology and think of us as primitive. This will lead them to underestimate us and our abilities. In their overconfidence, they will think us easily impressed and even more easily conquered. We can use that to make them doubt their assumptions while listening in on their thoughts and gleaning knowledge about them that will help us avoid the snare of their supposed technological superiority." She turned to Bobalo. "Captain, do you have a vessel suitable for a diplomatic mission?"

Bobalo nodded. "I can get one."

"And what will stop the invaders from shooting this ship down like they did the last one?" Lector demanded.

"I will take care of that," Eropa declared.

"How?" her father asked, frowning. "What do you plan to do, Eropa?"

"Command my double."

"Absolutely not!" Nikodamus shot up from his chair. "I forbid it!"

Eropa turned to him. "In this, you are the Mahal, not my father, and *I* am the Matriarch's Voice, not your daughter," she reminded him. "You have no power to stop me from doing anything."

Nikodamus sank back into his chair. "Will someone please speak to my stubborn daughter and tell her she does not need to do this."

No one spoke.

"We must all do whatever we are able to, Father, and I can do this." Eropa raised her voice to be heard by everyone in the library. "There is another piece to my plan which involves all of you. It is important. The aliens must not know that we have telepathic abilities or about any of the Rhune's higher esoteric practices. They cannot find out that we can read minds, each other's, or especially theirs. We need them to be unaware that we are listening to their thoughts--that they are telling us things they probably do not want us to know and they would never tell us on their own. If we use this ability wisely, we can know their plans ahead of time. We will know their weakness as well. We will gain access to the information they hope to keep hiding from us. This advantage--if kept secret--is exploitable and may give us what we need to keep our world and our freedom.

"As we know nothing of them, so they know nothing of us," Eropa declared. "But *our* ignorance will not last, while theirs must."

"It won't work. Someone will slip up and tell them," someone among the tables argued.

"Or they will do it intentionally to gain favor for their house. We cannot possibly control every man, woman, and child," Lector pointed out.

"But, for a time, we can control who speaks with the aliens," Eropa declared.

"Yes, we can do that." Nikodamus nodded. "This will allow us to gain vital information from them, costing us nothing outside of discretion."

"But the truth will come out," Miratha protested. "And when it does: any trust built between us will be completely erased."

"There will undoubtedly come a point when we will have to explain more about ourselves and our culture to the invaders," Eropa conceded. "But by then, we will know so much more."

"It is worth the risk," Nikodamus giving his daughter his support. "And who knows how this will play out. They may never need to know. Let us see who these aliens are and how things unfold," Nikodamus suggested. "It is nearly dawn. I suggest you seek your beds, my friends, before our midnight gathering raises more questions, we are unprepared to answer. It will be a long day, I expect. The Pira and Captain Bobalo will contact the aliens, and I will see to the arrangements for a reception and feast to greet them. You should all prepare to be in attendance," he concluded the meeting.

The Voices of Ebulon spoke quietly to each other as they shuffled out. Aless Mc'Larick, however, lingered as Bobalo joined the Pira.

"This reception will not go down well in Little Taiba. You're going to feast the invaders who killed our boys?"

"You must make them understand that we are trying to stop the loss of many more lives," Eropa cautioned. "No one truly wins a war."

"Quoting Wei Tei?"

Eropa smiled. "Borrowed wisdom is still wisdom if you understand its principles."

Bobalo inclined his head in a gesture of respect. "Your shuttle will be waiting for you at the docks whenever you are ready, Pira."

"And the pilot?" Eropa inquired as he turned to leave. Bobalo paused. "It cannot be you, Tai," she said quietly. "We need you. *I* need you. If anything went wrong and you were killed, there would be no holding back the Free Men. We cannot fight them in an open battle, but you know how to fight an effective underground war if it comes to that."

"I can't ask one of my men to take on a mission because it's too risky for me, Eropa. You know that." Bobalo shook his head. "That's not my way."

"And yet I still ask. You said you would do anything. Begin by honoring this request. You cannot die, Tai Bobalo. We need you and your family alive."

CHAPTER THREE

"So, I should not send Quinn either?"

"Surely the Bobalo men are not the only good pilots in the resistance?"

"There are others," Bobalo conceded. He took his leave, following the last of the Voices out of the library as Nikodamus approached his daughter.

"Is there nothing I can say to dissuade you from this course, daughter?" he asked.

"Nothing," Eropa replied.

"Well, you are your mother's daughter." Nikodmaus kissed the top of her head. "Ah, here comes Frevin. Perhaps he can talk some sense into you."

"Frevin would not even try," Eropa bristled. "Because he trusts my judgment. Frevin has always supported me..."

"Yes...*supported* you, Eropa, but know it for what it is: loyalty, not love, and do not confuse the two. They are not the same thing." Nikodamus joined the stream exiting the library.

Frevin glided to her side, his frail figure hidden by the yards of material contained in a Voice's official robes. They were old friends, maybe more, but *"Eropa,"* Nikodamus' words were fresh in her ears-- *"Loyalty--not love."*

Frevin took her hands in his own, holding them so gently, it was as if he were afraid to touch her, and yet his hands were smooth and soft as a baby's, while her own had callouses from long hours of training with weapons.

"Will you escort the aliens to the reception?" Eropa withdrew her hands from Frevin's.

"I would be honored," he accepted quickly. "Anything you would ask of me, Pira. You must know by now that I am yours entirely to command."

Aless watched Eropa recognize and dismiss her friend's obvious burning ambition.

"I need whoever makes this first contact to be comfortable sharing with me, mentally," the young Rhune explained. "I need to be able to see and feel everything they do."

"Of course." Frevin agreed.

"I know what you think of him, Lady Aless, but who else--among our court--is going to let me do this?" Eropa asked Aless privately, noting

her attention on the conversation. Aless half expected the Rhune to shut down the link between them, but she did not.

"Who indeed?" Aless replied. Few would freely allow a Rhune such access to their minds. Most would be terrified. Whatever problems are created by decisions we made today would have to be dealt with tomorrow.

"Would your meditation group help as well?" Eropa asked. "It might be useful to have them escort the Double as far as the alien ship's force fields, just as a show of support. I do not expect problems, but the last time I met my Double, Hagriva was with me."

"Anything you need," Frevin agreed. "If it eases the task and your father's concerns. And the Mirs' Trove? I could approach them in your name as well if you wished?"

"No," Eropa said quickly—perhaps too quickly--as Frevin's mask of diplomacy flickered for a moment, revealing…what? Disappointment? Frustration? "That is not a task that can be delegated to someone else."

"Of course." Frevin nodded, his face--once again--composed and benign of any high emotion.

"Have your friends meet you at the Taiban landing fields."

"We are honored to have been asked," Frevin bowed gently.

"He wants more," Aless warned Eropa.

"It does not matter right now what any of us wants, as individuals, Lady Mc'Larick. There is no time for such personal considerations," Eropa declared. *"And if access to the Mirs' Trove is to be requested, that will be done by Hagriva or myself. The Temple Masters will never grant such access to anyone else."*

CHAPTER FOUR

"To cross The Void, you must lose, then find yourself." (Attributed to Faed Ballatyn; The History of the Rhunes; Compiled in the Second Age.)

It was nearly dawn as Eropa climbed the stone steps to the old barbican tower. The treads were smooth, sanded, and polished by generations of soft soles passing over them, but few entered the confines of the aged tower now. Built on a peninsula overlooking the warm, southern sea; the old keep had dominated the region when each clan-hold was the center of a fiefdom, each lord, a king. The rise of Rhune influence had ended the territorial wars that had divided Ebulon into a warring patchwork--and with the end of war and raiding--the need for the clans to live in fortresses had also ended. The archway that had once connected the original Mc'Larick clan keep to the barbican tower had fallen and become garden stones when Feross Mc'Larick was still in short pants.

The Rhune Sisterhood had brought new teachings and new ways to Ebulon. Clan disagreements were no longer left to escalate into petty battles. Tribal differences were now brought before the Council of Elders, the clans' Voices tasked with settling disagreements through negotiation and consensus. Situations that could not find peaceful resolutions came before the Mahal or the Matriarch.

When the decision was made to move the capital from the cold north to the more hospitable southlands, the Mc'Laricks found themselves in possession of large tracts of prime land, the sale of which had funded their wealth for generations. Sales were made to accommodate the ever-expanding footprint of Iredipa Palace and sales to other clans who wished to have a presence close to leadership in the capitol. As the surrounding city grew, there were sales to merchants, landlords, farmers, and laborers. The major guilds also felt the moving of the capitol required them to maintain some kind of presence.

CHAPTER FOUR

Of the original Mc'Larick fortress only the barbican keep remained, a seldom visited stone structure, enclosed by an abandoned courtyard, hemmed in by the newer, more elegant wings and add-ons to the palace.

Little had changed since Eropa's mother had claimed the barbican as her workspace. The young Rhune pushed aside the tapestry that served as a door and entered the room at the top of the stairs, navigating canyons of stacked books and book serpents made of book towers that had spilled across the floor.

Glass jars and stale herbs, powders, tinctures, and congealing oils gathered dust on the shelves carved into the stone walls. Healing and divination tools cluttered a knife-scarred wooden table.

Eropa lifted a broken chair that had fallen into the narrow pathway and placed it on a pile of other cast-off furniture gathering dust. She went to the window and drew back the shutters.

The scent of fresh bread, tea, and spiced eggs wafted up from the city.

A rooster crowed.

A door slammed.

A cart's wheels began to rumble across the paving stones of the early morning city streets. A tradesman's day had begun. Palace and city slowly awakened, unaware that their world had changed.

Eropa lingered, watching the sun edge over the Mir Mountains, bathing Iredipa's white walls in the pink and gold of a new day.

Did my mother ever stand here at this window and watch dawn rise over the city? The young Rhune wondered. *How could she have turned her back on Ebulon if she had ever truly seen its beauty?*

Nikodamus' public explanation that his wife's death had been a tragic accident had extended even to his daughter, but with a five-year-old's ear for truth, Eropa had not accepted it.

Dupira Rhune had been a distant, pre-occupied mother, committed to her work. The many risks she took in pursuit of that work had endangered her daily, ultimately costing her life.

If Ebulon had mattered to her—if I had mattered--she would not have been so reckless or pushed herself so hard. That was what Eropa told herself, in private moments when no one else might hear her thoughts.

"Some lines are difficult to see until after they have been crossed," Dakmira's words echoed Eropa's fears.

"She is her mother's daughter," Eropa had overheard others say or think it many times. The assumption that Eropa was destined to repeat her mother's mistakes rankled--as if a parent or ancestor's mistakes were somehow genetic and inheritable. As if other people knew her better than she knew herself.

They do not, Eropa proclaimed.

But there were similarities.

Dupira and her daughter were Rhunes, trained by the Matriarch, Hagriva. Both tended to keep to themselves, preferring to remain aloof and self-contained, rejecting joining the mainstream life at court.

Before her mother's death, Eropa had lived an inordinately free and unsupervised life for a child at court. Iredipa was not Alden Baird, an isolated ruin on the edge of a dangerous cliff. In the more elegant and civilized southern capital, there were hundreds of people moving about, day or night. Everyone had assumed that some arrangement had been made for someone else to watch the child when--in truth--no one was. Dupira was too distracted to notice this domestic detail, and Eropa was careful not to bring it to her mother's attention. Maintaining the pretense, young Eropa invented stories and tasks--for herself--that appeared logical to any adult who came across the five-year-old and took it upon themselves to question her. Most of these involved an excuse for going outside the palace walls and spending time in the woodlands beyond.

Distracted by her concerns over the welfare of the beings on the worlds that she visited, it simply did not occur to Dupira Rhune that when she went out of body, her small daughter slipped away from her play space in the tower room to go on her own adventures. Precocious to a fault, Eropa was careful not to draw attention to a situation that allowed her unique freedoms.

It was the evening of the third day after Dupira's cremation that Eropa was stopped by the sound of raised voices-arguing.

"I must leave tomorrow," a woman's, raspy contralto announced. "I will be taking Eropa with me."

Eropa tiptoed through the corridor connecting what had been her mother's rooms to her father's and peeked cautiously around the corner.

CHAPTER FOUR

Despite her diminutive size, the old woman who had been Dupira's teacher seemed to tower over Eropa's father, who sat in his chair by the fireplace with his head in his hands.

Nikodamus raised red-rimmed eyes to look at the Rhune. His face was stubbled by several days' growth of an unkempt beard. He had not sought a political position, but once he and Dupira were promised to one another, his quiet capability had gained the attention of the Ebulonian people, and he had been chosen as Mahal.

"Wait a few months--a year," Nikodamus pleaded.

"No. There is no time. It must be *now*, Niky. I cannot hold death off forever. I must begin to train her." The old woman's stance was inflexible.

Nikodamus shook his head. "She is too young."

"She is the only one with any hope of successfully accepting The Gift when I cross over," Hagriva insisted on the precedence of her agenda.

"There must be someone here at court who could tutor her for a year or two?"

Hagriva gave a dismissive flick of her hand. "I have been watching her. The child would outwit them before they had taught her letters."

"What about her grandmother, Adaya?" Nikodamus suggested.

Hagriva's mouth drew tight. "Adaya has made a vow. She will not leave the Hidling again."

"There must be someone!" the distraught father argued.

"There is not," the old Rhune insisted. "There is only me."

Eropa's tiny fists clenched at her side. Her father was a kind man, an important man, and the old woman was being mean.

"I am not lacking compassion for your situation, Nikodamus, nor *her* situation." Hagriva looked toward Eropa as if she knew the little girl was there. Eropa ducked back behind the wall and held her breath.

"I cannot cheat death forever," the old woman said. "I will try to live as long as the child needs me, and I am cognizant that there will not be enough time for everything she must learn, but there is no other option."

"Miratha Dum'Laiere..." Nikodamus began to suggest an alternative.

"No," Hagriva cut him off. "She has neither the temperament nor training. She would not be able to take in The Gift."

"And Eropa will?" Nikodamus asked.

Hagriva shrugged. "If we have time."

"And what if she is not ready when you cross over?" The Matriarch did not answer. There was a trembling in her father's voice when he spoke, "Do not name her, Mah Rhune," he pleaded. "Better not to have started if you cannot finish."

"And who would take The Gift then, Nikodamus?"

"One of your sisters will step up," the Mahal suggested.

The Rhune's facial muscles grew tight. "You know we cannot leave it at that."

"Because you are thinking like a Rhune. I am asking, as a father, for you to think like a being of compassion. Let my daughter learn the value of life before you show her how to dissect it into pieces."

Hagriva drew a long breath in and let it out slowly. "I know what people say about me, Nikodamus; I am too old, I am out of touch, my health is failing, and I have used questionable magics to prolong it because I cannot accept giving up my control of this world. And they are not wrong in this respect; three hundred years is a long time to live, even for a Rhune. But none of that changes the reality of what is required for Ebulon and the other worlds that Dupira and I have looked after to remain free. Eropa must be trained."

"Like you trained her mother?" Nikodamus lashed out.

The old Rhune sighed into a long silence. "You cannot blame me more for Dupira's fate than I blame myself, Nikodamus. I should have known. I should have seen that she was in trouble. It was my responsibility, but she was skilled at creating and maintaining her mask, and I missed the signs."

"I admit to some responsibility in this as well," Nikodamus said sadly. "I knew she pushed herself, but I had no idea how hard. No one knew. She hid it well."

Eropa peered out from behind the corridor's corner. The old woman was looking right at her. *"There is one who knew,"* she spoke silently, allowing Eropa to hear.

The little girl once again retreated. It was true: she had known how often her mother went out of body, but why would she tell anyone? For her, each such event meant freedom. How could she have known that Dupira was putting herself in danger? Yet now that she had been led to understand, she could not help but find fault within herself.

"Did I kill her out of selfishness? Is my mother dead because of my little games--because more than anything, I wished to go play in the forest?" child Eropa asked herself, feeling a wave of guilt wash over her.

"You are a child. You cannot blame yourself," the Matriarch said *kindly.* But tears continued to roll down Eropa's cheeks.

"I promise that I will do everything in my power to teach Eropa not to repeat her mother's mistakes," the old Rhune promised Nikodamus, emotionally causing her voice to break. "But your daughter will be without my counsel for more years than she will have it, and she will need all the strength and confidence I can give her to make her way forward once I am gone."

"How will you teach her to live when, having lived so long yourself, you have forgotten the joys and sorrows of common life? Nikodamus muttered. He looked up at the Rhune, barely taller than himself, as he sat and she stood. "Eropa's education cannot be only spells and incantations, Hagriva. To lead well, she must understand the motivations of others and know how to live with them."

"A highly over-rated skill in my opinion." The Rhune sniffed. "Leading others does not require cohabitation."

Nikodamus had found the opening he had sought. "Is it your intention then to raise my daughter entirely in seclusion without the company of others of her generation? There has not been a Rhune school in Alden Baierd for over a decade."

Hagriva threw up her hands. "I have no time for stroking clan egos through the coddling of the talentless daughters, and neither does Eropa," she protested.

"And yet, by not doing so, you leave her more vulnerable than ever," Nikodamus pointed out. "Eropa is not you, Mah-Rhune. Our people will not tremble when she speaks or look over their shoulders when they imagine they may have drawn her attention simply by some misdeed. The days of ruling by fear here have passed. Eropa will need the people's willing loyalty, or she will not keep it."

Hagriva scowled but agreed, "I can see if any of the clans have a daughter they might wish to have trained."

"Thank you." Nikodamus graciously inclined his head.

"Meanwhile, you must go back to work, Mahal. The pain of your life partner's passing will not vanish, but neither will any of this." She indicated the mess of papers on the desk. "A world looks to you to govern them. You must resume your responsibilities."

The next morning, Eropa left with Hagriva for Alden Baierd.

Eropa folded the barbican's shutters back into place, blocking out the rose-gold morning.

It had been fourteen years since Dupira Rhune had become trapped across The Void; fourteen years since Eropa's mother was forced to merge her spirit with Duvrome Dmoledon while her body burned so that it would not weaken her spirit.

Somewhere, across the Void, on another world, another plain of existence, my mother's spirit still lives. It was a strange and lonely truth but one that she had learned from. She would not repeat her mother's mistakes, leaving her people and those she loved unprotected to benefit strangers on some distant world. No. Whatever the arrival of these strangers meant for Ebulon's future, Eropa Rhune was in charge of her own destiny—her own decisions. If some trick of the universe had conspired to collide her world with that of these intruders, she would aid or confound it, but it would be her choice.

When the task before her was safely accomplished, she would ask her former teacher, Bruhar Pranseas, if he knew of anything stashed away in their Trove of Discoveries that might be useful against these intruders if the need arose. Eccentric minds filled their rosters of the Scientific Society of Mirs, many of them makers of gadgets of esoteric purpose. The creation of weaponry had been banned on Ebulon for centuries, but if such a thing had happened, Pransease would know about it. Perhaps a Mir or two had created something finally useful under the present circumstances. Two Mirs who might be able to help her came to mind: Mithra and Malbuis Mir, both elders, respected in their fields. Eropa would ask her father to approach them.

Reaching above the door lintel, Eropa removed a sheathed sword from the hooks suspending it. She ran her fingers across the symbols of protection stamped into the leather scabbard, then pulled the blade free of its sheath. Casting the scabbard aside--a second set of symbols etched into the blade was revealed. Eropa began circling, bending, and sweeping, changing the sword from hand to hand; a slice, a swing, a block, a break; she moved through the pattern of movements, the blade becoming brighter as her skin did, the glow spreading from her hand into the sword's blade.

Breathing hard, she stopped and raised her arms into the air, palms down, and sealed within her body the energy she had gathered from the universe.

And now to begin.

Lighting a candle, Eropa kindled a fire in the grate, casting incense into its flame. The blue smoke wound its way through the room.

Digging through the piles of books, Eropa pulled out a heavy, wax-spattered volume. Opening the flaking leather cover, she turned its pages with such care that the paper might have been dragonfly wings.

"Hmm. Agiar, agair... Ah, here it is." Seating herself cross-legged on the floor, the sword bridging her lap, Eropa reviewed the recipe.

"Does no one ever dust in here?" Dakmira Keesch grimaced as she drew the door tapestry aside, holding it gingerly between her thumb and forefinger.

Eropa shrugged. "The mice and I do not care."

"I have come to help." The consort brushed off her hands. "What can I do?" She glanced nervously at the sword on Eropa's lap.

Had the Keesch woman even been back to the old barbican tower since the night Hagriva had ordered her to remove Eropa from her unconscious mother's side?

"You did not bring Miratha?" Eropa teased the Keesch woman.

Dakmira snorted. "That one would not come within fifty yards of any real magic. And she calls herself a Rhune."

"And you are a Keesch, so tell me again, why you are here?"

"I may not be a Rhune adept, but I can follow a recipe." Dakmira defended her intentions.

"And you are an exceedingly good healer, but what will take place here is not a healing, Dakmira."

"I am not leaving." The Keesch woman took the book from the floor in front of Eropa and began gathering ingredients, muttering to herself.

"Meaning that my father asked you to help, and you cannot refuse him. Will you help with the incantation as well, or would that be pushing your ethical compromise too far?"

Dakmira examined the words written on the page beside the ingredients. "I can do that. I hear you will speak to the Mirs about the Trove?"

"If Hagriva does not," Eropa replied.

"What is going on, Eropa? How could this have come upon us without warning?"

Eropa shook her head. "I do not know."

"Do you know the Mirs have something that could save us?"

Eropa shook her head. "No. We cannot place our faith in some unexplored vault of technological wizardry."

"But someone should begin looking," Dakmira suggested. "In case there is something." Eropa nodded. "I will ask your father to send one of his Mir friends. Perhaps Malbuis." Eropa nodded again, her focus clearly elsewhere.

"When I indicate that I am ready, contact Frevin. He knows what to do."

"I hope by the Mother's Grace that Hagriva is paying attention," the Keesch woman muttered.

"Hagriva is always paying attention." Eropa loosened the fastenings on her robe and removed her under-tunic, baring the pale green peaks of her breasts and sculpted torso. "And I am not an apprentice anymore, Dakmira. I have done this before. I am…"

"I know who you are, and I know who your mother was," the consort snapped. "And she is not here. If you get into trouble over there, I cannot help you."

"You can," Eropa disagreed. "You can help simply by being here, Dakmira. If you agree, I can weave the sound of your heartbeat into the spell. It will be my anchor to this place, helping me find my way back."

"My heartbeat." Eropa nodded.

"Are you able to do that?"

CHAPTER FOUR

"Yes." Dakmira turned away and began to mix the agiar. When she was done, she warmed it over the candle flame, chanting softly, adding a bit of her energy to the mix. She poured the slurry into a cup and set it in front of Eropa.

'"Sit there." Eropa pointed out a spot opposite her. "And do not leave the circle no matter what happens."

Reducing her physical functions to a subsistence level, Eropa began to elevate her spirit from her body, adjusting her focus to enter another plane. Picking up the cup of agiar, she tossed back the bitter brew. Her head wrenched back, fingers spreading like talons as her body began to glow white-hot, flooding with magic. Bright, white, light worms moved beneath the surface of her skin, blazing so that she glowed, her face, arms, and chest tattooed with light moving in a changing array.

"Begin," Eropa commanded.

The Keesch woman began to read.

"Mah Rhune heblow ah. Seis Rhune Mae. A-eee home etwaya rah. I-ee hoove etwaya rah, umbaaa aaaah aaaa." She repeated the last word over and over again.

E.F. Winters

CHAPTER FIVE

"Wisdom is a deep well; learning a shallow puddle." (The Truths as Spoken by Wei Tai: First Matriarch, from the History of the Rhunes; compiled in the First Age.)

Eropa's spirit appeared on a wide, barren plain stretching the horizon in every direction. Heat waves shimmered above the cracked hardpan as hot as the sunless white-hot sky. Eropa clutched her Glister sword and began to walk forward as the wind coiled and uncoiled her robes and hair.

This is an illusion, she reminded herself. I have no body here, no robes, no hair. They disappeared, her naked spirit moving forward, the energy sword tucked point up behind her arm.

At the far horizon, a speck of sand was caught up by the wind. It joined with three more, then more again, until it was a maelstrom spinning toward her. Coming near, it stopped, split open, and the Double stepped out.

"A dramatic entrance," Eropa commented.

The Double had chosen a male form on this plain, like and unlike Eropa in appearance. His eyes were green but narrower with many specks of gold, his lips even more full and sensuous, teasing a smile of derision. Where the Rhune was lithe and pale green, the Double's body was bronze and hard, his double-lidded eyes reptilian, and he moved as if stalking prey.

"Where is your 'keeper' little one?" The wide mouth curled into a crooked sneer.

"Why would you and I need some 'other' when we are two pieces of the same whole?" Eropa countered. "Such interference would only confuse our perfect understanding."

"Why indeed? And yet you try to hide the tension you feel." The Double raised the bare ridge bone, which would have been an eyebrow if he had not been hairless. "It makes me question whether you are brave or foolish?"

CHAPTER FIVE

"You need only to look inside yourself to know the answer. I am the Pira Eropa Rhune, the spirit of a hundred births. All of them remembered--yours included. Though I give you the courtesy of asking, I already know you will help me."

"You come as a supplicant but claim to know the outcome before I agree? It is foolhardy to test your future so dangerously in these dark times."

The statement piqued Eropa's interest. "What do you know of this darkness?"

"That it is both foreign and familiar, its scent, like a perfume in reverse, founded in a base of truth but overwritten by the stench of corruption. Instead of starting with bitter reality and adding on complex scents that build truth and transport the senses, this unknown alchemist began with a fair foundation, then overlayed it with rot and putrefaction. The base still exists, but its nature has changed beyond recognition."

"Can you name this alchemist?" Eropa asked. "Do you know from what world they hail?"

The Double's two-lidded eyes glazed over, the inner lids dropping to hide the reptilian irises. "They keep to the shadows and are therefore hidden to the light, but not to the darkness." The golden eyes opened. "I can tell you no more."

Eropa nodded. "We could be powerful allies, you and I. I have come to offer a bargain; my assistance at your request sometime in the future, for yours today."

The Double's eyes narrowed to slits. "Presumptuous when I could turn on you and take you for your power anytime. It would be no challenge," he said lightly.

"We share many traits, you and I," Eropa replied. "So, I recognize this same overconfidence in myself. I have worked hard to subdue this fault. You think yourself powerful, but I am Hagriva Rhune's heir and have the support of the Sisterhood. Do you truly imagine I would be easy to overcome with such alliances? And what advantage would there be in such a move when I am already offering to help you of my own free will? Mine is the better bargain for us both."

The Double crossed his muscled arms. "I am listening."

Eropa watched his eyes as she set forth her problem and explained what she needed him to do. Though the task of passing through the alien starship's shields was impossible for her, as a creature from another dimension, it would be simple for him. The Double's yellow eyes studied her as she spoke, his bloated lips relaxing into a smile of less derision and some modicum of respect.

"You have promise, little Rhune, and since our energies are so closely linked, your proposal pleases me. I grant you this favor, committing you to come to my aid at a future time of my naming, but I warn you, the favor I ask may not be easily accomplished."

Eropa inclined her head. "I will answer your call, brother."

"Then let us begin."

Nausea rose inside Eropa's physical body as the Double's astral form slid into it, and she moved into his. He would replicate her appearance, then remove himself. Any more than that, and he would be as unable to pass through the starship's shields as she had been. Eropa would hold and protect the Double's body until he returned.

"Summon Frevin," Eropa commanded Dakmira.

"Commander, an unusual reading just appeared on the planet."

"Explain, Lieutenant." Tartulon Kinsman, First Officer of the Lamdra, looked over his fellow officer's shoulder.

"It's an energy mass."

"A weapon?"

"Unclear. We're searching for a match, but there's nothing similar in any records from The Thousand Worlds. None of our previous scans registered this." Lieutenant Boradice lowered his voice. "How is that possible? This world is supposed to have limited technology, Tartulon, but if that's true, how do you explain this reading?" He pointed to his monitor.

"It has a biological component," Commander Tartulon deduced. "Is it possible that it's a life form?"

Boradice shook his head. "I don't know, but it's rising through the atmosphere and headed directly for us." The Lieutenant's fingers ran over the panel, checking and double-checking what was on his screen.

"Light of Death." Tartulon touched the panel in front of him. "Captain Yare, you're needed on the bridge immediately."

"On my way," a voice came back, groggy with sleep.

Boradice heard his friend's feet hit the ground.

CHAPTER FIVE

Somewhere in a disconnected part of herself, Eropa knew she was not on the desert plain of the Double's world; she was not really in the barbican, though a part of her was. She was not on her way to the alien starship, yet fragments of her were in each of these places. On the Double's world, she waited, her eyes veiled against the blowing sand by her other self's double-lidded eyes. With only the slightest shift in focus, she was able to see the particles surrounding her as matter: tiny, dull lights dancing in intricate patterns. She looked down at the million particles making up the Double's body. Though the sand particles were lifeless and dull with barely any glow to them, those making up the Double's body were incandescent. The dull stuff pressed up against the living matter, drawn by its warmth and brilliance.

All matter is drawn by that which is awake. Every living particle seeks its like, driven by the need to share sympathy. When sympathy is found, there is a joining, and both are strengthened. Like draws like, but without sympathy, there can be no joining. Order is achieved when chaos stops to listen and becomes harmony.

On impulse, the young Rhune blurred the edges of the Double's body.

Like a floodgate had opened, the dull particles rushed the bright ones—not just those closest, but all of them, everywhere, focused on coming to that space.

But there were too many.

Alarmed, Eropa retracted the Double's body back into solid form. The inanimate matter hit the Double, knocking it to the ground. Confused, Eropa shifted her focus.

"Where am I? What is this place?" she asked, her words swallowed by a dark vacuum.

"It is nothing," a voiceless reply came. *"You are nothing."*

"I am not nothing," Eropa's mind reasoned. *"I have a body. I live."*

Far ahead, a brilliant slash of light appeared in the darkness.

"There are no bodies here. There is only The Nothing and us. Join us, and you will no longer be alone."

"Stay away from the Crack between the Worlds," Eropa remembered Hagriva saying. *"The creatures that cling to its edge pretend to offer comfort, but their promises are lies."*

But in the Void, there was nothing else to focus on, and in the spirit world, where you focus, there you go.

"Join us, and we will keep you safe. Join us, and you can live forever." The starved souls clung like sea creatures on the rocks of a tidal pool, their deep need to feed stretching them into unnatural shapes. *"Come to us. Join with us,"* they pleaded, their hungry mouths working as if nursing some invisible teat.

"No..." Eropa's spirit hurtled through space, searching for a doorway to some more familiar existence. There were so many, each with its unique lesson along a separate but hauntingly similar path.

The invader's starship shimmered behind a curtain of energy.

And then there is you," Eropa felt a great need drawing her toward the starship's force field.

"Leave! You cannot be here!" the Double pushed Eropa out as he neared the charged particles.

Thick black smoke filled Eropa's vision.

"Frevin!" Dakmira called out mentally. *"Something is wrong."*

"You are the Pira Eropa Rhune. You are the Pira Eropa Rhune. Remember! Remember who you are," Dakmira shouted. "You are the Pira Eropa Rhune!"

"I am the Pira Eropa Rhune." Eropa repeated as the Double's desert world settled in around her.

"The mass is approaching our shields." Lieutenant Boradice blanched as he turned to Commander Kinsman. "It's coming through."

Perspiration beaded Tartulon Kinsman's forehead and the bridge fell silent.

"It passed through our shields like they weren't even there," Boradice said in a breathy whisper.

The men and women of the Lamdra crew turned toward the First Officer in frightened silence as if he could save them.

He could not.

CHAPTER FIVE

The spell broke when the bridge doors opened, and Captain Zeph Yare stepped onto his bridge, hair disheveled, eyes still puffy from sleep.

"Catch me up," he commanded his officers.

"I think your 'peaceful planet' is attacking us," Tartulon replied, his face set in anger and determination. "I told you we should have attacked them when their fighter fired on us."

"They barely have weapons," Captain Yare countered, his frustration under control, if just barely. He had won the argument over attacking the newly discovered planet--based on the fact that attacking it and potentially endangering resources was an unnecessary risk. They could not stand against a starship like the Lamdra.

"These readings can only be generated by an energy weapon," Boradice added. Zeph inclined his head toward his friend, acknowledging he understood the safe course.

"Very well. Power up weapons. Target the area identified as their capital."

"Aye, Sir. Gaining target," the weapons officer reported.

"Ten, nine, eight, seven, six," Boradice's countdown was quiet but steady.

Stripped of the armor of their superior technology, the Lamdra's crew faced their mortality, birthnaked.

"Five, four, three, two...." They braced for impact.

"Target acquired," the weapons officer announced then--without an explosion or any impact--a bipedal humanoid materialized on the bridge.

"Captain?" the weapons officer hesitated. "Shall I fire?"

"No. Hold." Zeph held up a cautioning hand, searching the data on Boradice's screen. "Lucha, you ran a full systems check?" he asked.

"I did. It said that everything is functioning as it should be."

"And this projection is coming from the planet?" Zeph suggested.

"No." Boradice shook his head. "There's no connection to any power source on the planet."

"None that we recognize anyway," Zeph suggested.

"It's more like the image *is* the power source," Boradice explained. Yare studied the apparition.

"Maybe they're not so primitive after all," he mused.

Despite the pale-green color of its skin, the alien apparition appeared to be female with pleasingly round, if not overly large, mammary glands in what Zeph felt through personal prejudice were the right places. In fact, all the curves of its body were, to his mind, passingly attractive. The heart-shaped face was rather flat in profile, but its oversized, deep, green eyes grabbed him, holding his attention.

"What do you think, Lucha?" Zeph asked, speaking in a voice that kept the question between them.

Boradice grunted. "Data aside, it looks like a girl to me."

A roguish grin curved Zeph's lip. "My thoughts exactly. Maybe she's got a sister."

Yare and Boradice had been friends since they were children getting in trouble in the streets of the United Front's Dome, and they had shared many intimate explorations of species across the Thousand Worlds. Traveling off-planet, one either learned to cultivate an open mind about desirabilities, or one went without intimate companionship, and that did not fit the reputation Zeph Yare, incorrigible scion of the Yare family, had earned for himself. The provocative promise of exotic aliens with previously only fantasized variations and proportions, function, and orifice locations had seduced more than one brash young man out of the Dome.

"We have underestimated these being's defensive capacity, "Tartulon insisted. "We should fire on them before they show us any more surprises."

"He has a point, Zeph," Boradice acknowledged.

Yare nodded. "I know he does." But he gave no order. "What is she waiting for?"

"I think she's waiting for *you* to say something," Boradice prodded.

"Right." Zeph ran a hand through his mussed hair and straightened his uniform. "I'm Captain Zeph Yare of the United Front's starship, Lamdra. And you are?"

The figure's vocalization began as a garble of unrecognizable syllables quickly morphing into an accented Common spoken in monotone.

"I am the Pira Eropa Rhune of Ebulon."

"It's speaking an archaic form of Old Common." Tartulon frowned.

Boradice raised an eyebrow. "They speak Common?"

"The root language of Common is very old," Tartulon explained. "Said to have originated with the early race that seeded the Thousand Worlds."

CHAPTER FIVE

Boradice rolled his eyes. "That's superstitious bullshit. The Thousand Worlds were not started by some mysterious super-race."

Tartulon stiffened. "The oldest records..."

Zeph interrupted. "Can we save the history debate for later? Look, you're free to bring me another explanation if you have one, Lucha, but for now, we're going with Tartulon's premise of a common root language. If you have any more bits of ancient history that might explain anything else about these people, Tartulon, bring them to me."

"You have approached our world without identifying yourselves or contacting us," the figure spoke again. "You fired on a vessel approaching our planet. How do you answer these allegations?"

"They fired first," Zeph pointed out. "We fired back in self-defense."

"The Taiban vessel was no threat to you," the alien female declared.

"We didn't see being fired on as 'friendly'," Zeph countered.

"Those who took this action are not from this world," the woman admitted. Their ways are not our ways, but they are our guests, so we are responsible. We apologize for their rash actions. The Council of Elders has considered your response and—as a gesture of peace-- decided to grant you an audience. Lower your ship's shields, and we will send a transport to bring you and your officers to the planet to meet our leaders, after which, there will be a reception to honor your arrival. Do not fire your weapons again." The woman vanished.

"Well, that was interesting," Zeph muttered. He raised his voice so that everyone on the bridge could hear him. "Officers and First Security Team, meet me in Shuttle Bay One by next span; dress uniforms. Tartu, you have the bridge."

"It is done." The Double appeared beside Eropa, his arrogance gone. A new affinity linked them. What he had felt, she had felt. Her danger had become his. They had faced the challenge and survived. Each had learned something.

Eropa felt stretched and thin. She could see the dull particles of the Double's world as it pressed at the weakening barriers that separated her from them.

"You are taxed, little sister," the Double cautioned, gently slipping in beside her. "Return to your world now. The task is done." He gathered her in and sent her spirit back to its own plane.

"Thank you." Eropa shifted her focus, slipping back into her body.

There were presences aboard the alien's ship that I could not identify--strong presences, well hidden. I sensed deep sadness and great pain," he added. *"Be careful, little sister, these beings live far from the path of the Truths."*

Eropa collapsed onto the floor of the barbican.

CHAPTER SIX

"When you know you know nothing, you are ready to begin. When, after years of study, you recognize you still know nothing, you will move toward understanding. (Wei Tai; First Matriarch, from the History of the Rhunes; compiled in the First Age.)

Zeph Yare looked out the starship's porthole. The view appeared as black fabric sprinkled with stars.

Yare leaned his muscular frame against the cold metal wall and sealed himself into the small cubicle he called "his."

It was a ridiculous habit of language. Temporary use of space within the six hard surfaces of a spaceship did not encourage ownership by those condemned to inhabit it. The apartment was brutally efficient, providing a sliver of privacy for the rare moments he could catch some sleep; that was all. If there was anything that Zeph Yare cared about, it wasn't here.

He thought of the Lamdra as "his" as well, but always with qualifiers. It was "his" as long as he maintained his position as captain, "his" until he returned to Paxlosis and the mission's financiers reasserted their claim of ownership.

Zeph threw himself onto the slab that served as a bed, giving in to the exhaustion that plagued him.

His captaincy had come under scrutiny from the start, and he maintained no illusions about the security of his position. He knew that every Consortium advisor was a spy, reporting back to their masters, their purpose on the mission, to make certain their interests remained paramount in every decision Zeph Yare made. He recognized that some of his crew were given positions above their skills. Written into the addendums of their contracts were bonuses compensating them for undesignated services. These men's loyalty was to whatever faction in the Consortium had secured their place, not to him. Not to the mission.

CHAPTER SIX

Zeph knew that when the powdered and pomaded merchants had voiced concerns over whether he would make the right decisions, what they were asking was, would Tennant Yare's son put their financial gain first, undisturbed by inconvenient, ethical qualms and humanitarian misgivings that he might have inherited from his father?

Zeph's mother had taken her son's part in a rare instance of familial loyalty. "I have provided more than half of the funds for this venture. I can always find other investors."

Zeph had never been able to navigate Morladja Yare's politics by any moral compass, but she was reliably ruthless where her interests were concerned.

The outshot of it all was there were a hundred ways Zeph could fail this mission and a hundred enemies waiting for him to do so, not because they bore him ill but because his failure would create a fissure in Morladja Yare's empire.

If the mission were a success, these same Consortium partners would see substantial gains to their investments, but their profits would never balance out the dangers raised by the gain in power.

Zeph did not envy his mother's colleagues' decisions about whether it was worse to have her as an ally or an enemy.

Publicly, Morladja had supported Zeph's captaincy. Privately, she had used his desire to head the mission as leverage against him, threatening to pull her support any time she felt the need to reassert power over him. Studying his every word and action and having him spied on to ensure his memories of his father held no surprises of conscience for the mission. In the end, her desire for power won; the Lamdra's success would be her own, sealing the family's position among the Thousand Worlds for generations to come.

Zeph got his ship.

Now, he laughed at his crew's jokes, joined in their games, outdrank and out gamed them all, desperate to prove that he was the first and best among them. And he was sick of it.

A few weeks ago, grumbles had begun among the crew. They had gone to space to discover new worlds and found none. With their dreams of returning home as heroes fading, there was talk that--failure or not--the mission was over, and they should turn back for Paxlosis.

It had taken every bit of goodwill that Zeph had banked to keep the Lamdra moving forward.

Then finally, unexpectedly, they found this perfect gem of a planet. More arguments followed, with the Consortium's representative, Holder arguing heatedly in favor of immediately attacking and colonizing the planet. Zeph had held his ground and won at least a temporary stay. Now, everything he had dreamed of was once again within his grasp.

CHAPTER SEVEN

"In one dark hour, the greed of a few wiped out centuries of knowledge." (Anonymous Taiban Freedom Fighter.)

Corin ap-Bobalo flipped the glass ball she was juggling to her hip, rolled it over her back, then down the other side of her body before catching it in the crook of her leg, ending in a coquettish pose. The smile on her face said, "Can you do that?" It was a good trick. One that had taken time to perfect, but the few visitors passing her in the market did not glance her way.

"Why am I even trying?" the young woman muttered, dropping the pose and catching the ball before it hit the ground.

It was the day before the Festival of Lights and the Iredipa market should have been teeming with life, but aside from the palace pages and cooks' apprentices scurrying through the streets, intent on their errands, the market avenues were nearly deserted. Corin made no claim to any psychic abilities from her Ebulonian mother, but even she sensed that something out of the ordinary was going on in Iredipa.

She wrapped her glass ball in linen and placed it in its basket. Her cousin Heldis had come by on her way to the cheese vendors to tell Corin that a meeting of the Free Men had been called. She was needed at home as soon as she could get away.

"I'm not doing any good here." Corin swept up the empty coin basket, dropped it into the larger basket, and headed home to Little Taiba. A hundred things would need doing before the Taiban refugee families descended on the Bobalo compound.

In the wee hours of the morning, a page from the palace came beating on the Bobalo compound's door, insisting that Eropa had sent him with a message for Captain Bobalo. Her uncle left shortly after and had still not returned when the family sat down to breakfast.

"I do not know why the Pira summoned him, so stop asking." Aunt Timee shook her apron impatiently when asked for the tenth time.

CHAPTER SEVEN

Corin and her five cousins shared suspicious glances across the rough, wooden, trestle table but let it go. Secrets were a serious matter among the revolutionary, fighting Free Men, and though Corin's Aunt Timee had married into the culture, she kept its traditions.

Uncle Bobalo will tell us all what's happening tonight at the meeting, Corin told herself.

Striding purposefully along the tree-shaded avenue that led north through the older Ebulonian clan estates, the young, half-Taiban woman headed for the western end of the bridge that crossed the river Mi'cosa, separating the Taiban District from the Ebulonian section of the city edging the palace to the north.

As Corin crossed the Mi'cosa, the tightness eased from her chest. The smells of Taiban spices and the wood smoke from the many cook-fires hung above the district's eclectic, hodge-podge of rooftops and curled around the crooked chimney stacks. The hyper-alert state Corin maintained when she was in Ebulonian parts of the city faded and she relaxed. This was home.

Where upper-class Ebulonians aspired to live in environments where silence reigned, the cultural fashion equating it with peace, The District, commonly known as "Little Taiba" was a raucous celebration of life. Children raced through the narrow, crooked streets, shouting as they chased a rusty wheel. Neighbors gossiped and greeted each other from their windows. Mothers scolded children--alcohol-sodden Free Men--too old or injured to fight in the resistance sang songs from the old world at the top of their voices as they leaned on their comrades of old.

The sounds of freedom. Sounds no longer heard on their home worlds in the Taiban Cluster.

In the two decades since the massacre of scientists in the Taiban worlds, known as The Purge, the population of Little Taiba had steadily grown. With no room to build out, the refugees had built up, sometimes resorting to top-heavy buildings that leaned into their neighbors as if trying to catch the latest gossip. Older structures often seemed to lean into the strength of more recent ones, like grandparents steadying themselves on a youngster's arm.

There was no privilege here--no wealth. Life among the Taiban refugees was precious, and they accepted it as it came with gratitude and appreciation for every little smidgeon of pleasure that sprinkled through the misery.

The original families who were more stable and established than the more recent arrivals, did not build fancy houses or move out of The District. Profits from any endeavor were plowed back into the community to help families and businesses and most importantly, to continue to sponsor missions into the Taiban worlds in hopes of one day freeing them.

The Taiban market served a different clientele than the market in Iredipa. In Iredipa, one could find choice cheeses and delicacies, fantastic arts, crafts, and fibers. The Taiban community's needs were more basic.

The center square of the marketplace narrowed at one end leading to and from the gate before the Mi'cosa bridge. Keeping to the north side of the square's perimeter, Corin passed the community's more established stores, mostly early refugees: Crochin and Son's Cartographers, Farnhold's Dry Goods, Humqualt's Machinery, and Moving Parts. Such permanent shops, all with living quarters above or behind, defined the central square where temporary tents and wagons were set up by less affluent craftsmen and farmers on market days.

Free Men gearing up for a mission, the administrator of a moon outpost, and even a moon-bound household, could find what they needed here. Besides foodstuffs, sales of weapons, maps, and devices to conceal information were always popular.

Crochin and Son's was a particularly important hub for the Free Men's missions. Cartographers and their ability to pass on current information were essential. Drop locations, contacts, and safe houses were continually changing. Misinformation carried a heavy potential for capture or death. The Crochin family's reputation had been earned through decades of close ties to the resistance.

Corin slowed her stride as three young Freedom Fighters came out of the store just ahead of her. No one would have mistaken them for anything else. Their heads were all shaved, of course, but the giveaway was in the way they moved, their awareness of their surroundings, and the clear, unspoken bond between them. Corin envied their closeness eager for the day that she too could join the fight.

CHAPTER SEVEN

On her mother's death, she had been taken into the Bobalo household and raised alongside her cousins by her mother's sister, Timee.

"She has her father's quickness," Bobalo's friend, Block, observed watching young Corin cross sticks with her cousin Quinn.

"But hopefully not his impulsiveness."

"For certain. No, I think she's got more of her mother in her than that," Block mused. "The girl has a steadiness to her--someone you can count on."

Bobalo's eyes followed his two older daughters, Heldis and Pem, as they crossed the courtyard, baskets of laundry balanced on their slender hips. "Corin is Timee's only sister's only child. Don't fill her head with notions of joining the movement. Timee would flay me in my bed."

Block shook his head. "Corin is not Heldis or Pem, Tai. When she's old enough to choose, her choices may not be Timee's choices."

"Corin knows her aunt's thinking on the subject." Bobalo took out his pipe and began filling it. "And she's a good girl."

"Aye," Block agreed. "Gratitude and respect will keep her from going against Timee's wishes as long as she's a girl, but what happens when she's older? If Corin decides to follow her father into the resistance, early training, the kind that makes survival and defense a reflex, will be all that keeps her alive."

Soon after, Corin was included in the daily training sessions with Quinn and his friends. When the Pira Eropa joined them as well, becoming Corin's sparring partner, the issue of Corin's future was silently settled. When she was old enough to choose, no one would stand in her way.

"Welcome home," Corin greeted the three fighters.

"It is good to see you, Corin," Vale, the tallest of the three replied.

"I thought you were going to sleep forever." Corin raised on tiptoe to plant a kiss on her cousin's cheek. It was not uncommon for returning fighters to sleep for days when they first returned from a mission. Once they left the small line of moons known as The String and entered the warlord's territory a sound night's sleep in safety was a luxury rarely available. She examined Quinn Bobalo's face. It was leaner, his arms more muscular, his dark eyes sunken, the brown curls and smiling eyes that had made him the object of many crushes, gone. A heavy sadness had replaced the smile. Corin rubbed his bald head affectionately. "What did Auntie say about this?"

Quinn grimaced. "It will grow back."

"Ald, Vale, it's good to have you back." Corin checked the size and location of the bandages and scars on her two friends. Their physical wounds were already healing, any injuries inside concealed behind the stoic composure they were working to maintain.

"Don't we get kisses, too?" Ald teased.

"Of course." Corin planted quick kisses on her friend's cheeks. Vale's solemn, blue eyes caught and held hers as if she were a lifeline he dared not let go.

"Why don't we have lovely cousins to greet us when we come home?" Ald complained.

"Because you had ugly fathers." Quinn put his arm around Corin's shoulders and drew her away. "I'm on my way home. Will you walk with me, Cuz? I'll see you two later." Quinn nodded to his friends.

"Aren't you coming to the meeting?" Corin asked them.

"We have things to do for the captain first." Vale and Ald hurried away.

Corin grasped the hand her cousin dangled off her shoulder. "What was that about?"

"I couldn't say," Quinn replied brusquely.

Corin gave him a sidelong glance but didn't pry. Free Taibans had secrets.

"We won't be here long--a few days maybe. Then we're headed back." Quinn told her.

Corin detected a bitterness at odds with her cousin's open, generous nature. "It was bad on Taiba, huh?"

Quinn's face clouded. "You can't understand until you've been there." He gripped her hand tightly. "I understand now why Mother never wanted any of you girls to go."

CHAPTER SEVEN

"She doesn't want any of us to go. She's a healer and Ebulonian, but we can't just ignore what needs to be done," Corin protested. "The homeworlds need to be freed."

Quinn nodded without committing any more. "I know you planned on joining once you were old enough, Corin, but it's not like the stories. There are no heroes and no glory. Fighting and hiding and being hunted every moment of every day, seeing the death and disease and misery-- changes a person."

"Not you. Not Vale," Corin insisted, wanting to say something encouraging.

"No, not Vale." Quinn grinned. "Vale was the same pool of calm there as he'll be on your wedding day and the day he dies."

Corin punched her cousin's shoulder. "You shouldn't tease poor Vale."

"I'm not. Men who fight together learn a lot about what's in each other's hearts."

Corin laughed. "Well then, maybe you should marry him. What about you, Quinn? Did you dream of some special person from here while drifting in your pod out in space?"

Her cousin's lips became a thin line. "No. There's no one here in Little Taiba for me, Corin," he said quietly, his eyes gazing away to the west.

Toward the palace, Corin thought. "Are you joking?" she said. "There must be a dozen girls just waiting to swoon into your arms if you'd only give them any sign of encouragement."

Quinn looked down at the ground. "I won't though, because none of them are anyone I want."

Corin and Quinn dodged a group of children playing in the street as they entered the Bobalo compound, happy to escape the problems of politics in the small concerns of peaceful life.

CHAPTER EIGHT

"Too many words clutter the brain." (Common Taiban saying)

The residences of the original Taiban refugees on Ebulon were compounds, each fighter's lands abutting those of their closest comrades. Coming from worlds where security was a constant issue, walls were built high, and gates were made to withstand an assault. Having spent the early parts of their careers as pirates and smugglers, the secret passageways, bolt holes, and false walls they built into their previous dwellings were imported to the new compounds on their adopted world.

The Bobalo neighbors were the first families Tai Bobalo had brought to Ebulon to settle the Crochins and the Farnhams. The grounds of Bobalo's residence occupied a half-mile squared housing--a military depot that had supplied and run a two-decade revolution.

But time had relaxed fears of imminent attack, and by the time Bobalo's eldest children faced adolescence, vines had been allowed to grow over the compound's walls. Most of the landing area had been re-purposed as orchard and garden space. With the introduction of Menander's new business of hiring Taiban vessels, wealthy Ebulonians were embracing the convenience of moving goods and themselves at a swifter pace. A public, centrally located, landing field had been created north of The District.

"Hello, Block," Corin greeted a giant of a man puffing on his pipe while he monitored the entrance from atop a barrel just inside the gate. His tall boots were worn thin at heel and toe, and his hair, beard, and clothes were unkempt. The weapons hanging from straps at his waist and thigh were all that could be described as well cared for. "How's the crowd looking?"

Block shrugged, "It's early, but I expect it will be larger than usual considering the circumstances." He took another puff.

Corin's aunt complained that smoking and drinking were the revolutionaries' greatest vices; even women were forgotten when Free Men got to chewing over old times and new strategies for the Resistance. The Free Taiban's community meetings retained the habits created by the need to live clandestine lives. Taibans were cautious folk, suspicious

CHAPTER EIGHT

of outsiders, and stand-offish to newcomers. So, representatives from each neighborhood attended community meetings, and strangers were not allowed.

"Gonna be a long one." Block poked at a pebble in the sole of his boot with his pocketknife. "There's talk in the city about invaders, warlords, and missing fighters."

Corin felt her heart jump. "Is it just talk, do you think?"

"Who knows?" Block removed the stone from his boot and tossed it, then caught Quinn's eyes and held them, a silent message passing between them. Not the kind Ebulonians sent, but something they both understood. "Come tell me when they're done. I'll be here."

"Thanks, Block."

Quinn started toward the family kitchen.

"You could save me some of your aunt's k'wilbus if you think of it," the old pirate called out as Corin hurried to catch up with her cousin. "No one makes k'wilbus like Timee."

"I'll set some aside for you," Corin promised.

After the bright sunlight outside, the kitchen seemed dark and cool, its tall stone walls drawing the heat up, away from the living spaces, its long rectangular windows grabbing any stray breeze that made it to the lowland depression where Little Taiba had been built.

"I see you have found our wandering one." Timee Bobalo swept two large loaves of bread into the oven.

Tai Bobalo's position as the recognized leader of the community came with a price. Every guest, no matter the hour, must be offered food and drink, and gossip would talk if quality or quantity was shirked.

"What can I do?" Corin asked her aunt.

"Pemmy went to the barn to feed the animals half a day ago. If you could find her, I'd be grateful." Timee wiped her hands on her apron. "Then join us. The captain wants us all at the meeting tonight."

Heldis entered, returning from the Iredipa market, a large cheese round riding her hip. Her long dark hair, curly like her father's and brother's, was twirled into two large sausage curls, her wide-set eyes, slanted and blue like her mother's, but appearing very different against skin that, like most children of mixed heritage, showed only a hint of green.

"I'm sorry, Mother, but this was the best I could do," the Bobalo's eldest girl announced. "The palace kitchen boys were ferocious. You'd think they needed every round of cheese and every bushel of fruit on the planet today. Apparently, there's some kind of event at the palace tonight. I was lucky to get anything at all."

Timee took the cheese. "It will do. Go wash. You too, Pemmy," she commanded as her younger daughter entered from the barn. "And tidy your hair. It looks like a goodnu's tail.

"I won't," the younger girl announced. Slight of figure, like her Ebulonian mother, the Bobalo's second daughter had hair as white and fuzzy as a field-ripe grass stalk. "I'll shave my head like Quinn. It's bad enough we have to work ourselves to death so that these old farts can yaw and smoke until the air turns blue. I'm not putting on airs for a bunch of pirates."

"Pemitai Bobalo, we do not call Free Men such names in this house," Timee scolded.

"And not all of them are old." Heldis swayed her hips as she stole a finger dip of softened butter from a bowl on the table. Her mother lightly slapped her hand away.

"And, do not be shaming me with your flirting tonight, Heldis." Timee shook her finger. "Pem, I hope you, at least, remembered to feed the animals?" Timee glanced at the door that separated the kitchen from the main room where the Taibans were gathering. "More than just the men are coming tonight," she cautioned. "The whole community has been invited."

"Wonderful." Pemmy rolled her eyes. "My hemline will be the subject of gossip all next week." She reached down and turned her skirt where her hem was torn.

Timee sighed. "Well, some things cannot be helped. Your dirty face, however, is not one of them. Wash it."

"Did anyone say what this event at the palace was, Heldi?" Pemitai asked.

"No."

The Bobalo family's two younger sisters, Nanscha and Mawli entered from outside, and their mother scooted them back out to wash up.

"The captain will no doubt explain everything at the meeting," Timee stopped the idle talk.

Tai Bobalo appeared at the door. The warm bread was in baskets covered with cotton towels, the soup was simmering, there was water for tea, and a large pot of cafit bubbled on the stove. The younger girls returned, and their mother gave them the once-over.

CHAPTER EIGHT

"Alright, let's go." Timee took Quinn's arm and led the girls into the big room.

The meeting room was both the family's dining room and living area during the short winter season, but it was little used the rest of the year, serving as convenient storage for unfinished projects and useful items without a home. Daytime rain being a rarity in Iredipa, the family preferred to gather in the kitchen or the courtyard. Tonight, however, the main room had been de-cluttered and swept in preparation for welcoming their guests.

When Timee led the family in, the room was already crowded.

The intensity of emotion hit Corin like a gut punch. The original families were present along with neighborhood representatives from different areas in The District. Many had brought their families with them, all of them breathing out hot, fear-ridden air. Word had gotten around that this would be an important meeting, perhaps a historic one, the kind that would be revisited in stories for years to come.

Heldis walked past her mother, crossing the room to stand by Woald Turgista's youngest boy, Toval. Their "understanding" had not been announced, but the girl's action was as good as a public declaration. Timee's face tightened. The families were old friends, but her daughter's boldness had forestalled her right to weigh in on the boy's character and soundness as a future mate for her daughter, and Corin could see that it did not sit well with her aunt. She searched the room for Vale, wondering if she found him, could she be as bold as Heldis and walk over and stand beside him? Was that even what she wanted? They were close. They had always been special friends, but did she love him that way? Did he love her like that? She suspected he did. She suspected she did not.

Bobalo addressed the crowd. "For years, we have kept Ebulon's secret. Free men and women have fought, been tortured, and died keeping it. Last night, four more young men made that sacrifice."

Nieda Turgista began to sob quietly. Tears swam in her husband's eyes and down young Toval's trembling chin. Heldis whispered something to him, and he whispered back. When she turned forward again, she looked troubled.

"I have asked you here tonight to sort out what we know is true and what we know is not before speculation overrides reason. A starship is circling Ebulon; that is true." Everyone in the room seemed to hold their breath.

"So, the warlords are here. They've found us." Hamuel Farnhold said softly.

"No, Ham." Bobalo shook his head, jingling the tiny bells on the ends of his braids. "The starship is not Taiban. These intruders are from another world--a world that we know nothing about—that we did not know existed until now."

"What are their intentions?" Jayq Jacoby, another of Corin's uncle's old friends asked.

"We don't know yet, Jayq..."

"How can you say that?" Woald Turgista cut Bobalo off. "My boy and his team are dead. I'd say that makes their intentions pretty damn clear." The crowd's tense silence burst into angry calls for justice and violence.

"What Woald says is true, partially." Bobalo waved his arms until the room fell silent. "But there is more to it. The vessel that was returning, Petre Turgista and his friends came up on the intruder's ship quite by surprise. Our young fighters would not have known anything about its origin, and we can only guess what was in their minds when they opened fire on the intruder's ship. Unfortunately, but understandably, the intruder's returned fire."

"They were almost home. They thought they were safe," Nieda Turgista, wailed. "We had Petre's place set for dinner." She turned and wept into her husband's shoulder.

"I am so sorry, Nieda... Woald." Bobalo's glance lingered on the friends from his fighting days, the last remaining comrades of earlier times. They had fought and planned a revolution together. They had history, difficult history, full of plots, promises, ill-gotten gains, and all the complications that women and treasure bring men forced to make a living outside the law. This new generation of fighters; the sons and daughters of the old families, were just starting down the path that would lead to the understanding of the sacrifices demanded by their cause.

"So, what's the plan, Tai?" Loosey Humqualt asked. "We've got a lot of men on missions on Taiba right now, but I could pull a few dozen together from men here pretty quick."

Bobalo shook his head. "Petre and his team knew the risks when they took their oaths."

"Their oath was to the resistance. This has nothing to do with that," Woald Turgista argued. "They weren't even on Taiba!"

CHAPTER EIGHT

"Petre and his mates fired first, Woald," Bobalo made each word deliberate. "Do you understand that? Because of what they did, the option for peaceful negotiations with these intruders is probably off the table, throwing everyone on this world into a war we can't win."

"Who said our boys fired first?" A thin, angular-faced female fighter demanded.

Je'anna Peru. A Turgista by blood. Corin remembered that Woald's brother, Harlan, had vouched for her to be brought to Ebulon because of some trouble on the home world. Corin had admired her when she first arrived. Now she knew better. She looked hard and mean as if whatever the trouble had been, she had earned her status as an outlaw, not just because she was a rebel, but because she had zero space or tolerance for anyone's needs but her own.

"The Pira Eropa witnessed the attack," Tai Bobalo replied.

Je'anna rolled her eyes. "Oh well, if the Pira said it, it must be true."

"Eropa Rhune is our ally. We live as we do because of the Rhune's support," Bobalo reminded her.

"Next time I take a dump in the community outhouse I'll remember to thank her," Je'anna snarled back.

Chuckles around the room made it clear that she was not the only Taiban who felt less than generous toward Ebulon's rulers.

"It's not perfect here, Je'anna," Bobalo countered, "but it's a damn sight better than Taiba, or have you forgotten?"

"Me, Cap? I remember like it was yesterday--oh, it was. But I don't remember seeing you there since…gee, how many years has it been?"

"Leave it be, Je'anna," Harlan Turgista reined the young woman in. "We all know why Bobalo can't go back to the Cluster."

"Hell, for the price on his head, I'd be tempted to turn him in myself," Saldo Murtevoy, a longtime business partner--going back to Bobalo and his friend's smuggling days--joked sarcastically. Though he had held the title of captain once, no one called him that now. "What's the plan, Bobalo? How will we fight these aliens?"

A murky character, Murtevoy instilled as much mistrust as respect. Corin had heard different stories of how Murtevoy had lost his ship; most seemed to agree on one point: he lost it under questionable circumstances, losing his entire crew in the process. Only after that had he joined the resistance.

"For now, we won't. The Pira has asked us for our patience," Bobalo explained.

Corin could see that her uncle was not happy with the idea, but she knew that if he had told Eropa he would get the Taibans to hold off, that was what he would do.

"The Pira wants some time to gather information before we formulate a plan."

Murtevoy snorted. "Since when does a Rhune know anything about battle strategy?"

"I think that four dead boys beat out a fool's hopes," Woald Turgista grumbled. "Fighters understand one thing: a fight."

"I understand the need to do *something,* and fighting is what we know, but the intruder's ship has technology beyond anything we're familiar with," Bobalo continued his support for Eropa's plan. "And the Ebulonians still hold hope for a diplomatic solution."

"Of course they do," Murtevoy quipped.

"You saw this ship?" Loosey Humqualt asked.

"No," Bobalo admitted. "I rely on the Pira's account."

Je'anna Peru snickered. "Hump me raw, Bobalo. Did you adopt the bitch?"

Quinn stepped into the open space of the circle, a hand on his dagger. "You will show some respect, Je'anna, or do you need someone to teach you the meaning of the word?"

"Oh, the puppy has teeth. Come here, puppy. I'll teach you things your daddy won't." Je'anna licked her lips. "I'll make you a real man."

"Je'anna!" her sponsor barked. "Apologize to Captain Bobalo or leave. Free Men may disagree, but we do it respectfully."

"I don't know why you brought me here, Harlan. I hate this place!" The girl glared at Quinn and Bobalo before flouncing out.

Bobalo looked over at the Turgista family, their last remaining son clutching Heldis' hand.

"Twenty years ago we made a contract with the Ebulonians, promising not to bring our war to their world. It was the first condition of our asylum, and we have taken pains to honor it, but last night that promise was broken when *our* men fired on these stranger's ship. We don't yet know if the damage can be repaired, but all of us need to think long and hard on what losing refuge on Ebulon would mean for us and our families."

Mothers held their children close, wiping tears from their cheeks before their little ones could see them and ask questions they did not want to answer.

CHAPTER EIGHT

"We'll know more about the aliens and their disposition after the reception at the palace tonight," Bobalo assured them. "I will call another meeting as soon as I know anything." The main door opened and Corin turned to see Vale slip in. "Timee, let us feed our guests," Bobalo concluded the formal portion of the meeting.

Corin followed her aunt into the kitchen to transport food and drink to their guests. Suddenly, Vale was beside her.

"Don't say anything, Corin. Please, just let me get this out." He took her hand and drew her outside. "All the time I was on Taiba, you were there with me, in my heart, in my mind. When it seemed like everything to do with goodness was gone, it was your goodness I remembered and clung to. We have been friends a long time, and I would never pressure you for more affection than you bear me and risk that friendship, but I have to know how to act--how to feel, and I don't."

"You mean with me?" Corin frowned. "You've always—We've always..."

"No, we haven't. I haven't." Vale shook his head. "I want more, Corin. I want us to be more," the young man's voice cracked with emotion.

For a moment Corin was not sure what to do, then she looked into her friend's eyes. He needed something right now, something to reassure him and connect him back to life. She could give him that, and it wasn't a lie. She didn't know what she felt. She smiled as she wound her arm through his.

"Let's get out of here before someone finds something else for us to do. If there's no tomorrow--we should at least be happy tonight." She pulled him out of the light from the kitchen and into the orchard.

CHAPTER NINE

"Your nature is Truth. It is in your bones and in your blood. Spill blood in the service of The Truths and watch them spread." (Anonymous from The History of the Rhunes: The Hundred Year War.)

Dakmira Keesch pinned a green silk scarf using amethyst cabochons to either side of the pointed cap, draping it beneath Eropa's chin, and teased the ends into folds down her back.

"You should be in bed, not playing political chess." She stepped back to assess the effect of her efforts. Traditional Ebulonian dress was fashioned in long lines fluted at the hem like petals and piped in a deeper maroon than the body--designed to mimic the flowers and vines that Ebulon's forest-dwelling ancestors had used when they first began to decorate themselves. "It seems my day is to be filled with doing things I am not comfortable with." Dakmira picked up a carved stone box. "Your father thought you might wear these." She held the box out to Eropa.

Eropa opened the box slowly. A necklace and earrings lay within. *Mother's wedding gift from Hagriva.*

"Father kept them here in Iredipa all this time? I thought Hagriva had taken them back to Alden Baierd and they were locked away in some dusty chest."

Dakmira sniffed. "That would have been sensible."

Eropa tilted the box to catch the late afternoon sun coming in the window. The stones greedily grasped at the beams as if being shut up in the box had starved them for light.

Dakmira sighed as she took the box from Eropa. Removing the earrings, she gently moved aside the draped silk and attached them to Eropa's ears. The young woman touched the dangling gems gingerly, making them swing.

"It is a shame they cut the original stone up into all these small pieces."

"The shame is that they did not grind the damn things into dust and scatter them to the wind," Dakmira disagreed firmly.

CHAPTER NINE

The stones set in the necklace and earrings were cuts from a larger power stone that had been gifted, by a tribal chieftain to his Rhune mistress centuries before. A volatile woman, the sorceress had been wearing the stone when she and her lover argued. She cursed the man; he burst into flames and died.

Subsequently, the stone had been cut into smaller fragments to lessen its feral power. The locations of the other pieces were lost to history.

Eropa fingered the gemstones. "Do they really not know where any of the others are, Dakmira?"

"No, and good riddance, I say." Dakmira took the necklace from the box and clasped it around Eropa's neck.

Eropa's breath caught as she looked into the mirror. The reflected face was her own and yet not her own. The costume Dakmira had chosen for the young Rhune gave her the appearance of being much older, accentuating a cool arrogance.

It is as if my mother looks out at me. Even the shadowed circles below Eropa's eyes were familiar.

"You are not her, Eropa," Dakmira gently admonished her charge. "You will not make her mistakes. You have told me that over and over."

Eropa nodded. "And yet the pressures I face now are much the same as those she faced trying to save those other worlds. How many times had she traveled out of body in the days before she was lost across the Void?"

Dakmira shook her head. "No one knows."

"Because she hid what she was doing, shutting herself away in the barbican day and night. Ignoring the needs of her body." Eropa remembered sitting outside the door at the head of the steps that led to the old tower, waiting for her mother to return.

Dakmira let her arms drop to her sides, stopping her efforts. "Eropa, you do not need to attend this reception. What you have done is enough. Let me send word that you are ill."

"No." Eropa lifted her chin stubbornly. "We need to know more. I must flesh out our foes, analyze their character, listen to their thoughts, and learn how they think. The hard part is behind me, Dakmira. I must only be present and observe, and this, I can do."

"Then you must go now. The aliens are nearly at the door to the reception hall." Dakmira went to the door and opened it, directing the pages waiting outside with a palanquin. "Take the Pira to the small door at the upper end of the grand gallery behind the Mahal's dais. And hurry. You have only a few minutes. She must be in place before the aliens enter."

"Stall the aliens, Frevin. Eropa is on her way," Dakmira spoke directly into the Mir's mind as the palanquin disappeared down the corridor.

The elegant arcade design of the Glass Hall rose to join the curved ceiling coming to a peak sixty feet above the polished, green stone floor. The banners of the major clans hung from angled spears attached to the half-walls of the gallery. Below, the namesake richly colored crystalline glass windows alternated with elaborate tapestries along the walls between each sea green arch. The late afternoon sun shone through, spilling color across courtiers' elaborate costumes, glinting in the spun-metal threads and gemstones as they floated in and out of the life-sized scenes in the tapestries.

Standing in a half-moon formation around the Mahal's high-backed chair, the Council Voices' faces were as somber as their gray robes.

Eropa entered through the small door behind them, taking her place beside her father as the mammoth stone doors at the far end swung open.

The court hushed.

The aliens stood in a vee, their sandy-haired captain at their head. His crew--in gray dress uniforms with plum striping--fanned out behind him. Physical beings. Fighters.

The alien captain led them forward, moving as a unit; the sharp click of their hard-soled shoes filled the chamber like a brutal invasion.

The alien captain's face was confident; his gray eyes fixed unwaveringly on Nikodamus Mir in his chair on the dais.

Frevin's robes flapped about his legs, fouling his steps as he tried to keep pace.

CHAPTER NINE

"Mahal Nikodamus Mir, may I present Captain Zeph Yare of the United Front starship, Lamdra," he glanced angrily at the alien as he tried to catch his breath.

"Thank you for receiving us, Mahal." Captain Yare inclined his head toward Nikodamus.

"We meet under unusual circumstances, Captain Yare," Nikodamus began. "Please be assured that the ship that fired on your vessel was piloted by young men inexperienced and shaken by your appearance here. They believed you to be one of our neighbors, the Taiban warlords, and acted rashly on their own. Their actions do not represent Ebulon or its government."

"It was an unfortunate introduction," the captain agreed, watching the Mahal carefully.

Yare's gaze shifted from the Mahal to Eropa, and the room around them vanished.

Eropa knew the alien captain, the feel of his energy, the sense of his inner spirit--but not as this person.

The past they had shared flamed to life--engulfing her in a vision. *They fell into a shared passion, his lips on hers, his need devouring her own. Her former lover's scent, his taste--she knew them well, the connection between them singular and intoxicating, but suddenly, it was not the lover she had known; it was the alien invader who she neither knew nor trusted. The corded muscles of her former lover's arms held her tight against him. His was the body of a warrior, his arms strong, but his kiss tasted of grief and loss.*

The vision held her fast. Eropa could not catch her breath, fear fluttering frantic wings within her ribs as the shadow of a distant past strove to obtain dominance over this life and the future. The path not yet chosen. The old expectations she had been raised with, and the future that this shadow-past desired fought each for their own vision. It stank of subjugation, not choice.

Eropa had felt this echo connection when she first encountered the starship.

She felt it now.

But that did not mean this alien's purpose would benefit her people. These were different lives. Neither of them was who they had once been.

"Only a fool accepts a vision at face value," Hagriva had warned Eropa many times. *"Discovering the truth of the vision requires disciplined non-attachment, an onion-like peeling back of the layers that come only with time and understanding. The naive choose to interpret a vision through their own wishful thinking, believing it portends a predestined future. Such thinking is dangerous, blinding you to the Truths that might be revealed."*

This is a vision, Eropa reminded herself. *Nothing more. And I am not a fool.*

The vision shattered, the Glass Hall, the court, and the alien crew reappeared, and the present once again settled its images around the young sorceress.

There you are. The alien's private thoughts blazed out to the entire court. *And even more fascinating in person. I'd like to find some dark corner and explore your private places.*

The hall clenched down on an unnatural stillness. Shocked by the alien invader's insult to their future Matriarch but afraid to show it, they revealed nothing, waiting.

Frevin's whole body had become stiff; his hands gripped into fists, his color high, his anger barely constrained.

"Control yourself, Frevin," Eropa commanded him silently. *"You cannot address his thoughts. You would reveal us. I do not care what he thinks about me. You should not either."* Eropa focused on her breathing, calming the turmoil within her.

The tensions in the hall compressed, the moment stretching on, and still no one spoke.

The Ebulonian courtiers shifted nervously, the soft rustle of their starched silks bouncing from wall to wall like the voices of unseen spirits murmuring from the arched ceiling and behind the pillars of the cavernous hall.

Some of the alien crew's hands began moving cautiously toward the weapons hanging from their belts, their eyes darting around the room trying to identify the source of the danger they sensed but could not see.

The future of two worlds teetered on the edge of violence that could begin in this room and define their histories going forward.

"And, of course, you have already met the Pira, Eropa Rhune, Captain Yare," Nikodamus's gracious voice broke the silence.

CHAPTER NINE

"I have." The alien captain took Eropa's hand and raised it to his lips, brushing the skin on the back of it with his warm breath. "And I am in awe of Ebulon's beauty." Still bent over her hand, the alien grinned up at Eropa as if there had been an assignation between them.

Untethered by the biological confusion his touch had set loose within her, she managed to glare at him as she yanked her hand away.

Nikodamus rose and casually positioned himself between Eropa and the alien.

"Come, Captain Yare. Let me introduce you to Ebulon's Council of Elders." With a subtle backward glance, he guided the alien away from his daughter.

The courtiers began to breathe, hundreds of private conversations assailing Eropa's mind. She shut them out. Beside her, she caught the angry glance Frevin shot at her before he hurried to join her father and the alien.

"He is not unappealing," Aless mused privately, studying the alien captain's muscular physique and unconscious good looks. His sand-colored hair only marginally cooperated with the notion of being combed, a hank continually falling over one eye. *"He has a poet's eyes, full of emotion and passion, and a decisive jaw. In another time, he would have been thought handsome."*

"He is dangerous," Eropa declared firmly.

Aless nodded. *"Undoubtedly. He is a fighting man. See how he marks the entrances and exits of the hall, and where each of our guards stands?"* The McLarick Voice chuckled warmly. *He puts me in mind of a scrawny cat that skulks outside our kitchens, all muscle, hunger, and desire."*

"He imagines we are mice he may toy with," Eropa quipped.

"And why would he not? By the Mother, look at them." Aless's mouth twisted in disgust. The Voices bowed and smiled obsequiously to the alien captain. *"They are all but rolling over and offering him their throats,"* Aless decried her colleagues' lack of composure. *"I do not think they understood the crux of your plan, Pira."*

Nikodamus, Frevin, and the alien approached the Dum'Laiere Voice, Miratha Dum'Laire. She tilted her head, batting her lashes, molding her painted lips into a simpering smile, at least twenty years too young for her face.

"Whatever is she doing?" Eropa demanded.

"Flirting." Lady Aless grunted. A faint glow shimmered around the Dum'Laiere woman. *"And she has donned a youth glamour to go along with that low-cut gown."*

"Why would she do that?" Eropa's fine brows furrowed.

Lady Aless sighed. *"She saw how he reacted to you. She seeks to gain a more intimate power over the captain."*

"The woman is without shame," Eropa proclaimed in disgust.

"The woman is without a husband," Aless countered. *"I wonder if Captain Yare would be quite so interested if he knew the true condition of those duggs, but if she is successful, this could complicate things."*

"She is not a Rhune, despite all her claims of secret training." Eropa dismissed the notion.

"But she is an experienced woman, and apparently, the alien is in need of one. Do not underestimate the influence gained through sexual intimacy, Pira," the older woman warned the young Rhune. *"For those who do not practice an adept's arts, it is the most powerful energy they experience, and many learn to wield it as you wiled Rhune practices. If Miratha Dum'Laiere forges a sexual alliance with this alien, her influence over him could become an issue."*

As if he heard them speaking of him, the alien turned away from Miratha, looking back at Eropa.

"I must find a way to get her alone, away from all the rest of them," his thoughts were like a claxon. Behind him, Miratha scowled.

Aless looked from Eropa to the alien and back.

"Glamour or not, it appears the captain's interest is fixed on you, Pira."

Eropa's chin went up. *"Are you suggesting I take him to my bed to prevent him from forming an alliance with the Dum'Laiers, Lady Aless?"*

"Only if you are interested in him, Pira."

"There is nothing glamoured about me." Eropa's expression hardened, and she turned her back to the alien, breaking their connection.

"Of course not. You are young, brilliant, and quite beautiful. You have no need for such devices," Aless assured the young Rhune. *"I don't suppose anyone has told you that before."*

CHAPTER NINE

Eropa dismissed the statement. *"No. It is entirely unimportant to the situation."*

"Apparently, not entirely," Aless mused.

Nikodamus re-directed the alien captain's attention, navigating him toward the banquet room where the celebration feast had been laid out.

Eropa visibly wilted, the exhaustion Dakmira had worked to temporarily abate using up the last of her energy.

Aless clucked. *"You are beyond weary, my dear, and if you stay, you will be seated beside the alien, expected to converse while reading his mind and not letting him know you are doing it,"* the elder Voice pointed out. *"After everything you have been through since last night, I question whether you are equal to this task."*

Eropa swayed unsteadily on her feet. *"I do not know,"* she admitted meekly.

"You are the Pira, Eropa, not a diplomat." Aless pressed the controls over her hover chair so that she was beside the young Rhune. "Fatigue makes you vulnerable. You are in no condition to spar with this man," she said quietly. "Tomorrow, we will have new information to discuss, but for now, you must rest. You have done enough. I will explain to your father and make apologies to our guest."

"Yes. Please do that, Lady Aless." With a last glance toward the dining area where the alien had disappeared, Eropa used the final shredded bits of her energy to slip through the small door at the back of the hall.

CHAPTER TEN

"The hubris of sentient beings is that their ability to think fools them into believing they are superior to other forms of life." (Hagriva Rhune from A History of the Rhunes compiled in the Third Age).

From a window on the starship Annihilator, Omrey looked out into space. Despite the emptiness, he could not forget the sight of Ra, the small planet—its crust broken and belching purple smoke.

We destroyed it. It was not much, but it was inhabitable, and now it is not. All because the spoiled son of a despot likes watching things blow up, and no one has the balls to stand up to him. Will there be no end to the carnage Paxlosis is held responsible for because of the Ceitonese under Dmow Tetpois' dynasty?

"It doesn't matter who found them, us or someone else," Shabus had argued when Omrey protested what was done to the small planet and its inhabitants. "The outcome for them was always going to be the same."

Omrey did not want to believe that, but the Thousand Worlds' agreements governing the treatment of other beings and their worlds were worthless out here in space as long as Yerga refused to stand up to his junior officer.

"I am surrounded by idiots," Omrey grumbled.

The captain of the Annihilator's shameless toadying to the younger Tetpois, Shabus, was indicative of everything wrong with their mission.

Was mental derangement basic in the genes of powerful Paxlosian families, Omrey wondered? Morladja Yare's reputation indicated she was as insane as the famously murderous Ceitonese leader. But where Morladja Yare's son was said to be a spoiled, self-centered libertine, Dmow Tetpois' truculent offspring seemed to favor more violent misbehaviors. The question Omrey kept asking himself--being forced to interact with Tetpois the younger--was how much behavior was learned, and how much was genetic. Either way, the root causes led to the powerful man who had sired him. Of course, he said none of this aloud, even in private. This was the kind of question that got people whisked off and dumped down a dark hole in the underground caves of Ceiton.

Fear, it seemed, was Shabus Tetpois' weapon of choice. He enjoyed pressuring the spineless Captain Yerga into questionable decisions, then watching him dangle like fish on a hook when they went wrong. Shabus enjoyed watching things squirm.

Omrey refused to kiss the younger Tetpois' ass, but he knew better than to challenge the Tetpois scion. No one on the Annihilator would stand up for him nor come to his rescue. They would do as they always did, stand by and watch while Shabus tortured whoever had the ill fortune to catch his attention, silently hoping that they would not be his next victim.

Omrey turned away from the window and walked the hundred feet to the containment area where the two last survivors of the small planet Ra were kept.

On entering, he smelled the creatures' peculiar scent; a combination of dirt, grass, animal musk, and whatever native spices they used in their food.

He passed the crewmen assigned to care for the captives who brought them food and cleaned their cell.

"Shit, they stink." The man held his nose as he passed Omrey.

Eventually, the creatures would have to be bathed, washing away the smells, the last link to their home world. But that was a task for another day.

Omrey stepped forward into the lighted area near the force field that separated the captives from their captors.

The male of the species was sitting in his usual place in the corner: his knees pulled up to his chest. His whiskers and the hairs on his snout were graying, his deep, brown eyes were heavy with grief, and it seemed to Omrey, deep with unspoken wisdom. The long hairs on the creature's head, once neatly braided, were now an un-groomed bird's nest of tangles. Nevertheless, Omrey found him to be a thoughtful creature--an animal of some intelligence, though how much had yet to be determined.

The female he was less sure about. She lay on the floor, as she had from the first, pretending to be unconscious. The monitors and the fact that she was not lying in her excrement told Omrey that this was not the case, but with eyes open or closed, she showed no interest in her new surroundings or her benevolent captor.

She is probably still in shock, Omrey excused her behavior, unwilling to entertain the thought that the creatures he had saved would not prove useful. If she did not come out of it and begin to adapt to her new life, the species could die. *I must take action to ensure that does not happen,* Omrey told himself.

Shabus interrupted, swaggering up to lurk in the doorway. "A genetic wonder, no question." His lip curled. "They stink, Omrey. Don't you smell it? Maybe you can't smell them over the smell of your hypocrisy."

Omrey turned to look at the younger man. Shabus' uniform did not have enough material to accommodate his blown-up biceps and blocky neck. His arms looked like they might pop open like overripe seedpods at any moment, and his neck looked as if it was squeezed from the tube of his uniform's stand-up collar.

Omrey smoothed his own finely fitted jumpsuit. Cut in the latest style, a full over-robe billowed and swished around him whenever he moved. He had two, both the same. They had cost him half of his signing bonus, but as a private contractor, it was important to set himself apart from the crew, and nothing said "man of importance" more clearly than expensive clothing. Omrey was contracted to use his mental talents to communicate with any alien beings the mission might encounter and to gain insight into their thoughts, culture, and traditions, intending to make recommendations about the viability of different beings for conquest and enslavement.

With little opportunity to exercise his skills, Omrey spent his time studying his shipmates, gathering information about their weaknesses, noting their mistakes, alliances, and rivalries, and storing it like treasure. Self-trained and self-promoted as a "psychic counselor" and anthropologist, it was Omrey's theory that language barriers could be overcome through direct mind contact. It was easy to fool the gullible. Without understanding how psychic phenomena worked or didn't, people assumed the psychic watcher knew things he could not possibly know. With a little talent, a little luck, and some good timing, Omrey had forged notoriety into a career. When the Annihilator's mission ended and the ship returned, Dictator/General Tetpois'

CHAPTER TEN

inferred patronage would bring customers streaming through his door. All he had to do was survive the general's son.

"Captain Yerga intends to gift the specimens to the Ceiton Institute for study," Omrey said, keeping any defensiveness from his voice. He had fed Yerga's bloated ego a bunch of nonsense about how the scientific world would honor him as a man of vision for preserving a newly discovered species.

"They look like fresh meat to me." Shabus eyed the captives as if they were already carved and on his plate.

"We can't eat them. They're sentient," Omrey pointed out. According to the guidelines of the original Pact of the Thousand Worlds, these creatures' culture had presented signs that should have marked them as candidates for alliance or colonization rather than the more radical "cleansing" that had taken place. Yerga claimed he had not intended to eradicate all life and that the chemical reaction between the Annihilator's weapons and the planet's geology had been entirely accidental and unforeseen, but Omrey doubted that. There were scientists onboard, specialists. Where had *they* been when the decision was made? Omrey made his case, but he was overridden. He suspected the same had happened to other voices of reason. A mission's contractors could advise, but none of them could match the influence of a Tetpois.

So, the small planet had been found and lost. Someone would pay, of course, some designated sacrificial offering who did not have a powerful family name. With resources among the Thousand Worlds stretched so thin, there was little interest in preserving a competing life form.

"There's only the two left." Shabus sized the furry aliens up. "If we eat them, no one will ever know if they're sentient."

I will know, you fuck. Omrey maintained his mask of blandness.

The male creature's dark eyes watched the two Paxlosians, moving as they spoke.

He is listening. What does he understand?

"Captain Yerga would be very upset if his scientific wonders turned up on someone's dinner plate." Omrey pretended to laugh as if enjoying Shabus' joke--and believing it was a joke.

Shabus snorted. "Yerga? He won't do anything." His cruel, wide mouth stretched into an unpleasant replica of a human grin. "They're always going to hate you, you know. They'll hate us too, but not like they hate you. We're just background. You may not have pushed the button that turned their little rock into a fireball--but you're the turd who kept them alive so that they have to remember the destruction of their world and everyone they ever knew--every day for the rest of their miserable lives--and they will be miserable. I guarantee it. Look at them, Omrey. You can see it in their eyes. They wish they'd died with the rest of their dog friends. You took that from them. That earns you a special kind of hatred. Isn't that right, dog-man?" Shabus taunted. The male specimen glanced over at the female, who remained as still as if she were already dead. "They're never going to forgive you for keeping them alive."

Omrey ground his teeth. *It should be you they hate.*

The male's eyes tracked from the heavy-lidded man in the doorway to Omrey.

"You'll see I'm right." Tetpois sauntered out.

Omrey knelt outside the containment area."*Do you understand me?*" He tried to project his thoughts toward the male's mind.

The creature blinked but nothing more. After a few minutes, Omrey's legs began to cramp, so he stood.

"I'll see you tomorrow. Perhaps we can speak then." He exited.

Grub woke up with the scent of his mother's flatcakes filling his wide nostrils. He reached out to pull up his sleeping hide, knowing his mother would call him when the first meal was ready, but there was no hide. And then he remembered; there was no bed--no mother, no flatcakes. Grub opened his eyes. From the darkness, two pale, blue eyes looked back.

"Go away and leave me alone, Bibi," he groaned, rolling over. A stick-like lump crunched beneath him; it was the ring reed flute his Uncle Gutte had given him for his name day. "Now look what you've done," he blamed the albino unfairly. Picking up the flute, he examined it. There was a small crack in the body near the opening. Grub placed the flute in his skin pouch and slung it over his shoulder.

"How Grub feel?" Bibi asked.

CHAPTER TEN

Grub turned his head, trying to see something--anything. A fierce pain shot through his right temple, and he moved his head back more carefully. It felt like it was filled with water.

"Where is my mother?" He wanted her to rub his head like she did when he was little and murmur soft reassurances. "Where is my mother, Bibi?" he repeated.

"Bibi not know," came the answer from the blue eyes.

Grub had been minding his own business, playing his flute when Bibi had appeared. He had come to regret stopping the other cubs from teasing the albino outcast. She had become such a pest, acting as if what he'd done had created a bond between them. Determined to hide from the clanless runt, Grub had run up a cliff-face path and into a cave. Bibi had followed. When he'd turned to shout at her to leave him alone and stop following him, he'd heard a loud crack--like the sky had split open. The blast of heat that accompanied it had knocked him to his knees. Bibi had been outlined against the cave's mouth, waving her hands as the roof collapsed.

He touched a furry hand to his head. A crude bandage--made of Bibi's waist scarf--was wrapped around it. He could smell his dried blood on it. The albino's hand touched his head cautiously, then pulled quickly away.

"What happened?" Grub noted from the sound of his voice that the walls of the cave were very close. "Where are we?"

"No worry, Grub," Bibi answered glibly.

"Bibi, what have you done?" he jumped to his feet. Reaching out, he touched both walls at once.

"This is not the cave. Where are we?" Splintered memories jabbed at Grub's cracked head. She had moved him. While he was unconscious, the creepy little albino had taken him from the outer cave to who knew where. Endless tunnels webbed beneath the mountains. Nobody knew where half of them went. The futility of his situation flooded through him. No one would ever find him.

Like most cubs, Grub had explored some of the tunnels close to the village, but if he were to try to figure out where they were, he would have to have kept track from their starting point. Grub sank back down onto the stone floor of the tunnel, feeling despair as the darkness crowded in on him.

"We're lost."

"Not lost," Bibi assured him. "Safe. Grub walk now? Bibi go slow."

Hungry, frustrated, and hurting everywhere, Grub could think of no other option than to hope Bibi knew where she was going, but he was not happy about it.

"How can you see in here?" he asked after stubbing his toe for the sixth time. Two glowing blue orbs blazed before him.

"Magic eyes see good." Bibi closed them, plunging them into darkness.

Grub frowned. Everyone knew females were forbidden to have anything to do with magic--everyone except Bibi. He wasn't sure whether to hope it was true so that she would find their way out of the tunnels or hope that she was lying because the alternative was too frightening.

Bibi resumed her confident stride, a pace that kept Grub's head at a low throb. Finally, he couldn't take it anymore.

"Bibi, stop. I can't tell which way is down, except that's where my whole body wants to go." Bibi looked back the way they had come.

"Sit." She sat beside him.

Grub didn't like touching her. He wanted to move away but his exhausted body refused to budge. After a few minutes, the warmth she gave off began to warm him, and he thought no more about moving.

"I'm starving and thirsty," he grumbled instead. "How much farther until we get home, Bibi?"

She reached over and tentatively placed her hand on his bruised toe. The pain drained away like water through a crack in a clay pot.

Grub stared into the darkness, seeing only the albino's glowing blue eyes. He wanted to ask her what she had done, then thought better of it. He probably wouldn't like the answer—that was assuming he could understand her childish gibberish. The ugly little thing probably didn't know what she had done was wrong. No one in the village paid attention to Bibi, or her crazy mother, Wan. If it took a little bit of magic to get home, then maybe that was okay, Grub decided. Once they got back, he could tell Uncle Gutte. Gutte would take care of it. Then Grub would make it clear that he did not want Bibi following him around anymore, and he would be rid of her.

"More walking," Bibi announced, getting to her feet. Her hands were mere inches from his aching head. If she touched it, would the pain go away like it did when she touched his toe? He was too proud to ask. Bibi took his hand and began guiding him slowly through the darkness.

It felt as if they had been walking forever when Grub realized the darkness had become a little less complete. At first, all he saw was the ghostly sheen of Bibi's silver fur before him, but bit by bit, the light transformed into a purple twilight, they turned a corner, the tunnel widened, and they were out.

But it was not anywhere Grub recognized.

"This isn't home," Grub protested. "Where are we?"

"Cave of Hollow Winds," Bibi announced.

Crouched as far away as she could, Urda turned her back to the Spirit Speaker and tried to ignore what he was doing. Gutte knew being so near the workings of magic made her nervous, but he also saw, how when he threw the ancestor's bones across the floor, she peeked over her shoulder. As soon as the rattling ceased, she turned around.

"What did you ask?"

"I asked about our village." Gutte's head slouched low his metal-collared neck dropped between his shoulders.

"What did they say? Please, Gutte Ra, tell me, even if it is bad. Knowing something is better than knowing nothing."

Gutte stared at the bones scattered across the floor. "Nothing. They said nothing."

Urda sat back. "Then it is true, the wall of fire has burned our village from Mother Ra's breast. Why should we live when everyone we love is gone?" She said the words like they had no meaning for her, her eyes dry, though Gutte heard her weeping during the silent nights since they had come to this strange place, muttering the names of her mate and cubs. She had always stopped crying when the pale-skinned, hairless ones came, lying still, pretending to sleep. When they kicked so to spray the floor with water, she scuttled to the back corner and bared her teeth at them.

"It was my fault, Urda--my failure." He dug his fingers inside the metal collar around his neck and tried to wrench it off. The gesture was futile. The ends of the collar had been fused on his initiation, making the metal into one complete circle with no end. A trickle of blood matted the brown hair where the Spirit Speaker's hard nails had gouged through the hide around it. "I am no true Spirit Speaker, and the gods have punished us because of it." Urda slid over beside him, her strong brown hands grasping his.

"Stop, Gutte. It will not come off. It will never come off, not until you die, and your body rots and the bones break apart."

Gutte's bottom lip trembled. "I should have died, not our village. Why did Boors leave us? He was a true Spirit Speaker. I could never do what he did—understand as he did. None of this would have happened if Boors had not abandoned us."

"You know why he left, Gutte. Everyone knew why." Urda spat on the hard floor. "Wan should never have let him come sniffing around her mother's cave. It was forbidden."

Gutte was not hypocrite enough to join Urda's admonishment of another for something he had enjoyed with Umma.

"And you are a Spirit Speaker, Gutte. You were chosen." Urda's round, brown eyes were as sincere as they were sad.

"I was only an apprentice, Urda. I was not ready." Gutte wrung his hands. "I needed more time." Tears wetted his fuzzy cheeks. "If Boors had…"

"Pah!" Urda interrupted him. "Boors is to blame. That abomination of a cub that Wan birthed proved that. Whoever heard of a white Cumin? That Bibi was a slap in the face to the spirits."

"You do not know what you are talking about, Urda," Gutte's tone was suddenly sharp. *"The future lies with Grub and Bibi,"* the old one had said. Whatever Boors and Wan had done, it was not Bibi's fault that she was born. "There is no law against a Spirit Speaker seeking pleasure. The laws only say that he may not claim the cub for his clan because he no longer has a clan. He belongs to all clans equally. The gods have a plan for Bibi, as they do for all Mother Ra's children."

Urda's thick black lips smiled smugly. "Now you sound like a Spirit Speaker."

"I have no one to serve but you." Gutte's brown eyes were muddy pools.

Urda's face fell. "I do not want my own Spirit Speaker." She crawled back to her spot on the floor and curled up.

CHAPTER ELEVEN

"Many fish swim in the stream of life. If you catch only one, it does not mean the others do not exist." (A discussion of philosophies attributed to Mo Tep Hunan; Third Matriarch. From the Book of the Rhune).

Nikodamus watched Yare as he sat taking in the details of the Mahal's study, the rich carpets, the shelves of leather-bound books, the fine paintings, and sculptures. Stretching his feet toward the fireplace, the alien captain sighed.

"You don't know how a man appreciates comfort after five years in space."

"I added a touch of onche." Dakmira handed Yare a steaming cup of tea. "It is a honey prized among our people. I hope you will enjoy it." She inclined her head politely.

The alien captain took a sip of the hot beverage. "That's different."

Dakmira smiled. "A polite way of saying you do not care for it, Captain Yare?" She reached for the cup. "Here, let me get you something else."

The alien pulled the cup in toward himself. "No. It is unusual, but I like it. Really."

"We say the more you drink, the better it tastes," Dakmira confided.

"It should relax him enough to talk easily but not enough for him to suspect that his inhibitions have been chemically altered," the Keesch healer informed Nikodamus privately.

"I will leave the two of you to talk." She disappeared into an adjoining room.

"So, tell me of your world, Captain Yare." The Mahal sipped his unspiked tea. He would need a clear head to keep track of the verbal and non-verbal communications he needed to monitor. "What is your planet Paxlosis like?"

CHAPTER ELEVEN

"It's nothing like Ebulon." Yare suddenly became preoccupied with the bottom of his cup and Nikodamus took advantage of the moment to slip into the alien's thought stream.

A series of dimly lit images presented themselves: an overcrowded city fallen into decay, its people gaunt, sickly, and in rags. Nikodamus saw their haunted faces as Yare had, looking up at him as he flew above their misery in the comfort of a small craft.

Out of reach of the contagion and dangers below, Nikodamus mused.

"The United Front is the governing body representing the larger portion of the population on Paxlosis. The smaller faction, the Ceitonese are a poor nation with little influence outside its people. The Front are strong partners of the Consortium that sponsored our mission, focused on expanding resources and technology," Yare pulled his focus back from his internal thoughts, shattering the images Nikodamus was seeing. "It's given us an advantage over some of the less developed planets among the Thousand Worlds."

Yare's words sounded rehearsed. "And those advantages have brought you here?" Nikodamus prodded.

"They've given us the ability to build a starship like the Lamdra," he agreed. "The Consortium is interested in cultivating trade opportunities, developing new markets—import contracts."

"Import contracts?" Nikodamus smiled from behind the rim of his cup. "Come, Captain Yare, let us be honest with each other, your starship is clearly a military vessel."

"Exploration is a dangerous business," the alien tried to sidestep the insinuation.

"A dangerous business for you, or for those whom you 'discover'?" the Mir asked bluntly.

The alien captain's body language tensed, his eyes losing their misty morning, gray promise, and becoming steely and hard.

I have struck a nerve, the Mahal thought.

Careful, Zeph. Nikodamus heard the man caution himself. *You argued against attacking this planet, don't force them into that position now.* When he spoke, his voice was moderated, the glint in his eyes controlled, but Nikodamus felt the anger hidden behind the control.

"Accessing new markets is not an act of aggression," said the alien captain.

"That would depend on the terms of the trade agreement," the Mahal replied unruffled. "And who would deny you whatever you asked with such a starship to back your will?"

"Anyone who felt they had the strength to resist a forced take-over, I guess," Yare suggested coolly. "But that's not you. I would like to believe that you understand the message behind the fact that though you attacked us without provocation, we did not fire on you."

"We did not attack you," Nikodamus corrected the alien. "And you obliterated that Taiban fighter."

"But we did not fire on the planet," the captain insisted. *Light of Death, any other ship's captain would have burned your green asses off this planet.* Yare ground his teeth.

He sees himself as a man of restraint. The Mahal considered thoughtfully.

"The actions of your 'guests', or whoever they are, gave us every reason to attack you. Our restraint should mean something, don't you think, Mahal?"

"We are here together," the Mahal replied.

"Our mission's primary purpose is to trade—to find partners with whom we can trade resources. Ebulon is in a good position to benefit from such an agreement. It could be very lucrative, not only for your merchants and your people, but for you personally, Mahal," Yare suggested.

Nikodamus raised an eyebrow. "Meaning that I could benefit, by supporting this arrangement?"

"You are Ebulon's leader. It is only right that you see some financial benefit. But of course, that can all be worked out in the details of our agreement," Zeph confirmed.

"I have no interest or desire to acquire more wealth than I have." Nikodamus's forehead wrinkled. "And forgive me, Captain, but I have always understood trade agreements to be based on mutual need. Ebulon is blessed with abundance. We need nothing. What exactly are you proposing that we trade *for*?"

"Our goodwill?" the alien shot back, his anger flaring.

And there it is. If he does not get what he wants, he is still willing to resort to force, Nikodamus surmised.

"And what arrangement did you make with the Taiban homeworlds?" the Mahal inquired strategically. The alien paused.

"We did not approach the Taibans. They have too many problems and nothing to offer us. We aren't interested in getting involved in that kind of trouble."

"The Taiban warlords would fight to protect what little they have, and you believe that we will not," Nikodamus summed up the situation.

"I have every confidence that if we fought these Taiban Warlords, we would win, but it is not worth the expense. The Taiban worlds are overcrowded and under-resourced already. Of course, that would not matter if we were here to take worlds," the Paxlosian declared. "But we're not."

Nikodamus set down his cup and stood. "I hear your words, Captain Yare, and they might give me more confidence if it were not for the militant nature of your starship's technology. It is a statement all its own and it says something quite different." The Mahal paused. "Believing that Ebulon could be easily conquered would be a grave error. While it is true that our sciences have taken a different path, it is not a *lesser* path. Do not imagine that we are defenseless," Nikodamus warned the alien.

Zeph's eyes narrowed. "I could have taken this world anytime, and we both know it," he forced the words through gritted teeth. "But *we* aren't threatening you."

"Right now, you are the only ones threatening us," the Mahal disagreed. Nikodamus reached into the alien's mind and dragged the memory of Eropa's Double's appearance on the Lamdra's bridge forward, forcing the alien to revisit the fear and doubt that he and his crew had experienced. He released the memory, allowing Zeph's control over the direction of his thoughts to snap back into place.

Yare blinked, disoriented.

"Do not allow your people to make decisions based on dangerous assumptions. Just because you do not see something you recognize as a threat does not mean there is no threat," Nikodamus cautioned quietly. "The Ebulonian Scientific Society of Mirs are quite prolific in their inventions."

"Peace is a luxury, afforded to those who are able to pay to enforce it," the alien said defiantly. The Mahal's nudge to remember Eropa's unexplained appearance on the Lamdra had weakened the alien's confidence, but it was not in the man's nature to back down. "Choose wisely and Ebulon could live peacefully for generations,

Mahal. Choose poorly and...." He did not finish the sentence. He did not need to.

"You suggest that we pay through trade for the privilege of becoming an occupied world?" Nikodamus scoffed. "My people will never agree."

"Then they don't understand reality, and it is your job to help them understand," Yare countered. "Freedom *costs*, Mahal. Its currency is lives and the Thousand Worlds are littered with the bones of those who overspent their accounts."

Mental images of a world cross-stitched by the blackened hulks of abandoned cities hit Nikodamus like a punch in the face. The beings who had once lived there had been scattered into a toxic, barren expanse, or lived pressed together underground in mutual misery. Was this Paxlosis?

Nikodamus ripped his mind away. Shaken, he breathed deeply to regain his equilibrium.

"The Ebulonian people will not accept a military occupation," he controlled his voice so that it did not betray how shaken he was by what he had seen.

"Then educate them," Yare advised. "Because, like your Taiban neighbors, most sentient beings have plenty of their own kind. What they lack are places to put them and ways to feed them."

Nikodamus studied the captain's face. A war was being played out within the young man. He did not know which side he would fight on. The Mahal needed to know where the Paxlosian's stood, but the more he saw of Yare's world, the more dangerous the path ahead seemed. The possibility of some avenue to peace was the thinnest thread. What could he say to convince the Paxlosian to take hold of the other end of that thread and commit to strengthening it?

"I know nothing of your world, Captain Yare," Nikodamus chose his words carefully. "As you know nothing of ours, but the Taiban refugees have taught us something of the horrors and destruction of war; families selling their own into bondage to eat for a few more months. Children living on the streets prepared to kill for a bite of bread. Murders take place on those streets every night, the bodies picked clean by morning. Flesh of any kind remains meat to the desperately hungry. And all of this exists because a few men want more—more than they could spend in three lifetimes." Nikodamus turned sad eyes to Yare. "No sane person wants war, Captain. Every day, I wake up hoping that Taiba's fate is not our own.

"You advise me to explain your version of reality to my people as if by doing so, it would convince them to accept becoming slaves on their world. This is not compatible with our nature, or our history. You ask us to embrace a trade agreement but offer no benefit. How can I suggest this to my people? You reply that it is my responsibility to convince them that it is too dangerous to remain unallied, that an alliance between our worlds will give them a kind of protection. This protection must be clearly defined and firmly agreed to. Then I can propose such an alliance. Then they will see a benefit."

"How did we get from trade agreements to an alliance?" Zeph asked.

Nikodamus sat back in his chair, his fingers steepled. "This trade that you propose. What do you think will happen here when the Taiban Warlords notice all this coming and going of starships--because they will notice. Despite the purge of scientific minds, the Taiban worlds went through a decade ago, the warlords will recover. They will build new ships, with better technology and if their attention is drawn to our part of the system, they will come here. What will become of this trade agreement then?" the Mahal asked. If it results in the destruction of the resources you seek, it will have no value at all. Any agreement between us must offer protection as well."

"I can't sell you weapons," Zeph declared.

"I did not ask you to. But an agreement that gives your sponsors a promising path to what will show itself to be a temporary financial gain because of the risks in play within our system, is a questionable asset. Dealing with all the challenges beforehand by offering a true agreement of cooperation, including protection of our partnership and its assets, shows forethought. It is well thought out. It has longevity.

"On our side, claiming to offer an agreement that has nothing to benefit us, looks like bad faith and, frankly, it has no chance of approval by the council Voices. But offer us an agreement that helps allay fears of the future threat from the Taiban worlds, and there will be Voices who support it; an agreement between two governments with a pact to protect each other in the event of an attack by an outside party, I could take to the council with confidence."

Zeph's brow furrowed. "What you're suggesting is beyond the scope of a simple trade agreement," he pointed out.

"I understand that. It is something much stronger, creating a greater bond between our people."

Both men gazed into the fire thinking their own thoughts, but Nikodamus once again joined his mind to Zeph's to hear the alien captain's thoughts as it turned over the possibilities.

"A treaty," Zeph muttered. The Consortium wouldn't like it. They would demand to know why he hadn't just taken the damned planet, but once they realized the wealth of what he had found here they would come around.

Once Ebulon's existence and its resources are made public, I'll be racing against every investor group that can come up with the funds to contract a starship and a Navigator. The Guild will become richer and even more powerful; the gatekeepers for every merchant who wants to do business here. But we will control the trade contracts. Without that, we could lose everything to them.

Yare's mind wandered to the document his mother's lawyers had created to cover any trade agreement not based on annexation. He had not paid any attention to the details of the document, but it existed. Morladja Yare left nothing to chance. *If I hold strictly to the specifics laid out in the document, she and her Consortium associates would have to support it, pushing through its ratification by the United Front's Presidium. And if Cyramus supported it, perhaps the Guild could be kept in line.*

"I fear I have been a thoughtless host," Nikodamus interrupted the alien's thoughts. "The hour is late, Captain Yare. An escort is waiting outside to take you back to meet the rest of your entourage. I invite you to return tomorrow. I will have someone take you to our marketplace." *Not Frevin,* he decided. "Afterward, we can speak again." Nikodamus rose and offered his hand to the alien. "Good night, Captain Yare."

CHAPTER TWELVE

"The Truths are not the easy path, but for a Rhune, they are the only path." (The Truths from The Book of the Rhune from the First Age.)

It was midday when Frevin found Eropa in the old barbican ruins. She was sitting on the floor amid stacks of old books and even older manuscripts. She did not look up from the book in her lap.

"I thought you would be with the alien today."

Frevin's mouth twisted. "And I thought you would be," he shot back.

Eropa looked up at him, one eyebrow raised. She felt Yare's presence the moment he arrived on the planet and continued to be uncomfortably aware of him. Whatever this connection between them was, it was not simple.

"Something is bothering you, Frevin. Would you like to tell me what it is?" she prodded him coolly.

"You are the future Matriarch, Eropa," Frevin declared. "What were you thinking, letting that alien barbarian fawn over you in front of the Court?"

"If you are going to be peevish, you may leave." Eropa dismissed him, turning her attention back to the book before her. She was no less annoyed with herself at how things had gone with the alien, but it was not Frevin's place to judge her, and she resented that he thought it was.

He recognized her cool retreat and stumbled over himself to regain the ground he had lost.

"Forgive me. I should not have said that."

"No. You should not. You should not have thought it," she reprimanded him. "We are friends, but I am still the Pira."

Frevin began to pick seedpods deposited by the wild grass outside from his otherwise immaculate robes.

"Your father asked Pliny Mir to escort the alien today."

"Pliny of the Ballatyn Clan?"

Frevin nodded. "That is the one."

CHAPTER TWELVE

He is a very pleasant person." Eropa nodded. "Captain Yare and he should get along."

Frevin sniffed in disgust. "I believe the Mahal finds my manner not deferential enough toward the alien captain."

"Huh," Eropa grunted.

The muffled sounds of the city beyond the walls drifted up through the shuttered window.

After a few minutes, Eropa asked, "You do not like him, do you?"

"Pliny? Of course, I do."

"No, the alien captain. You do not like him," Eropa clarified.

"Being the person who has spent the most time in the man's company, I believe I have the most informed opinion on his character." Frevin walked to the wooden shelves, feigning interest in the dusty bottles of tinctures and herbs. "Aside from his unforgivable behavior toward you, I find him arrogant, egotistical and rude."

"I begin to understand my father's decision." Eropa returned to scanning the book in her lap. "What would you have me do, Frevin, burn the man to ash like the Rhune mistress who used the bloodstone because she was angry? How would that serve our cause? We cannot afford to openly declare to these aliens that we know they are our enemies."

"So, he gets away with it," Frevin snarled.

"You would hold him accountable for thoughts he believes were private." Frevin began to protest, but she held up a hand stopping him. "Captain Yare is a stranger without an understanding of our culture or abilities," Eropa reminded the Mir. "And he is ignorant because we chose to keep him so, because, at the moment, it serves our needs."

"But you are the Pira!" Frevin exploded.

"And therefore, not to be thought of as a woman?" Eropa stood and faced him defiantly.

"That is not what I meant," Frevin spluttered, backing up.

"Explain what you did mean then." Eropa stepped over the piles of books and placed herself in front of him, blocking his way. "Have you ever imagined kissing me, Frevin?"

"I would never," he stuttered. "It would be disrespectful without..."

"Without asking permission?" Eropa finished for him. "And yet you have thought of marrying me?" Frevin's eyes widened. "Do not bother trying to deny it. We have known each other since we were children. I am not unaware of your family's hopes for our relationship. We get along well enough. We have shared interests. Some people see us as being well-suited. In all the years we have known each other, you have never treated me as anything other than your friend and Pira—until last night."

"I have the deepest respect…"

"As you should, but a Rhune is not only a sorceress. She is also a woman, with a woman's needs and desires." Eropa returned to her place amongst her books, resuming her search.

"The issue is complicated," Frevin tried to defend himself.

Eropa did not look away from her reading. "Not for Captain Yare."

The Mir scowled. "Do not tell me that you have been taken in by this barbarian's posturing. I can understand Miratha and those simpering court women, but you…?"

"She what?" Dakmira entered. "What are you doing here?" the consort asked Frevin as she set down a tray of fruit, biscuits, and tea. "Is he bothering you, Pira?"

"Yes. Please, make him go away."

"I was just…"

The Keesch woman stopped him with a look. "Leave her be, Frevin. Everyone knows what you thought about the alien and Eropa's meeting yesterday, but she did nothing wrong. I would hope, as her friend, you would remind anyone who says differently, that yesterday the Pira performed very demanding practices, possibly saving the lives of everyone on this planet, and that anyone who speaks badly of her because of the alien's missteps should be ashamed of themselves."

Eropa raised her head. "People are talking. What are they saying?"

"Forget about it. You cannot separate fools from their gossip, Eropa." Dakmira opened the shutters. Eropa winced, squinting at the brightness. The Keesch woman clucked her tongue. "Too much magic."

"Do you know what she is doing up here, Dakmira?" Frevin demanded.

CHAPTER TWELVE

"Arguing with you?" Dakmira glanced at Eropa. "What are you doing, Eropa?" The Rhune did not answer, continuing to study the book in her lap.

"Look at what she is reading," Frevin insisted. "She is looking for a spell."

Dakmira selected a book from the mountain sprawled at Eropa's feet, read the title, then traded it for another.

"What kind of spell are you looking for, Eropa?"

"The kind that would save Ebulon if we needed it. Something to do with disappearance or transformation, I think," the Rhune answered vaguely.

"Is there such a thing?" Dakmira asked.

"I do not know." Eropa picked up a new book and flipped it to the table of contents. "That is why I'm looking."

"But even if you found such a spell, it would take a monumental amount of energy, and the disruption of the Balance would be enormous. It would last for generations." Frevin and Dakmira exchanged concerned glances. Life-threatening magic was life-threatening on both sides. "You would have no idea of the consequences or what you might be setting in motion."

"I know what is in motion now," Eropa contended. "And if our situation degrades and we need a new strategy, whether a spell is entirely safe or not will be irrelevant. If we live, we will deal with the consequences. But we need to know our options." She and Frevin silently measured each other, not as the friends they had been but as the individuals they were becoming under the strain of the new developments affecting their world.

Dakmira changed the subject. "Your father has sent Mithra Mir's partner, Malbuis, to work on gaining access to the Trove."

"A collection of dusty old relics with toothless sprockets and broken wheels," Frevin jibed. "There's nothing of any use there."

"Malbuis seems to be of a different opinion," the consort disagreed. "But we will see." She glanced at Eropa. Preoccupied by her task, the Pira did not appear to have heard any of what had passed between Dakmira and Frevin. The consort walked to the door and held aside the tapestry. "I think you should go now, Frevin. The Pira and I have work to do."

"You would serve her best by helping her remember who her true friends are. She will need to know in the days to come," Frevin muttered as he crossed the threshold and descended the stairs.

"You will need to watch that one," Dakmira warned the young Rhune.

I know, Eropa thought to herself. Her entire world had become a desert of shifting sands. How was she to know who remained an ally, and who had been seduced by the chaos and opportunities of the moment to seek a new path?

CHAPTER THIRTEEN

"Invisible is what the sightless agree to call that which they have no eyes to see nor words to describe." (Attributed to Abrana Ballatyne in The History of the Rhunes Compiled in the Third Age).

The Mir who met Zeph at the shuttle landing on Ebulon introduced himself as Pliny Mir. Smiling broadly, the dimpled, round-faced diplomat announced that only a small number of Zeph's party would be allowed to accompany him to the market. The rest, along with all weapons, must remain on the Paxlosian shuttle at the docking area.

"It is a precaution reflecting peaceful intentions," the Mir explained apologetically. "The Taibans are not allowed to carry weapons in the marketplace either. No one is."

Zeph, Lucha Boradice, and the mission's accountant, Holder, headed off accompanied by a small palace honor guard.

"You have arrived on a most auspicious day, Captain Yare." The Mir's generous nature was reflected, not only in his face but in his more than average girth. "This is the last day before the Festival of Lights in the floating city of Auhora Whimlan, and the market will be well stocked. I hope you will take the opportunity to attend the festival while you are here. It is one of our most beautiful cities, especially during the festival."

"I'm not here to see the sights," Zeph replied, still disgruntled by being required to leave his weapons and men behind.

"Of course. You must have a great deal of important business to attend to," the Mir inclined his head in acquiescence.

The Iredipa marketplace was rich with sound and color. Carts and vendors' booths in double-sided rows crowded the entrance of the established stores that bordered the wide, tree-lined street. Hovering disks followed wealthier patrons--carrying their purchases--while working folk relied on baskets, carts, or small wagons pulled by short-legged ponies to move merchandise.

Pliny Mir led the three Paxlosians through the busy market, a hover disk to carry the samples Ebulon's merchants gifted the visitors followed. Zeph found the Mir had not exaggerated the wonders of the market. The displays of textiles, wheel and sprocket inventions, produce, and finely crafted items of whimsy and beauty were vast. The Paxlosians were astounded by songbirds housed in nearly invisible floating cages; enabling them to fly freely within a designated area, as by shimmering fabrics that looked as if they were made of exotic bird feathers so light they undulated like water at every hint of a breeze. Even Holder was in awe.

"See how the cage disappears?" The merchant directed the Paxlosian's eyes. "The wires are as thin as thread, only visible when the sun glints off them just so. It is also sturdy, of course,sturdy enough to contain small to medium-sized songbirds, that is."

"I suppose there's no real reason to house a large bird in this way," Zeph mused.

"Exactly. They do not sing, so why would you want one flying about the room?" The merchant laughed.

"But what keeps the cages from floating away?" Holder asked, fascinated.

"I cannot say, Honored Guests. The cages are a Mir invention," the man explained. "My family has held an exclusive contract with the inventor since my grandfather's day, and our shop is the only place you can purchase this marvel. You will not find it anywhere else in the market."

"A Mir makes them?" Zeph looked to Pliny. The Mahal, Nikodamus, bore this title: Mir. His first guide, Frevin, had it at the end of his name as well. Even this new guide, Pliny, was a Mir. Zeph felt he did not understand the title.

"The members of the Scientific Society of Mir have varied interests," Pliny explained. "There are many different guilds within the society, each dedicated to a particular discipline, but we are all connected, as learning tends to be. Some Mir inventions are practical and some more whimsical in nature." Pliny indicated the floating cages.

"But none are weapons?" Zeph questioned.

"As a diplomat, Captain, I am not privy to what mechanical inventions may or may not have been invented by other guilds," Pliny sidestepped answering.

Lucha sidled up behind Zeph, speaking quietly. "I think we're being watched."

"We're strangers from another world, Lucha. It would be odd if we were not," Zeph dismissed his friend's concerns.

"This is more than curiosity, Zeph," Lucha objected. "With only two of us and no weapons, I'm feeling very exposed."

Zeph quickly scanned the immediate area. "Stay alert."

An iridescent flash from a market stall drew Zeph forward, and Boradice followed.

Three booths down, a merchant displayed a selection of different colored gauzy fabrics, all in hues of blues and greens, resembling water with bubbles floating on the surface. Zeph squeezed a bubble between his fingers.

"That'll empty purses on Pax," Boradice commented, allowing himself to pause in his monitoring of the marketplace. Zeph released the bubble, and it popped back into shape.

"Empty theirs, but fill ours," Zeph agreed. A breeze lifted the fabric causing it to lose some of its bubble covering.

"What happens in a stiff wind?" Lucha asked wryly.

"There's not enough air circulation under the Dome to worry about that," Zeph reminded him before turning to the merchant. "How is this done?"

"Magic." The merchant winked. "A very old Rhune makes it for us..." He suddenly stopped mid-sentence, terror changing his features.

Zeph frowned and looked around. Pliny had moved to his side and would have been in the merchant's line of sight, but that was not an explanation for the Ebulonian man's sudden fear.

"The material is surprisingly strong for something that looks so delicate, is it not?" Pliny looked at Zeph innocently, stretching the cloth, then letting it snap back in place.

"It is yours." The merchant bundled up the bolt and placed it on the hover disc. "A gift, courtesy of the Weavers Guild."

Zeph was thanking the merchant when Boradice growled.

"Here comes trouble." Lucha placed himself between Zeph and a group of brightly clad men moving toward them. "Taibans--and they have weapons."

Their holsters and utility belts were empty, but there were conspicuous bulges beneath their clothing that indicated they were not rule followers, nor were their intentions peaceful.

CHAPTER THIRTEEN

The Taibans spread out at a signal from a broad-shouldered man in the center of the group--with gray feathering his temples--making a line of themselves across the width of the street.

"I hate stupid rules that can get me killed." Lucha slipped a knife from his sleeve.

"Are these your men?" Zeph asked the aging broad-shouldered Taiban.

The Taiban crossed his arms over his chest. "We answer to no one. We're Free Men, every one of us, and Free Men answer only to themselves."

"That's good to know." Zeph turned back to examine the merchandise on the table before him as if dismissing the Taibans' threat. A cocky kid with a shaved head stepped forward from the line.

"You're new here, so you won't have met any of our kind yet." Zeph realized that the "kid" was not male but female. "And there sure as death wouldn't have been any Free Men up there at that fancy reception they gave you yesterday. We figured we should introduce ourselves, face to face, so you know who we are and there's no confusion about it later. We ain't Ebulonians."

"I can see that." Zeph could smell the fight coming. It was in the Taiban's sweat, the ripeness of their breath, the way their chests heaved in shallow, fast breaths. They were getting ready, building their courage, preparing to spring.

The gray-haired Taiban's mouth twisted in a sneer. "And we aren't peaceful. We fight for what's ours and don't look kindly on those who might be thinking they can take that away from us."

"But nothing here is yours," Holder argued. "You're just refugees: squatters."

The Taibans stepped forward.

"That one's got a knife..." Holder shouted. Zeph pushed the accountant behind him, knocking Pliny off balance. Lucha lunged forward to block the fist of the man beside the knife wielder, then spun for a back slice. His hand never struck its target. The man froze mid-movement. Meeting no resistance, Lucha fell forward until the cobbled street stopped him.

Zeph tried to move to help his friend but could not. He, too, was frozen. His eyes were the only exception, and they rolled around, trying to see whatever he could.

Everything was frozen. Not a dismayed pause sort of frozen, or a surprised hesitation, but a hard, unnatural, gravity-defying stoppage. The knife-wielding Taiban stood, defying gravity, balanced on one leg with his weight forward, ready to stab Zeph.

Movement on his left caught Zeph's attention, and he rolled his eyes in that direction.

A small, cloaked figure moved at the edge of the shadow cast by a building. A deep, green cowl and cloak hid head and face. A long hank of white hair tumbled over one shoulder. The mysterious newcomer turned their head toward Zeph. He felt a tingle run through him. Then in a blink, they were there in front of him. They had not walked. They had just disappeared from where they had been and reappeared forty feet away. The woman, or what Zeph took to be a woman, was tiny in stature, barely reaching his chest, but her size bore no relation to the impact of her presence.

Zeph's heart thundered in his ears, his throat and mouth dry as the desert surface of Paxlosis. The woman's green-skinned hands and furrowed face glowed with strange symbols that moved beneath the surface of her skin. When her skeletal hands reached for him, Zeph felt his insides cringe, but there was nothing he could do but allow the trespass.

The old woman turned Zeph's body one-half turn, moving him out of range of the knife-wielding Taiban. Standing on tiptoe, she raised a hand to the level of Zeph's face and, using two fingers, pulled his lower lids down, looking deep into his eyes.

"I know you," a voice spoke inside Zeph's head. *The last time we met, you betrayed her. Will you do it again? I wonder, for you are not that same man, only connected by your past to him, as she is connected to the lives she lived before, and this time you have come in search of answers."* She paused, then released Zeph's eyelids. *"When you understand the questions, find me."*

As the woman backed away, Zeph's body began to shake, melting back into a human statue frozen in the marketplace.

The crowd began to move.

The Taiban's knife thrust came forward, missing contact-- Zeph was no longer there.

The Taiban stumbled, caught himself, and his friends laughed.

CHAPTER THIRTEEN

The Taibans turned around and began to saunter down the thoroughfare as if nothing had happened, the encounter entirely erased.

"What was that? What happened? Where did she go?" Zeph asked, finding his voice.

"Who?" Lucha asked, getting up off the ground.

"There was an old woman here, with white hair...," Zeph stuttered. "And lights under her skin."

"There is no one like that here," Pliny said quickly.

Was it too quick? Zeph spun around, focusing on the Mir.

"You know something. You saw something." Pliny looked flustered and cast his eyes down to the cobbled street.

He saw her. I'm sure of it, Zeph reassured himself. *And he knows who it was.* But even as the thought formed in his mind, the memory faded. Zeph was sure he had lost the thread of…something, but he could not find it, and then it was gone.

"What would you like to see next, Captain Yare?" Pliny smiled.

CHAPTER FOURTEEN

"What affects one world affects all worlds. What affects one spirit affects all spirits. This is the meaning of The Balance." (Attributed to Wei Tai: First Matriarch in the Book of the Rhune.)

A shadow dropped from the belly of the Lamdra's shuttle and held, crouched close to the ground.

When no one challenged him, he stood, brushed himself off, pulled the hood of his dark cape over his head, and casually removed his gloves. Folding them meticulously, he inserted them neatly into an unseen pocket inside the black coat partially hidden by the equally black cape.

On every world among The Thousand Worlds in the Paxlosian System, among those worlds officially recognized by the Shadowmasters Guild, a fabric was woven functionally. There were also places where the threads of that fabric had worn thin, making the world vulnerable.

The contractual agreement for which Spectre was accountable required him to identify the weak threads within the Lamdra mission and unravel them.

Spectre's position within the guild did not give him the freedom to inquire as to the reasoning behind his assignment. He understood that a constantly changing imbalance of power was in the Guild's interest.

On its face, his was an unusual assignment, surprisingly broad in scope, blatantly weighted against the United Front, and unaccountably lacking in detail. Spectre believed that beyond the goals of whoever requested the contract, allowing greater control to compound within the Yare family presented a threat to the Guild's influence. This hypothesis informed his previous decisions regarding actions to be taken during the Lamdra's voyage, ultimately leading to larger strategies Spectre foresaw based on undermining Zeph Yare's success.

CHAPTER FOURTEEN

With no data available on the Ebulonian city's layout, Spectre entered the city--turned right, then right again, building a grid in his mind. Always listening to the snatches of conversations he picked up building another kind of map, piecing together the challenges and weaknesses of this new world, and showing Spectre the way forward. Somewhere there was a key, a person who could be manipulated, pressed to renew an old grudge, or removed entirely, and this action would effectively destroy any chance of success the Lamdra mission had.

The Shadowmaster's skin color did not give him away in Little Taiba as it would among the green-skinned Ebulonians, but the Free Men and their families had their quirks--notably a penchant for color and the Shadowmaster's entirely black costume and unfamiliar face marked him as a stranger in the close-knit community, where strangers were shunned.

People turned their backs or stopped talking as he approached. They scowled and watched him until he passed out of earshot.

Disappointed but aware that he could not afford to miss being well settled on the shuttle before its crew returned, Spectre headed back toward the landing area.

Heated voices from a crowd blocking one of the intersections that adjoined the Taiban town square drew his interest, and feigning casual interest, he drew closer.

"The Ebulonians don't have the guts to fight, but *we* do," a young man shouted. "We should blow these intruders out of the sky!"

Bobalo told us to wait..." someone in the crowd protested.

"Bobalo is old and a coward, and he's making cowards of the rest of us!" the hot-tempered youngster berated them.

Interested, Spectre lingered at the rear of the crowd as a young Taiban woman pushed through to the center of the argument, two young Taiban men flanking her.

"Stop, Toval," she demanded. "Everyone understands your need to avenge your brother, but maligning the captain will not get you what you want. What would Heldis think?" the young woman tried to reason with the angry youth.

The young man bit his lip, but he was prideful, and there were many eyes on him.

"Heldis will understand, and if she does not, Corin, well, then it's better we know it now, " he declared defiantly.

"Old men in their rockers argue for peace," a cocky young woman with a shaved head supported the angry youth. "Bobalo should step down and get out of our way!"

There's a thread worth investigating. Spectre maneuvered for a better view.

"The only leadership the Free Men know, and trust is Tai Bobalo's," the other young man on the girl's right growled. "That is as true today as when he brought your families here."

The bald woman sneered. "Got a nice chunk of property for it too, didn't ya', Quinn? It looks to me like you Bobalos live pretty good here."

"Better than the rest of us," the young man Spectre heard speak first muttered.

The young fighter, Quinn, stepped toward the shaved-headed female, but his companion, Corin, stopped him.

"Careful, Quinn. We have enough trouble right now."

"*I'm* not causing trouble, Bobalo is," Quinn replied.

"Oh, come on, you all think it even if you don't say it," the shaved-headed female prodded the crowd. "You've lost the stomach for a fight, and this proves it."

"And who do you propose could take his place, Je'anna?" Quinn Bobalo countered. "The Ebulonians aren't going to listen to anyone else. No one else has their trust."

"They don't listen to him now!" someone shouted. Spectre could not see who.

"Free Taiban's trust is with their brothers and sisters, not outsiders." Je'anna thumped her fist against her chest. Others repeated the Free Man's gesture.

"My father *made* you Free Men," Quinn growled.

"No one means any dishonor to your family, Quinn." An older man joined the young people at the center of the crowd. "No one's forgotten what the captain did for us." He eyed the crowd sternly. Some looked embarrassed. More than a few left the square, muttering to those who, like them, were choosing to leave, but the stubborn and disillusioned stayed, their jaws clenched.

"Tai Bobalo is…"

CHAPTER FOURTEEN

"Je'anna, hold your tongue." The older man turned on her. "You're out of line."

"I don't give a damn about lines, and I don't give a damn about you, old fart," Je'anna shot back.

Quinn was on her in a blink, and sides were quickly taken through the scuffling of the dirt, making a dust storm that hid the action.

Spectre marked it all, making mental notes he could recall and review later to use in planning nuanced strategies.

He saw nothing that suggested the Taibans possessed the technology to challenge the Lamdra, but then he did not need the Taibans to win. He only needed them to disrupt the mission.

"Break it up! Break it up!" Two gray-haired fighters plowed into the fight, separating bodies left and right. The other old man helped them until two groups faced each other with the older men in between.

"Go home," one of the men shouted with an air of authority. "Some of you have a meeting you're expected at." With ink-stained fingers, he pointed to a shop sign that read "Crochin and son's cartographers."

Some of the young men began shuffling toward it, Quinn Bobalo among them. The older man stopped him.

"I'm going to ask you not to come in on this one, Quinn. They're not likely to speak freely if you're there, and we need to know what they're thinking."

Quinn nodded, walking away with Corin.

Spectre lingered, waiting for the crowd to disperse, then approached the cartographer's shop.

He listened for sounds within--and heard nothing. He tried the door, but it was locked. He peered through the front window. The main room of the shop was empty.

Walking around the side of the building, Spectre found an alley running alongside the "L" shaped structure. Boxes and crates were stacked high in the cobbled yard behind the building. The Shadowmaster did not see the Taiban Freedom fighter until the young man stepped in to block his path.

"What are you doing here?" the Taiban demanded.

Spectre spun around, hesitating only a split second while he considered the safest lie.

The fighter shook his head. "Too slow. Let's try again. Who you are, and who's your sponsor?"

"I'm nobody." Spectre's hand rolled a dart from his pocket into his hand. "I'm new--just arrived..."

The Taiban shook his head. " You're too old to have been in that bunch, so you didn't 'just arrive,' at least not on a Taiban ship." The man's eyes narrowed.

Spectre lurched forward. The Taiban fighter blocked his path, sweeping the Shadowmaster's legs with his. Spectre arched his body mid-air, throwing his weight backward and changing his trajectory. The impact of his full weight jammed through his arms from palm to shoulder, scraping the skin across the cobblestones. He bounced back to his feet. The Taiban's momentum brought him forward, spinning into the air to meet his opponent, and his foot hit the Shadowmaster's jaw. The dart fell from his hand, clattering across the cobblestones.

Both men froze as the glass vial bounced, then rolled under a stack of crates.

The Taiban's eyes locked on Spectre's. "Now, I am curious. What was that?"

Spectre leaped into the air, his legs shooting out to the side. Pushing himself off the crates, he ran horizontally across the wall, over his opponent's head, and back out the alley's entrance on the other side.

The Taiban pursued him.

Catapulting himself forward, the Free Man tackled Spectre before he made the corner. Pulling the Shadowmaster back into the alley, he punched Spectre in the kidneys. Spectre folded, moved with the movement, then rolled, prepping a second dart. Coming back up on his feet, he lunged forward and rammed it into the Free Man's chest.

"Corin..." the young man whispered as his eyes closed.

Terk waited until the stranger in black left, then came out from behind the stacked crates. Standing over Vale's body, he reached down and pulled the dart from the young fighter's chest.

"Dumb shit." He held the dart up to the light, checking to see if there was any poison left. Reaching down, he pulled a handkerchief from Vale's pocket and wrapped the dart in it. "Clem, you little weasel, get out here," he commanded as he placed the wrapped dart in his pocket.

The younger boy crept out from behind the crates.

"Is Vale dead?" He stared at the body.

"Yeah." Terk kicked the body. "Playing hero, again. We're lucky he didn't get us killed, too."

Clem closed his eyes and turned away, gagging.

"Come on. Let's get out of here before someone sees us."

"We should tell somebody, Terk. We should get help or something." The younger boy's eyes kept shifting to the body.

"Who do you want to tell, Clem? Vale's dead. No one can help him now. And what do you think we should say? 'We were hanging around your meeting, and we saw this guy.' Who's going to believe us, a couple of kids fresh from Taiba with a dead body and an unbelievable story about a mysterious stranger? No, we aren't going to tell anybody about this. What we're going to do is keep our mouths shut. Do you hear me? Shut."

"I heard you; mouth shut," the younger boy repeated woodenly.

"Good. Now, let's get out of here before someone sees us." Terk checked around the corner before slipping out of the alley.

Glancing back at Vale's body, Clem followed.

Dinner at the Bobalo compound was a strained affair. Corin helped Timee get the evening meal to the table, heavy with guilt at the knowledge that Heldis' dreams of a life with Toval would soon be crushed under the weight of grown-up politics.

Corin could see that what had happened was bothering Quinn as well. A fight in the marketplace between Bobalo's son and the last Turgista boy was prime ground for Little Taiba's gossip. It wouldn't take long for word to get around.

Corin was about to make an excuse to leave and meet Vale when Jaque Jacoby arrived at the door.

"Something to drink?" Bobalo retrieved a jug from the sideboard.

"I won't say no," Jacoby sat at the table, folding and unfolding his heavy-knuckled hands.

"How did the meeting at Crochin's go?"

Jacoby shook his head. "We're losing ground with these new men, Tai. Their answer to everything is violence. If someone doesn't agree, kill them. Crochin and I tried to explain that everything they want is possible, but it will take time, and they need to be patient. Bringing in so many at one time will be a problem."

"We always knew there was a risk," Bobalo agreed. "But what was the option? Leaving them to be killed? If the warlords got them, they were at risk that way as well."

"Children, go on now. Let the grown-ups talk." Timee shooed the girls from the table.

The girls obeyed, except Corin who remained, quietly beginning to clear the table.

Bobalo poured Jacoby a generous mug of wine, refilling his own, Quinn's, and Timee's. He paused, then filled one for Corin as well.

"Don't let it go to your head," he teased.

"You've heard what Toval said in the square?" Jacoby asked his friend.

"That was grief talking," Timee defended the boy. "Toval doesn't believe those things." The kitchen door opened, and Heldis walked in. She sat beside her cousin, unshed tears swimming in her blue eyes.

Someone told her. Probably one of her younger sisters. Corin took her cousin's hand and squeezed it. Heldis squeezed back. She might look frail, but she was a Bobalo, and they were made of strong stuff.

"I'd like to give Toval the benefit of the doubt," Quinn said. "Our families have known each other a long time." He glanced at Heldis. "But that new one, Je'anna Peru? I think she meant every word of what she said."

Jayque Jacoby nodded. "She's a hot head, never knows when to stop. She's Harlan's, so she's a second cousin or something, but what Crochin and I saw tonight was beyond the Turgistas. The calls for violent action have support."

"Free Men have differences," Bobalo tried to make little of the noise. "We work them out."

"These men are not your old comrades from the early days, Da," his son warned him. "They were so young when Taiba cut out their hearts that they don't know something's missing," Quinn complained. "They're twisted, inside and out."

CHAPTER FOURTEEN

"That's the warlord's work," Bobalo argued. "In time, they'll see that it's different here."

"Unless it's not, because they can make it the same," Quinn argued. "Taiba *is* the warlord's now, Da. There's nothing else left anymore. The world you, Jacoby, and Crochin knew is gone, and whatever loyalty you feel is missing in this new generation. I've fought alongside them. You and your friends chose to fight because you felt you had to make a better world. These people fight because they *like* to. They enjoy killing."

Bobalo put a hand on his son's arm. "I'm sorry your first mission was so hard," he apologized. "You were lucky, son. You grew up here, in safety. You had enough to eat, a roof over your head, a bed at night, your family and friends around you. Struggling to survive does things to people's minds, no question.

"It's true our crew are all older now, wiser, I hope, and more cautious, but I'm not sure we were any different back in the early days than these new Free Men and Women."

"Deep thinkers and gentle folk don't usually take to thieving and pirating," Jayque Jacoby said wryly. "There was this time when your father…"

"Don't start telling him old stories, Jayque," Bobalo stopped his friend. "I'll look like a hypocrite for always telling him to be good."

Quinn grinned. "It's too late for that." He tossed back his drink.

Timee stood. "Someone's coming." She paused. "Something's wrong."

"Who's on the gate?" Bobalo asked suddenly.

Quinn hesitated, thinking about that. "No one."

"That's the last time that happens," Bobalo stated.

"It's Ald," Timee announced just before the young fighter ran through the door.

"Quinn…Captain," Ald gasped for breath. "You need to come now. It's Vale. Someone killed Vale."

Corin's legs went out from under her.

E.F. Winters

CHAPTER FIFTEEN

Remembering their many lives, the Ballatynes looked differently at the present, turning away from having children of their own to become the mothers of worlds. (Explanation of the Ballatyne clan's near extinction in the decades following Abrana and Faed Ballatyne, the sisters' magical feats, reinforcing the Rhune trend not to bind to a mate or bear children.)

After their morning at Iredipa's market, Zeph, Lieutenant Lucha Boradice, and the accountant, Holder, spent the afternoon going from one reception to another.

"I think we've met every person in the city, some of them twice," Lucha groaned as Pliny led them through the palace's spacious corridors.

"I didn't see the Pira Eropa Rhune at any of the receptions," Zeph commented. "Why is that, Pliny?"

The diplomat looked uncomfortable. "The Pira's responsibilities are not … social."

"So, then what are they?" Lucha questioned the Mir.

Pliny blinked, then frowned, clearly confused by the question. "She is the Pira."

"Well, that explains it perfectly," Lucha muttered. "There are plenty of interested females, Zeph. You should stop obsessing over the one who is not."

"I'm not obsessing," Zeph defended himself. "Merely being polite."

Pliny stopped in front of yet another door.

"Here we go," Lucha groaned. "I feel like the main attraction at a spectator sport." The Paxlosians steeled themselves for yet another entrance into another gathering of strangers determined to meet them and discover what they could get from the relationship.

Pliny opened the door, revealing an empty and spacious suite.

"Your rooms." The Mir made a grand gesture that encompassed the rooms. "Dakmira-Keesch thought you might like to rest and refresh yourselves in private after such a very long, public day. She and the Mahal apologize for the grueling afternoon, but once the clans began announcing these gatherings in your honor, there was no way to avoid attending without giving offense."

"I understand. Some things are the same on every world," Zeph said wryly.

The suite had a high ceiling, marble floors, large glass doors that opened to the palace's lush inner gardens, a sunken pool steaming with hot water in the next room, and an elegant table set for three.

Lucha removed the cover from one of the dishes, releasing a tantalizing aroma. He picked up a fork and began to sample the dishes.

Though an incredible amount of food had been showcased at the clan receptions, Zeph and his friends practiced caution, understanding the possible consequences of unfamiliar, rich foods and strange microbes on their digestive systems--and though none of them would have said they were hungry--the lure of the aromatic food was now too much to resist.

"Please, thank the lady for her thoughtfulness," Zeph replied.

"There are private quarters for each of you in the event you wish to rest before you eat and bathe." Pliny indicated a hallway leading off to the left. He turned and addressed Holder and Lucha specifically. "Someone will return you gentlemen to your shuttle whenever you are ready."

Lucha frowned. "Return us? What about him?" He looked at Zeph.

"I believe Captain Yare and the Mahal arranged to meet after dinner to continue their discussion. The captain will join your party later. Please, make yourselves comfortable." Pliny backed out, closing the doors behind him.

Lucha crossed the room and reopened them.

Two palace guards stood at attention just outside.

"Do you need something, sir?" one of them asked in a heavily accented Common.

"No, we're fine." Lucha closed the door. "I'm not leaving you here alone, Zeph," he announced.

"You worry for nothing, Lucha."

"That's what you always say, just before you get us into trouble," his friend countered.

Holder sat down at the table and began exploring the fare.

"Try this one." Lucha served the accountant a portion from the first dish he had sampled.

Zeph joined them.

"It seems like all the dishes I liked most today are here on the table." The observation seemed odd and a little unsettling.

"Real food." Holder smacked his lips before drinking from his water glass. "Clean water, lots of space. You could put fifteen families in this room." He made a circle with his fork, indicating the high ceiling and generous size of the room. "And would have back on Pax."

"Maybe, but I wouldn't want to defend it," Lucha added around a mouthful. "The security here would be a nightmare." He indicated the open glass doors and the floor-to-ceiling windows, all open to let in the fresh ocean breeze coming off the Silver Sea.

"It would cost a fortune, no question," Holder agreed. "I think I'll invest in a security company when we return."

"But you don't have to worry about that here," Zeph pointed out. "That's the charm. Ebulon isn't like Paxlosis or any of the Thousand Worlds. It's peaceful and safe and..."

"Abundant?" Lucha suggested.

"Yes, that too," Zeph agreed.

"Give it twenty or thirty years. You won't recognize the place," Holder cautioned, always ready with the downside of anything. "But it does look like we're going to be very wealthy men. How long did you say it would take us to get back to Paxlosis, Yare?"

"I didn't."

The accountant chuckled at the young captain's refusal to reply. "Come now, surely you don't think the Consortium is going to be satisfied with trinkets and textiles when they hear about all of this, do you? I thought you got this assignment because you were Morladja Yare's son."

Zeph bristled. "I got the assignment because I was the best man for the job."

"Of course. Of course." Holder's smile was condescending. "But anyone who can afford passage to Ebulon is not going to want to leave, and that will change things. Don't worry, Yare, you'll be rich enough to buy whatever piece of paradise you want, including that long-necked girl you're so interested in--as long as your mother doesn't get wind of it. I can't imagine Morladja Yare approving of a bunch of green-skinned bastard brats claiming the Yare name."

"Excuse me." Zeph rose from the table. "I think I've had enough." He stomped out into the palace gardens.

Tai Bobalo, Jayque Jacoby, Ald, and Quinn slowed as they neared the north end of The District's square, approaching Crochin and Son's. Woald Turgista was stepping down from a stack of boxes that had become an impromptu stage.

Ochre smudges of light-cast by the Free Men's torches--lit the dark side streets as people entering from different parts of Little Taiba met, mingled, and came together.

"There are more here now than when I came to fetch you," Ald reported.

Jayque Jacoby eyed the crowd. "Yes, but how many are here because they agree with the Turgista, and how many are here for the entertainment?"

"Petre Turgista made the same oath the rest of us did," Quinn said darkly. "The same oath that a thousand other Free Men have made. His life was no more valuable than theirs."

"All dead sons are heroes," Jacoby repeated the adage.

Je'anna Peru jumped up onto the boxes that Woald had just vacated.

"You've heard from the grieving family. You know what they ask," she shouted. "Revenge!"

The crowd surged toward the landing docks, echoing her rallying cry: "Revenge! Revenge!"

"This is not good." Bobalo and his friends began to run into the crowd.

It was twilight, and Ebulon's early moons graced the sky, hanging like colored lanterns in the twilight, casting the magic of their pastel glow over the already beautiful gardens and transforming them into something Zeph had no vocabulary to describe.

He strolled along the paths, taking long, deep breaths saturated with the scent of flowers and spices, leaves, and dirt. A few times, he heard footsteps passing on the other side of a hedge, but no one approached. He basked in solitude as he might have basked in the steaming bath in the suite the Mahal's consort had arranged for them.

How long has it been since I was alone with nothing between me and a real sky? Zeph pondered. *Since we were living on Adairis before Father died,* he didn't think often of his childhood on his father's hunting moon. The memories were too painful.

Coming around the corner of a hedge--the garden path swelled into a circular courtyard. A large, wide-branching tree grew at its center.

Someone was circling it in slow, deliberate movements. A cascade of dark red hair whipped through the air as Eropa Rhune spun and reversed direction. Placing one foot in front of the other on the ground--in a most precise fashion--she extended the slender sword in her hand toward the tree.

Zeph stepped back behind the cover of the hedge, watching from where he would not be seen.

The young woman whirled, cutting high then low, slicing the night air. The sword blade sang.

So, not entirely peaceful, it seems. Zeph continued to observe. *This is a dangerous woman,* an inner voice warned. *Any reasonable man would walk away.*

"But then, I have never been a reasonable man," he muttered to himself. He frowned. Something moved beneath the Pira's skin, glowing designs like archaic symbols made of light. He could not think where he had seen the designs before, but they seemed familiar.

The colored beams from Ebulon's moons seemed to fold into Eropa's silk robes as they whipped and whirled around her, flying out and striking the air like lightning bolts. The faster her movements, the brighter the glow beneath her skin became, the sword in her hand mirroring the increased intensity until it looked as though she wielded blue flame, slicing the air here... then there.

Stars scattered in the Rhune's wake, tiny worlds pulsing in and out of existence, all in thrall to the Rhune's presence.

CHAPTER FIFTEEN

"Who are you?" Zeph asked silently, fear and excitement dancing together in his belly. *"What kind of being gathers universes and dances with stars?"*

Time warped as he watched, lost in awe, his senses suspended and numb to the reality around him. Yet inside, he felt alive in a way he could not remember since first experiencing the wonders of a natural world on Adairia when a bee gently landed on his hand, and he felt the hum and buzz of its wings.

Zeph shook his head and looked around as if waking up.

The Pira stood before him, her green-eyed gaze fixed on him.

He cleared his throat. "You're the Pira Eropa Rhune, right? We've met before."

"Yes, Captain Yare. We have," the young woman's voice slipped over his senses like silk.

"Call me Zeph." His voice was low and throaty. Her face washed in the pastel moonlight--he could see how young the Pira was, something he had not recognized before. He stepped toward her, their shadows merged, and he calculated the wisdom of stealing a kiss.

"That would not be proper," the Pira informed him, taking a step back. "After all, you are the captain of a great starship, while I am merely an alien. It is hardly the recipe for a friendship."

"So, we are to be friends then?" Zeph smiled, trying for charming with a hint of suggestion that there might be something more.

"History may not yet have decided if we are to be enemies, but we are most certainly not friends," she replied curtly. The glow beneath her skin faded, leaving them in the last, deep, blue fade of twilight.

He took her hands. "We could change that... spend some time together... get to know each other better."

The Pira pulled her hands from his as a palace guard approached.

"Captain Yare, the Mahal requests you join him in his study immediately." A half dozen more guards filled in the space behind the first.

"What have you done?" the Pira hissed.

"Zeph." Zeph turned as Lucha joined the group.

"What happened?" he demanded of his friend. "I leave you for twenty minutes..."

"It wasn't *me,*" Lucha protested. "I wasn't the one out here in the moonlight romancing their Pira," his friend scolded.

Zeph turned back to Eropa, but she was gone.

Pliny pressed to the front of the Ebulonians. "Ah, good. You see, Lieutenant Boradice, your captain is fine. Now, please, come with me. We must move quickly if we are to reach your shuttle in time."

"In time for what?" Lucha demanded as the guards surrounded him. His hand moved to his holster before remembering his weapons were left on the shuttle.

"I will explain as we walk. Mister Holder is on his way and will meet us at the shuttle. Captain Yare, the Mahal is waiting for you."

"I'm going, but he's not?" Lucha planted his feet, his arms crossed over his chest. "I'm not going anywhere without Zeph."

"I am sorry, Lieutenant, but I must insist," Pliny stood firm. "Captain Yare will be perfectly safe here in the palace."

"Great, then we can be perfectly safe together," Lucha dug in his heels.

"You do not seem to understand," Pliny blurted. "Every moment you delay increases the risk your shuttle and weapons could be taken from the landing docks."

"Taken? By whom? Explain yourself, Pliny," Zeph commanded.

"The Taibans hold you and your men responsible for the deaths of their comrades. They are bent on revenge, and right now, there is a large group of them moving toward the landing fields. We have sent additional guards, but if there are too many Taibans--they may be overwhelmed."

"I thought the Taibans were your allies? Nikodamus assured me that you had them under control," Zeph said stiff-jawed.

Pliny cleared his throat. "I cannot say more, Captain Yare. This is a discussion for you and the Mahal."

"Go on, Lucha. Make sure that Holder and the others get back to the ship safely," Zeph decided. "I'll speak with Nikodamus and send for a shuttle once we've straightened things out."

Lucha nodded. "Watch yourself, Zeph." He allowed Pliny and the guards to lead him away.

CHAPTER SIXTEEN

"Trust is built layer upon layer and lost in a single falsehood. (Anonymous Taiban phrase.)

Clemmet's head ached, and his stomach felt like it was eating itself.

When Quinn Bobalo's team first approached Clemmet on the streets of Taiba, they promised they could take him someplace safe, but that had been a lie. There were no safe places. The proof was Vale was dead.

Terk's insistence that they not tell what they saw in the alleyway behind Crochin's made no sense. It was out of character for Terk to avoid taking credit for anything, and something like discovering Vale's murderer would seem like an opportunity to the older boy. Why was he insisting on secrecy? What was Terk so worried about? What they were doing in the alleyway wasn't wrong. It was just a game they played back on Taiba, seeing which one could find the most secret way into a building.

Clemmet lay on his back under a vessel used to tow the engineless pods catapulted into space in Ebulon's direction from the farthest outpost in The String and picked up when they got close.

He liked the landing docks. He liked the things mechanics talked about: gears and engines and the inner workings of mechanical devices. He liked that the men at the landing area listened to his questions and answered them thoughtfully. They even listened to his ideas for improvements when he had them. Here, he didn't feel dismissed because of his age. Here, the worlds of science and mechanics, theory and practicality met. It was a stable, reliable world where broken things could be fixed and re-made into something better. It was comfortable here, and working with his hands helped calm Clemmet's nerves.

Looking up into the tow's underside, Clem adjusted the work lamp Loosey Humqualt had provided so they could see up into the insides of the ship.

CHAPTER SIXTEEN

Loosey Humqualt; imagine, Clem thought to himself. Screwloose "Loosey" Humqualt was a legend from the Free Men's early days, a self-educated mechanic, inventor, and sometime engineer. It had been his idea to use the tow and pod system to bridge the gap between the outer moons in The String and Ebulon, making travel between Ebulon and the Taiban Cluster possible. The journey remained risky, but the pod and "catch" system enabled the Taibans to build lives on Ebulon while continuing to support the resistance to the Taiban warlords.

Clem heard voices shouting and footsteps approaching fast. He peeked out from beneath the tow and saw a group of palace guards rushing a Paxlosian man onto a nearby ship.

"Get us in the air," the alien officer ordered.

"Where's the captain?"

"He's staying on the planet for now," came the brusque reply. "We're ordered to return to the Lamdra immediately."

Commotion at the gate drew Clemmet's attention. Taibans were running across the field toward the same Paxlosian shuttle.

"Go now!" the leader of the palace guards shouted, pushing the man inside as his fellow guards positioned themselves to protect the alien ship.

The shuttle's door began to close, and Clemmet wondered how it would take off with the palace guard all around it. The shuttle's engines had a soft, low hum, not the high screech of metal parts being forced to move synchronously at a speed that would wear them through.

"They're murderers! Stop them!" The Taiban mob pushed at the palace guard's perimeter. The shuttle shot straight up into the air, hovered, then disappeared into the night sky.

A few Taibans split off, making for small vessels, but most just stared at the spot in the sky where the Paxlosian shuttle had vanished.

"They may have got away for now, but they'll be back, and we should be ready," one in the group said.

"Ready to kill them," another added. It was not a loud statement, but Clem was close enough to hear.

Tai Bobalo's big friend, Block, arrived, leaping onto the wing of the tow that Clem was under. The big man's steps against the metal sounded like thunder.

Clem scrambled out the opposite side.

"What do you think you're doing?" Block roared at his fellow Taibans. "The captain gave his word we would not take things into our own hands. He gave his word...*our* word!"

"Go back to your nap, old man," a youth heckled.

Clem craned his head to see who had spoken so rudely. The youth's head was shaved in the style of a Free Man fighter, but Clemmet knew him. He was not old enough to have gone to Taiba yet.

"No one cares what you old farts think." The youth smirked.

The man beside the kid turned and punched him, laying the kid out flat.

"Show some respect," he growled. "Block here was fighting for this movement before your ma was old enough to bleed. Free Men can speak their minds, but we respect our elders."

"Say what you want about me," Block drew everyone's attention back to him. "I don't care. But I'll take down any man that says a word against Tai Bobalo. The only reason most of us aren't dead on Taiba is because he hunted us down, got us cleaned up, and insisted we could build better lives. But for that to happen, oaths had to be given, loyalties promised."

"Yeah? And how many more of our boys have to die before Bobalo does something about it?" someone in the back of the crowd shouted.

"Who said that?" Block's eyes ran over the crowd. "What fucking idiot said that?" No one moved.

"Come on then. Let's go for it." Je'anna Peru pushed her way forward. "Get down here, Block, ya' big ass kiss."

"Stop, Je'anna." Her friends tried to pull her back. "Don't act crazy. You can't fight Block. He's five times your size."

"The Free Men demand justice for the death of one of their own!" Je'anna shouted. "The Paxlosians have to pay!"

"Justice!" the crowd repeated, cheering.

They blame the Paxlosians for Vale's murder. Clem realized. The man in black might have been Taiban or Paxlosian, but Clem knew which he believed the man was. *We should have said what we saw.* Once again, Clem questioned Terk's reasoning and motivation.

"An idiot in command sends his men into a fight unprepared and gets them killed. Those of us who are still alive after twenty-five years of fighting know who kept us alive," Block declared.

CHAPTER SIXTEEN

"Oh, for the God's sake, will you shut up already about all the years you old guys fought together?" Je'anna complained. "I'm sick of hearing it. No one cares about back *then*. We want to know what you're going to do *now*?"

"Have you got something to prove, Je'anna, or are you just so messed up inside that you need to slide a knife into someone to feel alive?" Block goaded the young fighter. There was no reply. "That's what I thought." He spit on the ground. "Go fuck yourself. Some of us have been fighting all this time because we were trying to do something that matters—make a better world. You just fight because you want to kill something."

Shouted arguments agreed with Block's statement. Then, the crush of bodies parted, and the crowd went silent.

Tai Bobalo had arrived.

A general in all but name, Tai Bobalo, had forged a revolution out of a bunch of barroom boasters, cutthroats, and pirates, giving them hope for a better future. There was a reason he was the unofficial voice of the Taiban refugees. For a quarter century he had been recognized as the movement's de facto leader.

He jumped effortlessly up onto the bow beside his friend, the bells on his braids jingling.

"Justice will come," Bobalo's throaty baritone sang out. "The laws of the Free Men and the laws of Ebulon demand it. But revenge? That was never part of the agreement. Oh, we thought about it a lot in the early days. We were filled with anger for the lives of our friends and our families. Like you, we were angry about what they took from us, angry over the injustice of our meager lives. So, we stole from the warlords, took their ships, their cargo, sometimes lives--anything to hurt them back. They branded us 'pirates', and we wore the title proudly, but then the bairns began to come, and we started thinking about what we were doing. We could never hurt them enough to make up for what they had taken. We had to stop them from taking it, not just from us but from all Taibans. We decided we wanted more than a drunken brag told twenty years later. We wanted our freedom back...freedom for us and our children. Freedom became our new treasure."

Clem listened to the history--his history, and it made his chest swell with pride. These were his people.

"Some of you have enjoyed this treasure long enough to know its value," Bobalo went on, "You've grown businesses, homes, families--things we never dreamed possible when we started. Others of you are too new yet and don't understand the cost or the value of a Free Man's true treasure. I'm not here to tell you what to think or how to live. I'm no warlord. I'm not a lord of any kind. I'm just the guy who got here first and talked the Ebulonians into letting me bring others like me, promising them that we'd be good citizens who would add our talents to their world, not cause trouble or take away from the quality of their lives. Loosey engineered the pods and the tow system. Maybe he should be up here."

"You're doing fine, Tai," a nasal tenor sang out from the back of the crowd.

"I never tried to set myself up as any kind of an authority here. I'm a ship's captain, that's all. But when more folk started asking to come here with their families and wanted to join us in our fight, we decided that we needed oaths to keep our secret so we could all be safe. You all took that oath, not to me. You made it to everyone here and many more back on Taiba. Without them and the trust we put in one another, we're just refugees squatting on a world that doesn't much want us.

"Now I hear that some of you are thinking about breaking those oaths." Bobalo shook his head, and the bells tinkled. "I don't know what that means for Little Taiba, or for those back in the Cluster, or for the outposts in The String. Truth to tell, I don't even know how to go forward in a world where our oaths are meaningless. How can we build anything, a revolution, a team, or a building on a 'maybe'? 'Maybe' I'll meet you at the appointed time and place. 'Maybe' I'll bring the weapons I agreed to bring. 'Maybe' I've given you the right information about the safe house. 'Maybe' I'll have your back when we're attacked." Bobalo's dark eyes pierced his audience. "I can't trust a *maybe*. I'm not interested in sticking my neck out for someone who doesn't have the character to hold to their word: someone who isn't committed to following through with what we all agreed to do together. We held up our end, me and Loosey, and Jayque and Crochin. We made a safe place and brought you here."

Clem's eyes teared up.

CHAPTER SIXTEEN

That's what Terk wants me to do: break my promise. And wasn't not speaking up as bad as saying something you shouldn't?

"But we let these oath breakers in." Bobalo's face reflected both regret and acceptance of a harsh reality. "And now we can't just ship them back to Taiba. If they're willing to break their oath while living here where they're safe, what will they do once they're back in The Cluster where your next breath can be a negotiation? Some of these oath-breakers are among us now. They might be standing next to you. The hard truth is they're a part of us, even if they aren't true to us.

"Some of you have ideas about how we should go forward. Good. Come to the next community meeting and share them. That's what meetings are for. That's what Free Men and Women do. You think that Jacoby, Crochin, and I are getting too old to lead this community? We feel it. Our bones cause us pain every day, and when they don't nearly cripple us, our memories do. We've seen more death than any man should--a lot of death faces have come and gone. So, we don't disagree. We want to see new leadership coming up, but where will come from? You.

"So, when you're looking around, wondering who the oath breakers are, I want you to also think about who the next leaders among you might be. Maybe one of them will figure out how we should deal with those who would break faith with our cause but whom we can't trust to leave. Maybe one of you will come up with a way to get the Ebulonians to treat us better or figure out how to get these aliens to see us as something more than refugees on a planet that's not theirs. I hope so because I do not have all the answers." He walked to the edge of the wing and jumped down.

Toval Turgista walked forward until he faced the aging captain.

"We just need to know that you're going to do *something,* Captain." His voice quavered with emotion, but he was determined to be heard.

"Look around, son. My record of *doing things* is all around you." Bobalo gestured toward Little Taiba. "You were born here in my dream. You and your brothers grew up in it, and every time we lose one of you, a piece of my dream dies with them."

"You are our captain, Tai, in the air or on land," Harlan Turgista thrust his hand at Bobalo. They clasped forearms. "Steel to the heart;

I stand by my oath." Harlan thumped his chest, touching the hilt of his knife with the other hand.

"Steel to the heart," Bobalo and Block repeated both phrase and motion.

"Steel to the heart," Clem echoed along with most of the crowd.

"Gods, all this talking has made me thirsty." Block broke the mood, joining Bobalo on the ground. Loosey and a few older men sauntered up to join them. As the crowd broke up, they headed for the pub across the way. It had a picture of a metal heart on it with the words: "The Hard Pumper Pub" scrawled in a rough hand below.

I should tell them. I should tell them now. Clem started to follow. A hand gripped his shoulder.

"Where are you going, kid?" Terk's eyes were hard, little slits in his ferret-thin face.

"Nowhere," Clem lied, glancing after Bobalo and the others.

E.F. Winters

CHAPTER SEVENTEEN

"Illuminating the way was a beginning, but the people needed to be able to find their path even in darkness." (A History of the Rhunes; compiled in the Second Age.)

Zeph and Pliny entered the Mahal's audience chamber, accompanied by a pair of palace guards. The room was not nearly so grand in scale as the Glass Hall where the reception was held, but it still impressed. The pieced-together red, stonework floor was not perfectly even, the irregular shape of the pieces lacked the precise craftsmanship evident in the larger hall. The red-brown, fluted columns that held up the ceiling were scarred by time and scorched at their bases by fire. The indigo ceiling was painted to look like the night sky with crystals embedded in the plaster representing stars. The rougher nature of the architecture and craftsmanship showed in the imperfect outline of the narrow windows, each slightly different as if the artist had been experimenting as the project progressed.

The thick panes of green glass--held in the deeply recessed window casements--had many bubbles and inclusions, though they presented a certain fantasy element and rustic charm, the flaws left no question as to the level of skill of their artisan.

The Mahal sat at a round table where a dozen or more might be seated. A single bald man in deep green robes held him in earnest conversation while a few Voices, recognizable for their gray robes, mingled among courtiers in jewel-colored garb. Though the clans had feted Zeph throughout the day, not one spoke to him now. Neither would they meet his eyes.

"What's going on?" Zeph asked Pliny quietly.

The Mir cleared his throat. "I cannot say."

Zeph frowned at the obvious evasion. "You cannot or you will not? Please be clear."

"I, too, can see something has changed in the courtier's attitude toward you, but I have been with you and your people all day, Captain Yare, and I assure you, I understand the reason for this change in behavior no better than you. I suggest we practice patience and wait for the Mahal's explanation."

Nikodamus continued speaking in hushed tones to the green-clad Ebulonian. The man turned, marking Zeph's curious examination of him. Beneath the calf-length tunic were full-cut pants, cloth-wrapped leggings, and obviously handmade woven sandals. Seeing the man's face, Zeph decided it was unlikely he was naturally bald, but instead, his head was shaved smooth--not only his head but all facial hair, including his eyebrows. A high forehead sloped unbroken to a nose which was hooked slightly at the tip. The entire surface of his skin was etched in elaborate art imitating tree bark. Vines climbed up from beneath the neckline of the green tunic to encircle the hairless man's neck, looping over his left ear before branching out across the face and skull, scrolling over the textured bark design.

The tattooed man turned back to Nikodamus, offered a subtle obeisance, then glided rather than walked toward the door. Not a whisper of cloth--not the pad of a single footfall accompanied him.

Zeph thought of the inner spring of an old watch his father's gamekeeper, Hazzlebutt, had shown him the spring wound so tight the moment the old servant let it go, the energy contained within it exploded out of its wound state.

"You see what happens if we wind it tightly and then release it?" Hazzle had explained. He began to re-wind the mechanism. "But if we control that unwinding...." This time he did not release the gadget but inserted a small screw, holding the wheel-wound strip of metal in place. "It powers the watch to work as it does."

Every person in the room watched the vine-decorated man as he exited through the doors.

"Who is that?" Zeph asked.

"That is Master Pranseas Mir, the head Monk of the Aum Lung Temple," Pliny explained.

"A Mir monk?" Zeph asked, surprised.

"There are many sects of Mirs," Pliny replied. "A select group represents an order of monks practicing the old traditions. They rarely come among us here in the outer world."

"I thought Mir's were a scientific society," Zeph said.

"The Art is the first science, a science of nature. Its precepts are the foundation of our earliest culture and the base upon which most

Mir sciences were built. Come, Nikodamus is ready for us." Pliny led the Paxlosian forward.

The Mahal studied Zeph for a long time—so long that Zeph began to feel uncomfortable.

"I am finished for the day, Captain Ochette. Let those who are waiting know that I will hear no more petitions today," the Mahal directed the captain of his guard. "Thank you, Pliny. I will take custody of Captain Yare now," Nikodamus indicated that the diplomat should leave as well. Pliny inclined his head toward the Mahal, then Zeph before exiting, his footsteps echoing from wall to wall, and floor to ceiling, in clear contrast to the Mir monk's silence.

"Mir monks," Zeph muttered, shaking his head.

"You seem surprised," Nikodamus suggested.

"I've never known a man who claimed knowledge of a god to be so fit." Zeph chuckled.

The Mahal did not smile. "It would not occur to them to claim such a thing. Their order has nothing to do with old notions of gods or any power greater than what a person of commitment may attain." The Mahal shook his head. "There is much about us you do not understand, and words alone will not be enough to change your understanding." He sighed. "We will retire to my study." He rose, going out a small side door, leaving Zeph no choice but to follow.

Nikodamus led Zeph down a series of corridors before entering an unremarkable service entry that came out in the Mahal's study.

"You may make yourself comfortable, Captain." Nikodamus gestured to the chair he sat in the night before.

"I think I'll stand for now. I'm not sure I'll be staying long. Do you want to tell me what's happened, or am I supposed to guess?"

The Mahal crossed to the fireplace, gazing into the red-orange flames.

"A few hours ago, a young Taiban Free Man was found dead in an alley in The District." Nikodamus turned from the fire's glow, throwing his face into shadow. "What can you tell me about this, Captain?"

"Nothing. This is the first I've heard of it, and I don't see what's it got to do with me, my men, or the safety of my shuttle."

"Murders are not common on Ebulon," Nikodamus replied.

"If you are inferring that my people had something to do with this, my people and I have been escorted or under guard the entire time we've been on this planet," Zeph pointed out defensively.

"No quiet reconnaissance missions, no secret fact-finding infiltrations among the locals? Come now, Captain." Nikodamus gave Zeph a knowing look. "I am not so naïve as to think that you have not engaged in some kind of intelligence-gathering effort."

Zeph shook his head slowly. "My people are accounted for, either aboard the Lamdra, waiting at the shuttle, or with me, just as you requested, Mahal."

"I would like to believe that, Captain, just as I too would like to believe our discussions have been honest, laying a foundation of trust between us, but in the two days since you arrived, there have been three violent deaths. People are demanding that someone be held accountable."

"By people, you mean the Taibans?" Zeph clarified.

"Yes." Nikodamus nodded.

"Do you understand the nature of these people you host?" Zeph asked, inferring that Nikodamus did not. "Because I've seen their world. They are violent, waging a desperate underground war on the despots that reign over them."

"You have viewed them from afar. It is unfair for you to judge. The Taibans fight for their future—for their freedom. This has forced them to be violent, but they are not violent by nature. They are like you and I, doing what must be done to preserve their race. You do not know them at all," Nikodamus challenged him.

Zeph shrugged. "Maybe not, but I think more of your people think like I do than like you, and they're not going to risk their safety and prosperity over a bunch of Taiban hotheads. It's not in their interests."

Nikodamus bristled. "A life is not disposable."

"The first two Taibans you held to our account opened fire on *us,*" Zeph reminded the Mahal. "That's not an act of diplomacy."

"Neither is murder," Nikodamus stood his ground.

"Our hands are clean."

Nikodamus studied Zeph. "We will see. The Mirs are analyzing the toxin that killed the latest victim. If the substance is unfamiliar to us, the conclusion will be that it is of Paxlosian origin. If it is, the

Taibans will demand justice." Nikodamus paused. "You seem unconcerned, Captain."

"The Lamdra is a starship: the first of its kind, a technological marvel. Anything the Taibans could do would be a flea bite."

"You are both our guests," Nikodamus reminded Zeph.

"And hopefully, they will act like guests," Zeph countered.

"And will you?" Nikodamus demanded. Zeph did not answer, staring down the Ebulonian leader.

"We've done nothing wrong," he said finally.

"If this murder is indeed not you or of your making, then who could be responsible? Is there another power at work here that you have not identified, Captain Yare?" the Mahal suggested. "Someone who would benefit from your mission's failure?" Nikodamus walked to the sideboard and chose a thick amber liquor, pouring a portion into two goblets. He offered one of the goblets to Zeph. Zeph hesitated, then tossed the contents back while Nikodamus sipped his, considering the list. It was a long one—somewhat shorter when you reduced it for those who had the resources to affect an outcome so far from Paxlosis. The Consortium had spies among the Lamdra's crew, but, as he had said, his crew's movements were accounted for. Zeph's mother had many enemies, some of them were--no doubt--also her colleagues: people of means who would be uncomfortable with the added power that Zeph's mission's success would bring the family. Most of these colleagues, however, were heavily invested in the mission and stood to profit handsomely from its success. Working against themselves seemed unlikely, no matter how much they disliked Morladja Yare.

"I cannot think of anyone," he admitted.

Nikodamus walked to his desk and picked up the treaty.

"I have read the document you sent. I do not think the supporters of your mission have an interest in a treaty. They talk of allies as if they were vassals. It is the height of hubris to assume that in every conflict you will prevail."

Zeph shrugged. "They're confident in the Lamdra and its captain, but you're right, a treaty would probably not be their first choice. But then they are not here. They can't see what I've seen. I'm confident once they understand what Ebulon has to offer, they'll come around, but we must hold to the letter of their requirements."

CHAPTER SEVENTEEN

"We speak with certainty in public, then pray in private that the future will not make us liars," the older man said as if reciting the source of some old Ebulonian wisdom. "But the truth is, neither of us can make a promise, and know with certainty it will be kept by others. What we do here, Captain, you and I, is an act of faith; faith in those we represent, but most of all, the faith we place in each other."

Zeph looked away. As the captain of the Lamdra, he spoke for Morldaja, the Consortium, the Presidium of the United Front, and his government; people he did not agree with or admire, people he did not trust. But he had accepted this mission and agreed to act for them.

I asked for this treaty and therefore this ridiculous marriage, he reminded himself, *because it was the only way to get what I wanted, my captainship.*

"This is our best option," he assured the Mahal, feeling exposed under the Mahal's intense study.

If he brought back enough marketable goods, his share of the profits would allow him to cut ties with Morladja. He could become his own person; a power in his own right; able to make the changes he saw were needed beneath the Dome. But to do this, he needed the power the mission's success would give him.

"And these people in this Consortium, they truly believe a marriage between families is needed to seal such an agreement?" Nikodamus asked.

Zeph grimaced. His mother made certain he would not take this path lightly, requiring he be bound by any agreement he sought with allies. Several purposes were accomplished by this: it consolidated the Yare family's control over the trade attached to the agreement and it meant Zeph would never have a wife who would supplant her power over him. It was a master gesture on the part of the manipulative woman. A political treaty bride would never hold Zeph's affections, but he would be obligated to uphold and abide by the arrangement to protect his financial interests.

Zeph walked to the sideboard, filled his glass, and began to drink it, more slowly this time. He let the warm, velvety liquid slide down his throat. "This is very good. What do you call it?"

"Ver'cout. I will send a barrel back to your ship with you. There is something that puzzles me, Captain. Why you? If this marriage is meant to create an alliance between our two worlds, why--and I mean no insult, but why designate a mere ship's captain? Should not our bride be marrying someone of higher status?"

Zeph cleared his throat. "The Consortium prefers to keep things in the family," he explained a bit embarrassed.

"I understand. You promise to look out for their interests, and they give you a starship."

Zeph scowled. "No one *gave* me anything."

"No, of course not, you earned it I am sure, but it does help explain things."

"The union of two powerful families is a common practice among The Thousand Worlds," Zeph tried to shrug off the broader implications of the stipulation.

"It is barbaric," Nikodamus stated flatly.

"*War* is barbaric," Zeph corrected. "A peaceful, political solution reinforced by the union of two powerful families is a civilized compromise. The woman will be well treated, I promise you." He avoided going so far as to promise that she would be happy. "Whatever personal reservations you have, I suggest you set them aside. I'm not looking forward to being married to a stranger either, but if it's what I have to do to make this happen, I'll do it. You said the Voices need to agree, Nikodamus. Ultimately, this accomplishes what we both want: your people remain autonomous, mine get access to your resources."

"You must have wanted this command very badly to have agreed to bind your future to someone you do not know, someone you might never care for," Nikodamus mused, swirling the ver'coute in his glass. "Forgive me, Captain. I am assuming life partner commitments are based on affection in your culture."

"It happens," Zeph agreed. "Not so often among families where there are dynastic considerations."

"The need for intimacy is found outside these political partnerships?"

Zeph chuckled, "Oh yes."

"This gives me much to think on," the Mahal said, moving to the window.

The aura around Ebulon's colored moons reached out toward each other across the dark velvet sky, barely blending at their farthest

CHAPTER SEVENTEEN

reaches. It was beautiful, but also sad, like lovers who could see each other but never touch.

"I think it would be best if you are not seen in the city for a few days, Zeph." It was the first time the Mahal had called him by his given name. "We need to give the situation and the Taiban's emotions time to cool down a bit."

"I'll have a shuttle sent down to take me back," Zeph agreed.

"I have a different proposal," Nikodamus suggested. "The annual Festival of Lights begins tomorrow in Auhora Whimlan, a glass city floating on a lake lit by millions of lights: it is a wondrous sight. The journey will give you a chance to see more of our beautiful planet and its many resources, as you like to call them. The Pira Eropa Rhune is going. I will arrange to have her meet you there, and she can be your guide."

Zeph was going to beg off, but as soon as the Mahal mentioned the Pira, he found himself agreeing.

"Great. That sounds great."

"Then it is settled." Nikodamus walked Zeph to the door and opened it. Frevin Mir waited outside with the palace guard.

"Ah, there you are, Frevin," Nikodamus greeted him. "Thank you for coming. I am afraid there is a last-minute change of plans for tomorrow. I am asking the Pira to act as Captain Yare's guide to the festival."

The Mir's face remained a polite mask. "We will be honored to have his company."

"You misunderstand me, Frevin. I need your services here for the next few days. The Pira will escort the captain alone. Well, not alone." Nikodamus smiled. "There will be thousands of people there."

Zeph caught a subtle tightening in the Mir's placid features.

Is he jealous?

The idea that the lukewarm Frevin Mir might have some claim on the mysterious Pira struck Zeph as ludicrous, but it might explain why Frevin was removed as Zeph's liaison. Frevin Mir had certainly made himself unpleasant enough, and thinking back on it, Zeph realized the Mir's unpleasantness increased about the time Zeph began asking questions about the Pira.

"Eropa will be leaving very early in the morning and will already be there by the time you arrive. I will let her know to expect you in

Iredipa tomorrow evening. Good night." Nikodamus indicated that the palace guard should escort Zeph back to his guest quarters.

"What are you doing?" Frevin whispered as soon as he and Nikodamus were alone. "You cannot throw Eropa to this alien as if she were a piece of bread you can toss to a starving man to keep him complaisant."

"If you must be angry with someone, Frevin, please, be angry with me. This situation is not of Captain Yare's making."

"You saw what happened when he and Eropa met at the reception. Everyone did. Why would you put her in that position again? And you're sending her alone? Who will protect her from him?"

Nikodamus raised a questioning brow. "You think Eropa requires protection? Eropa is a Rhune adept trained since childhood in their lineage, and The Arts by Master Pranseas himself. Who could possibly be more formidable than her? You? You offer her nothing that she does not already have. It is precisely because of what I saw between Eropa and this alien that I am arranging this time for the two of them to meet without all the trappings of ceremony and responsibility. Nikodamus walked to his desk and slid a sheaf of papers under other documents, but it was too late. Frevin had seen the treaty's emboldened subtitles.

Cold fingers gripped the younger Mir's gut. "You send Eropa away with this man to further some political agreement? How could you use your daughter..."

"You overstep yourself." Nikodamus's eyes flashed. "Your boyish fantasies around my daughter play no part in the strategies our world is grappling with. They are beyond your and your family's ambitions. Whatever you wished for, it was never to be. It is over."

"Forgive me, Mahal," Frevin apologized quickly. "It is not my place to question your intentions. I am blinded by my respect and affection for your daughter-..."

"Whatever happens or does not happen between Captain Yare and Eropa, will be her choice, Frevin, and hers alone."

"If you truly knew her, you would know that was not true, not when the safety of her people is at stake." Frevin tried to dampen his

CHAPTER SEVENTEEN

anger and frustration. "She will accept any solution that protects us, no matter what the cost to herself."

"A fault inherited from her mother," Nikodamus acknowledged. "My intention is to shield her from those responsibilities, at least for a few days. She should form her own opinion of Yare, without these added burdens."

Frevin smirked. "By the Mother, you think she is going to like him, this alien."

"I think she may love him," Nikodamus corrected. "At least I hope so."

Frevin's hands squeezed into fists. "She could not."

"What we witnessed at the reception makes me believe differently. There was a connection…"

"Only a desperate man would cling to such a vague hope."

"Then I am a desperate man—a desperate father who wants what is best for his child." Nikodamus sank into his chair by the fire. "I have lived the life you wished for, Frevin. I walked beside a Rhune. No one understands the opportunities or the price that is paid better than I. And it is true it makes you seem to shine more brightly in the minds of other people, placing opportunities in your path you would not otherwise have, but it does not change who you are." The Mahal waved a dismissing hand. "And perhaps you are better suited to such games than I have been, but the lure of an adept's practices is a terrible and unrelenting rival. Magic never gives up."

Frevin sniffed. "A Rhune's work comes first. I understand that. I would never stand in Eropa's way."

"Which is why you would lose her, as I lost her mother," Nikodamus said sadly. "Eropa's best chance of not following in Dupira's footsteps lies in a strong attachment to someone unwilling to share her with that Rhune world—someone who will fight to keep her focus here in this world. I was not that man for Dupira. You are not that man for Eropa."

Frevin's nostrils flared. "I have read this alien's mind. He cares nothing for her. Eropa is the latest of many conquests he finds pleasure in luring to his bed."

"And if these days together cannot change, then that will be an end to it," the Mahal declared. "But they will be given this chance. I want your word, Frevin, that you will not speak to Eropa about this, that you will stay out of the way and allow things between her and Yare to unfold without your interference."

Frevin's jaw tightened. "I have never been less than completely honest with Eropa."

Nikodamus held him in a cool gaze. "If you believe that, then you are lying to yourself."

Silence built a wall between the two men, dividing them, utterly.

"I will have your promise," Nikodamus repeated. "Or I will have you confined and your mind blocked." Captain Ochette entered, standing by for the Mahal's command.

"She will not learn about this from me," Frevin promised.

CHAPTER EIGHTEEN

"The Truths are a guide, but each individual chooses their path, which is the nature of life. " (Anonymous; From the Book of the Rhune.)

Distracted thoughts filled Frevin's mind as he walked out of the palace and into the city. This off-worlder was unraveling plans Frevin and his family had worked toward since he was a boy.

The Ner'ansetts were an old clan, not as wealthy or powerful as the Dum'Laieres, or the Mc'Laricks, but respectable. Frevin's mother was not of the first line, but his uncle Wallish learned of his nephew's budding friendship with the Pira and ensured Frevin's education and position were the best the family could offer. Regular visits to the remote castle at Alden Baird, on the thinnest of excuses, became commonplace. Wallish's support assured the family's ability to pursue the friendship without an awkward appearance of need. Frevin attended an elite school and was apprenticed well within his chosen field.

Practicing an expression of benign wisdom and working to master the art of cooperative discussion did not decrease his ambition nor his goal to follow Nikodamus' path to a position of authority. He carved out a place for himself in the public eye as a rising star and the Pira's close friend and confidant. The Mahal's misguided plan--how to gain the alien's favor-- threatened to destroy it all.

Frevin paused in the middle of the boulevard, frowning.

An unusual energy was in the air. He scanned the way, seeing nothing. Whatever had been there was gone, with only a faint mental pattern remaining; the unusual signature was too unique to be missed by the sensitive. Frevin began to follow the fading thread.

Up one street and down the next, he followed the strange vibration until it brought him to the landing area north of town.

His eyes wandered over the Taiban ships in the field. The Lamdra shuttle was gone, and the Paxlosians were forced to flee before a Taiban mob. The unsettling energy, too, had disappeared.

Whatever Nikodamus wants to believe, these aliens have not come to make peace. Frevin could not be sure the energy's disappearance and the Lamdra shuttle's leaving were connected, but it was a possibility he could not dismiss.

Frevin considered his options and formed a new plan.

The Dum'Laiere estate predated the Palace of Iredipa by centuries, its architecture reflecting a time when territorial wars required monolithic living spaces with arrow slits and narrow, defensible windows and doorways. The location had been a residence long before the Dum'Laiere's conquered the original Bract inhabitants, killing or driving them away and cutting down the forestland to build a defensible castle.

The Mc'Laricks also claim coastal lands as the old races retreated deeper into the remaining forests, the boundary between the clan territories being a point of continual contention between them.

A substantial add-on to the original Dum'Laiere keep and walled bailey, including kitchens, a guardhouse, and a great hall, were constructed during a decade of peace brought on by a brief intermingling of the two families. Within a few generations, the old keep was declared too uncomfortable and isolated, and it was abandoned by the first-line family members, falling into disrepair as poorer third-line relations used parts of it as multifamily dwellings and livestock housing.

The first line Dum'Laiere only returned to rebuild the property when the Council of Elders decided to move their base to Iredipa, decades after the Great Peace.

Frevin was led through the old guardhouse and shown into a narrow stone room on the ground floor of the original tower. Soot-streaked walls marked pre-Rhune torch-sconces, now out of use. Hovering, a single large glow globe threw white light over the stone walls and floor. An inhospitable space, barren of décor, the room had not a jot of furniture, forcing him to stand while he waited. The lady of the house had little interest in making guests brought to this room feel welcome.

With nothing else to do, Frevin looked around. The high stone walls of the old tower now rose unfettered to the roof. The remnants of the old wood beams that once supported floors above were cut flush to the rock walls, leaving him feeling as if he stood at the bottom of a well.

Iron hinges groaned with the weight of the heavy inner door as Miratha Dum'Laiere entered. Hands folded across her taut corset, her lips pursed in her habitual expression of disgust, she examined Frevin.

"My curiosity is piqued, Master Mir. Why have you come?"

Frevin cleared his throat. "Forgive me, Lady Dum'Laiere, but I have information I thought you would want to hear."

"Go on."

"This was not an easy decision, but I felt--under the circumstances--I must tell you…"

"I am not interested in the history of your justification for coming to see me, Frevin Mir. Nor am I interested in the inner twisting of your tortured soul. Just say what you have come to say," she commanded him impatiently.

"Mahal Nikodamus and the Paxlosian captain are discussing a treaty between our worlds."

"So, the Mirs have found Nikodamus something he can use against the aliens in the Trove? Something to use as leverage?" Miratha demanded.

Frevin shook his head. "We have heard nothing about Malbuis Mir's search of the Trove yet. Though you might be interested to know that Master Pranseas had an audience with the Mahal today."

"There are too few temple monks to make any difference to the Paxlosians," Miratha dismissed the news.

"Nikodamus does not intend to fight the Paxlosians, I tell you. They are making a treaty between them. He plans to use Eropa to secure it."

Miratha's eyes narrowed. "Use Eropa how?"

"I only caught a glimpse of the document," Frevin admitted. "Historically how has any young woman been used to seal an alliance? He cannot do that, can he? As Mahal, he cannot negotiate a treaty without including the Council Voices."

"No, he cannot," Miratha scowled.

"He claims what he's doing is in Ebulon's interests. I fear he is being unduly influenced by the alien and is not seeing the Paxlosian's true intentions, Lady Dum'Laiere. That is why I have come to you."

"And you were right to do so, Master Mir. Tell me what you know." Miratha's smile cold and ruthless.

CHAPTER NINETEEN

"A Rhune's reasoning is only understood by idiots and Rhunes: (Common Ebulonian pejorative, generally shortened to *"Only idiots and Rhunes,"* a dismissal of anything the person making the statement does not want to bother trying to understand.)

For Braum Dum'Laiere, middle-aged, plain, with claim to neither charm nor wit, Miratha Avlec was a good match. Her rumored connection to the Matriarch made her much more desirable as the connection would bring the family prestige that had eluded them for many generations.

Claiming a shared ancestry with Hagriva through Hagriva's sister's line, introduced by third-party members hoping to avoid the appearance of her suitability being sold to the family and distancing her from backlash if her expectations came to nothing.

During their first winter, Braum became ill. The clan's matriarch, Cora, pointedly reminded Miratha that as their union had not produced a child, the alliance was on a trial basis. If Braum did not recover, Miratha would be expected to return to her clan.

Miratha nursed her new husband back to health and produced an heir before Braum succumbed to ill health.

As baby Dora grew, it was soon evident that the child took after her dull-witted father and would do little to raise the family's prospects. Belittled and downtrodden by her mother's glittering self-interest, little Dora was not allowed to attend school, her health being declared too fragile. She was not permitted playmates--there being only a handful among the clans deemed "worthy"…and it being decided it was not in the family's interest to let Dora's inadequacies become common knowledge as it might hinder her future matrimonial prospects. By the time Dora reached adolescence, her tutors were quietly dismissed with the excuse that it was unkind to continue trying to force the girl to learn things she was incapable of.

With complete control over her daughter's inheritance and the clan's investments, Miratha settled in to mold the future she imagined

CHAPTER NINETEEN

for herself, firmly at the reins of the Dum'Laiere fortune.

Anyone who knew the woman saw her manipulations for what they were, but Miratha had taken pains to ensure the Dum'Laieres did not know her. By the time they realized the depth of her ambition and how deeply embedded she was in their affairs, it was too much trouble to do anything about it. The truth was, Miratha had a knack for business, and aside from Braum's brother, Kirk, who managed the family's vast agricultural holdings, no one else was interested.

For her part, Miratha mostly ignored the Dum'Laiere country "cousins", second and third-line family members who lived and worked on the clan estates run by Kirk, but as the clan's Voice, she was required to consult with them. So, once or twice a year, she made the trek to the country to keep up the pretense. She showed up and spent a day or two so she could pretend to have listened to their concerns while they avoided her, pretending they had not, and everyone was happy.

"Gwillem," Miratha summoned the old manservant. "Make inquiries about increasing our house guard."

The old servant's brows knitted. "The Dum'Laiere clan has remained at the current staffing level--quite effectively--for decades, Lady."

"And now we need more," she spat back. "Is this a problem?" As a shirttail Dum'Laiere, like many older household staff, Gwillem had been with the family far longer than Miratha. She often suspected the cousins of informing on her to Kirk, but there was no getting rid of them. They were like the stones in the foundation of the old tower. No matter how rough and unattractive, they remained eternal.

"How many shall I say we are looking for, Madam?" Gwillem's tone and expression were unfailingly civil but not servile.

"A hundred." *Let Kirk chew on that for a while.* "And send Fratianne to me."

Too attractive not to be noticed, even in the plain clothing required of a servant, the half-Taiban, Fratianne's long hair was pulled back into a thick rose-gold braid that hung like a rope down her back. It was understood that her placement in the Dum'Laiere household was temporary, a steppingstone necessary to put her physical beauty on display where it could attract the kind of attention that could change her position. Both women leveraged that understanding according to their natures.

"Lord Lector arrived while you were with your other guest, Lady," the servant girl informed her mistress. "He is waiting in your salon."

"I will attend to him later. I am sending you with Dora to Auhora Whimlan to meet her future husband." Miratha led the young woman into an adjoining room and unlocked a bureau, removing a small bag heavy with coins. "I rely on you to keep her from making a fool of herself and disgracing the family. You will need this." She dropped the bag into the girl's hands, then brought out a small box revealing its contents: a needle and vial. "Get close to Yare. Seduce him, if necessary, but I need him in an isolated area where there will be no witnesses before the festival is over. Do you understand?" The girl nodded. "You have ambition, Fratianne, looks, and maybe some talent for this sort of thing. This is a chance to prove you have the determination to succeed." Miratha reached into the deep pocket of her dress and pulled out what appeared to be a small stone. "Take this. When you have Captain Yare alone, put it in contact with your skin. I will have men standing by."

"I won't let you down," the girl promised.

"See that you do not. You cannot go dressed like that. Choose some dresses from my closet and alter them if necessary. I will not want them back."

Fratianne exited, and Miratha opened a hidden door in the wall and slipped into the corridor behind it. It let out in her private salon.

"Lector, thank you for waiting."

"I thought you were brushing me off," Lector grumbled. "Your maidservant said you were entertaining a visitor."

"My maidservant needs to hold her tongue," Miratha complained as Lector began kissing her neck, leaning in to include the mounds of her breasts pushed up above the edge of her neckline.

"Do not be cross with her. She is such a pretty little thing."

Miratha pushed him away. "Fratianne is not your type, Harscham. She has no money and no position."

"A temporary situation, I am sure."

Miratha's eyebrows went up. "Are you making an offer?"

"Certainly not. I have my hands full." Lector grabbed Miratha's buttocks through petticoat layers and padding, pulling her to him. Miratha twisted free. "What is the matter? Has something ruined your mood?"

"I have had disturbing news," Miratha informed him.

"Ah, gossip!" Lector grinned. "A vice that rivals the pleasure of all others."

"We are going to need more wine." Miratha chose glasses from a wine cart and poured.

From a small window in the Taiban vessel, Miratha watched Alden Baird castle rise beyond the hunched ruins of the old capital. To the south and east, the green rolled swell upon swell like the soft mounds and curved valleys of a woman's body. To the west and north: the cliffs dropped off and fell a thousand feet to the stormy North Sea. In summer, twilight lingered past dawn; in winter, it was dark before dinner.

The ancient grounds where the castle stood sentinel, indifferent to its human abandonment, were on a high bluff marking the continent's northernmost point. Not a glimmer or glow brightened the blind windows. The Matriarch was either sitting in the dark or was not home.

Until a century ago, the castle at Alden Baierd had been the center of Ebulonian politics, but society had moved on, the desire for grace and ease evolving into a taste for easy living. The comfort of Iredipa's southern climate had begun a renaissance in open, airy architecture, as well as new fashions that matched the temperate climate, birthing the culture of etiquette founded on the pretense of spiritual and mental evolution.

The Taiban shuttle landed where the open moor became cluttered by broken foundations, the remnants of a once thriving city pocked by perseverant, green vines and hardy grasses in nature's bid to regain dominance.

The Taiban pilot opened the shuttle door and extended a short ramp. Miratha exited the ship.

"I weren't hired to go to that witch's tower, so don't ask." The man went back inside his ship and pulled the ramp in behind him.

Miratha picked her way through the warren of lichen-covered stones, tumbled low walls, and sunken steps. The geometric shapes of ramparts and towers pushed together like blocks, their spines dragged down by time, their proud pennants tattered to shreds by the elements. With an entire castle to choose from, Hagriva had taken up residence in one high tower.

Supported by half-rotten girders wrestled into position as braces, the stones were slick with algae. The remains of a rot-eaten staircase clung to the inner walls of the tower, its broken treads like missing teeth. A rivulet of water trickled down the wall to pool in a noxious puddle on the ground. Miratha minced around the edge, wrinkling her nose in distaste.

"The damn place is a death trap. Crazy, old bird," she mumbled. "What does she prove by living this way?" Miratha's last visit to Alden Baierd had been eighteen years before when she had come to plead for recognition of her daughter's bloodline. Her eyes rose to follow the broken staircase.

I am not climbing that.

"Mah Rhune," she called in a treacle-thick voice. "It is your granddaughter, Miratha, come to visit." A stair tread broke off, landing with a splash in the puddle beside Miratha's satin slipper. Stripes of smelly sludge slid down her silk skirt. "It smells like a pig sty in here." She held her nose as her temper began a slow burn. This rebuff was intentional. Nothing the Matriarch did was random. "Mah Rhune, please talk to me," Miratha pleaded. "I only ask for a few minutes--a few words. You would grant as much to any of your people, why deny me, your own flesh and blood? Our disagreements are nothing compared to what we have in common."

Silence.

Stubborn witch.

"Just listen to me then. I bring you news the Council of Elders does not know. Nikodamus has negotiated a treaty with these aliens, bartering away your precious Pira. If his plan succeeds, Dupira's daughter will become a treaty bride and return with the aliens to their world, never to return to Ebulon. You will lose her, Hagriva, your last student," Miratha taunted. "And you do not have time to train another.

CHAPTER NINETEEN

But I can stop this. Recognize me and my daughter, and Dora will take Eropa's place beside the alien. Eropa will stay, and we will both have what we want."

Water trickled down the walls, plopping into the puddle at the bottom of the stairs. Wind whistled through cracks between the stones, but that was all.

"Damn it, old woman, I know you can hear me!" Miratha shouted in frustration.

Silence answered. Miratha pulled her cloak around her.

"Very well. I will do this without your help." She stomped out of the crumbling tower.

The wind tugged maliciously at her clothing as she ran back to the shuttle, and she thought she heard it laughing.

CHAPTER TWENTY

"Strength is in belonging." (Common Cumin saying. Anonymous.)

Bibi called it The Cavern of Hollow Winds, but Grub felt no wind. It was big; their entire village could fit inside the hollow space. Variegated layers of red, pink, ivory, and gold sandstone ribboned the walls in smooth, undulating waves moving freely between walls and ceiling. Four tunnels led into or out of the cavern, one on each sandstone wall. Of those tunnels, one ended at a wall after only a hundred feet. Another linked up with its southern neighbor, and the remaining two twisted and turned in utter darkness, their smells warning of dangers along their paths.

There was a small spring of good water in the cavern.

Protected by the debris of a broken-down wall, spring water collected in a pebble-lined pool. Sand and silt collected muddying the water, but once Bibi scooped the debris out, it was drinkable, and if they were careful, they had a source of clean water.

An irregular shaft in the cavern's ceiling lent the space a daytime twilight that fed a patch of soil formerly used as a garden. Bibi found tubers, smaller and less sweet than those grown in the Cumin village but recognizable as related to the cultivated variety. They built a fire, cooked, and ate a few. Feeling revived, Grub began looking around, visually tracing the circular patterns of broken walls surrounding the abandoned garden. They were very like the temporary huts the Cumin built when they traveled.

Sweeping the red sand and debris away, Grub discovered faint markings carved in the stone. Slowly, he backed out.

This is a sacred area. He scanned the area, worried. *We should not have trespassed.*

Uncertain about what to do to compensate for his mistake, Grub was about to call Bibi, then stopped himself.

She would be no help. Females know nothing about magic.

Magic and ceremony were the exclusive territory of male Cumin. A female's power came only through her link with Mother Ra and focused on things like planting, raising cubs, or caring for the elders. Females who got too close to ceremony turned into demons. Cumin stories were full of cautions about females who ignored this common wisdom and ended up abandoning their mates and cubs to pursue the secrets of the spirit world. Cumin mothers who indulged in magic bore misshapen cubs, or no-color cubs, like Bibi.

"Mother Ra chose female to serve her through their bodies," Grub's father and uncles instructed him. "This is symbolized by the hemp string skirts they wear to cover their mother's cave. We serve through our hearts and minds. That is why we wear string shawls that cover our hearts."

Grub had overheard his mother and aunts whispering about Bibi's mother, Wan, and how she invited Boors into her mother's cave. When Boors suddenly left the village, everyone blamed Wan and Bibi, the little albino that was proof of Boors' and Wan's guilt.

Grub's aunt declared, "The Spirit Speaker ran away because he was ashamed of what he had done," but Grub remained confused. When he repeated this to his Uncle Gutte, the Spirit Speaker did not seem to agree.

"Ignorant Cumin pretend they know how the gods want us to act when they know no more than anyone else. It makes them feel important to tell other Cumin how to live." Though Gutte was a serious Cumin, Grub had never seen him look so sad. "Too often, Cumin mask their wishes by claiming they are the gods' desires, but the gods do not punish innocent cubs for the mistakes of their elders, Grub. Prejudice is a cruelty of small minds, not a judgment of the gods."

Grub did not know if he agreed with Gutte, but he wished his uncle were here with him now. There were many things he would like to have asked the Spirit Speaker.

Grub pulled hairs from his head and placed them on the carved circle.

"Forgive me, ancestors. I meant no disrespect in entering your space. And please, if it is not too much trouble, could you help us find the way home?" Grub did not know if this was a good way to speak to the spirits, but there was no one to ask, so he hoped it would be accepted.

That night, while they ate tubers, Grub told Bibi what he had found.

"Don't you see, Bibi, if there is a sacred circle here, this cavern is for ceremonies. Someone will come, and then they will find us and take us back home."

Bibi did not share his excitement.

"Circle is old, Grub--very old." She curled up to sleep.

"Lots of sacred things are old. That does not mean they are not used. What would you know about it? You are just a cub and a female one at that. You do not know anything about the spirit world." Grub lay down on the other side of the fire with his back to her.

The next day, Bibi announced she thought they should move to the old village.

"We cannot do that." Grub was shocked by the idea. "The circle--it is a sacred place."

Bibi frowned. "It is close to the garden. It will protect us."

"The dead spirits who live there will be very angry," Grub protested. "They will rise up and kill us in our sleep."

Bibi frowned. "Why spirits be angry with Bibi and Grub?"

"Because we moved into their sacred village."

She thought about this. "Grub is afraid of spirits?"

"I'm not afraid of anything. I respect the way things are done, is all, and moving into a dead spirit's house is not the way we Cumin do things." Grub puffed out his chest. He did not want to admit he was afraid of anything, especially not to Bibi. "Why should we move camp anyway? We should be leaving to go home."

Bibi eyed the patch of sky visible through the hole in the cavern ceiling. "Not time."

Grub's eyes narrowed. "Why not?"

"Grub needs rest," Bibi demurred.

It annoyed him that she didn't mention she might need rest.

"And who are you to say it's not time, Bibi? I am the male." Grub popped open another tuber, pressing the ends together and sliding his thumb along the seam.

Bibi sniffed the stale, mineral-scented air. "Not time." She rose and walked away from the fire, disappearing into the cavern's hollow bowl.

CHAPTER TWENTY

The little albino was the most frustrating and uppity female that Grub had ever met, with her stupid baby talk and strange ideas. She was always trying to make it seem like she knew things, but she never explained how or why. She lived as she always had, doing what she pleased, without respect for the authority that was his by right of age and the superiority of his maleness.

"When we get back to the village, I will tell Gutte how she's been practicing magic. Then we'll see who knows things." Grub sat down on the cavern floor, pulled his ring reed flute out of the bag at his waist, and began to blow into the slender tube, but nothing melodic came out. His impatience mirrored in its shrill squeal, and he quickly abandoned the effort, stuffing the flute back into the bag.

During the next few days, Bibi showed no sign of preparing to leave the cavern. Bored and restless, Grub forgot the mind-numbing darkness of the tunnels and decided to stop waiting.

"What do I need her for?" he grumbled. "If she wants to stay here, let her. But I am going home."

Bibi claimed to have led them here to the cavern, but if that was true, why couldn't she take them back the more he asked her questions, the more he realized she avoided answering.

She's lying. How could she have known where the cavern was? A female would never have explored so far alone. "She is pretending so she will seem important." But if they could stumble in--Grub was sure he could stumble back out.

Despite Grub's warnings, Bibi had taken to sleeping in the old village near the west tunnel. Standing staunchly on his moral superiority, Grub remained in their original camp, refusing to budge, meaning they spent most of their days on their own. Grub told himself he did not mind the arrangement; his company was better than the misguided albino's. Once he settled on the idea he would return to the village on his own, it suited him to have Bibi out of the way. He would make preparations, and she would never know until he was gone, and it was too late.

Grub pictured Bibi returning to the village weak, hungry, meek, and contrite. He would have been back for days before she returned-- his return celebrated by the entire village. He would appear before her, well-fed, wearing the fine gifts given to him by his family in honor of his return, and she would stand drooping before him, humbled, because they both knew she had lied to him. Grub replayed different versions of the scenario several times, Bibi's remorse growing each time until she fell at his feet and begged his forgiveness, vowing to be his slave and never questioning him again.

Grub smiled as he stuffed the roots he was gathering into his pack. With his simple preparations nearly finished, he climbed a boulder and looked out over the cavern.

Bibi was nowhere to be seen.

Grub always imagined she sat in her camp or somewhere nearby, napping like a cub or merely doing nothing. Now, he had to question that thought. He scanned the cavern more closely.

The albino was not here. Grub climbed down from the boulder and began to walk the cavern's perimeter, looking into corners and behind boulders. He checked by the creek and inside the dead-end tunnel. Bibi was nowhere.

She's left. Grub's heart began to pound. She was lying to him. She knew the way out and had been leaving every day since she brought him here. Grub sat back on his hunches, his mind racing.

"When she comes back this time, I will see where she comes from. Then tomorrow, I will know which tunnel to take. Grub climbed back onto the boulder that gave him the best view and settled down to wait, rage smoldering in his belly.

By late afternoon, he was fighting to stay awake. Movement in the west end of the cavern brought him alert.

Bibi crossed from the west tunnel to her camp in the old village. The reason for her choice of campsites was clear--she was sneaking out while she kept him here as her prisoner.

"No more." Grub peered at the dark mouth of the west tunnel.

When they first arrived, they entered the cavern from the south tunnel, but they had traveled for what seemed like the better part of two days. "The west tunnel must be a more direct route."

At dinner, Grub let Bibi burn her fingers pulling the roots from the coals, and did not offer help. He watched her moving about in the firelight. With no one to shave the hair behind her ears: a fine silvery down was growing on her head. It glistened like the soft down of ripe seed pods. What would such white hair look like grown long and dressed in clan braids, he wondered? But of course, Bibi's hair would never be braided. She had no clan--no tribe. She could not grow her hair long.

"I have decided it is time to go home," Grub announced, surprising even himself. Bibi looked up at him and blinked. Grub felt a rush of power witnessing her surprise. "We will take the west tunnel," he taunted, watching for her reaction.

Bibi's ear tufts quivered, her pale eyes as round as full moons. "No." Her voice was a shredded whisper, shimmering with fear.

"Why no?" Grub longed to toss her lies back into her face. A Cumin might use words to avoid the truth when necessary, but telling an actual lie made you less than Cumin. "Why no, Bibi? Tell me why I should not take the west tunnel and go home?"

Bibi's lower lip trembled, her mooneyes filling with tears. "West tunnel bad," she stammered.

"How do you know that?" Grub leaned toward her; his fists clenched. Instead of being cowed, the little albino seemed to gain strength from his bullying.

"Bibi knows," she declared, matching his forcefulness.

Grub sat back, grinding his teeth. "Then which tunnel should we take to go home?"

Bibi jumped up and ran to her camp. Grub stayed where he was. So, this was it. She would not admit her lie. He would have to go alone.

Grub stood and made his way to the edge of the abandoned village, placing himself where he could see Bibi.

She was digging a small pit outside the outline of her camp facing the tunnel. Grub watched as she finished digging, then stepped back into the sacred circle. Dipping her hands in what appeared to be water held in a clay-lined basket, the albino wetted her fur. When her entire body was damp, she crawled into the pit and partially buried herself. Picking up a wooden pole--he had missed--lying on the ground, she dug one end into the dirt, positioning the other, pointed end, toward the west tunnel.

She made herself a spear to guard the tunnel so he could not get away. Grub cursed himself. Giving her another chance was stupid. Angry with himself for having given away his plan, Grub trudged back to his camp, lying down by the fire. He tossed and turned. The image of Bibi's blue eyes swimming with tears would not let him sleep. In all the time he had known her and the hundreds of slights he witnessed her bearing, he had never seen her cry, but tonight, she seemed unable to do anything else. Why?

Grub woke in the gray light just before dawn. The fur along his spine stood up, the hair in his ears tingling as he slipped along the cavern wall.

Bibi was still sleeping beside her spear in the dirt. For a moment, Grub considered waking her. She was only a cub, after all. Then he thought of home and his family and how she kept him away from them. Silently, Grub tip-toed past her and into the tunnel.

I am going home.

CHAPTER TWENTY-ONE

"Sweep the dust in your mind out the door and close it before seeking understanding." (Anonymous Ebulonian saying attributed to the Keesch; undocumented.)

Vale was not just absent, off somewhere on an errand or mission. He was gone, and he would not be coming back.

Corin walked the alley behind Crochin and Son's, making small circles, hoping that understanding what had happened to Vale would ease the ache in her chest.

It felt right to keep their physical relationship private, but it reduced Corin to being just one more friend, and while a friend might be sad, they were still expected to do chores and keep up with the routine of daily life. Immoveable grief was for family and sweethearts. Corin was still unsure how to define what was evolving between her and Vale.

"I'm not seeing anything back here," Quinn called out from behind the crates stacked against the map merchant's back wall.

Corin stooped to dig a small piece of glass from a crevice between cobblestones, her eyes blurring with tears she refused to shed.

She sensed Quinn at her side. "You don't have to do this,"

"I need to do *something*."

"You could cry," her cousin suggested.

"It doesn't help, and your mother is starting to watch me with a worried look on her face."

"You should tell her the truth. There's no shame in loving someone, Corin. Vale was a good man."

"I will not be one of those poor, forlorn girls who are whispered about because she lost her man? Oh, what will become of her?" Corin made a face and faked a gossip's high-pitched voice. "Like because someone we cared about died, we'll never live again. It's just stupid. Vale and I weren't like that." Corin tried to will away the tears that welled up in her eyes. She could see no comfort in being defined by other people's pity.

CHAPTER TWENTY-ONE

"We will all miss him. Come here." Her cousin pulled her into a hug. At first, she fought his kindness, remaining stiff and rigid, but Quinn Bobalo was not easily put off. He kept quietly holding her, asking nothing, offering nothing but his silent compassion, like a blanket warmed by the kitchen hearth, and gradually, the ice wall she had built began to melt.

"They're all gone: Quinn, my father, mama, and now, Vale. " She leaned into Quinn, sobbing into his shoulder. "Don't I get to keep *anyone*?"

"You still have us, Corin, Mother, Father, me, and the girls. We're not going anywhere," Quinn promised.

"That's not true," she shot back, pulling away from him. "You're going back to Taiba before the end of this moon's ring. Vale told me so. Why, Quinn? Why do it when you know you're worth more there as meat than as a person?"

"Stop, Corin," Quinn said sharply.

"You wanted me to feel something. Well, this is what I feel: angry."

Before Quinn could reply, they realized they were not alone. The newly salvaged emigrant genius, young Terk, stood at the entrance to the alley.

"What are you doing here?" He eyed them suspiciously.

"We're looking for clues." Corin took a step back from Quinn, straightening. She dragged her forearm across her cheeks and tossed her head back defiantly.

"Crochin and them been all over this place." The skinny, sharp-faced boy's eyes were flinty slits. "Didn't find nothing. Ain't that right, Clem?" He turned around to address someone behind him.

A much shorter, sweet-faced boy with freckles sprinkled like russet stars across his nose and straw-colored hair peered out from behind the older boy.

"Yeah." The younger boy's clear, blue eyes shifted from the barrels in the alley to the stacked crates, lighting finally on a nondescript spot on the cobblestones a foot and a half from where Corin stood. Perspiration--like a glass circlet bound about his head-- beaded his brow, some braking, trickling rust-colored rivulets down his fear-paled face, like water-thinned blood. Terk jabbed the younger boy hard with an elbow, and Clemmet's stomach spasmed as he winced, bending forward, sucking in a quick breath. Still, he did not cry or call out. He was well-practiced.

This had happened before.

Corin shifted her gaze, confining her scrutiny of the boys to her peripheral vision.

Nervous and twitchy, Terk reminded her of a rodent with his small, slitted eyes, large front teeth, and defined overbite.

He seems worried about something. He was keeping close to his young companion, his fingers fiddling, hands opening and closing as they almost reached out to pull Clemmet closer every time he stepped away. *As if he thinks--at any moment--Clemmet might try to run off,* Corin mused. *Like a cat with a mouse.*

She sidled over to Quinn. "You know these two, right?" she whispered.

"Yeah. My team brought them out of Taiba." Quinn frowned. "Why?"

"I don't think they just casually showed up here, Quinn. They're here because we're here. That boy, Terk, is worried about us--about us and the younger one."

"Clem?" Quinn shrugged. "They're just new, Corin. They hang around sometimes. They don't know many people here yet. It's natural that Terk would feel protective of Clem. Clem's a good kid, smart, but good too. If we can find the right people to take him in, he just might be able to let go of the nightmare that was his life before." Quinn smiled at the younger boy, his affection for Clem obvious.

Terk saw it, too, but it did not make him smile.

Corin walked away.

"We thought maybe the others missed something," she said, re-examining the ground around the crates. Maybe you'd like to help us?"

"Terk never misses anything," Clem boasted, nervousness making him talk too fast. "If he sees it, he always remembers it, like he took a picture or something."

Terk shot the younger boy a look that said, "Shut up."

"Well, it's true, Terk. You just remember stuff," Clem whined like a whipped puppy.

"You've been here before, right, Clem? Did you see anything strange?"

The boy's eyes bugged out like an insect's. "No. I didn't see anything." He shot a fearful glance at Terk. "I mean, I wasn't here before--not ever. Neither of us was. We were at the metal yard, looking for parts." The phrase, however disjointed, had the ring of being well-rehearsed. His eyes darted again to the older boy. A practiced blank masked any honest reactions. Clem was not a good liar. He needed Terk for that.

Quinn placed a hand on Clemmet's shoulder. "You're not in trouble, Clem. Corin was thinking: maybe you noticed something the others didn't, is all?"

Clem's eyes went to the spot on the cobblestones. "I told you; I didn't see anything."

It's as if he's seeing something that isn't there, something we don't see, Corin thought. *Maybe because it was there but isn't anymore.* She and Quinn looked at each other, sharing suspicion in a silent exchange. When Corin turned around, Terk's expression was dark and readable. It froze her blood.

She forced a smile. "What about you, Terk? Maybe you saw something no one else did?"

"Me?" Moments lapsed as the boy went very still. Then, just as suddenly, he blinked and was back. "I'd have to think about that," he hedged.

Had questioning him triggered his memory talent? Whatever he had seen, he wasn't saying.

He's been interrogated before.

Quinn hadn't mentioned anything about the boy's past on Taiba, but that wasn't unusual. If Terk had been the prisoner of one of the warlords before he was brought here, Quinn and his team would have known, wouldn't they?

Unless Terk didn't tell them. Unless there was a reason the boy kept that piece of his past secret.

A cold chill ran through Corin, and she turned to study the awkward teen. Ferret-faced, his skin red with inflamed pimples, his heavy brows gave him the appearance of an eternal scowl. His eyes meet hers, glaring back, accusingly from behind the screen of greasy hair.

"You should keep Clem away from here, Terk," Quinn admonished. "It's not good for him to dwell on this stuff."

"Yeah, 'cause he's got such a gentle nature and all," Terk sneered.

"Come on fart face, let's go read you some nursery rhymes." Putting an arm around Clem's slender shoulders, he steered the younger boy out of the alley, whispering into Clem's ear. Clem winced and tried to pull away without success.

"But I don't want to go back, Terk," Corin heard him mutter as the two disappeared into the street.

Corin walked to the spot that Clem had been so focused on.

"This is where they found him, isn't it? This is where Vale died?" Quinn nodded. "Yes."

"Clem knew that," Corin declared. "He just lied to us about what he'd seen here. Why would he do that?"

Quinn shook his head. "He wouldn't. Clem's a good kid, Corin. He wouldn't lie about something so important."

"And Terk? What about him? Is he a good boy?" Corin challenged her cousin's adjudication of the new refugee's character.

"These kids have had hard lives, Corin. Trust doesn't come easy to them, and you're a stranger," he tried to excuse the boys' behavior.

"At the meeting the other night, Terk was studying the faces of the fighters. I thought it odd, but I couldn't think why it bothered me, but what Clem said about Terk's memory means something. It puts the pieces together. I think he was memorizing the faces of all the Free Men."

"It's not a crime to be smart," Quinn cautioned.

"No, but those boys were raised on Taiba, where it might as well be," Corin argued.

"Look, Corin, these kids spend years figuring out how to survive in the streets. If they're good liars, it's because they need to be. We can't expect them to suddenly act like other kids just because we brought them here. It takes time to let go of old habits and build new ones."

"I think we need to find out if what Clem said about Terk's memory is true," Corin insisted.

"Terk will share his gifts when he's ready--when he trusts us. Interrogating him isn't going to help. If we did that, we'd be no different than the warlords. He's a kid, Corin. They're both just kids."

But there's something wrong with that kid, Corin decided.

CHAPTER TWENTY-ONE

"We should tell Quinn, Terk," Clem said cautiously as they walked from the market.

Terk stopped in the middle of the street. "Tell him what, Clem?"

"About the man we saw--the one who killed Vale."

Terk's eyes grew hard. "We didn't see nothing."

"But we did," Clemmet insisted. "No one's going to get us in trouble, Terk. Quinn will vouch for us. He'll know it wasn't us who did it, and them knowing who did this could be important."

"You want a family, don't you?" Terk demanded. Clem nodded. "Do you think anyone is going to choose a liar for a son? Because as soon as you open your mouth and tell what you saw in that alley, that's what you'll be to them: a liar."

"I'm not a liar," Clem declared.

"Really? You saw Vale get killed in the alley, but you didn't say anything."

"Because you told me not to."

"That's your story? *I* stopped you? *I* forced you not to tell?" Terk shook his head. "It's weak, Clem. They won't buy it, and I won't support it. And what do you think will happen to Quinn if you get labeled a liar? He vouched for us. Do you think he'll thank you for making him look bad on his first mission? Whatever we do reflects on him, Vale, and Ald, so if we're liars, Quinn and Ald will lose trust and respect. If that's what you want, then go ahead, Clem. You're such a selfish little fart. Ruin their lives; ruin yours. But leave me out of it."

Clem hung his head. "I'm sorry, Terk. I guess I wasn't thinking."

"That's right, you weren't because that's what you need me for. That's what you've always needed me for." Terk thumped Clem's head. "Your brain is so full of gears and gadgets; you've got no idea what goes on in the real world."

Clem knew it was true. He was no good with people--except other mechanics. Regular people had rules about how they worked together, but Clem could never figure out what they were. He wanted to. He longed to understand. Sometimes he thought he had figured it out, but then Terk showed up, and Clem saw he was wrong.

CHAPTER TWENTY-TWO

"A Rhune does not surrender." (Anonymous; dated to the Hundred Year War.)

Traveling north at the pace of an Ebulonian windcraft, the differences between Paxlosis and Ebulon could not have been more exposed. A verdant landscape of forest and field veined by the silver ribbons of rivers and streams unfolded before Zeph in a never-ending vista of wonder, the planet's beauty unencumbered by man's trespass.

From the window of the shuttle that first brought him to Ebulon, he had marveled at the acres of virgin forests he had seen. Now, traveling through it, he experienced it more intimately. Ferns unfurled their fiddled heads lit by shafts of sunlight that sliced the dense green, dust motes danced suspended between heaven and earth. Moss hung from the ancient trees in ghostly tatters. Vines had become woven into delicate sheets of living lace. It was like the difference between looking at a beautiful woman from afar and intimately exploring her body, the scents, the textures, the entire landscape revealed. And yet, amid all the beauty, Zeph felt a foreboding. The forest disquieted something deep and unrecognized within him as if just as he studied it, some ancient primordial consciousness was studying him back.

"Does this place have a name?" Zeph asked his escort.

"The Silverleaf." Pliny Mir's face mirrored the calm reverence that Zeph was feeling, absent the uneasiness. "It was once part of a larger forest, which covered all of Ebulon," the Mir explained. "But for many generations, the different pieces of it were separated by cultivation.

Zeph bent his head back to view the high canopy.

"Proximity to human activity has substantially changed its nature in this area. The original forest is known as The Hidling; a name derived from the old language, meaning forest."

"You have so much history. I envy you that." Zeph again felt an upsurge of the strange new sense of loss that he had begun to experience since he'd come to Ebulon. It had never occurred to him that something was missing from his culture, but now he saw that it lacked any historical anchor, outside the Rain of Death that had chased his people under the Dome.

"Some Mirs are passionate about history and keeping records," Zephs's guide explained.

"Is there anything Mirs don't do?" Zeph asked.

"Of course. And we specialize but we are encouraged to research and further our culture's understanding of any area that strikes our interest."

"There are no female Mirs?"

"Muras." Pliny nodded. "Few come to court and fewer remain. They prefer a scholarly life of few distractions, as do many of my brethren."

Both men fell into a reflective silence, watching the scenery.

The windcraft made a soothing, whooshing sound and Zeph leaned back, giving in to the fatigue stalking him.

When he woke, they had left the Silverleaf, the sun was setting, and the bright orange moon, Thai, had risen. Its brilliant shades of gold and orange were softened at the edges by a soft purple wash that fanned out from the horizon like a starburst into the clear sky.

"I don't think I will ever get over my amazement at the constantly changing beauty you experience here every day living under an open sky like you do," Zeph confessed, his eyes bright with the reflection of the sunset.

"There is a peace to it," Pliny agreed. "It is good that you recognize how special Ebulon is. It gives me hope that you will also see the importance of protecting it."

Zeph stiffened. "It's your Mahal and his council who need to understand," he countered. "The agreements that are needed to guarantee Ebulon's future are theirs. I've done my part."

"Of course," Pliny nodded.

The windcraft sped across open meadows. Rising above the curve of the land, a glass city built on the tip of a peninsula came into view.

"There it is, Auhora Whimlan," Pliny announced proudly.

Zeph felt the visceral beauty of the stunning landscape before him in his entire body, like weightlessness had engulfed him.

Surrounded on three sides by a large body of water, the city sparkled with hundreds of thousands of lights. Backed by the vibrant sunset, reflected in the surrounding bay, the effect was doubled.

Dock-connected rafts webbed out like spokes across the bay radiating from the center-city enlarging the city to many times its normal size to accommodate festival visitors. Each of several hundred rafts held a dozen pavilions serving as temporary guest quarters.

The windcraft glided to the edge of the furthest rafts.

"This gentleman will guide you to your tent quarters, Captain Yare," Pliny handed Zeph over to an official. "The Pira will meet you in the morning. I hope your time here is memorable." He got back in the windcraft and silently floated away.

Zeph could not think of anything to compare to this because nothing was silent in his world.

"Please follow me, Captain Yare," the city official indicated they would walk down the docks.

Zeph and the official passed other representatives leading other latecomers to their tents. Some nodded. Others were too caught up in the delight of their affairs to notice anyone else.

Hundreds of watercraft from simple rafts with canopies to floating palaces, were sailing into moorage for the evening. Soft music and gentle laughter greeted them from across the water.

"I am sorry you have missed the first day," the official apologized. "But they say, it does not matter when you come to the festival, as long as you come." The man stopped outside a large tent, holding the flap aside for Zeph to enter.

The tent was comfortably furnished with a thick pile carpet and a liberal collection of jewel-colored pillows lined up along the back of a wide platform divan. A stack of blankets on a trunk at the end of the divan made the divan into a bed. A formal dining table and chairs were provided and an array of fresh fruits, cheeses, bread, wine, and water were set out to welcome him.

Two sets of loose, robed clothing the Ebulonians favored were laid out over one side of the divan.

"The clothes were the Mahal's suggestion. He thought you might prefer to blend in," the official explained. "Taibans often attend the festival, so your skin color will not give you away."

"So, no one knows I'm here?" Zeph asked, a bit alarmed.

CHAPTER TWENTY-TWO

The man smiled. "Officially, you are not, but it is hard to keep a secret on Ebulon." The man bowed and exited.

Zeph took one more turn around the tent, then drifted to the open door and out onto the dock.

The sun had gone down, erasing any detail below the tree line of the forest across the bay, but Ebulon's moons cast their colors over the slender crystal spires of glass.

As if responding to an invisible cue, thousands of light orbs and candles came to life. Zeph watched the glow spread through the city.

There was so much space here, he marveled. *I could walk away right now—and start a new life as anyone--anyone but myself. The Consortium, Morladja, no one would find me. I could leave behind everything everyone else has piled on me and be my own man-- live my own life.*

He had often felt that others had written his story for him. What would it be like to change all that and write it himself?

"But without your family's reputation and wealth, what would you do?" a small voice shattered the fantasy. *"You have no practical skills. You cannot build a house, plant a garden, or hunt for food. And as soon as you ask for help you will be found."*

I am the Lamdra's captain, Zeph reminded himself. *I asked for the position and I'm responsible for those onboard.*

And if he disappeared, his crew would assume the worst, and Ebulon would suffer.

Other beings would pay the price for his freedom. The treaty and its marriage were not a great option, but it was what he had.

The next morning the Pira Eropa greeted Zeph at his tent door. Her deep red hair, undressed and curling down her back and over her shoulders, looked maroon in the sunlight, her pale green skin washed out to almost alabaster. The gauzy, many-layered, dress she wore was iridescent green and blue, glistening like dragonfly wings. Zeph had chosen to wear his own pants and a simple white shirt, with his uniform jacket casually thrown over it. When he saw the Pira, he considered pulling her into his tent and down onto the bed instead of going out to see the lights, but the look on her face hardened, warning him that such an action was premature if not an outright mistake.

"You'll be my guide today, *all* day?" he asked, grinning.

As long as you behave yourself, Eropa said, silently. "We will see how it goes. You may find diversions you desire to undertake on your own."

"I doubt it," Zeph declared.

It was a beautiful day, a cloud-free blue sky spread like a bright awning overhead; nothing like the best day under the Dome could come close. With the sun sparkling over the mirror-smooth bay waters surrounding the glass city, boats and barges crowded with revelers had taken to the water in a grand migration, preparing for another day of festivities.

People hailed each other, swam, or ferried between crafts. Flushed-cheeked children snatched treats from tables heavy with special holiday foods.

Water cycling acrobats and jugglers peddled between the floating islands that formed into groups as friends and families tied off their watercraft to one another. Simple or intricate in design, every vessel was festooned with flowers. It was almost enough to take his mind off the exotic young woman at his side.

"Tell me, Captain, what is your world like?" Eropa broke the silence between them.

Zeph paused, uncertain if she was genuinely interested or just making conversation. What should he tell her? It felt somehow embarrassing to admit to his world's plight but before he could decide if there was a tactical reason not to answer, he found himself speaking.

"Crowded...dirty. We've lived under a protective dome for hundreds of years, space to live in is expensive. It's nothing like it is here on Ebulon." He waved his hand at the open expanse all around them. "There's no land for growing things. Any real food is grown on smaller planets among the Thousand Worlds and imported so only the rich can afford it. Common people eat synthetic foods."

The Pira stopped, her brows knitting. "Why must you live under this dome?"

"The surface of Pax--Paxlosis was poisoned during the Rain of Death," Zeph explained. "An attack by the rival governing faction on Pax."

CHAPTER TWENTY-TWO

Profound grief etched new lines on the young woman's face.

"So, your purpose here is more than exotic goods?" the young Rhune surmised. "Your world needs resources to replenish it? You should have explained this before. It is important."

"Why?" Zeph asked.

"The Truths tell us that all life is connected. When your people struggle, it affects us here, and every other world. When we take steps to help you, it helps all worlds and all life. It is the right thing to do."

"Well, if it helps us get a better trade deal, I'm all for it," Zeph said glibly.

A young Ebulonian woman carrying a tray of food moved down the docks toward them, her ample hips sashaying from side to side.

"Fresh bread and buns, rolls, and tasty twirls for you, friends," she offered Zeph a flirtatious smile along with a sample. He opened his mouth, and she placed the warm bread in it. Honey, sweet and sticky, dripped from his lips.

"Delicious."

"You will not find anything better to satisfy your hunger here today. That is, if it is food, you are hungry for." The young woman winked, resuming her hip-swinging as she walked on. She looked back over her shoulder to see if Zeph was watching. She smiled to find that he was.

"You know, you are free to accept such invitations," Eropa informed him. "Especially at the festival. That is, as long as the invitation is serious."

"You don't think she was serious?" Zeph teased.

"I think she was very serious about selling buns, but if she was sharing pleasures with every customer, I think she would be selling a different kind of bun." The Pira smiled.

"Do that again." Eropa looked at him quizzically. "Just now, you smiled."

"It is no wonder to smile, Captain Yare." Eropa frowned.

"It is when you do it." He reached for her hand, but she moved out of reach.

"The way you talk." She shook her head. "It is discomfiting. Do not try and make me into something I am not, Captain Yare. I am a Rhune, and the Pira; that is all."

"You're not like any woman I've known before," Zeph insisted, feeling the truth of the words as he spoke to them. She was something he could not describe—a surprise he had never expected to find. He felt different when with her—more alive, more himself.

She let his comment sit between them like a gift she was deciding whether to accept. He had intended it as a gift. Now he realized that perhaps she did not see it that way.

"I got a lot of invitations to, as you say, share pleasures at the palace in Iredipa," he boasted. "But there's only one invitation that interests me and that young woman seems uncertain if she shares my interest."

"You are very forward. Are all Paxlosian men like you?"

Zeph thought he saw a smile lingering at the corner of her lips.

"Only the bad ones, and when are you going to start calling me, Zeph?"

"I have not decided," she responded flatly.

Zeph laughed. "Did you just flirt with me?"

"No," Eropa retorted. "Certainly not. Rhunes do not flirt."

"I don't know. I think you just flirted with me and here I was about to give up hope. Well, you *have* to call me by my name now."

"Why is that?"

"It's a rule," Zeph stated. "Once you've flirted with someone, you have to call them by their given name."

Eropa sighed. "I fear it would only encourage you."

"Then you'd better stop smiling, too, because nothing has encouraged me so much for a very long time." He caught Eropa's hand and coiled it around his arm. This time she did not withdraw it.

"You are not as bad as you pretend. These things you make light of are not bad to say if you actually mean them."

Zeph stepped back and her arm slipped away, putting space between them. *Mean it? Mean what? I wasn't being serious. This is just a game. I'm Morladja Yare's son. I can't afford to let anyone see inside me.*

He watched as Eropa's face returned to the unreadable blank it had been when they

started the day. In only one breath, the few feet between them had grown back to being as wide as the universe.

CHAPTER TWENTY-TWO

He should have felt relieved. He had defined his boundaries; making it clear that sharing pleasure was something he sought but serious emotions and commitments were out with him. So, why did he feel so rotten?

Eropa sat down on the edge of the dock, removed her slippers, and moved her feet back and forth through cool, clear lake water.

Zeph stood by, awkward and hot in his jacket and boots, uncertain what to say or do to regain the casual familiarity he had just crushed.

A shrill voice burst the silence.

"Captain Yare!" A young woman in an alarmingly pink dress flounced up the dock toward them, flushed, curls, bosom, and ruffles bouncing. Some misguided hairdresser made a cone of brown curls on top of her head, the whole affair melting into a nest of bedraggled worms that hung down on either side of the young woman's face and over her slouching shoulders in the heat and humidity.

"Captain Yare, I am Dora Dum'Laiere," she gasped, heaving for breath. "I am so happy we have finally found you." A plump hand tried to press the beribboned hairworms back into place. "We simply could not get a dressmaker to attend us, and that fool of a hairdresser moved like a snail."

"I'm sorry, but have we met?" Zeph eyed the tilting tower of curls.

The girl blinked. "I am Dora Dum'Laiere."

"You met her mother, Lady Miratha Dum'Laiere at the reception; the Voice of the Dum'Laiere clan," Standing, Eropa explained.

A second young woman joined them.

"And this is my 'friend', Fratianne." Dora scowled at the new arrival.

Zeph felt a familiar warming. Dora Dum'Laiere's companion was as stunning as Dora was plain. Her voluptuous proportions overflowed a bodice cut to reveal far more than her creamy-skinned throat. A wide sash accented a waist that bloomed into sumptuous hips. Unlike Dora, the newcomer wore no petticoats to hide what lay beneath the clinging silk dress.

"Fratianne Lobah." The girl offered Zeph her hand along with a lovely view of her pushed-up breasts. Her dark, brown eyes, lushly fringed with long, golden lashes, snapped with insolence and intelligence. This was Zeph's type of woman and they both knew it. "I hope you are taking advantage of Ebulon's many distractions." The young woman tossed back a loose strand of bright, red-gold hair, exposing her round and unblemished décolletage.

Dora Dum'Laiere stared, her mouth slack.

Zeph released Fratianne's hand.

"Please say we will see each other again soon." Fratianne batted her golden lashes. Leaning in, she added, "Later perhaps, when you have less company." She slipped a folded paper into his breast pocket, her fingers lingering lightly on his chest.

"I have arranged dinner for us, Captain," Dora stammered. "Mother said we should get to know each other, since..." She stopped mid-sentence, her eyes wide.

"Since...?" Zeph prompted. "Since what, Miss Dum'Laiere?"

Dora leaned toward him. "You know, since our futures will be so closely entwined." She batted her lashes, intimating he should understand her hidden meaning.

Zeph's stomach tightened into a ball. Was this girl to be his treaty bride? He did not know what her relationship to Nikodamus might be, but he could think of no other explanation.

"Unfortunately, I'm already engaged for the evening." Zeph took a firm hold of Eropa's arm and wound it through his before pulling her away down the dock. "I thought you were supposed to be looking out for me," he whispered as they made their getaway.

Eropa looked back over her shoulder at the two young women. "You were in no danger."

"If you believe that, you don't know anything about men and women," Zeph scolded her.

CHAPTER TWENTY-THREE

"Who knows a Rhune's mind? Not even herself. (Common Ebulonian saying. Anonymous. Undated.)

Only a quarter of the clan Voices remained in the city when the call came for an irregular meeting of the Council of Elders. Less than half who heeded the call could be described as neutral. Miratha made certain her allies were present, the room weighted in her favor.

Lady Aless watched the Dum'Laiere Voice mentally tally her colleagues as they arrived.

As the stream slowed a silent signal passed between her and Lector.

Miratha stood. Patting her upswept coiffure, she smoothed her dress, her eyebrows raised haughtily above her dark, heavily lined eyes, painted lips poked out in a conspicuously constructed pout.

"I apologize for calling you away from your families," she addressed the council. "But a matter of urgency has come to the attention of some of our members and it must be addressed without delay. We have learned that the Mahal, Nikodamus Mir, has been holding secret negotiations with the aliens outside of this council."

It was a startling statement. Nikodamus' meetings with the alien captain were not a secret, but the inference that something had transpired beyond the Council's tacit understanding had the desired effect on the members; the Dum'Laiere Voice had her colleague's attention. It was short-lived for at that moment Nikodamus entered, his footsteps echoing as he took his place among them. Miratha waited until he was seated before continuing.

"These private 'negotiations' have come to a result, apparently." Miratha paused. "A result that we have not been a party to and have had no part in forming. Which brings me to the question: Nikodamus Mir, when was it that we made you emperor?" All eyes turned to the Mahal, but Miratha had no intention of allowing him to answer. She unrolled a document from the table before her. "How long were you planning on keeping us in the dark before you told us of this secret 'treaty' with the aliens?"

"My discussions with Captain Yare were private, but hardly secret since you all knew they were taking place," Nikodamus defended himself. "I was acting on the council's instructions, drawing the alien out to discover the Paxlosian's purpose."

"And yet you did not think to share what you discovered with anyone," Miratha flared back.

"It would have been premature. The only member of the council I shared my progress with was Frevin Mir." Nikodamus' eyes sought the young diplomat, his accusation unmistakable. "As the chosen representative of the Ebulonian people, I do not represent a single clan. I represent the entire planet. This is my concern. When there is something solid for the clans to consider, I will bring it to the council."

Miratha began to read from the document in front of her. "A suitable female member of the ruling house of Ebulon will marry the Consortium's designated representative and return with him to Paxlosis, sealing the partnership between our worlds. The 'ruling house'? Did you interpret this requirement as indicating the Ebulonian representative would be from your own house; the Gilreedys? A minor house at best," she sneered. "Explain to the council your efforts to have your daughter, Eropa Rhune, wed to this alien because I do not understand the logic behind it."

"In my discussions with Captain Yare, Eropa's name was never linked to this position of bride-advocate, and any hypothetical connection would have nothing to do with my family line. Eropa is her mother's daughter; a daughter of Rhune. Her standing as a member of the leading family of Ebulon would be based on her relationship with Hagriva."

"The defense of your innocence rolls easily from your tongue, Mahal, but actions speak more truly," Miratha declared. "You sent her to Auhora Whimlan with the man."

"I did," Nikodamus admitted. "Acting as his guide gave her an opportunity to get to know the alien captain—to listen to his thoughts and reveal himself. I explained this to Frevin Mir. I think he resented the arrangement, for reasons we can all understand."

Miratha's lips puckered in a look of disgust.

Frevin scowled.

"Does your daughter know about this hypothetical treaty?" Miratha demanded.

"No. For the same reason that you did not. There is, as yet, no need."

Confused discussions broke out among the Voices. A sinister smile played at the edges of Miratha's lips. She did love winning. She raised the copy of the treaty.

"The document goes on, referring to the Mahal and his family." She lowered the sheaf of paper. "It appears the alien is acting under the belief that you are Ebulon's ultimate authority. How do you explain that Nikodamus?"

"It was the decision of this council to keep them in ignorance of many of the specifics about our people and our world. I saw no reason at the time to alter the alien captain's misunderstanding. I do not share it, however."

"I suggest that you understand very well the result of your actions, Mahal. You have seized the opportunity to mislead Captain Yare into believing that you are Ebulon's supreme authority with the intention of setting yourself up as such and benefitting from this new position," Miratha accused. "Have you mentioned the Matriarch and her role as our true leader? Does Captain Yare have any idea that you serve entirely at the whim of the people?"

"Hagriva has chosen not to reveal herself. I am following her lead," Nikodamus explained. "The alien's assumptions can be corrected once the situation has been stabilized but right now, we need him to see the benefits of a treaty enough that he wants it as much as we do. That was my task, and the path that I have pursued."

Lady Aless raised her chair above the crowd's heads. "And you have our thanks, Mahal." Lady Aless inclined her head in acknowledgment of Nikodamus' efforts. "We asked you to draw out the alien captain with the hope that by doing so we would gain information to support the Pira's plan to convince the Paxlosians that we are more valuable as allies than as conquered people. Discussion of a treaty is progress."

"Progress?" Miratha raised her voice. "Progress based on unsustainable lies is nothing but an illusion. Nikodamus's only power is as arbiter of this council, and he has clearly been manipulating the alien to change that."

CHAPTER TWENTY-THREE

"Nikodamus Mir has been a trusted servant of the people for sixteen years," Aless disagreed. "He has consistently put the needs of our people before his or his family's, proving himself worthy of our trust in whatever actions he deems necessary."

"Men often lose sight of their ideals when power and wealth are at stake," Lector spoke up.

"Some do it as regularly as they lose sight of their own asses," Aless snapped. "But this mahal is not one of them."

Snickers skipped among the scattered minority who were not Miratha's supporters.

"We should have been represented," Lector insisted doggedly.

"We *were*," Aless reminded him. "The Mahal is the Voice of the People. He represents us all."

"And I have tried to do it well," Nikodamus defended his position. "I took advantage of opportunities as they were presented. It was my hope to have something definitive to bring to you regarding our options, but we are not there yet."

"Our options," Lector once again inserted himself. "Have you approached the Mirs about what might be useable in The Trove and if they will allow access?"

"It is a step we should look at," Nikodamus agreed, "But we are not yet prepared to approach the Education and Ethics Administration with a request. What would we ask for? We do not know enough," Nikodamus answered. "I have discovered useful information about the Paxlosians however." He explained, "Captain Yare is answerable to a Consortium of influential merchants and powerful families residing in an area they call The Thousand Worlds, of which Paxlosis is a major planetary power. This consortium has put protocols in place to maintain control over Yare, and his mission but he chafes under what he sees as the injustices of their views. Still, he insists that their criteria must be met for the treaty to hold. He desires the treaty. This motivates him almost exclusively, but he has begun to see us as his allies and the Consortium as a group that stands in his way. We can use this in our favor."

"So, the Pira's plan is succeeding," Aless declared.

Nikodamus nodded. "Yare has seen the value of peace and recognized the need to protect our resources and goodwill, but we will have to abide by the terms that his sponsors have laid out."

"Your excuses do not matter, Nikodamus. This is something we should have been a part of!" Lector shouted. "You should have come to us and discussed what was being proposed."

Nikodamus clenched his fists. "I was working to stop an alien attack and then a civil war. I am sorry, Lector, but I did not have time to stroke your ego as well. By the Mother, have you all forgotten the fears that were voiced in this room only a few days ago?"

"It is you who have forgotten." Miratha's tone was icy. "You have forgotten who you are."

"The aliens have only been here a few days and look what has happened to us," Aless interrupted.

"The problems in the Quarter are worrisome. People do not feel safe. We're discussing increasing our houseguards," Bren'harrow announced.

"Truly a sad day for Ebulon." Miratha sighed, glancing at Lector, and giving him a subtle nod that served as a prompt.

"That is why I feel compelled to call for the Baraq Ta," he took the cue. "The weighing of the people's grace against the Mahal Nikodamus Mir."

There was stunned silence. It had been two hundred years since the vote of no confidence had been used to remove a Mahal.

Lady Aless frowned, troubled. "A weighty matter and one that should not be taken lightly or decided by only a few. A majority of the council must be present for this vote."

Miratha's fists clenched the stiff satin of her dress. "The Voices are scattered to their clan holds. We cannot wait to call them back. We have the required number. We should vote now."

Aless scanned the room.

"Shall I help you count, Lady Mc'Larick?" Buckley Bren'harrow offered, snidely.

"This matter should not be hurried," Lady Aless objected. "There is always time for truth."

"A vote has been called for, Lady Mc'Larick," Bren'harrow pointed out, overrunning her objections. "The time for debate is over."

Nikodamus stood. "It is unnecessary. I never sought this position, and I have no desire to keep it if I have lost the people's trust."

"Don't be so quick to walk away, Nikodamus," Aless cautioned. "You have forged a relationship of trust with the alien captain. That relationship and the alien's belief that you can and will uphold the treaty you negotiate may be all that stays his hand from aggressive action against us. If Yare perceives weakness in our leadership and a division of loyalty and direction among us, he may re-think this."

"And if the alien is so strongly invested in Nikodamus, personally, what is to stop Nikodamus from complaining that he is being pushed out and urging the Paxlosians to step in to keep him in power?" Bren'harrow demanded, playing on the mistrust Miratha and her colleagues had created.

Aless glowered. "Nikodamus would never do that."

"Members of your clan killed their kin for less," Bren'harrow shot back.

"Nikodamus is not Hector Mc'Larick," Aless argued. "And though the role of the Mahal is important, the Matriarch remains the final authority on all decisions on Ebulon."

"For now." Buckley Bren'harrow snorted.

"You disagree, Lord Bren'harrow?" a voice joined the discussion from the dark recesses of the room.

Hagriva Rhune, Matriarch of the Ebulonian people, walked forward, the Voices quickly rising to their feet as she passed. The scent of nervous sweat burst into the air, eyes shifting, hands twitching and trembling. How long had the sorceress been present? What had she heard? What had they said? Worse yet, what had they thought? Were their most private doubts over Ebulon's course revealed, their hidden ambitions laid bare to the Rhune?

Tiny silver moons studded the cobalt blue outer robe that billowed behind the petite woman, the under-dress beneath it patterned in overlapping circles of gold embroidery with jewel-colored galaxies stitched into the background. Her long cobweb-fine hair was loose, a sign that she had come prepared for spell-making. Miratha's co-conspirators glanced quickly from one to another then cast their eyes down, their thoughts blocked--except from a Rhune.

The ancient sorceress stopped her determined march before Bren'harrow, locking her stone-cold black eyes on him until he joined his colleagues and lowered his gaze.

"Matriarch, we understood that you were…not well," Lector said carefully.

"And as usual, your understanding is imperfect, Harscham, because, as you see, I am here, and in good health with my faculties reasonably under control." Her half-smile had the glint of a midnight moon reflecting in an executioner's blade.

Lector bowed his head quickly. "We are overjoyed. You are most welcome, of course."

The matriarch's cold eyes judged and convicted him. "I doubt it, but I will show up." Her chuckle was low and throaty. "I will show up."

A shush of air from Aless Mc'Larick's chair accompanied her as she approached the Matriarch.

"Welcome, Mah Rhune." The Senior Voice leaned far forward, the Matriarch meeting her halfway so Aless could reach the sorceress' cheek for a quick kiss. "Your council has been missed."

The Matriarch squinted as she scanned the room. "A questionable statement these days, Aless, but it seemed like it was time to make an appearance." Completing her dramatic navigation of the room, she planted herself beside the Mahal's seat. "I understand there is some business to be completed?" she prodded the gathering. "It is true that not so long ago, leadership on Ebulon was decided by mortal combat," she addressed the council. "Though why anyone would want to return to those days I cannot fathom. Ebulon has thrived in peace. The old way meant that good people died, regularly, people like many of you with strong consciences and intelligent minds, but who did not have strong arms and martial skills. Intelligence and conscience mean little in a decision-making process based on the strength of a sword arm. Your ancestors knew this from experience when they chose a new path. Peace gave us leaders who thought and considered their actions, leaders with integrity and wisdom." She smiled at Nikodamus.

"But as with all life, the cycle moves forward then circles back and what was sought and learned becomes lost and reviled," the old Rhune's voice rose as if chanting a storied myth, or reciting from the Book of Truths, a sense of dreamy poignancy tingeing the words as if she were talking more to herself than those in the room. She shook off her melancholy and turned her black, bird's eyes on the clan Voices. "Some of you have begun to look longingly back to those old days when strength and power were based on the wealth of your clan coffers and the skill of your warriors. But none of you remember the realities of the violence."

The scent of anger spiced and mingled with the scent of fear as Miratha's allies tried for invisibility--quiet in thought and word, knowing the Rhune could pluck their innermost thoughts from their minds or read them off the surface of their skin.

"It is easy to mock wisdom as ineffectual when it is ignored. Too many Ebulonians mouth the Truths these days without understanding or the desire to apply them to their lives. Therefore, The Balance teeters." The old Rhune studied the Voices' faces one by one. Some trembled, the bountiful cloth of their expensive gray robes shimmering like quaking leaves in the wind. Others turned their faces away, too crippled emotionally to manage more than standing upright.

"And what will Ebulon choose?" Hagriva asked, musingly. "I wonder. You know not the nature of the beast that you would again invite among your people," she muttered. "You have lived too long apart from its stalking ways and cannot remember how it prowls and attacks without regard for human importance or wealth, taking the young and innocent as often as the strong and powerful, the brave as often as the cowardly, the intelligent as often as the fool, the righteous as often as those with ill intent."

"We are people with free will," Miratha declared arrogantly.

"You are." Hagriva inclined her head in agreement. "And if you choose to return to plotting and killing that is your choice. " Hagriva turned to Nikodamus. "Nikodamus Mir, are you prepared to fight Harscham Lector for the position of Mahal? I assume that it is you, Harscham, who covets Nikodamus' position?"

Lector began to protest. "I did not…"

"Do not perjure yourself," Hagriva stopped him. "I know well your desires in this matter."

"I have a proposal for you Miratha," Hagriva consulted the Dum'Laiere Voice privately. *"I will give you what you have desired, but you must agree to send Dora to me at Alden Baierd for as long as I decide her presence there is necessary. Do not ask me why. I will not answer. Agree or not. It is your choice."*

"I have no wish to fight for something that was given as a gift of confidence," Nikodamus replied to the Matriarch's question. "Please release me from my position, Mah-Rhune, and I will happily return home to my village."

"You still call it home, even though you have not been there in over thirty years." Hagriva smiled, toothlessly. "And there it is, the reason the people chose Nikodamus Mir as their Mahal. He does not desire power. Therefore, they trust him to vote in their interests, not his own. Congratulations on your negotiations with the alien, Nicky," she offered the side note. "Getting the Paxlosians to recognize the value of retaining Ebulon's autonomy is a worthy accomplishment."

"*Even if it did require betraying your daughter, and myself,*" she added, addressing him mentally.

"*You are angry with me,*" Nikodamus replied in the same manner.

"*I could work up to it.*" Hagriva turned her attention to Miratha. "I need *your decision,*" she pressed.

"*Dora will attend you at Alden Baierd for as long as you require,*" Miratha agreed.

Hagriva resumed speaking to the council.

"The Pira's initial strategy has been successful. By not revealing ourselves fully, we remain a mystery to the aliens while we learn more about them with each day that passes. I have an announcement to make," the old Rhune declared. "I recognize Miratha Avlec Dum'Laiere as the most recent descendant of my bloodline."

Miratha's eyes shone like copper coins lit by the bright rays of sunset.

"*Understand me, Miratha, whoever bears the title of 'Matriarch' in the future, The Gift will pass to my chosen heir,*" Hagriva cautioned her.

"*I am your blood,*" Miratha said. "*You have just declared it publically.*"

"*My blood, but not my choice. Let this go, child. You would not survive,*" Hagriva cautioned. "*The Gift would destroy you.*"

It was a victory with a defeat buried inside, and Miratha's cheeks burned scarlet for both.

Hagriva returned her attention to the council Voices. "Now, let us finish the business at hand, the Baraq Ta. Lector?"

"Mah Rhune, I was only... "

CHAPTER TWENTY-THREE

"I know what you and Miratha were doing, Harscham." Hagriva sat cross-legged on a pillow on the floor. "Pretend you have the balls to finish what you have started."

Lector licked his lips. "The call for the vote of no confidence has been made," he called out. "Please signify your vote by stating 'Baraq Ta' if you wish to make a vote of no confidence or 'I have confidence' if your clan continues to support Nikodamus Mir as Mahal."

Beginning at one side, each member weighed in in turn.

"Baraq Ta." Bren'harrow glowered.

"Baraq Ta," Morestad, McAlburn, and Wallish Ner'ansett fell in line.

"I have confidence," Aless Mc'Larick cast her vote. She was not the only one. Though there had been an effort to stack the room against Nikodamus, with the Matriarch present, those who were not firmly aligned with Miratha, wavered, refusing to make such a public stand against a man who had the Matriarch's support and changed their vote.

When the voting was done, Aless turned to Hagriva. "The vote is equally divided among those present. It is for the Matriarch to cast the deciding vote."

"'Those present," Hagriva repeated. "A telling statement. It is unfortunate that so many Voices have missed this historic moment, and fortunate that *I* did not." The Voices fidgeted like naughty children caught in misdeeds. "The Mahal, Nikodamus Mir has my confidence and retains all rights and responsibilities of his position. Let that be the end of this farce." Hagriva focused her hard, black eyes on Lector then Miratha. "Ebulon has bigger problems than the clans' petty bickering. I would encourage you all to ask yourself what kind of person takes advantage of instability in their government to further their agenda at the expense of millions of lives. We are done here." The moon and stars on her robes swirled around her as she strode out of the room.

CHAPTER TWENTY-FOUR

"To struggle is to embrace the lie of non-change; let it go." (Mo Tep Hunan: Third Matriarch; undocumented.)

By late afternoon, the victors of the day's aquatic competitions were declared, their victory stories set down, and triumphs celebrated. The shining waters of the bay lapped softly against the docks and watercraft, gurgling in the air pockets; a lullaby to the sun-kissed children napping in their parent's laps. As the sun lowered below the shadowed forest, limning the far bank, the day's heat released its grip, leaving the festivalgoers basking in the balmy summer's eve.

The city's lights came on, reflecting with the stars on the dark water, making the sparkling city seem to float in the night sky on the dark water.

Light orbs outlined white sand paths that curved through the city streets, white-walled canyons with strings of lights crisscrossing above them. Below, fine white sand sparkled like diamond dust leaving its sheen on everything it touched.

Zeph turned in a slow circle that began and ended at Eropa, then took another swig from the wineskin someone had gifted him.

"You might want to go easy on that," Eropa cautioned. "It's heavy with onche' honey, a popular relaxant."

"Oh? Your father's consort, Dakmira Keesch, introduced it to me the night of the reception. I love the stuff." He made another circle while composing a message; *Found paradise—staying. Why didn't I think of this before? I can look after the family interests just as well from Ebulon as from Pax, which may be better.* Suddenly, he could think of no reason to leave, and so many to stay. Oh, Morladja would rant and threaten to withdraw her support if he did not return, but with Ebulonian trade under his control, she would not be able to hurt him. He no longer needed her. He could make his way-create his position, and once he'd proven the project's worth, his mother would come around.

CHAPTER TWENTY-FOUR

Zeph braved a glance at Eropa. If she was a little more aloof than earlier, she was no less charming. The fine sand sparkled on her skin, hair, and in the folds of her clothes, her impossibly large eyes catching the flames of a hundred lights.

I could stay here and never leave. Zeph's drunken mind caressed the idea as if it were the most tender part of this strange young woman.

Somewhere in the city, music began to play, and people began to drift toward it.

"The concert has started. Shall we go?" Eropa asked.

"Your desires are my own, Pira," Zeph said with mock gallantry, reckless in his drunkenness.

"Follow me." Eropa kicked off her shoes, bundled her skirts, and ran down to the water's edge. "I know a shortcut." Zeph followed her. A canoe sat abandoned on the shore. Eropa steadied the small craft. "Go on. Get in."

He winced as he waded into the bay's shallows, water flooding in over the tops of his boots. Clambering clumsily over the side of the canoe, he toppled into the bottom.

Eropa laughed. "I think that you have never been in a boat."

"Not since I was very young." Zeph worked to untangle his legs. "Water under the Dome isn't used for boating, but my father had a small hunting moon with a pond." He righted himself, found his balance, and settled in as Eropa maneuvered the canoe smoothly across the bay—the ripples from the canoe's passing fracturing the city's reflection in the glassy water.

Letting the small craft slip through the water in silence, Eropa rested her paddle across the canoe's gunwales as they rounded the inland side of the peninsula. "Have you ever seen anything so beautiful?" she whispered, looking up at the shining city.

"Never," Zeph replied, looking at her.

A soft shushing accompanied the canoe's prow sliding onto a new beach.

Zeph jumped out, sweeping Eropa into his arms and suddenly he was enveloped by her presence, the sweet pine and moss scent of her, the way she sparkled, sand glittering in her hair and on her skin, Auhora Whimlan's lights shining in her eyes. Her face was only inches from his, her mouth so close that her breath tickled his chin.

Before he thought about it, he leaned in and kissed her.

For a moment Eropa's body softened to his, then suddenly went stiff.

"Eropa?" Zeph pulled away looking into her face.

Her body went limp, her eyes as lifeless as a cadaver's staring back at him.

"Light of Death!" Zeph's arms dropped to his side. The Rhune began to collapse onto the sand. Instinctively he reached out to catch her but as he did, her form vibrated apart, pixilating into thousands of particles, shimmering, and fading.

His fingers closed on empty air.

Zeph let out a primal scream as his mind splintered.

Morladja Yare was a bad mother…a bad person; everyone said so, though they weren't supposed to talk about her. Tennet did not want his young son burdened by knowledge of his mother's terrible deeds, but they talked anyway when they thought no one was listening.

Zeph liked living on Adairis much better than living with his mother under the Dome. Here he could run and play outside in the woods, and swim in a real pond. Hazzle had taught him to fish when the pond was stocked.

Tennet Yare was not always there on Adairis, but the staff, guided by the steward-gamekeeper saw to its running, including Tennet's young son, Zeph.

Zeph was a child, living on Adairis, his father's small hunting moon. Tennet Yare had flown him to his hideaway retreat after taking the child from his mother's house. She had just killed her lover.

Zeph's memories of his mother were of a cloud of black hair, a rosebud mouth that was always screaming, and her angry, violet eyes.

The memory darkened. Zeph's father was dead, and his mother was coming to get him.

The cook told the gardener that Morladja had killed Tennet, but it was confusing because Zeph had also heard the other servants

CHAPTER TWENTY-FOUR

talking about Tennet dying in "an accident." How could his mother have killed his father if it was an accident?

"I don't want to leave, Guerin." Young Zeph sniffled, wiping his nose on his sleeve as he sat perched on a stool in the kitchen. "I want to stay here with you and Hazzle, and Old Burn."

"I'm sorry, young master, but your father, bless him, is gone, and that means your lady mother now controls everything. What was his is now hers and there's no getting around it."

"Even you? Even Hazzle?" Zeph demanded.

The housekeeper's lips pressed together into a tight line. "In a way of speaking," she said tartly. "Anyway, she is coming to fetch you, and you know how she is about having her way. I'm sorry. I truly am, Master Zeph, you're a good boy and we're all fond of you but there's nothing for it but that you get your things together and steel yourself to go."

As Zeph shuffled from the kitchen, he stole a loaf of bread. He would not go to his room. He would not pack. He turned the corner and climbed into the old dumbwaiter he often used as a secret fort.

"I will hide until Mother gets tired of waiting and leaves," he declared. Once she was gone, he and Hazzle and the staff could go on as they always had. Even if his mother sent away the rest of the staff, Hazzle would never leave Adairis, no matter what Morladja did.

Zeph moved cautiously through the house using the dumbwaiter shaft to keep out of sight, uncertain who he could trust now that Morladja was mistress.

"Where's the boy?" his mother's sharp bark splintered the house's quiet.

"'Hiding somewhere I s'pose." It was Hazzle's voice that answered. "He likes to..."

"I know what he likes," Morladja snapped. "He's my son. Find him and bring him to me."

Zeph held his breath. People rarely opposed his mother, and when they did, they never won. It might take years for her to get her revenge, but eventually they paid.

Hazzlebutt had always been Tennet's man, but if everything that had belonged to Zeph's father was now Morladja's, did that mean that Hazzle belonged to her as well? Would the old gamekeeper betray his friend's son to the woman who probably killed that friend?

"If I knew where he was, Lady Yare, I would bring him to you, but your boy was pretty upset about his father's death, and he run off right after. We haven't seen him. We're worried about him, we are, but we don't know where he is."

"You've lost my son?" There was an icy threat in the question.

"It's more like he lost himself, Ma'am. I'll look for him again as soon as we're done here, but I knew you would expect an explanation, so I wanted to be here when you arrived. Maybe you could tell us where he is. You having those motherly instincts and all."

"Bring Zeph here to me, now!" Morladja exploded. "That's an order!"

"I think you're misunderstanding something about our situation here, Lady Yare. I don't take orders from you," Hazzle corrected her calmly.

"I own you!" Morladja's voice cracked like a whip.

"No, Ma'am, you don't. I was Tennet's man," Hazzle explained. "And now I'm young Master Yare's; me and this moon, deeded and titled. You can ask that lawyer fellow, Prudim. He's got the papers. Adairis will be held in trust for Master Zeph and I'll look after it 'till he's grown."

"You can't do this," Morladja spat viciously.

"I didn't." Hazzlebutt defended himself. "Master Tennet set it all up. Now, I think it's time you left. Adairis isn't safe for a woman like you."

A shiver ran through Zeph. Hazzle had been brave, but he knew his mother. She would not let this go. She would make Hazzle suffer, and now there was no one left to stop her--not until he came of age.

Suddenly Zeph's hideout did not feel safe; nowhere did.

Hunched on the dock in the shadow of a tent, Zeph took a long draught from his wineskin, wiping the dribble from his chin with the back of his hand. He stopped and stared at it. It was a grown man's hand, not a child's.

He had been dreaming. But why relive those memories? He hadn't thought about his father's death in years. He tried hard not to in fact. It was too painful.

CHAPTER TWENTY-FOUR

That was the beginning of the end of everything.

Hazzlebutt had done everything he could to protect young Zeph, but the old gamekeeper was no match for Morladja. Before the week was out Zeph had been found and sent back to live with her under the dome.

Eventually, Hazzle's life, too, was forfeited to the war between Zeph's parents, another "accident". Zeph had tried his best to bury that part of his childhood as a reminder of what his life might have been if his compassionate father had lived and been allowed to raise him.

So, why was he remembering it now?

The girl, Eropa, had been going to listen to a concert. He was carrying her to the beach. They had been so close…and then he kissed her…" Zeph's mind went blank. *"Don't think about this,"* an inner voice warned.

He bent over the water and vomited into the bay. Fumbling with the fastenings of his shirt, he ripped it open in frustration. His thoughts twisted and turned as if trying to free themselves from the spit they were turning on. *Don't think. Don't think. You can't think.*

Zeph dove into the water, swimming furiously to banish all thought.

Finally exhausted, he dragged himself out onto a far dock and collapsed.

The cool night air brushed Zeph's face and chest. He opened his eyes and stared up at the dark sky, stars scattered through it like bright jewels that defined a depth beyond the mind's ability to grasp.

"Where am I?" His muddled, drunken mind could not understand what he was seeing; a sky ruled by two moons. "Not Pax," Zeph decided. "Not Adairis." *This is Ebulon,* he remembered. "I am very far from home. So far away that I may never get back." Zeph lay on the dock, gazing at the foreign sky until he passed out.

Eropa's perception of her surroundings fluctuated more and more rapidly until the illusion of continuity held and her atoms completed the act of reassembling.

The air was chill and musty; the shutters closed against the sea air though the ever-present sound of the waves crashing against the northern cliffs could not be shut out.

Even in the dark, she knew the space; the small, stone-walled room that had been her bedroom since she first came to Alden Baierd when she was five. Using her intention, Eropa lit a small glow globe shattering the darkness, revealing the cobwebs and mouse droppings endemic to any space in the castle ruins where the continuity of human habitation had been broken.

The sparse room was as she had left it less than a year ago. Country clothes considered too casual and worn were tucked away in a wicker trunk at the foot of the plain, narrow bed. Mud-encrusted Garden clogs sat neatly beneath the bed's edge. A spare temple-style practice uniform hung limp, like a discarded shadow on a hook behind the door.

She no longer lived here or slept here; she had been banished, sent to Iredipa to take up the mantle of the duties for which she had been trained--a final training ground for her future as Ebulon's Matriarch.

Finding her knees shaky, the young sorceress sat down on the edge of the raincloud-gray wool blanket covering the cotton-filled mattress and focused her mind on calming the trembling that infected her body.

Why am I here? Her mind asked.

The scene in Auhora-Whimlan flooded back.

Zeph kissed her.

A delicious warmth rushed through her body, pushing out any strength she had left, sinking her forward onto the floor.

So many disparate emotions--each more intense than the one before raced through the channels within her body.

The sensation was wonderful…and terrifying.

"The man is a threat to us--an enemy," an internal voice warned her. *"You cannot allow him to gain the slightest edge of influence over you."*

Eropa understood the foundation of that thought. It was the classic Rhune hardline taught to the young; *protecting your power is your primary concern.* She remembered Aless Mc'Larick warning her about the power of chemistry between a man and a woman. Eropa had dismissed the elder woman's advice as well-meaning but ignorant of

CHAPTER TWENTY-FOUR

a Rhune adept's true experience. Eropa realized now how incomplete her understanding had been.

Why had Hagriva never explained this aspect of physical being to her? As many times as her teacher had warned Eropa about the dangers of releasing your control, she had never spoken of how Eropa's own body might be used against her, or how tantalizing, exciting, and confusing love-play, and the motives behind it were. How did a Rhune manage to navigate romantic relationships? It explained a good deal about why so many avoided such entanglements.

This alien is a threat to us--an enemy, the inner voice continued to spew rhetoric advising mistrust of the alien captain, warnings based on fear and ignorance, not on character.

It was true, Eropa did not know Yare well, but during the time they spent together his actions had never felt evil. Was he so skilled at being disingenuous? Could he truly hide such dark motivations from a Rhune?

Frevin believed the worst of the alien captain, but Frevin had his motivations. Though it was Nikodamus who voiced that Frevin's interest in Eropa was political, not personal, Eropa had recognized the truth in her father's words. And at some level, she must have recognized something. She had never allowed her friendship with Frevin to reach a physical level of intimacy and yet, when Zeph Yare appeared, Frevin became jealous, possessive, and controlling. She had never been concerned that Frevin would try and steal power by sorcerial means, but his willingness to use her for personal gain was cause for caution. They had known each other a long time and there were weaknesses in him—weaknesses she could forgive as a friend, but not as a potential partner or a future Mahal.

And what about this Zeph Yare? What weaknesses would you be willing to forgive in him?

Logic played no part in attraction.

The look on Zeph's face as she disappeared suddenly snapped into place.

Disassembling was an aggressive act of self-preservation, something undertaken by a Rhune under threat—an act meant not only to allow escape but to unhinge the enemy, providing time and space for the Rhune to complete their escape without being followed. The action had accomplished that. She effectively shredded the foundations of reality on which his worldview was built, crumbling reason.

The consequences of her action dropped like a weight in Eropa's stomach. Not only had she thrown the alien into a state of shock, then abandoned him she had revealed the existence of the abilities she demanded the Council of Elders keep secret…abilities the Paxlosians would find difficult, perhaps impossible, to accept. It was an act of sorcery without the camouflage of rudimentary technology.

They will hate and mistrust us from now on, Eropa realized.

"And it was my fault."

She needed to repair the situation, but how? Whatever she needed to do, she could not do it from here in Alden Baierd. She needed to return to Auhora Whimlan.

The Rhune stripped off her dress, letting it fall in a puddle on the floor, and donned her practice clothes. Wrapping the bindings around her legs and torso, she threw on her hooded cape, centered herself, and disassembled.

A fresh breeze rippled the surface of the bay surrounding the glass city. With the steadiness of a clock's pendulum, water slapped the underside of the wooden docks' honeycombed framework. The lights of the festival city still twinkled, but many had sputtered or been put out as the city's inhabitants sought their beds.

But for the rhythmic slurping splash of water, the susurra of the wind swaying the tall, fir trees on the far shore, whispering in her ears, the city had become silent.

Finding Zeph would not be difficult. Though his energy was confused and thready, a part of her remained keyed to his presence.

Eropa's leather-soled boots padded softly over Auhora Whimlan's deserted docks. Black against black, she moved like a leaf on the lake, counterbalancing the gentle rise and swell of the lake, using the height of a swell to leap from one puzzle piece of the connected dock to the next, matching her breath and movements to the wind, her mind empty, not thinking—only moving, each step, leap, and pause a perfection of precision.

CHAPTER TWENTY-FOUR

She found him lying passed out on a dock in the string of the outer ring surrounding the floating city.

He stunk of sour wine and onche'.

Kneeling beside him, Eropa gently moved aside the lock of brown-gold hair that had fallen across his face.

A deep gash scarred his mind.

He might be foolish and ignorant of how The Truths and the multiverse worked but he was not evil.

Point by point, Eropa touched places on the alien's neck, wrists…forehead, helping to calm his nervous system and restore balance. Surely when she explained her mistake, he would forgive her.

"I am so sorry." She lay a cool hand against the alien's flushed cheek.

Zeph's eyes flew open. For an instant he saw her and began to smile, then before another breath had passed, his gray eyes turned to hard-iron bitterness, the muscles of his face setting in grief and anger.

"What are you doing here?" his voice was gravelly and harsh like heavy rock dragging across gravel.

"I came because…I wanted to…" Eropa stammered, uncertain what he remembered or what to say. "I was afraid you might be hurt," she blurted out finally.

"Get away from me." Zeph stumbled to his feet. "*Who* are you? *What* are you?"

"I am the Pira…"

Zeph stopped her. "That's not what I mean, and you know it. What did you do to me back there on the beach?"

"You will be fine," Eropa assured him. "You are just very drunk."

"That's how you're going to play this, eh?" Bitterness bled through each syllable. "Try to convince me that I'm so drunk I was seeing things. What about The Truths, Pira? Everyone else must follow them, but you can just pick and choose?"

"Please. You just need to rest. Let me help you back to your tent." Eropa stepped toward him.

"Don't touch me," Zeph growled stepping back to maintain space between them. "I know what I saw, Eropa—I don't understand it, but I saw it, and tomorrow when I've sobered up, I'm still going to have seen it. So, there's no point in trying to pretend that I didn't. It's insulting."

"I should not have left like that," the sorceress apologized. "I was just…surprised."

"Surprised that I kissed you?" Zeph demanded with caustic sarcasm. "But isn't that why you were sent here, to soften me up so that your Mahal could get what he wanted for his treaty?" He snorted. "I don't think things turned out the way he planned, did they? Don't worry I'll be sure to tell him how you truly helped me understand your people."

"I should not have come." Eropa turned to leave.

Like a striking snake, Zeph lunged forward, grabbing her wrist and pulling her back hard against his chest. "We're not done, yet, Pira," he hissed into her ear, his face nuzzled deep in her hair.

Eropa felt the warmth of his breath tickling her ear, her neck, and her will began to melt like butter. She rolled her arm, reversing his grip, struck his right elbow with her left palm, and pushed her shoulder into him, knocking him off balance and breaking away.

Yare flew six feet before hitting the dock, his head thudding against the boards.

Watching him recover, Eropa waited with her foot pressed against his throat for his head to clear. The symbols glowing from beneath her skin lit the darkness around them.

"We have given you every opportunity to do the right thing here," she warned him, her voice low and threatening. "But do not mistake where you are, Zeph Yare. This is not your world. It is ours. Its rules are not your rules. They, too, are ours. Do not push us too far."

She slowly removed her foot from his windpipe, then, in a cyclone of sparks and swirling dark cloth, spun away, leaping across the water, a disappearing nimbus in the dark.

Dawn broke, and a gull's raucous cry woke Zeph. Feeling the boards of the docks pressing against his back, he opened his eyes.

Fratianne twirled one of her golden curls around her finger. "I thought I'd have to search the whole city for you, but here you are, practically at my doorstep."

Trying to sit up, he failed miserably. "Light of Death, my head feels like it's been crushed."

CHAPTER TWENTY-FOUR

"Wine and onche' are quite fun at first. Not so much afterward," the Taiban servant girl commiserated.

Zeph tried again to sit up. The effort wasn't worth the pain. He shut his eyes against the day's brightness.

"Damn. I'm in no condition."

"No condition for what?" Fratianne asked coyly.

"Anything." Zeph groaned. Something was tickling his chest. He opened his eyes. The girl had left off twirling her hair and was now twining the curly hairs on his exposed chest. "What are you doing, Fratianne?"

"Seducing you."

"Come back tomorrow."

"Tomorrow will be too late." She settled beside him. "I have a proposition for you."

"I'm not interested."

"It's not that kind of a proposition. I mean, it might be later, if you want, but it doesn't have to be. Listen, the way I see things, we are perfect for each other; you have questions, and I have answers," she announced glibly.

"My mind's a little fuzzy right now, Fratianne. You need to say what you mean."

"Pay attention, Yare." The Half-Taiban girl leaned over and thumped his forehead, causing him to see stars. "The next few minutes could define your future. The problem is that you're not asking the right questions. For example, what are the Ebulonians doing during those long silences in their conversations with you? Don't you get the feeling you're missing something? Wouldn't you like to know what?"

Zeph held very still, willing the nausea that came with the dip and rise of the docks to calm, but her words were beginning to filter through his alcohol-sodden brain.

"I'll bet you're going to explain it to me," he quipped.

She snorted. "That's not how this is going to work. I'll give you something you want then you'll give me something I want."

"You don't have what I want, Fratianne."

"I do." She straddled him. "You just don't know it yet."

Zeph frowned. "Get off of me."

She leaned in and began to whisper in his ear. Zeph could not catch all of what she said, but he caught enough.

"Stop. You're coming off desperate, and that's never a good negotiating position. Reading minds is a parlor game, Fratianne. It's not real." Zeph pushed her off and sat up on the edge of the dock.

Fratianne straightened her gown. "On your world maybe but this is not your world, and you need to stop making decisions and acting on them like it is. Telepathy is mostly how Ebulonians communicate with each other. Think about it, Yare. It explains a lot."

Zeph began to re-visit his conversations with Ebulonians starting with Frevin Mir's almost instant dislike.

"Those talks you had with the Mahal in his study? He was picking your brain. I hear he took a particular interest in your relationship with his daughter." Fratianne gave him a knowing grin.

"His daughter?" Zeph looked confused.

"The Pira."

Zeph felt like he had been spun around and propelled forward without a breath in between.

"Eropa is Nikodamus' daughter?"

The Taiban girl's eyes widened. "You didn't know that? By the Mother, you're such an idiot."

"But that can't be." Zeph could not accept what she was saying. "Nikodamus had dozens of opportunities to tell me that."

"And yet he didn't," Fratianne pointed out. "Ask yourself why?"

Zeph was certainly doing that. "And this mind-reading thing, Eropa has that?"

"Are you seriously asking me that? She's a damned Rhune--she's the worst. And not just a Rhune, she's the Pira!" Zeph blinked. "You're in so far over your head here, Yare. Look, you need someone on your side who can help you understand your opponents and what's going on here: me."

"And you're offering to do that out of the goodness of your corseted, little heart?" Zeph suggested, skeptical of her answer.

"No. There's a price. I want you to take me with you when your ship leaves."

"I can't do that," Zeph declared.

"Of course, you can you're the captain. But you're trying to win a game of strategy without knowing how to play or what the rules are. These Ebulonians: Mirs, Rhunes, they're not like us. They *know* things, like magic and..."

CHAPTER TWENTY-FOUR

"Wait, what did you say?" Zeph thought his mind had wandered and he had misheard her.

"You don't know what a Rhune is, do you?"

"They're some kind of group or guild," Zeph improvised.

Fratianne shook her head. "They're sorceresses."

Zeph made a face. "You mean witches?"

"Oh, they're much more than mere witches," Fratianne assured him. "They're the Keepers of the Truths, a powerful psychic sisterhood that spans universes and dimensions."

"You don't believe that shit, do you? I thought you were a sensible girl," Zeph scoffed. "Witches aren't real, Fratianne."

She smiled at him. "Again, what world do you think you're on? This is not Paxlosis. It's not even Taiba. It's Ebulon, and the rules are different here. Let me help you, Captain Yare. Take me with you. I'll make it worth your while." Her smile took on a suggestive tone.

Zeph refused to let her distract him. "The laws of science don't change from world to world. These Rhunes have made themselves out to be something important so they can wield power over the ignorant, but magic isn't real."

"How did the Pira get onto your ship with your shields up and no shuttle? Yes, I know about that. People talk around servants like they aren't there, but being half Taiban doesn't make me stupid. What the Pira did defies the rules of your science because it isn't scientific. It was magic. I know things, Yare. You don't have to fumble around in the dark, guessing. Let me help you." She walked her fingers up his thigh to his groin, snuggling in against his side. "Besides, wouldn't it be nice to have a warm, willing woman waiting for you in your cabin at night during that long trip back to Paxlosis?"

Zeph moved her hand away. "You don't want to go to Paxlosis, Fratianne. You'd hate it."

"You don't know shit about what I want or hate." She sat up. "You think Ebulon is a paradise? Not if you're Taiban or half Taiban. We're barely tolerated here. Every minute of every day Ebulonians make sure we know we're not as good as them. They think that all Free Men are crazy, living for some fantasy future when we'll all go back home to Taiba and be free. But Taiba is not my home. I was born here. I never lived there, and I'm tired of waiting to be seen as a person. I want to live free now and not as some second-class citizen."

"It won't be any different on Pax," Zeph argued.

"Just get me there. I'll do the rest. I won't ask you for anything, I promise. I'm good at making my opportunities."

"The answer is still no."

Fratianne's expression changed. "Okay, have it your way. Just remember it was your choice." Wrapping one hand around the back of his neck, the other came out from under her dress. Zeph felt a sharp jab in his neck, and a liquid numbness began to flood his veins. "You should have said yes," she whispered as his vision faded.

CHAPTER TWENTY-FIVE

"Hardship vanishes with acceptance of what is and the nature of all things to change." (Common Ebulonian saying. Undated. Attributed to an anonymous Mir.)

"**H**ow could you, Fratianne?" Dora stomped her foot. "Captain Yare is *my* fiancé-mine!"

"Dora, people are staring at us," Fratianne tried to calm the fractious girl.

"What do I care? I am a Dum'Laiere. Who are they? Nobody. You have embarrassed me and my entire family." Dora sniffed haughtily. "Did you not understand? If I were you, I would not bother to unpack when we return because Mother will most certainly fire you when I tell her what you did."

Fratianne grabbed the girl by the elbow and hurried her out of the main current of traffic, flinging her into a side street.

"She won't, because I was following *her* orders."

"You are lying," Dora proclaimed weakly.

"Captain Yare didn't know anything about your 'secret arrangement', Dora, because there is no secret arrangement. There's nothing between you and him--no agreement, and no plan. Nothing."

Dora blew her nose. "I know, no one is supposed to know…"

"No one knows because she made it all up!" Fratianne exploded in frustration. "You need to wake up, Dora. Your mother made it up."

"Why would she say it if it was not true?" Dora whimpered.

"I'm sorry to say this, but your mother doesn't always have your best interests at heart." Fratianne sighed. "If you tell her I said that I'll deny it."

Fratianne pushed Dora and she stomped off, leaving Fratianne to follow.

Dora entered their tent and threw herself onto the platform bed.

CHAPTER TWENTY-FIVE

"I am ruined," she wailed. "Word will get around, and everyone will know. They will all laugh at me. Why would Mother do something to shame me like this?"

"She did warn you not to tell anyone."

"People are so cruel." Dora sobbed into the pillows.

Fratianne sat down beside her, awkwardly patting her back. "I'm sorry. I shouldn't have said those things. Please stop crying, Dora."

The girl's wails slowed to sniffles, then stopped. Sitting up, her tear-stained face red and swollen, she asked, "Is there really no engagement? Mother was just pretending?"

"I heard her talking to Lector Harscham. You're not the only one being manipulated. The Mahal is arranging for Yare to marry the Pira, but neither of them knows yet. Yare wasn't faking his confusion. He doesn't know anything about your mother's plan."

"But she 'told' me Yare and I were to be engaged. You heard her."

"She'll never admit it, Dora, and no one is going to take my word over hers," Fratianne pointed out. "Even if I was stupid enough to confront her, which I'm not. Face it, Dora, neither of us has the power to take on your mother."

Dora straightened her shoulders. "Thank you, Fratianne, for being so honest. It was brave of you since you are only a servant, and it could cost you your position. Still, I am glad you told me."

"Look, as rich Ebulonians go, Dora, you're not bad. You're almost eighteen. All you have to do is hold on for a few more years, and Miratha won't have control over you anymore. You'll be in charge of your fortune and destiny. You can do that, can't you; hold on a few more years?"

Dora frowned. "I turned eighteen three months ago."

Fratianne blinked. "You're eighteen?"

"Yes. I think I know my birthday."

The Taiban girl's lips widened into a grin. "Then your mother has no more control over anything you do, Dora. You're the Dum'Laiere heir. You're really, really rich. You can do whatever you want."

"But how can that be?" Dora looked confused.

"For years, she's been telling everyone you're simple," Fratianne explained.

"I am not," Dora insisted.

"I agree, but is there anyone who will support you if you were to stand up to Miratha?"

Dora considered that. "My Uncle Kirk, maybe. My grandmother Cora would take my side if I could explain to her without mother's interference, and she believed me." An impish smile curved between Dora's dimpled cheeks.

"What are you thinking?" Fratianne prompted.

"I am thinking, if I am an heiress, that we should go shopping." She grabbed the Taiban girl and pulled her out the tent door.

CHAPTER TWENTY-SIX

"Holding to a comrade who has no honor is like carrying an empty water skin in the desert; it is a weight you cannot afford to bear." (Attributed to the Taiban Leader "Warin the First" undocumented.)

Sitting with his cheek pressed against the side of the Taiban vessel he was working on; Quinn twisted his arm around and wriggled it deep inside the working parts.

"Where's Terk?" Quinn loosened the brackets on the balancer he was replacing. "I thought he was looking after you until you go to your new family."

Clem shrugged. "I'm used to looking after myself."

"I've got it." Quinn pulled out the glass balancer. The tube's interior was dark and cloudy. "I knew it had blown," he said. "I swear that I heard it go. Hand me that new tube, will you, Clem?" With the new balancer in hand, Quinn began to twist his arm around again to get it in place.

"If you slide the balancer in at an angle up past the polls there, then set it down on the tumbler, you can take your arm back out and reach back in again over here at a better angle," Clem offered.

Quinn frowned. "Are you sure? Because if it falls…"

"It won't," Clem assured him. "There's a ledge inside that it can sit on. You can't see it from here, but it's there, trust me, and the body of the drive makes a wall behind it. It can't fall."

Quinn peered into the engine's dark recesses. "Okay." He set the glass tube down cautiously and pulled his arm out. Quickly going back in as Clemmet directed, he retrieved the tube, turned it, and slipped it into place. "That was easy. Thanks, Clem."

"With Vale gone, you have an opening on your team, right, Quinn?" Clem asked awkwardly.

"Yeah, I guess we do." Quinn continued checking, sliding his thumb and forefinger along rubber tubes and wiring systems to feel for problems he could not see.

"Are you thinking about offering it to Terk?"

Quinn stopped working. "He's kind of young, and he doesn't have any training. Why? Would it worry you if your friend went back to Taiba?"

Clem looked away. "No. I just wondered if he was the right person."

"No one can replace Vale," Quinn agreed. "We were like brothers, Vale and Ald and I."

"That's important for a team, isn't it?" Clem remained thoughtful.

"It is. You need to know that you can absolutely trust each other with your lives because, most of the time, that's what's at stake." Quinn went back to checking the ship's soundness, then added, "Terk does know the area and the people, so that's something in his favor, and the people there know him because of what he did for you kids. That might be worth having him along."

Clem had been on the run, hiding from the Intelligence Squads since he'd gone off on his own. Fingered as a "smart kid" from the mandatory tests at school, the I.S. had been turning up in the neighborhood more and more frequently where he lived with the other kids Terk called "his kids". Clem had worried that he was going to have to move on or risk getting caught.

Terk set himself up as a sort of big brother to a group of street kids, Clem included, claiming he "looked after them", and kept them from being preyed on by thieves and slavers, but Clem had seen things that made him question how protected they were with Terk. It was not something the kids talked about, but they knew they were being used. Kids who talked about it had accidents or mysteriously disappeared. Nothing said about Terk was private. The older boy somehow always knew.

When Quinn's team found Clem and offered to take him away from Taiba, Terk quickly included himself in the offer, talking about how he was being hunted by the I. S. and how he was worried that, as the I.S. drew nearer, he was putting the other kids at risk. He made it seem like it was Terk that the warlords were hunting, and Clem was only an afterthought.

Once the team agreed to take Terk, he insisted that before he left, he got the little he ones was looking after out of the city to a safe place. It was a good story. So good it made Clem feel better even though he was sure it wasn't true. If there was a safe place, why hadn't Terk taken them there before? Why now?

Terk took the kids away and returned a few days later, alone with more money than Clem had ever seen. He tried not to think about what that might mean. Suspicions weren't facts and thinking bad things about someone who had helped you stay alive was ungrateful. Still, the thought that Terk had done something bad with the other kids haunted him.

"Whatever you think he could do to help, it's not enough. You should take someone else," Clem said to Quinn in a rush of honesty.

Quinn stopped what he was doing and studied the shy boy.

"Do you want to tell me why?" Clem shook his head. "Do you have someone else in mind?"

"What about your cousin, Corin?" Clem perked up. "She's a good fighter, and you trust her."

Quinn's features darkened. "I'd trust Corin with my life, but I won't take her to Taiba."

"Find someone else then, someone you can trust," Clem repeated.

"And that's not Terk?" Quinn quizzed him.

Clem's face went white. "I didn't say that."

"No, you didn't," Quinn agreed.

Terk was rambling across the field toward them.

"Is this punk bothering you?" he ruffled Clem's hair as a greeting.

"Not at all," Quinn replied. "He's good company."

Terk glared at Clem. "Not telling you how to do your job, is he?"

"No, but he does seem good at fixing things. That's a knack that could come in handy," Quinn complimented the younger boy.

"Yeah, back on Taiba, Clem and I were always fiddling with mechanical stuff, taking things apart, putting them back together," Terk lied. "But you know what he'd be really good at? Flying. He just understands ships." Clem studied his shoes. "He wouldn't say anything, of course, because, you know, back on Taiba, if people know stuff like that about you, you get a price on your head for being smart. Clem and me both got prices on our heads. Don't we, Clem?"

Quinn stole a glance at Clem. The boy was trembling.

"You're here now, Clem. You don't have to worry about that. You're safe."

"Not since the Paxlosians came," Terk disagreed.

Quinn frowned. "That's enough, Terk."

"What? You want me to lie to him like he's some little kid?" Terk made a noise of disgust. "You can't just cover up problems with shiny lies, Quinn, not with kids like Clem. They know too much. They've seen too much."

"Is that what you think we're doing here, lying to you?" Quinn demanded.

Terk shrugged. "I don't know, it seems like you Bobalos don't tell half what you know, but Clem and I aren't stupid. We see things, and if they don't add up, well...." He turned to Clem. "Right, fart-face?"

Clem looked from Terk to Quinn and back again. He wished what Quinn said about Ebulon being safe was true, but it wasn't. Vale was dead. He scooted out from under the ship and shuffled away.

"Lay off Clem," Quinn warned Terk quietly. "He'll have a new family soon. He shouldn't have to think about that stuff."

"He's not some glass teacup," Terk retorted. "Clem's tough. He had to be, or he wouldn't be alive."

"Look, Terk, Clem has a few years left to be a kid. Let him have that. It's not much, but he deserves it."

"Yeah, 'cause he's so special." Terk's lips were twisted in disgust as he walked away.

The refugee community could treat the cuts and scrapes of those newly arrived from Taiba. They could fill their bellies, give them shoes, clothes--even give them an education and a family if they were young enough, but they could not change their past. Those who arrived with families and the young adapted most successfully, but in the past several years, the refugees were forced to make a change in the criteria for transport to Ebulon. These later arrivals came without ties behind them and little interest in ties going forward. They lingered at the edges of society, judging it with hard eyes and harder hearts. Brawlers by nature and survivors by trade, their activities for the rebellion had gotten them marked on Taiba and evacuating them had been the compassionate option. But these rough men and women had never had the luxury of having a life plan or goals beyond the next meal, the next mission. The idea of working for something that might bring you comfort in some hypothetical future was beyond their experience and grasp. Take away the fear, the bare-knuckle survival, and the Taiban warlord's fist hanging, over them, and they still only saw a world governed by those ever-present factors. They had no idea what to do with a world of possibilities and so, they did what people do when they do not understand something; they belittle it, label it false, and try to tear holes in its fabric.

Suspicion and a lack of confidence kept them isolated, migrating eventually toward others like themselves. Incapable of adapting to a culture that did not feast on the gore of its belly, the new refugees were bitter and dissatisfied.

Clem was young. A family had agreed to adopt him. He would have a place here. Terk, Quinn feared, would never fit in.

Terk waited outside Loosy Humqualt's offices for the mechanic to close shop. The old mechanic came out, waited as several of his employees joined him, then locked up. The group of men ambled down the street, other workers joining them, talking, and joking.

Terk sauntered along behind, his hands stuffed deep in his pockets.

The group passed the local pub and entered an unmarked warehouse beyond it. Something was going on, and he wanted to know what.

After loitering for a quarter of an hour, the slow stream of Free Men stopped. Terk casually walked the building's perimeter, looking for a way inside. A small, second-story window left partially open was all he needed. He climbed the brick wall with the help of a drainpipe, pressed the window open, and wriggled through onto a stack of crates inside.

The warehouse was crammed with wooden crates and old body parts for Taiban pods and shuttles. Terk flattened to his belly and crawled forward until he could see over the edge.

"A fucking warlord pays his men better than this; a mud hovel on a planet you have to almost die to get to. Ebulon's a prison, not a paradise." Je'anna Peru crossed her arms over her chest. "And I'm sick of these pansy-assed rich Ebulonians' superior attitude. This isn't what we were promised."

"Did you get hit on the head, Je'anna? 'Cause you've got a serious case of amnesia." Tommy Makepeace was an ugly son of a whore, with a crooked nose and a long knife scar that stretched over his mouth from nose to chin, but he was a good fighter and a steady hand, and people liked him, unlike the prickly Je'anna. "You seem to have forgotten, you don't have no options. People risked their lives to bring you here, and don't you forget it."

"I didn't ask them to," Je'anna retorted.

"And why did you have a price on your little bald head?" sarcasm-soaked Makepeace's every syllable. "Oh yeah, I remember, you shot your mouth off to one of Admiral Whort's fucking guards. You're done on Taiba, Je'anna. No warlord's ever going to let you work for them. Ebulon is all you've got. You may not have a feather bed to sleep on, but you sleep safe at night."

"Tell that to Toval's brother," Je'anna shot back.

Eyes flitted to the Turgistas, aware that she was poking at wounds that were still raw. The attendance of the Turgistas told Terk a lot about the politics of this group.

"You've got a black heart and a foul mouth, girl." Loosy's Humqualat's lover complained. "You're too damn new here to be making demands." The man had the face of a horse but the body of a god.

"These sheep need Bobalo's permission to scratch their butt, but I'm not laying down just to be taken advantage of," Je'anna refused to be talked down.

"This isn't about Tai Bobalo," Loosy interjected. "We're here to figure out how to get the Ebulonians to take us seriously, not fan grudges between Free Men." The refugees didn't like people talking bad about Captain Bobalo, especially the old guard, but that was starting to change with the population. There was grumbling, and if you were talking about the Taiban community on Ebulon, Bobalo's name could not be avoided.

Terk crawled closer to the edge of the crates and raised his head to bring more of the speakers into view. Besides the Turgista clan, Makepeace, and his friends, there was the Humqualt contingent, and another group clustered around the ex-captain, Saldo Murtevoy.

"As far as the Ebulonians are concerned, this is not our world and never will be, "Tommy Makepeace said. "We're intruders just as much as the Paxlosians are, but with less to offer."

A door on the far side opened and Quinn Bobalo's mate, Ald entered. He crossed the room and stood with the Turgistas.

Ald has changed camps.

"We have allies among the Ebulonians who have stood by us," Loosey argued. "If they hadn't, we wouldn't be standing here. If we start making trouble, we could lose their support."

"To make change, you need political power," Loosy's lover spoke up. "And we don't have any."

"I had an interesting meeting the other day," Saldo Murtevoy edged forward from his corner. "Several members of major clan houses approached me wanting to know if I could hire and train house guards for them."

"How many are they looking for?" Harlan Turgista asked.

"A few will ask for a couple of dozen, two or three will hire a hundred or more for each of their clans. More than it takes to guard a house." Saldo smiled smugly.

"They're hiring their own armies?" Loosy looked alarmed.

Saldo shrugged. "They're scared something's about to go sideways. It seems like an opportunity to me. They feed us, train us, gear us up, house us in barracks together. I've already begun recruiting. Maybe some of you know fighters who'd be interested?"

"Why the hell would I want to guard some green-skinned bastard's pile of rocks?" Je'anna challenged him.

"Because you like to fight, you need to eat, and it's a way for us to take some power for ourselves," Saldo replied. "The Dum'Laiere's want me to train two hundred in the first group. The Bren'Harrows will at least match that. The Mc'Alburns will start with a hundred, and The Harbines haven't given me a number, but they won't want to be seen as second best."

"Each group will be independent, under a separate command?" Makepeace asked.

"In theory, but in practice, they'll be hired by me, their captain is handpicked by me, and they'll answer to me," Murtevoy said smugly.

"The captain won't like it," Ald spoke.

"Maybe not privately, but how can he object? We're building bridges, helping our Ebulonian allies," Saldo satirically mocked the truth with a half-truth. "And Free Men and Women have the right to make a living. Send me fighters who are friendly to our cause. Steel to the heart." Murtevoy led the traditional gesture, thumping his chest.

CHAPTER TWENTY-SEVEN

"A cluttered life keeps the traveler close to home." (Common Ebulonian saying attributed the Keesch, Anonymous, undocumented.)

Dora Dum'Laiere was furious. Fratianne had gone somewhere and not returned, leaving her to do for herself.

"There is no one to do my hair, no one to get my breakfast, and no one to do up these damned buttons," she complained. "I will have her thrown out into the streets." Dora stomped over to the travel chest at the end of the bed tossing the fussy, girlish, old, pink, and blue gowns onto the floor. The mountain of discarded dresses lay like vapid victims, un-gently used. Anger rose inside Dora; anger at the dresses' girlishness, the satin shine that highlighted every fleshy roll of her mid-section, accentuating her youthful chubbiness, but especially anger at being imprisoned in a false childhood by her mother.

Dora scooped the offending clothing up, marched out onto the dock, and threw the dresses into the bay. It felt good.

"I am done with all of it." She marched back inside, retrieved a bag of coins from the bottom of the chest holding the rest of her clothing and belongings, and began dragging the chest across the floor. Outside, she pushed the chest, dresses, and all, into the water. Puddles of blue and pink satin floated up, their material darkening until finally waterlogged, they sunk. Dora felt wicked and wonderful.

"No more. I will decide now what I want, what I wear, and who I marry."

Back inside, she unwrapped the new gown she purchased after learning she was mistress of her own destiny and fumbled her way into it. She brushed her hair with a vigor she would have raged at anyone else for, but Fratianne had still not returned.

"I suppose I will have to find breakfast myself. Well, that cannot be too hard." Dora took the bag of credits and headed out. Tying the tent flap shut, she saw the note from her mother pinned to it. It would be "spelled" so Miratha knew when she received it. She did not touch it. "I have no interest in talking to you today, Mother," she hissed at the piece of paper as if it were Miratha herself. Dora would blame lack of a response on distance, her unreliable telepathic abilities, the distractions of the festival, and the incompetence of messengers--she might even tell her mother the truth.

The revelation that Miratha had been lying and manipulating her to maintain control over Dora's birthright had snapped something deep within her. Dora found she cared as little about her mother's wrath as she did about Miratha's goodwill. She had been a pawn but no longer. She would make her own decisions now.

"Good morning." Dora greeted the people she passed by as she strode confidently down the docks. Miratha would never have spoken to any of them, insisting they were too far beneath her exalted station, but Dora no longer felt bound by her mother's sense of propriety. It was a new world, and she was ready to explore it.

People here were much nicer than in Iredipa and the Dum'Laiere heir found that without her hair twirled and tied into elaborate knots, she could move her head freely, indulging her natural curiosity, something her mother hated.

Without her middle cinched into breathless immobility, she could move without experiencing the chronic shortness of breath that had plagued her from pre-pubescence on.

Without servants to interface with the world for her, Dora was forced to interact with those around her, and despite their lower status, she found this exhilarating.

She examined the vendor's breakfast goods as they passed by with their trays. Choosing what she wanted--rather than finding fault with what was brought to her--gave her an excellent appetite.

She had always believed shopkeepers and vendors to be a sour-tempered lot. Miratha was always complaining about them, but this morning everyone seemed utterly charming and eagerly helpful. Dora tipped the juice maker handsomely.

Perhaps it was coming to the Dum'Laiere manse and having to deal with Miratha that made Iredipa's merchants so sour. Perhaps it was Auhora Whimlan and the festival itself that made them so helpful. It was truly an amazing place, where people were encouraged to feel free and happy.

Embracing her new adventure, Dora explored whatever took her interest. No one asked where she was going, or when she would return. No one commanded her to do or act a certain way and no one reminded her of her duty to her family name. What had begun as an inconvenience quickly became a charming day full of insights into herself and others.

"This shade is perfect for your coloring, Miss. See?" The young woman at the ribbon stall held up a mirror for Dora. "The teal color brings out the flecks in your eyes."

"I will take two," Dora announced.

"Are you enjoying your stay at the festival?" the sweet-faced girl asked as she deftly twined the ribbons into Dora's hair.

"I am, thank you. In fact, I am enjoying it so much that I am thinking about taking a residence here." Only as she said it did she realize she could do that if she wanted. Her mother and grandmother might fuss but Uncle Kirk would stand up for anything that put space between Dora and her mother. "It must be wonderful to live here all the time." Dora sighed, dreamily. "Everyone is so charming."

"Well, if you do return, be sure to come and see me again." The girl smiled as she finished weaving the ribbon into Dora's hair.

"Thank you. I will." Dora had never had such a pleasant invitation. The shop girl had no idea what an important person Dora was. She had only bought two ribbons--something any girl with a few coins might do, and yet the girl did not shun or scorn Dora because she was not witty, or beautiful. She was nice simply because she wanted to be.

Dora lunched in a small café looking out over the bay and realizing she was no longer angry with Fratianne. She sat on the dock, watching people pass, wondering about their lives. No one cared that her hair was not done up in the latest style, or that splashing water might ruin her new dress. The concerns that had ruled Dora's life had become unimportant.

"Dora Dum'Laiere, is that you?" a voice yanked Dora from her contentment. "My dear, what are you doing here?" Lady Bresna was near to expiring from heat, dressed in the most extravagant Iredipan fashion with heavily embroidered brocade piled in layer upon layer. Bresna Bordent was a friend of Dora's grandmother. Bresna's faded flaxen hair was spiraled into a staked twist on top of her head from

CHAPTER TWENTY-SEVEN

which wired and beribboned braids curved out like butterfly wings, making her broad face seem even wider. The older woman looked so hot and uncomfortable, Dora thought she might faint.

"Look at her, Bordent." Bresna's husband, Lord Bordent, dressed in equally fashionable discomfort, stood awkwardly by his wife's side. Bresna's nose wrinkled as she took in Dora's bare feet. "Why, you have totally embraced the freedom of the festival! How brave of you."

"You are the brave one, Lady Bresna." Dora laughed. "How can you stand it, dressed in court fashion in this heat? No one tortures themselves with those stuffy styles here. You really should take the opportunity to frequent some of the city's marvelous shops. Their designers are absolute artists with fabric. They do not just keep up with trends, they make them. The newest styles are here weeks before they come to Iredipa, and the Iredipan designer's interpretations seem so conservative. Do you not agree?" She made a face. "Watered down for the older more sedate clientele, I suppose. It is like second-hand fashion, really."

Bresna, who considered herself quite the harbinger of fashion, pursed her lips into a pickled pout.

"I have been a patron of La Heggesse for decades." She sniffed, fluttering her fan before her painted face.

"I remember. It was you who helped make La Heggesse popular by introducing her work at court. Forgive me, Lady Bresna, I had forgotten." Dora played to the woman's vanity, gambling that Bresna's memory of the conversation would discard any evidence of her unorthodox behavior in favor of Dora's flattery. "Sadly, Heggesse is no longer the daring clothier she once was. All those tired cuts and drab colors. She needs to return to her roots for some fresh inspiration. Why only this morning, on my way to breakfast, I thought I saw her walking toward the Rue de Clannier."

A frown passed like a fleeting cloud across Lady Bresna's brow. "What a coincidence, Bordent and I were just on our way to the Rue now to peek at what is coming in for the new season," Bresna declared. "What do you think of the Clannier designers, Miss Dora?"

"Very fresh—very young." Dora declared. "And it is Lady Dum'Laiere now," she corrected the older woman. "I have reached my majority and am mistress of my fortune now."

"There's a plucky, young woman." Bresna's husband, a plump partridge of a man with ruddy cheeks and eyebrows like hedges, gave Dora an encouraging wink. "Perhaps you would like to accompany us," he suggested wickedly, knowing that she would not.

"A splendid idea," Bresna agreed.

Dora mentally weighed the value of the Bordent's goodwill and the coins in her purse.

"I think I will since our plans for the afternoon seem so well aligned." She picked up her shoes. "What is the benefit of being an heiress if you never spend anything on yourself?"

"Such a shame your mother is not here," Bresna said, eyeing the shoes in the younger woman's hand as if they were the result of some bodily function that was better kept private.

"Yes, is it not?" Dora replied without an ounce of sincerity.

E.F. Winters

CHAPTER TWENTY-EIGHT

"Beware of those who claim wisdom, telling you they know. They know nothing." (Wei Tai; First Matriarch from the History of the Rhunes compiled in the First Age.)

Spectre rarely walked among the Lamdra's crew, but when he did, he was in disguise. He knew the passageways, air ducts, and unintended byways of the inner ship like other people knew their own hands. He knew which areas were shielded and could not be scanned and which had high-energy signatures that would mask his presence.

He spent the years during the Lamdra's exploration of space studying the interactions of its crew, their loyalties, and the men's character, skills, and failings. He identified groups and identified pawns. He knew who was best suited to a task and how to manipulate them into doing it without realizing someone else was pulling the strings.

Most Guild contracts were specific, seeming unconnected events involving short-term goals that played into long-term outcomes known only to Guild leadership at the highest level. Each request for services was vigorously vetted and accepted if the expected outcomes supported the guild's master plan--a plan a hundred years in the making. An assassination, a theft, an abduction, a coup: the future of the Thousand Worlds as seen by the Shadowmaster's Guild, was a complex puzzle with success counted, not in lifetimes, but in centuries.

Logic demanded that for the guild to survive, their services must be in demand. A peaceful, prosperous network of equal worlds had no need for Shadowmasters. Without a need, the Guild's influence would dry up and their coffers with it.

Some contracts were designed to chip away at a world's weaknesses. Others forced a change in leadership. A missed shipment could dismantle a business deal that unhinged a government. The

CHAPTER TWENTY-EIGHT

Shadowmaster's Guild understood that empires and fortunes rose and fell on little things: scandals, affairs, finances, a death.

Wealthy clients spent heavily to preserve what they had. New players were eager to take advantage of any chance to topple an old family and take their place.

A Shadowmaster was trained to follow orders without asking questions or requiring answers. For an agent to be given the smallest hint of what part their task might play in the larger picture was a mark of honor indicating favor and the possibility of earning a place at the top among those who knew the secrets that mattered.

Spectre's assignment to the Lamdra was the first sign that his efforts were noted and he was being watched and considered for greater things. Suspicion, fear, and obfuscation were as much a Shadowmaster's tools as his darts and poisons, but Yare's refusal to grant his crew shore leave on Ebulon was complicating the Shadowmaster's progress. He could only go down to the planet when a shuttle traveled between the Lamdra and Ebulon, and in stowing away he constantly ran the risk of discovery or being abandoned. By his evaluation, his handling of his discovery by the Free Man behind the cartography shop was clumsy, but fortunately, it had worked out in his favor, seeding distrust between the Taibans, the Paxlosians, and the Ebulonians. The Taibans were certain the Paxlosians were responsible. The Ebulonians suspected the same but refused to admit it for fear of offending the leadership of the powerful starship.

Intent on the first phase of a new plan, Spectre climbed through the jungle of wires, tech, and tubes, squatting behind a grate in an air duct inside the walls to the level five pub, listening to the men on the other side. To Spectre's chosen pawns, he was just another faceless crewman, a voice in the crowd, a whisper in the night. He had already tried once and failed to turn the Lamdra crew against their captain, but this new plan took the crew's persistent loyalty into account and used it.

Yare's absence provided the Shadowmaster with the perfect opening.

Spectre's new victim was a chronic gossip, the kind of man who longed for recognition but had neither the brains nor the courage to earn it. Staging a conversation that fed his target an irresistible pudding of verifiable facts mixed with useful fiction, then sat back confident that the man would re-cast himself in the role of eyewitness and generously spread the word.

"What would you expect them green devils to say?" Spectre's puppet tossed back his drink. "They're not likely to admit they took the captain away and cut off his balls now, are they?"

"He's probably just getting the lay of the land, so to speak," another man grinned into the bottom of his cup.

"The lay of *someone* you mean," his neighbor joked.

"And here I am stuck looking at your ugly mug," another jostled his neighbor with an elbow. Back slapping and knowing laughter followed.

Zeph Yare's exploits were legendary among his crew. His mother was a rich bitch, but Yare was one of them.

"Do you think that's why they took him?" A young man, his beard still spotty and fine on his jawline, chewed on a toothpick. "He was being too friendly with some local?"

"Couldn't say." Spectre's man shrugged. "But they stripped his weapons off him, took him under guard, and he didn't come back. Come nightfall, Boradice and that Holder fellow came running back with a bunch of them green-skinned guards, and we're ordered to take off without the captain." The men nodded, muttering comments to their neighbors. "Ask around," the technician defended his story. "There were others who saw it same as me. When we took off, there was a mob of those Taibans trying to shoot us down."

The young toothpick chewer snorted. "Dumb bastards."

"Who gave the order to leave without the captain?" someone asked.

Spectre's man shrugged. "How should I know? I'm no officer."

"The Lieutenant would know," one of the men suggested.

"And the F.O. would have to know," the technician added. "He probably authorized it himself."

"That damned stiffed neck wouldn't tell you there was a snake on the crapper unless there was a regulation saying he had to," the old mechanic complained.

"Maybe he saw a promotion in it for him," Spectre's man suggested.

The young man slammed his drink down on the bar, startling the others.

CHAPTER TWENTY-EIGHT

"Boradice would cut off Dante Tartulon's privates and feed them to him before he'd let Tartulon steal the Yare's command," the young man said hotly.

The old mechanic rolled this around in his head. "If something's going on, Boradice will put it to right. You can count on it."

"Maybe he don't know," Spectre's man said as if on cue.

The others exchanged nervous looks that said a lot without saying anything.

"Just be ready to move when the time comes." The mechanic drained his mug and stood. "And trust me, boys, it's coming." He shuffled out.

Spectre smiled. At some point, a truly successful rumor campaign took on a life of its own. The art of a campaign of rumors was placing the intended stories with the right people, making them have just enough truth appear credible, nudging events just the right amount. When that pivotal point arrived the instigator's job was to resist further meddling and allow events to unfold on their own. Pushing too hard bore the potential of revealing the instigator's hand.

CHAPTER TWENTY-NINE

"A Rhune may light the path, but the people must move their own feet." (Anonymous: often attributed to both Wei Tai and Mo Tep Hunan, undocumented.)

Dora felt awkward standing alone at a ball knowing no one. She had never attended such an event, but it was not what she had expected. In fact, it was boring.

She bought a new dress, a blue silk washed with sunset colors at the hem with a pearlescent sheen. The designer had analyzed Dora's figure and suggested the style, a raised waist with a softly gathered skirt that just skimmed her hips. The neckline cut so that Dora's shoulders were bare and only gave a hint of cleavage, which the dressmaker claimed was beguiling yet modest. She had returned to the ribbon vendor and added flowers that matched the new gown, and the girl added a few flourishes that dressed her hair for evening without appearing stiff. The entire process took minutes, and there was not a sagging curl in sight.

Dora spent her afternoon at the baths indulging herself, then returned to her tent to find the recalcitrant Fratianne just waking up. The servant girl made some lame excuse about staying out partying that Dora barely heard, but made no argument when Dora declared she was going to the ball alone, cheerfully helping Dora dress.

But Dora had been at the ball for an hour and had not met anyone in the least interesting. She wished she were out on the docks with the common people, swishing her feet in the water and watching the sunset as the festival lights came on for the last time this season.

"Dora! Oh, Dora, my dear! We are over here." Lady Bresna called across the room, motioning for the Dum'Laiere heiress to join them. Dora tried to pretend not to see her only to find herself blocked in by the imposing figure of Faliese Bordent.

Lady Faliese's approach was barge-like with streamers of magenta and orange silk floating from the topsail that was her hair, piled high with fake additions to increase the effect.

"Dora Dum'Laiere, what a surprise. I have not seen you since... Well, you had just learned to walk. Your mother has positively kept you under lock and key so that none of the other clans could get a look at you. But now here you are." Faliese exhaled wetly. "I have someone you simply must meet." She stepped aside. "Frevin Mir, this is Dora Dum'Laiere,"

"Lady Dum'Laiere, it is a pleasure." The Mir bowed over Dora's hand. Refined and somber in manner, he smelled like beeswax, all honey, flowers, and warm wax. "What a beautiful gown."

Dora blushed.

"Frevin is a particular friend of the Pira Eropa's," Faliese primed the conversation.

"We were childhood companions. It is common knowledge and not noteworthy," he downplayed the connection.

"I recently met the Pira," Dora said. "She is here with the alien captain." Annoyance flashed across the Mir's face.

Faliese raised an eyebrow. "You do not approve?"

"It is not my place to approve or disapprove of the Pira's actions," the young diplomat answered.

"Then it is the alien whom you dislike?" Faliese baited him.

"I have had the opportunity to spend more time in the alien's company than most and have had the opportunity to observe how his mind works. I will say, my observations have led me to believe his values and character are very different from ours."

"But that is exactly why the women at court find him so intriguing," Faliese wheezed. "Taking such a creature into your bed would be tantamount to making love to a tiger."

"Or a hero from the old times," Bresna added.

"I am merely a man of my own time, I fear." Frevin inclined his head.

"Being an accomplished Mir is an achievement all ladies appreciate," Faliese corrected him. "Do you not agree, Miss Dum'Laiere?"

"Lady Dum'Laiere," Dora corrected her. "I am of age now therefore the title is mine. But yes, I agree Lady Faliese, a Mir of accomplishment is a fine thing."

"You are very kind." The Mir smiled at Dora.

She felt a flutter in her chest. This Mir, with his self-contained manner, striking blue eyes, and silvery blond hair, was someone an heiress would be proud to have at her side.

"I should ask you to dance, if only for the opportunity of being alone with you, Lady Dum'Laiere, but then I would be sure to make a terrible impression. I fear I have no talent."

Dora smiled. "Among so many people we would hardly be alone. Perhaps a stroll in the garden?"

"Go. Go," Faliese shooed them away with her fan. "Nothing important will happen here in your absence."

The Mir gestured for Dora to lead the way. The crowd grew close, and she felt his hand gently touch her waist guiding her through. With no corset and only a few thin layers of silk between them she could feel his warmth. It was dizzying.

"Is your family here with you?" she asked, raising her voice above the crowd.

"No."

It was the logical opening for him to sell himself as a good match and follow by reciting his lineage. It was what was expected, but Frevin either did not know that or considered it unnecessary to explain himself. Dora decided that she did not care.

"But you do have a family?" she teased.

"The Ner'Ansetts. Your mother and I serve on the Council together."

Dora raised her eyebrows. "You seem very young for a Voice."

"I am newly named a diplomat," he explained.

"That is much more of an accomplishment than being a good dancer." Miratha could hardly object to a fellow council member unless, of course, Frevin had opposed her on some favored issue. Then Dora might like him even more. "Of course, the Dum'Laieres are one of the oldest families," she bragged. "And when my grandmother passes, I will take her place as head of the family."

"I am sure you will be as formidable as you are gracious," Frevin said, politely. "But what of love, Lady Dum'Laiere? Family and position are all very good, but they do not make life worthwhile or keep one warm at night."

"Love is not often considered in dynastic marriages, Frevin Mir," Dora spoke plainly.

"But certainly, as a modern woman who is in a position to choose for herself, you can give it that place in your own life at least, if not for others?" Frevin suggested.

Was he flirting with her, presenting himself as an option, then suggesting she insist she choose a partner herself rather than be ruled by strategic alliances decided by her family?

"You try to make it sound simple. But I do not think it is as easy as that," she demurred.

"Everyone will be loved by someone." The young Mir declared.

"Is that true?" Dora asked dimpling.

"I believe so," Frevin Mir said smoothly. "I hope so."

Dora was inexperienced socially, but not in matters of intimacy. Thinking her simple had one advantage, it had made it easy to convince stable boys and gardeners that they could share a tumble without fear of being reported.

Dora imagined what it would be like to have Frevin's soft, manicured hands against her bare skin, instead of the rough sandpaper grabbing and clenching she had endured from her low-born lovers.

They stepped into the moonlight-drenched garden. The white sand pathways rippled in the bay's breeze, while shadow and light snaked along the folds of the carved statues' robes scattered around the grounds.

"It is a shame the festival is over. I would like to have spent more time and gotten to know you better." As soon as she said it, Dora knew she had said too much and been too forward. "I am sorry. I did not mean to make you uncomfortable. As the Dum'Laiere heir, my world has been rather small and isolated, and becoming Lady Dum'Laiere has brought challenges along with its opportunities."

"And what does your mother think of these new 'opportunities'?" the Mir asked.

When Dora returned home, there would be a reckoning. She needed allies. "She does not like them at all," She answered truthfully. "Do you leave tomorrow then?"

"I hoped to leave tonight," Frevin replied. "I came to the ball expecting to meet a friend and make arrangements to travel back to Iredipa, but I found you instead."

"You could return with me," she suggested. "Please, say yes. I have a hired ship, and your company would make the trip so much more pleasant."

"I would be in your debt," the diplomat agreed.

"Then it is settled." Dora linked her arm through his and began strolling back to the party. "Meet me on the beach at the tip of the peninsula in an hour. Will that give you enough time?"

"Of course. I will not keep you waiting," Frevin assured her.

Dora watched him walk back inside, his robes billowing softly behind him. She would not care if he did.

E.F. Winters

CHAPTER THIRTY

"Stop lying and pretending to plug your ears. You know the Truths when you hear them. " (Attributed to General Parish Mc'Larick during the Hundred Years War.)

Zeph inched toward consciousness; his eyes weighted like an iron statue. Within sight but out of reach, ripples undulated the flickering light that filtered through the bottle green water, meters of it pressing him against the bottom of a lake or a river, he did not know. Through the curtain of his eyelashes, he watched the light dance across the surface far above where he lay, calmly drowning.

For the most part, he did not care that he was drowning. It was the sort of fact you either fought or accepted, and since he could do nothing about it, he went for the latter. Inexplicably, the chemicals that controlled his emotions shifted, awakening a spark that tugged and teased him from the twilight of helpless acceptance.

With painful awareness taunting him, Zeph cringed into the shadows, hoping he could hide, and it would pass him by. He could not bear living with its chiaroscuro of opposites fighting back and forth over the middle ground of his psyche. Hope, fear, denial, longing—bouncing between opposites had exhausted him until he embraced the numbness of complacency.

Some part of him recognized that this was someone else's goal, not his, and he was being manipulated into this place of beaten-down hopelessness, but merely knowing did not give him the strength to fight back.

Zeph gritted his teeth and tried desperately to become heavier so the powers that wished to move him would give up and let him lie at the bottom of the green water. Still, the buoy of awareness would not be denied, and it lifted him slowly up toward the rippling surface.

The closer the light came, the more his lungs burned, tortured by the anticipation of taking a breath. Though in this they were at odds,

CHAPTER THIRTY

his lungs fought for it—for life, his diaphragm spasming, the vacuum in his airless throat choked by rhythmic bursts.

He was nearly there. In the light. In the air.

A shadow moved between Zeph and the light, and hands were placed on either side of his head.

No!

He struggled against their forceful grip, spluttering and gasping, complacency ripped from him like a blood-congealed bandage left until it was fetid and brown, grown into the wound's cavity. Suddenly desperate for awareness, Zeph struggled against the hands that refused his freedom.

Steady and deliberate, the energy exuding from the hands wrung out the Paxlosian's mind, pushing him back down to the bottom, and holding him under the water.

Slowly numbness seeped in through his pores taking his body, then his mind. The heaviness flooded through his limbs as his mind took what it still had and fled deeper into recesses strange to it.

Zeph lay beneath the green water, watching the light glint over the ripples far above him, detached, dozing.

And then the cycle began again.

Zeph's eyes felt like sand had been poured into them before they were glued shut. He grimaced, squeezing his eyelids to scratch the unbearable itch before peeking through the encrusted slits, his body tense…waiting.

Waiting for what? He asked himself.

To be pushed down beneath the water, his mind replied.

You are on dry land. You are breathing air. Both reassuring facts. *It makes no sense to think you will be pushed underwater.*

The image of his shadow torturer flooded Zeph's mind. His heart raced, frantic breaths gut-punching his newly returned awareness with the much stronger memory of being pushed down.

"You are awake. Good," a woman's voice snapped Zeph back into focus. A dark plum blur moved into view, the fine, perfumed material of a full skirt swishing near his left ear. "We were beginning to worry." Zeph noted the "we" and wondered who "we" were.

His right leg began to cramp and instinctively he tried to change position to relieve it, finding he could not move, as were his arms, legs, and torso being strapped down to the surface beneath him. He tried again, applying greater effort but only managed to add stabbing pains in his head and an itch beneath the straps that held him.

The purple blur fluttered a hand, and the weight holding Zeph down vanished. With his head still spinning, he managed to push himself up to a sitting position.

The plum-clad woman came into focus.

"Lady Dum'Laiere." Zeph grimaced as pain shot through his head like an arrow. "Where is the other one?"

"There is no one here except you and I, Captain." Miratha smiled. It seemed forced.

"There was…someone else," Zeph declared.

"You are mistaken."

Zeph was sure Miratha was lying but decided not to argue the point. He had many unanswered questions, and he hoped to get a few answers before he offended his hostess into defensiveness.

"Where am I?" he started with the most innocuous one.

"My home," Miratha replied.

Zeph massaged his temples, hoping to stop the pain. "In Auhora Whimlan?"

"In Iredipa," she corrected.

Zeph's forehead wrinkled; his head cocked to one side. "I don't remember leaving Auhora-Whimlan. How did I get here?"

Miratha sighed. "You were quite the worst for drink. My men say that while they were rescuing you, you hit your head."

Zeph squinted up at her. "*Rescuing* me?"

"You do not remember?" Her eyebrows arched condescendingly. "You were attacked by Taibans on the docks at Auhora Whimlan. Some of my people were nearby and interceded. They are a vengeful lot these Taibans, primitive and uncivilized. Apparently, they blame you for the recent deaths of some of their fighters."

"I don't remember any of that," Zeph muttered. "What I do remember is your girl, Fratianne, sticking me with a needle." Though, admittedly, the details were fuzzy, Zeph knew he had not been so drunk that he misremembered his encounter with the servant girl.

CHAPTER THIRTY

"One should be careful about drinking too much onche', Captain Yare," Miratha said, cooly. "Particularly when you are unaccustomed to its effects." Her tone was measured, benign, and infuriatingly patronizing.

"Your daughter, Dora, was there too." Zeph frowned. "Though that was quite a bit earlier."

"Yes, she mentioned meeting you. An obedient young woman, my daughter, Dora, malleable and undemanding. It is unfortunate that you two did not have a chance to become better acquainted. She will make a good mate for the right man. But there is time enough for that. You are here now and safe, and that is what matters," Miratha declared.

The statement was trivial enough, but Zeph felt like he was being herded toward a trap.

"I wasn't in danger," he claimed.

"You have been in danger ever since you arrived, you simply did not recognize it," Miratha warned him with a cryptic smile.

"Odd that you didn't say anything to me about this before."

"The Pira said we were about to be invaded," the Dum'Laiere woman excused her actions. "She and Nikodamus swore us all to secrecy while they isolated you and gleaned information to use against you in their planned attack."

Zeph did not buy it. "That doesn't sound like Nikodamus. He and I shared quite openly what we wanted for our people," he defended the Mahal.

Miratha pursed her lips. "You more than he I think, since he was listening in on your every thought," she retorted scathingly. "What you term a 'talk' was an interrogation, Captain Yare. He asked you leading questions which you answered, revealing what he wished to know about you and your world."

"Are you saying that he read my mind?" Zeph demanded, his face flushing.

Miratha nodded. "An ethical violation that any person of honor would never engage in--certainly not with someone they expected would become their ally. Nikodamus put you at great risk in sending you off to Auhora Whimlan exposed and unprotected. But then, perhaps that was his intention. I cannot say. My colleagues and I, however, believe that you are far too valuable an ally to be placed in such danger."

Eropa's comment about Miratha Dum'Laiere's ambitions ghosted out from the fog keeping Zeph's thoughts from clarity, but he had the distinct feeling that he was seeing evidence of those ambitions now. He needed to understand more.

"When we met at the reception, you mentioned you were related to someone called the Matriarch?" he prodded Miratha.

"Yes." The woman folded her hands inside the long, flowing sleeves of her over-gown. "The head of the Rhune sisterhood on Ebulon. I am her most recent descendant."

Zeph caught an air of barely veiled arrogance in the declaration. "And her heir?" he inquired.

Miratha inclined her head.

Zeph's eyes narrowed. "I understood that was the Pira Eropa's position."

"Because you were encouraged to think that," Miratha snapped back. "The truth, however, is more complicated." The woman paused and re-gathered her composure. "You have been lied to since you arrived, Captain Yare, but by revealing what has been hidden, I am confident you will see the situation more clearly and we can come to a mutual understanding."

Zeph wasn't sure he liked the sound of that, but he answered, "It's always good to hear more than one point of view." Managing to stand, Zeph took steps toward the only door in the small room. "But right now, I need to check in with my crew. I should also let the Mahal know that I'm safe."

His legs stopped working, suddenly becoming as solid and still as stone.

"Neither of those things are possible," Miratha informed him. "Officially, you are still at the Festival of Lights. For now, your true location must remain secret. The Taiban District buzzes like a nest of angry wasps. They continue to hunt you. If it were known you were here, it would put us all in danger—most especially you."

"My absence will be noticed," Zeph warned her.

Miratha raised an eyebrow. "The Pira left Auhora Whimlan early the morning after your drunken escapade. Interestingly, just before the Taibans attacked. One must wonder about the timing." She shook her head, perfume pouring off her. "Difficult though it may be for you to accept, Captain Yare, you have been betrayed." She opened the door. The small room they occupied was at the top of a narrow, utilitarian staircase just under the eaves of the roof. There was a landing with two other doors on either side of this one which presumably led to other rooms. "Let me know if there is anything you require," Miratha tossed the offer over her shoulder as she and her skirts and perfume swished out.

"I *require* returning to my ship," Zeph stated aggressively, intending to stop her.

Miratha paused. "It would not be safe."

"So, I am a prisoner here?"

"You are a *guest*," she accentuated the last word, setting her thin lips into a determined line.

"On my world, if a person is unable to leave when they choose, it begs a different definition," Zeph matched her stubbornness.

The Dum'Laiere woman's eyes burned with smoldering anger. "You have been reckless in your alliances, Captain Yare," she informed him curtly, her eyes narrowing. "Perhaps your time would be more productive if you spent it considering the choices you have made that landed you here. Many futures depend on it, including your own." She shut the door behind her.

Zeph looked around the small, spare room. He seemed to be alone, but he did not feel alone. A shadowy presence lingered--one not entirely unfamiliar. He remembered the will physicalized in the hands that had pushed him down, a woman's hands he realized now. Miratha's?

No.

Zeph shuddered, then opened the door and checked outside.

"If you will come with me, Captain Yare, I will take you to more comfortable lodgings," the uniformed servant announced.

Zeph started to follow her down the narrow stairs, glancing back over his shoulder at the door to the room next to the one he had been occupying. A sliver of light escaped from beneath the door, blocked for a moment as someone moved between the light source and the wooden door.

We were not alone. He followed the servant down the stairs.

CHAPTER THIRTY-ONE

"The Balance is infinite, not negotiable." (Wei Tai; First Matriarch from A History of Rhunes Compiled in the First Age.)

Miratha despised country life. The only thing she despised more was traveling to the country for her visits as the Dum'Laiere clan Voice. It seemed patently unfair that she had to go through the charade. She had given the Dum'Laiere's what they wanted: Dora, a First-line family heir. They owed her.

They have no idea the lengths I had to go through to get a child from Braum.

As unlike his older brother as a man could be, Braum's younger brother, Kirk, was the controlling authority over running of the clan's rural estates. Rugged as stone, Kirk was a man who loved manly things and manly people. His lover, a gentleman farmer from a neighboring estate, was a distant relative of some kind, like most of the region's residents. Where Braum had been fleshy, distracted, and ill, Kirk was focused, intelligent, and hard. Conveniently for Miratha, he hated court life, the city, and politics, preferring livestock, orchards, grain fields, and hard manual labor. He managed and sold crops and livestock and made certain required services were available in the region. Despite their mutual prickliness, Miratha recognized that Kirk was the key to support from the rural clan. If Kirk approved, the others would follow.

A hired Taiban vessel brought Miratha to the edge of the Dum'Laiere estate, where she met a local driver and carriage. Though she would have preferred the ease of being delivered to the door of the house, arriving in a spacecraft would only widen the alienation between her and the country folk she pretended to represent.

From the carriage window, Miratha viewed the fields and orchards. The estate looked well-tended, and she knew from the figures in the bank ledger that it was profitable. They were enjoying a good year. Miratha understood nothing about what it took to produce the commodities they sold, the sale of which provided the city branch of the family with their comfortable lifestyle, but once reduced to numbers on an account sheet, she understood success. Kirk was not a man she could undermine or replace. She needed him as an ally.

The carriage rolled over the crest of the hill and into a slow decline that took them down into the valley where the estate manse rose, its red roofs bright against the green fields and orchards. The team of horses slowed to a trot, continuing along the lane leading to the big house. Miratha craned her neck to see up to the top of the old castle on the ridge behind it. The old stone structure was occupied only by Cora Dum'Laiere, Braum and Kirk's mother and the matron of the clan. Out of date, free of all modern conveniences, and impossible to heat, the old-style fortress had nostalgic connections bound up in memories of the old woman's childhood. A doughty, cheerful chatterbox, Cora Dum'Laiere was well-liked both in and out of her clan.

"After I am dead, you may do what you like with the old house, but as long as I live, it stays," Cora had declared. No one argued.

As Miratha's carriage pulled up to the front door of the manse, the workers in the front yard began to run toward the barn.

"They are going the wrong way, the ninnies." Miratha pursed her lips. "They are supposed to run toward a guest, not away from them." She could only hope they had gone to notify Kirk that someone important had arrived.

She waited for the carriage driver to come around and open the door for her. When he did not, she gave him an unkind mental nudge. He obeyed, embarrassed and red-faced. He clumsily opened the door and turned down the step so she could disembark in her dainty shoes and fancy dress. Miratha gave him the agreed-upon fee and no more, then let herself into the house.

The house smelled of fresh bread and summer grass, with a base note of barnyard. She looked over what she could see from the foyer as she removed her gloves. It would have been easier to use the house's condition as a barometer of the family's wealth if Kirk had more interest in maintaining the Dum'Laiere reputation. Running a finger over a wooden cabinet revealed a track left in the dust. The carpet fringe was worn away, and the chandeliers were as dull with dust as the furniture. She would have to purchase suitable replacements and have them sent out.

Miratha turned to find her brother-in-law standing watching her.

"Ah, my dear brother." All satin and perfume, she swept toward him.

"What are you doing here, Miratha?" Kirk sidestepped her embrace.

"Why, I have come to see you, of course," she blinked in a show of confusion.

"Because we are so close?" He eyed her with practiced suspicion.

"You never visit Iredipa, so I must come to you." Kirk crossed his arms over his chest and waited. "And I have matters to discuss with the family." Kirk raised his eyebrows. "I am their Voice, after all," Miratha reminded him, her manner falsely sweet.

"Only because none of us cares about the games you play at court," Kirk said bluntly.

"I know how dedicated you are to our welfare," Miratha flattered her brother-in-law. "You work so diligently here so that we may all live comfortably. I do appreciate your sacrifice."

"It is no sacrifice. As I said, I prefer it here."

"Actually, I have come to get your advice," Miratha continued.

"If you want advice about crops, I can help you, but if you are here to ask about anything outside of this estate, you have made a trip for nothing," Kirk declared.

"You know the hearts and minds of the people here."

"I speak for no one but myself." Kirk refused to be flattered.

Miratha ran a hand over the smooth satin of her full skirt. "Well, like it or not, people look to you for leadership."

"They look to me to set the price of grain and give rulings over boundary or livestock disputes. I do not tell them what to think, Miratha."

Miratha's color rose, but she curbed her anger. "How did you come to have such a suspicious nature? Your brother was such an open-hearted, trusting man."

"My mother had to cut my brother's meat for him until you volunteered for the job."

Miratha thrust out her lower lip. The childish expression did not suit her aging beauty. "When will you set aside this enmity between us and let us be friends again?" she asked petulantly.

"We were never friends, Miratha."

"We could have been. We still could be." She batted her eyes, conjuring a subtle musk scent. "Have you ever been with a woman, Kirk? Some things are worth experimenting with at least once."

Kirk moved closer to the fresh air coming in through the window. "I have no interest in discussing my love life with you."

Miratha dropped the pretense. "We should at least recognize that we are allies. We have common interests: the family, its future, its good name."

Kirk grunted. "It is unfortunate that Braum did not see you for who you are before you dragged the Dum'Laiere name into every political drama that fine little nose of yours could sniff out."

"You think I have a fine nose? How gallant of you to notice. Most men only see a woman's breasts." She looked down at the two round globes nearly popping out of her boned bodice. "It is good to know that you have an eye for a good woman, even if it is only artful appreciation."

"You are hardly a good woman," Kirk growled.

"The Dum'Laiere's were a footnote until I married your brother, rural merchants with a yellowed history of better days," Miratha's temper finally flared.

Kirk's eyes narrowed. "And so, you reveal what you really think of the family."

"I brought this clan back into circles of influence and power," Miratha boasted. "I gave them importance and breeding. I gave them an heir with a desirable heritage."

"I hope you are as proud of your little doll when she grows up and bites your hand."

"Dora would never do that," Miratha snapped. "She is a dutiful child who respects her mother's wishes."

"It is the one thing that I hold against her," Kirk smirked.

"You are impossible!" Miratha huffed. "I am trying to be serious, and all you want to do is to show how clever you are. I realize that insulated as you are here among your cornfields and sheep, you know nothing about what is going on in the world, but the situation on

Ebulon is changing very quickly, Kirk, and if the Dum'Laiere Clan is going to survive, they are going to have to change with it."

Kirk frowned. "You are referring to the arrival of these aliens."

Miratha's finely penciled brows rose in two balanced, artful arches. "So, you have been paying attention? When you did not reply to my message, I wondered if you remembered how to read."

He shrugged. "I keep up, with or without your messages."

Of course, Miratha reminded herself. Kirk had spies who would inform him.

"The alien's arrival is a singular moment in Ebulon's history." Miratha began to pace nervously. "And it presents the kind of opportunities that come once in a thousand years, opportunities that have the power to change political cultures and the fate of great families." She faced Kirk. "Nikodamus is a Gilreedy; a no one. He would not have been heard of outside his little village hamlet if he had not married Dupira Rhune." Miratha lifted her chin. "But I am Hagriva's descendant, and Dora is my daughter."

"Dora?" Kirk repeated in disbelief. "Are you speaking of the same Dora you have been telling everyone for years, is incapable of making a decision and therefore cannot take care of her affairs? What kind of insane plot are you conjuring up for my niece?"

"Dora does not need to be brilliant to marry well." Kirk frowned. "The history of our world is changing, Kirk, and I refuse to let my family—my daughter, be written out of it. It is incumbent on us to safeguard the family, and for that, I will need your help." Miratha paused, making sure she had her brother-in-law's attention. "The family needs to hire and train a large private guard."

"How large?"

"Think in terms of a small army, though of course, we will not call it that," she demurred.

Kirk blinked in an unconscious display of noncomprehension. "The council will never allow it."

"There can be no issue with us employing house guards," Miratha deflected his concerns. "And that is all we will ever admit to. Whether being trained or merely housed, they will always remain separated. No one will know their true number because we will not let them be seen gathered in one location. They will be divided and rotated between the town manor and the country estate unless we have need of them all."

CHAPTER TIRTY-ONE

"It is a singularly aggressive move, Miratha." Kirk shook his head slowly. "If the other clans find out…"

"They won't say a thing," Miratha cut him off. "The Bren'Harrows and the Mc'Alburns have already begun hiring to increase the number of their guards, and others will follow. With so many of the major houses taking the same action, who would dare protest?" Miratha flicked her hand dismissively. "No one of any consequence."

"And what is the actual purpose of these 'guards'?" Kirk asked suspiciously.

"You are always so suspicious, Kirk." Miratha smoothed her skirt again. "They will do what guards are always hired to do, keep the family and its property safe."

"But why so many?" Kirk persisted.

"It is a safety net," Miratha explained. "Since the alien's arrival, the city has become an increasingly dangerous place. Political power shifts from day to day--not only among our people but among the Taibans as well. Tensions are building. Eventually, the situation is bound to come to a head, and who knows what will happen then? We need to protect ourselves."

"The Bren'Harrows and the McAlburns you say," Kirk mused.

"Yes. They have already begun hiring," Miratha repeated.

"If you want to be able to move these men into the city quickly without being noticed, we will need to buy more of the Taiban transport ships as well," Kirk pointed out. "We can begin by buying some used ones. Perhaps Menander would consider letting us purchase some of the older models he used when he first began hiring out."

Miratha nodded. "I will say that they are for the family. Dora is getting older. She will be stepping out into a more active social life…"

"Will she?" Kirk looked hopeful.

"Don't be ridiculous." Miratha swatted his arm. "Dora can no more socialize than a cat can." She changed her tone, becoming once again more serious. "The situation in Iredipa is fracturing, Kirk. No one knows what is going to happen with these Paxlosians. And the Taibans? We should never have allowed those brutes to stay. We will rue the day we did, mark my words."

"I have been asking Mother to come and stay here in this house for months," Kirk admitted, worried. "But you know how she is. She refuses."

"Try again," Miratha urged him for reasons of her own.

"If it truly is so dangerous, Miratha, you and Dora should not stay there. You should come here for your safety."

Miratha raised her eyebrows. "Both of us? That is an interesting invitation."

"Do not make more of it than was meant," Kirk cautioned her.

Miratha pursed her lips. "You are such a bore, Kirk. Anyway, I cannot leave court right now. There is too much to be done."

"Shall I ask Gwillem to oversee the hiring?"

"No." Miratha began to remove her traveling gloves. "I have a man for that."

Her brother-in-law nodded. "We have stores enough to feed the extra mouths and plenty of seed set aside for planting a large crop next season as well. We've had good harvests the last several years. Our accounts are good," the businessman in the Dum'Laiere farmer assured Miratha. "I will look at a few of our investments, and we can talk again in the morning about how much we can afford to spend before we would need to cut back on expenses. If we need to protect our investments, these guards will need more than hay forks." He paused. "Promise me, Miratha, that this is not just another of your little manipulations. Is there an actual threat?"

"Change is coming, Kirk. We can get ahead of it or be run over."

"The Dum'Laiere's will not sit in the road and wait to be run over," he declared his position.

Miratha cocked her head to one side. "Then I am in your hands." She batted her eyelashes.

"Neither my hands nor my bed, woman," Kirk replied, but there was less annoyance than usual in his tone.

As Miratha began to climb the stairs, he walked to the open door and looked out at the hip-high grass rippling and swaying like a green ocean, the backs of mares and an occasional foal's head rising from it like islands.

"I will send one of the girls up to check your windows," Kirk called up after her. "There is a storm coming."

CHAPTER TIRTY-ONE

"Truer words were never spoken," Miratha muttered under her breath.

CHAPTER THIRTY-TWO

"Spirit is not measured by importance." (Anonymous Spirit Speaker.)

Bibi tested the point of her sharpened stick between her finger and thumb, then returned her eyes to the west tunnel's entrance. She hoped that by partially burying herself in the sand, she was camouflaged from anything that might be looking at her from inside the tunnel. She used guano collected from the tunnel walls and steeped it into a tea, to mask her scent. She shook her head, blinking her eyes half a dozen times. All her work would be for nothing if she fell asleep.

"Please don't let them come here." She hoped the beast would stay in its part of the maze of tunnels.

The days seemed long in the cavern. It was exhausting constantly dodging Grub's questions and suspicions. The job of keeping the two of them fed fell to her as a female, and she managed the small supply of tubers and water conservatively so that they would not run out. Grub would have used it all up in a few days.

"That was all the tubers you roasted?" Grub wiped his mouth. "I'm still hungry. You should have roasted more."

When she explained that they needed to save as many of the tubers as they could for planting so the tubers could grow more of themselves and they would have some to eat in the future, he had not been able to understand at all.

"Why would they need to do that?" he demanded in disdain. "We'll be going home in a day or two."

Sometimes she wanted to scream at him, but she held her tongue.

She wished Grub was not so angry with her--that sometimes they could just sit and talk. If he could accept her, even a little, things would be better between them, but he could not seem to.

Bibi did not miss the village. Aside from Grub, Gutte-Ra, and Bibi's mother, no one had paid any attention to the albino cub, except to scold, hit, or push her away. Bibi desperately hoped that she would not have to be the one to explain to Grub what had happened to his family. Even though it was not her fault, he would never forgive her. Grub was just that way.

Most days, once Grub became distracted by his projects, Bibi slipped out to explore the tunnels, trying to find the way to her father's new village on the far side of the mountains.

"Ancient One, if you can hear me, please tell my father t we are here and he should come and get us," Bibi whispered, several times a day. "Please, tell him. His name is Boors."

But the days and nights added up, and no one came. No one answered anymore either.

Bibi had never been to Boor's village, but he had told her about it when he brought her to the cavern after they began secretly visiting.

It had been easy to get away. No one noticed when she left or asked where she'd gone. Wan had not died yet, but she lived in a world of her own, trapped inside her head.

"Bibi Ra, why do you still talk like a mewling cub?" her father asked one day.

Bibi liked the way her father called her by her proper, grown-up name, using the Ra suffix.

"Not knowing few words." She squinted one eye against the sun to look up at him, wondering if it was true that by becoming her father he lost his powers. It seemed very unfair. Boors knew a lot of things and Bibi was proud to be his cub, even if she could not have clan braids. "Not much talking for Bibi and villagers."

Boors frowned. "The other Cumin don't talk to you?"

"They shout; 'get out', 'go away', 'don't touch'." She absentmindedly rubbed a hand across the shaved places on her head. "They call Bibi a 'bomination'," she struggled with the word.

Boor's face turned a muddy red and he muttered something under her breath she did not understand.

"Then you must become a very good listener," he told her. "You must be like a shadow, so they don't notice you, but listen to everything. Then you can practice the words you hear until you can speak them perfectly."

Their lessons took on a new urgency after this. Boors introduced many new subjects, teaching his small daughter what she needed to know as a member of a village, but also what she would need to know to survive on her own. He tested her understanding, like in a real school.

"Why do I learn this?" she asked one day, emboldened by his kindness. "Other cubs not learn this."

"Spirit Speakers are taught many things," her father explained. "Things other Cumin have forgotten, but someone needs to remember."

Bibi wished she had asked her father if he was a seer and saw the future. Maybe when she saw him in his new village, she could ask.

Bibi wriggled from her sandy hollow, stood, and brushed the sand from her silver fur. A pale twilight lit the cave. In some places, the dried sand stuck to the dung tea she had rubbed over her fur, and now those places itched. She scratched herself making a poof of dust and wrinkled her nose. She needed to wash before breakfast.

The small pool of water that gathered in the spring would have been the place for a real wash, but Bibi had made Grub agree to keep that spot for drinking water only. All washing was done downstream of the pool. Bibi lay down in the tiny trickle of water. It was barely enough to rinse the caked sand off her back. She turned over on her stomach, splashing the water onto her arms and legs, sniffed her fur, and sneezed.

Maybe the dung tea worked too well. She did not want to smell like one of the beast's allies all of the time. Then again, even if she got the smell off of her now, come nightfall she'd have to put it back on. Grub wasn't likely to come near enough to notice anyway.

Rising from the creek, she shook, then began to climb the bank to stir the coals of the cook fire before digging tubers for breakfast.

As soon as she was within sight of the cook camp she knew something was wrong. The camp had been stripped bare. Bibi's heart sank.

Grub had left the cavern.

There were only two tunnels that he could have taken that would not have required his immediate return: the one they had come in from in the south, and the west tunnel. Bibi's stomach knotted. She padded back to her campsite and examined the dust outside the tunnel mouth. Grub's prints were clear.

He had taken the west tunnel. That was why he had asked her about the tunnel last night. He had seen her coming out and decided it must lead back home. But he did not know what she knew. He did not know about the beast. If she did not find him quickly, he would know about it soon though.

Bibi raced to her camp, grabbed her spear, and splashed what was left of the dung tea over her body, rubbing it over her fur.

I will need another weapon. She pulled a medium-sized pole from the lean-to she had begun to fashion to protect her bed. Racing across the packed dirt, she thrust it into the coals and waited, perched on her haunches. Her stomach grumbled at her demanding the breakfast she had promised, but there was no time for breakfast now. Still, she would need her strength. Leaving the pole to harden in the fire, Bibi leaped from rock to rock, landing in the old garden. Stubby fingers uncovered a good-sized clump of tubers. She had been saving them, but she had no time to sift for smaller ones. Shaking off the dirt, Bibi returned to the fire, retrieved the pole, then went back to her camp. Stuffing the tubers into her belt pouch, she picked up her stick and headed for the west tunnel.

As Grub's confidence waned, his progress slowed. When he started, he had paused at each intersection, checking for air drafts, thinking that once he was out of the tunnels, he would be able to recognize where he was from Ra's terrain. He just had to get out of this horrible tunnel. His firestick had burned down to a stump and gave off only the dimmest light, but one tunnel seemed much like another, and with no sense of direction and no idea which way home might be, Grub soon realized he was lost.

It was so much easier following Bibi, letting her make decisions, then blaming her if things didn't work out. Maybe he had been too hard on the braidless albino.

Grub sniffed the air, wrinkling his nose in disgust. The tunnel smelled worse and worse as he went along. The stone walls themselves seemed to stink. He moved the stubby firestick close enough to examine the rough walls. Dried yellowish-brown droppings painted the rock walls in dripping stripes.

"Ouch!" Grub tripped over a stone and dropped the firestick. Instantly he was plunged into darkness. Backing up until he could touch the wall, he began to inch forward.

Something whistled past his ear. Grub stopped, smelling a new scent.

A rock bounced against the stone floor.

"Sh," Bibi hissed close by.

"Bibi?" Grub could not decide if he was relieved or annoyed that she had followed him.

"No talking," she whispered. "It listens. It will hear."

Grub held very still. "What do you mean, 'it'? I don't hear anything."

"'It' does." Bibi wrapped her small hand around Grub's and began pulling him back along the tunnel the way he had come. "Hurry," she whispered.

Grub pulled his hand away. "I'm not going anywhere with you. I'm tired of this game. I want to go home."

"Shush, Grub! No talking." Bibi again took his hand, tugging him along behind her.

"Stop it!" He yanked away, carelessly throwing himself back along his original path. He struck the wall, scraping his leg against the tunnel's rough surface.

A low rumble rolled through the throat of the stone tunnel.

Grub stopped "What was that?" The sound repeated, bouncing back and forth between the rock walls, the floor, and the ceiling. "Where did it come from?" It was hard to know its source or the distance it had traveled. Bibi once again grabbed Grub's hand, pulling him frantically along behind her. He did not resist her but kept turning his head to peer into the darkness behind them. "What was that, Bibi?"

Around one corner, then two. Grub could discern a slight glow ahead of them. Behind the third corner, two firesticks lay on the floor: Grub's dead one, and a second stick, its fire only an ember. Bibi picked up both sticks, blowing on them together, she reignited Grub's stick.

"You tried to hit me with a rock, didn't you?" Grub accused her as he retrieved his, now burning, firestick.

"Shush," Bibi hissed again. "No talking. West tunnel very bad place, Grub."

"A bad place? Really? Then why do you keep coming here?" he challenged her.

Bibi thrust her face into his. "To save stupid Cumin cub."

CHAPTER THIRTY-TWO

"I am not stupid, and I am not a cub." Grub stuck his chest out. "And I don't need a mewling like you to save me from anything. I know all about your little game, Bibi. You like it in this terrible place. You don't want to go home. You don't have any family, and you don't want me to have any either. You don't want to share me, but I am not yours. I will never be yours. Do you hear me? Your lies will not work on me anymore."

"I hears you, Grub. The whole mountain hears you." Bibi held the firestick aloft and sniffed the air. Grub followed suit.

"Smoke and ashes, you stink, Bibi." Grub made a terrible face.

"Hush." Bibi pulled him farther down the tunnel.

When she stopped, her blue eyes blinked in the dark. "Stink," she muttered. "Must fix Grub's smell." She handed Grub her firestick and began smearing her hands in the yellow stuff that streaked the walls.

"What are you doing?" Grub gagged, sure that bad spirits had possessed the little albino. Bibi reached over and began wiping the yellow goo off her hands onto his fur. He slapped them away. "Stay away. Don't touch me with that stuff." He began backing away.

Bibi continued to move forward, her hands outstretched. "Grub must smell bad."

"No. Don't come any closer."

Bibi lunged at him as he turned and ran down a side tunnel.

"Grub, stop!" Bibi raced after him.

Grub did not stop. He did not know where he was running, only that he was determined to get away from the she-demon that chased him. Panicking, his foot struck an uneven spot on the floor of the tunnel, and he fell. The firestick clattered and rolled on the floor, the ember breaking off and rolling to one side. Grub grabbed the stick and held it to the dying ember, hoping the wood would ignite. Before more than a splinter of red started to glow, leathery feet were padding toward him. He blew on the tiny spot of glowing red and kicked the fading coal down the tunnel before him, running on, feeling his way with his hands on the tunnel walls.

Breathing in short, shallow gasps, he did not notice the stench in the air until his lungs demanded a good solid breath, but when Grub stopped to take a solid, deep breath, he doubled over, coughing.

And then he was running again.

A roar shook the tunnel.

Grub dug in with his toe claws to stop himself from moving forward.

The smell was everywhere.

Hearing Bibi's panting breath come up from behind him, Grub turned to see her blue eyes looking up the tunnel ahead of them. They were round with horror.

"What was that?" he wailed.

"The beast," Bibi's voice shook. "It smells Grub. Beast not eat in long time, and Grub smells like dinner." She resumed smearing the yellow feces on him.

"That's disgusting," Grub groaned, but this time he did not resist her efforts.

"Beast's friend's shit," Bibi explained, cryptically. "Better to be friend than dinner."

Grub was shocked. How did she know who this beast's friends were? She must have been down these tunnels many times. She must have been close to this beast and its allies--close enough to watch them, study them, and know their ways.

"Why didn't you tell me about this?" he demanded with wounded pride.

Bibi grunted. "Grub not talk to Bibi--not listen to albino, female," Bibi copied Grub's arrogant tone. "Grub only argue." She wiped the last of the muck off her hands onto her thighs.

A breath-heavy growl came slithering up the tunnel throat. Bibi placed a chubby finger to her lips, cautioning silence. Her eyes winked out, and Grub was alone in the tunnel, the darkness eased only by the sliver of red flickering in and out on his stick.

"Bibi?" he whispered. "Where are you?"

The smell was getting stronger, and Grub breathed through clenched teeth to keep from vomiting.

A slow moisty hiss warmed the tunnel's air, heavy with the putridity of flayed flesh and inflamed intestines.

Grub shut his eyes tight. *I'm going to die.* Once again, he felt Bibi's small hand wrap around his, and once again, she began silently drawing him back along the tunnel.

"Shh."

CHAPTER THIRTY-THREE

"It is not weakness that draws us to a world, but strength of spirit."
(The Book of Rhune.)

Grub ran down the tunnel, imagining claws scraping his back. He pushed down the scream that clogged his throat and forced his lungs to take another gulp of the stifling air, then risked a glance over his shoulder. Beyond the small circle of light cast by Bibi's firestick, there was only darkness, but he knew it was there: the beast.

They inched along like the shiny beetles Grub used to poke with sticks. Their tiny legs would move as fast as they could, but it was never fast enough to get away from the giant casually menacing them. Forced to move deliberately while danger stalked you made its own kind of madness.

"A little more and we be out of Beast's tunnels," Bibi whispered in his ear. "If you can hear me, Ancient One, please help us," she added. "We are in most terrible trouble."

She ran her hands over the muck on the walls and patted herself down again, paying special attention to her armpits and crotch.

"Now you."

"We smell bad enough." Grub wrinkled his nose. "I'm going to be sick."

"Better sick than dead. Cannot smell like Cumin. Must smell like Beast's friends." Bibi did a peremptory rub down of guano over Grub's arms, back, and belly, stopping short of more personal areas, waiting awkwardly.

"Ashes and dirt, you are stubborn, Bibi." Grub wiped his hand over the cave wall and patted his groin.

"Now we go." Bibi started off again.

They kept moving, cautiously and silent. The beast followed.

There was no way to tell how long they traveled, but at some point, they realized they had left the portion of the tunnels that were marked by the beast's ally's droppings. The scaly scratching and the

CHAPTER THIRTY-THREE

sharp click of claws on stone did not stop following the Cumin through the hollow darkness.

"Why does it not go back?" Bibi peered behind them. "Beast never comes so far." She paused, holding her firestick high.

Lines of dried blood clumped Grub's legs where he scraped them when he fell.

Hope drained from Bibi's face. "It follows Grub's blood scent."

Grub swallowed hard. He had been on hunts with the older males and understood what she meant; the beast was starving. It had picked up the scent of Grub's blood, and it would follow it back to the Cavern of the Hollow Winds.

"The tunnels by the cavern will be too small for it, won't they?" Grub asked hopefully.

A smelly blast from the beast's empty belly pushed around the last corner, enveloping them in a cloud of decay and rot.

"Run!" Bibi pulled Grub forward and they raced down the tunnel, pursued by the scrabble of a hundred knives being sharpened against whetstones.

The pace was reckless and unforgiving, Bibi's chubby feet making a steady pat-a-pat while Grub stumbled and slipped repeatedly.

"Slow down, Bibi," he wheezed out of breath. "I can't see where we're going.

"Jump now!" she shouted.

The floor disappeared beneath Grub's feet, air whistling past his ears.

I'm falling, he realized just before he struck the ground. A sharp pain stabbed his side.

Without hesitation, Bibi hauled him to his feet and pulled him back into motion.

They took a sharp corner at a run and Grub felt the muscles in his arm stretch and pop. He ran on.

"On your belly! Duck! Slide!" Bibi commanded.

Grub threw himself to the ground, feeling his shoulders scrape the edge of an opening at the base of a wall. He scrambled to his feet on the other side. Bibi was a pale outline in the inky blackness. In the next instant, she was colliding with him, wrestling him to the ground.

"Bibi, what are you doing?" Grub tried to fend her off, dropping his firestick. She pushed his arms out of the way, parting the fur over his ribcage.

"Fresh blood," she groaned.

Grub sucked in a painful breath as she stretched the skin near the wound. "Something stabbed into me when I hit the bottom of the shaft."

"Grub very brave." Bibi picked up her firestick, gently knocking it against the stone wall so that only the strongest part of the ember remained.

Grub shook his head. "No, I'm not. I…"

"Grub must be brave," Bibi cut him off. Kneeling beside him she stuck the firestick onto the new wound to cauterize it.

Grub sucked in a breath, ready to scream, but her hand covered his mouth.

"Do not!" she warned.

He understood. The pain echoed off his bones, but he kept it inside himself. The smell of burning hair and hide circling added another layer of stench to the young Cumin. Bibi's watery, moon eyes flooded over into little tear waterfalls.

"Bibi is so sorry, Grub. Never want to hurt Grub."

"I'm the one who should be sorry, Bibi." Grub apologized. "You are only doing what needs to be done." He took his firestick and rolled it over the scrape on his knee.

"The beast may be big and hungry and scary, but it's not going to get us. We are Cumin. We will live, Bibi, and we will find our way home." He took the little albino's hands and placed them over his wounded knee. "Please, Bibi Ra, heal me. Uncle Gutte told me when you have a gift you must use it when you are asked. I am asking you now to help us both so that we may live."

Bibi focused on his injured knee. Grub felt a prickling that became a shimmer, and the pain faded. Bibi moved her hands to the cauterized wound on his side. It was like a cool stream flowed across the heat in the wound.

When she removed her hands, the glow from her eyes was dimmer, and her face looked drawn.

"Bibi, I…"

CHAPTER THIRTY-THREE

A snuffling noise behind them sent them scurrying to the far wall. The beast had caught up. With their backs pressed against the rock wall, Bibi and Grub watched in terror as a huge, scaly snout bumped up against the crack under the wall where they just came through. Inhaling bits of dirt and rock, the beast sucked air into its gaping nostrils. Its exhale sent debris clattering across the floor to the Cumin's feet.

Their eyes locked as the huge snout snuffled down the length of the crack. It reached Grub's firestick and stopped. Lunging forward, the beast butted its head furiously against the rock wall that separated it from its prey. A mouth lined with broken, knife teeth opened, and a mucous-coated blue-gray tongue snaked out. Wrapping itself around the stick, the tongue pulled the firestick under the wall.

A moment later, it rolled back through the opening, clattering across the floor.

The beast barked, sneezed, and snorted. It paced back and forth along the wall's length, but it did not leave. Hunger was its master, and it could smell meat only a few feet away.

Bibi held up her firestick, searching the walls above them.

"There." She pointed to a corner of the ceiling.

Grub could just make out a faint point of light that might be an opening. Sliding along the wall, they moved below it.

"You first." Grub made a stirrup of his knitted fingers and boosted Bibi up to the first rock-shelf. Scrabbling and grasping at every crack and bump, the plucky female climbed up, pulling her stick up after her.

Grub looked back at his firestick lying discarded a few steps from the wall.

"Grub, come on," Bibi called from above.

"I'm coming," Grub assured her, but he did not begin to climb.

"What are you doing? Leave it!" She read his intent as he sprinted for the stick.

Grub's hand locked around the stick just as the beast's snout hammered hard into the crack. Grub yelped, jumping like he'd stepped on a live coal, the beast's tongue shot out, mopping the floor with thick, gray slime.

"Grub, watch out!" Bibi screamed as the slimy protrusion twitched and wriggled closer and closer to Grub.

The young Cumin stabbed the tongue with the firestick, and it slithered back under the door, trumpeting in pain, pounding its bulk into the walls shaking like an earthquake.

"Grub climb now!"

Grub backed toward the wall and planted his stick against the niche where it met the floor preparing to vault to the first shelf. The seared flesh of his wounds felt like they were being ripped open.

"It's coming!" Bibi shouted as three scaly fingers with scythe-like claws swept the floor. Snagging the end of Grub's firestick, he missed his trajectory and hit the wall. He grabbed whatever he could to stop himself from falling to the ground.

"Reach up." Bibi's arm stretched down to him, grabbing one arm and tugging at it.

"Not that one..." Grub felt his shoulder muscles tear as Bibi leaned back, puling him up onto the ledge. The firestick disappeared under the wall.

Bibi gripped his arm again and began to pull him to his feet.

"No!" Grub protested before he blacked out.

He regained consciousness, looking up at Bibi's worried face.

"Grub? Grub, wake up," one little paw jostled his chest.

"I'm awake. I'm awake, Bibi. Let me be. I'm all right." He struggled to sit up, cradling his injured arm, but the world seemed to be moving in circles, and there were flashes and stars.

"Not all right." Bibi sat back on her haunches. "Grub foolish." Her words were harsh, but Grub could see by the glow from her firestick that she was relieved.

"Grub alive," he pointed out, feeling strangely alive and exhilarated.

"Come. Must keep climbing." She turned and began the next leg of their ascent.

The stone around them continued to shake as the beast pummeled them, trumpeting its anger.

"I hope that gives it a terrible headache," Grub muttered unsympathetically. "Doesn't it ever give up?"

"Cumin is good dinner," Bibi stated.

CHAPTER THIRTY-THREE

"Right." Grub bit his lip, climbing and powering through that pain, which seemed to be everywhere. Bibi made the second ledge, and with help, Grub made it without further injury.

A gravel and rock pile in the corner was easier to navigate, and soon, the Cumin were looking through the small hole at the ceiling into another larger cavern.

"It's a long way to the floor," Grub voiced his misgivings. Double the height they had climbed on this side, a debris-covered shelf would be their first descent. From there, they would have to see what presented itself.

Grub gestured for Bibi to go through the opening first. Wriggling after her, he kept his injured arm close to his body, using the other arm to ease forward. He stood up on the other side, felt a rush of air, he was pushed forward, and struck from behind. Falling into Bibi, the Cumin tumbled toward the edge. Grub grabbed Bibi and flattened himself, making his body weight stop their rolling. He grabbed Bibi's firestick, jumped to his feet, and began whacking at their attacker. Not much larger than a big rabbit, the creature dove and grabbed at Grub's hair, yanking out hanks of it with its claws.

"You leave him alone!" Bibi jumped up, flailing her arms at their winged attacker. Now outnumbered as well as outweighed, the creature retreated, flying to an outcropping above the Cumin. It watched them with yellow eyes.

"I have heard the hunters tell stories about these big bats." Grub eyed it suspiciously. "They steal the eggs of other animals and sometimes carry off mewlings. I thought they were supposed to be shy creatures that preferred to avoid Cumin villages.

"Beast's friend," Bibi surmised. "And this, not Cumin village." Bibi sat down watching the oversized bat, the beast alternately trumpeting and banging against the wall.

"Not safe to stay here," Bibi commented unnecessarily.

"Do you think the beast could break through?"

Bibi shrugged. "It will die trying."

Grub nodded. "All right, you go down first. I'll fend off our flying friend."

Bibi held the firestick over the side of the cliff, searching for the best way down to the next ledge, leaving her firestick for Grub, she knelt at her chosen spot, and slipped over the edge.

The beast's friend took to the air squawking violently, its attention focused on Bibi. Grub picked up Bibi's firestick and batted the creature to the far wall. The bat slid to the floor, stunned.

"Hurry!" Bibi urged.

Grub dropped the firestick down to her and climbed over the edge. Bibi was almost down to the largest ledge when their attacker came to. With a screech of absolute fury, it went for Bibi, teeth, and claws bared.

Bibi leapt the last few feet landing on a pile of old leaves and grass. Grabbing the firestick from the rock shelf, she lifted it, ready to defend herself. Grub was right behind her.

"Yuck." Grub pulled his hand away from his butt. Thick orange yolk dripped from his hand. "What is this? Eggs?"

"A nest." Bibi realized. Three eggs lay crushed within the twigs and grass of the nest as a thin tendril of smoke rose from where the firestick had kindled the dry grass.

The bat shrieked, dropping onto the nest and beating at the fire with its wings. Its actions having the opposite of its desired effect, fanning the flames. The fire spread quickly around the circle until the entire nest was engulfed.

Grub pulled out a large twig and stuck it into the flames until it caught. The Cumin braced themselves for a new attack, but the bat creature had forgotten all about them. Smoke was filling the upper reaches of the cave.

"Let's go." Grub and Bibi slid down the rock incline that sloped from the nest to the cave floor. Adrenaline erasing both fatigue and pain and they leaped from boulder to boulder, putting space between them and the burning nest as quickly as they could.

When they finally slowed, the beast's trumpeting had faded along with the smell of smoke.

Grub stopped. "Do you have any idea where we are, Bibi?" There was a faint light, not enough to be sure of what you were seeing, but enough to make you think you saw something.

Bibi shook her head. "Bibi never been here."

They were in unknown territory with no idea which tunnel would take them back to the cavern or out from under the mountain.

"Well, we aren't going back that way."

CHAPTER THIRTY-THREE

They kept walking, taking any path that allowed them to keep moving forward, walking until walking became stumbling. Their throats were parched, their feet aching, legs numb. When they came to a place where a trickle of water snaked in under a wall, they stopped to rest and slake their thirst. Grub produced a handful of tubers from his belt pouch, and they chewed the fibrous root gratefully.

"If we were back at the Cavern of Hollow Winds, would you know the way back to the village?" Grub asked after a while.

"No," Bibi replied. "If Bibi knew, we would have gone that way and would not be here."

Grub told himself he was prepared for any answer, but he was not.

"But if we worked at it, and were careful, you could find it, couldn't you, Bibi? That's what you were doing in the west tunnel before, wasn't it, trying to find a way out?"

"A way out, yes." Bibi dropped her head. "Ra shook, Grub, and tunnel by Cumin village fell down." She acted this out with her hands. "That way is gone."

Grub remembered the caves shaking and the tunnel beginning to collapse over his view of the Brittlegrass.

"But we could still find another way. We could get back. We know the village is at the foot of the mountains. Once we get out of the tunnels, we can figure out where we are. They will have noticed the cave has collapsed, and they'll have parties out looking for us. Uncle Gutte will know. He saw me from the Spirit Speaker's cave just before the shaking started."

"Gutte cannot save us," Bibi whispered.

Her certainty infuriated him. Despite all they had just been through together, once again, she placed herself in the position of standing in his way of going home. "Why can't he save us, Bibi?" Grub demanded. "You keep telling me we can't go back, but you never say why."

Tears clouded her moon eyes. "Everything changed. Way back closed." Her voice was flat and emotionless.

"All right," he agreed. "We'll start looking for a new way as soon as we get back."

Bibi rose wearily and started walking. He could hear her muttering quietly, "Ancient One, please...."

He felt like he was walking in his sleep in a nightmare of darkness. Then the walls hung back, scooping out to the sides in long curves. The cavern fanned out, and they stood beneath a large stone dome.

Grub stopped abruptly, every instinct in him on high alert.

A fresh air current at their backs had blocked the smell, but now it hit full force; death slept here.

Bibi scanned the bone-littered floor, seeing beyond the small circle of the firestick's light. Grub squinted into the darkness, making out the gruesome piles of skeletons, their bones drawn against the shadows.

"Is this the beast's cavern?" he whispered terrified.

Giving Grub a sign to wait for her where he was, Bibi padded forward. Returning quickly, she announced, "Beast not home. Still hunting Cumin." Whether the creature would be gone for hours or was on its way back, they could not foresee. "Quick and quiet." She pointed across the carnage-riddled cavern.

Grub followed cautiously, using the fading stub of the firestick to skirt around bones and debris, keeping close to the wall as much as boulders and debris allowed. The piles became large and sprawling, forcing the Cumin nearer the center of the cavern, into a space swept regularly by the beast's tail.

Closer to the center, gristle clung to fresher bones, vainly trying to hold form and identity. Ragged bits of hide hung over broken ribs. Beads, twisted sinew, and rotting bits of cloth recognizable as Cumin adornments still circled snapped necks, hanks of kin braided hair, twisted hands, and mangled feet, the tarnished wealth of a simple people. Grub held his arm to his nose, hoping to block the foul smell, and got a lung full of guano stink. His gagging and coughing punched a hole in the silence.

"Shush!" Bibi hissed from the darkness.

Breathing through his mouth to avoid the smell, Grub followed as Bibi wove through the beast's boneyard.

Grub spied a good knife, scooped it up, and tucked it in his pouch. When he found another, he took it as well. He could gift it to Bibi.

As he was stowing away the second knife, the firestick's light glinted off a large oval stone. Grub stooped to pick it up.

CHAPTER THIRTY-THREE

Its cream-colored surface was pearlescent, smooth to the touch, and patterned in delicate swirls that seemed to move and change as he rolled the stone back and forth in his hand. It was of a good weight, not light, the feel of it somehow comforting as if imbuing him with renewed strength. Grub stuffed the stone down the front of his tunic, cradling it against his belly, and hurried to catch up with Bibi.

CHAPTER THIRTY-FOUR

"The Truths may be braided or woven but not twisted." (Mo Tep Hunan: Third Matriarch from A History of the Rhunes compiled in the First Age.)

Omrey studied the Cumin specimens, considering the little he had learned from them. The female continued to be surly and withdrawn, while the male showed himself to be both curious and intelligent. The vocabulary of the male, who identified himself as something that sounded like "Goota," was growing quickly--his understanding proving to be beyond what the other Ceitonese expected.

"It is a shame your kind were wiped out," Omrey complimented the male Cumin. "They would have made an excellent workforce."

Much of Omrey's time with the Cumin was spent teaching him the games of strategy that he enjoyed; a ruse he used to casually ask about Cumin culture. When they were engaged in these sessions, the female scowled at them from a corner or pretended to sleep. She made no attempt to learn. If Omrey came near her, she snarled and showed her teeth.

"Why does your female not speak to me?" Omrey asked Gutte one day as they played.

Gutte shrugged. "What would she say? You and I play games. We talk your talk. There is no place for her in these things."

"But she talks to you?"

"Of course." Gutte nodded.

"What does she say?" Omrey leaned forward, interested. "What does she think about all of this?"

A mask came over Gutte's face, his eyes cast to the floor. "I cannot share this. You must ask her yourself."

"But she won't talk to me. So, it is left for you to tell me," Omrey urged.

CHAPTER THIRTY-FOUR

"I am a Spirit Speaker, Master Omrey. I serve," the Cumin declared flatly. "What is said to me is private."

Omrey looked up from the game and frowned. "Whatever you were before, Gutte Ra, you are no longer a servant."

Gutte touched the collar around his neck. "I am a Spirit Speaker. I will always be."

Omrey offered to remove the metal collar, but the Cumin refused.

Omrey lowered his voice. "You are the last Cumin male and Urda is the last female. I saved her so you can make little Cumin cubs."

Urda growled, eyes blazing, giving Omrey pause. Perhaps she was learning.

"You have made a mistake," Gutte explained. "She is not for me."

"You won't mate with her?"

"No." Gutte shook his head.

"But there are no others. If you refuse to mate, your race will die."

Gutte's eyes took on a faraway look. "This is not the Cumin's future."

Omrey jumped up from the table and began to pace the small cell.

"Why are you being so stubborn, Gutte?"

Urda slunk back into her corner, trying to make herself very small.

"Urda is a good Cumin. I am a Spirit Speaker, for us to mate is taboo."

"Are you saying that being a Spirit Speaker, you have been celibate?"

Gutte hung his head. "No."

"So, you have mated before?"

"Yes," Gutte replied softly.

"Then what is the problem?" Omrey demanded.

"It is forbidden," the Spirit Speaker repeated.

"Before perhaps but all that has changed now. I freed you," Omrey boasted. "You can be a real Cumin male. Those who kept you from it are all dead. They can judge you no more."

"Some things cannot be changed." The Cumin's lips set in a sad smile. "To Urda, I will always be Spirit Speaker."

"You would end your species over some foolish superstition?" Omrey persisted.

"If it is what the gods intend for us," Gutte declared.

E.F. Winters

Omrey's eyes narrowed. "Apparently, you are not as intelligent as I thought." He stomped out.

"I am sorry, Gutte," Urda spoke softly. "Sorry you cannot become the great father of a new Cumin village."

"They would only have enslaved our children. Better that we are the last," he answered sagely.

"You never wanted to be a father?"

Gutte sat down beside Urda, thinking of Umma and the unborn cub he had made with her. "Once, but you know that could not be."

"Umma's cub was yours?"

Gutte nodded.

"I am sorry." Urda leaned her head on his shoulder, and they sat together silently lost in their memories.

The door opened and their pig-skinned captor re-entered, followed by three others of his kind. One carried a device they had used to stun the Cumin in the early days of their captivity.

"Tranquilize them both," Omrey ordered the man with the device.

"Gutte!' Urda shouted as a dart struck her belly. A second dart quickly followed and Gutte slumped down beside her.

"If I say you will have cubs, you will have cubs." Their pig-skinned captor was so close his saliva splattered Urda's face. "You are alive because I saved you and you're in no position to refuse me anything. Take her over there," Omrey commanded the guards accompanying him.

Hands clamped around Urda's ankles, and she was dragged to the far corner of the cell.

"Hold her."

The pig-skinned one's helpers pulled her legs apart and cold, impatient fingers pulled aside the soft fur that covered her mother's cave. Prying apart the tender lips that had once become plump with love play but were now shriveling as Urda's years of fertility were left behind her, Omrey brought out a smooth hollow tube from under his coat.

"You didn't think I was going to leave this to chance, did you?" he taunted her.

CHAPTER THIRTY-FOUR

Urda tried to kick and bite, growl and scream, anything to stop what was happening to her, but her body would not move, frozen by the substance in the dart.

"I took care of all possibilities before you were allowed to wake up." Omrey slammed the cold white tube into her mother's cave. She could feel the male seed spurting inside her.

No! Urda cried out silently.

"Apparently, it's no harder to milk a Cumin's seed than it is a man's." Her captor leaned over her. "Feel that you sanctimonious bitch? That's a taboo being squirted into your belly. You think Gutte Ra's cub is not good enough for you? Well, you've got it now, and you'll carry it, too, because if you try to do anything to get rid of it, I'll have you tied hand and foot until it's born. Then I'll do it all over again to get another one. I don't care about your prejudices and superstitions. I don't care about your comfort. Your one purpose here is to bear Gutte Ra's cubs. So, you can make this easy on yourself or you can make it a misery. I don't care." He yanked the tube back out of her without regard to the fragility of soft flesh grown thin with age, tearing further the small flesh rips made moments before. "We're done here."

Urda lay looking up at the harsh white lights as the pig-man's footsteps faded.

CHAPTER THIRTY-FIVE

"Loyalty based on fear is a betrayal in waiting." (Anonymous saying from The Hundred Years War).

Glancing out his third-story window, Zeph paused. For a beat, he glimpsed Miratha speaking to a rough-looking, gray-haired Taiban at the entry to a large open staging area just south of where Zeph was housed. People in street clothes and House Dum'Laiere uniforms were in the background repeating weapons drills.

Taibans, he noted as the window glass clouded. Zeph snuck a look at the surly house guards in their ill-fitting uniforms. The house guards, also Taiban, who tailed him throughout the day rarely spoke. He did not know their names. The house servants who tidied his rooms had more intelligence and better manners, but Zeph used the small pieces of information he was able to glean together to gain a broader picture of Ebulon's social and political situation--one that went beyond the carefully curated image the Council of Elders, the Mahal, and the Pira were working to present. There were undercurrents here, stress not only between Taiban's and the Ebulonian natives, but between the clans and their government. Miratha's disillusionment with leadership was not a singular case. He was not meant to see what he saw outside the window. Was Miratha's conversation with the Taiban man what he should not have seen, or was it the training of the two dozen house guards, all of them Taiban?

Zeph wondered how that came to be with mistrust of the Taiban refugees so common, but he understood there were Taibans who wanted to kill him, Taibans who were willing to rescue him for a price, and Taibans who could be paid to keep him prisoner.

The Taibans are for sale, and they are not unified and of one mind. He wondered who, besides Miratha, was buying.

Despite her claim that he was free to move around within the boundaries of the estate, Zeph was sure that not only was he constantly guarded, but he frequently sensed the presence of the mysterious woman who had held his consciousness within the illusion of the green pool.

She watches me.

Whenever Zeph approached an area that he was not meant to see, the window he was viewing it from suddenly clouded, the door he was trying to enter was locked, or he was inexplicably transported back to some earlier "approved" point in his explorations. His dull-minded Taiban guards acted as if nothing had happened, suggesting their minds were being tampered with, and Zeph could not say how many times he tried the experiment before he realized what was happening. Experimenting, Zeph re-traced his steps, again seeking out the forbidden location, finding the pattern would simply replay in a loop until he gave up and made a different, more acceptable choice. Whether the Paxlosian's stubborn exploration of the occurrence was a test of his warden's will, or he was taking advantage of a rare opportunity to make a statement against being so controlled did not merit his examination. He filed away what he learned and did not speak of it. Certainly not to Miratha.

The game they played required both jailor and jailed to pretend that she was not holding him against his will, and he was not spending his days surreptitiously searching for a means of escape.

Despite the shock of learning about Eropa's abilities and the mistrust he felt initially, Zeph found he thought about the Pira a lot.

Had Eropa tried to see him again before she left Auhora Whimlan? Did she know he was not there? If so, she assumed he'd returned to the Lamdra, or, as Miratha inferred, she knew about the attack? It was possible no one realized yet that he was missing, his crew included.

"She's a Rhune sorceress. They're the worst," Fratianne claimed, describing the Pira.

If what Fratianne said was true, and Rhune magic was real, could a Rhune alter other people's realities? If so, where did truth end and manipulation begin, and how would anyone on this world know when they were acting of their own volition and when they were being manipulated? Zeph finally understood the division between the Pira and her people he had wondered about.

He thought back to that last night in Auhora Whimlan.

E.F. Winters

She came apart in little bits of light, then vanished. He shuddered involuntarily.

Every interaction between them played in his mind over and over again, every thought and desire he experienced as his own, questioned. Could any of what he thought he felt be real? She could have been playing him as a puppet since the beginning, and yet he wanted so badly to trust her.

Which, in itself, is suspicious.

Even without the strange loop effects Zeph experienced in various parts of the Dum'Laiere manse, it felt as if one room led into another, with long formal galleries in the abandoned wings relegated to housing clan memorabilia: torn battle flags, pennants, old weapons, and portraits of Dum'Laiere Clan ancestors. The older the art, the more alien the ancestor appeared, with the earliest ones dressing in clothing that looked more like leaves, long, stick-like fingers, and hair that looked like the tight, curly green moss Zeph had seen on dead wood in the rain forest Pliny and he rode through on the way to Auhora Whimlan.

Once again, Ebulonian's access to so much space, they could ignore it and a rich historical past caused Zeph to reflect on his people's lack of either.

When the Rain of Death forced the dome dwellers' ancestors to take refuge under the dome's protection, they left with little more than the clothes on their backs, creating a huge gap in information about what had gone on before.

A generation later, those who prospered or were able to protect their wealth embraced a fashion for collecting relics from the old world. Scavenged illegally from the polluted wastelands, the desperate poor were easy marks for middlemen who had connections with the wealthy. With the promise of pay, the desperate poor ventured out into contaminated lands to bring back items of interest from Paxlosis' past. When the objects were delivered, the traders placed them in airtight containers to shield themselves and their buyers from any contamination. The danger it posed to the unfortunates who had obtained the piece was dismissed as a risk they knew about and willingly taken.

Even when it became common knowledge most of those recruited sickened and died, the poor beneath the Dome were so desperate, they were not dissuaded. One successful trip could feed a frugal family for years. Life had a price on Pax, and there were always bargains to be had.

Zeph had flown over the remains of old Pax outside the Dome, looking down on the tortured girders, broken bridges, and burnt-out shells of the abandoned cities. He had also seen the tracks in the desert left by the "mutant" descendants of those who were left out of the Dome, designated as too "contaminated" to be allowed entry. The logic at the time was that they were doomed to die anyway, so there was no point in wasting resources on them.

But they had not died.

Beyond any Dome dweller's expectations, those who were contaminated and their descendants had stubbornly lived on, successfully reproducing so that new generations had claimed Paxlosis' surface as their own.

It was an awkward legacy for their Dome-dwelling cousins who viewed themselves as superior, and now they were paying for their hubris. The very structure that once protected them was betraying them, the plasteel disintegrating under years of residual bombardment from the chemical leftovers from the Rain in the Death environment. The contamination the Dome was designed to keep out had been seeping through the cracks for decades, creating health problems among the poor who lived near the Dome's walls. Diseases resulting from poor nutrition and polluted water have long been a problem among the dome-dwelling poor, but in the last few decades new diseases have arisen; diseases that eat at the flesh and undermined a person's DNA.

Evidence of contamination was now being seen near the center of the Dome. No one could say how long it would take before the Dome Dwellers were forced to evacuate, but scientists warned privately that plans should be made for such a move within their lifetime.

And here was where the true irony came in. Without immunity to the toxins still left in the environment above ground, the Dome Dwellers could not live on the surface of their world. Even if the poorer sector of Dome Dwellers who might have gained some immunities due to their long exposure over decades, knew nothing about living anywhere except beneath the Dome, and were not equipped to survive in the desert eating the meager mutated plants and animals the mutants survived on.

This was why the Consortium purchased a starship with the new technology, paid the exorbitant fees the Guild asked for a Navigator, and sent Morladja Yare's son out into the multiverse on the pretense of seeking new trade opportunities. Paxlosis needed a backup plan. And Zeph Yare needed a way out of the Dum'Laiere madhouse.

Zeph lowered his arms and the voluminous sleeves of the robe Miratha's steward was helping him with, puddling at his toes. He raised them and the many yards of material bunched up at his elbows.

"How can anyone do anything wearing clothes like this?" he demanded.

"They cannot," the steward replied. "That is the point, Captain Yare. People who need to *do* things cannot afford this fashion. To embrace it you must be wealthy enough to be useless."

"Impractical and inconvenient," Zeph muttered.

"Fashion for the idle." The steward smirked.

"When is my uniform going to be repaired?" Zeph asked. Miratha had promised it would be returned to him as soon as the seamstress was finished, but Zeph had little faith in Miratha Dum'Laiere's promises. His uniform would make him too visible and easily identified as Paxlosian, and she had no intention of sharing his whereabouts, still clinging to the belief that given time, he could be convinced to support her camp.

Zeph tore off the cumbersome robe and threw it across the room.

"I can't wear this." The shirt beneath, though snug across the chest, was acceptable, as were the loose-fitting pants. "Your mistress will just have to deal with me being unfashionable."

The steward bent to retrieve the pile of material. "Mi'lady merely wishes you to be comfortable during your stay."

"So, she keeps saying," Zeph grumbled.

Just as Miratha maintained the pretense that her actions were in Zeph's best interests, he held up the pretense that he was listening to her speeches focused on trying to convince him that she and her allies were the future of Ebulon.

CHAPTER THIRTY-FIVE

Neither of them believed the other, so the relationship did not improve.

The last time she mouthed her usual drivel about being concerned for his safety, she ran a hand across the bed in his quarters. The suggestion did not escape him, but Zeph continued his practice of ignoring her invitations.

"I'll feel comfortable when I've talked to my crew and let them know I'm safe," he retorted, continuing his demand to communicate with his ship.

Miratha's eyes flashed with annoyance. "There is no way to contact them."

Miratha was not a patient person, and Zeph took some small pleasure in stripping whatever she had from her, exposing her as the angry, vindictive, and bitter woman she was.

"What about the device left in my tent in Auhora Whimlan? Has that been found? You said you would inquire, Miratha."

Miratha made a gesture as if she were flicking the subject away. "The festival tents have been dismantled, their contents stored in a warehouse until next year, Captain Yare. This device could be anywhere among all that bedding."

"It would be obviously foreign," Zeph pointed out.

"It is a prodigious amount of bedding." Miratha glared.

I know you have it, Zeph fumed silently, knowing she could hear him.

His inability to fight his way out of his palatial prison, protect himself, or communicate with his crew made him feel exposed in a way that, as a person of means on Paxlosis, he was not accustomed to.

Had Miratha confiscated his communication device when she had him "rescued"? Was it her plan to offer to return it to him later at some key negotiation point, or did she intend to keep the device indefinitely, turning it over to some Mir for study? If the device has been found in his tent in Auhora Whimlan, wouldn't whoever cleaned up have reported it? Pliny, Nikodamus, or someone official from Iredipa would have started asking questions about Zeph's whereabouts.

Unless Miratha got it first and bought the finder's silence.

One evening Zeph came downstairs to await the summons to dinner in the library and found Dora there.

"You may wait outside," she informed his guards, haughtily. Closing the door on them, she turned and smiled shyly at Zeph.

An awkward silence held the room hostage.

"Are you reading my mind?" Zeph asked her finally.

"No." She winced. "I am trying to think how to apologize to you for my behavior in Auhora Whimlan. It was a cruel jest my mother played, telling me that we were engaged."

Zeph cocked an eyebrow. "You think she meant it as a joke?"

Dora shrugged. "I have found that things work out better if I do not examine my mother's intentions too closely." She smoothed her dress in a gesture eerily reminiscent of her mother. "I have made a few changes since we last met."

Zeph reassessed her. "More than a new wardrobe, I'm guessing?"

"Oh yes. My visit to Auhora Whimlan turned out to be quite enlightening. Much more so than Mother realizes, but I expect that to change soon. Very soon." She grinned wickedly, quite changing her round child's features to something that foreshadowed an older woman—not beautiful, not serene, but handsome with a sharp intelligence. "I am sorry for having embarrassed you in front of the Pira, Captain Yare."

"So, you *were* reading my mind," Zeph teased.

Dora made a face. "You do think so very loudly."

Zeph frowned. "How does someone 'think loudly' or quietly? A person just thinks, don't they?"

"Not here. To an Ebulonian, your thinking is like shouting." Dora sat, carefully spreading her skirts. "It is hard not to hear and nearly impossible to keep track of a conversation."

Zeph frowned. "Why is that?"

"Well, there is just so much going on." Dora opened her eyes wide and made a pretense of being overwhelmed with a string of tiny shakes of her head. "There is the line of dialogue that is being spoken out loud with its subtext, and then there is the internal dialogue streaming from your mind. I can barely decide which to address, and I cannot imagine I am alone in this. And then there are so many bloody words," she exclaimed. "How do you sort through all the clutter?"

"I had no idea. It sounds like I should be apologizing to you." Zeph chuckled. "So, tell me, how does a person think 'quietly'?"

Dora stood, her rose-colored gown rustling softly as she strolled the room. This new, more sophisticated look revealed the Dum'Laiere scion's pale green, softly sloping, shoulders and a fair amount of skin at the throat and chest, indicating a certain female abundance could be expected with maturity. She stopped by a side table offering a selection of crystal decanters, chose two crystal glasses, and poured a deep amber liquid into each.

"I had a Mir tutor for a time," she confessed, bringing Zeph her offering. "He taught me that the trick to keeping your private thoughts private was to keep the stream of those thoughts close inside you, like secrets. Avoid letting the words become strung together into full-fledged thoughts." She looked to Zeph. It was obvious from the quizzical look on his face that he did not understand. "You see, Captain, words are like herd animals; they like company, and thoughts are rather like the Brask and the Bosk of old, they rely on words to dress them up."

"I have no idea what that means," Zeph admitted.

"You do not know Ebulonian history. Of course. I am sorry." She paused, then tried a new tack. "The tutor gave me assignments to practice. One was not letting words form into sentences in my mind but instead, as they rise, scatter them about like fallen leaves. Naturally, you want to know where they land so you can go back and bring them together when you're alone and it's safe to fully examine your thoughts.

"For those witnessing you practicing this technique, it may seem like you are unfocused or dull-witted. This is particularly true if you are young, and your mother has already put it about you are both of these things. Then it seems like confirmation. But it is completely accepted that a Mir or Muras or someone highly educated will mumble some unspecific reply when they are keeping their true thoughts private." Dora sighed. "There is a tradeoff. At least there has been for me." She smiled embarrassedly.

"It seems very unfair," Zeph commented, feeling the prod of guilt for his early judgment of the girl and her lack of intelligence.

"It does," Dora agreed. "And, looking back, I realized it was an odd thing to teach a young girl who was supposed to be too slow to learn. I am sure my mother never agreed to it." Her pale brows knit together, giving her a musing look but it did not last, and she quickly discarded the moment of ennui. "However, my Uncle Kirk has never been afraid of my mother. He has always supported me."

"You think he arranged the tutor's strange lesson plan?" Dora nodded. "A good kind of relative to have." Zeph raised his glass, saluting her and her absent uncle.

"Right now, every word that pops into your brain joins a train of other words with one thought rolling into the next, going on and on. Trying not to listen to this indulgence of thought is absolutely exhausting. Try instead to keep your attention on one thing at a time, focused on the moment.

"You explain your people's communication etiquette better than anyone so far in all my weeks here. Do you have any other hints?"

The young woman tilted her head to one side and looked at the ceiling. "Well, first of all, stop making up stories in your head about what you are seeing and hearing. Tuck all of your insights away like treasures to take out and consider later, when you are alone. That will save you and those around you a lot of embarrassment, not only from inappropriate thoughts but from poorly considered statements that could hurt you later." Zeph nodded thoughtfully. "Oh, and never lie," Dora added. "You are terrible at it."

"I beg your pardon. I was considered quite a good liar in my youth," Zeph protested.

Dora shook her head. "On Paxlosis maybe, but not here. Because we hear your thoughts. So, we catch you right away. You could try for half-truths when you need to lie. That way what you are saying is only partly a lie so people will have to figure out which is true, and which is the lie and that will take their focus away from what you are saying and doing for a time."

"I will try. Thank you, Dora. You are quite a good teacher," Zeph complimented her. "Maybe you could give me more pointers while I'm here?"

Dora looked uncertain. "I do not know. It takes a lot of practice, and I am not good at mind-reading." She perked up. "But then if I were, it would be second nature to me, and I would never have needed a tutor, and I would not be able to explain it. It makes Mother angry that I am so dull-witted, but honestly, she is not much better. When I was little, I used to test her," the young heiress whispered confidentially. "She hardly ever 'heard' my thoughts."

"She seems to rely on that other woman for that," Zeph suggested cautiously, uncertain if Dora would open up about Miratha's mysterious watcher or whether this would shut her down.

"Rusch?" Dora made a face like she'd tasted something rancid. "You have met Rusch?" she seemed surprised.

"We've had dealings," Zeph dodged.

"Yes, well, I have my tutors, and mother has hers," Dora cloaked the statement in as much mystery as she could muster. "I am not supposed to know that Rusch is anything but a laundress," she confided. "But I have seen her and Miratha plotting and whispering together. She is no servant."

"Then who do you think she is?" Zeph encouraged her to gossip.

"Her teacher, like I said. She's the one who taught Miratha what Hagriva would not."

"A Rhune?"

"Well, not a *real* Rhune," Dora clarified. "I do not know where she came from or where she learned what she knows, but mother never names her publicly. She cannot. Both of them take pains to keep her identity and presence here a secret. If Uncle Kirk knew she was here in the house, I think he would throw them both out into the street. But then Kirk would make me go with him to the country, so…" She shrugged. "When I was little, Mother thought that if she could not hear me thinking I must not *be* thinking." The wicked grin returned, blue eyes twinkling with mischief. "You might find this surprising, Captain Yare, but pretending you don't think is much harder than just going along thinking like everyone else."

"Then why go to the trouble?" Zeph asked. "What possible advantage can there be in having your mother and everyone else believe you are not as smart as you are?"

Dora shrugged. "Lower expectations gave me time to do what I wanted."

"And what was that?"

"Have fun, of course."

"And your mother never figured out you were faking it?"

Dora shook her head. "Not yet, but she will soon," she boasted. "Do you have a mother, Captain Yare?" Dora turned the focus on him.

"Oh, yes."

"Like mine?"

"The similarities are frightening," he commiserated.

The door opened and the Dum'Laiere's manservant, Gwillem, entered, announcing dinner.

Zeph expected it would be a very interesting dinner.

E.F. Winters

CHAPTER THIRTY-SIX

"What hardship could there be in sharing a body when we are all one? My sister is myself." (Faed Ballatyn from a History of The Rhunes, Compiled in the Second Age.)

Lucha Boradice charged into the level four bar like a bull, his feet crunching shattered glass as the crew moved quickly out of his way. The air was rife with the stink of stale alcohol, sweat, and blood.

"What the hell is this?" he demanded.

A gray-haired crewman wiped his face with his sleeve, glancing sideways at his friends before speaking. "Just letting off some steam, Lieutenant."

"This kind of 'steam' could land you in the brig, Birse." Lucha scanned the bar. Except for the crewmembers in the far back, everyone, men, and women, were on their feet ready to join the ruckus that was about to happen. "It's gonna be hard for me to convince the F.O. to recommend shore leave if you can't keep yourselves in check onboard the ship," Lucha hoped a little reason would settle things down.

"Dante Tartulon can kiss my ass," someone grumbled.

"What was that?" Lucha searched the crowd in the direction of the remark. No one spoke or indicated who had spoken, after a while, he let it go and continued, "Well, clean this up and we'll say no more about it."

"Maybe you could settle something for us, Lieutenant?" The older crewman, Birse, sauntered forward. "It's about the Captain; about what's happened to him."

"Nothing's happened to him." Lucha frowned. "He's in negotiations on Ebulon."

A short-cropped, kinky, orange-haired female stepped up alongside Birse. Not many women had signed aboard the crew, the weight of child and elder care still fell more heavily on those of their gender, but jobs beneath the Dome were scarce, and the possibility of

CHAPTER THIRTY-SIX

bonuses made the long mission more appealing. There were not many, but they were not a novelty.

"Those green bastards tell you that?" she challenged Lucha.

Lucha did not answer.

"That's what I thought."

The man next to her spat on the floor. "It's a damned cold man who sits by and does nothing when his friend's in trouble," he grumbled.

"And if I thought Zeph Yare was in trouble, I'd be the first to do something, but he's not," Lucha insisted.

"That's what we said, isn't it?" Birse gave the man a friendly slap on the back. "We knew you'd never let anything happen to the captain," he assured Lucha.

"But you're not in charge, are you, Boradice?" the woman rebounded. "First Officer Tartulon is." She paused. The strait-laced Tartulon was not popular with the common folk among the crew, which was most of them.

"Let it go, Punch," Birse cautioned the woman under his breath.

"I won't." She glared at him before turning back to Lucha. "So, when was the last time you heard from the captain?" she asked pointedly.

Now Lucha hesitated. He had his concerns about Zeph's prolonged silence, and though he kept reminding himself that this wasn't the first time his friend had disappeared between the sheets for a few days, something wasn't feeling right about his long silence. Zeph was so obsessed with this mission being a success, he wouldn't do anything to endanger it. This absence didn't add up.

"Make no mistake, Lieutenant, we're all of us loyal to Captain Yare," Birse declared. "It just doesn't sit well with us that nobody's doing nothing when the captain could be in trouble."

"Except he's not in trouble," Lucha repeated, hoping it was true.

"We've heard otherwise," Punch countered. The crowd of men stood firm behind her.

"Those green-skinned bastards arrested him the night the rest of you came back," a boy Lucha recognized as being called "Rail", pressed forward. "And now they're holding him hostage, right?"

Lucha's brows drew together. "Where did you hear that, Rail?

The kid looked embarrassed. "Everyone's saying it."

"Everyone who?" Lucha demanded.

The crew hesitated to answer. No one wanted to be the one to out a fellow crewmember.

"I heard it from a technician who works on level five," someone spoke up.

"Yeah, that's the guy," Rail agreed.

"Does this crewman have a name?" Lucha asked.

"Maybe something like Bratten?" Others were nodding.

"And he heard it from a guy who was there on the shuttle," Rail jumped in.

"No, Bratten was the guy on the shuttle," someone else disagreed. "He saw it himself."

"*I* was on the shuttle," Lucha said. "And it didn't happen. Somebody's playing you."

"Could be." Birse scratched at the end of the day whiskers on his chin, unconvinced.

"The Ebulonians are trying to convince Zeph that we shouldn't attack them because as long as they're left intact, their resources can make us all rich. How would arresting him fit into that plan?" Lucha pressed.

"Maybe he got himself somewhere he wasn't supposed to be?" Punch smirked.

"It wouldn't be the first time," an anonymous voice in the back joked.

"I'm not going to speculate on the captain's private life," Lucha declared. "First of all, because he's my friend, and second: because he's the captain." He fixed them with a glare that settled them down.

"They took your weapons from you when you landed though, didn't they?" Punch pointed out.

"They didn't 'take' them they asked us to leave them on the shuttle," Lucha corrected. "Weapons aren't allowed in their marketplace."

"You were disarmed and then the captain was taken away under guard," Punch summed up the basic facts.

"We were *escorted* by palace guards, that's not unusual for foreign visitors, but no one was arrested, and no one's being held hostage," addressing each point of misinformation.

"So where is he?"

CHAPTER THIRTY-SIX

"I told you; he stayed behind because he wanted to keep talking to Ebulon's leader."

"That was days ago," Birse pointed out. "Where is he now, Lieutenant? Why hasn't he come back to the ship?"

"I don't know," Lucha defended himself. "He's working out the details of some deal. These things take time."

"But you've heard from him?" Birse persisted.

Lucha avoided answering. "Look, I see how the situation looks suspicious, but do you honestly think that if Zeph had been taken hostage, something wouldn't have been done about it?"

Punch looked around at her fellow crew members, taking a silent vote. She raised her chin and replied, "Maybe the F.O. wanted a promotion."

Lucha clenched his jaw. "Dante Tartulon is a tight-ass rule follower, not a mutineer."

Confusion ran through the crowd when the Lamdra's First Officer entered as if on cue, a score of security guards at his back.

Dante Tartulon was tall with the kind of body and bearing that pulled off a skin-tight one-piece uniform. He also had the stiff neck required to hold up the long nose he used to look down at everyone. Below a broad forehead and receding hairline, dark-circled, deep-set eyes made him look eternally stressed. "Lieutenant Boradice, what's going on here?" he demanded shortly.

"Just breaking up a little rough play, Sir," making light of the situation.

Tartulon took in the damaged room. "Who is responsible for this?" his cultured voice boomed out over the crew.

"Let this go, Dante," Lucha cautioned in a low voice.

Tartulon's mouth tightened. "Lieutenant, you will address me as F.O. or Officer Tartulon, while we're on duty."

"Why? Because the men don't know our real names?" Lucha retorted. "They've probably figured out our secret handshake by now."

The humor was not appreciated.

"That's enough, Lieutenant." There was a warning in the First Officer's voice, but Lucha was not hearing it.

"Lieutenant Boradice was just trying to keep the peace, FO.," Birse joined the effort to de-escalate the situation.

"That isn't his job, crewman," Tartulon rebutted coldly. "It's mine."

"Just figured that out, did you?" Lucha muttered.

"Security, take Lieutenant Boradice to the brig," Tartulon commanded. Lucha blinked in surprise. "A starship is not a party venue, Lieutenant, and insubordination toward a higher-ranking officer will not be tolerated. It's that sort of behavior that breaks down discipline, leading to chaos. Perhaps a few hours in isolation will remind you of the importance of maintaining order on board a starship, and give you some respect for authority, your own, and those above you. Navrat," Tartulon addressed the junior officer. "See that he gets there and report back to me."

As security officers stepped to either side of Boradice, a quiet buzz began to build among the crew.

Tartulon was losing popularity points he did not have.

"You will accompany us, Lieutenant," the lead security officer announced.

"I will," Lucha agreed. "If only to prove my respect for the normal chain of command aboard the Lamdra."

Navrat Tila gave Lucha an apologetic smile and fell in with the security detail.

"Just come along nice and easy, Lieutenant," the guard closest to Lucha whispered as they marched him down the corridor. "As soon as we have the ship secured, someone will come and let you out."

"What?" Lucha stopped, forcing the whole security team to do the same. "No."

"Keep moving, Sir," the security lead Tonk urged Lucha.

"Listen to me. I've heard the rumors, but they're just not true. Zeph's not being held hostage," Lucha repeated. The guards pushed him toward the lift. "Tartu!" he shouted back over his shoulder. "I need to talk to you. Tartu!"

They were now far enough apart that his fellow officer could ignore him, and Tartulon did.

The lift door closed.

"You need to stop this, Tonk," Lucha continued to try and alter the course he saw developing. "If you do this, it will be a permanent entry in the ship's records, and we'll all have to live with the consequences of that."

"This is not some unconsidered impulse, Lieutenant Boradice," Tonk said. "If there is not a problem, someone should have stopped the rumors long ago, but it's too late now. The situation's been discussed, and decisions were made."

"With the goal of helping Zeph," Lucha pleaded. "But this is not helping him. It isn't helping anybody. You need to stop it because it's not just us who will suffer. Bonuses? Gone-forfeited. How will you feed your families? Who will hire you? You won't be heroes when you get back to Pax, you'll be disgraced—an embarrassment to your family. You'll be lucky if you can get a job cleaning shit in water reclamation."

"We're not mutineers," Tonk stated.

"It doesn't matter what you tell yourselves, or what I think, or even what Zeph thinks," Lucha countered angrily. "If you replace the authority on this ship, it's mutiny. Tell them, Navrat."

"The Lieutenant's right," Navrat spoke up. "If what you're planning is mutiny, it will go into the mission records, and everyone found to have been involved will lose their bonus. It's in the contract."

"We're not going against the captain," one of the guards argued. "We're saving him."

"The only people you're helping are those who are looking for an excuse to claim we failed," Lucha argued.

Tila lagged toward the back of the group as the security team delivered Lucha to a cell.

"We'll be back soon," Tonk promised quietly.

"Don't bother. I'm not going anywhere." Lucha sidled over closer to Tonk as he spoke. "I was put here by the authority of the commanding officer of this ship and only he, or Captain Yare, can release me. Unless there's someone else in charge now?"

Suddenly, Lucha moved forward, and before anyone knew what was happening, he had Tonk in a lock with his weapon pointed at his head.

"Navrat, take their weapons." He backed out, keeping a firm grip on Tonk. Looking completely confused; the younger lieutenant obeyed. "I was Zeph Yare's friend long before I was any kind of officer. If he's in trouble, I'm the guy who'll lead the way to get him out of it, but I won't stab him in the back, supporting a mutiny on his ship that will destroy this mission. Get in." Lucha indicated to the security team that they should enter the cell. "You should join them, Navrat. I don't want it to be said that you helped me."

"What are you going to do?" Tila asked.

"Try and straighten this mess out."

"I'm having a hard time telling whose side you are on, Boradice," Tonk complained.

"I'm not confused about it at all," Lucha tossed back. "I'm on my friend's side, you know, Captain Zeph Yare. Now you men can just sit in here and stew over your misdeeds until I get back with the captain," he parroted Tonk's earlier words back to him.

Navrat stepped forward. "Take me with you, Lucha."

"No," Lucha denied the request. "I can't be sure how this will come out. I never planned on a career with these people, so if it goes badly, it won't matter to me, but it wouldn't be fair to mess your chances up, Nav." Boradice was walking toward the exit, about to engage the fourth wall security lasers when the brig's doors opened. Six more crewmen entered. They did not seem to notice the incongruity between the positions of the security team and the prisoner.

"Lieutenant Boradice, come with us," the sergeant in charge of the newcomers commanded.

"Why?" Lucha squinted, suspicious of the sergeant, whom he knew to be one of Dante Tartulon's brown-noser sycophants, a fleshy Dome dweller who wore non-regulation jewelry on both his hands, whose surname Lucha could not remember. The crew only referred to him as "ring-finger".

Tonk frowned. "I was ordered to bring the Lieutenant here and lock him up, Bindover."

"Looks like you did a good job of that," the man noted sarcastically. "And now I've got new orders."

Tonk looked up from his communications device. "Fighting has broken out on level three."

"Shit." Lucha was close enough to backhand Bindover, knocking him out as he shouted, "Weapons!" to Navrat, indicating the need to return the security team's equipment to them. Taking advantage of the moment's confusion, Lucha quickly disarmed the newcomers, motioning them into the brig while the security team pivoted out. "Take him with you." Lucha chucked his chin toward the unconscious

CHAPTER THIRTY-SIX

form of Bindover.

Navrat approached Lucha. "You can't leave the ship now. You have to stop this, and you're the only one they're going to trust."

Lucha looked at the security team, now standing beside him outside the cell. "This is one crazy day." He sighed. "You claimed you were loyal to Zeph. I'll give you a chance to prove it. Help me restore order. When things are stabilized, we'll send a shuttle down to the planet for Zeph, agreed?"

Tonk nodded. "Agreed.

Lucha led the mutineers from the brig at a sprint.

CHAPTER THIRTY-SEVEN

"An action removed from the events that created it is ripe for misinterpretation." (Attributed to Dom'pliece Ballatyn at her trial; the Hundred Year War.)

Navrat Tila piloted the Lamdra shuttle over wide swathes of wilderness that gradually became cultivated lands. With the Lamdra's other officers focused on stopping a mutiny, Navrat decided to take action on his own. If he could get Zeph Yare back to the ship, reassuring the mutineers that their captain was safe, the threat would be over. One person might not make much of a difference aboard the Lamdra.

Zeph had not exaggerated Ebulon's resources were beyond the comprehension of a Paxlosian raised beneath the Dome. Navrat Tila had not realized how beautiful a healthy planet could be, and he found himself gaping at the abundant flora of the landscape below.

"And no one's living on any of it," Navrat whispered amazed. For the first time, he saw the wisdom of not giving the Lamdra crew shore leave. On a world like this, a man could walk away and never be found.

A light fog clung to the south coast area, spindle-topped towers poking up through the spun-sugar fog marking the palace's location. Tila made his plans based on Lucha's report that there was no defensive network in place to flag his approach as long as he stayed away from the Taiban run landing fields.

Slowing the shuttle as he entered the fog, he kept a close eye on his instruments. Coming in low, he navigated so that he would be near the landing field.

The wispy fog allowed only intermittent views below. Navrat looked closely for a likely landing site. Suddenly, the dense forest stopped revealing a meadow in their midst. Estates edged the meadow on one side while forestland surrounded it on the other three. A half mile to the south was a larger, lit clearing set near the mismatched farrago of the Taiban District's rooftops.

Navrat hovered the shuttle above the smaller field, slowly lowering it. Quickly shutting down the engines, he reached forward and pressed the panel that opened the main door. The smells of dirt and organic matter teased his nostrils.

Walking down the shuttle's ramp, Navrat was soon knee-deep in grass stalks beaded with raindrops, their heads bent, heavy with moisture. He pressed the control in his hand, closing the ramp and shutting down the small ship then plunged forward.

Keeping his peripheral vision sharp, the Paxlosian officer hurried to the cover of the forest and headed south toward the palace spires he had seen from the air.

As soon as the young officer Navrat Tila exited the shuttle, Spectre unscrewed the mechanic's access panel and lowered himself from the shuttle's belly into the grass beneath it, moving mindfully through the damp field grass, aware that he could be observed from a number of the second and third story windows of nearby mansions.

Yare's absence from the Lamdra had been a happy accident, working in the Shadowmaster's favor, but getting caught on the wrong side of the attack he had worked so hard to make happen would not help him. He needed to get into the city, learn what he could, and return before Tila did.

Unlike the Dome city-state where Navrat Tila was raised, the Ebulonian capital sprawled. Because of his uniform, there was no question of blending in. Navrat was immediately recognized as an intruder. He tried to look as if he knew what he was about and where he was going, a task made easier because of the height of the palace's towers. Plenty of natives stared at him, but no one stopped him until he got to the palace gates.

"I'm here to see your Mahal," Navrat announced to the guards. "I have an urgent message for him from the Lamdra."

The guard noted Navrat's uniform and frowned. "Is he expecting you?"

"No," Navrat admitted, "but he'll want to see me."

"I will notify a diplomat." The guard continued standing where he was. Within minutes a rotund Ebulonian came hurrying out of the palace.

"I am Pliny Mir, the diplomat assigned to liaison with the Paxlosians." He wiped the perspiration from his face. "You are asking to see the Mahal, Nikodamus Mir?" The man seemed nervous, though he hid it well.

"I did," Navrat replied. "Lieutenant Navrat Tila of the U.F. Lamdra," he introduced himself. "But we could skip that step if you would take me straight to Captain Yare."

The round-faced Mir paused before saying, "Please, follow me, Lieutenant."

Spectre climbed the hill north of the shuttle. Rambling mansion estates, larger than the United Front's Presidium's Palace, crowned the top of the ridge, old houses with high rock walled gardens, elegant roof lines, and private orchards. Within minutes he was in the city, blending in among the carters delivering lumber and other goods, Taibans, idling or rushing to complete errands. Activity seemed to center on a pair of gates up ahead. Spectre ambled over to get a better view.

The back gates of a large estate stood open, supply wagons and workmen moving quickly in and out. Inside the yard, dozens of Taiban men were lined up drilling in fighting techniques. Badges in the same orange and black as the uniforms of those who trained them were pinned on their jackets. More men with similar badges or uniforms stood watching. Spectre stepped up behind a cart and joined the stream of trade people going in the gate. A cue of Taibans was lined up to sign a book in return for payment of local credits. Spectre followed the other tradesmen beyond the training yard. Carpenters were busy remodeling old stables into barracks, while merchant's agents instructed carters where to stock goods being brought in. Spectre sauntered up to a callow youth.

"Are you joining up?" Spectre asked casually.

The boy looked longingly at the line. "The Dum'Laiere's are paying better than any of the other clans, but my ma won't have it. She says it dishonors the captain." He shouldered the bag of dried goods and trudged off.

CHAPTER THIRTY-SEVEN

Spectre took one last look around and headed back the way he'd come. He had a lot to think about.

Clem was tromping through the woods with Terk lagging somewhere behind him when he was drawn up by the unexpected sight of a Paxlosian shuttle parked in the middle of the meadow just beyond the wood's edge.

There was no one nearby. The meadow was silent except for the buzz of insects and the rustle of grass moved by the breeze.

Clem marveled at the shuttle's design as he walked forward. The material sheathing the ship's body reflected its surroundings so that it almost disappeared into the greenwood.

A panel in the shuttle's underside suddenly swung open and the man in black dropped to the ground. Hunching low, he scanned the surroundings.

Clem ducked, his heart racing.

Terk came up behind Clem. "What are you doing, dumb head?"

"Get down!" Clem pulled the older boy down beside him.

"What are you playing at?" Terk tried to rise.

"Stay down. He'll see you," the younger boy hissed.

Terk's eyes narrowed. "Who'll see me, and why should I care?"

Clem peered cautiously over the tops of the tall grass. The man in black was climbing the hill on the far side of the meadow, headed for the gate that led to the street above.

"Vale's killer. He's right over there, walking up that hill." Clem pointed.

Terk raised his head enough to clear the grass and stood.

"You're imagining things."

"I saw him," Clem protested. "A Paxlosian dressed in black like the man that killed Vale just came out of that shuttle."

"Just because he's wearing black doesn't make him Vale's killer," Terk pointed out the flaw in Clem's logic. "Look at that ship. It makes those Taiban clunkers look like scrap metal. A Taiban ship couldn't land in a space ten times the size of this meadow. Come on, let's get a closer look." Terk began to make his way through the tall grass.

Clem hesitated. "What if someone else is inside?"

"We're just a couple of kids. There's nothing wrong with just looking." Terk stuck his hands in his pockets and continued ambling forward through the meadow.

Clem's life as Terk's satellite was nearing an end. Their tacit pact of protection and obedience was based on the need for survival in a chapter now closed. Clem had a family who would look after him. Terk, however, was too old for such a placement. It was decided that he should live in a group house with other young men. He said he didn't mind—that he preferred his independence, but Clem could see that Terk resented Clem's new family and his loss of power over the younger boy because of it. Still, it was hard to break old habits.

Clem rose and began to follow Terk through the meadow to the shuttle.

"Hello? Is anyone in there?" Terk called out. When there was no answer, he grinned. "See? We're clear." He walked around the other side of the ship, examining it.

Clemmet ran his hands along the vessel's underside, fingering the places where the sheeting panels joined together. No warning bell sounded. No one came out to tell the boys to shove off. Clem pulled out his penknife and pried open the hatch that the man in black had dropped from. It opened easily. Grabbing the edge of the ship's body, he hoisted himself up into the compartment. Pulling his legs in, he crawled toward a second interior door and went inside.

Raised patterns in geometric designs covered panels on either side of the crawl space where tiny lights blinked in a synchronized repetition. Clem could almost hear the ship whispering its secrets in a language both foreign and familiar. He wished he had more time. He was sure that if he did, he would understand how this amazing ship worked.

He ran his fingers across the raised design of the panel. If he could copy the diagram and show it to Loosy Humqualt maybe the Taibans could build a new kind of ship. Clem liked the idea of repaying the kindness of the Free Men. If he could do that, he would no longer be merely another faceless refugee among hundreds. He'd be a person of worth, someone who mattered and belonged.

Clem studied the diagram, trying to set the details in his mind, but the more he examined it, the more he realized the pattern's complicated depth. If he forgot some key component, would what he remembered be rendered useless? He did not even have paper.

CHAPTER THIRTY-SEVEN

What he needed was Terk's photographic memory. Terk wouldn't understand anything about the image he stored in his brain, but he could draw it out so that Clem could figure it all out. But would Terk help him? Clem hesitated, his belly tightening. With Terk, everything had a cost, and Clem could not allow the older boy to hold his plan hostage.

Clem rolled up his sleeve and took out his penknife. Using the tip of the knife, he scratched a rough copy of the diagram into the skin of his forearm.

Navrat tried to ignore the sense of being overwhelmed by the breadth and scope of Ebulonian architecture which continued to amaze him not only for its sweeping beauty but also its waste of space, focusing on mapping the many turns he and the Mir took traveling through the palace's halls.

They stopped before a tall door, indistinguishable from many others they had passed in the same hall.

"Lieutenant Navrat Tila of the Lamdra," the young diplomat wheezed as the door opened revealing a distinguished man in dove-gray, woolen robes. "Lieutenant Tila, this is Ebulon's Mahal, Nikodamus Mir."

"Thank you, Pliny." Nikodamus turned his attention to the young Paxlosian. "We have not met before," he noted. "You were not at the reception."

"No," Navrat found his voice.

"The guards at the gate indicated you seemed most anxious. What can I do for you, Lieutenant?" the Mir asked.

A cold sweat trickled down under Tila's uniform. "I need to see Captain Yare immediately."

Nikodamus frowned. "I do not understand. The captain returned to your ship several days ago."

Navrat felt his insides go cold. What game was this they were playing?

"If that were true, I wouldn't be here," he declared firmly.

The Mahal shared a glance with the plump diplomat, Pliny. "I assure you, Lieutenant, we had every reason to believe that Captain Yare was back aboard the Lamdra."

"Six days ago, Lieutenant Boradice and Mister Holder returned on the shuttle we sent down. Captain Yare did not return with them. We were told that he stayed behind to negotiate with you, Mahal, so naturally, I am here to ask you where he is."

"We met, as you say," the Mahal explained. "The following day he went to a festival in another city. When he left, we understood that he returned to his ship."

"So, you are saying that you do not know the captain's whereabouts and cannot produce him?" Navrat reiterated. "Before you answer, Mahal, consider how this looks from the perspective of the Lamdra's crew."

"I assure you I am as dismayed by Captain Yare's apparent disappearance as you are," the Mahal declared. Whatever else he might have been going to say, he did not.

The young woman who had appeared on the Lamdra's bridge entered the room. Tila's heartbeat began to gallop, his vision blurring.

The young woman lightly touched his arm, and the world steadied.

"Why have you come?" Her voice was soft, but there was an irresistible command to it.

"I-I came to get the captain," he stuttered.

"Because he is not on board the Lamdra."

"Yes," the lieutenant agreed.

"And you believed that he was here on the planet?"

"Yes."

"And he is needed on the Lamdra."

"Yes.

"I see that you are afraid—Why? What is it you fear?" the woman demanded.

Navrat did not want to say, but the feeling of being compelled was too strong. "There are problems." He clamped down as if he could stop the words.

"Explain," the young woman prodded.

Navrat's breath was shallow and fast. Sweat beaded on his forehead and the fuzz of his upper lip. He did not want to answer, but he was unable to lie to the Ebulonian woman, even though he wanted to.

"The crew thinks you're holding the captain hostage," he blurted out, feeling as if someone was prying open his mind.

"We are not. But if he is not with you and he is not here with us, then where is he?" She turned to the Mahal and Navrat's agony stopped.

CHAPTER THIRTY-SEVEN

"I'm not leaving without him," he declared defiantly.

"No, of course, you are not," she said dismissively. "You are fine, Lieutenant Tila. Sit down over there by the fire and wait until I decide what to do with you." She pointed to a chair facing away from them.

Navrat sat as directed, outwardly compliant, but inside he was seething.

Who were these beings that could do such things? Had they done this to Zeph? What about Lucha Boradice and Holder? They had been down here on the planet for most of the day. Had their minds been infected or were they still miraculously their own? Could any of the men who had come in contact with the Ebulonians be trusted?

I need to warn Tartulon, Navrat thought. He tried to reach into his coat pocket for his trans and found he could not move. *The crew is right.* He struggled with the frustration of his helplessness. *We should attack this planet, wipe out these monsters, and take their world before it's too late.*

CHAPTER THIRTY-EIGHT

"In the end, a single drop breaks the dam." (Anonymous: Common Taiban Free Man saying.)

"**H**ey, fart face, where are you?" Terk shouted. "Where'd you go?" He would find the open cover soon.

Clem opened the main hatch of the ship, standing at the top of the ramp as it lowered to the ground.

"You're a clever monkey." Terk strode up the ramp, pushed past the younger boy, and headed for the cockpit. Clem followed, careful to keep his arm from brushing his body. Terk examined the command console in the cockpit. "What do you think these do?"

Clem sat in one of the chairs. "Make it fly, turn it, tell it to hover," he answered vaguely. His head was spinning, and the cuts on his arm stung.

"I've got that, smart ass, but which does which?"

Clem turned the chair to face away from Terk. "I don't know," he lied, noting the blood beginning to streak down the sleeve of his shirt.

Terk touched a panel, and it lit up with a whirr and a beep.

Clem whipped back around. "You shouldn't do that, Terk."

"Why not?" Terk touched another screen, then another, adding to the colors that lit his ferret features. He flipped some toggles, and the engine came to life.

"Stop. Someone will hear."

"Out here? Don't be stupid, Clem." Terk continued touching things.

"You're going to get us in trouble. Here, come look at this circuit panel I found." Clem tried to distract his friend. "There's a diagram here of the whole system."

"You think too small, turd. Why should I care about some picture when I can see the real thing in action? Come on, Clem. Don't you want to see this thing actually run?"

CHAPTER THIRTY-EIGHT

Clem's sleeve was wet, and he felt like he was moving when he was standing still. He sank to the floor and waited for the wave of nausea to pass. When he returned to the pilot's console, the ramp had been withdrawn and Terk was again fiddling with the panel controls. Clem's throat constricted.

"What are you doing?" he squeaked, his throat dry.

"Taking this shuttle. We're going to be really rich, you and me, Clem." Terk's eyes gleamed with greed.

"We can't," Clem stuttered. "We'll get caught. Where would we hide it?"

"We're not going to try to hide it, we're going to take it to Taiba."

Clem's eyes grew wide and round with fear. "We-we can't, Terk. The Paxlosians, they'll blame the Free Men. They'll attack Ebulon. People will be killed--our friends..."

"Friends? You mean those idiots who kidnapped us and brought us here? They'll only be getting what they deserve."

"You don't need to do this." Clem pulled up his sleeve, exposing the notes he'd carved into his skin. "We can build our own ship. See?"

Terk looked at Clem's arm, and his mouth twisted. "You're a creepy little brat, aren't you? But you do what needs doing. I admire that."

Clem shook his head. "We don't have to live like that anymore."

"What makes you think that? Because they gave you a bed and a teddy bear?" Terk snarled. "That doesn't mean shit. Those weaklings who want to play house and make you their little doll can't protect you from anything. What do you think they're going to do when the Paxlosian attack? Quake in a corner sniveling, that's what. Nothing's changed. I'm the only one who can protect you, Clem."

But it has changed! Clem wanted to wail. But Terk would only take it as another sign of weakness.

"We won't make it to Taiba. They'll catch us," he said quietly.

"There's not a Taiban ship on Ebulon that can touch this thing for speed." Terk grinned, certain that Clem had come around as he had always done. "And by the time any of the Paxlosians figures out it's gone; we'll be too far away for them to do anything about it. You and me are destined for the easy life, Clem. There are folks in the Cluster who'll pay us enough for this technology that we could buy our own fucking planet. All we have to do is get this thing there.

"We're just a couple of kids. The warlords will take the ship and kill us," Clem argued.

"They won't!" Terk shot back.

"What's to stop them? A couple of orphans with a ship like this? We'll be dead the first time we have to stop anywhere."

"Shut up!" Terk spun around and slapped Clem across the face. "Shut up. I won't let them do that. Now, sit down and fly."

"I don't know how to fly this," Clem protested.

Terk's beady eyes narrowed. "That shit might work on some people, but not on me." Terk pulled a gun out from under his jacket and pointed it at Clem. "Fly the ship, genius boy. You and I are going to Taiba."

In that moment, everything Clem had been given--hope, a family, a sense of belonging--all vanished.

That's the problem with having things; they can be taken away.

"I don't want to go back." A sob caught in Clem's throat.

Terk grabbed him by the collar and dragged him to the control panel, and dropped him into a seat. "I don't care what you want. Fly."

"How Terk? Even if I could figure out the controls, think logically. We don't have charts to navigate."

With his free hand, Terk pulled a large, folded paper from inside his jacket and tossed it at Clem. Clem unfolded navigational charts used by the Free Men. "You didn't think I was spending all that time hanging around Crochin's for the company, did you?"

Clem looked out the front window. The twinkle of lights from Little Taiba were visible now just above the treetops. He took a deep breath, put his hand on the control stick, and raised the shuttle into the air.

"That's my boy." Terk looked pleased.

Aless Mc'Larick did not become Senior among Ebulon's Voices merely by outliving her colleagues. She earned the position through decades of proving herself to be smart, tough, and fair. She did not suffer fools well. Life was too short to clutter it up with people you did not give a damn about just because they had the audacity to impose themselves upon you, even if they were family. Aless had relatives she did not allowed to visit her for years, and it caused her not one moment of regret.

Her chair hovered a foot above the rain-slick cobbles, gliding through the empty street bordered by handsome townhouses and gated estate entrances. As she traveled, she indulged herself in peeking in on her neighbor's lives, enjoying the little slices of life she caught glimpses of: families finishing supper, children being herded off to bed, grown-ups settling in for the evening. The simplicity of the scenes bonded her to her fellow Ebulonians without the awkward encumbrance of being forced to socialize with them as individuals.

An afternoon rain left a woody scent on the air, and as she drove her chair along the wrought iron fence that separated the woods backing the estates on the south side of the street, Aless took in a healthy lungful. She was nearing the entrance to her own house when she sensed movement in the shadow of the building and stopped, hovering in place.

Strange. She looked but saw nothing. Perhaps it was Hally's young man, Roald. Aless considered the dramatic nature of her great-granddaughter. The girl seemed to thrive on adventure, and at her age, a boy without family connections was the definition of adventure. Hally's mother did not approve, of course, but Aless had no objections to the boy. The clans needed some new blood from time to time.

Aless reached out mentally to reassure Roald that she would not give him away, but the mind she touched was more than unfamiliar. Its nature was strange, precise, and yet mercurial, with dark corners and hidden layers.

"Who are you?" She squinted into the shadows. The shadowy figure did not move. "Stop cowering there in the dark. I know you are there. Come out here and show yourself." She nudged her verbal command with enough magic that the stranger would be unable to resist.

And yet he did resist.

How did they do that? Who are they? Aless' curiosity was piqued.

An engine whined from the clearing in the nearby woods, raising the figure's agitation. Aless moved her chair closer.

"Stop skulking and come out here," she spoke directly into his mind. She felt a spike of alarm flicker in the stranger's mind.

He had not expected her to speak to him in that way.

He is not Ebulonian, Aless realized. *And not Taiban.* He was something else.

"Who are you?" Aless asked again.

"I am no one. I am nothing. I am not even here," the stranger chanted mentally.

"You are someone, and you most certainly are here. I can hear you thinking. Show yourself," again she compelled him to obey. The stranger took a reluctant, stiff-legged step closer then a second.

The man was dressed all in black, with black gloves covering the skin on his hands, his face hidden in the deep folds of a black hood.

"You have made a mistake. I am not who you think I am. Let me go on my way," he muttered through clenched teeth.

"No," Aless refused. "What is your name?" The figure continued to move toward her. "What are you doing outside my house? Do you know who I am?"

"It doesn't matter," the man hissed. "Because I am talking to a dead woman."

With a quick, fluid movement, he was before her. Aless felt a sting in her chest. The man disappeared down the street behind her as she slumped in her chair, numbness spreading through her body, stopping her heart.

Clem slammed the Paxlosian shuttle's fly stick forward, skimming the tops of the trees around the meadow and tossing Terk to the back wall of the cockpit.

"Careful, you little shit!" The older boy scrambled back to his feet.

Clem pulled the stick back sharply, reversing direction, once again toppling Terk.

"Stop that, you fucking idiot!" Terk scrambled forward on all fours and elbowed Clem out of the way, taking control of the stick. Without resistance, Terk's momentum doubled the power of the control stick's forward motion. The ship's engines raced, and it shot up into the air, driving Terk to his knees. Fighting against gravity and the ship's momentum, Terk struggled to climb back to his seat, reaching for the ship's controls.

CHAPTER THIRTY-EIGHT

"No! No! No!" Clem pounded Terk's hand.

"You fucking traitor." Terk smashed Clem's fingers with the butt end of the gun. "Let go. Let go."

Clem's grip began to fail as the bones in his hand fractured. He released the controller, swung his chair around, and kicked Terk back against the bulkhead.

Reaching forward, he flipped a switch on the shuttle's console. The engines began to slow, then faltered, before they began to fall from the sky.

"I am sorry," Clem thought as the shuttle crashed into a wall on the north side of Little Taiba, exploding in a ball of fire.

CHAPTER THIRTY-NINE

"In the mirror of The Truths, you will see your true self." (Anonymous from the Book of the Rhune.)

"**T**ake this seat here beside me." Miratha Dum'Laiere gestured to Zeph. "Dora may sit on your other side."

Dora did not take the suggested seat, seating herself instead on the opposite side of the table. But before her mother could do more than frown, the young woman was up and out the door. "Excuse me."

"My apologies for my daughter's lack of manners, Captain," Miratha tried to cover her confusion with a polite veneer.

"It's not necessary. She's young. She's still trying to figure out who she is," Zeph dismissed Miratha's concern.

"I do hope she does it quickly and in private." Miratha sniffed. "Dora does not yet fully understand the uniqueness of her position as a young woman of the First Line in a clan as old and powerful as the Dum'Laiere's, but she will. With the clan behind her, Dora will be a most sought-after partner."

As if Miratha's statement was a premonition, the dining room door opened, and Dora re-entered, proudly holding onto the arm of Frevin Mir. The Dum'Laiere matron's eyes darted between the two guests. It was not hard for Zeph to imagine smoke coming out of her ears.

"I did not realize that we expected a second guest," she addressed her daughter icily.

"*My* guest," Dora corrected her mother. "*I* invited him. I believe you both know Frevin Mir?"

Fratianne appeared, hurrying to set an additional place at the table.

Frevin noted Zeph's presence, quickly unwinding Dora's arm from his. "Forgive me, Lady Miratha. I fear this is an intrusion," he offered nervously. "Perhaps I should return another time." Dora grabbed his arm, forcing him to remain at her side or create a scene that would put a blot on his reputation.

"Do not be silly, Frevin," she scolded. "We are all friends here. In fact, I would venture to say that there are few with a greater understanding of the true situation here on Ebulon than we four."

Zeph did not need to read minds to measure Miratha's displeasure. The woman glared daggers at Frevin and her daughter.

An awkward silence settled over the table; a silence Zeph realized indicated a nonverbal conversation was taking place that he was not a party to.

Dora winced, clenching her jaw as if the intensity of her mother's mental scolding was causing physical pain, but there was no evidence of retreat on her willful face. Her plan in bringing Frevin here would not only reveal her independence, but--as Frevin loyal to Nikodamus--would force him to inform the Mahal about Zeph's presence at the Dum'Laiere estate. Unable to risk it being revealed that she was keeping Zeph against his will, Miratha would be forced to let Zeph go.

"Frevin and I met at the Third Night Ball in Auhora Whimlan," Dora pattered on. "Lady Faliese introduced us. His family is the Ner'Ansetts. You know some Ner'Ansetts, do you not, Mother?"

"Of course," Miratha answered. "Wallish Ner'Ansett is a Voice on the council."

Frevin nodded. "A quiet, thoughtful man. Many claim that good listening is what makes a good Voice. Those with that quality seem more focused on representing the interests of their people and less interested in promoting their own."

"Well said, Frevin," Dora gave the Mir a besotted look of admiration. "Frevin has been teaching me all about politics and the law. He has opened my eyes to much I did not understand before," Dora declared, an insincere smile glossing the double meaning of her words. "I cannot think of anyone whom I trust more to advise me, including those in my own family." The steel behind Dora's eyes belied the dimples in her round face. "You remember, Mother, how you sent me to Auhora Whimlan to meet Captain Yare, telling me that story about a plan for him and I to be engaged? Frevin helped me understand why you would say such a thing."

"You are too kind, Lady Dum'Laiere." Frevin gave Dora a humble nod.

Miratha's shoulders and neck stiffened as Dora giggled. "Lady Dum'Laiere is my mother, Frevin. I am just Dora."

Frevin blinked in a confusion that smelled of insincerity. "But you are the Dum'Laiere heiress, Dora. When you reached the age of majority, that title became yours. Your mother's title is now 'Matron'."

Zeph thought Miratha was going to lunge across the table and scratch out the Mir's eyes.

"You are so good to explain these things to me, Frevin. I am sure I will rely on your advice for years to come," Dora simpered, throwing a triumphant look at her mother.

Fratianne re-entered and commenced serving the first course. On making her way around the table to Zeph, she spun around quickly, and her skirts swept a piece of Zeph's tableware to the floor.

"Pardon, sir." She knelt to pick the fork up as both of their heads ducked under the table, she hissed, "Be careful. That Mir is the one who told Miratha about the treaty." She straightened up. "I will fetch you a clean fork, Sir." She hurried from the room.

Sitting back up, Zeph tried desperately to keep his thoughts scattered and not let them form the accusation he wanted to scream at the disloyal Mir.

Miratha's gaze fixed on Frevin. Was she trying to work some private angle with him?

Their alliance was not public. Frevin would not want it to be. It had to be destroyed, and Frevin would embrace that rather than be called out as the traitor he was.

"It's good to have people whom we can trust surrounding us," Zeph said. "If Frevin Mir is that person for you, Dora, you cannot go wrong with him beside you." He turned to Frevin. "You and Matron Dum'Laiere have been working together on the council for some time now, haven't you? You must have partnered on many projects before this."

"I am newly pledged to service," Frevin hedged.

"But you are trusted by the Mahal and the Pira? You were assigned to liaison with us, which indicates some confidence in your loyalty. It was kind of you to step aside when the Mahal asked you to relinquish your place beside Eropa in Auhora Whimlan and allow me to go in your place."

Dora's brow wrinkled.

Zeph hoped he had raised enough doubt in the Dum'Laiere heiress' mind--about Frevin's sudden and convenient appearance in her life--to force the Mir to take action and prove his support of Dora.

If he was so offended by my interest in Eropa that he was replaced as our liaison, what is he doing here with Dora Dum'Laiere? Zeph thought as loudly as he could.

Everyone at the table froze, the air suddenly lead-heavy.

"Being as you are so close to the Mahal, Frevin Mir, would you mind delivering a message to him for me?" Zeph asked.

Miratha nearly dropped her fork.

Frevin hesitated. "Your liaison is Pliny Mir now, Captain Yare," he pointed out.

"But Pliny is not here. You are." Zeph knew the Mir could not reasonably refuse his request without raising Dora's suspicions and branding himself Miratha's creature.

"I am at your service." Frevin inclined his head. "What message would you like me to convey?"

"I'd like to remind the Mahal how delicate the line between failure and success can be. I did what he suggested; I went to Auhora Whimlan with his daughter, but the outcome was not what he hoped, I think. I have evidence of other factions whose agendas work against our plans for a peaceful treaty. My hopes are quickly diminishing."

Frevin rose. "It seems you will have the opportunity to deliver your message in person, Captain. The Mahal asks me to bring you to him immediately."

"But we have three more courses," Miratha protested. "Surely you have time to eat?" No one believed she was worried about the food.

"My apologies for cutting our dinner short, Matron Dum'Laiere, but unfortunately, we must take our leave."

"It's been an education." Zeph nodded to his hostess. He gave a quick wink to Dora and followed Frevin to the foyer that led to the street.

"I cannot allow this," Miratha declared. Frevin and Zeph did not stop. "At least wait until I can summon men to escort you. For your own safety, Captain Yare, you should not walk the streets without protection."

"I think I'll risk it," Zeph shot back, not stopping.

They were on the top step outside the door when an explosion lit up the sky to the southeast.

"That was in the District," Frevin said as the sky over Little Taiba flamed orange. He and Frevin began to run.

CHAPTER FORTY

"A thought is as inconsequential as a passing breeze until you put the force of a tornado behind it." (Attributed to Dom'Pleice at the start of the Hundred Year War. Undocumented.)

Heat waves rippled the darkness above Little Taiba, a dirty orange smudge bleeding the sky. The smoke blocked Ebulon's early moons, the refugees' screams riding its back. Searching desperately for the faces that would make them grateful that only their homes were being destroyed while residents of the District shouted into the chaos. A lucky few found their loved ones clinging to them like heavy driftwood on a storm-tossed sea.

Corin sloshed through the muck as pump wagons rushed past. Torrents of water poured down from air-born Taiban ships dumping loads onto the burning city.

Street by street, the skyline of Little Taiba was collapsing. If the situation between the Taiban factions, the Paxlosians, and the Ebulonians were fraught with tension before, the sudden, unexplained fire set everything to unravel into one huge catastrophe.

Corin pushed her way through the crowd.

I need to find Uncle, or Quinn, or someone. The stink of sewage and old wood burned her eyes.

Somewhere nearby, a small child wailed. Corin spun around, seeking the source. A toddler stood alone in the mouth of an alleyway--her face dusted by soot, tear tracks striping her cheeks--crying for her mother.

Corin scooped the child up, holding the little girl close to her chest to shield her face from the searing heat of the burning buildings. Corin could feel the little heart thumping against her. *How can anything so fragile survive this?* she wondered, looking at the horrific scene around them. Where were her parents? Where would the child be safe? Was there such a place?

Everything was falling apart.

CHAPTER FORTY

Corin's eyes tracked south and east toward the Bobalo compound. "There's fighting at the west gate!" someone shouted.

"Fighting? Who's fighting? It's a fire, for the Mother's sake, not a brawl." Corin's voice was like paper embers in the roar of the flames, but in her gut, Corin knew it didn't matter. The event was taking Little Taiba's residents to the brink and dumping them over the edge.

"They were closing the south gate when I came through," she overheard a man tell his wife and children. "We'll have to hurry, or we'll be trapped." The children clutched their mother's legs as the father took the baby from her arms.

"They wouldn't. There are women and children—old people," the woman let the sentence drift into uncertainty.

"I no longer know what anyone will or will not do," her husband said sternly. "But I will not risk our family."

Corin grabbed the man's arm as he brushed by her. "Who did this? Who is closing the gates?" she demanded.

"Does it matter?" He yanked his arm from her grasp. "If they lock us in, we'll burn alive." He led his family into the crowd heading west.

Settle down. Stay calm. Corin's mind fought the panic rising around and within her. Where was Bobalo? Where was Quinn? Were the girls and Aunt Timee safe at the compound? The sky to the east looked encouragingly dark.

Holding the little girl tight, Corin pressed through the crowd, trying to angle to the east.

Whirlpools of humanity tossed strangers together and tore families apart as the panicked refugees struggled to reach the west gate before it closed.

"Let us through!" Corin pushed against the tide, clutching her breathing bundle, but again and again, the crowd swept them west.

Living obstacles tripped and entangled her feet, throwing her off balance and forcing her to step wherever she could to remain upright. Seeing an opening, Corin tried to cut back to the edge of the mob, hoping when the street widened, she could peel away and again make for the Bobalo compound. Then, something struck her on the side of the head. She staggered into the man behind her.

"Keep your feet, girl." He steadied her. "This is no place for you," he added, seeing the child in her arms. "You're not a fighter, and this is about to become a battle zone."

"Why is everyone talking about fighting? What's going on? This is a fire, not a war!" Corin tried to find some reason.

The man put an arm around her shoulders and pushed through the human flood until they reached the edge.

"No one knows what this is," he said gruffly. "Go home, if you still have one, and find someplace safe to hide." He disappeared into the crowd.

Corin shifted the child's weight to her hip and looked around, getting her bearings.

Nothing looked right. The backs of the buildings on the east side of the street were entirely engulfed in flames, while their front yards, with their little makeshift stake fences, remained untouched, black soot butterflies dancing among sparks that winked on and off like fireflies.

"Mailie!" A woman emerged from the river of people.

"Mah!" The child gave a choked cry and vaulted into her mother's arms.

"Thank you." The woman buried her face in the little girl's curls.

"Find someplace safe, if you can," Corin urged her.

The woman nodded, and then mother and daughter vanished back into the crowd.

Corin jogged over to the stake fence in front of a burning building and pulled two of the stakes from the ground. Checking their balance, she took her new weapons in hand and began zigzagging between the flaming walls, heading east.

Fire blocked her route one way; rubble blocked it another. Again and again, she was forced north and west until she found herself at the gate beside the Mi'cosa bridge.

Refugees streamed through the gate, filling anything that would hold water. An old woman struggling under the weight of two buckets fell in front of Corin, spilling water over the ground.

Corin ran forward. "Let me help you, mother."

The woman leaned on Corin's arm, allowing Corin to guide her to a turned-over crate. "Are you hurt?" Corin asked the woman as she lowered her gingerly to sit.

"Just let me catch my breath." She looked back at the fire, and her eyes glazed over. "The stairs were burning before anyone knew that anything was happening." The old woman's cataract-filled eyes shone with milky tears. "By the gods, what have we done to deserve this?"

"This is a fire, Auntie, not a judgment on the Free Men," Corin declared. "The gods don't punish the good for the deeds of the bad."

The old woman looked up at her and smiled wanly. "You are very young. It happens all the time."

"I don't believe that," Corin stated stubbornly.

"You'll see in time," the woman disagreed softly. "Leave me. I'm fine. I just need a moment."

A shout of protest rose from the crowd behind her, and Corin turned.

The gates were closing.

"What the hell is going on here!" Tai Bobalo's voice thundered over the heads of the crowd. Block was opening a path through the frightened mass of refugees for the Taiban captain. "We're fighting a fire. We need water. Who told you to close these gates?" Bobalo bellowed at the men positioned at the gate's controls. "Open the damned things up!"

"We don't take orders from you," a man on palisades shouted down.

Bobalo raised an eyebrow. "So, what son-of-a-bitch do you take orders from?" he demanded.

"Son of a bitch, Saldo Murtevoy, that's who," the man shouted back as if it were a challenge.

"Saldo doesn't have the authority to give that order," Quinn protested.

"Apparently, someone disagrees with you, son." Bobalo raised his voice to be heard by the man on the gate. "I need to talk to Saldo. Can you get him for me?"

The man began to discuss Bobalo's request with his companions.

Block grinned as Corin joined them.

"Finally. Are you all right?" Tai Bobalo asked his niece. "We were looking for you."

"Yes." Corin nodded. "And Auntie and the girls?"

"The fire hasn't spread that far east," Bobalo assured her. "But the situation is deteriorating quickly. I need you to get to Eropa and tell her what's happening."

"What is happening?" Corin asked. "I heard that there's fighting. Whose fighting while the quarter's on fire?"

"The factions are queuing up and not to talk." Bobalo's eyes narrowed as he studied the men on the wall.

"And you think Saldo's behind it?" Corin frowned, unable to believe that any of the Free Men or Women would risk so many of their own people's lives.

"Can you get to Eropa, Corin?" her uncle repeated his request.

"Of course," Corin agreed.

"Good. Quinn, go with your cousin."

"I don't need anyone to go with me," Corin protested. "Quinn should stay here and help you."

"That was not a request, Corin," Bobalo snapped. "It was an order from your captain. This is not the world you know, and these are not the men you think they are. Their blood is up, and no one is thinking clearly." Bobalo turned his attention to the next problem. "Ald, I have a mission for you as well."

"Let's go, cousin." Quinn and Corin rushed off.

CHAPTER FORTY-ONE

"Words may be misunderstood. Intentions rarely are." (Attributed to Rensean McWraith in the opening days of The Hundred Year War.)

The smoke rising from The District alarmed and angered Miratha. Dora's clumsy reveal of--Zeph Yare's presence at the estate--to Frevin had her temper at a boiling point. Now, she had lost control of her prize. Problems in the District coming to a head were not helpful. The question was, what alterations had to be made to her plans?

Each of the Dum'Laiere's three stables were converted to sleeping quarters for members of the Dum'Laiere house guard. What were formerly stalls, were furnished with cots, and the larger open floor was converted to an eating space. The former carriage house was now officer's quarters. Meninger, a Taiban merchant, used his shuttle service to remove and stable the horses.

Though Miratha approved the contracts for carpenters and carters, food, blankets, new uniforms, training equipment, and weapons, with the many other distractions demanding her attention, she only casually noted the constant dust rising from the stable yard as everything formerly equine was transitioned to military use. She felt no need to monitor such mundane arrangements. That was what Saldo Murtevoy was hired to do.

Her lack of attention did not infer trust of the Taiban mercenary, the Dum'Laiere Voice had no illusions about the man's character. In fact, Willem's efforts to vet the man had resulted in multiple sources reporting the man's continued bitterness over losing his command a decade past, leading Miratha to suspect he harbored ambitions beyond his station. Nevertheless, he offered a quick and easy answer to the clan's needs.

Right now, she needed more information about what was going on.

CHAPTER FORTY-ONE

She checked her hair and smoothed her dress before stepping into the practice yard, wincing at the dust that immediately dulled the sheen of her satin dress, and coating her slippers.

Small groups of men lingered in the old stable yard, some in the new Dum'Laiere house guard uniform, others too new to have been costumed with anything other than placards bearing the Dum'Laiere sigil in the clan's colors worn over their rough clothing. A few bore only rough facsimiles of the sigil on a makeshift armband or pinned to their shirt or vest.

The yard was oddly empty considering the number of Taibans on the family's payroll. Miratha's eyes narrowed.

A satin-covered arm snaked out and grabbed a boy who had the misfortune of passing within her reach.

"Where is Captain Murtevoy?" she demanded, gripping the boy's shoulder.

"I-I don't know, Lady," the boy stammered.

A scream sailed over the wall that separated the Dum'Laiere estate from the Bren'Harrow's to the west, whipping Miratha's head around.

"What was that?"

"Apparently, there's some trouble in Little Taiba. A fire, I'm told."

Miratha spun around to face Saldo Murtevoy who had come up behind her.

"Let the boy go." His eyes focused pointedly on her fingers digging into the boy's shoulder.

Miratha's ire rose at being given orders by a man who was essentially hired help, but there was no mistaking the threat in the mercenary's "suggestion".

"Get back to work." She pushed the boy away from her so hard he stumbled and fell. Murtevoy's eyes narrowed, but she smirked primly, her nostrils flaring as if she smelled something unpleasant.

"Is there something you need, Lady Dum'Laiere?" the mercenary captain growled.

A group of five Taibans came around the corner of one of the stable buildings. They bore no evidence of being affiliated with her house guard, other than, they were on the property. Their muscular, unwashed bodies smelled of sweat and foreign spices, their manners and laughter low and raucous. What had she been thinking, letting these wild, uncivilized men into her world? The family might rent their weapon arms but putting a bit of material with the Dum'Laiere insignia on their chests did not make them loyal to her.

Another scream sailed across the wall and glass shattered this time to the east.

"Where is everyone, Captain Murtevoy?" She heard the tension in her voice. It was pitched too high and tight, revealing her fear. She smoothed her dress again, a habitual gesture she used to calm herself. "There are two hundred men on my payroll and yet I see a dozen?"

"A dozen men patrol the estate's perimeter," Murtevoy replied. " Fifty are off duty. Another hundred training in the countryside and two dozen are looking at the problem in Little Taiba."

"I do not care what is happening in Little Taiba. I want every man available here, protecting this estate."

"Keeping the District's problems within the District is important for both of us," Murtevoy stated.

"I am not paying for your politics," Miratha countered.

"You are paying for my advice and experience."

Miratha snorted derisively. "Your experience as a strong arm. If you think you were hired to think, you are mistaken. You are to listen and pass on my orders."

"Strategic autonomy is in my contract," Murtevoy's explanation smelled like defiance.

Miratha blinked. Had she really agreed to that? Probably. All the clans had. It did not seem like a problem at the time, but she saw the error now. She examined Murtevoy with a more discerning eye.

"I admire a man who makes the most of an opportunity. I have another you might find interesting."

"I'm listening," Murtevoy declared.

"It is not generally known, but Captain Yare is in the city, possibly on his way to the palace, or the landing fields. If some far-seeing individual were to act quickly, they might intercept him." Miratha took a deep breath, so the fullness of her bosom strained over the edge of her bodice--then giggled like the foolish woman she was --but not so that the plump flesh jiggled suggestively. "A person with a talent for strategy might find advantage in having possession of the

Paxlosian captain," she suggested, looking elsewhere to give the impression that her suggestion was only casually mentioned.

"You want me to bring him back here?" Murtevoy asked.

"Certainly not." Miratha snapped. "I am a member of the Elder's Council and a clan Voice."

"Meaning you can't have anything to do with Yare's 'interception'. I understand." Murtevoy's smile revealed a quiet, underplayed cruelty. "I heard you already had him."

"You should not listen to gossip, Captain Murtevoy." She gave an indignant sniff. "Forget I said anything. I want you to send a dozen men to the palace. As you say, the District's turmoil may spill over into other areas of the city. Chaos is a breeding ground for violent change and the presence of our men could make the difference in the night's outcome for the Mahal…and all of us." She gave him an intense look, willing him to hear words she was not saying, then quickly retreated to the safety of the main house.

"Captain Murtevoy!" Ald, one of Quinn Bobalo's team members approached at a run. "Captain Murtevoy, I've a message for you from Captain Bobalo."

"Not here," Murtevoy led the young fighter to the officer's quarters. The carriage house had been furnished with cast-offs from the mansion, giving it an air of aged gentility, furnishings far beyond anything any Taiban possessed, except perhaps for Meninger whose shuttle service had become such a success.

Adjutants and minor officers in crisp new Dum'Laiere uniforms hurried in and out of side rooms.

"All of the gates in the District, except one, have been secured, Captain Murtevoy," one of the officers informed the Taiban Mercenary as they passed through. "Only the Mi'cosa gate remains open."

"Explain that?" Murtevoy demanded.

"Bobalo has people there insisting it stay open, because they need access to the river to fight the fire that's burning."

"Captain Murtevoy." Ald stepped forward. "Captain Bobalo sent me to get your help with this. The fire—it's running too fast. We can't stop it. We need more people. Bobalo asks you to send help."

Murtevoy examined the young man. "My people are contracted to protect the interests of the Dum'Laiere Clan. We're under no obligation to assist the District."

"But they're Taiban," the young man looked shocked. "Surely you could spare a few--?"

"No, I can't. My orders are to pull my people out of Little Taiba. Bobalo's inability to control his people is not my problem, but they're posing a threat to the clans. My people are needed here to protect the Dum'Laiere estate. Tell Bobalo I can't help him."

"You have men positioned in every clan," Ald declared boldly. "Hundreds of them—more than anyone realizes. You can spare a few. Please."

"Whatever you've heard, I don't give orders to anyone but the men here on this estate," Murtevoy declared. "Why don't you go ask the clan guard captains for help? You'll get the same answer, though. We're done believing in Bobalo and his cronies' promises of a better future. We're creating our future, our way, on our terms."

"Please, Captain Murtevoy," Ald pleaded. "Little Taiba will be destroyed."

"'Not my responsibility." Murtevoy began to pull on a pair of expensive leather gloves. "I know you admire the old man--hell, we all do, but dreams have a spoil date and Bobalo's are moldy and stale— not fit for eating. It's time for a new dream, not in some faraway future back on Taiba, but here today on Ebulon. You're a decent fighter. You should join us."

"I knew you were bitter, Murtevoy, but I didn't realize you had no heart. People's homes are burning, and you could help, but you won't because you can't get past the fact that Tai Bobalo is a better man than you are, and everyone knows it." The boy spun on his heels and rushed out.

"Damned idealist," Murtevoy muttered.

CHAPTER FORTY-TWO

"The Rhune who moves mountains on a whim will stumble on a pebble." (Mo Tep Hunan: Third Matriarch, From the Book of Rhunes.)

Nikodamus walked to the window out of sight of the Paxlosian who, Eropa bound to silence and sent to sit by the fire.

"Frevin has found Captain Yare," she informed her father. "He is with Miratha." Her gaze remained unfocused, her mind elsewhere, listening to a voice not in the room.

"Do not worry, daughter," Nikodamus assured her. "Yare will recognize Miratha's machinations for what they are."

Scanning the room Eropa's eyes lit on papers strewn over her father's desk, her attention caught by the unusual quality of the paper and printing of the documents on top.

Eropa picked up the strange document examining it. "Frevin said…" She did not finish, her eyes burning with the sting of tears. "I cannot believe…you would not…not ever. You are my father."

Nikodamus turned and saw what she was holding. "Put it down, Eropa," he said quietly.

Stunned disbelief strained the young sorceress' features.

"This was your plan--the outcome of your negotiations with the Paxlosians? *This* is what you want for me—for my future? To be forced to leave you--to leave my home?" Eropa's hand shook so that the papers shivered like leaves. "What about my duty as a Rhune, Father? What about my responsibility to our people? I am not just some first-line daughter to be married off to seal some contract between clans. I am the future Matriarch."

The sudden change of plans that kept Frevin in Iredipa-- Zeph's mocking courtship--suddenly took on new meaning and made terrible sense.

"'We must each play our part'." Nikodamus's sad eyes begged her to understand.

CHAPTER FORTY-TWO

"And you have decided this is to be mine." Her fingers released the document. It fluttered to the floor like a flock of white feathered pigeons floating to a landing, resting at last on the stone floor.

"From the beginning, our plan was to find a path that did not include war and the destruction of our world or the death of our people. We were all searching for that path--even Yare," Nikodamus reasoned calmly. "This treaty, flawed as it is, does that. It does what we need it to do, Eropa. It protects our people. It appoints you to protect our people. This is a way forward where before we could see none. It is what we hoped for."

Eropa shook her head, unshed tears glistening in her eyes.

"Not me. You have conspired to barter away my future, my inheritance, my happiness."

"Not that, daughter--not ever that," Nikodamus objected. "I witnessed what happened between you and the alien when you first met, and it made me believe that you might find happiness with this man. I sent you to Auhora Whimlan to give you a chance to explore that possibility."

Eropa looked at him coldly. "How dare you."

"I made no promises, Eropa. I told him nothing. He does not know you are my daughter or that you might be this treaty bride."

"Might be?" Understanding dawned within a mind that felt as if a great thunderstorm of permanent darkness was building a mere breadth of a blade's edge away, and when her heart stumbled, as she was sure it would, she would be swallowed whole, the storm's violence shredding her into a million dark spider's silken threads, its chaos becoming her body. "This is why Hagriva recognized Miratha as her descendant," the young sorceress muttered. "She did it so Dora Dum'Laiere could be the treaty bride and seal this agreement."

"And you could remain here." Nikodamus nodded.

"But when you sent me to Auhora Whimlan, you did not know what Hagriva would do." The features of Eropa's face became tight, her eyes as hard and sharp as her bitter accusations.

Pain rippled across her father's face. "You said we could not fight them, that if we tried, we would lose. You were searching for an answer from magic that could have required your sacrifice. Why is this different?"

"Because that would be my choice," Eropa declared, her voice unnervingly angry and unnaturally controlled.

"This would have been your choice as well, but following this path meant that you lived. It was an honorable compromise."

Eropa's eyes were twin flames of bright green fire. "I am a Rhune. We do not compromise." She exited in a whirlwind of silks and charged energy, fracturing the air around her.

Zeph had only taken a few strides when Frevin appeared alongside him.

"I need to get back to the Lamdra," Zeph announced. "Can you arrange a shuttle?"

"No," Frevin resisted. "This starship of yours is like a harlot, obeying any hand at the helm. We cannot risk another mistake like when they fired on the Taibans."

"Captain Yare!" Fratianne ran up to them, a wrapped bundle held to her chest. "These are yours. Dora found them." She gave Zeph the bundle.

He opened it. Wrapped inside was a gun and holster. He buckled the holster on. "There was a trans unit--communication device--a small silver box?"

Fratianne blinked. "This is all she gave me." She rounded on Frevin. "Stay out of my head, Mir!"

"You have a strange way of serving your mistress." Frevin accused her.

"And you of serving your Mahal," the servant girl flared back. "I wonder what the Pira would say if she knew how you betrayed her father's confidence. Poor Dora has no idea that it was you who plotted with her mother to capture Yare. Just whose side are you on, Mir?" She paused. "Oh, I know; your own," she finished harshly.

Frevin's color rose. "You little Taiban half-breed, you understand nothing!"

"Typical. No one else knows anything."

"Stop, Fratianne," Zeph interrupted the argument. "We have more important issues than your petty bickering. Can you get me to the landing area, Fratianne? I need to hire a ship."

CHAPTER FORTY-TWO

She hesitated. "The District is a mess, Zeph. It's not just the fire, something else is going on. The clan's house guards are streaming off their estates, marching toward Little Taiba."

"To help with the fire," Zeph finished.

Fratianne shook her head. "I don't know. I just don't know, but we can't know who's in control of the landing fields or what their hoping to do."

"You see? We have to go to the palace," Frevin repeated. "It is the only place you will be safe."

"I will be safe on my ship," Zeph declared, his frustration showing.

The Mir dropped his eyes. "We cannot be sure of that."

Zeph scowled at the Mir. "I can."

"There is some question about who is in control of your ship," Frevin announced." Zeph wanted to punch the smirk from his face. "Until we are certain that order has been restored aboard the "Lamdra, we cannot risk…

"Order will be restored when their captain returns!" Zeph shouted. "You think telling me this will make me stay here? I need to get to my ship. All of these people, my crew, I am responsible for them."

There was another explosion, this one nearby on one of the clan estates.

"When you are safe, Captain Yare, we will find a way to contact the Lamdra, but right now, we need to get you off the street and someplace where you are not in danger of being killed at the whim of some Taiban ruffian mob who thinks you killed their friends," Frevin insisted. "If you are taken by these men, riled up as they are, you will be killed with no thought as to the consequences for their people. What do you think your crew will do then?"

The Mir's reasoning was sobering.

Fratianne took hold of Zeph's arm. "You know how much it hurts me to say this, but he's right, Zeph. If you're killed, none of us have a future."

"Okay," Zeph agreed reluctantly. "We get to the palace, then we contact the Lamdra. That's the deal."

"Yes," Frevin agreed.

Eropa's energy lit the corridors of Iredipa's palace as she ran from her father's rooms. The sound of hairline cracks radiating through the polished stone floor were born from each contact of the Rhune's tiny feet, ricocheting from wall to wall down the long, empty, stone corridors. The Rhune's power striking the stone with a force beyond explanation. The web-line ruptures grew as she moved. Web overlapping web, fogging the stone's dark sheen and sculpting its clear lake-like surface into a violent landscape of crushed stone upthrusts pulling crystalline fissures as she passed.

The symbols of her ancestral power raced under her skin without pattern or restraint, the glowing veins scalding her as if the magic within her was combustible and would consume her from the inside out,

Eropa approached the tall, broad doors at the corridor's intersection and threw her arms out to the sides. Rebounding against the walls, her power split the thick wood apart as if it were as brittle as thawing ice and not made of trees that were hundreds of years old and as thick as man's thighbone. The doors pulled from their hinges, their bases thudding against the abused stone beneath it like a drum of thunder, adding its booming echo to the screams of the stone as its once smooth, peaceful surface is ripped and scarred like living skin.

The tops of the huge wooden slabs fall together, pausing to lean one against the other in a moment of grief before toppling one last time in successive roars of destruction to lay at last against the ruined bosom of the floor.

"Prepare a windcraft for me," Eropa gave a mental command to the guards at the front gate, not withholding the intensity of her energy or sparing the delicate cells of their brains.

"I am going home."

Corin thought she knew Quinn's skills, but the time he spent on Taiba in the Resistance had seasoned his youthful daring into skills that balanced speed, daring, and caution. If he sensed someone approaching, they sought cover. At blind corners, Quinn scouted ahead. They sprinted down long, open roads, and slunk cautiously through narrow spaces between buildings, scrambling over walls as they worked their way toward the palace.

"If we get separated, when you get to the kitchens, take the servant's stairs that go up until you get to the level with the green marble floors," Corin explained.

Quinn squared his jaw. "We are not getting separated."

"But just in case we do." A tall stone wall blocked their way. "It's part of the old city wall from before the palace was built." Corin indicated the section of white stone. "If we run along the top for two hundred feet we can drop onto the other side. We'll be one street away from the palace grounds. Go left when you get to the top, toward the market."

They scaled the wall and dropped off into the narrow pedestrian path on the other side. So narrow that only hand carts could navigate it, the cobbled path sandwiched between two pale, gold, stone walls, double the height of a person, felt like a trench despite the established neighborhood and its desirability. Close to the palace, it was popular among palace officials.

They were running down a long straight stretch when Quinn suddenly rolled into a recessed entry, pulling Corin in after him.

Quinn put a finger to his lips as three men turned the corner, entering the same walled walkway they were traveling.

"Do you believe they would do such a thing?" conversation drifted toward them. "Where is the precedence?"

"There is none," a second voice replied. "But then, we have never been under such a threat before."

Corin and Quinn flattened themselves against the back wall of the portico they had slipped into, blending with the shadows.

The men continued down the walkway, talking as they did.

A metallic squeak from the door behind Quinn and Corin warned them that the entryway had a purpose and people who used it. They were about to be discovered.

Quinn leaped up into the grillwork above, crawling through to the topside, quickly lost in the foliage.

The door behind Corin opened, catching her in an escaped shaft of light.

"Hello?" a round-figured Ebulonian exclaimed in surprise as he stepped into the doorframe.

"Pliny, were you expecting another guest?" Two white-haired Mirs leaned forward to look over his shoulder.

The young Mir looked confused. "Mithra, is this one of your students?"

An explosion rocked the city, and the four strangers stood staring at each other. The men from the walkway joined them.

"What are you doing here, Taiban?" one of them demanded harshly. "You have no business in this part of the city."

"Probably a Taiban spy," his companion muttered.

"Oh, leave off, Bren'Harrow. She's just a girl," the man the others had referred to as Malbuis scolded.

"Go on, Quinn. Go." Corin hoped that her cousin realized she could not avoid this delay, and he must go on without her.

She took a breath and calmed herself. "I am Corin Ap-Bobalo, niece to Captain Tai Bobalo, the Pira Eropa's sparring partner," she addressed the other elder Mir. "Please, Master Mirs, I am in need of your help. There is trouble in the District, and I must contact the Pira."

The anger inside Eropa held her in a strangling grip, twisting her thoughts into pathways from lives lived long before, pathways of darkness and power she had not explored in this lifetime. She did not know how to control the fierce power within her, its dark and bright energy scalding compassion and reason from her. The claim was made that the Pira remembered a hundred lives, but she did not remember them all at once, and she had not always been enlightened. The history of sentient kind and their allied species was not a smooth lake. It was a flowing river, muddy and turbulent in bad weather. Uprooting trees and scouring banks, it swept away lives.

There was no justification to excuse her father's betrayal. She had been foolish to believe his protestations of fatherly affection.

If someone loves you, they do not lie and manipulate you for their own purposes.

If Nikodamus had been honest and told her the truth, would Eropa have agreed to go to Auhora Whimlan with the alien?

CHAPTER FORTY-TWO

It was uncertain, but at least it would have been her decision. Her father should not have treated her like a blind pawn.

And what about Zeph?

Eropa reconsidered every smile, every touch that passed between them. Had it all been motivated by this hidden agenda, each moment designed to soften her, make her more malleable to the terms of this demeaning treaty? Nikodamus had said the alien did not know she might be the treaty bride, but how could she believe him? Even Dora Dum'Laiere had known. Had Nikodamus blocked Yare's mind to hide the truth from his daughter?

I should never have let the alien get so close. That was a mistake, Eropa told herself, pleased that by disappearing, she had changed the situation and claimed her power. The Paxlosian deserved what he got.

Outside the palace, heavy smoke hung over Little Taiba; flames were consuming buildings in the northern part of the city and had begun to lick those further south.

Eropa looked at the burning slum, but from within her seething anger, it meant nothing.

She climbed into the windcraft and sped from the palace.

There were few Ebulonians on the road, all of them furtive, frightened, and in a great hurry. As the Pira neared the Bren'Harrows estate, she could hear people beating on a door. At the next estate, the gates were wide open, one off its hinges. House guards came running out, their arms laden with expensive décor and art items, their pockets heavy.

Eropa ignored them.

Nearing the Mi'cosa bridge, Taibans swarmed from the District's gates, wailing and crying.

Molten anger simmered through the Rhune, the slow burn destroying the links to the many expectations, rules, and interpretations she had been given as Truth.

The patterns beneath her skin began to change, becoming darker, ruddier.

The destructive strength and fierce, indomitable energy of the burning city drew the sorceress forward, its turmoil calling to that which raged within her, its source feeding her primal anger.

Eyes dilated and fixed, the Rhune's skin glowed fire red as she walked across the bridge toward Little Taiba.

The gates slowly began to close.

"Eropa!" a voice called out behind her. She looked back over her shoulder. The alien, Zeph Yare, was running toward her.

"Eropa!" another voice joined his.

Frevin. She recognized him.

People were shouting as they rushed to get in or out of the burning city.

"They're coming! They're coming!" they shrieked. "Close the gates!"

Her feral eyes glowing, Eropa turned her back on the two men and ran forward, vanishing into the melee.

CHAPTER FORTY-THREE

A speaker of the Truths is less important and as easily discarded as the match that lights the fire." (General Andreen; A History of the Rhunes; The Hundred Year War.)

Two guards stood sentry at the Cook's Gate. Quinn slowed his pace and walked on nonchalantly, his hands in his pockets, saluting the guards as he turned into the kitchen gardens. The guards gave him a cursory inspection and let him pass. If he were already inside the palace walls, the guards at the outer gate would have checked him.

Quinn stepped through an open arch in the breezeway that connected the Cook's Gate to the kitchens and ducked inside. The kitchens were staffed nearly every hour, but dinner clean-up was over, and tomorrow's bread baking had not yet begun. Quinn scanned the room until he found the stairway that connected the service levels to those above, he edged his way to them, and started climbing, grabbing a stack of linens--as an alibi--in case he met anyone coming down.

He imagined going to Eropa's rooms many times before, but never under these circumstances. He was not blind to the differences in station between them. When Eropa accepted a partner, if she did, it would not be to the half-Taiban son of a pirate. As a friend and trusted fighting comrade, Quinn could share some part of Eropa's life, and he would be there if she needed him; today, tomorrow, or twenty years from now. However, if he exposed the secrets of his heart, he would either be banished, or an awkwardness would linger between them. He made his choice. He would take the crumbs that fell from the table as long as it meant he could stay in the room.

Quinn reached the palace floor paved in green marble.

"Through the hall with the clan banners, you'll come to a large sweeping staircase," he played back Corin's directions. *"At the top, go right. At the tapestry of the old city, turn left. Eropa's rooms are down the hallway on the left."*

CHAPTER FORTY-THREE

Quinn paused outside the doors. There was no guard, no page, but the doors matched Corin's description. Fourteen feet high with a sculpted relief of vines and leaves carved into the burnished wood, they made him feel small and insignificant.

"Eropa?" His light tap sounded like the scratches of a giant rodent skittering across the stone floor. Emboldened by the urgency of his mission, Quinn cautiously opened the door and slipped inside. "Eropa?" he hissed.

The early moon cast pale light through the lattice shutters, shining across an empty bed nestled in an old tree. Quinn was following the wall to see if there were any other rooms where Eropa might be when he saw a moth disappear through an illuminated picture. He crossed to it, and lifting his hand, touched the surface. There was no surface. His hand went through just as the moth had.

Silently, Quinn stepped through the projected picture and into a corridor concealed behind it.

Drawing his weapon, he approached the other end. A curtain of translucent light showing it, too, was concealed. Quinn moved stealthily toward the muffled voices coming from the room ahead until he stood just behind the cascading light of the second holographic inage, looking through it into another room.

It was handsomely appointed, with many shelves filled with expensive-looking books. There was a large, carved wooden desk with a chair behind it that looked like it had been recently occupied. The crackle and glow suggested a fire in an unseen fireplace. The knees of a woman's blue silk dressing gown were all Quinn could see of what he took to be the Mahal's consort sitting in one of two high-backed chairs facing the fire, all but her knees hidden by the large chair back. The other chair curved around someone wearing gray pants with a lavender stripe up the side.

A Paxlosian, he thought, wondering if it was the alien captain himself.

The Mahal, Nikodamus Mir, stood by the outer door, speaking to someone outside who Quinn could not see.

"The Taiban's have overrun the neighborhoods nearest the District," a voice said.

"Let me know as soon as the young man arrives," the Mahal instructed the guard.

Percussive feet tramping through the hall interrupted the quiet scene.

Soldiers, Quinn deduced, fingering the weapon strapped to his thigh.

"Mahal Nikodamus," he called out softly.

Nikodamus turned toward the hidden corridor. "Who is there?"

"Mahal Nikodamus?" a harsher voice twisted the Mahal's attention the opposite way toward the outer hallway.

"Yes, I am here."

"An old friend sends their greetings," the voice growled.

Before Quinn could move, the Mahal staggered back from the doorway. As he hit the floor, the two palace guards fell across the threshold beside him.

Quinn leaped from behind the wall as a woman in her dressing gown streaked by him, falling to her knees beside the fallen Mahal.

"Nikodamus!" she cried out as a pool of blood circled her knees, soaking into and staining the pale blue silk of her robe.

Quinn positioned himself at the foot of the injured Mahal shooting at the quickly retreating Taibans.

"Quinn!" Corin's voice came from the hallway behind them.

"I'm here!" he called back. There was a blinding blast of magic, and she was through the door, ready to fight beside him.

With flashes of magic continuing to hamper the Taiban's escape down the outside corridor and more guards arriving every minute, bodies were piling up, hampering their defense. They needed space to maneuver.

"Dakmira Keesch, pull the Mahal's body back into the room so we can protect him," Corin tried to get the distraught woman's attention. Dakmira looked up, tears streaking her face.

"You are too late." Her chest heaved and she lunged from the floor into the Taiban closest to her, fingers scratching at his eyes.

Shrieking in pain, the man fell back, taking the Keesch with him. A Taiban grabbed her head from behind and sliced a knife across her neck, opening the artery. The Dakmira sank to the floor.

Corin grabbed a long sword off a dead guard and launched herself over the dead, skewering the Keesch woman's killer. Breathing heavily, she spun around, ready to face her next challenge, but there was no one left.

CHAPTER FORTY-THREE

The three Mirs: Mithra, Malbuis, and Pliny--who had accompanied her to the palace--slowly came out from behind the corner they used as cover, staring at the carnage.

White-haired Malbuis was the first to recover. "The Mahal?" He stepped over the bodies, his long beard wafting with his movements.

"There." Corin pointed.

Pliny and Mithra followed their friend's lead, discretely picking their way into the bloodied room. Malbuis put his hand to the Mahal's neck.

"He is dead," the elder Mir stated, his voice shaky.

The Mirs looked dazed.

"Blessed Mother." Pliny wetted his lips. "How could this happen?"

"I got in," Quinn pointed out. "Apparently, others did, too."

"We need to get these bodies out of sight and clean this up before anyone else arrives." Mithra's clear blue eyes held his partner's, a look of collaborated caution passing between them.

Pliny looked confused. "But surely it is our duty to--"

"It is our duty to protect our people, " Malbuis stopped him. "Someone just murdered the Mahal--someone that appeared to be Taiban."

"They're wearing clan badges." Quinn pointed out.

"Dum'Laiere," Mithra identified the sigil. "These men are members of the Dum'Laiere clan's house guard."

"Private army, you mean," Quinn corrected.

"Even powerful houses do not have private armies on Ebulon," Pliny exclaimed.

Corin pulled a clan insignia from one of the dead men's jackets. "They do now."

"They are house guards," Pliny asserted.

"A few dozen men are a house guard. A few hundred are an army," Quinn disagreed.

One long white eyebrow peaked up on Malbuis' face. "What are you saying, young Boablo?"

"The Bren'Harrows, the Dum'Laieres, the Harbines, the Naran'setts, they've all been hiring all the men they can recruit," Quinn replied.

"Mercenaries," Pliny muttered.

"The Dum'Laieres." Corin pulled off a roughly made armband.

Mithra shook his head. "Anyone could make such a crude badge. Miratha Dum'Laiere is far too clever to send assassins wearing her clan's colors. That in itself indicates it was someone else."

"Maybe they figured they wouldn't meet any resistance, just a quick in and out," Corin suggested.

"Or they did not plan on leaving any witnesses," Quinn added.

"Hubris," Malbuis muttered.

"They needed the badges to get in," Quinn suggested.

Malbuis seemed to fold inward. "It's too poorly planned for Miratha," he counseled.

All five looked at the carnage, considering the consequence.

"This cannot become public," Malbuis said cautiously. "Not yet at least. We need time to figure out the purpose and power behind it."

"Whoever they are, they will be expecting a report," Quinn pointed out. "And when they don't get it…"

"They will be left to wonder, which gives us the advantage for a period of time, because we know and they do not," Mithra surmised.

"It's not like whoever sent them can announce their men are missing and ask around," Corin added wryly.

"The first man said something just before he struck Nikodamus," Quinn remembered. "His words were 'Greetings from an old friend.'"

"That could be almost anyone," Mithra said.

"It's not Bobalo," Corin defended her uncle. "He sent Quinn and I to tell Eropa what was going on in Little Taiba and ask her to assure the Mahal that the Taibans causing the trouble were a small number of renegades and did not represent the population."

"Anyone who knew Nikodamus will know that Bobalo has been a friend and ally for years," Mithra agreed. "But there are some who will use accusations to further their agenda, and we cannot discount the power of their narratives in the presence of such fear."

"And after years of fighting for recognition, the Matriarch has just named Miratha as her descendant," Malbuis added another piece.

Pliny peered toward the corridor that connected the Pira's chambers to her father's. "Where is Eropa?"

"She was not in her rooms," Quinn informed them.

A disconnected, unfocused look came over the younger Mir's face. "She is not answering me. Her mind is blocked," he stated.

CHAPTER FORTY-THREE

"Someone find out how these men got access to the palace. Corin and I will go find Eropa." Quinn began to run down the corridor.

CHAPTER FORTY-FOUR

"Magic is chaos harnessed by intention." (The book of Rhune.)

Murtevoy's mercenaries entered the battle believing themselves to be the predators, only to find they were prey: a Rhune's prey.

The flames burning Little Taiba fed on the fear its inhabitants breathed out, dancing with the shadows they cajoled to revelry while luring them to violent ends. Eropa, too, took her place at the burning table of the fire's feast, embracing the Dance of Death. No Rhune cautions played in her head, no caution at all. Seeing through the filter of others' eyes long dead, she abandoned herself to the fury inside, holding nothing back, saving nothing for tomorrow, not even sanity. The Pira, eyes ablaze with an intoxicating madness--that made her every choice a statement of her belief in her invincibility--was a streak of dark amber light flitting through the streets and alleys, killing every mercenary who stumbled into her path.

Double-grip to single-handed-slice, spin, thrust; they fell like hollow stalks before a hurricane wind, a wind that was the blind power of a Rhune unrestrained.

Firearms were ineffectual against her. She sensed the shooter's intent before their decision to aim was made. She was anger in motion, a flood for unleashed, with no consideration of destruction or its consequences. The whirling Rhune warrior was everywhere, then nowhere, cutting a throat, gutting a stomach, severing an artery, then gone. Fire and bloodlust were on the menu, adrenaline making her body sing with power.

An axe-wielding Taiban stumbled out of a knot of fighters. The stench of his living carcass was viler than the bodies already dead whom he trod over as if they were pebbles in his path.

Eropa did not ask herself whether he was on one side or the other of this civil riot, where neighbors were fighting neighbors. Some of the Taiban mercenaries wore the uniforms of the clans they were contracted to; others did not, and who could tell which was which?

CHAPTER FORTY-FOUR

The battle-raged creature that was loosed, did not care to stop and consider such details. One death was like another, and death came to all. One movement, one death, leading to the next and the next leaving a grotesque ribbon of bodies weaving over the burning landscape.

Her long auburn hair had long ago fallen from its braid, creating a tangled aura around her head, tumbling down her back. Her silk tunic and pants were sprayed with blood, her slippers and legs coated with mud, and the excrement left behind by the dead. The Pira planted her feet in a wide stance and gave the brute her fair warning, two fingers pointed toward the blackened sky, but she did not want him to take her warning. She wanted to end him.

Leering manically, the Taiban strode toward her, his fat stomach jiggling. The girth of his waist told Eropa that he had no discipline. The way he moved, swinging his axe at the empty air, told her he was not a warrior, only a bully.

"Come here, little man," she taunted him.

"You won't be smiling when I do."

"But I am smiling," the Pira countered. "Because I will warrant that your fighting is as toothless as your infantile grin," she nudged him to action.

The fat man lifted his weapon and threw his weight forward, stumbling clumsily. It was a brawler's choice, having no finesse or skill.

Eropa deftly stepped aside to let his weight take him past her. Gathering energy, she sliced her glister sword clean through the man's thick neck. The fatty skin split open, blood spurting across the hump of his wide, sloping shoulders. Eropa stepped back to avoid his flailing arms as he sailed past, his head rolling away until it rested finally in a low spot. His lumbering body fell into the mud.

"I see you started without me." Corin stepped into her place beside Eropa. Looking down at the waxy-skinned, fat man she made a disgusted face. "I always hated that ass."

Corin... A shadowy, half-formed memory of a connection to humanity, distant and fragile, tugged at the Rhune's tortured mind, she struggled to sort her confused emotions toward the young woman.

"I'm here to fight beside you as we always practiced, Pira," Corin assured her friend.

"As am I." Quinn took his place on Eropa's other side.

"We will fight together, as we were always meant to," Corin offered her hand to Eropa. Still uncertain, Eropa took it, feeling a cooling trickle of emotion that had no share of death or bitter destruction flowing through her from the grip. The Taiban's presence felt like Ebulon, grounded and balanced, casting a soft misting rain over the rage that consumed the Pira.

"As we always will," the young male Taiban on her other side added his pledge, a prediction speaking of gratitude and the strong bonds of friendship.

She was not alone Eropa's mind grasped at her friend's peace. Quinn and Corin were here with her, ready to fight alongside her. Eropa could not remember what she was fighting for, but tenuous memories of the many hours she and these two compatriots spent training and laughing together pushed back at the rage that was consuming her.

"You came to a battle with only a sword?" Eropa teased her friend.

Corin shrugged, "I'm out of ammunition. No one told me when I left the house this morning that there was going to be a fight."

A breath closer to herself, the Eropa settled in to face their foes.

Swords drawn, the three friends stood as a unit. They knew each other's fighting styles, strengths, and weaknesses as well as they knew their own.

"The battle is heated there, and our friends are pressed. We should move." Eropa conjured a fog, using it as cover to overtake mercenary fighters who had moved forward from the main groups.

The three flowed across the terrain, interconnected pieces sensing the thoughts and movements of the companions beside them, feeling the threats around them.

A breeze blew a hole in the magically conjured fog, and there stood the Paxlosian Zeph Yare. Eropa's sword arm faltered. It had never happened before, but she had not sensed his closeness.

His eyes found hers. He breathed in and held that breath.

"Light of Death, look at you." Eropa could feel the pull of him, his warmth, his heartbeat--the very life within him. *"Who are you?"* he marveled silently. *"What are you?"*

"I am the parchment upon which you will write the treaty that saves two worlds," she jabbed her reply into his mind, bitterness

dripping like poison from a viper's fangs. Then she remembered Hagriva had recognized Miratha. Yare's treaty had nothing to do with her.

A heavy sword blade arched from out of the fog, slicing down towards her. She reached out to bring energy from the ground below her, but nothing happened.

The energy did not respond to her call.

She had no magic.

Death formed as a brutal blade sliced the air, raised above her.

Recognition sparked a flicker of regret in her as she thought of her father, whom she loved and whom she knew loved her. She thought of the friends here beside her who would mourn her, Hagriva, once again abandoned by her student but too late this time to start again, and then there was the alien standing there wreathed in the fog—a man who might be her great love if only she were brave enough and he could find enough pieces of himself to give her something.

It will not be. Not in this life.

The sword's edge descended toward her.

And then Quinn was there inserting himself between Eropa and her death, blocking the mercenary's strike. There was a moment of struggle, Quinn twisting the assailant's blade from his hand by means of leveraging his and the sword was released, flying through the air to land in the mud and muck. He gaped as Quinn's sword ran him through.

"Quinn...." Eropa gasped her gratitude.

Quinn pushed his opponent off his sword, then, taking a few staggering steps back, collapsed to the ground. A red bloom spread across his chest, his expression changing like a sudden sunset, determined bravery becoming relief then, settling into something harder as he recognized the significance of the bright life's blood painting his shirt: understanding.

I am dying. I saved her, but that was all I could do. It was all I could ever do, Eropa heard her friend's thoughts. *She would never have loved me as I loved her.* Regret splattered across Quinn Bobalo's last moments coloring it violently like paint's clawed fingers flinging itself from a dropped bucket.

"I am so sorry, Eropa. I was too late," he wheezed, air rushing into places it was not meant to be and leaving places it should have remained. "I failed you," Quinn whispered hoarsely, barely able to form words.

"You have never failed anyone, Quinn Bobalo," Eropa insisted. "Least of all me." Eropa glanced to where Corin fought, unaware of her cousin's impending death. *"Corin,"* she shouted into her friend's head. *"Quinn needs you!"*

"But I did," Quinn managed to choke the words out. Those that followed were harder, and he winced with the pain of saying them out loud. "Your father is dead…and Dakmira."

The words created no image in Eropa's mind. Only a blank; registering nothing. She could not even think about them now.

Quinn is dying!

The reality of the immediacy of her friend's death pierced her torment like the sudden slap of arctic water, propelling her from the consuming darkness into the shock of deep grief.

Quinn was dying here, now, in the community his father started, as it burned down around them.

A shadow fell across Quinn's body, blocking the leap and fall of the flames that had been flickering over his familiar face

"Eropa, behind you!" Corin shouted off to their right.

The Rhune sensed the bulk of the large man moving toward where she knelt beside Quinn. With her back exposed to him, she was an easy target but that, too, seemed unimportant. "Eropa, move!" Corin's voice, a few steps closer, shrieked, and the young Pira knew Corin was coming to her aid—to *their* aid, hers and Quinn's, not knowing that it was too late. Quinn was already gone. Corin would throw herself at this Taiban brute, and her life, too, would be forfeit.

Corin stumbled to her cousin's side, grief streaking the grime that could not cover her fears.

"Quinn!" Her knees hit the ground hard, desperation reaching out, her hands fluttering over her cousin's still body like moths, searching his wounds, "Stay with me, Quinn."

Eropa could not move. She could not think. She had no magic to fight with no energy to rise to her feet and raise her sword either to protect her friends or herself frozen.

CHAPTER FORTY-FOUR

"So be it. We three will pass through the veil and cross the Mother's Meadow together then," she sent him a silent promise.

What had he said? Her father, too, was dead… and Dakmira?

Even the long-lived Hagriva would soon rest in the Mother's embrace, and then there would be no one. What was left for her to live for when it was so hard? No. The world was changing too fast and demanded too much. She could not keep fighting. She did not want to.

Corin lay across Quinn's body sobbing, begging her cousin-brother not to leave them—not to die, but her pleas fell on dead ears.

The sour sweat of the Taiban wielding death enveloped them, his hot, heavy breath moving the small curls on her head as he grunted with the effort of raising his weapon.

An explosive crack attacked the Rhune's eardrums, like a blast of thunder splitting open an aged tree to expose its heart. Blood and brains rained down around Eropa and her friends. The Rhune blinked.

Part of the Taiban man's skull landed beside Quinn's body, rolling to a low point before stopping. A partial bowl, a portion of its grisly contents remained.

Zeph Yare had easily tracked Eropa, even though he feared he had lost her a few times as he fought in her wake through The District. The fire's glow made it challenging, but whenever he lost her, he had only to search for a distant glow in the shape of a person. Oddly, the color of the glow was different than before, a muddy amber with dark blotches like spilled ink and swirls that looked like her body trapped black smoke and was trying to find a way out, her presence transformed from a sub-vocal hum that defined calm to a galloping percussion carving a path of death. The Pira that had been had become unrecognizable, or maybe he did not known who she was, for this woman was chaos and terror, justice and glory, each murder artistic and graceful, each spray of blood and viscera horrifying and breathtakingly beautiful.

Zeph could not say why he followed the Rhune into the battle in The District. Wasn't he supposed to be mad at her? Hadn't she used him badly, led him on then, whacked him the first moment he showed her he was vulnerable? He could not think of any logical reason he should forgive her for what she had done to him at Auhora Whimlan—for how she and her father played him. And yet he did.

If some piece of Eropa's mystery had been revealed showing her to be not only intelligent and beautiful but powerful and dangerous, the alternative, Miratha Dum'Laiere, had proven to be the type of manipulative, power-hungry bitch, he already knew only too well. Given a choice, a Rhune governed by defined secretive ethics was preferable to yet another woman twisted by bitterness and thwarted ambitions who was bent on grasping power beyond her control.

The longer he followed her, however, the weaker his justification seemed. The meditational form he viewed her practicing in the garden as if it were a dance became something quite different. Unleashed, Zeph viewed the Pira's dance from afar. Spinning and swirling, swinging her thin-bladed sword as she leaped in airborne arcs of incredible height and power. Somewhere, she picked up two satellite fighters, the three of them moving as one through the Taibans they somehow identified as opponents.

She did not need his help—she might even skewer him. Though his views had undergone an alteration over the last week, it was uncertain how she viewed him, particularly if she learned he was at the Dum'Laiere's. Still, when he saw her, he had to follow. He could not say why.

And then the moment came. Unexpectedly, while fighting Eropa he suddenly froze, like one of the desert-dwelling mutants caught by a skit out on an open dune. Zeph, too, froze for a moment certain he was seeing her last moments as a swirl of the suspicious local fog hid her and her attacker from view. The fog parted, revealing the male twin of the Taibans who fought alongside the Rhune falling to the ground, having used his own body to shield Eropa from the attack.

She was spared.

Zeph began once again to breathe, but in battle, moments of relief are rare and brief, and another Taiban nearby turned toward the pair of stilled warriors.

Still, the young sorceress did not move—did not act.

Why doesn't she do something? Zeph thought silently. She had powers. She could *do* things--amazing, wonderful, terrifying things. And yet she did nothing, kneeling silently, stunned by her fallen friend like any young woman might.

CHAPTER FORTY-FOUR

The strange fog began to lift, twirling away and vanishing into the chiaroscuro of bright flame and dark smoke.

The female Taiban was nearby just recovering from winning her own latest deadly duel. She saw her friends' situation and ran forward, jumping across the bodies of the dead, focused on intervening.

She won't make it in time, Zeph realized.

The Taiban standing over Eropa was a giant of a man dressed in filthy clothes with a crude clan badge pinned to his soiled leather vest with tree-trunk arms that dwarfed his tiny head. Zeph thought his head looked like a piece of shriveled fruit someone had sat on top of a boulder for target practice.

He raised his weapon and fired. The rotten fruit and juices of the man's skull rained down onto the Taiban boy's death scene.

The giant boulder frame fell with a thud, his partially intact skull rolling forward to settle nearby.

Eropa turned and looked at Zeph. Her eyes were wells of fathomless green water the flames of Little Taiba reflected in them, or maybe the flame was from inside her, and the other was merely a convenient explanation his brain was providing because it did not want to recognize the extra-ordinary experiences of this world and its Pira.

Even considering the possibility was entirely new for the Paxlosian captain the poignant despair carved into every line of the Ebulonian Pira's pale green face wrenched his heart.

He thought her strong and indomitable--a force of nature to herself--but that was also an illusion--magic's lie. Despite everything she knew and was, Eropa Rhune underneath it all, was a young woman who suddenly looked very alone.

She needed him.

Zeph made his way through the detritus of bodies and their final excretions; blood, urine, feces, and brutalized flesh until he stood beside the young women and their fallen friend. Breathing hard from the exertion of getting to her side quickly, he stood with his arms hanging uncertainly at his side. He had started feeling so certain only moments ago, but now that he was here he, suddenly did not know what to do.

Unworthy words rose within him but stuck in his throat.

Surely, such sacrifice and grief deserved a moment. Yes, that felt right. So, he waited silently, a self-appointed guard standing over the grieving young woman. Their shoulders shook, their ribs shuddering. They whispered last moment promises and begged the young man and their alien gods to change the unthinkable outcome of the last few minutes that changed their lives and stolen his. Zeph did not listen, trying to make himself invisible. This was private stuff—private moments, not meant for an alien stranger, however well-intentioned.

Scanning the area around them for threats, Zeph noted the remnants of a crashed shuttle by the North wall. The flames around it were dying, but it had definitely come from the Lamdra. That was a story he would have to unravel later.

How did I ever imagine this was going to be easy? He chided himself as he continued to scan the area. He felt the female Taiban's eyes studying him and let it be. To her, he represented everything that had gone wrong in the past few weeks–everything that threatened the world that gave her people refuge. He could not expect her to trust him.

The battle had moved on, but the space the fighting trio cleared would soon be re-inhabited. Waiting as long as he dared Zeph finally cleared his throat.

"He's gone, Eropa," he said, not unkindly. He caught the Taiban female's eyes. "I'm sorry, but you can't stay here. We need to go." The Pira continued to sit catatonic beside the young man's body. "She's taking this hard," Zeph observed. "Were they lovers then?"

The Taiban woman fixed him with her brown eyes. "It is not your place to ask or mine to answer." She paused. "We have been family for years. It is not only Quinn's death that weighs so hard on her but Nikodamus and his consort as well. Quinn must have just told her. You have a lot to answer for, Captain Yare."

"I did not come here to hurt anybody. I came for peaceful trade." The young woman raised one eyebrow. "You cannot hold me responsible for all of this," he protested.

"Good intentions, even if they are sincere, do not change the result. It is as you see." She looked around at the evidence.

"Nikodamus dead? Light of Death. I can hardly believe it." Zeph's breath felt heavy, his chest like a stone.

CHAPTER FORTY-FOUR

"Over here!" a voice came down a nearby alley.

Zeph squinted, trying to see through the sooty smoke. "Whoever that is, they'll be here soon."

"Eropa cannot fight anymore," Eropa's friend replied, again scanning the area, this time looking for an avenue of escape.

"She shouldn't have to." Zeph leaned down and lifted the young Rhune into his arms, where she huddled, her face pressed against his chest. "If you're coming, it has to be now," he called over his shoulder as he carried the Pira from the battlefield.

CHAPTER FORTY-FIVE

"*It can't be undone by words or wishes*": A Common Taiban phrase often shortened to "words or wishes," leaving the rest of the phrase understood.

"**W**hat happened to her back there?" Zeph glanced at the young Taiban woman half running beside him to match his stride. "She stopped fighting even before your friend could have told her about her father."

"Her magic failed," Corin said.

"How can that happen? Zeph asked, hurrying across the bridge. "I thought she was supposed to be special, being the Pira and all."

"Eropa is many things," the young woman replied. "But invincible is not one of them." Frevin was hurrying toward the end of the bridge, preparing to intercept them. "Be very careful what you say to this one. Frevin Mir has great ambitions. You need to be suspicious of everyone right now, but particularly someone like him. We cannot be sure where his loyalties lie. I think you should know that the men who killed the Mahal wore Dum'Laiere badges."

Zeph stopped abruptly. "How do you know this?"

"I was there. Quinn and I went to the palace to find Eropa and ask for her help with the fire. We arrived in time to catch the intruders and fight them, but not in time to save their targets. I'm Tai Bobalo's niece, Corin Ap-Bobalo. Quinn is…was my cousin," her voice broke as she said his name. As Frevin intercepted them, Corin stepped between them, her face stern, her body language unapologetically protective.

The Mir took in the threesome. "I planned on going to the palace but apparently that is no longer an option. Events indicate it might not be safe. We need someplace to wait until the situation settles down."

"Not the Dum'Laiere's," Zeph stated. "I won't go back."

"No." Frevin nodded. "I have asked Dora to meet us at the landing area. I asked her to hire a shuttle to take us to the Lamdra."

"And you trust her?" Corin clearly did not.

"Dora is not her mother," Zeph assured the Taiban.

Corin shut her mouth, falling in with Zeph who began to follow the Mir north through the city toward the landing area.

"There's one more thing you should know, Captain Yare," she muttered between tight lips. "One of your men was there in the room when the Mahal was murdered."

Zeph's face registered shock but he covered it quickly. "Was he…injured?'

"He was not in the battle," Corin explained. "He was just present."

Zeph nodded. "Thank you."

Dora and Fratianne were waiting for them within sight of the area's entry.

"What is *she* doing here?" Dora demanded, unnerved by Eropa's inclusion in the group. "You did not say anything about the Pira coming along, Frevin."

"I did not know," Frevin assured her quickly. "We found her in Little Taiba. She has taken in a good deal of smoke and is not conscious. We could not just leave her there, Dora."

"No. Of course not," Dora agreed reluctantly, but the way she stomped off toward the airfield made her feelings on the subject apparent to all.

"We do not know to whom these men at the landing field owe their allegiance, Dora," Frevin cautioned her. "So, tell them whatever story you like, except the truth. We need to avoid them knowing that Yare and the Pira are among us."

"Fine. Just follow my lead." Dora sauntered forward. "These people are with me," she announced to the guard in an alarming impression of her mother. "Come along, everyone. Our shuttle is waiting." She sailed past him.

One of the Taibans eyed Eropa. "What's wrong with her?"

"Smoke inhalation," Corin answered. "Her estate is near The District and everything there is burning. It's quite terrible."

The man examined the rest of the party. "You two aren't Ebulonian," he indicated Corin and Zeph. "The flight request didn't say nothing about transporting Taibans."

Dora scowled. "What is this? Why are you questioning me like this? I have never been questioned like this in the past when I hired transport from Menander's. I booked the largest shuttle available so I could take my friends to the country where they will be safe—is that it over there?" She pointed to the largest shuttle in view. "And I paid an exorbitant sum to do it. I do not expect to be questioned by some Taiban ruffian about my guest list. Who is your master?"

"Dora, dear," Frevin tried to get her attention.

"I'm a Free Man," the man snapped. "I don't have no bloody 'master', and if you don't answer my questions, you aren't going anywhere."

"Perhaps we should just take a breath—" The Mir took her arm. She yanked away.

"And by what authority do you imagine you are going to stop me?" she taunted the Taiban archly.

"By the authority that I'm *here, bitch.*" The Taiban pulled his weapon, an older model percussion gun common among the lower classes around the Taiban Cluster. With The Purge resulting in the deaths of most of the Cluster's scientists and engineers, new armaments had not become available to the public for over a decade. These old models were all most folk could afford.

Dora's face fell, but she only had one example to draw from: Miratha's.

"I will report your impudence to Silas Menander."

"The price is higher for bitches."

Dora blanched.

"Blessed Mother!" Fratianne cried out, clutching her belly. The group turned and gaped at the moaning servant girl who suddenly looked very pregnant. "I am sorry, Sister, but I think the baby's coming."

The guard looked from the green-skinned Dora to the pale Fratianne. "You're her sister?"

"Half-sister," Dora improvised. "The birth threatens to be very difficult and dangerous for both mother and child. Look, I am sorry if I have spoken rudely to you, but I am so terribly anxious over all of this; the fire, the riot, my friend passing out, and now the baby coming." She pulled out a handkerchief and dabbed at her eyes. "I am not myself."

Zeph thought she might be more herself than he had ever seen her.

"Ah!" Fratianne doubled over, clutching her belly, feigning pains that buckled her knees. Frevin caught and supported her.

"Please, we need to get her somewhere she can lie down at least. She could have the baby at any moment. There is always a lot of blood and…things. I know, maybe we could use your little station-hut there?" Dora suggested with vile innocence.

"No!' the guard looked nonplussed by the idea of having the masculine territory of the guard's hut transformed into a birthing room.

"Well, I suppose it would be less than ideal," Dora agreed. "There is a healer in the north, near my country estate, who everyone swears by. I am hoping she can help with the birth, but we must get her there and that means getting us all into that shuttle over there," Dora gave the guard a solution to his problem all wrapped up neatly. All he needed to do was say "yes" and step out of their way.

The guard turned his attention to Frevin and Zeph. "And who are you two in this little drama?" he asked, still suspicious but clearly thinking about it.

"I am her husband." Frevin lied, indicating Fratianne.

The guard's focus went to Zeph. "And you?"

"He is my manservant," Frevin replied before Zeph could answer. "And this one is my personal bodyguard." Dora indicated Corin. "For the Mother's sake man, stop asking questions like this was a cocktail party and let us board!"

"When I'm done getting to know you all," the man sneered.

"Very well, I am Dora Dum'Laiere, and what is *your* name?"

"None of your concern," he back-tracked quickly.

"You are absolutely correct. It is not." She and the guard glared at each other, neither flinching. They had reached a stalemate.

"Let us go on our way," Frevin said under his breath, in a controlled, authoritarian tone. The guard's expression went slack, and he stepped out of the way.

"Go ahead. Your pilot is on board."

Zeph gave a questioning look all around as they began to walk. "What was that? Another Ebulonian ability no one told me about?"

"Do not talk. Just keep walking," Dora commanded.

They were crossing the open landing green headed for the shuttle when a dozen Taiban mercenaries stumbled through the gate.

"Don't look around. Just keep moving," Corin urged.

"Stop!" the man at the head of the new arrivals called out.

"Do not stop," Corin countermanded the order.

"Stop them!" Taibans dressed in clan uniforms began to run forward trying to cut them off. "Don't let them board!" the leader shouted.

Perimeter dock guards moved to join the chase as two dozen of Tai Bobalo's loyalists swept in the far gate led by the man himself.

Corin paused on the shuttle's ramp.

"Stay with them or come with us, but decide now," Zeph shouted as the others disappeared inside.

"I go where Eropa goes." Corin followed.

The shuttle shot into the sky as the loyalist and mercenary forces collided on the landing field below them.

Zeph set Eropa down on one of the bench seats in the passenger area. She slid to the shuttle's window. Pulling her knees to her chest, she leaned her head into the crook they created.

The others chose their seats quietly, trying not to hear the small, stifled sobs coming from the Rhune sorceress, trying to pretend their attention was on the drama below.

Zeph heard every labored breath, every heartbreaking gasp but he knew there was nothing he could do. She had not protested as he carried her, clinging to him like a single cable, that was all that remained between you and being lost to open space. His shirt was damp where she wept against his chest, but whatever attraction had flamed between them, the last night on the dock at Auhora-Whimlan, had been snuffed out. The most he could do was try to help straighten this mess out now that she was alone.

CHAPTER FORTY-FIVE

He was grateful when Corin slipped in beside her friend. She said nothing, just sitting close enough that Eropa would know she was there, letting the tears mark tracks through the soot on her cheeks.

There was so much going on here that Zeph did not understand, but he understood loss. After his father died, Zeph lost Hazzlebutt, in a manner of speaking. The wily old gamekeeper eventually returned to him in a new form, but losing the two men who had created a life for him on the small hunting planet--the two men who were responsible for teaching him how to be a person--had utterly devastated the nine-year-old boy. It had molded his approach to relationships, which was to avoid them becoming serious. Trust, like permanence, were things he did not believe in, and did not seek.

"They are losing," Eropa broke the silence.

"How can you tell?" Zeph asked.

"I hear their despair."

Corin grasped her friend's hand and gripped it tight. "They'll be alright. Uncle knows what he's doing. He won't let them fail."

Eropa looked at her friend. "Does he know about…?" She let the question dangle, not speaking Quinn's name.

"I don't think so," Corin said leaning on her friend's shoulder. "Not unless someone found him. Not yet."

"Yare, you must ask the pilot to contact the Lamdra to let them know you are on board this shuttle," Frevin said. "They have to know you are coming, or they could shoot us down, like before."

Zeph nodded and walked forward to the cockpit.

"Can you give me an open link? I need to contact my ship and identify us," he told the Taiban pilot.

"I'm sorry, sir, but we're not allowed to initiate that kind of communication. And we don't have that kind of range--"

Corin was in the cockpit before he finished. "Veremy Jacoby, do you know who these people are--who you have on board?" she demanded.

Young Jacoby glanced toward the cabin. "I know you, Corin."

Corin pointed. "That one over there is the Pira Eropa Rhune, the Matriarch's heir. This man here," she indicated Zeph, "is the captain of the Paxlosian ship that we're trying to make sure doesn't fire on us or attack Ebulon. That one in the fancy dress is a Dum'Laiere, and the man beside her is a Mir and a member of the Council of Elders. These are the dammed people you'd ask permission from, so just call the dammed Paxlosian ship."

The boy shrank three inches. "Jeesh, Corin. You don't have to yell."

"It's been a rotten, terrible day," Corin said blinking back tears.

Zeph waited for her to tell the Taiban pilot about Quinn's death. She didn't. Some things were just too personal to share in a hurry.

Zeph stepped close to Corin. "Thank you, Corin. I think we've got this now." He looked back at Eropa, still curled up by the window. The Taiban gave a subtle nod and returned to sit beside her friend. This time, Eropa's hand reached out, clasping Corin's.

"I am so sorry, Corin. It was my fault," Zeph heard the Pira confessing. "It was all my fault." He turned back to the young pilot.

"Please, open a channel and contact my ship. I'll take full responsibility." Young Jacoby began making adjustments then stopped, his hands hovering over the com array. "What's wrong?" Zeph asked. "Are we close enough? Do you have enough range?"

The young man shrugged. "I can't say for sure. This isn't something we do."

"Well, give it a minute and then try again," Zeph said.

Veremy Jacoby did, but the result was the same. "Still nothing."

"That can't—that doesn't make sense," Zeph blustered, frustrated.

"It does," Eropa said quietly appearing in the door behind him. "They will not answer. They cannot because they are not there. There is no longer a starship orbiting Ebulon," Eropa declared. "The Lamdra is gone."

CHAPTER FORTY-SIX

"When the Rhune's uncovered the secret to traveling between dimensions, worlds warped around them."

A steady stream of crew members fed the brawl in the corridor outside the bar on level three. It was unclear to Lucha if the new arrivals knew why their friends were fighting or if they just saw an opening and jumped in. The Lamdra crew had been cooped up shipboard for a long time and recruiting had been heavy in rough neighborhoods, where signing on to an open-ended mission into uncharted space had seemed more like an opportunity and less like a risky venture.

When a group splintered off from the main mass of bodies and headed for a lift, Lucha realized that although he expected the situation to burn out like any bar fight--ending in broken noses and swollen lips-- if it was allowed to spread to the bridge, it would make things far more problematic.

"Stop them," he ordered the security team stacked up behind him, pointing to the crewmen fighting to maintain their newly acquired position as they waited for the lift. "We need to contain this thing," he mumbled, worriedly.

"Too late for that." The team leader snorted. "If you'd wanted to stop this, you should have been honest with the crew days ago."

Lucha pinned him with a steely glare, "I didn't know about this days ago. Did you?" The question was also an accusation, and the security team leader looked uncomfortably shamefaced. "We cannot let them get to the bridge," he declared, ignoring the man's discomfort. He meant it to come out that way but dwelling on blame served no purpose. He dreaded to think what the Navigator might do if mutineers took control of the bridge. "Have your teams get control of the lifts—all of them if you can. No one goes to the bridge, except me or the F.O."

"Dante Tartulon is not stepping back onto that bridge," the team leader growled.

"The F. O. is not the enemy here!" Lucha exploded. "The situation is."

CHAPTER FORTY-SIX

The Security leader shook his head. "Him and men just like him who uphold the unfairness have always been the problem--thinking we're not good enough or smart enough to know when we're being robbed of the rights to a decent life, hoarding every resource for themselves."

"Dante Tartulon is a working-class grubber, just like you and me. He's not a rich snob."

"Then he should know better! He should be fighting with us, not trying to shut us up and locking you away!"

"You want things to change, you have to learn to recognize when you're being manipulated and when someone's actually trying to help you," Lucha argued. "A mutiny is not going to help any of us. You said you trusted me but you're still following the path that some nameless crewman set you on. Who do you trust? This invisible gossip or Zeph's friend?"

The team leader spoke into his com and his people fanned out around the edges of the area, half going in each direction until they held positions on either side of the lifts on the opposite end of the corridor.

Lucha found Tartulon in the fray, and dodging and shouldering a path through the tumult, approached his fellow officer. A capable boxer, Dante Tartulon had already thrown his punch when he recognized Lucha.

"Boradice! I'm sorry—" he paused, remembering. "I will not allow a mutin..."

"Don't even say it," Lucha stopped him. "This is not a mutiny, Tartu. It's a drunken brawl. 'You understand? It's a brawl."

Tartu shook his head. "People have been injured.

"Any deaths?"

"I don't know," Tartulon replied. "This is terrible. How could this happen? I am supposed to be in charge. Zeph will never forgive me."

"He's a pretty forgiving guy," Lucha tried to calm the frantic First Officer. "Look, people pick fights, Tartu, they trip, they get hot-headed--there are accidents, but a brawl is not a mutiny. A mutiny has to be reported. A mutiny stains the entire mission and has consequences for everyone."

Tartulon mulled Lucha's unspoken suggestion over before nodding.

Lucha turned his weapon's meter down to zero, pointed it at the ceiling, and fired. The reverberation was deafening.

"Every one of you bastards stop now!" he shouted.

The Security Officer echoed the Lieutenant's command and Dante Tartulon ordered the same for the men under his command.

"Line up," Lucha barked. As much out of habit as obedience, the bedraggled and bloody crew began to fall into a haphazard line. "Line up, I said!" He glared a crewman into place. "If I have to beat the shit out of every one of you, I will, but if I do, someone's going to pay for my bruised knuckles." He walked the emerging line until he got to the end then turned around and started back. He stopped and rubbed his jaw. "Well, I feel better. How about you, Tartu?" Lucha grinned with the uninjured side of his mouth.

Tartulon shook out his hand. "Have you got a plasteel plate inside that cheek?"

"Nope. You got me a good one." Lucha continued to work his jaw from side to side. "I don't think I've had such a good fight since Zeph and I..," he stopped himself. "I better not. That file might still be open back on Pax." Lucha stretched his shoulders and faced the line of the crew. "Okay, so we all got a little stress worked out of our systems. Maybe not in the best way, but it's done. What do you think F.O. Tartulon, shall we call for a post check in, say quarter span?"

"I'm good with that." Tartulon took the lieutenant's lead.

Lucha turned to address the men lined up in the corridor. "The captain's been notified that you're a bunch of lovesick girls threatening to break up with him if he doesn't show up with flowers, so he'll be back on board soon. The F.O. understands you've been cooped up here for a long time and that the situation has stretched tensions to unreasonable levels. Like most of you, he came up through the ranks, so he understands how hard it can be cooped up on a ship so long with nothing better to look at than your ugly faces, so he's giving you a break on this, but no officer can run a ship without a crew he can count on. If you're injured or near someone who is, get them to the medic, otherwise, we expect you to be at your assigned posts at check-in within twenty minutes. If you are, that'll be the end of this. If you're not, you'll spend the return trip in the brig facing charges which, according to your contracts, means your share of the profits is forfeit. Seems a damn shame, but actions have consequences.

"Get to your posts now. You've got a sixth of a span."

The line broke as crew members hurried off to quarters or posts.

Lucha gestured to the security team. "The bridge, gentlemen."

CHAPTER FORTY-SIX

The Lamdra's officers and a security team entered the lift to the bridge. The star-scape window that doubled as a projection unit was a black star field from one side to the other, just empty space.

Lucha lowered his voice. "Did you order us out of orbit, Tartu?" Tartulon shook his head. "So, where's the planet?" Both men's eyes tracked to the stairs that led to the Navigator's bubble and Lucha groaned. "We are so screwed."

"Why have you summoned me?" Hagriva Rhune glared at the gathered Rhunes surrounding her in multi-tiered circular galleries.

"Because you do not show up unless we do," one of the Rhune Councilors retorted brusquely.

Hagriva shrugged. "I do not see the point. We both know what the other has to say. Bringin' me here to repeat what you have already heard merely wastes everyone's time."

"That is not your decision to make."

"Is it not?" Hagriva bridled. "Unless they have been changed recently, The Truths declare that we have free will."

"Only the willful would make such an infantile argument," Hagriva's first interrogator sat back in her high-backed chair, tucking her pointed chin and crossing thin arms over her equally unsubstantial chest.

"Free will exists within boundaries," the prune-faced Rhune beside the thin one clarified with simpering condescension as if the Ebulonian Matriarch were a naughty child.

Hagriva's eyes glinted like sun on a knife-blade. "You forget yourself, Nomis. I know the many minds of those who have given us The Truths. I knew some of them personally. Age has given me experience, not senility."

"It is hard to tell by the way you act." Nomis smirked.

Her sister Rhune threw her a warning look that cut off whatever Nomis was going to say. "The Truths must remain paramount," she addressed herself to Hagriva. "The sisterhood must speak with one voice."

"When have we ever spoken with one voice, Anglin?" Hagriva demanded. "Lively discourse over the meaning of a phrase or the true author of a teaching has ever been the Rhune's way."

Anglin's mouth drew into one thin-lipped line. "Privately perhaps, but not publicly. Uncertainty is dangerous, Hagriva, and questioning only encourages it. It cannot be tolerated. It will not be. Too many worlds have been lost. We lose their confidence."

"We lose power, you mean," Hagriva accused. "That is your real concern."

"You say it as if that were a bad thing, but power is how we save worlds, Hagriva," Nomis interjected.

"Spreading knowledge is how we save worlds," Hagriva corrected. "The Truths teach beings to embrace the best in themselves. We do not order them to believe or understand as we do. We do not force, coerce, or control."

"Of course not," Nomis sniffed, her thin, pinched nose and pointy chin raised into the air, a beacon of her arrogance. "We are enlightened beings."

"A self-proclaimed enlightened dictator is still a dictator to their people. What are you really afraid of?" Hagriva looked at the gathered Rhunes who looked away, glancing quickly at others before masking their emotions and shielding their thoughts. Hagriva made note of the many empty seats in the Council circle of tiers. "No Ombra are in attendance today. Where is Honor Searhigh? Honor Bergha?"

"Gone," someone in the upper tiers blurted. "They are gone."

"Honor Bergha has not yet returned from her travels."

"And Honor Searhigh?" Hagriva questioned the council.

"They don't know" another anonymous voice spoke from the distant upper tiers.

"Is this true?" Hagriva did not need to ask it, but she needed a moment to wrap her head around what she was hearing. "Has someone been sent to look for them?"

"You rub salt in a raw wound, Hagriva. Be careful," Anglin spoke in a quiet tone meant only for the lower tier's ears.

Ebulon's Matriarch frowned, ignoring the warning. "And have you spoken to their kin?"

"We cannot find them," Nomis said.

"They are gone as well," Anglin replied reluctantly.

"The harassment Bergha spoke of," Hagriva mused. "Nests had been robbed--their mating grounds stalked by hunters."

CHAPTER FORTY-SIX

Anglin perked up. "Did she tell you where these breeding grounds were?"

The Ombra had always been secretive about the locations of worlds that their kin visited for nesting and mating."

"We must know, Hagriva. We cannot help them if we do not know where to go, and we need them."

"Because without them you cannot visit other worlds or dimensions except astrally," the old Rune surmised.

"It hampers our efforts" Anglin tried for understanding. "How can we spread The Truths if we cannot physically appear and work beside the beings we are trying to save?"

"You can no longer convince them you are gods, eh?" Hagriva smiled deviously. "This is your concern when our friends are being brought to extinction?"

"You are in no position to question us, Hagriva Rhune," Nomis' patience vanished, her temper flaring. "You are called here because you have made mistakes, and the sisterhood cannot afford you making more."

"Make yourself clear," Hagriva retorted.

"I can name many but let us start with Abraya Rhune."

"You declare a sister finding her own path a mistake, merely because you do not understand it. I admit that I too have made that mistake."

"A mistake, you admit it? And what about Dupira? You have lost your last two most promising students," Nomis accused.

"Adaya is not lost. She follows The Truths as she understands them."

"She is more like a Keesch healer than a Rhune adept."

"And what excuse do you give for Dupira's loss?"

Hagriva's whole physical demeanor sagged. "That I am responsible for."

Nomis' face registered her victory. "You must send Dupira's daughter to us. We will complete her training. She cannot become another mistake."

"Her training is complete," Hagriva stated. "What more would you have her learn and from whom?"

"That is not your concern."

"It is. Dupira died trying to be the perfect Rhune, imagining that she must make amends for her mother's choice. She did everything we train young adherents to do, focused all her energy on the worlds within her care—sought new worlds and brought them under her tutelage. It was too much. There was no Balance. I will not allow the same for Eropa."

"The completion of her education will be our responsibility. There is a convergence of energies about this daughter of Dupira's. It must be studied, her character molded, her actions guided. This cannot be left to you."

CHAPTER FORTY-SEVEN

"Resist? You ask me why I did not resist? To resist you must still be alive." (Anonymous survivor of The Purge at the Scientific Conclave in the Taiban Cluster.)

From Menander's air-borne shuttle, Corin watched the sky lighten as the light of Ebulon's sun flowed across the flatlands of the southern peninsula, a soft gold light that awakened the white walls of Iredipa, its spearpoint towers, and the signature stained-glass dome of the Council of Elders' Library.

The juxtaposition of pristine beauty with the black, smoking ruins of Little Taiba carved a hole in her heart. It was not that she could not understand the bitterness of the Taiban men and women whose impatience had broken out into a riot.

No one in the shuttle commented, all looking out the windows to see what they could as daylight revealed the night's effects. Struck by the damage, or perhaps privately grateful that their homes were safe within the protected parts of the city, each seemed to consider what had been stripped bare and what it meant for them personally.

Eropa's losses were her own, though some of them overlapped with Corin and her family. The Pira's guilt over Quinn's death and whatever had occurred before it that led to her failed magic was hers alone. She no doubt felt compassion for the Taiban refugees, but her life had not been disrupted as theirs had. She still had a home, resources, and purpose.

The feelings of the servant girl, Fratianne, were unclear; her lovely face was hard to read, and Corin knew nothing about the young woman aside from their shared mixed heritage and that she claimed some dubious connection to Yare.

The Paxlosian captain's brows were furrowed, his mouth hidden behind a fisted hand, a man imprisoned by confusion. His starship, his men, his responsibilities were all one and missing, without any hint of why, where, or how long that status might remain. Like some of them, he did not yet know the extent of his loss and could only worry and wonder.

The Mir, Frevin, and his simpering companion, the Dum'Laiere girl, Corin dismissed completely. Privilege would see that neither truly suffered.

Anxious to return to his family and find out how they had fared, Veremy Jacoby agreed to drop the strange collection of passengers off at different locations, as long as the location was safe for the shuttle to land. After some argument, the Dum'Laiere's spoiled scion, Dora, gave up her demand to be flown immediately to her family's country estate, persuaded by the Mir to spend the night at an apartment a family member owned on the far side of the city away from where The District's violence had spilled over. Though Corin suggested that Eropa come with her to the Bobalo compound, the Pira flinched as if struck stating that being responsible for Quinn's death, she could not intrude on his family's grief and further put them out by assuming they would host her.

"I will return to the palace," she declared, stubborn as ever. Yare announced he would as well, it having been revealed to him that one of his officers had arrived there to speak with Nikodamus before the Mahal was killed, and that there was no reason to expect he was not still there.

The Dum'Laiere servant girl merely said, "I'll go to The District, with Corin."

"The landing field might not be safe," young Jacoby decided. "But I can land on the old strip at the Bobalo compound. Will that be close enough for you?" he asked, glancing back at the young woman nervously. She really was very pretty, Corin noticed, with her odd coloring, nearly white skin, so like Pemitai's, red-gold hair, and fair-day blue eyes. Fratianne made some non-verbal sound indicating agreement, her attention on the smoldering ruins below.

Corin followed her lead.

The north side of Little Taiba--closest to the wall that separated the town from the landing area--had been reduced to its foundations. Closer to the market square, where brick was the more common building material, charcoaled cut-out walls--staggered like ridge-backed reptiles--curled around dark treasures of smoking debris, collapsed roofs, and upper stories fallen into sharp-angled architectural mounds. Layers of paper-thin ash moved with each shrug and flick of the wind's whim revealing half-melted household objects twisted into parodies that mocked human investment in collecting things for a future that was an illusion.

Death seeped from every corner and alley of the ash-crumbled devastation, the soot-glazed profiles of human memories mixed with decaying flesh adding a grotesque texture to the smooth clay mud that coated the streets and gutters while a few feet away, mere steps across a bridge, birds still chirped in green-leafed trees shading lush lawns.

Surrounded by the shattered dream that was their city it was not hard to understand how the refugees might look toward Iredipa and frown, their hearts hard, keenly aware of the inequity of their lives.

The refugee community staggered under the realization of the lives lost. Everyone was hurting and everyone was looking for someone to blame. The lines between Bobalo loyalists and Murtevoy's mercenaries and their supporters were quickly defined; if a Taiban believed that violent action was the only path forward, demanding immediate social changes and legal equity, they supported Murtevoy, despite the damage to Little Taiba. If they were still willing to be patient, believing as long as they continued to show they were good, hard-working folk, time would change their host's prejudices against them, they remained loyal to Bobalo and his friends. Disagreements were mostly verbal, but words did lead to blows and small fistfights continued to erupt throughout The District and still, parts of the community pulled together as they always had. Those whose homes were spared opened their doors and shared what they had.

"It is our way," a red-eyed Timee told her children. "We fight and die, eat and starve together. That is how it has been here among us for the past twenty years and it is how we will survive now."

"Some of the people taking food from us turn around and curse Father's name," Pemitai complained.

"It is not about what *they* do, Pem. It is about what *we* do," her mother reprimanded. "And we must act according to our consciences."

Exhausted by the sleepless night, their eyes red and burning from crying, the Bobalo girls worked silently through their grief over their brother's loss dutifully sorting through clothing, blankets, dishes, pots, and pans--anything that could be of use to those who lost their homes.

"Give away anything that we do not absolutely need," Timee instructed her daughters. "If we haven't used it in the last month, someone else probably needs it more."

But whatever they gave, it was not enough. It would never be enough. Still, the distraction of keeping busy on a task and the sloughing off of material possessions now recognized as unimportant was a kind of salve.

Having returned to her family, Corin lay on her bed staring at the ceiling, hammered by emotions of guilt, anger, and resentment. Every part of her ached, inside and out, but she knew she was fortunate. She was alive. She still had a bed, a ceiling, food to eat, and most of her family was alive. Examining her feelings honestly, she was forced to admit that she vacillated between compassion for Eropa, facing grief alone without the warmth and affection surrounding Corin, and resentment toward her friend for the part Eropa played in Quinn's death.

It was not what Quinn would have wanted. She knew that and she needed to find a way to come to peace with her cousin's decision.

"I know she is not perfect," Quinn explained once when Corin scolded him for treating Eropa as if she were something untouchable and far above him. *"But she is important, like Da is important—to the bigger picture of things."*

"If Uncle is important, you are as well," Corin pointed out. *"You are his son, trained by his side since you could walk. You know everything about the movement, Quinn. You are as important to us as Eropa is to her people."*

Quinn shook his head. *"Eropa's influence will go beyond the Ebulonians, Corin. She will work to save worlds we will never see or know about. That is what a Rhune does."*

Corin did not argue. She could not. She was not immune to the feelings of admiration and loyalty that sparked in the heart of her cousin. It was a heady feeling being in the inner circle of the future Matriarch, but there had been times when she resented the assumptions of deference due the Pira—sometimes including Eropa herself. More than once Corin found her loyalty toward her cousin and her friend at odds. Quinn Bobalo was a good person—better than any hand-wringing Ebulonian, and Quinn should not feel that he was unworthy of Eropa's affections.

And yet he had. Weighing his worth, Quinn Bobalo had decided his death was more useful to Eropa than his life.

Could she, Corin, set that aside? The half Taiban wondered. Was remaining Eropa's friend disloyal to Quinn, or did it honor his sacrifice?

Pemitai shuffled into the bedroom the girls all shared, two facing rows of beds bumped up against the walls with simple, clean cotton quilts smoothed over them. The Bobalo's youngest's white hair was dark gray and stiff with soot. She threw herself onto her bed beside Corin releasing a long sigh, her hands crossed over the charcoal and dirt-stained shift.

"How long do you think it will be before mother asks us to double up?" the haggard teenager asked.

"One pregnant mother or old lady," Corin replied. "We could be sleeping on the floor by the end of the week. So, sleep while you can, little cousin, because I snore."

"I can't believe Quinn is gone," Pemitai said, the words both wistful and hollow. "He's our big brother. I expected he would be here to protect us, forever."

Corin moved over to her younger cousin's bed and wrapped her arms around her. A sob caught in Pemitai's girlishly flat chest.

"Every time I start to wake up and remember I wish as hard as I can that this will all turn out to be a dream and everything will be like it was before, Petre and Vale and Quinn teasing us and laughing like they did before they went to Taiba."

"It's a good wish, Pem." Corin held the younger girl until her sniffles calmed to a sleeping breath.

Bobalo's bulk filled the kitchen doorway. In the space of breath, he crossed the room, lifting his wife into his big arms, bending her into him like a blade of grass.

Their heads folded together like a pair of spring buds, they wrapped their arms around each other, the flouered prints from Timee's hands leaving white marks on her husband's soiled clothing.

"Where are the girls?" he asked, his voice gouged and rough. The stink of battle coming off him filled the kitchen. "Has Corin returned?"

Timee stopped his questioning, placing two fingers on his lips. "Corin is fine. Veremy Jacoby brought her in just after dawn," "Nanscha and Mardeth are finishing wiping down the larder. Pem is sleeping."

"And Heldis?"

Timee's expression tightened. "She has gone to see Toval."

Bobalo's face took on a darker aspect. "Timee, the Turgistas have changed their alliance. They have aligned with…"

"They won't hurt her," his wife interrupted. "She's practically family to them."

"Except that she's not," Bobalo said gruffly. "And now, she never will be. Toval is dead, he said tersely. "The Turgistas chose their side and they have paid."

"There is no 'they', Tai Bobalo," Timee flared. "There is only 'us', and since when did losing a son become a sign of retribution? Retribution at whose hand? Gods that you no longer believe in? You were never so foolish, Tai Bobalo. We lost *our* son. What was *our* fault? Should I be angry with you because you trained Quinn to fight, or with the Pira because he believed her life was more important than his own? How would any of that help us?"

The great warrior's eyes flooded with grief, and he gathered his tiny wife back into his arms.

"Oh, Timeee, our son, our beautiful son is gone." He burrowed his face in the hair at the crown of her head, wetting the brown strands.

"Where did such bitterness and anger come from?" Timee whispered. "We have worked so hard to help the new ones—brought them out of the misery of the Cluster, freed them from the Warlords--shown them new possibilities for their future."

"The blame for this is not entirely our own," Bobalo said, his dark eyes going even darker so that they looked as black as his curly beard and braided hair. "This thing between Saldo and me has been there since he lost his ship."

"That was not your fault," Timee cautioned.

Bobalo shook his head and the tiny gold bells tingled, the sound enhanced by the thick cob walls. "It doesn't matter. He blames me."

"Because he does not have the character to accept responsibility for his own decisions," Timee defended her husband.

"We always knew there was a risk in bringing in so many new people so quickly. We hoped we could do better, but Saldo's actions forced them to a head."

Timee sighed. "We made decisions without knowing his plan."

"Or that the Paxlosians would come when they did," Bobalo added.

Timee closed her eyes, damp lashes moistening the tired circles beneath her eyes. "I would never have imagined such evil could come here."

"Men in the throes of battle rage do things they would never do if they had half their sanity."

"I would not count too much on anyone's sanity right now," a new voice joined the conversation.

Bobalo pulled back from his wife's embrace to stand on his own as Jayq Jacoby and Block entered.

"Timee, will you get our friends something to eat? I need to fetch our wayward daughter," Bobalo announced.

Block stopped him. "I'll do it, Tai. Feed this old man, Timee, and try to coax him to get some sleep." Block retraced his steps.

"I'll get word out that there's to be a meeting," Jayq offered. "We need to know who stands with us and see if anyone understands what Saldo is looking for in all this."

Their friends left as quickly as they had come. The couple were once again alone but sorrow crowded the kitchen.

E.F. Winters

CHAPTER FORTY-EIGHT

"Grasp not for answers, but for the understanding that will help you know what to do with them." (Traditional Rhune teaching, anonymous.)

"You cannot wait for someone else to save you," the Ancient One's throaty voice pierced Bibi's sleep.

"You're back! Oh, please, Mah Rhune, please, do not leave me again. I need your help. I am only a very small Cumin...barely more than a cub, and I cannot stop Grub from..."

"You must." The tickle of Hagriva's mental voice felt very weak. "My time in this life is short, Little One."

"But you are a spirit. You can't die," Bibi tried to sort out this confusing statement.

"I have a body, and it is very old. Once I leave the flesh entirely, time will not be the same for me as it is for you. Years may pass for you in what for me will only be a moment. You must rely on yourself and your own good heart."

"I do not have a good heart." Bibi's blue eyes filled with tears. "I am an abomination."

"Who has said this to you?" the spirit demanded.

"The Cumin in my village."

"They are ignorant gossips and you must forget their cruel words for you, Bibi Ra, are a blessing. Someday you will be named the mother of Ra."

Bibi shook her head. *"That cannot be."*

"It can. All you need to make this so is there inside you."

"I do not know how to find it," Bibi protested.

"Sit in silence. Empty your mind and open to the wisdom of the multiverse. Do it often. When you learn to hear, you will find what you seek." The voice began to fade. "There are others whom I have taught. You will recognize your sisters by the mark of my touch." A series of images of a small, much younger, smooth-skinned being like Hagriva with long red braided hair; sequences through Bibi's mind. "*I will send help if I can.*"

Bibi woke, picked up her spear, and faced the west tunnel.

Grub's eyes popped open, bringing him abruptly from sleep to waking. Something brushed against his ankles.

Bibi was crawling around him, tying him up with a rope of braided grass.

"What are you doing?" He tried to pull his legs away. She held them down firmly.

"Tying you up," she replied.

"Stop it, Bibi! This isn't funny." The little albino pulled the rope tight. Grub reached down to free his legs, and she deftly looped his hands, tying them together as well. "Bibi, I don't like this game," Grub complained. "I am not playing. Set me loose."

She ignored him, finishing the job before announcing, "Bibi will come back."

"You're leaving?" Grub's voice rose an octave. "You can't leave me like this. Where are you going?"

"Stop screeching like a spoiled mewling, Grub. Something might hear you," Bibi warned.

Grub looked toward the west tunnel. "You can't leave me tied up and defenseless. What if the Beast comes? What if one of those flying things followed us back here?"

"Play dead." Bibi walked away.

"Bibi, come back!" Grub shouted. But she did not.

Grub rolled over onto his side. Despite Bibi's healings, everything hurt. "Why should I care if she goes back into the tunnels alone?" he grumbled. "Stubborn, stupid female."

Unable to do anything except stew, he eventually drifted back to sleep.

When he awoke, Bibi was squatting beside him, holding fresh-baked tubers and a gourd of water.

"Eat." She held a tuber to Grub's mouth.

"Untie me first." He pouted.

Bibi fixed her eyes on him. "No."

E.F. Winters

"You can't keep me tied up all the time," Grub argued.

"Only way to keep Grub out of trouble," she disagreed. "Grub is hurt. No good for walking. No good for fighting. Can't run. Grub is angry, Cumin. This makes him dangerous. If Bibi unties him now, Grub won't be tied up again."

"I am not dangerous," Grub declared vehemently.

"No? Grub doesn't listen to anyone but Grub. Grub goes down the west tunnel or any other place he wants without thinking what could happen, what could be there. Grub acts like a big, male, Cumin boss who knows everything and Bibi knows nothing, but *I* got us to this place. *I* kept us safe and made sure we had food to eat and water to drink. You would have eaten it all on the first three days and bathed in the water. All you do, Grub, is cause trouble."

He blinked. "Bibi, you spoke like a grown-up Cumin."

"Do not change the subject. We cannot go on like this. We know about the Beast, and it knows about us. We must make some changes."

Grub tried to look contrite. "Okay."

"What do you mean, 'okay'?"

"I won't do those things anymore."

Bibi remained suspicious. "What things?"

Grub hesitated. "I won't uh...argue and I won't go where you tell me not to." Bibi sat back on her heels. "I've learned, Bibi. I really have. I understand now." The albino raised an eyebrow. "Well, I might argue a little if I need you to understand my point of view, but if you think I'm wrong, you can just argue right back and tell me why your way is better, and then I will agree." Bibi did not look convinced. "Friends don't just follow, Bibi, they go together. They do things together and they rely on each other, like in the village, or how we did yesterday," Grub tried to explain. "We worked together to escape from the Beast and its allies." Grub sensed her wavering. "We should be allies; you and me."

Bibi frowned. "I don't need somebody to go with me. I am quiet and small and have magic eyes. Grub's only got male bossiness."

"Grub's got..." Grub stopped himself. "Grub is...I am strong and a great hunter...well, a pretty good hunter, for my age," he adjusted the brag sheepishly. Bibi snorted. "Bibi, think about the hunters when they are going out on a hunt. They do not go out alone, do they? Why not?"

CHAPTER FORTY-EIGHT

"Meat animals be heavy."

"So, it takes several men to help the man who makes the kill bring it home, and for that, they get a share, but there are other reasons."

Bibi frowned. "What reasons?"

"Because if there is trouble, they are not alone, there's someone to help them, like you helped me yesterday, and I helped you." He plowed on, "Bibi, you can't just keep wandering around by yourself with no one to help you."

"Why not? Bibi alone before. Bibi always alone."

And suddenly, Grub understood. Bibi didn't understand the idea of relying on someone else because she never had anyone to count on. Wan had been odd since Bibi was born. The albino was on her own from the time she could walk. None of the villagers spoke to her; they just talked to each other, and she just happened to be there. That was why she didn't know how to speak or act like a proper Cumin. Bibi probably didn't miss the village. Why should she? She was never a part of it. Like a ghost walking invisible among them, all Bibi ever knew was her mother, and Wan was crazier than a bullood.

Grub felt ashamed of his people and himself. They pushed Bibi away because she was different. Only Bibi refused to die. Instead, she grew strong.

"Was it when you were alone that you found this cavern?' Grub asked.

Bibi hesitated before answering, "Yes."

"All right, have it your way." Grub nodded. "Go alone into the caves if you don't trust me. I'll wait here and hope you change your mind and feel differently tomorrow." Bibi stared, taken aback by his sudden change. "But please, try to be careful, Bibi Ra, because if something happens to you and you don't come back, I will be helpless and unable to do anything. You will probably die, and I will slowly starve to death."

Bibi's shoulders sagged. "Don't want Grub to die. Bibi will...*I* will be careful, and I will come back."

When Grub awoke in the morning, water and food was set beside him and his hands were unbound...Bibi was gone.

Free to move around, Grub found he didn't have the strength to do much more than shuffle to the creek and lie in the cool water. By the time he returned to his bed, he was shaking.

E.F. Winters

Bibi returned mid-morning, looking happier than she had in some time.

"Did you find something?" he asked, stretching his taut muscles.

"Many tunnels," she replied enigmatically, as she repeated the ritual touching of his sore places.

"But did you find something special? Something new?" he persisted. "Tell me, Bibi."

"I walked. I looked at new tunnels like all the other tunnels," she stated, confused about what was expected of her.

"Sit," Grub commanded. She sat tentatively. "Now tell me what you saw, and smelled, and felt. Cumin do that with each other. It brings them joy."

"Grub and Bibi will do that?" she asked, her brows knitting. Grub nodded. "We will feel joy together?"

Grub nodded.

Bibi beamed. "Bibi--" she stopped herself. "I will be a good listener, Grub. My father taught me that was important."

"Your father?" Grub frowned. "Bibi, do you know who your father is?"

"Boors," she announced, unembarrassed.

"You are certain?" There had always been rumors and accusations about Boors and Wan, but neither had ever admitted the liaison as far as Grub knew.

"I am," Bibi stated firmly. "He taught me. He showed me this place." Grub stared at her, flummoxed by this new information. "Now we be allies, Grub will teach me to speak good Cumin words?"

"Yes." Grub nodded, thinking about the larger meaning of Bibi being the offspring of a Spirit Speaker. "And when we go back home, everyone will see what a good teacher I am."

Bibi stood and walked away.

"I will never understand her," Grub muttered.

CHAPTER FORTY-NINE

"A smile does not make a friend. A sword does not make an enemy."
(Common Taiban phrase used mostly by the Free Man movement.)

As the long eventful night progressed, the three Mirs who were involved in the discovery of Nikodamus' murder--Malbuis, Mithra, and Pliny, along with Captain Ochette of the palace guard--focused on ferreting out and untangling evidence about what had gone on and who had done what leading up to the riot and Taiban fire. They were certain they were linked, although they could not prove how. Malbuis Mir, being an old friend and former teacher of Nikodamus and known to have engaged in late-night philosophical discussions, sat vigil throughout the latter hours of the night, while the others left for errands or their apartments, though it was certain none were able to rest.

When Zeph and Eropa returned to the palace just after dawn, the Pira quickly retired to her rooms, exhausted and in need of solitude, while Yare's priority was to check on his young lieutenant, who had been in Nikodamus' chambers when the Mahal was attacked. Ascertaining that the Paxlosian officer was not physically injured and there was nothing more he could do for the bewildered young man, Zeph waited to rejoin the Mirs. The ruse that the Mahal had invited him and the Mirs to discuss the complex situation surrounding the previous night's events provided a background for a lengthy gathering.

Pliny arrived escorting a generous breakfast from the palace kitchens, which the members of the group fell on gratefully as their schedules over the past 12 hours had been short on opportunities for such comforts, and being under stress and having gone without sleep, they were in need of energy.

During the earliest hours of their evidence gathering, the Mirs found that many of their questions required a frustrating amount of waiting; waiting for someone who had *not* been up all night to wake

CHAPTER FORTY-NINE

up and come to work, waiting for some bit of research to provide insight, or waiting for an interview to be completed and reported back. The temptation to send a page to fetch a potential interviewee from their bed needed to be resisted as unnecessarily drawing attention to their activities. A compromise between the urgency to know and minimizing suspicion was key.

Breakfast had been served, and lunch was expected when Pliny returned, accompanied by Captain Ochette, a hopeful smile on his round face. "Captain Ochette, please share what you have discovered," he prompted the good captain.

"Last evening, shortly after your man from the Lamdra arrived, Captain Yare, a message was delivered to the lieutenant on duty."

"A message from…?" Mithra interrupted briefly.

"The sign and stamp were of the Lady Miratha Dum'Laiere, Master Mir," Ochette stated.

"And the message?"

"A statement saying that due to the situation in Little Taiba, House Dum'Laiere was sending a dozen of its house guard to assist with the protection of the palace."

"Ah." Malbuis steepled his pointer fingers, leaning his forehead against them in a gesture of concentration. "So, because of this message, these additional guards were expected when they arrived."

"Yes," Ochette confirmed.

"And you assigned them to a post?" the elder Mir sought clarification.

"Lieutenant Shorvas, did, yes. I was looking into the Taiban situation at the time. Shorvas assigned the Dum'Laiere team to the Horse Gate, where he felt we could use additional coverage."

"And?" Pliny prompted.

Ochette's eyes shifted nervously. "The men arrived and were given their assignment, but when Shorvas returned for his shift today, he informed me that the Dum'Laiere men never reported to the lead at the Horse Gate."

"Because they had other orders," Zeph muttered. "And those orders did not include guarding the Horse Gate."

"Were they 'truth read' before being given entry to the palace grounds?" Mithra asked.

"No, Lord Mir." Ochette looked a little embarrassed and more

E.F. Winters

than a little angry. "That is not a skill we see among today's recruits."

"Explain, please, Captain Ochette. It is important we have as much information pertaining to last night's events as possible."

"Openings in the guard are mostly filled by referrals from the Voices," Ochette said, showing some reluctance. "They are seen as desirable entry-level positions for young men in the second or third lines of their clans, and it has become common for openings to be used by the Voices as a means of repaying favors or rewarding loyal service. This practice has diluted the quality of the recruits, but what has had an even greater effect is the trend among those clans who have retained a militaristic subculture to train their young people in exhibition fighting." Ochette's mouth twisted, showing his distaste for the trend.

"They have no practical fighting experience," Mithra concluded.

Ochette let out a sigh that was more of a whuffle, his shoulders sagging. "No. We have a training program, of course, and they are required to practice and remain fit, but the habit of choosing 'flashy' moves and putting on an impressive show to gain admirers among other young people at court has been difficult to change. Real fighting is messy and not very romantic-looking. And then there are the requirements for recruits. There have not been any around esoteric skills in decades, nor have we been allowed to add them to the training roster. I have brought this up to the Elders who sit on the standards committee, but they have shown a strong reluctance to change the requirements in a way that might make it more difficult for them to award positions. Any criteria that would make it less likely that a Voice's candidate could be guaranteed to pass have been soundly voted down."

"So, the palace guard are for the most part inexperienced, undertrained, and have a sense of entitlement. Do I have that correct, Captain Ochette?" Mithra asked for clarification.

"I do not mean to malign my men. They are not a bad lot," Ochette tried to temper his statement. "The changes that are needed, however, cannot happen without support."

"And those who should have supported them have failed them because they were complacent," Mithra surmised the feeling of the captain.

"It is understandable, there has never been an attack in Iredipa before," Ochette agreed. "But then the clans have never hired outside mercenaries to create their private armies before either."

"Armies?" Mithra queried.

"They've tried to hide the numbers, but between the four major houses who hired extra guards, they trained and armed hundreds of Taibans."

"And the 'loaned' guards from the Dum'Laiere's were Taiban?" Malbuis asked, keenly interested. Ochette nodded. "We cannot dismiss the Taibans as the instigators of Nikodamus' murder."

"That makes no sense," Zeph spoke up. "The District was nearly burned to the ground, hundreds were killed in the fire and the fighting... I was there. The Taiban community was the victim here. What motive would they have for killing Nikodamus? He supported them."

"If you were there, then you know the Taibans are no longer a unified group," Malbuis reminded him. "The community has splintered into factions."

"Because the Dum'Laiere's and the other clans have pushed them, promising rewards," Zeph argued.

"These are things we must look at," Malbuis acquiesced. "But a thorough investigation must include analyzing this division among the refugee population. What is the cause? Who supports it? If there is a leader, who is that, and where were they that night?"

"Captain Ochette," Mithra returned to the thread of the discussion having to do with the unprepared state of the palace guards. "Who sits on this committee to whom you made this situation of lack of preparedness known?"

"Buckley Bren'Harrow, Harscham Lector, McAlburn, Aless Mc'Larick, Miratha Dum'Laiere."

Mithra's smooth, beardless face remained neutral. "The Lady Miratha knew about this weakness in the palace guard," he surmised.

Ochette nodded. "Yes."

"And do you see a connection between her having this knowledge and sending guards to the palace last night?"

"I am a soldier. It is not my position to make such connections," Ochette sidestepped the question.

"Of course." Mithra inclined his head toward the stolid captain. "But if you were in a situation where you needed assistance again, would you feel comfortable requesting help from House Dum'Laiere?"

Ochette did not hesitate. "No."

"Are you able to explain why?"

"Mercenaries have unknown loyalties. I have no confidence in those the clans have hired. It is not that they are Taiban. There are many Taibans whom I respect and admire, but these men were not screened for loyalty or character. Who are they accountable to? Considering the amount of looting and the attacks on Ebulonians, they are not loyal to the houses that hired them. And since the clans hired them, armed them, and then put them in positions of trust, I question the clan's motives."

"Someone gave those men that order," Zeph mumbled.

"Exactly," Ochette agreed. "And lives that were under my care were lost because of it."

"We will find out who is responsible for this, Captain Ochette, I promise you," Mithra Mir assured him.

"We need to know the intention of everyone asking to enter the palace," Malbuis Mir declared. "Pliny, you were a student of Padear Pranseas, correct?"

"Yes, Master."

"Are you able to contact the Padear directly?"

The younger Mir's face lost some of its roundness when he grimaced. "He has many duties…"

"And the monks do not like getting involved in politics," Malbuis finished. "Yes, I know, but this is a unique situation. This cannot be an official request, as the only one among us who has any official authority is the Pira, and she is understandably distracted."

"Pranseas would be more likely to grant the request if it came from Eropa," Pliny suggested.

"This is not the time to press her," Malbuis said quietly. The others murmured agreement, and Pliny nodded his assent to contact the Padear.

"If you're uncertain, this Padear will agree, what about Frevin Mir?" Zeph asked. "He reads minds." Pliny bit his lip, looking as if he was on the verge of saying something, but stopped himself. "What? What is it?"

"I think it unwise to count on Frevin Mir's cooperation, Captain

CHAPTER FORTY-NINE

Yare," he spoke cautiously. "You said that he was present with you and the Pira when you made your escape?"

"Yes," Zeph acknowledged.

"So, he knows about the Mahal's death," Pliny let the statement sit, unembellished, unexplained, before continuing, "The question we must ask ourselves is who else knows now? Who might he have told? From what you have shared, it seems that Frevin Mir has been playing a game of mysterious loyalties. The present situation represents a unique opportunity for a man of his ambitions."

"He is my kinsman, and yet I agree with Pliny Mir's assessment. He will not let this opportunity go by."

"No one has heard from him, have they?" Pliny asked. None of them had.

"He will not ally himself with us," Mithra declared.

"But if he was going to tell someone, wouldn't he have done it already?" Zeph asked.

Mithra held his hands out, palms up. "Perhaps he has, and we simply do not know about it yet."

"He holds back because of Eropa," Pliny put forth his theory. "Frevin will not make an openly hostile gesture that might offend the Pira as long as he believes she supports us. He still has hope she will favor him in his desires, political or personal."

"Well, he's hedging his bets on that then, because he's been cozying up to Dora Dum'Laiere," Zeph snarled.

Mithra, the more politically and socially savvy of the Mirs, frowned. "Explain, please, Captain."

"They met at some ball at Auhora Whimlan," Zeph waved his hand, indicating he didn't know the unimportant details. "And apparently, they've been seeing each other ever since. She brought him to the dinner as a surprise guest the night of the riot. That's why he was there. Not because Miratha had invited him. She was livid that he was there, but Dora's crazy about him. Frevin's coached her on limiting her mother's influence over her since Dora's reached her majority, reducing Miratha's control."

Mithra raised one crescent eyebrow. "Livid indeed. But we should not count Miratha out so easily. She is still the Dum'Laiere Voice and Hagriva's recognized descendant, which gives her status on her own."

"And of course, we have yet to see how the treaty details play out," Pliny said. They all looked at him expectantly until he explained. "Everything to do with the treaty and who will benefit from it on this side is in limbo until we know what has happened to the Lamdra."

Eropa walked through the electric illusion-curtain that masked the corridor between her rooms and those of her father as Zeph asked, "What's the Lamdra's return got to do with Miratha?"

The Pira had changed from the blood and dirt-encrusted clothes she wore yesterday, clutching the pale, green silk dressing gown as if her grip on it was life itself. A single braid of tight ringlets hung down her back, ending at the gentle curve of her spine. Downy corkscrew curls had escaped the braid, making a red-gold halo around her head. Her face was the color of a spring leaf but as emotionless as a death mask, except for her green eyes, bloodshot and red-rimmed from crying.

The Mirs traded looks that Zeph could only interpret as *proceed with caution.*

"Ah, Pira," Mithra smoothly turned to the young Rhune. "Our hearts are lighter seeing you are recovering."

But it was Malbuis who went to the sorceress' side.

"Please know, Eropa, that you have not only our support and loyalty as our Pira, but our sincere promise to assist you in any way we are able. You are special to us, not because of your position, but because you are our dear friend's daughter, and he loved you very much. He lives in The Mother's embrace," the elder Mir lowered his head as he said the words.

"He lives in the Mother's embrace," Eropa repeated with the other Mirs, her green eyes, watery pools of sadness.

"We were going over what we have learned and what questions still need answering," Mithra explained. "Did you happen to hear from Frevin Mir? He has not joined us."

Zeph silently applauded the Mir's tact.

"He is seeing Dora Dum'Laiere safely back to her people's country holdings this morning," Eropa said quietly. "I expect that will take some time."

"No doubt," Mithra agreed as knowing looks crossed between the Mirs and Zeph. "And have you come across any demanding thought or question that it would ease your mind to know the answer?" Mithra

CHAPTER FORTY-NINE

moved on, recognizing that the young Rhune had joined them to be distracted from her grief.

"Did Miratha have my father and Dakmira killed?" she asked, green eyes blazing beneath a bank of dark lashes.

"We do not know yet," Mithra replied.

"Then, no." It was less than a whisper--barely more than an exhale and every instinct in Zeph told him to scoop her up again and take her back to her rooms where she could grieve and heal, but he knew it would be seen as presumptuous…a trespass. He had no place in her life.

"What has the Lamdra's return got to do with the treaty?" Zeph repeated his question, hoping to move the focus away from the Rhune.

Pliny gave a big sigh. "It is the wording. If the treaty is accepted as it is now, the Mahal and the Council of Elders will be officially recognized by the Paxlosians as the governing authorities on Ebulon. The Matriarch will not be seen as having any governmental power. Hagriva and her position as Matriarch are never mentioned in the document."

The group sat silently, considering this new information.

"Meaning that the Matriarch would potentially have less, or perhaps even no influence over policy decisions," Malbuis walked them through his thoughts.

"Outside of spiritual matters, yes," Pliny confirmed.

"And giving strength to the argument by certain clans that the Rhune's time of ruling on Ebulon has passed.

Zeph's eyes flew to Eropa, the blood draining from his face. "That was not my intention."

"But it is what the treaty says," Pliny held fast.

"I-I didn't write it," Zeph stuttered. "And those who did, didn't know what they were saying." He leapt to his feet and began to pace. "It was written before we even found Ebulon. It's just a trade document," he pleaded. "It wasn't meant to change a government. It's just about trade and finances."

Mithra smirked. "What do you think government is for, Yare? Bringing in wealth, deciding who has wealth, adding to people's wealth, spreading wealth, or at least pretending to, because that can gain you more influence and power, which can gain you more wealth."

Malbuis touched his partner's arm, silently calming him. "I never knew you to be such a cynic, my love."

"This result is not my doing. If the clans are interpreting it like that…twisting it like that, that's not me. I'm not a politician. I'm not a diplomat. Nikodamus knew that," Zeph tried to disabuse the notion that the treaty was about anything other than trade. "I knew nothing about your culture or the structure of your government when Nikodamus and I talked about this."

"But he did," Mithra said. He stood at the Mahal's desk and picked up the discarded copy that Eropa had tossed there before she stormed out. "There are places in this document where particular names and titles were to be filled in. Not once did Hagriva Rhune's name appear. Nikodamus could have given you any name. He could have pointed you in a different direction, corrected your suppositions. But he did not, and now we will never know why." Mithra held up the treaty. "But this is the version of the treaty that was in place when he died, and it represents his best efforts on our behalf. That will have significance to our people."

"Particularly those who have felt constricted under Rhune rule," Malbuis suggested.

Yare turned to Eropa. "Eropa, please, I did not know…I did not understand…"

Green eyes flashing cold fire, the Pira spun on her heels and swept from the room, disappearing through the light screen.

Mithra cleared his throat. "Pliny, please reach out to Padear Pranseas and request the loan of two dozen monks capable of truth reading, not in a private room under controlled circumstances. They need to be able to read people's intent while they are present in a public area," Mithra directed.

Pliny brought his attention away from the electric curtain where Eropa had disappeared and back to Mithra.

"He will want to know why," the Mir said simply.

"Tell him you will explain everything as soon as you are able, but that you need the assistance immediately."

Zeph jumped up from the table and started for the electric curtain.

"I need to talk to Eropa."

"Not now, Captain Yare." Malbuis stopped him. "It is best that she face this in small doses."

"But I can explain!" Zeph protested, his face flushing scarlet.

CHAPTER FORTY-NINE

"Can you though?" The old Mir's voice was gentle, his eyes compassionate. "Can you really?" The Mir's question seemed to have a much deeper meaning than the words indicated. Zeph felt them digging into him, as if true answers were spilling from his body like blood from a wounded artery. His strong jaw was clenched; his fists contracted into tight balls by his sides.

They were right, he *did not* know. And he hated it. He was on a strange world with strange rules, and Fratianne was right, he needed help understanding what to do and not do…the mistakes he had already made. Nikodamus, the man whom he had come to think of as a friend, who had provided him his only anchor here was gone, and whatever Zeph sensed between him and Eropa was gone as well though he acted as if it was still there, but she was always moving away just out of reach.

Were these Mirs helping him now that Nikodamus was gone? Why should they? Their loyalty was to their people…to Eropa. There was no one here with any reason to take Zeph's part, and he couldn't fly away and leave the whole mess behind, because his ship was gone.

His ship was gone, and he might never leave Ebulon.

CHAPTER FIFTY

"The ripples that emanate from unnatural manipulations affect The Balance on all worlds, because all life in every realm is connected. Those ripples cannot be controlled." (Rhune quote: anonymous.)

Having viewed the damage to the clan estates along the river near The District from the air, did not prepare Frevin for seeing it up close. Estates closer to the Mi'cosa Bridge appeared deserted, their gates ripped from their hinges, rock walls breached and tumbled open. The clans who had bought in to Murtevoy's plan for protection had fared the worst. When the trouble began and the Taiban mobs attacked, their illusions of superiority and invulnerability were breached along with the gates; the mercenary Taibans were already within their walls.

Frevin felt anger heating his chest.

How dare these Taibans attack them? We welcomed them as guests and supported their cause. How dare they turn on us for our kindness? Frevin never felt strongly one way or another about the Taiban refugees before. He was aware that Eropa had nurtured some connection among them—something to do with her training. It never seemed of any importance, and he certainly did not know any Taibans personally, but the events surrounding the riot had revealed that he was in common with Ebulonians who had long spoken against granting the revolutionaries safe haven.

Frevin could see guard-pairs patrolling the avenue between the closest clan estates and the river. There were not many.

Across from him in the shuttle, Dora nervously clasped then unclasped her hands.

"Most of the trouble was confined to estates that were closest to the District," he tried to reassure her. He had slipped a mild sedative into her drink last night so she would sleep, giving him enough quiet to consider his situation.

Nikodamus was dead and distracted by that event, Eropa remained distant and unresponsive to Frevin. If he was truthful with

CHAPTER FIFTY

himself, this were the situation since the Paxlosian's arrival, and though his hopes had been sparked by the Pira's sudden return from Auhora Whimlan, her coolness seemed to only be getting worse no matter what he did.

It was a disappointment to himself and his family, who had invested heavily in the promise of a partnership between him and the future Matriarch, but he could no longer count on the connection. As the foundations of their culture and government shifted and crumbled beneath their feet, Frevin recognized he needed another way to get the power and position he so badly desired.

There were factions. But who should he ally himself with?

Aside from recognizing Miratha's claim of descendancy, Hagriva had absented herself, embracing a reluctance to take part in Ebulonian politics and the Council's decisions. The power of the major clans was once again on the rise, and discomfort with Rhune leadership was being spoken about openly in some circles.

Dora Dum'Laiere, as the heir of her clan's first line, had the potential to grant someone connected to her political and financial position and power. And she was gullible. It had taken Frevin no effort at all to work himself into a position of influence with the young woman—an influence he could retain the rest of their lives, whomever they partnered with.

None of this boded well for Eropa's future. The next Matriarch might become a mere ceremonial figurehead with little power to affect decisions on Ebulon. The situation did not suit Frevin's ambitions.

And now there was this Taiban girl, Corin's, claim that Miratha was responsible for Nikodamus's murder. If this were found to be true—if she was formally charged, association with her would be tantamount to political poison. Even being remembered as having supported her could damage a person's future.

And yet she was a formidable woman. Those who stood in Miratha's way were effectively removed or neutralized. Was it possible she could still emerge from all of this unscathed?

"I heard that the Bren'Harrows and the Harbines have both fled the city," Dora interrupted the Mir's thoughts, returning him to the shuttle bringing her home. "They say the Taiban mercenaries hired to protect them turned on them."

Frevin offered a strained smile. "There are a lot of rumors right now, Dora. Repetition does not make something true." He patted her hand. He had convinced her to return to the family estate in Iredipa, rather than going to the country, assuring her that her mother remained in residence. She might resent her mother's control and be angry at her for her lies, but Dora had been reliant on Miratha for everything in her life up until a few weeks ago. It was not so easy to erase the habits formed during those decades.

Dora slid forward to the edge of her seat, looking out the window at the city below, signs of tension increasing in her as they drew closer to the Dum'Laiere manse.

"I can hardly imagine how awful that would be, having people you trust attack you."

"I am sure there is a lesson for us all in it. It seems clear they were misguided in placing their trust in such an unworthy race," Frevin commented.

He felt Dora turn and study him, but she made no comment.

The outer walls of the Dum'Laiere estate came into view, its manicured avenue making a ribbon through the grounds. Dora let out a long, relieved breath, biting her lip. There was no sign of damage or violence. The moment the shuttle touched down, she was out the door, running up the front steps.

Sweeping through the reception foyer into the house proper, she called out, "Mother? Mother, I am home."

Frevin quietly entered the mansion and closed the door as Miratha came out of the library.

"And still your new friend is with you. How kind of you, Frevin Mir, to dedicate so much of your precious time to my daughter. I cannot imagine how we will ever repay you for such attention."

But I am certain you have a plan. She primly inclined her head toward Frevin, her eyes remaining as cold as Arctic stone.

"Matron." Frevin returned the gesture with a measuredly less indication of respect.

Miratha's body tensed. The Mir's message was clear; the dynamic between them had changed.

"Dora's safety is important to us all," Frevin replied. "You were not attacked?"

"No." Miratha sniffed. "Some of my neighbors' vetting processes were less thorough. Thankfully, we experienced no such laxness on this estate."

A smart dog does not defecate in its own den.

Frevin turned to Dora. "Dora, would you mind getting me something cool to drink? I find the ash in the air has parched my throat."

"Of course." Dora looked perplexed but scuttled off to the kitchens.

"Nikodamus is dead," he told Miratha.

Miratha's eyes grew wide in what appeared to be genuine surprise. "What?"

"And Dakmira-Keesch. They were attacked in the palace last night by Taibans. Your hand is suspected."

Miratha had not recovered when Dora returned.

"Both?" the Dum'Laiere Voice managed to vocalize something from her shock.

"Yes." Frevin nodded. "Nikodamus and Dakmira were both murdered last night."

The glass in Dora's hand tilted sideways, the contents spilling across the floor.

"Foolish girl," her mother scolded her. "Summon a servant to clean this up." Dora did not move, but Miratha had already turned her attention back to Frevin. Her hands were trembling. "I feared this. I sent assistance, hoping to avoid it."

Frevin's eyes narrowed. "What kind of 'assistance'?"

"I sent men to help guard the palace during the riot."

"You expect me to believe that? Why would you try to protect him when you have been working for years to get him out of your way?"

Dora was aghast at the accusation. "Frevin, how can you say such a thing? Mother would never..." she stopped mid-sentence. "You did not do this, did you, Mother?" she asked.

Miratha's eyes flashed. "Certainly not."

"I have been loyal..."

"Loyal to whom and by whose definition?" Frevin demanded. "You have been belittling the Pira and trying to undermine her and the Matriarch's influence for years. You kidnapped Yare and held him captive, concealing it while you worked to undermine his agreement with the Mahal and turn his allegiance to you. You tried to unseat

Nikodamus, calling for the Baraq Ta—something that has not happened in generations! I would not be surprised to learn that you were responsible for manipulating the Taiban fire and riot to weaken Nikodamus's alliances."

Miratha squared her shoulders. "They were always Murtevoy's. It was to him they gave allegiance. We were all duped by this Murtevoy," she sneered. "He was a master manipulator who exploited our fear and promised security, an arrogant and ambitious bastard whom I was forced to censure more than once for taking action in our name without my permission. We had words about it that day, in fact, and I warned him not to abuse my trust by directing resources we were paying for to further his agenda."

"You mean among the Taibans?" Frevin asked, his interest perking up. Miratha nodded. "Do you have proof that Murtevoy was responsible for the Taiban riots?'

Miratha tossed her head. "I do not know if it reaches a level of proof, but early on, I caught him redirecting our guards to The District during the fire. He seemed very keen to get the gates all closed. I demanded that he return our men to the estate immediately, and he appeared to agree." She sniffed, smoothing her dress. "They were hired to protect the Dum'Laire clan and estates after all, not to interfere in Little Taiba's politics. Why he would desire such a thing anyway is beyond me."

Dora sank into a chair. "By the Mother's grace, you have destroyed us."

"Closing off The District could have appeared like an act of loyalty, protecting his clients if it had worked. It might even have helped ingratiate him with that element among the clans who have remained obstinately anti-Taiban."

"But he did not succeed. They did not protect their clients," Miratha argued. "The Taibans ransacked a half dozen estates near the river.

Frevin shrugged. "You do not change the nature of people merely by giving them new clothes and a wage. But can the identities of the Taibans who broke into the estates actually be proven? The clans do not wish to look like fools. They will distance themselves from this. There will be an effort to blame other Taibans—unemployed Taibans who were not hired," Frevin surmised.

CHAPTER FIFTY

What should we do, Frevin?" Dora asked.

Frevin smiled, a smile that outwardly said she should not worry, he would handle things, but that inwardly was in recognition of his own success. Despite accusing her mother of treason, Dora Dum'Laiere still trusted him.

E.F. Winters

CHAPTER FIFTY-ONE

"The beliefs and outlooks of a spirit that has lived in the flesh are molded by their physical experiences, prejudices, and the dogma of their time. If a spirit has never experienced physical life, it will know nothing of life's challenges. Either way, their knowledge is flawed." (From "Lessons to Other Worlds." Author/compiler unknown. Attributed to Hagriva Rhune)

With the landmark buildings and wooden street signs gone, The District was unrecognizable. The snaking, nonsensical cross-grid had been so changed that navigation required Corin to use distant focal points; the Mi'cosa bridge to the northwest, the roofline of clan estate mansions directly across the river to the west, the dome of the Elder's Library and the spiral turrets of Iredipa palace to the south, and the Mir Mountains to the east.

Mud hovels and repurposed metal parts scavenged from spaceships had long defined what passed for housing on the steep slope to the south, separating the curve of the Mi'cosa river channel from the more affluent section of the city near the Elder's Library. Here, the land fell off sharply, and only the poor were motivated to build on it. Composed of space-tech salvage, the fire had found nothing of interest to consume here, leaving the poorest of the poor with a semblance of shelter.

The riot and fire were only a day in the past, but the time seemed much longer. Soot stains climbed the lower third of Corin's wide-legged trousers. Ash and smoke coated her hair. They were in her nose, embedded in every wrinkle of skin around her joints, and caked under her nails.

She didn't care. No one cared anymore. People were too focused on survival and politics.

Corin walked through what was left of Little Taiba, suffering the many slights, the gossip, the sneers, the shoulder pushes, even surreptitious gut punches. She knew the other girls were experiencing

CHAPTER FIFTY-ONE

it too. She saw the bruises they hid beneath their clothing. None of them talked about it. That would make it too real, and somehow it felt like the shame was theirs.

Corin bit her tongue and pushed on toward the Bobalo compound. If she stopped to call out every physical trespass or argue every false statement, she would never get anywhere. How could anyone with a brain align themselves with Murtevoy and his mercenaries? It required blatantly ignoring the facts about what Saldo and his street-soldiers did, and how many were killed due to their actions.

The justifications for this were numerous—all of them lies.

Corin felt betrayed—felt that her uncle and the Bobalo family were being betrayed—and anger raged inside her, urging her to lash out. It was unthinkable that those for whom they had done so much could turn on them this way.

She passed Block, standing armed and alert at the gate, and nodded in silent greeting. She was too tired to talk. Too wound up and distracted to sleep. So, she washed the soot and smoke from her face, arms, and hands and then tried to pry the black, charcoal-clotted clay from the soles of her boots. No one needed the extra work of trying to clean the stubborn stuff off the floors or the stained spots the dark charcoal would leave behind.

There was no one stirring, so she made her way to the family's garden to see what it might offer.

The pickings were slim. The problem with harvesting for need was that what was picked early was a little small and underripe, reducing the harvest. However, the family had given away as much as they could spare and more, nearly emptying their pantries. Now, they needed to fill in with what was growing. It would be a rough year for everyone in Little Taiba. There would be no harvest of overflow and no preserving this year.

As she searched through the foliage for hidden vegetables, trying to focus on the growing things and ignore the horrendous pictures that kept flashing through her mind, Corin wondered how Eropa was doing, alone in that big palace. Of course, she was the Pira, so she wasn't really *alone*--except that she was. There were people all around her, but not people who cared about her like family. With Nikodamus and Dakmira gone, the only person left in the palace from Eropa's

E.F. Winters

support was Frevin Mir, and she seemed to have finally recognized him for the uppity ass that he was.

Eropa was surrounded by hundreds of people, but she had no one.

"At least *she* has enough to eat," Corin muttered, tossing the spindly carrots into her gathering basket, realizing that her friend was despondent and probably not eating, and ashamed of the edge of resentment that crept into that last thought.

She's my friend, and she was Quinn's friend. It isn't her fault Quinn is dead. But maybe it was. Corin had been focused on her own fight during Quinn's last minutes. She had not seen Eropa, and Eropa had not communicated since they all were dropped off by the Menander boy at their various points at dawn.

It weighed on Corin.

In every mixed-up part of yesterday, Eropa was there, like a key. The center or a pivot point of events. How much the Rhune shaped those events and how much she had been merely caught up in them like the rest of them was a huge question mark in Corin's mind. She could not stop thinking about the old saying from the Book of the Rhunes that claimed that worlds warped around a Rhune. Was it a natural thing? Worlds warped because of a Rhune's presence, and the sorceresses themselves played no part in the alteration, or did the Rhunes *do* the warping?

It seemed to Corin that it mattered. It mattered to her right now because Quinn was dead.

Feeling like she had been drowned, then wrung out and tossed aside, Corin carried the gathering basket into the Bobalo's big kitchen. Her aunt, Timee, was sitting at the big kitchen table, her head hidden in her cupped hands.

"Auntie?"

"I'm fine, dear." Timee wiped her cheeks with her apron. "Just a moment, you know—feeling overwhelmed by everything. So many dead."

"And Quinn," Corin said softly, putting the basket down on the table and going to her aunt.

"And Quinn." Timee held onto her niece, her thin shoulders giving a shudder before she recovered herself. Sitting up straight, head high, she wiped fresh tears away. "It is only to be expected in times as bad as this."

CHAPTER FIFTY-ONE

"Have there ever been times as bad as this before?" Eropa asked, appearing outside the doorway. Timee moved to stand. "Please do not get up." The Pira motioned the older woman to stay where she was.

Timee looked up at their unexpected guest. "It is not always the number of dead or the scale of suffering that tips the balance," she replied. "Some losses are just harder to accept; maybe because they seem so personal." Her voice broke.

"I wanted to come before, but I could not find any justification where it was acceptable to ask you to pay attention to my feelings when your own are what is important," Eropa explained, her face heavy with sadness. The whites of her eyes were veined with red, swollen, and puffy, a mirror of Corin's and Timee's. "And still I had to come." Her voice caught. "I understand if you turn me away. You have every right to, but I cannot get away from the shadow of grief over my friend, your son's loss. The guilt over my part feels like I am being stabbed over and over again. Guilt bleeds from every part of my body, and I cannot hide it. I must speak the truth. It was my fault."

"Please, come in and sit, Pira," Timee gestured, her tears responding to those of the Rhune. Eropa did, each of the women struggling with the weight of their emotions and the shattered shards of lives that, on the turn of a moment, had changed too much to bear.

They sat in the high-ceilinged kitchen, imprisoned by a voracious silence that devoured their words before they could speak them aloud.

It was Timee, with her compassionate nature, who finally broke the spell.

"It is very hard to bear the burden of feeling responsible for someone's death, even when logically you could not have stopped it."

"But I could have!" Eropa despaired. "I should have."

Timee reached out and touched the younger woman's hand. "I cannot say anything to relieve this thing you are carrying in your heart and head—this guilt. I was not there. I am sorry."

"You should not be apologizing to me," Eropa responded almost angrily.

Timee's lips curved into a subtle, sad smile. "I am a Keesch by training," she explained.

"I did not know that."

"My desires have always been to provide healing, and the Mother knows there is always a need for it." Timee sighed. "You see, I, too, bear a burden of guilt that cuts me. We told people they would be safe here on Ebulon—that they could have a better life." Tears sparkled in her brown eyes.

"And you have done everything you could to make that happen," Eropa tried to soothe the older woman's worries.

"That is not how it feels." Timee paused. "In the early years of the rebellion, we lost a lot of people because they just launched themselves into space from the farthest outposts, hoping we would find them. No one knew they were coming, and there was no one to catch them." Her eyes glazed over like a fish caught in a net, but hers was a net of her memories. "They had no real information to guide them, just rumors. It was important to us to keep our secret. But they had heard there was a community being built where it was safer, and if you could get there, you could join it. You just needed to find the right people. So, people began to ask around on the outlying worlds in The String. And, of course, that made us more secretive, because any one of them could have been agents or spies for the warlords.

"Many of those who were trying to find us never spoke to our people, but others who claimed to be connected to the movement took advantage of our secrecy to prey on the desperate. The payments they demanded for the false coordinates they gave devastated families' finances.

Hearing about these enormous sums and unwilling to take the risk of being turned in to the warlord's people, a bounty had been put on anyone caught trying to leave with a larger amount for someone trying to escape with or send a child away, some did not try to find help. They simply bought any pod they could afford and had it shot out into space, hoping we would find them.

"Back then, if we knew to expect a pod, they sometimes went astray. If they lost momentum too far out in space, we could not catch them. But most of the problems happened because we did not know a pod was coming."

"And yet they still came," Eropa prompted.

Timee nodded. "This was right after The Purge, and families were desperate to hide their children from the warlords. They were willing to risk everything. So, they made their way to the furthest outpost they could get to and climbed into a pod, hoping someone would find them before they ran out of air.

CHAPTER FIFTY-ONE

"I remember one pod--Jayq Jacoby found it. He went out to catch some returning fighters, and he came across this stray pod. It was small, only rated for one person, but when it was opened, there were three inside: a young mother, a little boy, and a baby girl. They were all dead, of course, because as small as the children were, there had only been air for one. I can still see the children's little faces cuddled up against their mother like they'd fallen asleep in her arms. They could have floated out there in space forever if Jayq hadn't found them, and I felt so sad. They would never wake up because they did not know where to go, and we found them too late." Tears glistened on Timee's green cheeks.

"So, you started reaching out and bringing in more refugees," Eropa concluded. Timee nodded.

"And got a lot of black-hearted bastards," Corin added sourly.

"Many of the men you now know as community leaders started just like them," Timee chided her niece. "People become what they need to become to survive in the world they are born into. We three are fortunate, Corin. We were born here. We cannot judge these people. We do not understand what they have lived through."

The only sound in the kitchen was the three women's breaths-- too soft to disturb the quiet, softly holding them together like a ribbon holds the wrapping on a gift.

It was a gift, Timee's story; a gift from the older woman to the younger; a gift of history lived, precious and personal, providing an opening for a sharing that could include forgiveness of self and others.

"Please, accept my apology," Eropa's voice faltered. "And try to forgive me. Quinn died because he stepped between me and the sword that would have killed me," she confessed, her voice quivering on the edge of emotion. "I do not know what happened, but when I reached for it, I could not touch The Source, and the magic I counted on was not there. It failed, and Quinn paid for that failure." The Rhune shook her head, dashing tears away with the back of her hand. "I did not ask him to—I did not want him to. I wish he had not done it, but I cannot change it. The truth of it remains, and no excuse I can give removes my responsibility. I know that words will never be enough to compensate for his loss, but I had to say how deeply sorry I am." The face she turned to Timee Bobalo was constricted by heartbreak and remorse.

"He loved you," Timee said softly.

"I wish he had not," the reply seemed ripped from the Rhune's breast. Timee's fine, arched brows wrinkled in a silent question. "Because then he would not be dead." A sob caught in the Pira's throat.

"You cannot have known Quinn and truly believe that, Pira." Timee seemed to grow taller; her back was so straight. "You grieve, as we do, because you loved him as well, though I do not claim to know what form that love might have taken. But my son chose a warrior's path, Pira, and this is the reality of all mothers who bear such men-children, and why our hearts break every time they step out of our sight. Quinn might have died for anyone, a Free Man or Woman, a child, or an elder. A pod could have malfunctioned, or the food in a cache could have gone bad. My son's life was at risk every day, but he chose to die for you." Timee studied the face before her. "If you would honor his gift, prove you are the person he believed you to be and stand by his people."

"I will," Eropa nodded. "What do you need?"

"Right now, food, blankets, and building materials," Timee listed practicalities. "Some tents would help as a temporary measure. There are not enough buildings with roofs to shelter everyone, nor enough food among us to feed them all. And then there will be political considerations. Things are being said about why this happened. Accusations are being tossed about, everyone waiting to see who will be holding the blame when things finally explode."

"There will be a new Mahal," Eropa said. "I cannot speak for them, but you will continue to have the Rhune's support." Timee inclined her head in thanks. "Have your people ask at the palace for Pliny Mir. He will see that you have the supplies you need." Eropa rose and went to the door. Corin followed her friend. Lingering in the doorway, she watched Eropa walk alone across the compound's grounds toward the gate.

"It feels strange that a Rhune struggles with guilt and sadness just like the rest of us, doesn't it?" Corin muttered. "I always figured that having a greater understanding would insulate them from that because they would know how all the pieces fit together--why some live and some die." Corin turned back to the kitchen. Timee found work in which to bury her sorrows, measuring the ingredients for tomorrow's bread.

"It is a good sign that she still feels these things. If someone with her power did not, that would be something to worry about."

Corin sat back down at the table, watching her aunt knead the dough for bread. "I feel so lost, Auntie. Like, The Balance has shifted. Vale and Quinn are gone. Little Taiba is destroyed..."

"Little Taiba is *not* destroyed," Timee corrected her niece adamantly. "The buildings may be gone, but the community will survive, we will rebuild." Timee glanced out the door. Twilight was descending over the Bobalo compound, but she could still see Eropa's outline as the Pira slowly crossed the compound grounds. "She is not well, you know, your Pira. She hides it, but beyond her struggles with guilt over the deaths of Quinn, her father, and Dakmira—and she does feel guilt over all of them, there is something more, a darkness of spirit that I have never seen in her before. She said her magic failed."

"Yes." Corin nodded.

"This darkness is at the root of that. It cannot simply be ignored. It will not heal itself. It must be dealt with, Corin, or it will consume her."

"What can be done?" Corin asked, worried for her friend.

Timee shrugged. "This is the realm of high magic, niece, and I am a Keesch, not a Rhune. I can see the illness, but I cannot heal it." Timee's attention lingered on the young sorceress as she approached the compound's gates. "Do you think it is safe for her to travel alone with everything that is happening and her magic being so unpredictable?"

Corin snorted. "She's the Pira. And anyway, she's just going back to the palace."

"Is she?" Timee dropped the bread dough onto the table and began kneading it. "I thought she said she was going north."

"She didn't say that." Corin hesitated. "Not out loud anyway." The point of her aunt's question became clear. "But that is what she's planning to do, isn't it, Aunt? She's going north to Alden Baierd."

Timee nodded. "I believe so. She will be alone there, with only old Hagriva to talk to, which is to say she will have no one at all because the old Rhune is hardly in her body anymore, they say. She sees to the welfare of many worlds, and her energy is not what it was. Her time is running short."

Niece and Aunt exchanged a look, understanding passing between them.

"I can't leave the family right now," Corin despaired, feeling once again the split of her loyalty between her family and her friend. "Quinn has just died, and Little Taiba is barely hanging on. We need every spare set of hands we can get just to feed people."

Her aunt's subtle smile returned. "We are a large family, Corin, the Bobalos and their old comrades, and the Pira has pledged more resources to help us. We have many hands here, but who does she have?"

Me, Corin answered silently.

"Catch up with your friend before she gets too far. I will explain it to your uncle."

Corin ran to her room quickly, tossing sturdy travel clothes, her favorite knives, a sharpening stone, and the small kit of survival equipment she had been taught to always pack. She was adding every type of small weapon she could fit when she heard her uncle's voice coming from the kitchen.

He is safe. Relief soothed her worries.

Smiling, she exited through the low open window and ran to catch up with the Pira.

The table in Nikodamus' apartments where the Mir's and Zeph had sequestered bore the look of an embattled miniature town, the structure created by used dishes and glassware, some stained with wine, some still bearing remnants of the food that had designated their purpose. It was fast approaching the cycle of a day since Nikodamus' death. They had uncovered some significant facts. They had many agreed-upon suspicions, but they could not declare with certainty who had killed the Mahal of Ebulon, and there were no more short-term investigations that might yield that information.

The room slid into an exhausted silence.

I think we are done." Mithra breathed. "There is nothing more we can do right now."

CHAPTER FIFTY-ONE

"The time has come. We must inform the council of the Mahal's passing," Malbuis voiced what they were all thinking.

"Once we do, everything we have done will be called into question," his partner warned.

Malbuis nodded. "And Ebulon's future will pass into the hands of whoever seizes leadership. But we did not do this because we wanted to govern. We did it because we believed it was the best way to stop whoever was responsible gaining what they were after and hold them accountable before they covered up the evidence."

"Who do you think the council will follow?" Pliny asked. They had received word a few hours ago that the senior Voice, Lady Aless McLarick, had been killed the same night as the Taiban riot and fire.

"Lady Aless could not have been removed at a worse time," Mithra muttered.

"They will not support Lector, surely." Pliny made a face.

Mithra shook his head. "Harscham's ambitions are too naked and self-serving. He makes noise, but they know him to be a boastful dullard. They will be frightened. They will look for comfort, someone who can lead now but maintain continuity by continuing as the next Mahal. They will want someone they believe has enough visibility and support with the common people to win their vote. That is not Lector."

"Even if Miratha backs him as her creature?" Pliny inquired.

"Miratha's influence is gone," Zeph declared. "Descendant of this Hagriva or not, once they know what she's done, no one will dare be allied with her."

"And what exactly has she done, Yare?" Mithra challenged him.

Zeph blinked. "What do you mean? She drugged and kidnapped me and held me against my will. She had Nikodamus killed…"

Mithra shook his head. "We cannot prove this."

"I lived it. I was taken from Auhora Whimlan and imprisoned at her estate," Zeph spluttered.

"Miratha will tell a different story," Mithra pointed out.

"A lie, you mean," Zeph shot back. "Her maid told me everything…"

Mithra cocked his head to one side. "The Taiban servant whom you claim helped Miratha drug you so her mistress could spirit you away. You think she will be believed?"

"She was forced to do that!" Zeph argued.

"A member of the Dum'Laiere house staff is not going to give evidence against the family," Pliny informed Zeph. "Even if she agreed to, it would never happen. The clans have traditions about loyalty and ways of dealing with those who break with those traditions. Severe, permanent-end-to-the problem ways," the Mir emphasized the words to make his meaning clear. Zeph thought the wealthy on Pax and the wealth on Ebulon were not so different after all, despite Ebulonian pretense.

"Then we talk to Dora," Zeph argued. Mithra raised an eyebrow.

"Whatever her differences with her mother, a Dum'Laiere of the First Line is not going to damage her clan."

"Frevin was there," Zeph tried again, his stubbornness kicking in. "He was a guest at dinner the night of the riot. *He* can verify what Miratha was doing."

Mithra shook his head. "Frevin is unlikely to take such a bold move. He has yet to decide what side he is on."

"And from what you have said, he could verify that you were a fellow dinner guest, but he could not speak to the circumstances under which you arrived, or why you remained there," Pliny pointed out.

Zeph didn't answer, saying instead, "The men who killed Nikodamus and his consort wore Dum'Laiere uniforms. The Bobalo girl, Corin, saw that—*you* saw that."

"Crudely made sigils hand-sewn onto street clothes." Malbuis dismissed the idea. "Easily faked."

"Come, Yare, only a fool would send in assassins wearing their clan sigil or send a message to the guard announcing they are coming," Mithra tried to bring Zeph to a place of reason. "And Miratha is no fool."

"You think someone set the Dum'Laiere's up, Mithra?" Pliny asked.

Mithra received a silent agreement from his partner before he replied, "It is possible."

"I don't believe this!" Zeph exploded. "Miratha Dum'Laiere is responsible!"

"We are only saying what the Council will say. We cannot accuse her without solid proof," the elder Mir attempted to mollify the Paxlosian. "She is the Voice of a powerful family, and no one can remove her from that position except the clan. So, unless they take that action, she will continue to retain a certain amount of influence."

"And if we did accuse her, and then are proven wrong, she will use it to gain sympathy among the other clans," Mithra explained.

"Her allies would exploit it," Pliny stated.

"And if she is guilty, she has been working to cover up any evidence as fast as we have been working to find and save it, because she knows that we are looking," Mithra went on.

"Frevin," Zeph harumphed grumpily. "Where is Eropa?"

Pliny hesitated. "She is not in her rooms. It does not appear that she has been there in some time."

"Have the guards been alerted? Did anyone see her leave?"

Pliny snorted, "Not unless she wanted them to. The Pira is accustomed to coming and going as she pleases."

"Except that someone has just murdered her father and we don't know who or why yet," Zeph snapped.

"Eropa can take care of herself."

"Then why is the Bobalo boy dead?" Zeph demanded angrily. "If there's one lesson I've learned during this last death-saturated day, it's that magic is no guarantee of safety. It's a lesson I would recommend you learn." The Mirs had the grace to look humbled. "Captain Ochette?" Zeph summoned the captain of the guard from his post outside the door. "Have you seen the Pira?"

"She left the palace before nightfall."

"And you did not tell anyone?" Zeph demanded angrily.

Ochette gave the alien captain a level look. "She is the Pira. Whom should I have told?"

Zeph rearranged himself, letting go of the alarm and frustration of the situation. "She left. Can you share with us where she went?"

Ochette hesitated, but Pliny saved him the awkwardness.

"She went home to Alden Baierd."

"How do you know?" Zeph asked.

The Mir shrugged. "Where else would she go but the place she thinks of as home?"

"Will she be safe at this Alden Baierd?" the alien captain demanded.

"The two most powerful women on the planet live there," Pliny answered without answering.

"I'm not talking about magic. I'm asking if there are physical protections there to stop someone who might wish the Pira harm." Zeph turned back to Ochettte.

"No," the captain of the palace guard replied reluctantly. "Since the seat of government moved to Iredipa, Alden Baierd has become a deserted ruin, except for the Pira and the Matriarch and an occasional monk staying at the nearby temple. Padear Pranseas could be called upon to keep a watchful eye, perhaps…assign some monks to stay at the old temple if no one is there currently. He was the Pira's instructor in martial arts when she was at Alden Baierd."

"Pliny, has the Pranseas replied to you about providing monks who can truth read?" Malbuis asked.

"He has agreed to our request," Pliny confirmed.

"I will explain the concern and ask him as a personal favor to protect Eropa," Malbuis said.

"One more nail in our coffin when the Council learns what we've done," Mithra cautioned.

"I see no reason to inform them." Malbuis sniffed, his bushy white brows arching the wrinkled skin of his face into a thin parchment. "They are council elders, not emperors."

They had tried to discover truth surrounding the Mahal's death before important facts could be covered up but going forward, they would be viewed as covering up the most important facts; the Mahal Nikodamus Mir was dead, murdered in his rooms in the palace and though those who had wielded the weapons were also dead, the identity of who had sent them remained in question.

The Mirs had known from the beginning that their subterfuge must be revealed, and there would be a cost for their decision to carve out these hours could cost them. Without Eropa standing beside them to immediately dispel questions over their motives, those intentions were vastly more vulnerable to ungenerous interpretations by their most ungenerous peers, and their decision could cost them those peers' trust, their positions, possibly even their lives.

"Miratha and her supporters will be alert for any misstep," Mithra said.

Pliny nodded. "And Frevin. The Mother help us if the two of them ally. But Miratha will be brought to justice, Captain Yare. She will pay for her actions."

"I'm not worried." There was a storm in Zeph's gray eyes.

CHAPTER FIFTY-ONE

The loss of life claimed by the fire and subsequent riot was tragic, but that was not the end of Little Taiba's woes. The aftermath caused a second wave of deaths that all but crippled the small community. Elders, the injured, the frail; all succumbed in the face of the demands required for survival. Connections that held up commerce and the cause for two decades were obliterated. Bobalo and his loyalists, trying to provide humanitarian aid, were overwhelmed. Trust, when it existed, was as fragile as spider silk.

Little Taiba's problems were Spectre's salvation. He worked alongside Taibans trying to save their homes, their families, their livelihoods. Devastated and grateful, no one asked about his connections. What was important now was that the man was there to help them during the fire and was there still, continuing to help. That was enough.

The Shadowmaster created a background story for himself, using only the dead, just in case.

A new person emerged from the ashes of the smoldering city: Free Man Jaeger. Quiet and hard-working, he kept to himself, seldom smiled, and never boasted. People noted his sinewy strength and quiet capability and made assumptions about who he had been before; assumptions that Spectre neither confirmed nor denied. Their stories put flesh on the bones of the bare bones back story he had puzzled together, anchoring his invented truths in additional layers of fabrication stitched and held together by the dead. Some of what the gossips invented for Jaeger, Spectre owned. Other bits he discarded as too showy, substituting humbler versions more in keeping with his new persona, but he rarely corrected misinformation. It did not matter that the citizens of Little Taiba did not know his truth from theirs; *he* needed to.

Myths began to grow around Jaeger like weeds, and Spectre let them grow. Scything them down would only reveal bare ground he did not wish to have examined.

People he helped were quick to want to return the favor, and Jaeger was regularly invited to share a meal, the use of a thin blanket, or a dry corner to sleep in.

E.F. Winters

Spectre let his beard come in, and his short, cropped hair began to grow. Picking up found bits and pieces from among the rubble, he added the credibility of personal items to Jaeger's story, complete with stories about each of them: a blue stone earring from the ash of a burned-out apartment explained as a memento of his long-dead mother, an unremarkable pocketknife he could claim was from his uncle.

He pushed the post of the blue stone earring through the cartilage of his ear, ignoring the pain and the popping noise it made as it stabbed through. A Shadowmaster could not afford such a statement of individualism, but such small details were important to his sense of costume as a Free Man.

Walking through the district, Spectre observed the divide between Bobalo's loyalists and Saldo Murtevoy's mercenaries and their allies, trying to see it all through Jaeger's eyes, listening with Jaeger's ears. The tension provided the texture to every conversation; each side blaming the other for the fire's devastation and the riot that had grown from it, who had sided with whom, who had done what and for whom, and who could or could not be trusted. The constant churning of the story added to the uncertainty everyone felt.

The Iredipa palace guard began making appearances in The District, asking questions about Saldo Murtevoy, who had slipped them at the Dum'Laiere estate.

"Someone has to be blamed, and they've assigned Murtevoy the part--the Clan's part in it be damned!"

"But they hired and controlled their guards, didn't they?" it was argued. "They ordered Murtevoy's men into The District. That makes them responsible, don't it?"

"Ebulonians are never going to admit they did anything wrong," another argued.

"The Taibans hired to work for the clans were Free Men and Women. They should have disobeyed their orders before attacking their own."

"They were trying to put down a riot."

"They shut the gates! They made the riot."

Neither side would accept the other's view.

But the question foremost in everyone's minds, Ebulonian and Taiban alike, was what would happen now?

CHAPTER FIFTY-ONE

People watched the traffic on the streets. They watched each other, and they kept one eye on the lights in the sky.

"Might as well be back on Taiba," Spectre heard them complain.

When he left the Lamdra, Spectre had been confident that mutiny was imminent, but he had not planned on not returning.

Without a means to get back on the Lamdra and no information about what was happening on the starship, time seemed to crawl.

Like a man lost in the desert, the Shadowmaster thirsted for any bit of rumor or hearsay about Yare or his starship. There were mirages everywhere: Yare had been seen on Ebulon. He had fought in the riots. He was imprisoned in the palace. He was dead, and all the other sightings were attempts to cover it up so that the Paxlosians would not attack.

Spectre threw himself into playing Jaeger and waited.

E.F. Winters

CHAPTER FIFTY-TWO

"Shun the present; become the future." (Taiban warlord propaganda slogan encouraging the sale and recruitment of intelligent children after The Purge.)

Clemmet crawled from the wreckage of the Paxlosian shuttle, a foul, chemical smoke stinging his eyes and throat. Inching away, he dragged himself through the stinking mud. Movement on his left drew his fogged attention, and he raised his gaze from the wreckage to a phantom limping away through the smoke and flames.

The last of his strength fled; Clem lowered himself onto the mud-slick earth and wept.

"I did it. I crashed the shuttle. I stopped him." There had been no time to think about it or the consequences, but he had to stop Terk. And he had, hadn't he? The image of the limping figure disappearing into the smoke closed its fist around his haze-infested mind. When he decided to crash the shuttle, he accepted that he would die. Waking up was part of the plan.

Clem opened a swollen eye and blinked. His view of the world was reduced to a few square inches visible from one uncovered eye, framed by the frayed gauze bandages swaddling his head. Drifting in and out of consciousness, the young genius relived the events leading up to the crash, interrupted by flashes of the few moments of semi-lucidity that followed. Had he seen Terk staggering away from the wreckage, or it just been shadows and smoke?

Other voices brushed Clem's ear, hushed whispers, moans of pain, nightmare cries, and by these signs, he knew there were others in the room, injured as he was in body and spirit.

Silent healers moved between the cots, whispering in soft, pastel-colored voices, spreading soothing ointments that smelled of honey and tangy, tree-bark oils, their breath tinged by tinctures and the scents of their lives in the outside world. He began to identify them by their

CHAPTER FIFTY-TWO

scents as they moved around the room: warm linen, rosemary, bread, vanilla, each one unique.

As the cycle of days and nights drifted forward, Clem's sense of the presence of others in the room became less dense. Some left to go home with their families. More did not.

"We cannot save them all."

Sometimes Clem floated in a half-conscious space between waking and sleeping and imagined that he heard Terk speaking nearby.

"It was a terrible thing. So many injured. So many dead," the older boy's mimicked commiseration sounded false and flat.

It couldn't be Terk, he told himself. *Terk is dead. He died in the crash.* That was the whole reason behind his actions; Terk could not be allowed to take the shuttle to Taiba and sell it to a warlord, betraying Quinn and the Taiban rebels who had saved them from the warlord's hunters.

Clem pushed away the haunting image of the injured figure limping away from the wreckage. Terk was dead. Pain was just muddling things in his mind.

But something else had happened, Clem realized. Something that he had missed. He first noticed it in the snatches of conversation between the healers; there had been a fire and a riot, and Little Taiba had suffered badly. He tried to listen, but nothing was said about a crash or a Paxlosian shuttle. And then one day, he opened his good eye, and Terk's weasel face was leaning over him, filling Clem's narrow view.

The older boy's smile was a malicious rictus. "There you are, you old faker."

Terror flooded through Clem. Terk was alive, and he had found him. Clem tried to move on his cot or call out, but he was tied down, his mouth muffled by gauze.

I am completely at his mercy. Only Terk had no mercy. *Please, let me die. Please, please,"* Clem prayed to no god in particular. Clem would never tell anyone what he had done, but if there were an advantage in it for him, Terk would. *I need to disappear. I need to go somewhere that he can't find me.* Clem's mind flitted from impossibility to impossibility, but there was no escape.

E.F. Winters

"I can't stay now, but I'll be back." Terk vanished from the frame of Clem's vision.

He'll be back. He'll be back. Clem's mind continued to pound at the barriers of his helplessness. His injured body was a prison he could not escape. And then a new realization cut through the fog.

If Terk was indeed alive and not a hallucination, then he had been at the infirmary before, which meant that he had not been able to leave Ebulon.

I can still stop him, Clem realized. *I can still keep him from returning to Taiba. I have to live.*

Clemmet began to refuse the sedative tincture that Bread and Vanilla brought him to relieve his pain.

"You should at least have a little bit," Vanilla advised Clem the second time he refused his dose. "You're badly burned, and one of your hands is broken. It's really going to hurt without this." She had unwrapped his head enough to free his mouth to take the tincture, but it did not change his limited field of vision. He turned his head to bring the girl into view.

She was a wild waif, white hair bushing out from her head. She had the wide, flat face and the almond eyes of an Ebulonian with pale olive skin common to half Taibans.

"I'm Pem." Her eyes crinkled when she smiled. The dusting of freckles across her pert nose was only a shade off from the gold flecks in her hazel brown eyes. "Would you like me to get a piece of paper and a quill? Your family must be very worried."

A happy reunion with his family was a naive fantasy that Clem had dismissed weeks ago. Any notion of reuniting with his new, adoptive family had died with Terk's appearance. Terk was dangerous. Clem could not afford to have a family or connections the older boy could exploit. The couple that had adopted Clem would find another orphan, one more deserving of their compassion. Clemmet, the boy they had taken in, needed to stay dead.

"Can you tell me who your people are?" Vanilla Pem asked.

Clem closed his eyes and turned his head away.

"I'm sorry," she muttered, misunderstanding his reaction. "The fire took so much from us all." Tears brightened her golden eyes. "My brother Quinn died in the riot that night, too, and so many others."

CHAPTER FIFTY-TWO

Quinn? Clem re-examined the girl's features. She was lighter-skinned than Tai Bobalo's son, but there were similarities in her features. He tried to remember how many sisters Quinn had and if he had ever heard their names.

"I'm sorry." Pem wiped her eyes. "I shouldn't talk about my troubles." She stood. "If you change your mind or need anything, just ask for me."

"Well, there he is." Terk stood at the foot of Clem's bed. A slender bandage wrapped the top of his head, and his arm was in a sling, but aside from that, he seemed much like his old self--too much like his old self. Clem felt like a turtle trapped on its back, unable to flee its torturer.

"Do you know each other?" Pem looked from one boy to the other.

"We've met," Terk sidestepped.

"Do you know his people then?"

"No," Terk lied.

Pem offered her hand to Terk. "I'm Pemitai Bobalo."

"Callum Gorick." Terk took her hand, smiling like she was a sweet he'd like to unwrap and gobble down.

Clem tried to speak, but it came out as a faint groan with a bit of mumbling on either end.

Pem laughed. "All right. I'm going, I'm going. Excuse me, Callum, I need to fetch my impatient patient some soup." She hurried off to the kitchen.

"Well, aren't you the lucky devil?" Terk sat on the edge of Clem's bed. "You live through an accident, a fire that levels a city, and a riot that kills hundreds, and end up in a cushy bed with a pretty little Bobalo to nurse you back to life. There is no justice." Terk leaned in close to Clem's ear. "I know what you did." He sat back up. "I won't tell, of course, at least not now--unless you do something stupid. You keep my secrets, turd face, and I'll keep yours. Just like old times, right? Nod your head like a good boy to show that you understand."

Clem nodded.

Quinn Bobalo had been good, brave, and honest, and he was dead.

Terk was none of those things, and he was alive.

Terk was right; there was no justice. The world was broken.

Pem returned with a bowl of broth. She propped Clem up with pillows. "Let's see if we can get you started on the road to recovery, shall we?"

"I'll leave you to it." *I'm watching you,* Terk mouthed from behind Pem. He added a smile that made him look like a rabid rodent.

Clem accepted Pemitai's help, spoonful by spoonful, forcing himself to finish the soup. He needed to eat to get well. He needed to get well so that he could kill Terk.

E.F. Winters

CHAPTER FIFTY-THREE

"A teacher unwilling to be surpassed by her student teaches nothing worth knowing." (Hagriva Rhune, from A History of The Rhunes, compiled in the Third Age.)

Eropa followed the narrow path that ribboned through the green-gray moor-grass, following the cliff edge above the North Sea a few hundred feet from the tower that Hagriva and Eropa always used as a common room then paused, feeling the cold breath of the North Sea's mist on her cheeks, the strength of the harsh North wind pushing against her.

Within the white moon's quarter of Dupira Rhune's death, Hagriva had brought five-year-old Eropa to Alden Baierd. In keeping her word to Eropa's father she again invited the clans to send their most promising daughters to the old capitol for schooling as Rhunes. But there were concerns about the safety of young girls working under the tutelage of the legendary but aged Rhune without a younger, balancing influence present. What kind of magic was the Matriarch employing to remain alive for what for others experienced as multiple generations? And what would happen when she finally lost her battle with death and those powers were released?

A scant dozen families found a daughter, granddaughter, or niece to spare, families who already had Rhunes in their bloodline, or those who were blatantly ambitious.

Some of those who came had begged to be allowed to go. A greater number pleaded against what felt like exile from their lives.

Eropa thought about that brief time when she had been part of a school, a group of other girls. But she had never been like them. The youngest among them by far, she had known more about magic and less about life. They found her odd and said so. Whenever Hagriva introduced a new practice or concept, Eropa understood it and could apply it immediately. She did not know how to apply understanding

CHAPTER FIFTY-THREE

she could not grasp to making friends. Magic, she understood. People, she did not.

Eropa's fellow students came from major houses, minor houses, and families with no position or wealth. The Matriarch brusquely informed the girls that none of that mattered now; they were all equal. The girls, of course, knew better. Those born to wealth and privilege adjusted slowly the first year, continuing to lord their status over the other students. But Hagriva had a reputation for being a demanding teacher, and age had not increased her patience. By the end of the first year, any girl whose work was deemed "unsuitable" by the old Rhune's standards was sent home without justification.

In the second year, the hierarchy of wealth and family was finally replaced by a hierarchy of talent as the conceits of the outside world faded in light of the single-minded focus required to become a sorceress capable of altering the natural order and shifting the Balance.

When they left and the "school" closed, leaving Eropa and Hagriva alone Sometimes however, the desire to succeed outweighed ability, for not all things having to do with magic could be taught.

Blethann Bren'Harrow was the oldest of the second-year girls. She had arrived the first year certain of her own superiority and by her second year was obsessed with the future she imagined for herself as a great and storied Rhune who also represented a major clan.

Family and learned charm had obfuscated Blethann's shortcomings before Alden Baierd, masking deficiencies of character with delusion and denial. It was a common failure among those in her privileged world.

But Alden Baierd was not her world.

The Matriarch watched Blethann manipulate the other girls cognizant of Blethann's efforts to ingratiate herself with the Matriarch through gifts and compliments. Hagriva was a stone. She had taught generations of girls, guiding them to maturity as Rhunes. She watched Blethann and waited to see if the change to a deeper understanding would come.

Then one night, Blethann was missing at dinner. A search throughout the old castle and the caves below ensued. Blethann was found in a tower room, her green skin purpling, her tongue swollen and lolling out the side of her mouth, eyes rolled back in her head. Her heart did not beat so much as skipped, then rested. Hagriva shooed the girls out and worked through the night but whatever dark world Blethann's spirit had gone to, it could not find its way back.

The Bren'Harrows came, railing about Hagriva's unfitness to be given the care of young people, but there was no reversing what the girl had done. Fed by the Bren'Harrow's public blame, the other girls were quickly removed leaving Eropa the Matriarch's only remaining student. It was a relief.

Hagriva was far more attentive as a teacher than Eropa's own mother had been and Eropa was both an eager and singularly precocious learner. She went to Iredipa to visit her father when he asked her to, but she did not like being at court. The quiet life of Alden Baierd where the Balance was constantly supported by the weft of their daily lives was much more peaceful, and easier to understand.

Word soon spread that the Matriarch's last student was special. With the rise of the young Pira's star, Dupira Rhune's place in history faded to a footnote, and a new reason to visit the northern castle arose.

Whenever they visited, they shivered and complained about the northland's eternal twilight and misty, moisture laden air, bragging about how early their families had moved south to Iredipa, as if this somehow proved their line's superior intelligence.

Eropa did not agree.

Life in Iredipa was too easy; the same gentle breeze blowing off the Silver Sea, the same golden sunlight day after day. And it seemed to Eropa that an undemanding climate molded people who were self-indulgent to the point of indolence, while inclement weather, which required a person to work hard to survive, bred character. People needed to face nature's power to remind them that there were powers they had no control over, powers greater than themselves. A strong storm gave people something to pit themselves against, something to measure their strength by, to bond with others, and teach them the value of each day.

Earnestly explaining this theory to her teacher, Hagriva just shook her head.

"You have an active mind and a vivid imagination. It will be a challenge for you to learn the difference between what is real and what is your mind, playing."

CHAPTER FIFTY-THREE

"And what is the difference?" young Eropa asked, green eyes wide at the idea that these were two different things.

The old Rhune looked down at the tiny, piquant child, recognizing that her question was serious and deserved a serious answer.

"There is a feeling you get when what you are being told comes from outside yourself, but from the Source of wisdom that is The Truths. You will know it when you feel it and when you do, you must pay attention so that you remember the feeling so that you can never be fooled by your mind or someone else trying to trick you with lies.

The little girl's brows furrowed but she said. "I will watch for this feeling, mark it, and remember it, Mah-Rhune, so that I will not be fooled."

And yet you were fooled, the Rhune reminded herself in the present day. *You let anger and bitterness blind you, lost control—lost The Balance and took everything you know down a dark path that ended in the deaths of those closest to you.*

She sighed as she released that memory, returning her mind to her childhood. The curious and the concerned began coming to Alden Baierd spouting transparent excuses like they were asking for advice, or they were concerned now, the school was gone, the child-Pira would be lonely in her new isolation.

"Why do they come?" Eropa asked her teacher after a particularly annoying visit by a member of the McAlburn clan. "They did not have a girl at the school."

"Perhaps because they want to see this prodigy they hear so much about."

"Who is that?"

"You." Hagriva's chuckle sounded like an old hen clucking.

Eropa puckered her face up. "What use could 'seeing' me be?"

"Folk have peculiar notions, child, especially those at court. They believe that talking to others about seeing you makes them more important in other people's eyes. And of course, when they see you, you see them as well, and they harbor hopes that someday when you are older and take your place in Ebulon's governing, you will remember them from these visits and grant them some favor that gives them an advantage."

E.F. Winters

"I have heard them think that," Eropa admitted, glancing distastefully at the expensive doll the McAlburns brought her as a gift. "But it makes no sense. If I find them shallow and ridiculous now, why would I give them anything when I'm older and, one can assume, wiser?"

"They think you are like other children, naive and malleable."

"But I am not," the fledgling Rhune declared, without doubt.

"No, you are not," Hagriva agreed. "But being the Pira will not get you out of doing your chores. Go down to the old kitchen gardens and see if you can find any more of those little fingerling potatoes that we discovered last week".

Eropa had jumped up, grabbed a basket, and headed down to the garden, eager to please her teacher and equally pleased to get to dig in the dirt, hunting for growing things.

There was one visitor among those who sought the young Pira out whose visits did prove worthwhile. Lady Ner'ansett arrived with her children, ostensibly seeking guidance from Hagriva, and while the adults talked, the children played in the caves beneath the headland. The oldest boy's name was Frevin.

Seeing an advantage in the budding relationship between her son and the girl who would become Pira, Lady Ner'ansett began a pattern of visits, which had resulted in the friendship between the two children.

Eropa stood on the headland looking down at the waves, their crests frothing with seafoam, then listlessly began to retrace her steps back to the tower.

"I will be beside you, always," Frevin had promised even before his cheeks had fuzz on them. And he had meant it, then.

Eropa believed he had still meant it on the day the aliens arrived. But he had not said it since.

The boy who was once so eager to be recognized for something, had grown into a self-proud man who claimed to value Eropa's friendship but who had come to take her favor for granted, seeing in it a path, not to a deeper relationship, but to power.

Eropa compared Frevin's desires with Quinns and his declaration of love in his last moments of life. She had felt a deep kinship with Quinn Bobalo--even toying as a girl with a crush on the young Taiban with his thick, dark curls, broad smile, and sparkling almond-shaped

CHAPTER FIFTY-THREE

eyes. Quinn had always been open-hearted and generous, as committed as any storied hero, strong in both body and character. Frevin was none of those things. Cool, collected, arrogant and self-centered, their friendship had grown from her isolation and his proximity, but he never had a claim on her heart. As confused as Eropa was over this since the aliens' arrival, it was clear that Zeph Yare complicated everything.

There is no sense to my feelings for him, Eropa reminded herself, staunchly. *There is no soundness to it, and no future.* Whatever their relationships had been in other lives, in this life, they would not be together. Ally or enemy, had yet to be determined, but the alien must not be allowed to believe he could leverage her feelings into something she would regret. He and Dora would leave Ebulon and perhaps, over the years if he returned many years from now, she would see him again, but her life as a Rhune would have gone on just as Hagriva and her father and everyone else expected—nothing changed.

Except it had. Zeph Yare had lit a spark in her—the sliver of a flame that, alone amid the darkness of loneliness and responsibility was trying to burn back the howling gales of life lived as a political necessity.

And what will I do if my connection to magic does not return? she asked herself. *Without magic, I cannot be the Pira. And if I am not that, then who am I?* The constructs built around her since her mother's death were burned away the night of the fire, leaving her without purpose for the first time in her life.

The chill, crystalline air's seduction of the northern light on the cliff above the North Sea was a tenuous embrace, poignant promises whispering in the mist, while three hundred feet below, sibilant waves threw themselves against the cliff's foot with the reckless self-destruction of passion gone wrong.

How do people bear this emptiness and the longing? Aless Mc'Larick would have said that most people filled it with sex and sometimes love, but Eropa saw more problems there than solutions on that path.

A sorceress might fail the magic, but magic should not fail the sorceress. She turned her steps back toward the old ruins.

Nothing had been resolved.

E.F. Winters

Eropa climbed the puzzle of half-rotted stairs, feeling her body like a weight that bound her to her pain but when she lifted the iron latch on the heavy door a burst of warmth rushed at her from the fire in the stonework fireplace. The excitement that awakened inside her, eagerly greeting the fire's power made her feel nauseous, her skin itching as it took on a muddy glow.

"'Good walk?" Corin asked from beside the fire pretending to read.

"Yes. There's mist in your hair."

Corin felt her wind-brightened cheeks redden even more.

"You need not worry about me, Corin," Eropa teased. "There will not be sudden, unexpected dangers here. No one wants to come here anymore. They prefer to forget it exists."

"There's no sense tempting danger," Corin quipped. Of the three sparring partners, Eropa, Quinn, and herself, Corin knew herself to be the most cautious. She was the one who always waited and watched before making a strategic strike.

The round room at the top of the tower had open beams that burst from a center circle, like the spokes of a wheel where birds perched, their coos and chirps syncopating the rustle of feathers. Bundled herbs and dried flowers hung by their rooty ends above the painted red starburst fading on the thick hewn floorboards, the surface subtly undulated by the craftsman's tools. Wear-worn, only ghosts of the patterned colors remained. A spinning wheel, wool thread still attached to a spindle, sat on the far side of the room by the fire. A large black cast iron pot lay on its side near the hearth. Every article a piece of Eropa's secret life.

Though Hagriva had not deigned to make an appearance, Corin felt the Matriarch's presence everywhere. The birds that roosted in the rafters of the upstairs room they used as a common space, studied the young women with a suspiciously human interest. Feral cats whose path they crossed walking anywhere about the old, ruined castle stopped ratting to follow them, and Corin was sure she had seen one of the gargoyles atop a crenulated outer wall of abandoned fortress tracking their passing with its one good eye, its stone face having been half eaten away by weather and time.

"The Matriarch knows you're here, right?" Corin asked testily.

CHAPTER FIFTY-THREE

"She knows," Eropa confirmed, her usual quiet patience once again dominating all communications.

"And she knows what's happened?"

"Of course," Eropa agreed.

"Then why would she do this, Eropa?" Corin's brown eyes snapped. "Why would she treat you this way? I thought she was supposed to care about you."

"She does, in her own way," Eropa explained. "But Hagriva is not Aunt Timee. She was never a mother. She could not divide her attention enough. She has too many responsibilities for the beings of too many worlds."

"And their needs are all more important than yours?" Corin demanded.

"Yes," the Rhune replied. "If they were not, she would be here, Corin. I assure you."

But Corin could see that the Matriarch's continued silence had begun to feel like a rejection. She stood.

"I'll go see what I can find for us to eat in that mess you call a garden." The Taiban girl took her cloak from a hook before turning back at the door. "You're too hard on yourself, Eropa. None of us are who we were before all of this. We've all changed. How could we not? Okay, so you're not perfect, you lost control. Everyone makes mistakes."

"Not like that." Eropa shook her head. "I should have been better than that. I *am* better than that—or at least I thought I was, but the first time I'm faced with a challenge I lose, not only all control, but the ability to use magic or just act? What does that say about me, Corin?" She turned away, tears rolling down her cheeks. "I am not worthy of the trust that has been placed in me. I cannot do this."

"If you can't, then who will lead after Hagriva crosses over, Miratha? Whatever faults you may have, you're a damn sight better than Miratha Dum'Laiere. Aunt Timee says that our most important lessons don't come from the good times. We learn the hard truths from the bad times. I don't know what lesson you'll take from this, but it came at a high price. I hope you only have to learn it once." She left the Pira alone.

"I know you are here," Eropa reached out to her old teacher. *"Please speak to me. I need you. Something is wrong with me. My magic is gone, and I need to know how to get it back."* Eropa closed her eyes.

The birds stilled, the fire's flame softened. Enfolded in the warm silence, Eropa saw a shimmering thread of consciousness its visible end attached to the old spinning wheel in the corner. Strung across the room, it stretched out the door. Eropa reached out to touch it, but though it looked to her mind's eye like spider silk, it was not. She turned her wrist, wrapping the shining thread around her hand then rose, opened the door, and followed the thread down the decomposing steps. Corin was there at the bottom, holding the four ends of a piece of cloth sagging with a few handfuls of dirty root vegetables.

"You've found something." She set the cloth onto a stair and stepped in behind Eropa.

The thread led them into the hall of one of the many broken buildings of the once grand structure, archaic symbols narrating its great and glorious past in a language no one remembered.

They followed the thread to a stairwell, its stone rippled by ancient feet. They approached the entrance to an inner tower, the tallest remaining among the ruins. Climbing cautiously to the highest floor, they followed the thread to the right, passing through a gutted gallery onto a balcony that intersected a hallway where the outer wall had fallen away.

Corin looked over the side at the long drop below. A strong gust pushed her back.

"Stay close to the inner wall," Eropa warned.

They picked their way through the broken hallway, the wind stinging their cheeks, arriving finally at the shelter of an alcove on the far side. Intersections branched off to the right or straight ahead. Eropa followed the thread straight on coming out on a second parapet walk. From the high tower, below, the naked moor rose and fell in the fecund swells of a reclined woman, her swollen breasts and belly declaring her a mother.

What was left of the tower's walls was no more than a foot in height, and sometimes not even that. Eropa and Corin walked the length, holding to each other for ballast, harrowed at every step by the unfettered north wind. The parapet walkway ended in the dubious shelter of a partially walled alcove. The stairs inside brought the pair to a closed door.

Eropa tried the latch.

"Is it locked?" Corin whispered.

"Not by any man-made device." Eropa muttered something under her breath and made a sign with her hand.

The door swung open.

Hagriva lay on a bed, a glow lamp hovering above her.

"She's not…dead, is she?" Corin shuddered.

"No," Eropa assured her. "While her spirit walks other worlds, her body lies here in a state of suspension sustained by magic."

"And that's okay? I mean it's safe?"

Eropa nodded.

"She looks so old," Corin whispered.

"She should have crossed over from this life decades ago, but my mother died, and a successor had to be trained." Death had been the silent third in Eropa and Hagriva's relationship; one that Eropa had often been jealous of, knowing that someday it would take her teacher, always fearing that it would be too soon.

Eropa closed her eyes, murmuring in a language known only within the sisterhood.

"You are distracting me." Hagriva's voice spoke inside Eropa's mind. *"And I can ill afford it. There are things that must be done Eropa—things that I must do, while I still can."*

"Please, Mah Rhune. I need you."

"Go bother your grandmother, Adaya. She must answer your questions now," came the harsh reply.

"But something is broken inside me, and I need you to fix it!" Eropa wailed.

"Oh, so dramatic," the old woman chided her student. "Stop this indulgence, center yourself, and listen to what I am saying. I cannot give you this attention you ask for. It is not that I am unsympathetic, but I must focus on where I am and what I am doing right now. I have nothing to spare for you." The feel of her mental voice softened. "What you need is in the Hidling. Go to Adaya. She will know what is to be done. I have told her you are coming."

CHAPTER FIFTY-FOUR

"Beware the hand offering gold. Most men have two." (Anonymous
Taiban saying.)

Outside, the palace of Iredipa's security was finally seeing a
greater level of restriction, though it still did not approach the level
Zeph considered the norm for any leader's resident structure,
governmental or private business, on any of the planets he was
familiar with among the Thousand Worlds, and certainly far from the
kind of multi-level fortresses the wealthy lived in on Pax.

The Mir Padear Pranseas followed through on his promise to
Pliny and sent aid. Palace guards posted at entry points throughout the
palace perimeter were now supported by a temple monk who "read"
any wishing to enter.

Zeph felt only marginally safer with these pieces in place. As
soon as the Mahal's death was announced to the Council of Elder
Voices, the Mirs, Mithra, Malbuis, and Pliny, returned to their homes
to sleep, awaiting the expected summons from the Council. He found
himself feeling set adrift without their insights explanations. Though
he had only met the older Mirs because of their involvement with the
discovery of the attack on Nikodamus, he told himself that Pliny,
being appointed Zeph's liaison, would reappear soon.

He hoped it was true.

On the inside, the palace had become tomblike, silent, and
deserted, reminding Zeph of the deserted underground bomb shelters
he had explored among the ruins from the Rain of Death on Paxlosis
as a teenager. The uncertainty of the situation was too much for the
sheltered Ebulonians, and anyone who could have left court did.

Only the kitchens and housekeeping areas of the palace, the
corridors near the Elder's Library, and the clustered apartments kept
by the Voices and their staff still saw activity, pages hurrying between
clan representatives as each family strategized who to ally with and
who to oppose for the greatest gain.

CHAPTER FIFTY-FOUR

Knowing too little of the clan's histories, rivalries, and interwoven relationships to predict who would side with whom--and nothing about what any of that would mean for the treaty—or the structure of Ebulon's government, Zeph tried to note faces and listen to rumors, stashing them away for sharing with Pliny when he returned and could make sense of it all.

Zeph's lieutenant, Navrat Tila, remained troubled by his experience the night of the Mahal's murder. Fearful of Ebulonians, he was equally suspicious of his own motives, always questioning if someone was manipulating the thoughts and decisions of those around him, and on the first day after the attack, Pliny had arranged for a healer, Patisel Keesch, to attend him. Patisel was a middle-aged widow who dressed plainly, covering herself modestly, including her hair, which she wrapped in a full scarf. The Mir settled the woman into rooms beside the Paxlosian's suite and set her the task of minding him, hopefully coaxing the young man from his paranoia.

Understanding the inference that other people thought he needed help, when he didn't, and holding to the belief that he recognized a threat that they were blind to, Navrat refused to speak to his tender. Still, she showed up every day.

"If he won't talk to you, what do you do here all day?" Zeph asked the woman.

"I make tea, sweep the courtyard, cut flowers in the garden, and arrange them in the rooms. Sometimes I play music, or work in the gardens," Patisel replied calmly.

"And Navrat?"

"Watches."

Zeph's face screwed up into a quizzical mien. "How is that helpful?"

"We are creating a routine based on regularity, peace, and personal control. I arrive at the same time each day and do the same tasks in the same order. I ask nothing of him—not that he acknowledges my presence in the room nor speaks to me. I am simply here, sharing this space until I leave. Already, he shows signs of becoming accustomed to my being near and realizing that I pose no threat to him or his independence. His thoughts and decisions remain his own. No one is trying to change or influence them."

"And you hope this will do what?" Zeph asked.

E.F. Winters

"It will help Navrat Tila regain confidence in himself," Patisel explained. "There are signs of progress. Navrat has noticed when my watering urn is empty and fills it for me, though I have never asked him to do this. He does this only because he decides to, and it is in his nature to be helpful. He spends a good deal of time watching me work in the garden and seems quite interested in the progress of the plants. I expect that soon he will step up and begin to help more actively. There is a comfort in simple, peaceful, everyday tasks. Is there not, Captain Yare?" She did not seem to expect him to reply. "In time, he may confide in me, or he may not." Patisel shrugged her thin shoulders. "It is not important that I know what your friend has been through or what he is thinking, only that *he* does, and that he begins to overwrite the restrictive narrative he is playing in his head that defines himself as a powerless inhabitant of his own life. A return to balance will give Navrat Tila confidence, help him find his center, and regulate his thoughts and actions." Zeph nodded, thinking of his struggles after Eropa's abilities were revealed. Patisel cocked her head to one side, her cornflower blue eyes, a surprisingly vivid feature in a woman whose dress and appearance said she did not want to be noticed.

"I am sorry for your experience of this, Captain. The Keesch do not hold with the more aggressive Rhune practices," she suggested, with a quiet smile. "It is our belief that the inherent risks, both for the practitioner and for the ripple effects wrested on reality, outweigh the benefits. But then, our work is confined to our circles and our own world. So, perhaps it is unfair of us to judge."

"I was thinking too loudly again, eh?" said with a lopsided grin.

"You are learning." Patisel inclined her head, acknowledging the Paxlosian's efforts to change his habitual way of thinking and align himself more with Ebulonian etiquette.

"Navrat's struggle is not out of any weakness. He has good reason to question the events of that night, Patisel Keesch. I have questions about them myself."

Who was piloting the shuttlecraft when it crashed? Was it their intention to start the fire? So many questions. He caught the Keesch woman watching his face.

"Do you enjoy gardening, Captain Yare?" she asked.

CHAPTER FIFTY-FOUR

"It's not something people do where I'm from, but I appreciate the efforts of those who do." He indicated the lush gardens that framed the doorway leading from the apartment to the palace gardens.

"I have seen you out walking at twilight," the Keesch noted. "Perhaps this is *your* path to healing."

"I don't know. I do enjoy it, though," Zeph replied politely.

"I was surprised to see you here in your rooms today," she commented as she took up a nearby broom to begin sweeping the steps to the courtyard. They did not need sweeping, but it was part of the routine she had established, which Navrat had come to expect. "You are usually gathering with the Mirs and the Voices this far into the white moon's continuance."

"Not today," Zeph replied. "I imagine the council is playing catch-up about the events surrounding the Mahal's death."

"He lives in the Mother's embrace," Patisel muttered the blessing.

"Yes, he lives in the..." Zeph wanted to be respectful, but it felt strange repeating the words without believing in a great goddess mother who protected and nurtured all life. "Anyway, nothing's happening today," his voice fell off.

Patisel stopped sweeping. "Not true. The Elder's Council meets in the library as we speak."

Zeph opened his mouth to disagree, then stopped himself. The Keesch woman's certainty was unflappable. He spun like a tornado and stormed from the room.

As Zeph approached the great doors to the Elder's Library, two guards stepped in front of him, denying him access.

"I'm Zeph Yare, Captain of the U.F. starship, Lamdra." He tried to continue but was again barred entry. Zeph scowled. "What is this?"

"Our apologies, but we have been ordered not to allow you to enter while the Elder's Council is in session," one of the guards informed him.

Zeph became very still. "Ordered by whom?" he growled.

"The Voices of the Council of Elders," the man replied.

"Which one, specifically?" Zeph questioned him.

"Frevin Mir," the man answered.

"Frevin Mir is a minor diplomat. While I am the captain of a starship, making a treaty with your world. Do you think the Council of Elders wishes to offend me by excluding me from discussions about that treaty?"

"I do not know..."

One of the doors opened, and Frevin stepped out. His fine blond hair was brushed out, falling loosely about his shoulders, his gray robes were new and of a finer quality material, that floated above the floor as he moved. It was a calculated change, less clerkish and academic, more princely and leader-in-waiting.

"This is a council meeting of the Voices, Yare. You have no place here. You are not welcome." His nostrils flared, one side of his mouth curling in contempt.

The door opened a bit again, and Pliny slipped out, nervously hovering behind Frevin.

"Is the Pira in there?" The question sounded like the beginning of an interrogation, and Frevin's mouth puckered in contempt, but he did not answer.

"She is not," Pliny replied for him.

"And the Matriarch?" Zeph shot out.

"No."

"Why would you hold a meeting of this importance without one of them?" Zeph demanded. "What you all decide may not hold. The Council does not rule Ebulon, the Rhunes do," he stated, pointedly. "You see, I know that now, and you do too, and yet you're acting as if you don't. That seems either very foolish or very dangerous to me."

"The Rhunes are aware of recent events. If they feel it is important to be here, one of them will come," Frevin side-stepped the sorceress' absence.

"Eropa is grieving her father's murder," Zeph retorted.

Frevin inclined his head in agreement. "And needs time. The Council understands that. Nevertheless, the business of governing must go on. There is no time to sit back and wait. There are challenges to be faced, actions requiring decisions. We must decide what to do about the Taiban problem."

"The Taiban problem?" Zeph repeated, thinking it was not the Taibans who were the problem. "This is working out pretty well for you, isn't it, Frevin?" he said instead. "The experienced decision makers are all being killed, and here you are, only too happy to fill the gap." He leaned in, lowering his voice as if to impart a secret. "It

CHAPTER FIFTY-FOUR

seems that you and Miratha have more in common than you'd like to admit."

"Captain Yare…" Pliny stepped forward, placing a warning hand on Zeph's arm.

Zeph yanked it away.

Frevin's chin jutted up. "I am a loyal servant of my people."

"No one could think otherwise." Zeph's smile was entirely insincere. "Unless they knew about your late-night visit to Miratha Dum'Laiere after that last talk Nikodamus and I had, or this new relationship you have with her daughter, Dora. You're playing both sides to make sure you get what you want, no matter who wins this political battle."

Frevin barely flinched, but he flinched. "No one questions my motivations," he said, a little too loudly.

"But they should." Zeph's gray eyes blazed, but Frevin's glittered with a hard, steely malice.

"Without your starship, Yare, you are nothing," the Mir volleyed back. "Not a captain, not an ally, and certainly not a threat. How will you live when the council realizes the Lamdra is not coming back, and have you thrown out of the palace?"

Zeph's fists clenched and unclenched. Imagining strangling Frevin.

"Captain Yare…" Zeph took the warning from Pliny and relaxed his hands, resisting the urge.

"It will be back," he declared between clenched teeth. The space between the two rivals pulsed with barely constrained anger. "They. Will. Come. Back," he formed each word with deliberate care.

"For your sake, I hope so," Frevin's voice dripped with insincerity. "I think you will find life on a foreign world without status, family, or means…difficult." His robes whirled dramatically as he spun and re-entered the library, shutting the door loudly behind him.

"He acts like he's already the new Mahal," Zeph growled.

"The Council considers him uniquely qualified for the position," Pliny shared. "Believing, as the common people do, that he was close to not only Eropa, but to the Mahal and knew Nikodamus's heart and mind."

"But it's a lie!" Zeph shouted.

Pliny cringed, glancing at the doors to see if the outburst would bring anyone else out of the council meeting. It did not, and he took Zeph's arm guiding him away down the corridor.

"He's a pretender. He wasn't party to Nikodamus and my discussions, and he saw only one page of the treaty. Frevin Mir isn't thinking about how to resolve Ebulon's problems. He's thinking about how to get the clans to support him in the next election for the new Mahal. These people read minds. Why can't they see that he's lying?"

"Calm down, Captain Yare." Pliny lowered his voice to a whisper. "You are being watched, your actions reported. What you are saying could be construed as a threat against Frevin Mir and puts you in danger. People believe that those around them speak the truth," he continued in a more audible tone. "Lying is rare among our people. It would not occur to most that someone might be lying--unless that person had already proven untrustworthy." They exited the corridor, entering Zeph's suite. Pliny paused as he closed the windows and doors to the courtyard.

"The council is convinced that because of his relationship with the Pira, Frevin was privy to the Mahal's thoughts and plans."

"Only because he's lied to give them that impression." Zeph flopped down onto the overstuffed sofa like a sulky juvenile.

"And who knows more? You?" Pliny put on a mock-shocked expression. "They are not going to take your word over Frevin's. He is one of them: a Neran'sett, a member of the same clan as Mithra, and an elected Voice, and you are an outsider: an alien whom they still fear would like to invade their world.

"Eropa's mother chose an unknown Mir from an unimportant family as her partner. He was elected as Mahal, and he guided us wisely and graciously for twenty-some years. It turned out that he was not only a good man, but a good leader, probably because of the same qualities that drew a Rhune to choose him in the first place. Now he is gone, and our world is in turmoil. We've had rioting, a community burned and turned on itself, all within weeks of being threatened and nearly invaded by an alien power."

"That possibility is not off the table yet," Zeph quipped.

CHAPTER FIFTY-FOUR

"It is as long as you do not have a starship," Pliny flashed, glaring at Zeph. Zeph had never seen the Mir show such a temper.

"I didn't mean it." He looked contrite.

"Then you should not say it," Pliny warned, his feathers still ruffled.

"I am sorry, Pliny."

"There are pieces of this that you do not understand, Zeph. There have been factions whispering about wanting out from under Rhune rule for decades, but it was only after you arrived with your starship that their dream seemed imminently possible. Miratha was recognized as Hagriva's descendant while the Matriarch herself is generally expected to die any day now. Nikodamus Mir barely survived a Baraq Ta, then the clans hired and trained personal armies, though they called them guards. Those factions are no longer whispering," Pliny indicated by nuance that this was significant. "And the people are terrified. It is only natural that they would look for someone like they had before." Pliny paused. "We need a new Mahal."

"But not him," Zeph remained adamant.

The young Mir diplomat rubbed the back of his neck with one hand. "I have enjoyed being liaison to you, but please, Captain Yare, do not put me in a position where I would have to betray my people to take your part, because I will not."

"No. I would not want that," Zeph conceded.

"Then stop baiting Frevin," Pliny said. "If he wins this, and he very well might, you must be able to set aside your pride and work with him."

"He betrayed Nikodamus to Miratha. Fratianne heard him," Zeph reminded the Mir.

Pliny shook his head. "The treaty is no longer important because you are no longer important." Zeph's expression darkened, and Pliny plowed on. "Frevin is right on this; you have no ship, no men, and therefore no power. Without your starship, you cannot return to your own world."

"You think I haven't thought about that?" Zeph demanded. "I have."

"There are only two people for whom this treaty remains important: you and Miratha, and then only if Dora is the treaty bride. In this, you and she are still allies." Zeph groaned, but Pliny did not stop. "As long as Frevin continues to have hope that Eropa will accept him as her life partner, it is in his interest for the structure of our government to remain as it is: Eropa retains her place in line for the Matriarchy, and the most likely scenario is that he becomes Mahal."

"Why doesn't she just say it, so everyone knows the truth?" Zeph demanded.

"It is not the Pira's place to speak for or against a candidate. It would be seen as an interference with the people's free choice," Pliny disagreed. "And the moment she makes it clear to Frevin that she will not choose him, he will throw everything he has behind those who wish to end Rhune rule."

"She won't choose him," Zeph muttered.

Pliny raised an eyebrow. "You know this, or you only wish it?"

Zeph glanced sideways at the Mir. "I thought it was impolite to read someone's mind without permission," he grumbled.

"I do not need to invade your privacy to see that you have feelings for the Pira, but you must realize, treaty or no treaty, you and she will not walk the same path. Whatever his reasoning, Nikodamus' plan regarding his daughter and you died with him, but whether Ebulon's political charter is rewritten or not, will make little difference to Eropa. She will still be who she is: a Rhune, and she will continue to do her work, while you, my alien friend, will either be on your way back to your world with Dora or struggling to live as a refugee without position or power, or a way to sustain your needs."

"I can always rent out my services as a mercenary," Zeph joked.

"Trotted out to be put on display as an oddity at parties by some wealthy house?" Pliny shook his head. "I cannot see you accepting such a life."

Zeph grimaced. "You paint an unappealing picture."

"The Ballatyns are an old family. I know how things work here," Pliny retorted.

Zeph rubbed a hand through his sandy hair. "You're right. I wouldn't want that life. I'd rather disappear and live like a hermit in the forest, and fish and hunt for my supper."

"There are many ways to disappear on Ebulon," Pliny agreed. "But someone will always find you."

Zeph wondered if Eropa would be one of those who looked for him. Would she want to visit him in his forest hideout? She might prefer a small, humble cottage to palace life, but on examination, the emotions the fantasy brought up were still tinged with the doubts that continued to trouble him, and pining over something so uncertain not only made him look weak, but it wasn't fair to Eropa, who did not share his feelings.

Pliny brought him back, "You should consider moving out of the palace. You are too vulnerable here, and you have no allies. It is not safe. Of course, you are welcome to stay with me," he offered. "Malbuis and Mithra have also offered their home."

Zeph nodded. "Thank you. And please, thank them for me. I'll consider it." But inside, he was seething. *I need my damned ship.*

E.F. Winters

CHAPTER FIFTY-FIVE

"They will hunt us to our last breath. If we must die, let us die fighting as Free Men." (Warin Strongarm; called the "First Warin;" his son being the "Second Warin".)

Eropa and Corin took the windcraft that brought them to Alden Baierd south then east to the village at the crossroads. With a main street of thatched-roof houses and kitchen gardens cross-hatched by a dozen side streets of the same, a person could start in a field at one edge of the village and walk to a field on the far side in little more than a mile. The population had shrunk substantially since the capital moved taking with it merchants, tradesmen, and clan members living at or visiting Alden Baierd.

Before the capital moved south, the northern reaches were secure, providing the needs of travelers great and small. Those who were tied to the land remained, adapting to a less affluent lifestyle. Those who were truly Northern born had no interest in living anywhere else.

While the dwellings surrounding Alden Baierd were gradually dismantled, scavenged for building material for walls, pathways and courtyards, the village simply repurposed existing structures. A merchant's mansion became an inn. The old inn became a Keesch wayfarer's healing station. A large milking shed, no longer needed for the many cows required to produce large cheese rounds for the court, became the new guild hall.

The villagers living at the Crossroads had been casual observers of the young Pira Eropa's childhood, marking changes in her height and character whenever she came to purchase supplies not produced at the old castle. She had gone to Iredipa a year now and old-timers smiled and nodded at the young Rhune they considered one of their own, absent of the fear and mistrust she experienced in those who lived further south.

Eropa led Corin to the stable yard first.

CHAPTER FIFTY-FIVE

"Choose a few horses that look sturdy and intelligent," Eropa suggested. "Check them for soundness, body, and temperament, then try out the best and see if they handle well and you are compatible."

Corin's eyebrows knitted. "I've always just ridden whatever the stable boys brought me when we rode out together."

"Then you probably have an idea what you like and what you don't. Think of it as choosing a companion for the adventure ahead. Strong character and stamina are more important than a fine gait and a pretty neck."

Looking over the horses in the stable yard herself, the Rhune settled on a tall, sturdily built sorrel of no particular beauty, but with a kind face and intelligent eyes.

"His previous owner was a physician-Mir, My Lady," the stable owner made his pitch. "But when he arrived in the village, he himself was ill. Unfortunately, he died at the inn, leaving his bills unpaid. The gelding was sold to me by the innkeeper to recoup the cost of the Mir's room and care. I do not have the gift myself, but I was assured that the animal would respond to thought speech as readily as neck reining, or leg commands. He should be steady on both road and trail."

Eropa stroked the red gelding's neck, directing her thoughts to the animal. *"Can you hear me? What should I call you?"*

The horse jerked up and nickered, as if startled from a nap, then turned its big head and examined the petite woman beside him.

"The Mir calls me 'Ready Brother'," he answered.

"I am bound for the Hidling, Ready Brother. Will you carry me there?"

The animal eyed the hardened sap grip of the Glister Sword poking up from behind the woman's back.

"I must wait for the Mir. He will expect to find me here when he returns." The animal's agitation could be seen in the tensing of his muscles, the shifting of his eyes, and his quick, short breath. *"He has been gone a long time, but he will return for me, and I must be here when he does."*

"No one told you?" Eropa continued to stroke the long-legged horse with smooth, unhurried strokes. *"Your friend was sick. He did not get well. I am sorry. His heart beats no longer."*

E.F. Winters

Ready Brother's head sank low, his long neck stretched down. *"So that is why he did not return. I had begun to think I had done something wrong."*

"The fault was not yours; it was only his own frail body that kept him from returning."

The big, red gelding looked around at the stable yard, his dark eyes clouded by sadness. *"Then I am alone here."*

"Someone who needs a good horse will come along," Eropa assured him. *"They may buy you to pull a farm cart or ride you out to take care of their business."* Eropa prepared to move on.

"You asked me if I would take you to the Hidling," the gelding stopped her. *"I would."*

"You are not afraid to tread the deep wood?" Eropa asked.

The gelding glanced again at the Glister Sword. *"It is a perilous place. The Mir's travels took us to its edge more than once, but I was his companion for many seasons. I have no wish to return to being merely a beast of burden."*

"I am in need of a strong and faithful companion." Eropa took his face between her hands and looked him in the eyes. *"A steady friend, whom I can rely on."*

"I have been all of those things," the red horse said, proudly. *"And could be again."*

Eropa blew gently into the gelding's nostrils, leaning her head against his, forehead to forehead. "I will ride this one out," she told the stable owner. "And if we suit each other, I will buy his freedom. You say the Mir who owned him traveled in the area a good deal, do you have his original tack?"

"It was old and of poor quality, my lady," the stableman made a face. "But I have a fine selection you may choose from. Something bright perhaps, to match my lady's position and fine taste?"

"Something simple with no metal," Eropa countered. "We are bound for the Hidling."

The man's face fell. "Very simple then. I will look around. It is possible some parts of the old Mir's equipment were tossed into a corner. It was quite worn and weather-beaten." He walked to the back of the room where tack was displayed and began to dig through a barrel. "But I will not have two such bridles. Is the other lady continuing on with you?"

CHAPTER FIFTY-FIVE

"The plainest two that you have will do," Eropa assured him.

The man's eyes wandered to the beautiful workmanship of more expensive saddles and bridles that the Rhune could easily afford.

Eropa followed his gaze. "The Hidling," she reminded him. "I am not ignorant of the old ways, and I do not wish to offend and get off on the wrong foot." This far north, she did not have to argue that none of the ancient folk still lived to be offended. Here, the stories of sightings of the Ancient Ones were not so old.

Digging through old bits, halters, bridles, girth straps, and buckles, the stable owner fished out a simple, braided leather hackamore. Eropa found a second bridle hanging on the wall that had very little metal on it, and they turned to the question of saddles without buckles or grommets. Finding two wool felt pads with leather stitched on top and woven belly straps, the stableman took one to Corin who was narrowing down her choices while Eropa saddled and bridled the red gelding.

Climbing up onto the animal's back, she leaned down to one side and patted his thick, muscled neck. *"Ready Brother?"* The long-legged gelding settled in, dropping his head as if familiarity had reawakened his confidence. Eropa walked him around the paddock, assuring herself that horse and rider had an agreed-upon method of guidance, then indicated to the stable owner that he should open the gate. A quick walk through the village, testing the gelding's reactions to any startling noises or unexpected movements in the village, and Eropa guided the horse into an open meadow.

"Would you like to stretch your legs?"

An active trot through the fields was followed by a full gallop along the road and Eropa decided that Ready Brother had earned his name. He might be a bit out of shape from lack of exercise but that would be remedied by the days ahead. He was strong and sound.

"As I said, Pira, he is not the most handsome beast," the man apologized. "The Judge has a long-legged mare he purchased for his daughter he would be happy to sell to you. She is a beautiful animal, and I am sure she would meet with your approval."

Eropa swung her leg over and slipped down the horse's side. Her head barely matched the horse's withers. Warmed up and slick to the touch, Ready Brother's earthy scent spoke of easy days under open skies, reliability, and contentment; emotions Eropa had not felt in some time.

"This red giant will do."

The big horse's head came around and he nuzzled her shoulder, nickering softly.

"Trust comes quick with mind-speech," the stableman commented.

"If both parties are trustworthy," Eropa added. "Ill intent just as quickly becomes a liability."

"You're traveling companion is trying out a bay in the far pen." He directed Eropa to where Corin had chosen a spirited mare.

"If she likes that one, we will take them both." Eropa smiled. It was good to be among folk who weren't trying to manipulate her into anything more than buying their good wares.

They were walking back to the stable owner's office to finalize the sale when the man turned their conversation toward serious concerns.

"I beg your pardon, my lady, we do not hear much about goings on out in the world these days, but we have heard some disturbing rumors from the capital."

"Rumors from the capital are always disturbing," Eropa countered. "If they were not, no one would repeat them."

"Is it true that aliens have come to Ebulon to make us all slaves?" the man asked.

"It is true that they have come," Eropa confirmed. "But they will not make us slaves. The Rhunes will not let that happen. You know that."

"No, of course not." The man glanced at the Glister Sword on her back. "It is just that, well, we have no means to defend ourselves, and the Matriarch is seen very seldom these days."

"Of course. I remember an exhibit at the summer fairs when I was younger--a collection of weapons from the old times. It was a local collection, I think."

The man nodded. "The pieces are borrowed for the fair from Mc'Larick's."

"Are any of the weapons still useable?"

The man looked uncertain. "Might be some are. A Glister Sword has no issue with time, but metals are not so forgiving."

CHAPTER FIFTY-FIVE

"And are there craftsmen who study the ways and teach the skills?"

The man shook his head. "A few have the knowledge, Pira, but they are quite old."

"I will contact the Tye-aire Temple Mirs and ask them to send someone to you. Can you house and feed them?" The man nodded, but now he was frowning. "Perhaps you could encourage local bowyers and metal smiths to brush up on their skills and take on a few apprentices? Send word to Pliny Mir at the palace and he will take care of the fees and materials. The old arts are both beautiful and useful and it is important that they not be lost." She turned and looked at the stableman. "Do you understand me, Master Stableman?"

"I think I do, but I cannot say you have eased my mind."

Eropa sighed. "I would if I could, but there is no sense in pretending something that is not true."

"Do you think it will come to that, Pira?"

"Even a Rhune does not understand all the small choices that affect how the future is molded," Eropa replied cryptically.

"Even a Rhune who remembers a hundred lives?"

"Even she. But there is one thing such memories do make clear and that is that it is better to be prepared for something that does not happen than to be unprepared for something that does. I will have materials sent to the village." Eropa took up the big horse's reins and climbed onto its back. "I count on you to share what we have said without embellishment that might frighten your neighbors."

"It would take little enough to do that," he declared.

"Even so, a man of character does not seek self-aggrandizement at the cost of others' wellbeing. I trust that you are that man. Word your explanation carefully."

"'Ask no idle questions of a Rhune'," he muttered. "My old mam warned me."

"Be careful, my friend. The times become more dangerous."

"I will," the man promised. "And I will get our people ready, Pira, but what of herself there at Alden Baierd? Should we plan on protecting Mah-Rhune as well?"

Eropa's eyes tracked north. "Hagriva would not want you to waste effort on her behalf. Her days of needing earthly protection are nearing

E.F. Winters

an end. When she leaves this physical body, it will be a time of her own choosing."

"A sad day for us all. We look forward to your return to us here in the north," the stableman honored her with a subtle obeisance.

Eropa and Corin spent a few more hours in the village buying light provisions and with no more than bedrolls for comfort, they packed their saddlebags and Glister Swords and headed southeast down the old road.

The Hidling nourished a billion lives and a million beating hearts within its borders.

Before the clans, before the Rhunes, before sentient beings of human design evolved with all of their concerns about walls and boundaries and what belonged to whom, and who might take it, the Spinney, the Bract, the Bosk and the Voy tended the forestlands.

Born of the ancient forest's Standing Ones and their smaller, more fragile relatives, the ephemeral spirits of Ebulon's early races emerged, each species true to its biological source. At first, they had little substance, their bodies too delicate to see except from a certain angle in a particular light, and their forays away from the protective shells of their botanical hosts were brief. Playful and creative, these early ancestors began to don mosses, leaves, and vining flowers to decorate their translucent forms, beginning an evolution. As their spirits became braver, their fragile bodies became more solid and resilient, and their movements about the forest widened. Retaining traits of their original floral heritage, the various species might be slender, like trees, or boxy, like stumps and stones, their bodies becoming less transparent and denser. Hands and feet tended to reflect their root-like origins, covered with tiny root-hairs. Skeletal coverings diversifying from the soft, pliable coverings akin to skin and colored in some variant shade of new grass of the Bract and the Spinney, to coverings with the stronger texture of the Voy with a thickness, bearing a closer resemblance to bark or a burnished hide that looked quite like stone. The most fragile of these original inhabitants once coalesced into something more than spirit but less than flesh, became

CHAPTER FIFTY-FIVE

caretakers of the forest lands, nourishing the living heart of the Hidling.

A hundred generations further into the planet's history, a webwork of treetop cities with pathways between wove through the arboreal canopy of Heblon. A hundred more and a social strata unfolded dividing those who kept the gift of "sight" from those evolution had rendered "blind."

As centuries passed, the division of the original species widened, becoming two parallel civilizations; one keeping to the hidden tracts of the forests, the other taking up mastery of the meadows and bluffs where castle keeps could be built and defended. In their efforts to keep what they had and take what they wanted, border folk began crafting weapons and practicing the martial skills to wield them.

The forest folk were easy prey. Within half a span of their long-lived generations, most of the Bract and the Bosk either yielded to the might of the castle-bound border lords descended from the Spinney and the Voy or disappeared into the deep heart of the Hidling, relegated to myth.

It was here, in the deep shade of the ancient forest, that Adaya Rhune retreated when she turned her back on Rhune magic.

"The Rhune way is not 'our' way," she insisted passionately to her friend and teacher, Hagriva. "Rhune magic is not Hebelon's natural magic. It is an import from other worlds."

"The Truths belong to all worlds," Hagriva repeated a common Rhune saying.

"No. There is a difference in the magic," Adaya insisted. "And it is a profound difference."

"You sound like a Keesch." Her teacher's lip curled.

Adaya shrugged. "There is much to be said for the Keesch point of view. It is impossible to maintain the Balance if you indulge in this type of magic. It creates an imbalance in and of itself."

"This is not about magic, it is about that muscle-bound woodsman," the aging sorceress accused her friend.

"Do not blame Auger. This is my decision," Adaya defended the simple, honest man.

"So, bed him and get it done with. Spend a decade having babies and running barefoot in the forest. The magic will still be here when you have grown bored. You will always have a place among us. There is no need for you to run away from what you have worked so hard to become so you can experience love and motherhood, Adaya. This big pronouncement of refusal is unnecessary.

Adaya remained firm. "Auger and I will build our home and raise our family in the deep wood."

Hagriva refused to concede the loss of her student. "You have a duty to the sisterhood. As a Rhune, there are actions you are tasked with for keeping the Balance, Adaya."

"And I will do that; from the Hidling," Adaya's determination matched the Matriarch's stubbornness.

"What you seek in the old forests is no more, my friend," Hagriva warned. "The Bract and the Bosk and all their cousins are gone, and they took their magic with them, but the Truths are eternal. They hold the kernel of what the forest folk believed."

Adaya's eyes took on a faraway look, seeing something beyond Hagriva. "Perhaps, or maybe what I seek is not magic at all. Something in the deep wood is calling me, Hagriva, and I must answer. Perhaps what you think was lost is not yet entirely forgotten and can still be saved."

"I hope that is true," Hagriva released Adaya, with an aching heart.

Corin was not a talkative companion, which suited Eropa.

The first night, they set up camp within sight of the road and while Corin made a meager meal, Eropa fed and rubbed down the horses. After dinner she gathered reeds from the edge of a creek bed area and began to weave bridles to replace what they had purchased. When she was finished, she presented it to the red gelding who nosed the grass braid.

"I do not need this," he told her indignantly.

"I understand that, and I mean no offense, but riding without any means of visible control could be noticed. It would be best if we passed without drawing attention to ourselves. I ask you to wear it as a favor to me, Brother."

"For you then, Pira."

The gelding returned to nibbling grass.

CHAPTER FIFTY-FIVE

Eropa sat by the fire, her eyes searching the sky.

She felt Corin studying her. Her friend continued to stay close as they traveled, remaining watchful, but not intruding.

"Are you feeling any better?" Corin asked.

"What I feel is a great, dull nothing; like I have been cut off from life. Living like this is like being half alive." Eropa stared into the campfire.

"Perhaps it is a kind of blessing. To feel all the pain right now might shatter us," Corin declared. "Numbness is nature's way of buffering our grief. Bearable fragments of memory popup then burst, like a bubble. The sweetness of those memories somehow cushions the harsh finality of loss. I think if they were to come upon me all at once I might drown in it and drowning in sorrow is not an option for a Bobalo, or for the Pira."

"Am I still the Pira? How can I be without magic?"

"Power is not all that gives you value, Eropa. The adults in your life have a lot to answer for in how they raised you, if that is what you believe." Corin set out her bedroll and curled up in it.

On the third day out, black smoke rose over the trees to the southwest of the road.

"Maybe a farmer is burning debris or an old building," Corin suggested without confidence.

"Maybe, but I think we should camp farther off the road tonight," Eropa announced.

The next day, smoldering farmsteads blotched the rolling hills the road passed through. The countryside stank of bitter smoke and dead meat. Corin's mare and Ready Brother traveled on high alert, their ears forward, their heads continuously moving from side to side, wary of any source of danger.

"We are not alone on the road," Ready Brother warned Eropa well before either of the humans became aware that other travelers approached. Eropa pulled her companions off into a grove of trees to the side of the road and waited.

A band of Taibans came sauntering along, their noise and boisterousness declaring they had no fear of encountering anyone.

One drove a farm wagon pulled by a pair of draft horses loaded with the only items of value farms might have food or a string of livestock tied to the back of the wagon plodded along, grabbing a mouthful of greenery when they could. The marauders passed a jug of ale around between them.

"These dirt lovers are easy pickins," one bragged as they drew closer to where Eropa and her friends hid. "Keep at this for a few months, then find us a nice steading to hold up in for the winter and we could live like wealthy men till spring. Then we could start all over again. Those first few didn't seem to mind helping us out. Kind of generous they was."

"It's easy now because they aren't expecting trouble, but it won't stay that way," his ginger-haired companion advised. "Word will get out. They'll weapon up, and they'll be looking for us."

"They won't," the first man argued. "They're Ebulonians. They won't do anything."

"You shouldn't have killed that farmer by the river, Polson," the man walking beside the ginger admonished the first man. "Folk don't take well to killing."

"He came at me with a pitchfork," Polson protested.

"He was a farmer," the other man objected. "What was he going to do, stab you with it?"

"Yeah, he was gonna stab me."

"I'd have tried to stab you, too, if you was doing my wife right in front of me," the ginger muttered.

"Then maybe he should have turned around and not watched." Polson laughed. "I never had me a green-skinned woman before. Disappointing. 'Might as well have been putting my stick into a bag. It was like there was nothing there."

"Like doing a dead woman," the ginger's friend grunted.

"I didn't do no dead woman," Polson protested. "She was alive when I was doing her."

"I said 'like' a dead woman, not she 'was' a dead woman." The man glanced at the others to gauge whether they would stand up for him or let Polson have at him. The man driving the wagon spoke up.

"Shut up, the lot of you. What's done is done, and it can't be undone by words or wishes. We got what we needed, and we're moving on. Best not to make a habit of raping and killing though. The deeper they hate us, the harder they'll hunt us."

"I never did no dead woman." Polson kicked a stone in the road.

Eropa's skin was glowing, not the spring green and bright gold of natural magic but the muddy red brown that had pulsated through her on the night of the riots and fire in Little Taiba.

"Just let them pass, Eropa," Corin whispered. "There's nothing we can do for the farmer's family now."

Eropa drew the Glister Sword from her back and kicked up Ready Brother.

"Dammit!" Corin urged her own mount forward, a beat behind.

Bursting from the trees, the Rhune bore down on the Taiban ruffians.

The battle-hardened men were too experienced in guerrilla warfare to be fully taken by surprise, but at the moment they realized that two riders were bearing down on them fast, they also realized that the riders were women and dismissed them as any threat.

It was a costly mistake.

The dark connection within Eropa was ripped wide by the men's callous abuse. Sword and body glowing like a dark demon, the Rhune fell on her victims.

On her first pass, she sliced through the neck of the scrawny Taiban in the back of the wagon who was fool enough to stand up. Rough hands reached up to pull her from Ready Brother and she went with the motion, tumbling off the horse, landing on her feet. Squatting in a battle-ready crouch, she faced the mercenaries.

The nearest man was dead before he blinked.

Corin leaped off her mount and positioned herself at Eropa's right. A moment of grief rushing her as she thought of her cousin, Quinn, who would have closed the circle.

Eropa gave herself to the maelstrom inside her, violence feeding violence. There was no fire, or larger battle, to feed on, but dealing death was enough.

"*The dance of life is a tiptoe along the edge of death's blade. One misstep, and everything changes,*" Bobalo had often quoted to his students the old Tye-Aire temple wisdom of the monk Mirs. If either Corin or Eropa made a mistake now, both would die miserable, violent deaths.

Corin's Glister Sword did not glow with inhuman power, but she was a well-taught warrior. The ginger did not try to fight for his life, sacrificing himself to the inevitable. Corin followed up by taking out the wagon driver, followed by the ginger's friend.

The only man left was Polson.

"Mercy, have mercy," the pimple-faced young man whimpered, squatting beneath the wagon's front wheels in a puddle of urine. "We were hungry. We needed food."

Eropa, looking like a vengeful goddess, stalked toward him.

"And they needed their lives."

"Please, don't hurt me!"

Eropa pointed her hands at him, fingers spread wide. "I am not going to touch you," she sneered. The dark energy beneath her skin pulsated with her heartbeat, pound, pound, pound.

Polson's eyes bulged like a puffer fish, the veins in his temples welting to the skin's surface. He burst apart and the pieces fell into the dirt.

Corin stood, breathing hard and fast. The stock animals tied to the back of the wagon were huddled together, but the sun still shone, the birds still sang, and a breeze blew the stench of the dead men's final evacuations away.

Everything was as it had been before; except for the dead men littering the road.

Eropa staggered to Ready Brother and pulled herself onto the horse's back. Walking him around the back of the wagon, she cut the rope holding the livestock, doing the same for the draft horses harnessed in front.

"We're done here." She turned Ready Brother back onto the road.

It was miles before Corin broke the silence, her brow furrowed, her face troubled.

"They must have come out of Iredipa."

"Or one of the clan estates. Frevin said they've traced the roots of the riot to a Taiban named Murtevoy."

"Saldo Murtevoy; the chicken-livered traitor," Corin cursed. "There'll be others like these, and there's no one out here in the countryside to stop them. Whatever we've come here to do, Eropa, we need to do it and get back to Iredipa before everything is torn apart."

CHAPTER FIFTY-FIVE

They rode on, the silence of introspection turning into cautious listening.

By evening they turned off the main road and onto a narrow path heading toward the menacing shadow of trees that marked the boundary of the Hidling.

E.F. Winters

CHAPTER FIFTY-SIX

"The path of Truth is radical, not common. Therefore, traveler, do not pack common comforts for an uncommon journey." (Anonymous from the Book of the Rhunes compiled in the First Age.)

Piercing the bellies of the clouds, the treetops of the Hidling stole rain like a cutpurse takes a rich man's wallet, funereal moss draping its lower branches like ghostly sackcloth, branches that had not seen sunlight since before the first Rhune came to Ebulon.

Dew dripped slowly from the upper canopy to the thick, undisturbed decay of the forest floor. The travelers' breathing became soft, hushed, their faces caressed when air, rippled by iridescent wings fluttering among the fiddlehead ferns, moved.

Paired amber eyes blinked at the strangers passing, then vanished with a flourish of a ringed tail.

Beneath the Hidling's ancient trees, a twilight gray held sway. The rustle of a bird's wings was a rarity at the foot of the tree-giants, the winged ones preferring to perch in the sunlit canopy hundreds of feet above.

But if the primeval life of the forest had retained its storied sentience, it had not retained any affection for humankind.

"Turn back," a voiceless warning breathed from the gloom. *"Leave this place."* And still they directed their feet forward, foreboding squeezing their hearts, whispering fears plucked from human nightmares.

"Tell me again why we came here?" Corin's voice sounded like a gong in the vast quiet.

"To see my grandparents," Eropa replied softly.

"And they live *here*?" Corin looked genuinely puzzled. "Why?"

"For my grandmother's work. And no, it does not get better further in. Stay alert for me, Ready Brother," Eropa whispered to her stoic mount. "I need your eyes and ears now more than ever."

The red gelding fluttered his lips, head high, ears forward.

CHAPTER FIFTY-SIX

Corin's mount pranced, shying nervously at every movement and shadow, her hindquarters tucked and ready to bolt.

"Steady, girl." Corin trilled softly to the frightened animal.

Despite Eropa's warning that the mare's nerve could desert her if things became difficult, Corin advocated for the animal's purchase, arguing that the bond between rider and horse could make up for other weaknesses by either horse or rider.

On the road, the spirited mare performed admirably, aside from her determination to establish dominance over the older, less flashy Ready Brother, but once beneath the Hidling's canopy, she had begun to unravel.

"Perhaps we should walk the horses for a while," Eropa suggested, concerned over the mare's edginess.

"Are you sure that you can?"

"I have the strength to walk, Corin," Eropa gently scolded her friend.

"You do not," Ready Brother chided.

"But I will do it." Eropa slipped off the horse, careful not to let the depths of her weariness show.

Corin slid to the ground as well, shaking the stiffness from her legs.

"You know, you do not have to do this, Corin," Eropa advised her friend. "You could take the mare back to the Crossroads and wait for me. I can rejoin you there when I am done."

Corin's jaw tightened. "I go where you go." The mare began to dance, sidestepping and snorting.

"Run--run away," Eropa heard the animal's thoughts. She rested a hand on the mare's neck. It shivered, lowering its head, fear draining from its body.

"We cannot leave yet," Eropa explained to the horse. "*I must go forward, and Corin goes with me. You may return to the borderlands if you choose, but you will travel alone."*

"No, not alone! I cannot go alone." The mare took three steps backward, terrified. *"When you are alone, they attack."*

"What is it that you are afraid of?" Eropa asked the horse. *"What you see, or what you do not see?"*

"What I smell," was the mare's quick reply.

E.F. Winters

"Danger!" Ready Brother squealed as a huge cat jumped from the trees, its teeth barred, claws the size of sword blades, dug into the dirt.

"Leave this forest. You are not wanted here," its feline voice sounded like a tortured death.

The mare reared, pulled her reins from Corin's grasp, and bolted back the way they had come.

The big cat's eyes tracked the horse; its tail twitching, powerful shoulder muscles undulating, but it did not give chase. Its golden eyes returned to its chosen prey, Eropa. *"You should follow that four-legged piece of meat."*

"You mistake me," Eropa declared, her skin beginning to glow like burnished copper. "I am the Pira Eropa Rhune, the daughter of Adaya Al'Kandin and Auger Mc'Kinock."

"Two humans who should have known better than to whelp such a kit." The cat began to circle Eropa and her companions. *"You and your magic are not wanted here, Rhune."*

"I am the Matriarch's heir. This forest is full of my allies and friends. If I call them, they will come to my aid," Eropa said, confident that the great cat would back down and leave them unharmed.

"No one will come, Rhune," the cat growled. *"You feel wrong."* It sniffed her. *"You smell wrong. I will not give you the honor of eating you. Your body will rot on the forest floor for lesser animals to chew on."*

"I mean you no harm," Eropa remonstrated, her confidence waning.

"And yet harm dogs your every step, sucking the life from all you pass." The cat's eyes checked the ground at Eropa's feet.

A slow, curling darkness marked the Rhune's footprints leading back to where she had dismounted.

Eropa stared at the back marks. "I did not know," she stammered.

"A Rhune: the granddaughter of Adaya Al'Kandin and Auger Mc"kinock, and you did not know? I do not believe you." The cat prepared to spring.

"Do not turn your back or look away from it, Corin," Eropa briefed her friend. "Raise your arms high above your head and try to look big. If it attacks, stay on your feet and fight to your last breath. Do not run or play dead, or it will surely kill you." Corin slowly raised her arms high. "Whoever sent you has little regard for your life," the

CHAPTER FIFTY-SIX

Rhune warned the creature. "My question to you is, how much do you value it?" The plants at her feet were black and wilted, and the area of contagion bled out from her in an ever-growing circle.

The cat shrank back. *"You have no power, Rhune. You cannot harm me,"* it declared, but uncertainty showed in its golden eyes, which darted back and forth, seeking its escape route.

"Are you certain? You see what has happened here, where my feet have touched. When the rot reaches you, will you, too, wither and die?" Eropa demanded menacingly.

The cat cringed back from the Rhune, lifting a paw, then leaped, turned mid-air, and disappeared back into the forest undergrowth.

The ruddy light under Eropa's skin faded, and she swayed on her feet. Corin caught her before she hit the ground.

"You're not well, Eropa, and this place isn't making you better. It's making you worse."

"No." Eropa looked despondent. "It is me who is making the forest sick. We must get to Adaya's quickly, Corin." She stumbled to Ready Brother, but she no longer had the strength to climb into the saddle. Corin stepped forward and assisted her. Eropa lowered herself onto the horse's neck. "I am sorry, Ready Brother, but there is nothing for it now but that you carry both of us," Eropa whispered to the red horse.

"I'll walk," Corin deferred.

"No. We do not have the time," Eropa insisted. "*I* do not have time." The Rhune wound her fingers through the big red horse's mane. "Brother, I am going to show you the way. Remember what you see." She pictured her grandparents' homestead and the path they would need to take to get there.

"I will remember," the horse promised.

Corin vaulted up behind Eropa and took up the reins. "Alright, let's go then."

The darkness of night was smothering. Eropa had been unconscious for hours, but Corin held them in the saddle. Ignorant of where they should be and what dangers they might encounter. The red

E.F. Winters

gelding walked steadily on, following a path and direction unknown to the Taiban girl.

"I hope you know where you're going," she muttered to the big horse. She thought the forest dark before, but as the day faded to twilight, then on to midnight, she was obliged to revisit her definition of darkness. A sliver of starlight had become blinding.

What did the black footprints that Eropa's feet made mean, Corin wondered? Was Eropa draining the forest's life, or was something in her poisoning her surroundings? Neither option boded well for the Rhune's companions. Corin felt the numbness in her arms. Was it caused by her inability to change position for so long, or was it being in contact with Eropa? Was Ready Brother stumbling more now because it was dark and he was carrying them both, or was what was happening to Eropa seeping poison into the big horse? It stood to reason that if they were in contact with the Rhune, like the plants, they were at risk.

Growls, cackles, clucks, and ill-favored shrieks populated the wall of darkness.

"Gods, this place is a black pit." Corin hated seeing nothing. The only thing worse than imagining what was watching them was seeing the yellow and amber eyes peering out from the shadowy foliage. "Go ahead, watch us," Corin shouted at the slit-eyed creatures. "But keep your distance." She loosened an arm, hoping to reach back and draw the glister sword Eropa had given her, but she did not have enough hands to keep hold of the Pira, control the horse, and hold the weapon.

The path narrowed to a wildlife track, the fern fronds and bushes brushing against Ready Brother's legs as they moved past.

Corin felt the moist, panting breaths and smelled the feral scents of their observers. In the distance, a big cat shrieked, spreading its rage through the forest. Ready Brother stumbled, his entire body shuddering.

"Steady on now, boy," Corin said softly. The grating shriek repeated; a little closer. "Whoa." Corin pulled back lightly on the reins. The gelding tossed his head, letting her know he disapproved of her decision to stop. "I mean it, Ready Brother, whoa," Corin repeated, shifting her weight and pulling the gelding's head in. "I promise, I'll make this fast." She slipped off the tall horse's back, her leather boots thudding softly in the duff. Removing her cloak first, Corin worked to

CHAPTER FIFTY-SIX

get Eropa's off. Moving her arms brought discomfort, the sliding of the material over them making it even worse, but she did not stop.

Pain is temporary. Death is not. The Taiban girl traded Eropa's dark-green cloak for her own plain brown one, then, checking to make certain that the glister sword's pommel was free and accessible, she pulled a rope out of the saddlebags. Climbing back on, Corin scooted forward. The sleeve on the arm that had borne most of Eropa's weight bunched up, exposing ugly bruises and fierce boils. Any place that she had been in contact with Eropa felt raw. Ready Brother must have similar injuries.

"I am sorry, Brother, but we must go on." Corin twisted around until she could lift Eropa's torso to a sitting position. She wrapped the rope around Eropa and herself, then pulled the hood of Eropa's green cloak down over her brown hair. As long as the cat believed the Rhune might still be a threat, they had a chance. If it realized the Rhune was unconscious, they were done for.

"If any of these creatures strikes up a conversation, Brother, I am the Pira. Got that? It might buy us enough time to get out of this alive."

The big cat's wail sounded again, this time so close that both Corin and the horse jumped.

"Settle down. It's okay." Corin patted the horse's neck.

Tree branches cracked. Small trees splintered, announcing the approach of something large and un-catlike from their left. The roar of the cat came from the right.

"Run, Brother! Run!" Corin kicked the red gelding to a gallop. The gelding leaped forward, and Corin gave him his head, concentrating on keeping Eropa and herself in the saddle.

Snarls and growls whipped past in the darkness; the thud of heavy bodies shaking and swaying the forest foliage, and tremors shaking the ground. A swarm of large bat-like creatures flew across the path. The gelding lowered his head and plowed on, ignoring the leathery beat of wings against his head and body.

"Get away!" Corin struggled to keep her seat while claws scratched skin and ripped out hair.

Ready Brother veered to the right, running with the stream of fliers, gradually angling out of their path on the other side.

The exhausted horse settled back into a trot, his sides heaving.

"Good boy," Corin gasped, her breath coming hard and fast. "Eropa was right. You've got stamina and guts enough for three horses." She let Eropa's head and shoulders slip down onto her left side so that her friend's head rested on her thigh. Supporting the comatose Rhune under her left arm, Corin loosely tied off the reins.

An anguished cry skinned the air, then died in the distance. There was a crash followed by a thud, and a big cat's call of triumph.

"Whatever it was fighting, it won now, and that means it will be back after us," Corin told the gelding. "I have no idea where we need to go, so you're in charge, Brother. Take us where we need to go."

Weaving this way and that, the big red gelding eased once again into a run. Dodging trees, he jumped fallen logs, leaped creeks, and plowed determinedly up hillsides that closely resembled cliffs, recklessly plummeting down the other side.

Corin kept her head low and held on tight to Eropa.

Suddenly, the winged bat creatures returned, once again harrying them with their furry bodies and leathery wings. Ready Brother swung his head from side to side like a battle axe, biting at whatever came within reach of his big teeth. The creatures struck Corin, trying to push her from the saddle. She reached back, drew her sword, and began slicing at them.

A cacophony of clucks and clicks added to the soundtrack of the horse's hooves. Gangly creatures with undersized bodies and oversized heads took over the assault. Mirroring Corin and Ready Brother's path, the new invaders swung from tree to tree, whooping and cackling.

Corin glanced sideways, trying to get a good look at the acrobats tumbling through the trees, but the speed of their movements made them a blur.

The heavy scent of wet earth and fresh moss filled her nose, and she heard a chittering sound behind her on her right side. Turning, she could see nothing. Something fluttered in her peripheral vision on the left. Whipping around, she found a creature with a head the size of an infant's perched on Eropa's shoulder, preparing to pull the Pira's hood back.

"Hey, you, leave her alone!" Corin shouted. The creature turned and examined the Taiban girl with huge, bulbous eyes. Its thin lips stretched into a feral grin the entire width of its head, revealing a

CHAPTER FIFTY-SIX

double row of sharp teeth. It looked from Corin to Eropa then back, its eyes contracting to black slits. It growled, and Corin thrust the butt end of her sword at it.

"Get away from her, I said." The hobgoblin jumped to Corin's shoulder, nosed her hood aside, and bit the top of her ear.

"Ow!" Corin shook her head to disengage her attacker. It held on tight with its long-fingered hands and tiny, sharp teeth. Corin brought the pommel of her sword down on its head, disengaging it from her ear. "I mean it. Go away and leave us alone!"

The thing jumped from perch to perch, dodging the sword pommel's blows and snickering. Then it was gone.

Corin tugged the green cloak's hood back down over her head and re-gripped Ready Brother's reins.

Her ear stung like fire, and she could feel the warm trickle of blood dripping down the side of her neck.

Ready Brother slowed to a trot, then a walk, his coat steaming, his ribs blowing in and out like a bellows. He could not keep this pace up forever.

"Adaya Rhune," she focused her inner thoughts. *"I don't know if you can hear me, but Eropa is here with me in the forest, and she's injured. She needs you, but everything seems determined to keep us from getting there. Please, send help--a guide, something."*

"I think those creatures pushed us off course." She looked back over her shoulder. "Are we still on the path to Adaya's? I think that we need to go back." She pulled the gelding's head around. Ready brother made a circle, bringing his head back to where he had started.

"No, Brother, we have to go back," Corin tried again. The horse shook his mane and would not budge. "But we need to..." The big cat's cry stopped her. Corin leaned close to the horse's ear. "Okay. You decide, but I have a thought. Can you smell water anywhere nearby, Brother? Cats hate water. If we can find someplace with big water, maybe we can get him off our tail. Find us big water."

The gelding set off at a slow trot.

Corin and Ready Brother traveled through the night. Every few minutes, Corin re-sent her mental message, hoping Eropa's grandparents would miraculously hear her, but she knew she was no Rhune, and she had no confidence that what she was doing was anything more than talking to herself.

E.F. Winters

She did it anyway.

When the ghostly outline of the canopy above them indicated dawn, Corin began to relax. Even in the dark undergrowth of the Hidling, predators would hold to a pattern, hunting by night and sleeping by day.

As they went on, the forest canopy gradually thinned and got closer to the ground. The air warmed, and the great ferns and flowers gradually were replaced with more recognizable varieties. They came to a river and turned to follow it. Ready Brother refused to go in any direction but downstream.

The sun was high when they came out of the forest onto the lip of a valley. Corin breathed in the sunshine and the wide-open view. The river led them to a lake. An island rose in the middle of it.

"You've done it." She patted the gelding's neck. "We're safe."

Ready Brother took them around the lake's edge until they reached a copse. A large, sturdy raft secured to a stump floated in the lake's shallows. Corin scanned the landscape for the owner or anyone other than themselves that might be a candidate for crossing.

As they approached, a stick-thin man came out of a reed hut in the copse. He did not look like an Ebulonian of today, but he did not look alien either. He was something in between; something entirely new, or very, very old. Corin remembered the stories Aunt Timee told her and her cousins about the forest folk of Ebulon, now vanished. Still, stories lingered about people living close to the Hidling seeing one. Corin sheathed her sword and urged Ready Brother forward into a trot.

The stickman appeared to be as interested in Corin and the horse as she was in him. He scratched his head, strode over to a log, and sat, waiting for them.

"Good morning." Corin untied herself from Eropa and dismounted. The odd man's long, sticklike hands were braiding a heavy rope.

He rubbed the stubble covering most of his face.

"Caught yourself a Rhune, I see; rare, that is. 'Don't see many of their kind around here." His speech was slow, the intonation rolling gently like the rhythm of the water.

"I didn't catch her," Corin corrected him. "I'm taking her to her family, but we've lost the path."

CHAPTER FIFTY-SIX

"A difficult path is hard to follow." The ferryman squinted at the Rhune on the back of the horse. "Smart horse." He put down his rope and began to walk toward the lake. "Come on then. It's best you put some water between her and those who follow you."

Corin glanced back at the forest, then followed the man to the raft.

"Take him aboard." He waved Corin and Ready Brother on.

Corin led the horse onto the raft, untied Eropa, and laid the Rhune down on the deck. The man fetched a pitchfork of hay and dropped it onto the deck for Ready Brother.

"Here is some breakfast," the man muttered to the horse. "You look like you could use it. You are a big one." The man patted the gelding.

"I don't know how to pay you," Corin apologized. "We came through the Hidling so we have no coin..."

"Metal has no value here, no matter what color it is, or whose likeness it bears." He studied her. "You are Ebulonian and something more that I don't know."

"Taiban. I'm Taiban."

The odd man frowned. "Because that part of you is more important than the other?"

"No. Because that's what the Ebulonians call any of us who are only partly like them."

The stickman made a clicking noise. "Border folk are hard to understand."

"For me, too," Corin agreed. "So, if you don't use coin, how do people pay you to ferry them across?"

The man shrugged. "They don't. I enjoy being out on the lake. If someone wants to come along, I enjoy their company. If not... Sometimes they tell me stories. Sometimes they share their food."

"I have neither food nor stories," Corin confessed.

The stickman frowned. "Now you are just being selfish."

"No, I'm not, really," Corin stuttered. "I don't..."

"You are from the outside world, you are half Ebulonian and half something else, and you have just caught yourself a fresh Rhune, but you have 'no' stories?"

Corin thought about Little Taiba, the fire, the battle, Vale, and Quinn fighting and dying beside the Pira.

E.F. Winters

"Ah, I knew it," the man perked up. "I can see the stories in you. Come, tell me." He untied the rope and began to pole them across the lake while Corin began the tale of the burning of Little Taiba and the battle of the Free Men. They were near the island when the ferryman spoke again.

"You have had many troubles, Rhune Carrier, but you will face more before you sleep safely again." He eyed the water and the storm clouds that began to gather overhead. "Strong powers work to remove you from the Hidling."

Corin glanced at Eropa. The young sorceress had been unconscious during their flight in the forest, but as the wind stirred the lake, she also stirred. The old ferryman's eyes locked on Corin's.

"She senses the forces rising against her. There is no safety for you here."

"We're almost to the island." Corin looked ahead.

"It will be no different there," the man cautioned.

"But the cat can't go there. He won't cross the water," Corin stated her premise as if it were fact.

The stickman looked down into the water. "The Rhune's problems are much bigger than one caterwaul."

Corin followed his gaze. The dark, shadowy shape of a huge behemoth swam beneath the raft. It cleared the logs and leaped from the water, slapping its body down to make a wave that rocked the raft violently. Ready Brother squealed, stamping his feet as he slid on the wooden deck.

"Careful, Brother!" Corin scrambled to calm the horse and protect Eropa. Beneath where the Pira had been lying, the wood was black, soft, and rotting.

The ferryman's eyes narrowed. "What have you brought among us?" his anger mirrored the churning, swelling waters. "You border folk will never learn. We do not want your poisons here."

"She's sick. She isn't doing this on purpose," Corin protested. "We just need to get to her grandmother, Adaya's."

"Get off my raft, now!" The man's mood had changed as suddenly as the weather on the lake.

"I'll take her off as soon as we get to shore," Corin promised.

CHAPTER FIFTY-SIX

"No. Now!" the ferryman roared, rushing forward, pole in hand. Corin pulled the glister sword from her back and positioned herself over Eropa.

"You will not touch her."

"She is tearing the raft and everything around her apart. Don't you see it?" He pointed to the fraying and blackened rope lashings. They were unraveling. The stickman jabbed his pole at Ready Brother's chest, forcing the horse to back up.

"Please, just let us get to the island," Corin shouted above the rising wind.

"No!"

"Tell me how to get to Adaya's?"

"No!" The man continued to poke at the red gelding until the animal's back hooves were at the raft's edge. With a lurching roll, the logs tipped, and Ready Brother stumbled off. His terrified squeal ended abruptly when he hit the water.

"Brother!" Corin shouted, torn between helping the struggling horse and protecting the Pira. The horse's head surfaced, and he began to swim for shore.

"You can't just throw us off into the lake and leave us!" Corin turned her wrath on the stickman. "She's the Pira. You cannot just turn your back on her."

"The Rhunes have no hold on my kind," the man declared.

"You invited us onto your raft," Corin pleaded. "You asked us aboard. You owe us safe passage."

The man frowned. "On the far side of the island is a shoal that connects to the mainland shore," he gave in. "The waters are shallow enough to walk off the island from there. Look for the arched tree. Now go." The stickman pointed.

Sheathing her sword, Corin dragged Eropa to the edge of the raft and jumped off into the water.

E.F. Winters

CHAPTER FIFTY-SEVEN

"The Rhunes are transplants to this world." (Adaya Al'Kandin- ne Rhune to Hagriva Rhune; unverified. Anonymous author of "The Last Matriarch.")

The large creatures threatening to sink the raft circled close to Corin, Eropa, and Ready Brother, but they did not attack, keeping their distance from the Rhune.

Battered by wind and drenched by rain, Corin wrestled Eropa onto the beach, then onto Ready Brother's back. Shivering, she leaned into the horse's warmth. Pressing her face against his satiny hide, she sobbed out the fury and desperation that congealed inside her.

The red gelding's withers quivered, his breath coming in shallow pants that smelled of better days; horse and grass. Corin put her arms around his big neck.

"We can do this," her voice cracked with exhaustion. "There may be powers that don't want us here, but there are also those that do. We just have to hold on until they find us." She took up the wet reins and guided the gelding from the beach into the woods. As quickly as it had risen, the storm disappeared. The clouds cleared, and it was once again a sunny day.

The outer ring of the island's landscape was a windswept bluff covered by low grasses, large rocks, and stunted evergreens blown into odd shapes by lake winds.

Further inland, the forest reasserted its biology, but the rocky island soil could not sustain the growth on the scale of the rest of the Hidling.

Ready Brother's head hung low, his steps sluggish.

He cannot go much farther, Corin worried, but the travelers stumbled on, making for the island's interior.

Light filtered through the lacework of the sparse woodland canopy. Birds bickered, sang, and shrilled warnings at the stranger's

CHAPTER FIFTY-SEVEN

approach, and then the woodlands opened into a sun-drenched meadow.

Corin led the gelding to a large flat boulder, removed Eropa from his back, and then his bridle.

"I don't know how much farther we have to go, but I know we won't get there if you don't rest and eat." The Taiban girl lifted the saddlebags and felt pad from the gelding's broad back, revealing the bruises and sores the animal had from carrying Eropa. Corin sucked in her breath. "Oh, I am so sorry, Brother." She dropped the gear and searched the saddlebags for the healing ointment Eropa bought at the Crossroads. Treating the big horse's wounds took most of the contents of the small jar, but if they did not find help soon, they would not need it. Checking the horse's sides where Eropa's legs and arms dangled against him, Corin applied the last of the ointment.

"We'll be somewhere soon," she promised. "And when we do, I will make sure you are cared for properly." She pulled Eropa's staff from among the gear and placed herself at the foot of the flat rock where she laid Eropa out. Resting in the sunshine, Ready Brother grazing nearby, the hum of the summer insects lulled her fretting mind, and she dozed.

A woman's face hovered over her.

"Find two white birches on the south side of the meadow. Pass between, then keep straight on. When you find the arched tree, look for the stone Voy; the water path begins there.

Corin's eyes opened. Had she been sleeping... dreaming? *"Find two white birches."* She struggled to her feet and looked south. Two slim, paper-bark birch grew at the edge of the meadow. The sun was hanging low just above the trees. She had slept longer than she intended. Corin retrieved the horse and gear. Using both sleeping rolls as extra padding, she placed the blankets over the horse's back, then walked Ready Brother over to the rock where she had left Eropa.

The Rhune's eyes fluttered open. "Corin?" Her voice was barely a whisper.

"You're awake," Corin greeted her friend.

"Where are we?" the Pira looked around.

"On our way to your grandmother's," Corin assured her. "Do you think you could drink some water?" She retrieved a water bag from their gear and held it to her friend's lips. The small effort seemed to tire the Rhune, and she closed her eyes.

"This meadow... I don't recognize it," the Pira said, her voice the thread of a whisper. "Did Ready Brother remember the way?"

"Adaya has given us a new way. We'll be there soon." Corin helped her friend to Ready Brother's side.

The gelding flinched as Rhune's arms pressed into the raw spots on his back.

Eropa looked at him, confused, then read all that Corin had tried to hide.

"What have I done?" she muttered. "Have you injuries like this as well?"

"It's not so bad for me," Corin tried to make light of her wounds.

Tears welled in Eropa's eyes. "I did not know. By the Mother, I did not know," her voice broke.

"Hurrying to Adaya's is the best thing we can do for him now. Once there, we can heal his wounds." Corin hefted the saddlebags, took up Ready Brother's reins, and headed for the white birches. "Just a bit farther," she encouraged the gelding.

The golden leaves on the birch trees shivered as the travelers passed, dropping as if it were late fall instead of early summer. Corin set her jaw and walked on.

"Where now?" Eropa asked.

"We're to look for the stone Voy, whatever that means." Corin frowned.

"The Bosk, the Bract, the Spinney, and the Voy," Eropa repeated the opening line of an old poem still common among the villagers at the Crossroads. "The old races, the original inhabitants of Hebelon. Of all the forest folk, the Voy were most different; sturdy of body, stout and strong." A faint smile lifted the Rhune's countenance. "Like rocks. The old folk say that a Spinney might be mistaken for an Ebulonian of today, but the Bract: small, ethereal creatures, were ever only seen in glimpses. They never truly gained solid forms. The Bosk had a reputation for being quite wicked with sharp little teeth. Territorial in nature, they loved shiny things and delighted in preying on their less aggressive neighbors."

Corin felt the scab on her ear.

"So, they bite?"

CHAPTER FIFTY-SEVEN

"I suppose." Eropa shrugged. "What else would they do with teeth like that?" She pointed to a large black boulder in the shallows. "The Voy stone."

The boulder was the size of a person, with moss growing on its "head" except on the very top, where birds had used it as a perch, scratching it clean so that it looked like the Voy had been tonsured. Its rough, blunt-featured face frowned, its chin resting on knees drawn up against its belly.

The travelers searched the shallows around the rock until they found the underwater path, then set out anew.

They were well out onto the narrow up-thrust, with deep water on either side, when Corin caught Eropa studying the sky.

"The wind is rising."

"There was a storm earlier, but it passed," Corin explained without embellishment. Placing a hand on Ready Brother to steady herself, they picked their way slowly across the rocky underwater shoal.

The storm strengthened, the waves on either side of the shallow, watery path growing higher until they washed violently over the shoal. Soon, what had been navigable at knee depth turned into a brief swim before the water retreated, and still the waves rose, pushing more water in each swell, and sucking deeper troughs between peaks. Shivering in their sodden wool cloaks, hair and clothes clinging like a second skin, the travelers struggled on, swimming, stumbling, and swimming again.

"The swimming periods are getting longer," Eropa pointed out.

Ready Brother snorted and blew as the waves splashed against him, lifting his solid body off his feet.

"Climb up here with me," Eropa urged Corin. "We don't weigh anything in the water, but we need to stay together."

The water beasts that swarmed them before swam closer and closer as the water deepened, leaping and splashing on either side of the shoal.

"They will be able to swim over it soon," Corin warned, keeping a wary eye on their menacing escorts.

"And us," Eropa agreed. "But for now, the shallows still run between them, and we can use them as our guides." As if to taunt the

Rhune, the next wave pushed her and Corin off Ready Brother, spilling them into the water.

"Hold onto me!" Corin held tightly to the gelding's mane as his legs rhythmically pumped to stay afloat. When the wave pulled away, sinking them back into a low trough, his feet had lost the shoal.

One of the pods of water creatures swooped near, rolling its huge body. It slapped its tail against the water. The turbulence separated horse and riders. The pod swarmed the frantic horse, bumping him with their fatty bodies, circling and striking at him with their muscled tails. Ready Brother struck back with all he had, hoof and tooth. Shrieking, he bit into the waxy hide of the closest of his assailants.

"Leave him alone, you beast!" Corin kicked at the creature, her back against the horse's rump to provide leverage. Eropa was at his head, her fingers twined in his mane, her body hugging his withers. Her strength was failing. "Swim Ready Brother!" Corin shouted as she grasped the horse's tail.

The gelding snorted in short, powerful puffs as he swam for dry land, his mind too deep in the well of instinct to seek the shoal.

The travelers dragged themselves, waterlogged and exhausted, from the lake onto the mainland shore. Two Large birds were approaching from the West.

"Friend or foe?" Corin asked.

Eropa shook her head. "I don't know."

"Let's get off the beach. We're too exposed," Corin decided.

Seeking the shelter of the trees, they once more entered the Hidling.

The wind raked the trees, striking at the travelers with branches and cones, the forest howling in protest at their return.

"Climb on! Climb on!" Eropa urged Corin to join her on Ready Brother's back. Corin vaulted up behind the Rhune and gave the tall horse his head.

Small branches whipped their faces while larger ones tried to knock them from their seats. Vines caught at the gelding's legs and were ripped out by their roots as the red gelding found a deep reserve of strength within him and refused to be stopped.

The swinging creatures that had harried them before reappeared, now throwing rocks, pine cones, and thorn darts at the travelers.

CHAPTER FIFTY-SEVEN

"They're back," Corin lamented. "Pesky little things. One bit me."

"Bosk," Eropa said. "We must give them something."

"What?" Corin shouted.

"Anything."

Corin reached inside her shirt and pulled out a necklace on a thin leather string. Ripping it from her neck, she held it up high.

"An offering for our passage," she shouted.

There was a cackle and a cluck as a Bosk swooped overhead. The necklace disappeared from Corin's hand.

The attack went on.

"Okay, so peaceful bribery doesn't work. I know what will." She pressed her thighs into Ready Brother's sides and pulled her glister sword from its sheath. "Duck," she shouted to Eropa as she swung it over their heads.

Whack, the next Bosk that flew near fell. Whack, whack; the next two followed.

The attackers shrank back, chattering and shrieking angrily, but they stayed out of range, merely grinning at the travelers, displaying their sharp teeth.

Ready Brother galloped up the hill before them.

The caterwaul was crouched in the path, the irises of its yellow eyes swirling in optic opposites.

It lifted a paw, bunched its hindquarters, then stretched its lean body out long, preparing to pounce, teeth bared. It began to snarl, the expression of anger and dominance ending in a dismayed whine as a glowing orb flew between it and its prey. The orb exploded, banishing the darkness in a shower of white light as the caterwaul cowered.

Ready Brother slid forward. Scrambling frantically to avoid the falling sparks, he reared, tossing Eropa and Corin from his back. The sparkling lights fell and faded, and the forest went black.

"Eropa? Are you all right?" Corin called out.

The darkness growled.

Corin scrabbled on hands and knees, searching blindly for her Glister Sword. It ignited at her touch. Able to see where the unconscious Rhune lay on the forest floor, she planted herself over her friend, prepared to fight to the end.

E.F. Winters

"Run, Brother," she told the big gelding. "Save yourself if you can. I will hold them off as long as I'm able."

With a snort and a toss of his big head, Ready Brother joined her.

"Okay. So, we will do this together. If this is my death, I am proud to share it with you."

Yellow eyes whirling maniacally, blinked open, and the cat growled. The ground rumbled.

Another ball of light popped into existence from the nothing. As it exploded, a matched set of black draft horses pulling a wagon thundered forward through the cascading sparks.

"Ho there! We've found them!" the man at the reins called out.

CHAPTER FIFTY-EIGHT

"There are always some who will try to convince you that they recognize truth and you do not. Their goal is to undermine your instincts and experience. You must see them for who they are and not who they pretend to be." (Lessons to Other Worlds: author /compiler anonymous attributed to Hagriva Rhune.)

Zeph Yare, captain in name only of a missing starship, walked the streets of Iredipa, self-battered by questions. Where was the Lamdra? Why had it left orbit? Who gave the order for the starship to leave? What could possibly have been the reason? What kept them from returning? When would they finally appear? What would he do then? And the most disconcerting question of all: what would he do if the Lamdra did not return?

It gave him a sense of adventure to imagine living in the wilds of Ebulon, but when practicality put its bit in, he recognized that the only time he lived on a natural world ended when he was nine shortly after the death of his father, when Hazzlebutt, the small hunting moon's gamekeeper and the lodge's steward, was killed.

He has never chopped wood, or made a weapon, or used a weapon that wasn't a gun. He never cooked his food, killed, or dressed the meat of an edible animal, or grown anything.

"In short, I am absolutely useless," Zeph grumbled as he walked toward the Mi'cosa River.

Were there wild animals in those dense forests, or smaller, creatures less obviously dangerous but just as deadly?

Following Pliny's advice, Zeph left the palace, temporarily taking up a shared room with Navrat at the Keesch widow, Patisel's, while he figured out their next step.

But it was not only questions about the Lamdra that battered him. He worried about a lot of things—most of them things he could do nothing about in the situation as it was.

Eropa was prime among them.

Was she safe in the old ruin with only an ancient sorceress as company? The Mirs all seemed to think that, unlike a regular old person, a sorceress gaines power with age, not less. Zeph still worried. Eropa had been gone for days now. What could she be doing in an old ruin? How would she fill her days? Did she ever think about him? Did she know how badly things were going here without her?

Without consciously planning, Zeph's feet led him across the Mi'cosa Bridge and into the blackened remnants of Little Taiba. Finding himself at the north wall where the fire was said to have started, he scrutinized the metal lumps and curved plasteel remains of the Lamdra shuttle lying in a heap against the wall.

"A melted mess, eh?" A muscular Taiban in fire-colored striped pants and tall, red leather boots approached. The man's abundant black hair was pulled into a single thick rope made of many tiny braids with bells braided into them that tinkled softly as he walked. An older Taiban, impressively taller, though less bulky in build, walked beside the braided man, looking like a wren next to a parrot. The braided man offered his hand to Zeph.

"Tai Bobalo." The Taiban leader had a strong, confident grip, his steady gaze taking Zeph in. The Paxlosian felt weighed and measured. "And this old pirate is my friend of many years, Block," the Taiban indicated the lanky older man. Block gave Zeph a small nod but said nothing, and Zeph felt the same sense of scrutiny. Unlike his friend, Bobalo, Block made no pretense of acceptance before the judgment had come in. "And you are the Paxlosian starship's captain, Zeph Yare," Bobalo announced, pushing the words through the thick mat of his curly black beard.

"I am," Zeph admitted, finding he was unable to keep himself from smiling. Tai Bobalo was entirely unapologetically himself; big and boisterous with a wealth of humor and charisma that immediately put Zeph at ease. It was refreshing after the weeks of suspicion and maneuvering he had gone through. He felt his shoulders instinctively relax.

"Do you know what happened here?" Bobalo asked Zeph, looking at the shuttle's wreckage.

"Only that my lieutenant who piloted the shuttle landed it among some trees when he came to speak to Nikodamus, and then somehow it ended up here, wrecked," Zeph replied.

"A mystery for certain," Bobalo agreed. "But Block and I have been to the place it landed in the woods and done some investigating. We could shed some light if you were interested?"

Zeph nodded. "I'd be grateful."

Bobalo gave a small half-smile of acceptance. "There were four sets of prints in the field where your shuttle originally landed." He gestured northeast of the wall. "Two were the size of adults. The third was uncertain. It could have been a small adult, or a large child, but the fourth was definitely a child's footprint.

"So, my man and three others," Zeph summed up.

"The two adult prints leave the shuttle and never return."

"But then they couldn't return if the ship wasn't there anymore, could they?" Block added.

"My crewman, Tila, was at the palace. His business would not have been completed until after the shuttle was moved and crashed," Zeph clarified.

"Huh." Bobalo thought about this. "What about the other person aboard?"

"Lieutenant Tila says he flew alone. There was no second person," Zeph assured the Taibans.

"But there was a second set of footprints that began at the shuttle. So, someone else was on that shuttle," Bobalo corrected him. "Who might that have been, Captain Yare?"

"I don't know," Zeph answered honestly.

"Your crewman, Tila, must be lying to you, Captain," Block suggested.

"I can't imagine it," Zeph disagreed. "And there's no reason for him to."

"Since there hasn't been any traffic back to the Lamdra, you should be able to check the ship's records and see who's missing. Except your ship is…out of communication range." Bobalo's expression let Zeph know he knew about the Lamdra's mysterious disappearance—of course, he did. His niece, Corin, was on the hired shuttle when they found out.

"We can check it later, when the ship comes back," Zeph said pointedly. "Meanwhile, there's the question of who the two other prints belong to."

CHAPTER FIFTY-EIGHT

Bobalo continued. "The child-sized footprints and the second, larger prints that might or might not be a child's arrived together. They enter the field from the direction of Little Taiba, wait, hiding in the tall grass, then approach the shuttle. They do not leave."

"The adults do not return, and the young ones do not leave..." Block let the sentence hang.

"You think kids flew and crashed my shuttle?" Zeph scoffed.

"Very smart kids," Bobalo suggested. "And it ended badly."

"That's ridiculous." Zeph was not convinced. "How would they known how to fly it?"

"They didn't for long," The Taiban leader pointed out wryly.

Zeph forced himself to consider the possibility that this hypothesis was possible. "Do you think they could have survived the crash?" he asked, looking at the mangled and burned shell.

"We found no bodies," Block said. "But with so many injured or burned during the fire, their injuries would not help us identify them."

"The thing I find more disturbing is this question of the second passenger from the Lamdra."

Zeph frowned. "Why is that?"

"They leave the shuttle, walking north through the field toward the Ebulonian estates that border the wooded area and enter the street very near where Lady Aless Mc'Larick was killed that night by a poison dart matching one used in an attack on one of our fighters in an alley in Little Taiba the second night after you arrived." Bobalo's dark blue eyes were striking against his nut-brown skin, but Zeph did not like the accusatory way they were looking at him. "You need to seriously consider who this second person might be, Yare, because whoever they are, they are a murderer, and I do not think they are acting in your mission's best interests."

"And right now, they are either dead or trapped here on the planet," Block pointed out.

Zeph and Bobalo's eyes met in the same conclusion.

"They must be hiding out in Little Taiba."

"Where they would hope to blend in." Bobalo's grin reminded Zeph that before the man was a revolutionary, he had been a notorious and very successful pirate. "But come." The large Taiban slapped Zeph on the back, the weight of his hand like a slab of meat. "Join us for dinner. I have a story you should hear that will explain much about

E.F. Winters

Taiban history and our place in it, and perhaps make some sense of this short trip your shuttle took at the hands of children."

The Bobalo compound had been spared by the fire that heated things up the night of the riot, but not its after-effects. Crates, empty of supplies, were stacked in towers against the inner sides of the compound's walls or outbuildings, of which there seemed to be quite a few. A half dozen gaunt children, watched by haunted-eyed parents, played in a fountain at the back of the house.

Block dropped off at the gate, taking the place of another Taiban who then shambled away.

A tidy orchard had been planted in a wide strip behind the house, encroaching on what had once been a landing area. There was a large vegetable garden, and quite a number of outbuildings, including an old hangar—most of which looked unused.

Snaking lines of small, sleeping tents cringed away from the hot southern sun, ringed beneath the orchard's shade.

The Bobalo house itself was a large white block in the center of an open space. Long, narrow, open shuttered windows were cut into the three-foot-thick earthen walls coated in layers of polished white alise. Time had webbed them with flowering vines. The windows, like the door, were open and appeared to have no glass. The roof was flat and possibly usable as an open-air space.

Unfamiliar spices, cheerful chatter, and open, honest laughter accompanied the clink of pottery and metalware, coiling through the open doorways and long windows where the family was preparing for the evening meal.

Bobalo led Zeph to the kitchen door, where he introduced Zeph to his striking Ebulonian wife and two of his five daughters.

"You have a handsome family," Zeph complimented Timee Bobalo.

"Thank you." She picked up the basket of clothing she was sorting through and moved to another room. She handled running a household that was also the base for a revolution, raising five girls, herding a husband, his friends, and colleagues, and caring for multiple

CHAPTER FIFTY-EIGHT

refugee families, but something about Zeph's appearance seemed to have stretched her patience a bit too far.

"I don't think she likes me much," Zeph commented after she left.

"It is not you. She is angry with me. I have invited the man responsible for the death of some of our friends' children, the enemy by some accounts, and required her to feed him at her table. Timee has a good heart, but your ship's arrival is at the center of many challenges for our family and others, friends, and those for whom we are responsible here." He slapped his knee. "But I promised you a tale."

"A history lesson," Zeph corrected.

"You will find this is both in one." Bobalo flashed him a large, toothy grin. "A decade ago, the warlords instigated something we call 'The Purge.' A petition had been signed at a conference of scientists. In it, they vowed to no longer accept work on projects to be used against the people. The warlords learned of their intention, raided the meeting, killing most of the scientists. A generation of scientific knowledge, virtually wiped from our worlds within hours.

"The goal, to destroy all opposition to themselves, was poorly thought out, because now there was no one to build their war machines. Those men and women of science who remained alive, due to not attending the conference or leaving before the raid, were quickly captured and forced, through various means of torture and extortion, to work for the warlords. Every small act of resistance has a cost, and the scientists have been prone to 'accidents'.

"Realizing they had created a new problem, because those scientists left to them were aging, the warlords implemented mandatory intelligence tests in schools. Children who scored high were given scholarships to special science boarding schools. The propaganda being all about how it was an honor to have your child selected. Then rumors started circulating that families were being denied visits and told that their children could not come home. In the agreements they signed, parents somehow lost all rights.

"The high-scoring students were legally kidnapped.

"That didn't sit well with the public, and families who expected their children to be recognized as having high intelligence began to avoid having their students tested, even going so far as to remove them from school and hide them from the authorities.

"The warlords countered by offering huge sums to any parent, family member, school staff, or neighbor who provided them with the name of a child who would test well, more if they could deliver the child directly to the warlord making the offer. Children became a commodity, like bread, with people buying and selling them. They grabbed children off the street, they hauled them out of their houses, or from classrooms. Families with children who were certain to be a target became desperate, and our mission expanded to rescuing Taiba's future scientists and engineers."

Bobalo sat back and took a puff off his pipe. "We've been siphoning off Taiba's brains for years now."

"That's extraordinary," Zeph said.

"And still there are so many we have not been able to help. And now this. The Pira promised us supplies to help those who suffered loss in the fire. It comes in spurts—never enough and never until after it's needed."

"I am sorry for your troubles," Zeph apologized. "I was working with Nikodamus to make an agreement that would benefit all of Ebulon's inhabitants."

"He was an honorable man, unlike many of his colleagues."

"You fear changes with a new Mahal?"

"The persecution of my people has become both more common and more open." Bobalo raised both palms in a gesture of futility. "What will happen when they feel they have the support of their fellows in government, and there will be no consequences for these actions? Though they pretend at enlightenment, not all Ebulonians understand the Truths."

"They'll have to work something out. You're here. They can't just banish you and send you all back to the Taiban Cluster."

"I think they'd like to," Bobalo suggested.

"But that would be a disaster. Someone would talk, and the warlords would come. That wouldn't help anyone."

"There are other ways to decimate a population. Sometimes the food they give us is such poor quality that Timee refuses to give it out." Bobalo caught Zeph's eyes, holding them, saying silently what he was not sure he could say out loud. "It would be easy for such food to be contaminated."

Zeph sat back in his chair, shocked. "They wouldn't do that."

CHAPTER FIFTY-EIGHT

Bobalo took a long pause, giving Zeph time to think. "You can't think of one Ebulonian who would do such a thing?" his voice was a low, spiny whisper. "Not one?"

Zeph could think of several, and there are those among our hosts who would celebrate such actions. I agree that the clans are complicit in much of what has befallen you, Captain Bobalo. It was the hope of some of the Mirs and me that we could reveal the part they played in Nikodamus's death, hoping that those who were involved were unable to profit from it by making themselves positions in the new government, but I have little faith the council will take the kind of action needed." Zeph shook his head.

"You heard the council put a bounty on Murtevoy yesterday?"

"Then they will have him soon. At least they're doing something," Zeph grumbled.

"I do not think the Ebulonians will easily take Saldo," Bobalo disagreed. "Half the population thinks what he did was treason, the other half makes him out a hero who thumbed his nose at the clans. We're not much taken with authority, for obvious reasons, and Saldo Murtevoy tricked the clans into giving him resources, then turned those resources to his purposes."

"Against his people," Zeph added.

"They have a dozen excuses explaining that, and none of them hold Saldo accountable." The conversation paused.

"Do you believe the clans ordered the attack on Little Taiba?" Zeph asked, finally breaking the silence.

"If they did, they're never going to let Saldo be arrested. He knows too much. But he is not stupid. If the clans are responsible, he knows his life is forfeit to their conspiracy. That is why I think he will agree to meet with us."

"Us?" Zeph frowned.

"I have been thinking a lot about this, Yare. However misguided it might have been, Saldo wanted something from all of this: status, wealth---a future where he once again wielded authority. Manipulating it so his fellow fighters got positions among the clans, and he was seen as their leader, is a step, but it can't have been the ultimate goal. It is too small, and too much of what happened does not fit, even if you make accommodations for some of his people going rogue and being out of his control."

Zeph frowned. "What are you thinking?"

"I do not think the clans were the ultimate target customers. I think you were."

"Me? I've never met the man—I've never even seen him," Zeph protested.

"Yes, but he knows enough about what you're trying to do to understand that when you leave Ebulon, you will need to have some protection for your interests here. You cannot just fly away and expect to come back in five years or whatever it will be, and everything is still as it was. The political situation has been thrown into free fall here. Someone is going to have to look after your interests."

"And Saldo hoped that will be him?"

"He had a military force, trained and equipped, with the proven ability to act outside the two established groups: Ebulonians and the refugee Taiban community."

"The man killed his own people," Zeph expostulated. "He destroyed the community where he lived. How could he justify this? What you're suggesting, Bobalo, is…"

"Unthinkable?" the Taiban leader added.

"I know worlds where I would not be surprised by this, but not here." Zeph ran a hand through his hair. "He'd have to be unhinged."

"It is easy to believe the Ebulonians as a race are better than they are because some of them are that good, but like any society, they are not all the same," Bobalo said sadly. "And we Taibans are not from this world. We're products of the Cluster, where twisted minds bent on the destruction of anything or anyone that thwarts their will is brutally destroyed. Our people come with few possessions, but they carry heavy burdens inside."

"I thought this was paradise," Zeph muttered. "I thought it was a place where beings set aside aggression and greed, trading for grace and intelligence. Nikodamus made me believe that was who his people were." Disappointment and disillusion weighted Zeph's heart and spirit, like someone dear to him had died—and they had, but it was more than Nikodamus' death. An ideal, a dream he wanted to believe in, had died and taken his naivete with it.

"I am sorry," Bobalo spoke solemnly. "Nikodamus was a good man. I will miss him."

CHAPTER FIFTY-EIGHT

"I barely knew him." Zeph sniffed, trying to shake off the effect of the emotions. "But I admired him."

"Many did," Bobalo agreed. "Now we must try to hold together the alliances he built without him. The clans have people searching for Saldo. If they find him, any responsibility held by any Ebulonian or clan will die with him. The Taiban community will be blamed for everything, including our destruction. They are trying to push us into a civil war, Yare, and if they do, they will drive us off of Ebulon and back to the Taiban Cluster, or whatever outpost we can find to take us in." Zeph gave Bobalo a thoughtful but skeptical look. "It is in the agreement that we made between us nearly twenty years ago," Bobalo assured him. "The riot has already laid the groundwork for expulsion. Any further aggression could mark the end for us.

"If Saldo Murtevoy is taken by them, it will be the match that starts the next blaze. We need to find Saldo before they do."

"And I am the bait," Zeph revealed his understanding of Bobalo's plan. The Taiban leader nodded.

E.F. Winters

CHAPTER FIFTY-NINE

"Trying to define the Truths, you lose them. Trying to speak to them, you lie. But hear them in their natural voice and the universe will sing to you." (The Ballatyn's from the Book of the Rhune compiled in the Second Age.)

Blast marks blackened Iredipa's white walls, maelstroms of dark smoke rolling away from the burning city like black wheels in the sky.

The vision shivered and changed.

Rag-daubed children scattered like rats down alleyways between the filthy and crumbling bombed-out shells of old buildings.

"Taiba," Eropa deduced.

Her vision morphed into a third.

Those being pursued were stocky-bodied, fur-covered beings. A silver female looked back over her shoulder and into Eropa's eyes.

"Help us, Wise One," she begged. *"Help us. The Balance is broken. Help us, or the Cumin of Ra will surely be no more."*

The furry silver one's features and fur shifted to a thick, burnished hide, her head flattening out and rolling across the top until it became a bronze sculpted face, crowned by a scalloped forehead.

"You are the only one who can save us," the young female claimed.

Eropa felt the fear and strength that united each of the worlds in her vision, and the images changed again.

The city was dark, the sky above a lighter blur hidden behind a solid, dull barrier marred by algae patches. Tall buildings encroached on every side. Garbage was piled to the first story, clogging walkways, soaking up the sewage that ran down the gutters.

The purr of an engine drew her attention. A flying craft approached overhead. Through its large front window, Eropa could see Zeph Yare, his face lit by the console in front of him.

CHAPTER FIFTY-NINE

"Zeph's world beneath the Dome." The sense of despair exuded from every corner, every atom, the planet itself screaming in its death throes.

Eropa cringed. How could they live like this?

"We are all connected," she heard Hagriva say in her memory. "We tell ourselves that others are not our concern, and since life is a choice, we make it so we are not responsible for the results of others' choices. But the Truths teach us that what happens to one affects us all. When you understand this, you cannot back away from the fight."

Amid all the disorder and uncertainty that marked Corin's life since the alien's arrival, the simplicities of Auger and Adaya's cottage in the Deepwood were unexpected. Corin inhaled the scent of the flowers, herbs, and forest so unique to this place where the domain of tree and human overlapped.

She always felt more Taiban than Ebulonian, but being here, she realized this was as much a part of her heritage as Taiba—more so because she was born on the planet and had grown up on its soil. The Hidling's malevolence was absent from Auger and Adaya's little corner of the forest, leaving nothing but its magnificence and mystery. And yet she did not feel any danger. Eropa's grandparents had created a sanctuary in the Deepwood.

Ready Brother grazed on clumps of grass along the wicker-fenced yard. With the aid of one of Adaya's herb and beeswax ointments, the sores on the gelding's back and sides were healing, as were her wounds.

Eropa would also heal, and soon enough they would return to Iredipa, Corin reminded herself, wondering what they would find there.

Auger Mc'Kinock sauntered out of the house with his customary slow, rolling gait. The pace here in the Deepwood might be more easily measured by the slow, steady growth of trees than the quicker pace of the human heartbeat, and Corin wondered if, when she and Eropa returned, they would find they had been gone for years, not days. Looking at how time had so little effect on Eropa's grandparents, it seemed a reasonable possibility.

"Come, lass, and help me feed the critters," Auger called to Corin over his shoulder as he headed for the barn.

There was nothing she could do for Eropa now; that was up to Adaya, and it was good to stay busy. Corin trotted after the older man.

It was a tidy barn, smelling of hay and horses, everything in its place. There were a few goats, some chickens, some long-haired rabbits, and a long-legged woolly animal that Corin had never seen before. Not a bit of metal was used in any part of the steading, no nails, and no hinges, every part handcrafted by Auger from wood, leather, and natural fibers.

The house was a practical structure with a living roof of short mosses that shot up delicate pink flowers on invisible stems hovering over it like a halo. Clouds of butterflies and bees flitted among the flowers during the day, and moon moths took over the territory at night. The wood-framed windows were skillfully covered with translucent wing material gathered from large insects when they molted. Flowering vines climbed the walls and the chimney chase, curling around the fence posts and wickerwork gates. Crafted with a balance between care and whimsy, the yard and garden were as wild and charming as a bracken wood.

"It is something, what you've built here," Corin complimented Auger as she took the shares of hay for the two black draft horses, Bearnas and Baltair, and dropped them in their troughs.

"Nothing lasts like metal, but that is not the way here. Ninety percent of our time is spent fixing what's been broken, but it gives me something to do." Auger cracked a crooked smile.

They finished feeding, then headed back to the house.

"How is Eropa doing?" Corin asked as they climbed the steps to the porch.

"Ach, she'll be fine, thanks to you and that long-legged, red beastie. T'was not a small thing you did getting her as far as ya' did, Lassie."

"I was so afraid we would be too late," Corin admitted.

"Not to worry. Adaya has a healer's touch, and our girl comes from strong stock: Mc'Kinock and Al'Kandin. We're hard folk to kill."

"I don't understand, though, Auger. Why did the forest want to kill Eropa?" The question had bothered Corin for some time. "She's the Pira, and your granddaughter. Doesn't that mean something?"

CHAPTER FIFTY-NINE

"It is a forest, Corin." Auger tilted his head to one side. "It does not have human loyalties or motivations, but it does have a protective instinct, as do all living things. Eropa was infected with a sickness, and she brought that sickness with her. The forest tried to stop her from bringing that infection into it and endangering it. Once she is well, she will no longer be a threat."

"But how was she 'sick'? What happened to her?" Corin needed more.

"You would know better than I," Auger turned the question back to her.

"There was a riot and a fire in Little Taiba. Eropa fought in it. She saved a lot of lives," Corin defended her friend. "She was only doing what she had to."

Auger looked at her long and seriously before he spoke. "I think if that were all of it, she would not be sick." He went into the cottage.

"Walk with me," Eropa's grandmother suggested a week into her granddaughter's recovery. Eropa rose.

"If you like." Despite Adaya's recusal of Rhune tradition, she had grown up and been trained as a Rhune. A walk would not merely be a walk. "Where is Corin today?" she asked.

"I believe fishing was on the agenda today." The message was subtle; neither her grandfather nor her friend would be joining them.

Adaya led her granddaughter out the wicker gate into the forest, following a path Eropa could not see but Adaya knew well.

"Do you understand what happened to you?" Adaya asked as they walked.

"I understand my mistake," Eropa hedged.

"Well enough not to repeat it?"

Eropa bit her lip. "I hope so. Things have been difficult in Iredipa since the arrival of the aliens."

Adaya made a harumphing noise in the back of her throat. "That excuse is beneath you, Granddaughter. Decisions should not be made from fear, Eropa. It does not matter if it is fear for your people, fear for yourself, or fear of these intruders; the result is confusion and weakness." Eropa wanted to argue that she was not afraid, but her grandmother stopped her with a look. "When we are most tempted to lie to ourselves, it is most important that we examine hard truths. You define yourself as a Rhune, but you are much more. Life cannot be lived as if there were written rules that you can memorize. There is a natural order within nature's chaos, but its nature is to change, and to think we can control it is hubris."

"You cannot be more disappointed in me than I am in myself, Grandmother," Eropa said humbly.

"You misunderstand me, Eropa," Adaya scoffed. "I am not disappointed in you. You are not to blame for this. The failure lies with your upbringing."

"Please do not blame this on Hagriva. It is not her fault," Eropa was quick to defend her teacher.

"Hagriva was not alone in raising you. Nikodamus bears responsibility, as does your mother, who had you by her side for your first five years and did little enough," Adaya said tartly. "And then there is this Rhune insistence that they are the only ones who can truly interpret The Truths and who have decided they alone are the arbiters of what will maintain The Balance in the multiverse. Do not misunderstand me, Eropa, I have great admiration and affection for our teacher, but she is not infallible. She cleaved dogmatically to Rhune traditions and could not instill in you what she did not understand herself."

They walked on, immersed in their private thoughts, before Adaya spoke again.

"There have been disturbing changes among the many worlds-- changes that went undiscovered until their ripples became too broad and touched our shores. The greater effect occurs when we stop the pebble before it hits the water. It may be all but too late, and yet we cannot turn away and pretend the stone that fell in the pond and made these ripples had no effect, or we would not be Rhunes." Adaya smiled. "And whatever they say, your grandmother is still a Rhune, Eropa." She sighed.

"Our choices are our own. They affect lives far beyond our circle- -beyond this world even. The arrival of these intruders at this moment in time means something, Eropa. The Taiban unrest and many other events occurring on other worlds that we are not aware of are all connected--held together by the woven fabric of choice.

CHAPTER FIFTY-NINE

"The burden of decision will come to you soon enough, whether you are ready for it or not, and you will learn how fragile and mutable right and wrong can become in the doing."

"I understand," Eropa replied.

"I do not think you do," Adaya said sternly. "Hagriva has taught you to submit to duty, as she did, as your mother did, because for them, that was the Rhune way. But if you study the Truths in their original texts, you will see that blind obedience is not what they ask of us. Quite the opposite, they encourage individual thought, analysis, and interpretation. How else can they be truly 'multiversal'? Have you ever considered *not* submitting?"

Eropa looked shocked. "I could not do that. I am a Rhune."

"You have been trained in Rhune philosophy, but you are also an individual with free will. Have you never thought to ask who these invisible Rhunes are who demand your unquestioning loyalty? Have you ever examined the purpose that moves them?"

"I am not part of the Council," Eropa replied.

"But someday, you could be. The Council once openly embraced discussions of the differences in cultural understandings of The Truths. Now they demand that all worlds adopt one interpretation: theirs. It is not an understanding reached through the firing kiln of experience but dictated by those who have deemed their understanding is right and therefore everyone else is in error."

Eropa frowned. "Philosophers and academics enjoy debating the nuances of every word, but people need certainty, grandmother."

"Strict rules without flexibility," Adaya grunted. "That is the path you will hold to, granddaughter? Your mother worked herself to death doing her 'duty', then the Council had her body burned to protect the knowledge she possessed, destroying any possibility that she might return; the result of inflexible thinking."

Eropa felt her heart leap. "Was such a thing even possible?"

"Not without a body. By the time I heard about it, the deed was already done. If Hagriva and I could have changed the outcome, it was too late. The Sisterhood's leadership denied you your childhood, took your mother from you, then demanded you be removed from the care of your only remaining parent, your father. Why?"

"Hagriva needed to train me."

"At five?" Adaya arched a brow. "If it had been decided that you were to inherit 'The Gift' anyway, why did she need to force-feed hundreds of years of her own experience into a child too young to understand any of what she learned?"

"They needed to know that I could do it—that I was worthy," Eropa explained. Her grandmother's questions were unsettling.

"Ah, yes, there have been some problems: my perceived defection, your mother's overzealous reach. Mistakes, the Council calls them. Mistakes for which we have all paid and continue paying." Adaya stopped walking, studying her granddaughter's face. "Do you believe that someone else has the right to demand that we comply with 'their' beliefs and choose our actions to suit 'their' purposes without understanding them?" she asked.

Eropa remembered her sense of betrayal on discovering the alien's treaty stipulation with its humiliating marriage. She had not accepted blind obedience then. She had become angry, acted on that anger.

"It does not matter," Eropa replied, feeling the deep scars caused by her rebellion. "Sacrifices have been made. I will not dishonor them now."

"Spoken like a true pawn. Hagriva has done a good job with you." Adaya gave her granddaughter a mocking nod of respect. "Our great teacher has raised a good little lamb who will obediently walk to slaughter as instructed. Oh, I hear you silently protesting, but I ask you, why has Hagriva left you to struggle with the questions that haunt you, then sent you to me when she knew you would no longer accept her sidestepping? She knows what I will say to you. I did not blindly accept the path the Sisterhood set for me. I found my way."

"Because you met grandfather."

"No. That is a convenient excuse for the Rhunes, but it is not the truth. My decision was made before I met Auger. Hagriva and I were already arguing. I had been questioning the pursuit of power and higher magic when your grandfather showed me the Deepwood and its truth, and I fell in love."

"With him, or the forest?" Eropa teased.

Adaya smiled, a moment of nostalgia flickering across her face. "Both."

"Hagriva must have been livid."

CHAPTER FIFTY-NINE

"I had no idea that she possessed such an indelicate vocabulary, but then I suppose you have many opportunities to learn strong language in three hundred years of trying to manipulate the lives of others. But you need to know this, Eropa, despite Hagriva's initial anger and disappointment--and much of it was that disappointment-- she and I have become stronger allies because our paths diverged. When we have hard questions, we have a larger pool of knowledge to draw from. If I had stayed, I would have merely mirrored her knowledge--repeated her answers. Now, my understanding is my own."

"I am sure it is wonderful to live here among the trees, removed from the complications of people and politics, Grandmother, but this is not the real world," Eropa reproved Adaya.

Her grandmother laughed. "You think Iredipa and Alden Baierd are the real world? The center of power on Ebulon is not Iredipa or Alden Baierd, Eropa," Adaya argued. "It is here in the Hidling. The Deepwood was old before the first Rhune set foot on this world. Our people know that when they plant a seed, the planet nourishes it so it will grow and feed their children. Iredipa has no such power. Iredipa only grows greed and pretense."

"And Alden Baierd?"

"These days, Alden Baierd grows only moss. Without the Deepwood and the Hidling, Ebulon would die," Adaya announced. "In her last days, Hagriva understands that. That is why she sent you here to see me."

"It is all well and good to recognize the importance of the living planet, Grandmother, but someone still has to stop the bad people," Eropa said testily.

"And you know how to tell who they are?"

"Of course," Eropa insisted.

Adaya's smile felt condescending. "There is a difference between standing against something and fighting it, Eropa, a difference within yourself, and in the price that is paid for the actions you take. A Rhune is tasked with keeping The Balance, but first, you must know balance and imbalance, change and transformation. Making a decision is more than defaulting to the result of inaction."

They walked deep into the forest while they talked. There was a quiet only broken by the vibrating hum of bees, the wind shushing the grass at their feet, and the ruffled branches of the trees. A songbird warbled joyfully, answered by another, then fell silent only to be echoed somewhere in the distance.

Peace and contentment rose from the ground, enveloping grandmother and granddaughter like an invisible mist. Adaya's eyes changed, her focus floating away from reason and the conversation required of it.

"The heart of the Deepwood," she whispered, reluctant to break the natural song that surrounded them. "Come, after all this talk of difficulties, I would share some hope." She led Eropa through the dark pine trees, each step releasing a perfume from the duff on the forest floor.

They came out from under the dense canopy of pine into a grove of slender deciduous trees, with white bark glowing against the backdrop of the darker evergreens shielding it, its leaves fluttering black and silver against the white bark.

"This is the Deep," Adaya informed her granddaughter. "The heart of the Hidling."

The grove followed a pattern of radiating lines and concentric circles with an open aisle down the center that led to a clearing. In the clearing stood a single enormous white tree, larger than any tower Eropa had seen, its roots twisted into small rooms, tiny burrows, and a large hall. Tiny, white lights flickered in and out among the time-burnished roots.

"Move slowly and above all remain calm," Adaya cautioned Eropa as she led her to the base of the great tree. Peering over a trunk-sized root, smooth and gently twisted with age, she indicated Eropa should do the same. "Come closer. Look."

A scaled beast raised its huge head, turning swirling kaleidoscopic eyes on them. The scaly tail of the beast encircled a stack of glistening stones with pearlescent landscapes of whorls and swirls imbuing their surfaces.

"She will not hurt you as long as you do not threaten her clutch," Adaya assured Eropa. "This is Honor Searigh, a Windega, or Ombra, the Rhunes call them. The Sisterhood uses them to move between dimensions and worlds. The Ombra have sat on the Rhune High Council as far back as records go, but their numbers have dwindled recently as their breeding grounds have been invaded."

CHAPTER FIFTY-NINE

"Could not the Rhune protect these places?" Eropa asked. The Windega's head turned on her long neck, and she looked at Eropa, studying her. Eropa felt the whispering pull of the great beast and her magical clutch of many-colored eggs.

"Their location is unknown to us. The Windega have kept the location a closely guarded secret," Adaya replied. "Though they are beings of great power who have engaged with the Sisterhood for centuries, they remain barely known to us, not even where their home world is. Only a few Windega over the long span of time have deigned to interact with any of our allied species, and even among those, there is a question whether we understand their actions and motivations or they ours.

"The Hidling has not hosted a fertile female since the days of Abrana-Faed, before Hagriva was born," Adaya added softly, the softness of her face echoing Eropa's, a deep sense of wonder wrapped around a compelling desire to safeguard and care for the creatures. "Searigh was in great distress when she arrived," Eropa's grandmother went on. "Injured, exhausted, but once she settled in and the Deep Wood began to heal her, she dug out this burrow, made a nest, and laid this precious clutch." Adaya paused. "She arrived the same day the aliens did."

CHAPTER SIXTY

"Lighting the path was a beginning, but the Rhunes' charges needed to know how to find their way even in the darkness." (Anonymous. A History of the Rhunes: The Hundred Year War.)

Grub sat back on his heels and stretched his back and shoulders. He hated weeding, but between their growing appetites and the small animals that were raiding their cache, the Cumins' food supply was steadily dwindling.

He glanced at Bibi, patiently separating tuber clumps, setting aside half for eating and replanting the other half.

When Grub planted things, they died. Therefore, weeding had become his chore. When he complained about the futility of cultivating crops they would never see harvested, Bibi was conspicuously silent. Every suggestion Grub made about finding their way back home fell on deaf ears. Grub wondered sometimes if the little albino had any intention of ever leaving the cavern.

As agreed, he began to teach Bibi proper speech, the stories, and the social strictures of Cumin society. She was very bright, soaking up everything he told her, then pestering him with questions that he had never thought about until he thought his brain would crumble.

"No more questions, Bibi! I can't think anymore today. I'm not sure who is teaching whom," he grumbled.

She also remembered everything, catching him up on details he had neglected or changed from one telling to the next. The only thing he had to tell her twice was to leave him alone.

"Bibi, stop," he scolded her regularly. "You are starting to sound like an old aunty, always reminding me of how to do things."

And she would stop, for a while, never sulking about it, and then something else made her curious, and she started back up.

There were other changes as well.

Bibi was losing her chubby cub shape. Grub noticed how the silver fur across Bibi's back rippled like wind in new grass. Sometimes, when they wrestled in play or challenged each other to an

CHAPTER SIXTY

obstacle race, Bibi won, and it was not because Grub let her, though he would not admit it.

Now that no one was cutting Bibi's hair, it hung in a shimmering silvery fringe brushing her shoulders. In some lights, she was beginning to look like a real Cumin female, something that unexpectedly gave Grub a disquieting feeling as well as a brief spark of pleasure.

Of course, Bibi could not weave her hair into clan braids, even if she knew who her father was. As a Spirit Speaker, Boors had no clan, and Wan's clan never recognized the albino as one of theirs.

Bibi had taken to smoothing her fine, silvery strands with stubby fingers, a nightly ritual Grub found both familiar and comforting to watch, remembering the females from his household sitting by the fire to comb out their hair each night before re-braiding it.

Grub recognized changes in himself as well. His brown clan-braids had grown long, and a light, downy fuzz was beginning to shade his jawline. Back in the village, he would have been moving to the men's camp.

But the evidence of time's passage mirrored in their bodies did not change Bibi's mind about going home.

Whenever Grub pressed, she would sniff the air, looking up at the tiny patch of sky visible from the floor of the cavern, then say nothing.

"Why do you do that, Bibi?" Grub asked her finally. "What is it you are trying to smell?"

"Air," was her cryptic answer.

Grub took a deep whiff and wrinkled his face. "All I smell is old cave, but I do not see what that has to do with trying to find our way home."

The last time he asked, she surprised him, saying, "When the wind blows again, we will talk about leaving."

"When the wind blows..." He squinted up at the chimney shaft, chewing on the mystery of why the wind needed to blow. Several days into his anticipation, he realized the wind had not been blowing, and it should have been.

He realized he could not remember there having been any wind since they arrived at the Cavern of the Hollow Winds. In the Beast's tunnels, smells were pushed by sluggish air currents moving between levels, or by the creature's terrible breath, but there was nothing Grub would call "wind."

Like so many mysteries they lived with since they became trapped under the mountain, Grub was certain that if he had just one more piece of the puzzle, he would understand this.

"Why must we wait for the wind?" he challenged Bibi. "Why can't we go home now?"

Her blue eyes blinked. "Wind cleans Ra's air."

Grub jumped to his feet. "That does not explain anything. I want to go home, Bibi. I want to go home now." He stomped his foot.

"Do you know the way?" Her calm was more frustrating than if she had shouted at him.

"No," he admitted.

"Me neither. Here we have food, water, and no big animals hunt us."

"Except the Beast."

"It cannot come here. The tunnels are too small. We are safe in the cavern, but if we leave, we are not. We could become lost again, or the beast could find us, or those bat things could kill us."

"The wind will not change any of that," Grub pointed out the flaw in her reasoning.

"There is no place to go, Grub. We stay here until the winds come," she repeated stubbornly.

Bibi's vocabulary and Grub's cheek hair were not the only things growing in the Cave of the Hollow Winds. Every night when Bibi went alone to her sleeping place, Grub secretly took out his stone. He proudly presented Bibi with one of the knives he picked up in the beast's cave, showing off the one he kept for himself as well, but he did not mention his private treasure.

At first, Grub had kept the stone in a hollow carved out of the sandstone wall behind his sleeping space, but when they began to experience theft by small animals, he became afraid that his stone might be taken. Fashioning a sling pouch, he tossed some dried weeds into the bottom of the pouch and settled the stone among them, putting a few useful items on top so Bibi would not wonder why he carried the sling. All through his day, Grub felt the stone's warm weight nestling against his belly. He cared for it as he had seen Gutte care for the village's sacred relics, rinsing the dust off its surface, letting it sit

CHAPTER SIXTY

in a patch of sunlight from the cavern chimney when Bibi was not around, mumbling his private thoughts to it as if the stone were alive. He had never been good at secrets, but he kept this one. The stone was his, and he did not want to share.

Alone at night, Grub took the stone out, rolling it between his hands, feeling the deep satisfaction of it just existing. At night, he rested with the stone against the curve of his furry belly, enjoying its muffled hum. Sometimes, after Bibi went to bed, he placed the pearlescent stone near the fire and watched the stone's swirls snake around its surface. As his treasure grew larger and heavier, he took pride in the fact that it no longer fit in the palm of his hand, never questioning how it was that a stone grew, or hummed, or had warmth.

Maybe it is a magic stone, and I will discover how to use it and become a great Spirit Speaker, the young Cumin spun out a fantasy. Bibi's magic eyes would be nothing to his powers, and when he returned to the village, miraculously alive and grown, everyone would respect him. He imagined himself magnanimously announcing to the village that although Bibi was strange, she should be accepted in the village because he taught her the Cumin ways, and this made her a worthy female. Of course, she would have to abandon practicing magic, he reminded himself. Surely, she would be willing to do that to be recognized as a true Cumin? It was what she wanted most in the whole world.

One night after Bibi went to her camp, Grub was preparing for bed when he noticed a pair of round gold-flecked eyes watching him from beyond the fire's light. The eyes were too large for a rat or a squirrel. Grub slipped the stone beneath his tunic and curled around it, pretending to sleep. But he could not sleep. Why were the eyes watching him? Who did they belong to? It bothered him that the eyes seemed more intelligent than those of the small creatures they knew shared the cavern.

In the morning, Grub searched for tracks in the area where he had seen the eyes, but most of the area was hard rock, and the sandy ground around it showed only the small scratched footprints of mice and voles.

After that, the young Cumin grew more cautious, setting up traps around the food cache and keeping his treasure out of sight.

E.F. Winters

"I am sorry," he told his stone charge. "But there are animals who like shiny things, and I do not want you to end up in some smelly rodent's hole."

And all the while, Grub kept an eye on the chimney shaft.

They had been in the cavern for something over two moons now. The rains should have come and gone. The hot season should be over and frosty days be on their way, but day after day, the patch of sky they could see through the chimney remained a dull, dirty brown.

"I hate it here," he complained to the stone. "The seasons never change, but outside, it will be time to hunt. Every hunter will be needed, and then we must protect our stores from raiders. Bibi is stubborn and wrong-headed. She has always been that way. That is why she argues with me, but we need to go home."

Grub made a spear and began to practice with it. He was sure that Bibi watched him, and he secretly hoped she noticed how strong his spear arm had become, but she said nothing.

"She knows now that I am stronger than she is," Grub bragged to the stone.

"Cub make speaking noises to Sisirra's treasure?" a voice squawked in very un-Cumin-like sounds.

"Who's there?" Grub drew his knife from his belt and slipped the stone behind him. Edging himself to a better defensive position, he glanced to where the lump that was Bibi's sleeping form was some distance away.

"Cumin cub shouts to female Cumin, and he must show what he stole from Sisirra's cave," the voice said.

Grub's eyes narrowed. How did this intruder know he had stolen something? What did it know about his stone?

"Not 'yours'," the voice argued. "And not a stone."

Grub froze, his mind replaying his theft of the knives and the stone.

"Sharp sticks, worthless to Crarm," the voice reassured the Cumin. "But egg..."

"Egg?" Grub repeated. "I have no egg."

"You do; Sisirra's egg. You stole it from her cave," the invisible creature disagreed.

CHAPTER SIXTY

"A stone is not an egg," Grub grumped. "And I do not have any stinky old egg, so go away." Grub made a show of curling up to sleep, hoping the creature would take the hint.

One of the beast's big bat allies hopped forward into the fire's light. It had small pointed ears, a short, rounded snout, and black eyes. Grub scooted back against the short wall behind him, pushing against it until the hard rock pressed against his back.

"Guardians not bite… much." The bat creature opened its mouth to show a row of evilly sharp teeth. Grub was not reassured, but he did not want to admit it because then the creature would know that Grub had already fought one of its kind and burned one of their nests.

Grub realized the creature probably already knew all of this. That was probably why he was there.

Crarm studied Grub soberly.

"Kee's nest burned, her clutch gone." The creature made a motion like a shrug. "Tomorrow, Kee forgets. Next season she mates again and makes new clutch, but Sisirra's egg be special. Egg magic very strong; stronger than Kee's mother instinct. Guardians must protect egg. So few left now of Sissirra's sisters and brothers." Crarm swung his head from side to side. He came closer, making himself comfortable within the warmth of the fire. "Only one egg left on Ra-- maybe only one anywhere." He sighed, his breath making a rattling noise in his throat.

"Why are you telling me this? Go away and stop bothering me," Grub insisted, though he was beginning to think he might understand more than he wanted to. "Who is Sisirra?" he asked, unable to hold back his curiosity.

"You know." The bat thing roared and trumpeted, flapping its wings. Its claws shredding the air.

"Sh!"

Bibi sat up and looked toward Grub's camp, but he just ignored her, and after a minute she lay back down.

When Grub looked up from the fire, the Guardian, Crarm, was gone.

Grub lay back down, once again finding his thoughts kept him sleepless. Was it possible that his stone was a beast's egg? Now that Crarm and the beast's allies knew where the stone was, would they attack and take it back?

"Crarm's words all true." The guardian landed easily atop the short rock ridge above Grub. "Stop fear thoughts. Crarm not hurt Cumin cub." Though his smile remained as terrible as before, up close, Grub could see that his eyes showed intelligence and curiosity rather than anger and a desire to see everything as a meal. The big bat slipped off the ledge, sitting an arm's length from Grub. "Cub take good care of egg." Crarm stole a few inches closer.

"Stay where you are," Grub warned.

"Cub show egg to Crarm?" The bat cocked its head sideways to look up at Grub.

"I told you, I don't have any egg," the Cumin repeated defensively.

"Crarm been looking and looking. Followed Cumin smell. Been to cavern many times, seen egg."

"You went through our things!" Grub accused it. "You've been into our food!"

The golden circles that marked the ally's eyes whirled as he licked his lips. "Crarm hungry and roots good. Crarm like 'em." He smacked his thin lips.

"You stole our food!" His condemnation was clear.

"And you stole Sisirra's last egg," Crarm pointed out matter-of-factly. "Got more roots? Hunting very bad. Guardian's stomachs rattle like dried gourd." He poked out his shrunken belly and knocked on a rib.

"Doesn't Sisirra hunt for you?" Grub asked.

Crarm rolled back into the sand, snick snicking in some version of laughter for his species. "Sisirra hunt? No, Sisirra too slow and too lazy. Mostly, Guardians hunts and Sisirra eats, but hunting no good now." He sobered. "Big animals all gone from Ra. Mostly everything gone. Cub should be careful. Anything with a heartbeat sniffs around the tunnels," he warned.

Grub felt the stone's smoothness against his backside. He always knew it was special, but he did not understand why or what it was. His feelings about his stolen treasure were complicated, but if what Crarm said was true, then one day his "stone" would hatch into a baby beast. What would happen then? Would he be its first meal?

CHAPTER SIXTY

It would be better for everyone if it never hatched, Grub thought, but if he and Bibi left and went home, it wouldn't matter if the beast left a baby behind to roam the tunnels beneath the mountain.

"Show me the way out, and I will give you the egg," Grub offered.

"Show Crarm the egg," the bat countered.

It was hard for Grub, but he reached behind him and reluctantly drew out his treasure.

Crarm's eyes warmed, misty with emotion. "Sisirra's egg," he whispered reverently. "Crarm may hold it?"

"You won't try to fly away with it?" Grub demanded, forgetting that he had just offered to barter the stone away.

The golden irises rolled wildly. "Crarm never harm Sisirra's egg. Never."

"All right." Grub gently placed the egg in the cradle Crarm made of his wings.

The guardian looked up at Grub. "Cub good guardian."

Grub swelled with pride, trying to push away the feelings of loss that swept over him, watching someone else hold his mysterious charge.

Crarm carefully handed the egg back. "You take." Grub held the egg tight in the circle of his arms, pressing it against his belly. It began to vibrate softly and hum.

"Few Guardians living since day of the red fire," Crarm said, wistfully. "Many were outside hunting when fireballs fell from sky. After, only bad air outside, and everything burned: trees, grass, animals. Guardians who go out to check on friends don't come back." Crarm's brow furrowed. "Sisirra so hungry she's crazy with belly growl. Then she lays two eggs. Guardians try to go outside to hunt, but only a few come back. Tell sad stories before they die. Sisirra so hungry now she eats whatever she can catch, even us. Even one of her eggs." The Guardian looked sad. "Guardians hungry too, but Sisirra is big and Guardians are little and kept close by egg magic. Then Sisirra smells fresh blood of Cumin. She goes mad trying to hunt and eat cubs, trumpeting and banging rock walls. When she loses Cumin smell, she wanders tunnels, following old scents. She goes outside and breathes bad air." The words were spoken like a death sentence.

"The beast found a way out?" Grub's mind was filled with that single detail. "Can you show me?"

E.F. Winters

"No good outside. Everything burned."

"Maybe close to the cave entrance it is, but not everything is burned," Grub argued in superior certainty.

"Everything," Crarm repeated sadly.

"Not my village--"

"Cumin village gone, stubborn cub--burned," Crarm insisted. "Only bones there. If cub goes outside, bad air make him into bones too."

Grub jumped to his feet, holding the stone against him. "I don't believe you. You're just saying that to get me to give you this old rock. Bibi and I lived through the fireballs and the bad air, or whatever you say happened. Other Cumin will have lived, too."

"No." The Guardian rolled his head from side to side. "Ra burned all over."

"You're wrong!" Grub snapped. "Others will have gotten inside a cave, like we did, and the air is getting better. Bibi said we could go home as soon as the wind blows."

Crarm hung his head between his shoulder blades. "No wind coming. Ra is dead."

Tears welled in Grub's eyes. "No one lived? There's nothing?" The guardian shook his head, and his golden eyes were heavy-lidded. "My whole village is gone--my family?" And then he realized, this was why Bibi would not take them home. This was what she meant when she said their world was gone. Grub buried his head in his arms and sobbed.

The egg began to hum softly.

That night, Grub dreamed the nightmare that Bibi kept him from seeing when she blocked his view by pulling down the cave opening.

The huts were burning, the bodies of Cumin villagers lying everywhere, dead. Only the odd fortune that he and Bibi ran into the cave to explore had saved them. Then Bibi brought them to the cavern, knowing it was here because Boors had shown her. They lived because of Bibi, and even though he was mean to her, she had gone a step further, risking her life to find Grub when he did not heed her warnings.

He wished she hadn't saved him.

Grub woke with a shudder. His hand was resting on the egg. Its soft thrum soothed him. As he tucked the stone away in his pouch, his

CHAPTER SIXTY

fingers touched the ring reed flute his uncle, Gutte, had given him on his name day. Grub took it out and began to play a sad tune.

Bibi kept looking at Grub as she prepared hot water for tea and roots to break their fast.

"Grub's eyes be puffy," she noted. "Is Grub sick?"

"No," Grub answered sullenly. He did not want to talk.

"That was a beautiful song you played this morning." She began to eat. "I never hear this song before."

"I made it up from my own heart, like Uncle Gutte showed me—like a real Cumin would." Grub jumped to his feet. "But you, Bibi, will never be a real Cumin. You are an evil spirit in a stolen body." He used words he hoped would injure her and stab her to the core. "There is only one Cumin of Ra now--Grub. The others are all dead, because of you."

Bibi blanched.

"You never cared about them, did you? How did you know the fire was coming? You are an abomination, just like they said. You could have warned them; the mothers, the cubs--you could have saved them. Did you hate them all so much?"

"Bibi knew nothing about the fire coming. Bibi was just there, following Grub. That is all. We were playing, remember? I pulled the rocks down to keep us safe when the fire was coming."

"Why, when everyone else is dead?"

"To save my friend, Grub. I did not know the others would die, Grub. I just wanted to save you," Bibi wailed.

"You have done a terrible thing. I am angry that you made me live. I do not want to live with you." Grub marched away.

It was dark when Bibi came to find him. He did not realize that the day had passed while he lay there mourning his family, the village, and the life he expected to live.

"What you do with the life you have, you must decide for yourself," she told him quietly. "I will no longer get in your way." She turned and walked back to her camp.

Grub pulled his sling pouch around and took out the stone, cradling it in his lap, then he got out his ring reed flute and played

E.F. Winters

tunes he remembered from home, weeping as he struggled to find the notes.

Bibi was not at breakfast the next morning, nor did she come to the fire that night. After hours of too much thinking, Grub was glad of Crarm's company when he appeared.

"Got roots?" the Guardian asked.

"A few." Grub shared what he had cooked for Bibi, who was obviously trying to punish him by her absence.

"How's egg?" the Guardian asked around a mouth stuffed full.

"Good," Grub replied. "You know, I think it has grown. I wasn't sure before because, well, a stone wouldn't grow, would it? But now that I know it isn't a stone, I'm sure it has grown."

"Sisirra's egg grow big." The little creature grinned. "Cub take good care of it."

Grub glanced at the guardian uneasily. "I guess, you could take care of it better than I can, Crarm. I don't know anything about raising a baby beast." He imagined the egg the size of a full-grown beast cracking open and a very hungry monster picking up Bibi and stuffing her into its mouth.

Crarm rolled over backward, snick snicking. "Cumin mind pictures funny!"

"Babies are always hungry," Grub tried to justify his imaginative scenario.

Crarm stopped laughing. "Cumin cub take good care of egg. Egg must stay here," he announced as if it had been decided.

"But if it's going to become a baby beast, it will need to eat and drink beast-milk or something, won't it? What will I do? I don't know anything about beasts."

Crarm shook his head from side to side. "Few Guardians. We cannot feed hungry baby Sisirra."

"If everything outside was burned, how will anybody feed it, Crarm? There aren't enough animals left alive on Ra, and if it's going to have any chance of growing up, we're going to need to keep Sisirra's hungry little beast from hunting the animals that are left so they can make babies before we hunt them--lots of babies."

CHAPTER SIXTY

Crarm held up a tuber before chomping down on it. "Good plan. Baby Sisirra must eat roots. Grub smart mama."

"I am not its mama." Grub glowered.

Crarm gave a wicked, toothy grin. "It thinks you are. Egg purrs and purrs for you. It knows Grub's voice, Grub's heartbeat, Grub's smell and touch. Sisirra's egg bonded to Mama Grub."

Grub pulled the egg out of the sling and set it on the sand in front of Crarm. "Then you be its mama."

The creature shook its head. "Too late. Egg been with Grub too long. Sisirra's egg die missing Mama Grub. See?" Crarm pointed to the frenzied swirling on the egg's surface. There was an unsettled pace to the motion, as if it were searching for something. It began making noises that were not soothing hums.

Grub reached out and touched the luminous shell, and the patterns calmed. He pulled it to him, feelings of wonder and comfort filling him. The egg began to hum.

"Don't worry," he crooned softly. "I won't give you away." Whatever it was, stone or egg, marvelous magic, or monstrous beast, it needed him. "You and I are all we have now. Just the two of us."

E.F. Winters

CHAPTER SIXTY-ONE

"What you call magic is merely the work of an adept who holds the keys to reality, fitting them into the lock of chaos and turning that lock, harnessed by their intention." ("Lessons to Other Worlds" anonymous. Author/compiler unknown)

Spectre entered the yard of the man he was helping out in exchange for a room. The man's daughter, Thiel, was hanging out laundry and smiled as he walked inside the half wall of what had been a courtyard. Spectre liked the way the fresh-faced young woman moved, like the graceful swans that glided across the water in the pond near the Iredipa marketplace.

He dropped his head, keeping his eyes on the ground as he passed by. Thiel was fascinating, foolish, and kind, and everything about her made him uncomfortable, stirring feelings that were not only unfamiliar but unacceptable for his kind.

Sometimes, in moments of weakness, his mind tried to justify acting on these strange feelings. If he were stranded here for years, it would be easier to wait out his exile in the security of a relationship. Connections would support his disguise.

He watched the smiling young woman from beneath hooded eyes.

"A man with honest feelings for Thiel would walk away," an inner voice, Jaeger's voice, cautioned. *"In the end, whatever you choose, one of us will be betrayed."*

"There is no 'us'," Spectre reminded his alter ego. *"You are a temporary fabrication of necessity. You are not me."* He turned his back on Thiel's slender body and shining hair.

The guild taught, *"Those who master the self are fluid and without ego. They take up shovel or sword with the same ease".* It was a kind of permission test to be able to hide oneself deep within another.

Spectre settled himself into Jaeger, abandoning his plans for Jaeger's plans; his thoughts for Jaeger's thoughts, harboring only Jaeger's secrets and inner longings. Jaeger would keep him alive.

CHAPTER SIXTY-ONE

But deep down, Spectre would remain.
I will never become less than who I am: a Shadowmaster.

Zeph and Bobalo's visits continued in an observable pattern, waiting for Murtevoy to make contact. The attacks on the clan estates during the Taiban riot damaged what support the Taiban refugees had, and Nikodamus' murder added fuel to the growing anger and resentment against them. No one cared whose uniform the assassins wore, their faces were Taiban—their skin brown, not Ebulonian green. Speculations about clan involvement in the events of the riot, the fire, Alyss McLarik, Dakmira Keesch, and the Mahal's murders were ignored. Influence buried exploration of that narrative.

Little Taiba was becoming more deeply divided by the hour as the stresses of broken families, uncertainties of homelessness, hunger, and futures fed dissatisfaction and fear that quickly flared into street brawls between those who supported Murtevoy and those who believed he was a criminal. Brawls easily became neighborhood battles as groups of younger Taibans roamed the burned-out streets and alleyways looking for a fight. Those who supported Bobalo asked for patience and calm. Those who supported Murtevoy were done with that, insisting it was past time for patience, that they needed to demand their hosts give them equality and share Ebulon's abundance, or they would take it.

The Council, without Nikodamus' calming hand and in flux and chaos themselves, saw only a threat. Anti-Taiban sentiment was voiced openly, those who had long been against the refugees' presence, whipping up fear and mistrust.

It seemed to Zeph, watching from the outside, that the Council was determined to make as many mistakes as possible, assuring the Taibans, who saw violence as their only path, had plenty of examples to fuel their view and convert more of their fellow Taibans to their side.

"They will never willingly give us anything." Zeph heard it in the streets regularly, noting in dismay the fledgling government repeatedly ignoring any opportunity for negotiation.

E.F. Winters

Once the sun disappeared and the first moon appeared, a sinister element that preyed on their weaker fellows, took over the streets of Little Taiba, borrowing bravado from darkness and drink. More timid refugees retreated to whatever shelter they had, abandoning the bereft community to the hardest elements of the population.

Where fear and dissipation rule, safety and cleanliness fail. Zeph smelled the difference between the Little Taiba he had seen in his early days on the planet and the version he walked through now. Without a united labor force and with fear and violence stalking the streets, clean-up efforts struggled and stalled. Burned beams and refuse were piled high beside properties where efforts had started. Soon, streets were blocked as scavengers spread out piles as they went through them.

Soot clung to everything it touched, transferring to everything that touched it. There were few washtubs and less soap. Outside the rivergate, the water ran gray.

Zeph kept to Bobalo's plan, traveling back and forth from the widow Patisel's cliffside house to the east end of The District, where Bobalo's compound was located, and back at regular, predictable times. Though he was unsure who might be Bobalo's people, he knew they watched from market stalls, outside pubs, and from the shadows and rooftops, looking for the sparks threatening to erupt in violence, and waited for Murtevoy to appear.

Even so, when it finally happened, he was startled.

The man who stepped out from behind a burned-out building hid half his face behind a wrapped scarf, his clothes typical of a Taiban Freeman, of heavy, rugged cloth, serviceable with many pockets and accessories providing splashes of color that were easily removable. The stranger planted himself in Zeph's path.

"I hear you're looking for me."

"If you are Saldo Murtevoy, I am. I've been hoping to meet you." Zeph offered his hand. Murtevoy did not take it. The part of his face Zeph could see was set in a scowl with deep, weather-worn wrinkles that said this was his usual expression. Zeph could not see much else to give him any hints into the man's character. But this was clearly on purpose.

"A strange declaration from a man who dines with Tai Bobalo," Murtevoy said accusingly.

CHAPTER SIXTY-ONE

"I understood you dined with him many times yourself," Zeph suggested this fact spoke to a similarity between them: their relationship with Bobalo was a pre-requisite for business, not an indication of a close friendship. "It's not in my mission sponsor's interests to take sides in Ebulon's politics," he made his position clear. A ship passed overhead, and Murtevoy watched it until it passed out of sight.

"Those are not yours," Murtevoy muttered.

"No," Zeph agreed. "But they've passed and there's no reason to think they have any interest in us."

Mortevoy's eyes darted around both sides of the street before he bolted.

Block and Jayq Jacoby were in his path before he got more than a few strides in, stopping him. Within seconds, Murtevoy was hemmed in on all sides. He spun around, his eyes cutting into Zeph.

"Damned bastard. You think they'll thank you for this? They'll kill you just the same as me, just as soon as you're not useful to them." Bobalo strode out from a nearby building. "Come for the price on my head, Tai?" Murtevoy shouted before spitting into the blackened dirt at Bobalo's feet.

"I'm just here to help, Saldo," Bobalo reassured his old comrade. Murtevoy snorted. "We both know the Ebulonians would rather you were dead. You have a better chance of getting a fair hearing if you come with us. The facts about what happened need to be heard."

"Whose facts?" Murtevoy sneered. "Theirs? Yours? His?" He pointed to Zeph.

Again, a ship flew overhead, this time coming in low over the buildings. It landed in a wide section down the street.

"Your men?" Zeph asked Bobalo quietly.

"No." Bobalo's jaw was tight, the beard twitching with the muscles beneath it.

The shuttle door opened, and Captain Ochette of the palace guard came out, followed by a half dozen palace guards who quickly took up positions around Zeph, Murtevoy, and the Taibans.

"Saldo Murtevoy, you are wanted for questioning in connection with the murder of the Mahal Nikodamus Mir and his consort, Dakmira Keesch," Ochette announced.

"I had nothing to do with that, and you can't prove I did." Disdain stamped Saldo's face.

"The truth will be known quickly enough," Ochette stated as two temple Mirs also exited the shuttle.

Saldo went white. "I was employed by the Dum'Laiere clan. I was under Miratha Dum'Laiere's orders. The old witch made me do things! You know how they are," he appealed to Bobalo, then Zeph. "They have powers. They can make you do things that you don't want to do."

"When your mind is read, the truth will be known." Ochette motioned his men to take charge of the prisoner.

"Keep them sorcerers away from me!" Murtevoy tried to twist free. "They don't care about the truth. They don't 'read' anything, they just make things up." Murtevoy's eyes darted around the street, looking for an exit.

"Were you following me?" Zeph asked Ochette.

"I was asked to keep an eye on your activities," Ochette admitted. "You are far too dangerous a character to let wander around without supervision." Zeph thought he caught a hint of dry humor underneath the Captain of the Guard's stern exterior.

"And I bet I can guess who gave that command," he retorted.

Ochette did not look at him as he said, "I would not bet against it."

A small crowd gathered, but more than one saw what was going on and hurried away.

"You need to get him off the street," Zeph told Ochette, his voice low. "There are too many groups who would like to have this man in their control or see him silenced forever." Ochette threw him an alarmed glance. "Can you keep him safe?" Zeph asked.

"That is my intention, Captain Yare."

Zeph hoped Ochette was still the man he believed him to be and had not been persuaded to the cause of one of the clans in the past few days.

Murtevoy refused to walk, forcing Ochette's men to drag him toward the shuttle, his feet scrabbling in the dust, as he continued to shout his innocence, trying to rally the crowd to his defense.

"We'll have company soon," Zeph warned, watching the side streets.

CHAPTER SIXTY-ONE

A guttural cry from among the retreating guards pulled his attention.

Saldo Murtevoy was sinking to the ground.

Ochette, Zeph, Bobalo, and his men all ran toward the guards who circled tightly around Murtevoy. When they got there, the Taiban was already on the ground, blood pooling around him.

Bobalo turned Murtevoy over. A dagger was stuck in his chest, skewed sideways by the man's bulk so it would have gone in and then cut to the left.

The experienced, older men's eyes quickly made their way around the circle, stopping on a young guard whose dagger sheath was empty. The young man looked horrified.

"He grabbed the dagger from my belt and stabbed himself with it. By the Mother, I swear. I did not kill him. He did it himself."

"They've killed the captain!" the crowd shouted.

"They've killed Bobalo!" someone else took up the cry.

"Not Bobalo, Murtevoy. They've killed Murtevoy."

"Good riddance!"

Shouts supporting one or the other of the Taiban captains spread like a grassfire, people running from side streets to join the crowd, their cries mixing and dividing them until the factions divided, facing off from opposite sides of the street, the dust clouding the middle.

When the dust settled, both sides stood, sweating and angry, ready to fight.

"You bastards will pay for this!" The sides surged forward, pressing against and breaking through the smaller circle made up of the palace guards intermingled now with Bobalo's men.

"Get Yare out of here, now," Bobalo commanded indiscriminately.

"He's right." Ochette nodded. "Everyone into the shuttle." He jumped into action as the crowd swarmed forward, uncontrolled, moved by the mass of bodies pressing and pushing forward as the side streets continued to heave bodies forward.

A gun went off, and Ochette fell.

More shots followed, uniformed guards and Taiban Freemen in street clothes collapsing in poofs of dust, making petals of bodies set around Murtevoy's red blooming center. The mob rushed forward with one purpose: gaining possession of Murtevoy's body. As soon as they did, they began to retreat, disappearing amid wails of grief into Little Taiba's burnt remains.

"They killed Captain Ochette," a young guard who was standing close to the young man whose dagger was taken said. He was not much older himself, and he looked to Zeph and Bobalo for understanding.

"I'm sorry. He was an honest man. He did not deserve to die this way," Zeph offered condolences to Ochette's men.

"That Taiban, he took Jori's knife and-and stabbed himself," the young guard stumbled over the words, fighting to find reason in what he had just witnessed. "Why would he do that?"

Young Jori lay at his friend's feet beside Captain Ochette and the other dead, Taiban and Ebulonian, their bodies in odd-angled lines, their pooling blood coming together to make deep crimson deltas in the dark charcoal dust.

"He was afraid," Zeph said, thinking of Murtevoy's reaction to the temple Mirs and having to be Truth Read.

"A Freeman prefers to die fighting," Bobalo offered his own explanation. "You should take your dead and get them back to the palace," Bobalo indicated the waiting shuttle. "You can try and sort out what happened once you're safely back at the palace and someone is caring for your fallen." He gripped the young guard's shoulder in a soldier-to-soldier gesture of support. "Don't expect to make sense of it. A friend's deaths never make sense." He released the young guard's shoulder with a slight nudge to action, giving his men a silent command to maintain a perimeter for the Ebulonians while they worked.

Once jostled from their shock, the Ebulonian guards made short work of loading the shuttle and quickly took off, wary of the possibility of the mobs' return.

Bobalo and Zeph watched the shuttle fly over Little Taiba back toward the palace.

"Your friend Murtevoy knew exactly what he was doing," Zeph said to Bobalo, careful not to be overheard. "He's turned his death into a call to arms."

"And sealed the fate of us all, I fear," Bobalo growled. "I hoped it would not come to this, but we have worked too hard to build new

CHAPTER SIXTY-ONE

lives here to just be pushed off the planet. You didn't start this war, Yare, but you may have to end it. You may be the only one who can."

It was a truth that made Zeph uncomfortable.

E.F. Winters

CHAPTER SIXTY-TWO

"The Truths are eternal, not perfect." (Anonymous. The Book of Rhune.)

Eropa and Ready Brother traveled together one last time. While Eropa would return to Iredipa, the big, red gelding decided he would not enjoy being stabled among the palace and courtiers' high-bred saddlehorses in a large complex of barns and arenas but would prefer to stay with Auger and Adaya in the Deep Wood.

Auger and his team of draft horses set a leisurely pace through the Hidling, the narrow road and surroundings more dappled and bright as they neared the ancient forest's edge. Corin rode on the wagon bench beside Eropa's grandfather, soaking in the peace of the place.

"It makes me sad to leave." She sighed. "I have learned things about myself here, with you."

Auger grunted. "It'll do that. You seem to have gained an admirer, Corin." He squinted into the trees overhead.

Corin frowned, feeling the scab on her ear. "You mean that nasty little Bosk?"

Auger glanced at her ear. "'Put his mark on you, did he? That's interesting."

"Painful is what it was," Corin complained.

"You do not seem to understand the honor you were shown, lass. People talk about the Bosks stealing things, they're collectors, you see, appreciative of beauty, or usefulness—things they recognize as having worth. Few people have seen a Bosk bole, but it is a wondrous place, filled with things they have gathered. Sometimes those things continue as what they were before, but sometimes the Bosk rework them into fascinating objects."

"That does not excuse him from biting off a chunk of my ear," Corin grumped.

CHAPTER SIXTY-TWO

Auger chuckled. "I suppose from a Taiban's point of view it does not, but from a Bosk's that bite was a way to mark you as something special and worthy of their notice."

"You mean he bit me as a way to claim that he had collected me?" Corin scowled into the canopy above. 'I am no one's to be collected."

"Some things cannot be taken, only marked," Auger agreed. "But you should know that they are very protective of anything they consider 'theirs' by right of recognition of worth. In the Bosk world, you will forever be connected to that one Bosk because he marked you as worthy."

"That's weird." Corin resettled herself on the wagon bench and looked around nervously.

"I think it is fascinating," Eropa spoke up. Even on Ready Brother's back, her head was not at the same level as Corin's sitting aboard the oversized wagon, but it was close enough to be conversational. "And rather sweet," she added.

"You could do worse for an ally," Auger told Corin. "A Bosk does not mark an outsider lightly. It means he saw something in you, something special." Auger watched the canopy for some time. "Notice how he won't let any of the others get near us—well, *you* actually. We're merely present. He's been protecting us from being harassed."

Corin craned her neck to scan the foliage above. When she found the Bosk who had bitten her, he grinned, baring rows of tiny, sharp teeth.

"I serve the Mul'n Maith," the Bosk spoke mentally as he leaped from tree to tree to keep up with the wagon.

Auger grinned. "Mul'n Maith, eh? That's quite a title you've been given. As I said, they like shiny things."

"What does it mean, grandfather?" Eropa asked.

"Burning metal, liquid metal, and female, something like that. A reference to the fight you put up in the Hidling, no doubt," Auger explained.

"Perhaps 'Molten Maiden'?" Eropa suggested.

Auger nodded. "Aye, that's a good translation. Corin ap Bobalo, Molten Maiden of the Bosk." Auger and Eropa laughed.

"You're having too much fun with this," Corin chided them.

"Seriously, Corin. It is a great honor to be given such a title by an ancient race. You should be very proud," Auger assured her. "This

Bosk thought you very brave--a worthy opponent: glowing like molten steel. Shiny."

"A person is not shiny."

"Some are," Eropa disagreed. "And you, my friend, are one of them. I would not be alive if it were not for you, and Ready Brother." She patted the big horse's shoulder. "And for that I am eternally grateful." Auger nodded with satisfaction.

"We are quite proud to travel in such illustrious company, aren't we, boys?" he flicked the reins, clicking his tongue to hurry the pace of the two huge, black draft horses pulling the cart.

Corin was not the sort of person to push herself forward and did not seek attention, but as the Bosk noted, her character, loyalty, and commitment made her worthy of it. The half-Taiban continued to scowl, but Eropa thought she detected a hint of a smile when her friend next glanced up into the trees to see if the Bosk was there.

"I will miss the peace of being here," Eropa sighed, filling her eyes with the sun-bright and deep shadowed dapple of the old growth trees.

"Me too," Corin agreed.

"You know, you do not have to go, either of you. You could ignore these people's arrogant summons. They only have the hold over you that you allow," Auger offered sagely.

Eropa and Corin's eyes met, both recognizing that they had already decided.

"It is not as simple as that, Grandfather," Eropa declined the suggestion. "It might be that we could do that someday, but right now we have commitments we are obligated to see through."

Auger grunted. "A Rhune's reply."

"Not surprising since I am a Rhune," Eropa retorted.

"What's your excuse?" Auger asked Corin.

"She needs me. I go where the Pira goes," she replied.

"Can't argue with that," Auger gave in. "Don't want to try. Thank you, Mul'n Maith, for standing by our Pira."

"I merely fulfill the heart-pledge of my kinsman," Corin replied, thinking of Quinn. Her cousin would have done anything for Eropa if she let him. What she would allow Corin to do was yet to be seen, but Corin was determined to remain by Eropa's side, protecting her as long as it was possible. She never imagined living a life amid Ebulon's

CHAPTER SIXTY-TWO

politics, but if that was the price for honoring Quinn's memory and remaining true to their friend, she would wade those waters.

She looked into the trees and found the Bosk, squatting on a branch that overhung the road-pathway.

"When you return, you will come among us," it informed her. *"And we will teach you secrets that should not be lost."*

Auger gave Corin a quick, sharp look. Did he hear the Bosk too?

"I am not worthy," Corin declared humbly.

"Our race is scattered—small family groups whose generations are failing. We will not last, but it is our deep-held belief that our knowledge must. That will be your task, the task of the Mul'n Maith."

"I fear you have chosen poorly, my Bosk friend. I am only half Ebulonian and do not have the gifts of those who are full blood of that race."

"Your gifts are your own," the Bosk said. *"And I am not mistaken. You are who I have named you; the Pira's protector and more. If you do not yet see your worth, seek the path that will reflect your true self to you. Remain true to your vows and seek us out when one day you return to the Hidling."*

Corin pondered what the Bosk said. *"When one day you return to the Hidling."* That sounded as if she would not be returning soon, and yet, she could think of no reason her return would be so delayed.

When Eropa, Corin, Auger, and their four-footed friends reached the Hidling's tree line, a shuttle was waiting out in the field beyond the tree line. Sun-saturated, the brightness of the tall grasses, each one outlined in bright light and imbued with rays that turned them a brilliant, eye-stopping green, forced their eyes to close, their heads turning away.

Stopping well beneath the shade of the Hidling's outer edge, Auger eyed the metal shuttle from his bench on the wagon. "Be extra careful and on guard, my dears," he said. "Things that are clear to our hearts here in the Hidling get muddled out there in that other world."

"We will be careful, and we will look after each other and return soon." Eropa kissed her grandfather's cheek, then dismounted.

Corin made her goodbyes as Eropa stroked Ready Brother's thick neck, whispering her goodbyes. The stalwart gelding whickered back, bumping the Rhune with his nose before burying it in her shoulder. Eropa leaned into him, her eyes wet with tears.

"The best of horses. The best of friends," she murmured.

Ready Brother replied with an expulsion of breath so complete that his body sagged.

"He will miss you, but he will be safe and content with us," Auger assured his granddaughter. "His time of fearful adventures in the past."

"While mine, I fear, are just beginning." Eropa straightened, sliding her hand down the horse's long nose.

"When things settle down, you can always send for him," Corin suggested.

Eropa held her grandfather's gaze. "Where I must go, I do not think he can follow."

Tai Bobalo came out of the shuttle, and Corin leapt from the wagon bench, hurrying into a crushing hug against her uncle's bear-like chest.

Then Zeph Yare stepped out. His eyes were immediately drawn to Eropa's. Conflicting emotions crowd each other to be the one to cross his face. But he was no longer as naive as he once was, and his thoughts remained private.

Eropa stepped out from beneath the Hidling's canopy, away from Auger and her family, and walked determinedly across the sun-washed field toward the shuttle that waited to take her back to Iredipa and her responsibilities.

She stood before Yare, studying his face, and he hers, their thoughts guarded, the air around them sparking with charged energy.

"It's good to see you well again, Pira." He subtly bowed his head, in recognition of her position—not a word or thought indicating anything personal between them.

Eropa looked in his gray eyes, searching for it, missing it, but he understood his future and hers now, and he recognized that in this life, those futures barely overlapped. She did not know what she had expected, but it was not this.

"Captain Yare." She ducked into the shuttle, blinking as she once again passed into darkness.

CHAPTER SIXTY-TWO

"We'll update you on the situation on the way, but right now we need to go," Bobalo urged his niece inside.

Seating himself in the cockpit, he indicated that Corin should take the co-pilot's seat, leaving Zeph and Eropa alone in the passenger section.

"The Taibans have struggled since the fire and the riot," Zeph said impersonally. "There are shortages of everything, except hunger, blame, and bitterness, and the Council's decision to place blame for every problem on the Taibans has only encouraged more prejudice and increased the threat of violence."

Eropa blinked. "I left instructions. Pliny was to give them aid."

"He did what he could, but without you, he had little power. The new council leadership has not kept Nikodamus' promises to the refugee community."

"Frevin," Eropa said.

"Yes, Frevin," Zeph acknowledged. "He has completely forsaken the wishes of your father." Zeph hesitated. "You told him you would not choose him as your life-partner?"

Eropa turned and looked directly into Zeph's eyes. "I did. I will give much for my world, but I will not promise my heart when it is a lie."

Words and emotions crowded Zeph's mind, but though there were many things he wanted to say, he knew it was unfair to give them life by saying them out loud. Better to leave them in the half-life of silence.

"He has thrown in with those who resent the Taiban refugees and would end Rhune rule."

Eropa understood. "He ingratiates himself with the old clans that wish to regain power so they will support him in becoming the next Mahal."

"Yes. I am sorry, Eropa."

"Why should you be sorry? You did not make Frevin act as he has."

"But his dislike of me has certainly not helped. My presence has somehow goaded him all along, and I keep asking myself if he would have made other choices if I had not been here."

"You take too much on yourself, Captain Yare. Frevin's choices are his own," Eropa said firmly as Bobalo appeared from the cockpit.

E.F. Winters

"The Council of Elders has declared they will restrict Taiban movement to within The District. No shuttle flights, no trading in the markets, no foot traffic into Iredipa. Not for any reason. Taibans who have worked in the Ebulonian sector of the city for years cannot go to work. It feels more like the Taiban worlds every day," he complained. "Murtevoy was an egotistical ass, but he was no strategist, Pira. He did not plan and execute this whole uprising himself. I guarantee it. Someone else was behind this, acting through him."

"If you knew who, you would have said so. Whom do you suspect, Captain Bobalo?"

The big man shook his head, the silver bells attached to his braids tinkling with the motion. "I wish I knew, but Saldo is conveniently dead." Eropa raised a quizzical eyebrow. "We were trying to talk to him, but Ochette showed up with his men, and Saldo stabbed himself."

"Making it difficult to confirm who his allies were, and who led them," Zeph added. "The clans are working to erase every trace of their involvement, placing blame entirely on the Taibans."

"They will use the original agreement between us to banish us, Pira," Bobalo explained soberly. "And your friend, Frevin, supports them."

"I will speak to him," Eropa promised.

Bobalo shook his head, filling the cabin once again with the sound of tiny bells. "Things have gone too far. We did not want to interrupt your time with your family, but Murtevoy's death and these new restrictions have blown up. There will be a civil war between the three factions at any moment. We need to stop it, Eropa, and for that we need Yare's ship."

Eropa frowned. "I do not understand."

Zeph looked to Bobalo, then plunged on. "What you did when we first met, appearing on the bridge of the Lamdra without a shuttle, can you do that again?" he asked.

"Of course," Eropa replied.

"Even if we don't know the ship's location?" Zeph added.

"Yes," Eropa confirmed.

Zeph exhaled a breath he did not know he was holding. "I need to communicate with the navigator of the Lamdra as soon as possible and convince them to bring the ship back into orbit."

CHAPTER SIXTY-TWO

"Corin," Eropa called forward. "Land in the marketplace at the entrance closest to the palace kitchen."

"We will need weapons," Zeph suggested. "We may have to fight our way in."

"There are weapons in that locker." Bobalo indicated the wall separating the cockpit from the cabin.

"It will be tight for a Taiban ship to land there, won't it?" Zeph asked. Tai Bobalo had re-taken his position as pilot of the shuttle, the others standing behind him, weapons stuck into belts, boots, and hands, watching from the shuttle's cockpit as the ground raced toward them.

"It'll be fine," Corin said confidently. "The market's been closed for weeks. There won't be any stalls set up in the central square. It's plenty big enough to land in."

"There won't be any lights either then," Zeph stated.

Corin snorted. "Stop worrying, Captain Yare. There are good reasons my uncle is respected as a pilot. His skills are legendary."

"Stop telling stories, niece." Bobalo stayed focused on his task.

"But in this case, they are all true." Corin put a hand on Bobalo's shoulder as he brought the ship in close over the buildings surrounding the Ebulonian marketplace.

Zeph scoured the ground below. "It looks like looters have been here but moved on."

"There could still be stragglers," Bobalo warned. "And anyone near enough to see or hear us will swarm this ship the second it touches down. There are few things more valuable than it is right now."

"We can't lose the shuttle." Zeph looked to his companions for consensus.

"Agreed." Bobalo nodded. "I'll get you down, then move off fast and find somewhere close by to wait. Eropa can let me know when you're ready to be picked up."

The Pira nodded.

"Get as close as you can to the kitchen gate," Corin directed her uncle. "Then turn the shuttle so it protects us as we approach the palace."

Bobalo grinned. "So, you *were* listening during my strategy lessons with your cousin and his friends."

"I lived, ate, and breathed them, Uncle," Corin admitted. "I wanted nothing more than to join Quinn and Vale, gain your approval, and fight for our freedom on Taiba."

"Corin…" Bobalo started to apologize.

"Please don't, Uncle," she stopped him. "Everything is different now. I am not that girl, I am the Mul'n Maith, according to the Bosk, and I don't need anybody's permission to do what I know must be done."

"Pira, what have you done with my quiet, unassuming niece?" Bobalo teased, his eyes twinkling.

"It was not my doing, Uncle," Eropa countered. "It was the Bosk whose attentions made her so full of her own importance."

"A Bosk? Truly, Pira?" He shook his head. 'Are you sure you weren't seeing things?"

"It was a Bosk," Eropa said firmly. "There is no doubt. And it named your niece Mul'n Maith, Molten Maiden, because it thought she was shiny." Eropa grinned at her friend.

"I wish you hadn't told him that," Corin protested. "Do you know how much Taibans love to brag and tell stories? I will never hear the end of this." Corin turned to the others. "Call me whatever you like, but when I open this door, run, and don't stop until you get inside the palace."

Bobalo finished his circle, pitched the shuttle's approach from the east, aiming for the end of the thoroughfare closest to the kitchen entrance. As the shuttle descended, figures moved out from the shadowy overhangs of nearby buildings, tracking the vessel's trajectory.

"We're going to have company," Bobalo warned.

"We see them," Zeph said, regripping the unfamiliar Taiban weapon he was given.

The shuttle bumped and scraped to a stop, then Bobalo forced it into a sharp turn.

Corin opened the door. "Go!" She jumped to the ground, followed by Eropa, then Zeph. The engine's whine rose in pitch, and the shuttle climbed back into the sky amid a spatter of gunfire.

CHAPTER SIXTY-TWO

Zeph and Corin shot back, trying to provide a breadth of safety for the shuttle and covering Eropa's retreat to the protection of the palace walls.

The group reformed beneath the covered walkway that connected the kitchens to the market gate, the area ghostly silent, the stone walls shaded in shadow, the paved floor littered with debris.

"This way." Eropa led Corin and Zeph through the kitchen gardens.

Slipping silently through the back byways of neatly laid out plots, the gardens became less well-tended and increasingly wild in nature as they got further from the kitchens. A dark spike outlined against the moon-bright sky seemed to be the beacon Eropa was leading them to.

Where are we going?" Zeph asked, keeping his voice down in case they were followed.

"The Barbican. It is a small piece of the bulwarks left over from what was the original Mc'Larick fortress built on this land centuries ago," Eropa told him. The hair on the back of Zeph's neck pricked up, sending a shiver through him. "It has served as the foundation for many powerful spells," Eropa acknowledged his instincts to be wary of the stone tower. "But it will not hurt you." She took his hand.

As she climbed the stairs of the Barbican, her face transformed, softening, like a lover returning to where their heart dwelt. The light patterns beneath her skin began to glow subtly in the now familiar swirls and vine-like patterns, whimsical, playful, the designs moved like the wind, skipping and dancing.

A tingling warmth tickled Zeph's palm where their hands touched—the energy beneath her skin pulsing against his, as if testing to see if there was a doorway between them. He felt no fear but raised no barrier, and it respected the boundary.

No one said it in words, but Zeph understood from the looks and awkward silences that what Eropa was about to do for him—for all of them, really was not simple. Not even for her. She had done it before, but it was dangerous. And yet she walked toward the task in complete surrender and easy acceptance of the possibility of her death.

Zeph could not think of anything in his own experience to liken it to, except maybe making love. Yet, even in that most intimate act, he had never surrendered himself or indeed trusted.

E.F. Winters

Because you have never really made love or felt love. You have only had sex," Zeph recognized. *You have never been in love before.*

"What is wrong, Zeph?" Eropa's soft voice interrupted his troubled thoughts.

"In Auhora Whimlan…" he started awkwardly. How could he tell her what he was feeling?

She is needed here more than ever, Zeph reminded himself. *I cannot take her away.* Within the larger context of what was happening here on Ebulon, he recognized his feelings had no importance. The looming threat of the Taiban warlords, the tensions between the Taiban refugees and their Ebulonian hosts, the ambitions of Miratha Dum'Laiere, Nikodamus' assassination—each piece was important. Just not his piece. Eropa had unlocked a door to a new way of seeing and experiencing the world, and for that, he would always respect her, but she could never know how much more she had become or how strong her presence would always be in his heart.

"I need you to know I didn't know you were Nikodamus' daughter. I don't know why, but he never told me. I swear," Zeph stumbled through the words. "I never knew you might be the connection to the treaty. I found out when Fratianne told me after that night when you disappeared. Nothing that happened in Auhora Whimlan had anything to do with politics."

"Mostly, I think it had to do with a lot of onche'-laced wine," she replied with gentle humor.

"Yes, there is that," Zeph admitted sheepishly.

"But my reaction to your kissing me was unwarranted," she, too, apologized. "It was the result of my training--years of cautionary tales about maintaining control. And when you kissed me, I definitely did not feel in control. I regret what I did," she confessed. "And I would take it back if I could. But that is in the past, and we must focus on what is ahead of us." She slipped her hand from his, continuing to climb the stairs alone.

Zeph refused to revisit his decision to recognize the Mahal and the Council of Elders as Ebulon's government. He needed to do whatever he needed to do to make sure Eropa was able to remain here. It was the right thing to do, but thinking about leaving Eropa here and sailing away left an ache in his body like he'd fought hard and lost. It

CHAPTER SIXTY-TWO

was not the choice he would have made before when he'd sailed from Pax, but he was not that person anymore.

E.F. Winters

CHAPTER SIXTY-THREE

"The Truths tell us, 'Conceal the self among the stars'. When it is well and truly lost, you will find your way." (Quote from The Matriarch's Journal; The Book of Rhune.)

As soon as Eropa led Zeph and Corin into the room at the top of the tower, Eropa assigned them each tasks to prepare. First, the Agiar. She had faith in Corin's ability to follow the precise directions required in every part of the ceremony, but Yare's participation was an unknown. What they were about to embark on was what he would call "magic", and though he was more accepting, evidenced by his request to assist, he did not know what he was getting into, and his reaction could not be forecast.

She started him out with simple preparation tasks, hoping to reduce his anxiety and maintain enough familiarity with his perception of reality to keep him grounded.

Zeph settled in, accomplishing everything she asked of him, gathering herbs, fresh water, building up the fire, without question and with attention to detail.

When everything was ready, Eropa announced, "I thank you for your help, Captain Yare. The time has come for you to decide if you are staying through the more mystical pieces required of what we are doing. If so, you must remain the entire time, no matter what you see or feel—despite fear or discomfort. You cannot leave in the middle. It would be dangerous and put everything in jeopardy."

Zeph's brow wrinkled. "Everything; you mean it would jeopardize the outcome?"

Eropa nodded. "Yes, the outcome and myself." She could see by the set of his shoulders, the stiffness in his neck and stance that he was uncomfortable with that.

"We don't have to do this…"

CHAPTER SIXTY-THREE

"We do," she stopped him. "If there was another way, you would have already done it. Do not fret, Captain Yare. I can do this. I have done it before." Her eyes teased him.

"And what will I see or feel that I should be worried about?"

"That is uncertain." The sorceress shrugged. "Each person's experience is their own. The mind can create complex scenarios to deal with what does not fit its understanding of reality. You have some experience with this." Zeph nodded. "What will happen in this room will be at the least strange and at the most frightening. And it will go on longer," she warned him.

"What you're doing, you're doing for me," Zeph said. "The risks you're taking should be mine, but I can't take them. So, I'll do what I can. I'll stay," he declared.

"Good." Eropa gave him a reassuring smile. "Then I have something you can do for me. Corin, read this chant." Eropa handed her friend the book with the page open to the chant required to summon the Double. "Keep reading it, over and over again, until we are finished, and I have returned. The sound creates an energetic bridge that I will need to get over and back."

"And what do I do?" Yare asked.

Eropa fixed him in her gaze. "Your heartbeat will anchor me to this world." Corin started to protest, but Eropa raised a hand to stop her.

"How exactly will that work?" Zeph's tone indicated his uncertainty about accomplishing what she asked.

"I will connect to you and the sound of your heartbeat. Like a living drum, I will be able to use that connection to find my way back."

"Your way back from where?" Zeph frowned. "The Lamdra?"

"It is more complicated than that," Eropa explained. "You will see my body sitting here on the floor, but *I* will not be in it. My spirit— my consciousness must travel to another plane and negotiate an agreement with a being there who can do what I cannot; pass through the Lamdra's shields."

Understanding bloomed on Yare's face. "It was not you on the bridge."

"Yes, and no. It was my Double, an entity connected to me-but not me. Your shields will damage any energy bearing a signature from this plane, even something as small as the imprint of a spirit. I cannot say how long you will need to sit. I do not know how long it will take to get my Double's attention and agreement. Then the Double must find the Lamdra and its navigator. There could be problems with any of these steps, but this is what we must do to bring your ship back."

Zeph nodded. "Alright."

"I'm ready," Corin said.

"Then let us begin." Eropa sat, and the others settled into their places.

"Mah Rhune heblow ah. Seis Rhune Mae," Corin began to read the chant. "A-eee home etwaya rah. I-ee hoove etwaya rah, umbaaa aaaah aaaa."

Eropa's spirit walked across the desert playa that covered the surface of the Double's world. The vein-like cracked ground glistened with tiny mica particulates appearing wet as it arced over the distant, curved horizon.

The Double's arrival lacked the dramatic entrance of their previous meeting. Assembling his form from the sand, he approached, stopping within a few feet of her.

"You are foolishly stubborn, little Rhune. Go home before your presence is detected by hungry spirits." The Double examined her with reptilian eyes. *"You are not strong enough for this. You put us both at risk."*

"Asking me to delay is the same as telling me no," Eropa informed him. *"If you stay with this decision, many will die. I cannot accept that. If you will not help me, I will seek another who will."*

The Double's alarm at this declaration was subtly conveyed by his body language, not by his expression.

"The last time I did you a favor, you almost destroyed my body," the Double argued, *"and you were steadier then than you are now. I see a taint of darkness on you. What have you been doing?"*

"Fighting and winning. You see me free the taint now," Eropa argued.

"Barely."

"Times are difficult on my world."

CHAPTER SIXTY-THREE

The Double guffawed. "They are difficult everywhere since the world-straddling beasts have abandoned us. Travel between worlds has become nearly impossible. One can only put so much fear in a tyrant's heart when all you can do is appear like a ghost."

Eropa wondered if he was referring to the creature she had seen in the Hidling, but thought it best not to reveal what she had seen.

"You are trying to distract me," she accused.

"You have not been told of this?" the Double mocked her. *"Ask the old woman who teaches you. She knows."*

"I am not here about that. I have made my request. Name the price you will require for the favor I ask," Eropa persisted.

"Your firstborn son; your everlasting soul; a kiss from your red lips." The Double smiled roguishly. *"But your child could not live on this world, and your soul and mine are parts of the same, so kissing you would be like kissing myself, and where would be the fun in that?"* He laughed heartily.

"I only need you to deliver a message to the ship that you went to before," Eropa tried to sidestep his games.

The Double made a face. *"There is something wrong with that starship. I do not like it. It has the stink of death, and this dressing up in another's body offends me."*

"You only need to deliver a message," Eropa cut him off. *"How you look is not important."*

"These aliens' shields give me a headache," he continued to resist. *"Why do you not use one of their metal boxes?"*

"The ship is no longer in orbit around my world, and I do not know its location, but I must deliver a message from the captain to this navigator. If civil war on Ebulon tears the Rhunes from power and the Taiban warlords enslave those who remain, the sisterhood would not be pleased." Her eyes narrowed to green slits, as reptilian in nature as the Double's own. *"They might blame you for refusing to help me. Of course, you could gain their gratitude instead by helping me. Locate the Lamdra and deliver its captain's message."*

"What is the message?"

"Tell them Captain Yare is safe, and it is time to bring the ship back into orbit around Ebulon. Encourage them to do it quickly." The young sorceress felt the strong, organic connection between herself

E.F. Winters

and the alien captain. Stronger than anything she could have constructed of magic, it was a link that required no energy to maintain.

The Double felt it as well.

"At least your requests are not boring, little Pira. Very well, I agree," he said with a flip of his long-fingered hand.

No nausea accompanied the connection this time. Her body knew the puzzled pathway, and the pieces slid into place with ease. She settled in to wait.

Grief and fatigue lurked close behind every thought, and only will kept them at bay.

She heard Corin chanting and felt Zeph's physical warmth beside her in the circle, his heartbeat strong and steady.

My father, Dakmira, Quinn; so many of the grounding presences in my life are gone, she mused. And soon, Yare would leave as well. A deep sadness seeped from the broken pieces of the young Rhune's heart into the space around her, accepting her connection to Yare like a lost child accepts a stranger's hand, uncertain if they are their rescuer or their destroyer, but knowing their choices are few.

"Alone. So alone," the Void echoed back. *"Help us. You are powerful and we are in need,"* voices twisted pieces of her mind. *"You are a Rhune. You must help us."*

Eropa's awareness shifted, and she hovered before the dark well of emptiness that was the Void.

Spirits clung to the ragged edges of the Crack between the Worlds, their voracious mouths opening and closing like the greedy babes of a darkling race suckling on the teat of the universe.

"Leave loneliness behind and join us," others chanted.

"Solitude is a pebble on a Rhune's path," Eropa recited the adage. *"Those who can forget us are better off, for those who cannot die too readily and too soon."*

"But we are one, together, forever," the lost beings spoke like a choir in her mind. The attraction of such certainty held a powerful appeal, and Eropa drew closer.

"Help me, Mah Rune," a new voice vibrated the Rhune's core. *"Do not forsake me. I have no one else."* Hagriva's energy surrounded the little creature, and through it, Eropa recognized the silver-furred creature's plaintive plea, calling her from far across the multiverse.

CHAPTER SIXTY-THREE

This one must be on a world Hagriva has been helping, she realized, wondering where her teacher could be.

A powerful presence billowed like a roiling cloud of smoke from out of the Void.

The Hungry Ones cringed back, terrorized into silence.

"Well, you are a sparkly bit." The new arrival licked at Eropa, breathing in the young sorceress's essence, squinting one eye at her as if she scrutinized a specimen under a magnifying glass.

Instinctively, Eropa tried to move away.

"You cannot leave." The dark entity's power made itself into a ring shape surrounding the Rhune in every direction.

Something is wrong. Eropa tried to focus her thoughts, but they flew away, scattering into the never-ending darkness.

Tendrils of slippery, silver fog curled around her.

"Have you lost your way, baby Rhune?" the bodiless being mocked. *"Where is your mummy?"*

"My mother lives across the Void," Eropa's mind answered.

"One of my neighbors, then? Perhaps I know her. What is her name?"

"Dupira Rhune," Eropa's mind answered without thinking.

The presence bristled in alarm, quickly covering it with a deceptively calm, oily surface.

"Dupira Rhune's get? Oh, this is ripe. Two Rhunes, both trained by the great Hagriva, stumble into my web." The entity drew so close that Eropa thought it meant to breathe her in. *"Do you know what happened to your mother, little Rhune?"* Its eyes crackled and sparked. *"I ate her,"* the entity hammered its way into the forefront of Eropa's awareness. *"She is always there, a part of me. I feel her, hear her, and smell her every moment, day or night."* Eropa felt the being's victorious spite like a dagger, striking at her heart. *"I hate her! But still, there are rewards. I think I will eat you, too."* The voracious being's fog tendrils curled around Eropa, pulling her toward the mouth of the Void.

Eropa felt the core of herself resist, shredding into whisps, half-transparent, dissipating like the morning fog on Alden Baierd's rocky coasts as wind and sun burned it away.

"Mother!" she cried out.

E.F. Winters

"Dupira Rhune is dead," the entity shot back. *"Only Duvrome Dmoledon remains. I am all that she could ever have been and more, while all that remains of her is the knowledge that I gouged from her weak and dying mind. They made me promises, your Rhunes, and kept not one. They did not accept me and give me a seat among them. They shunned me like a parasite, and I am the host! I am the one who matters. But they will not ignore me after this. Not with two of their precious sisters under my sway."* Duvrome Dmoldedon resumed pulling Eropa's spirit into the vortex.

"Something is happening," Zeph said, starting to his feet.

"Stay where you are!" Corin pulled him back down. "You will not leave this circle," she growled fiercely.

Zeph sat, reluctantly, his mind racing over the possibilities of what he should do. All of them required the Taiban girl's cooperation.

"I could *feel* Eropa, Corin—I mean, before. But now I-I can't," he stuttered. "I think she's in trouble. I think she's gone too far."

"Then close your damn eyes, focus on keeping your heartbeat strong and sending it out to her—but you keep the connection," Corin ordered him.

"You don't understand, Corin. I can't *feel* her--I can't *find* her!" Zeph argued, his heart hammering against the walls of his chest.

Corin dug her nails into the flesh of his wrist. "Don't you dare say that, Zeph Yare. Don't you dare. Eropa trusted you—you, who haven't done one damn thing but make promises that you can't keep." The young Taiban woman sat back, visibly working to calm herself.

"Tell me what to do," Zeph pleaded. "I don't know what to do."

Corin took a few more deep breaths. "Fill every corner of your mind with thoughts of Eropa," she coached. "Memories, fantasies— whatever you can bring up that is strong and emotional. Don't just *offer* Eropa a path back. *Make* her come back. You will not lose her. Do you hear me? *We* will not lose her." The Taiban's loyalty was leonine, and it bolstered Zeph's confidence.

He began replaying every memory he had of Eropa; her first appearance on his bridge, their meeting at the reception, secretly watching her sweep stars and planets in her wake as she moved

CHAPTER SIXTY-THREE

through the strange dance she called "her practice", he infused his heartbeat with longing.

Feeling the thread between them searching unsuccessfully for her was as painful as any physical wound Zeph had borne. He reached out for the remnants of the thread that had been connected to her and gathered them gently, holding them close. Like a spider's untethered silk, Zeph followed the thin, stretched thread out into a darkness that had no markers and nothing by which to find one's bearings.

"Eropa! Eropa!"

What if I never find her? What if I've lost her forever? For a panicked instant, Zeph's will faltered, grief flooding through him, but then, instead of weakening him, the grief swept away the panic, replacing it with stoic determination.

Zeph connected his heart with his midsection, grounding the connecting thread between him and Eropa on his end.

This link between us has always been there, he realized. It was a pact between their spirits, a partnership.

It was what brought him to Ebulon.

"Eropa," Zeph reached out to her with his heart, strong and true, knowing her heartbeat would know his and it would guide her home. *"Eropa, I am here. Come to me."*

Zeph moved his awareness purposefully along the thread.

"Fill every corner of your mind with thoughts of Eropa...and get her back," Corin's words fueled his will.

And then there was tension again. The other end again became secured.

With a gasp of relief, Zeph willed his spirit to her, folding around her like a blanket of protection.

"I found you," he murmured, holding her close. "You're safe."

He felt the pressure of weight against his left arm, where Corin sat beside him, his sleeve oddly damp. Corin's chanting wavered and hiccoughed, tears falling onto Zephs' arm, where she buried her face.

The Double opened itself to the universe, searching until it felt the signature energy of the Lamdra. It was not only the crew that was distinct, it was the wounded nature of the vessel itself, its pain and regret bearing the faintest hint of sentient nature.

Almost alive. Not quite dead, the Double thought.

"Who are you?" a small, plucky voice challenged him.

Thinning himself out across space, the Double became nothing and slipped through the starship's shields. *"You were hiding when I came before."* He approached the nest-like home of his challenger.

"Where is the old Rhune?" the creature spat back. "I know you know her. I can feel her on you."

"The Rhune is not my concern," the Double informed the creature. *"I have come with a message from Captain Zeph Yare."*

"Go on then," the small voice commanded imperiously.

"The message is for the one he calls the navigator," the Double resisted.

"I am the navigator," the childlike being declared.

E.F. Winters

CHAPTER SIXTY-FOUR

"Live by the Truths or die by lies." (Attributed to Regard Mingal, Mir monk/priest, Uncle of General Andreen, whose Book of Thoughts is believed to be the inspiration for the laws governing the choosing of the first Mahal.)

"Why am I here?" Corin asked Zeph for the tenth time as the Lamdra lift took them up to the bridge level.

"Because your uncle asked that I bring you," Zeph explained. His previous explanation of "you'll see" was, apparently, not sufficient.

"That is not an answer," Corin retorted.

"It is all the answer you are going to get right now," he cut the conversation off abruptly as the lift's doors opened.

"Captain on the bridge," Tartulon announced as Zeph and Corin stepped off the lift. "Welcome back, Captain."

The bridge crew observed their returned leader closely, waiting for indications of how he would react to events that played out in their absence.

"Thank you for all you've done to hold things together, Officer Kinsman." Zeph's sign of support for his second in command was unequivocal. "And to the rest of you, as well," he acknowledged the bridge crew. "I cannot say how much value I place on your professionalism and loyalty. We've faced challenges during this mission, together and separately, but we have come through them, and what we've found here--what we are set to accomplish on Ebulon will be worth all the sacrifices." His eyes scanned the bridge stations, tracking to the stairwell that led to the pilot's bubble. "Tartulon, you have the bridge." He walked to the door outside the enclosed stairwell and palmed the identification lock, entering.

The spiral staircase was inside a dark, padded tube that ended in a clear roof that let starlight slide down to the stairwell's foot. Considered to be hypersensitive to stimuli, a navigator's environment was insulated against both sound and light.

CHAPTER SIXTY-FOUR

Zeph removed his boots, set them carefully aside, and began a sock-footed climb up the metal stairs to the landing above, where the navigator's bubble was accessed.

Zeph approached the communication terminal on the landing, his hands hovering over the keyboard. If the navigator felt he violated the terms of the Guild's contract, they could report him, resulting in a huge financial penalty, deducted from his profits from the mission. But in reality, if this conversation upset the navigator, a fine would be the least of Zeph's problems. The navigator had moved the Lamdra out of orbit without being given a command to do so. That was neither normal nor acceptable contractually, which gave Zeph leverage. But using leverage to manipulate a navigator, who was known to be very touchy about being seen to have made a mistake, or just human interaction in general, was a risk. A navigator held the crew's life in their hands every span, and being socially naive if not outright inept, if they became offended, they were known to react badly.

It wasn't that Zeph felt the navigator did something wrong, but by the rules, it was not correct and smacked of arrogance. It was easy to imagine the decision indicated a loss of confidence in Zeph's leadership. If it were the case, he needed to know about it and repair the impression if possible. He thought a lot about where to begin this conversation.

I have to know where we stand.

He was about to key in his message when words appeared on the screen.

Welcome Back, Captain Yare.

Zeph paused. Then keyed in a businesslike response.

We will begin the return trip to Paxlosis soon. Please plot the most direct, fastest route considering the crew and vessel's safety,

Do you have the figure for additional weight? The navigator's words appeared on the screen.

Zeph squinted again into the darkness, but he was unable to see anything inside the sealed glass room.

Not at this time. The specifics of trade negotiation and accumulation of merchandise were put on hold during the Lamdra's unexpected absence, he typed. *I will inform you when loading is complete, and the metrologist has calculated the final weight.*

He wanted to ask what happened, why the navigator moved the ship from orbit, if they were still concerned or thought it likely they would overstep in such a way again, or if they would outright ignore a command, but navigators were odd. Savants with a rare and very particular ability, great lengths were gone to in order to keep them satisfied with their extremely isolated lives. They were not only extremely well paid, but they enjoyed a constant flow of gifts from potential customers and the Guild itself. Every distraction and luxury was provided. This tended to make the social naïve, even inept navigators, very spoiled.

The direct questions Zeph wanted to ask could very well result in a defensive sulk, or worse.

Is there something else, Captain?" The navigator's message appeared on the computer screen. *You seem…troubled.*

The hair on the back of Zeph's neck stood up.

I wanted to thank you for protecting Ebulon in my absence. He spelled out his thoughts honestly but with care. *I was unexpectedly detained. I apologize if my absence made you anxious.*

The entire crew seemed disturbed by it, the navigator replied. *Do you think it likely that you will be 'detained' for such a length again?*

No, Zeph answered in text. *But to complete the mission's business here, spending some time away on the planet will be unavoidable. I do not wish to cause you or the crew additional concern, but there are issues that only I can address.*

I understand; you are the captain.

I am, Zeph replied unnecessarily, but it made a subtle point, reminding the navigator that decision-making was his purview. *But that is not to say that I do not value our unique partnership,* he added rather boldly. *We've both faced complicated and unusual situations recently. Going forward, I expect our path will follow more contractually common precedents.*

A reed-thin shadow moved in the heavy gloom inside the darkened glass walls of the navigator's bubble.

I will await the final weight figures, the navigator sent. She did not say that she understood he expected her not to act on her own again, but Zeph was barely within contract protocols for communication, and he did not want to push it.

CHAPTER SIXTY-FOUR

I will send them as soon as I have them, he typed. *Meanwhile, if you have concerns or become anxious, please reach out to me.*

Zeph retraced his steps down to the bridge's deck, feeling the attention on him from crewmembers who were looking at screens and read-outs. When he once again stood among his bridge crew, he ordered, "Prepare to fire weapons."

There was a split second of hesitation, followed by a well-rehearsed series of precision movements at the weapons console.

"What's going on, Yare?" Corin was beside him, whispering. He ignored her, focused and determined.

"Bring up a visual of the area identified as The District with a filter showing life-signs," Zeph commanded.

Corin's face went white. "What are you doing?" she demanded, so close her voice could only be heard by Zeph alone.

"Making a statement," he replied curtly.

"You can't fire on The District," Corin protested. "There are people there! They've suffered enough!"

"This is not an impulsive gesture, Corin. Bobalo and I have had long discussions about this and agreed, it needs to be done. Someone has to stop the fighting."

"This is not stopping the fighting. It's escalating it!" Corin argued.

Zeph shook his head. "No. It's stopping the petty squabbles by reminding them what a real fight would be like—not just Taibans but Ebulonians as well."

"Then where are the Ebulonian targets?" she shouted, too angry to be worried about what the crew heard or thought.

"This is the first round of strikes." Zeph turned his attention back to his bridge crew. "I'm looking for a few uninhabited targets, people. Give me options. He again addressed Corin, "Your uncle gave me some suggestions, but people move around, and avoiding the loss of human life is the goal here. You know the community, Corin. Can you point out targets?" The look in her eyes said he would be her first choice.

"Don't make me do this," she groaned.

"We can do it without you, but we don't know The District like you do, and we are more likely to make a mistake. We have to stop

E.F. Winters

the fighting, Corin," he reminded her quietly. "If we don't, the Taibans will be banished from Ebulon."

Her eyes burning, she pointed. "Here, here, here, and here." All the areas she pointed out had low biological readings. Some were on the outskirts. Most were in what was the center of town.

"Those readings are probably just rodents, right?" Zeph muttered.

"Of one kind or another," Corin muttered.

"Marks received and targeted," the weapons technician answered back. A compiled map with the darkened areas came up on the bridge's main screen.

"Three pulse strikes at each target point, focused on the outermost corners. Fire," Zeph commanded.

"Firing," the tactician echoed.

No one spoke as areas of intense heat blossomed on the view screen. The bridge crew watched in death-like silence. The separation between the eerie silence of the bridge and the chaos unleashed was its own kind of disturbing.

"Take us back to the wide view, giving me this entire side of the planet," Zeph commanded his gunner. "Enlarge the area north and west of The District." The image changed, showing vague collections of squares representing the clan estate houses on the edge of Iredipa city. "I want a small, focused burst just south of here," Zeph pointed out an estate house. "Followed by a second target here." He unfolded a crudely sketched map from his pocket, traced a road out of the city, located it on the screen, and pointed. "Here, in this field, should make the point." Corin looked at him quizzically.

"That's the Dum'Laiere farm, and their house in Iredipa."

"It is," Zeph agreed. "I want Miratha Dum'Laiere to understand very clearly that she's not going to get away with what she's done. I know, and I will hold her accountable, even if no one else does."

"What about Dora? That's her home, Zeph. She's taken your side—our side. She's helped us."

"She will just have to understand…or not."

Corin shook her head. "You do not understand the power of family among the clans. They may complain and fight violently amongst themselves, but if an outsider attacks one of them, they all rally to that person's defense."

"Miratha must be brought to heel, Corin."

CHAPTER SIXTY-FOUR

"Target set. Ready to fire, Captain," the gunner announced.

Zeph refolded the map of the Dum'Laiere country estates and gave the order, "Fire."

Zeph woke, blinking the sleep from his eyes, his body alerted by something, a sound, a breath of air, a whisper of cloth against cloth as thighs passed each other, carrying their owner creeping forward, or perhaps it was the soft rub of shoe leather on the stone floor.

He peered into the darkness, remembering where he was, not in his rooms beneath the dome, not in his cubicle on the Lamdra. He chose to return to the suite in the palace, hoping for two takeaways by the Council and locals: one that they occupied guest rooms, a reminder that their stay on Ebulon was temporary, and two, that though he could issue force, he had no intention of setting himself up as a conqueror, or a replacement for their Mahal.

Zeph sensed more than heard movement in the room. Holding very still, he kept his breath slow and steady: a sleeping breath, a breath of the unaware and unwary.

And then he saw her standing in the darkness, her green eyes sparkling, a faint glow behind them making them shine out in the dark room. Eropa. He sat up, and before he had taken another breath, she was across the room and in his arms, so his next breath was filled with her, the pungent scent of flowers and spices—none of which were familiar except for their scent on her.

Their lips crushed together in a bruising kiss that released them from years locked in isolation in one mad renting, igniting the fuel of weeks of denied passion quickly fanned into a conflagration that threatened to burn their two souls away.

Zeph did not know what would be left in the ashes. He did not care. His only thought was to be with her here in this moment, completely, a moment that he fervently wanted to last forever. She was a Rhune. She had magic. Surely, she could do that—surely, she would if he could only show her how much he loved her—how if she allowed him to be a part of her life, he would never take or demand anything but would only give to her.

E.F. Winters

"Do not make such promises, even silently in your heart," her voice warned in his head. *"That is the lie of love. We say we want nothing, but we want everything."*

It was true. He did want everything.

"And for these moments we have together, you will have it. All I can give." She reached up and slid her silken robe off her shoulder, exposing the flawless green skin, translucent as a dragonfly's wings, glistening with a sheen like a sprinkle of dust from distant stars.

She slid one leg down his, then the other, and they twined themselves around each other, blanketed by the night and the whispering silk of the bedclothes.

When Zeph woke, he was tangled in the bedcovers. A pale silvery dawn was just beginning to brighten the blue sky as the first day moon, Hylos, took over the sky from the fading blue tones of the night's last moon, Teagra.

He was alone, left to wonder if his night visitor had only been a dream. Did the bedclothes smell of Eropa or had they always smelled faintly of strange blossoms and exotic spices? Maybe it was just the soap the laundresses used in the palace.

When he saw Eropa, he would know.

He threw the covers aside, rising to stretch before dressing, unusually eager to start his day.

E.F. Winters

CHAPTER SIXTY-FIVE

"Do not proclaim who you are. Be who you are. It will not go unnoticed." (Mc'Larick clan motto attributed to Allistaire Mc'Larick.)

Who would stand in the position of influence in Iredipa was the question of the time. In the wake of Nikodamus' death, a changing chorus of characters stood to take the position and stumbled, their attention focused on placating the older, more powerful clans who, despite playing significant roles in the destruction of Little Taiba, refused to take any responsibility for the consequences of their actions in hiring, training, and arming the mercenaries. The clans, and therefore those vying for leadership, had no interest in addressing the Taiban refugees' problems. There was no will to work out a path to peace. The only changes they supported were those that gave them more autonomy from Rhune control.

Distracted by the jostling for influence, the Voices in the Council of Elders dismissed or ignored reports of bands of suddenly unemployed mercenaries harrying the countryside and small hamlets as they sought a way to get off Ebulon and back to their home worlds in the Taiban Cluster.

Zeph's message to Ebulonians and Taibans alike was unambiguous; he was in charge. He and his starship would enforce the order needed to find a path to a peace that honored all Ebulon's inhabitants, not only a few favored clans. It was not what Zeph wanted, but it was necessary.

The clans and much of the council were resentful of the Matriarch and her power over them; now they had a new power to contend with. They did not like it, but they knew they could not stand against his starship.

Remembering Nikodamus' cautions about the populace's unsuitability to becoming colonized, Zeph issued an official statement declaring that he would honor his promise and Nikodamus Mir's

CHAPTER SIXTY-FIVE

intention. The Paxlosian's role would remain as peacekeepers, while the divided factions worked out their differences, stabilized leadership, and established a foundation for an equitable future for all who lived on the planet. Persecution of innocent Taibans would not be tolerated, nor would violence on the part of the refugees.

The clans grumbled but sat back to wait out the foreign interference. In the face of Little Taiba's ruin, it was hard to argue that the poor treatment of the refugees contributed to the eruption of violence, many of whom lived peacefully alongside them for years.

The Paxlosian attack on the Dum'Laiere estates was held to be a statement of some guilt by that house--a warning to all the clans to behave.

The power dynamic having once again shifted, Frevin Mir appeared outside the suite at the palace where Zeph resumed residency. Though the hour was early, empty breakfast plates evidenced that those present, Pliny, Mithra and Malbuis, and Tai Bobalo had been there for some time. The new McLarick Voice, Lady Aless's daughter, the Bren'Harrow Voice, and Kirk Dum'Laiere passed Frevin on their way out. Stacks of paper littered the table, the bitter smell of old wine and stale tea dregs indicating that breakfast was not the first meal the group ate while poring over problems.

Zeph tried not to look smug at the younger Mir's discomfort, but he did nothing to ease it.

"I don't have time for you today. You'll get updated tomorrow with the other Voices," Zeph told him curtly. There was no sense in pretending they had any mutual regard beyond tolerating each other; their enmity was too public.

"I am not here to ask anything of you, Captain Yare," Frevin said. "I am here to help. The situation is a quagmire, but I can advise you, show you which clan member's requests should be addressed, and which are better ignored, for example."

So that you can still claim to have influence, Zeph thought ungraciously. "Mithra does that," he said out loud. It was equally dismissive. "He has decades of experience as a diplomat among the Voices and knows the alliances, old feuds, and the intricacies of working with old power." Zeph looked up from the sheaf of papers in his hand. "While you, I understand, are quite new to your position." Zeph turned his attention to the Voices as they took their leave.

E.F. Winters

The corners of Frevin's mouth twisted. "There is so much to be examined and considered, and as an outsider, you cannot understand the subtle layers at work here." Zeph looked at the Mirs and Bobalo.

"We'll struggle along."

"This stubbornness of yours will only make things more difficult."

Zeph turned cool eyes to the ambitious diplomat. "Maybe, but it will also keep our strategies from being leaked before we've smoothed out the details, undermining our efforts," he countered pointedly, alluding to Frevin's betrayal of Nikodamus' trust. Frevin's face went red. Zeph returned to examining the document in his hand. "When I figure out what you're good for, I'll let you know."

"You are making a mistake, Yare," Frevin said, his anger controlled but invisible. "I am to be the next Mahal." His chin went up.

"No one has voted yet, Frevin."

"You need my support," the young Mir fumed.

"And I assume I have it," Zeph replied with a smile. "As a close confidant of the late Mahal, you will certainly understand what I am doing. An Ebulon that supports all its inhabitants in comfort and security was Nikodamus' vision. I intend to honor him by upholding that vision."

"You are a fool and an interferer!" Frevin exited in a flurry of dove gray silk.

Zeph shook his head. "Stomping out like a spoiled child."

"If he becomes Mahal, he will hold this against you," Pliny said once the door had closed.

"Why should now be any different than any other day?" Zeph said flippantly. "He has borne me a grudge since the first day I arrived. I don't trust him, and I don't even like him."

"It is not necessary to like someone to work with them," Malbuis suggested sagely.

"It helps," Zeph quipped flippantly. "I like all of you."

Bobalo chuckled. "Until we tell you that you're going to have to do something you don't want to do. We'll see how much you like us then." He used his weight to press himself into a chair unquestionably designed for a more slender body type. "You'd think in a palace, they could afford more comfortable chairs," he complained.

CHAPTER SIXTY-FIVE

"They were not built for comfort," Malbuis informed the Taiban. "They were built to keep those who occupied them uncomfortable so the host could maintain the upper hand."

"Made for the snakes and eels of the palace court," Bobalo tried to wiggle his bulk into a more comfortable position.

Mithra's head jerked around. "I am a courtier and I do not consider myself a reptile of any sort," he proclaimed defensively.

Malbuis chuckled. "The captain did not mean you, Mith." He turned to Bobalo. "Whomever built that chair would never have imagined a great hulking bear of a Taiban would be invited into the palace to sit in it." Bobalo chuckled, giving the elder Mir a wink. Mithra scowled.

"Captain Bobalo is a Taiban, Mithra." Malbuis clasped his partner's shoulder and rubbed it affectionately. "They are an outgoing and playful people."

"We are," Bobalo declared heartily. "You should come to dinner at my home. I have daughters. It is very noisy." He laughed.

"You should go, "Zeph agreed, smiling. "Bobalo's wife, Timee, is a wonderful cook."

"We shall do that!" Malbuis accepted happily. Zeph noted that Mithra was visibly less excited about the prospect, but he had no doubt that Timee would win the straight-laced Mir over.

"Have your Freemen had any luck locating the mercenaries who left the city?" Zeph asked Bobalo. The ex-pirate stretched out his legs so the tips of his red boots peeked out from beneath his long, full-cut purple pants. The fine, butter-yellow cotton shirt was set off by a rust-brown, suede vest with elaborately embroidered edges. Zeph recognized Timee's work.

"I sent half the crews you assigned me to check the flight-ways to The String and the other half to scour the countryside. They'll report back by tomorrow morning."

Zeph nodded. "Good."

"I thought Taiban ships could not make it from Ebulon to any of the outpost moons in the String," Mithra commented.

"You are right, Mithra." Bobalo nodded. "But it's best to be cautious. The chance that some disgruntled ex-Freedom Fighter manages it, then goes off selling tales to the warlords, would be a disaster for Ebulon. We'll reel in any stragglers," he assured Zeph.

E.F. Winters

"And if these stragglers were caught marauding, what then?" Zeph asked.

"We space them," Bobalo replied.

Mithra's eyebrows shot up. "Truly?"

Bobalo laughed. "No, my Mir friend. We are not entirely uncivilized, but we had a community meeting, and that solution was brought up more than once."

"It won't help heal the rifts in your community," Zeph cautioned.

"Politics," Bobalo grumped. "They make you treat bad people as if they were good and good people as if they were bad. Sometimes I miss the days when if a person did something awful, I could just throw him out an airlock."

"However did you keep a crew?" Miratha sniffed.

"We hired good people," Bobalo quipped, his grin cutting through his full, black beard. "Zeph knows what I mean. Wouldn't everything be easier if you could just throw this Dum'Laiere woman out an airlock and be done with her?"

"It would," Zeph agreed.

"But it is not an option," Pliny inserted, giving Zeph a warning look.

"No, it's not." Zeph sighed.

"You worry too much," Malbuis told him. "Miratha cannot succeed Hagriva--not really. Not in any significant way. She would not survive the Matriarch's Gift."

"I don't understand. What is this 'Gift'?" Zeph asked. He learned there were a lot of advantages to having Mirs around; they knew lots of things, and curious by nature, they were eager to share what they knew.

"When a Matriarch passes, their chosen heir, traditionally a student of outstanding ability, inherits not only their title but a rather mysterious but powerful accumulation of knowledge. The scope of this knowledge is far beyond what a person could learn in a lifetime and is purported to be the combined knowledge of all the previous Matriarchs in that line. Because of the vast scope of this transference, the student's mind must be carefully prepared by years of specific practices to safely incorporate, or accept, this knowledge," the elder Mir explained. "Though Miratha claims to have been secretly taught by some unnamed mentor, there is no proof she was ever formally

CHAPTER SIXTY-FIVE

trained in Rhune practices, and she most certainly would never have been given the preparations to accept The Gift. Who would have taught her? If there indeed was some Rhune who taught Miratha, the woman would have been an outcast, or Hagriva would have known of her. It is extremely unlikely she would have received this level of training. She would not have known what was required to prepare Miratha for accepting The Gift safely."

"Safely." Zeph's attention was caught by that word. "That's an odd word for something that's supposed to be an honor."

"If the student is not capable of accepting The Gift, their mind may be splintered, their sanity unhinged, or their life forfeited." Zeph's frown deepened.

"Malbuis, your fascination with this subject is unsettling."

"Of course, everything we know is third-hand. You won't find a Rhune talking about it, and in truth, there have been no problems within at least the last three hundred years," Malbuis tried to speak to Zeph's concerns.

"You mean since Hagriva received The Gift from *her* teacher," Pliny clarified.

"So only one person," Zeph grunted. "It's not much of a present if it might kill you. Why would anyone want the damn thing?"

"Because it gives them power beyond what most of us could ever dream of," Malbuis replied.

"Unless you are a Rhune," Pliny piped in. "In which case, you have dreamed of nothing else your entire life."

"Pliny is a Ballatyn," Malbuis commented to Zeph conspiratorially. "Related to a famous pair of accomplished sorceress sisters in the Rhune hierarchy, so, even though he's not a Rhune himself, he *knows* things--things not commonly known outside his family circle."

Pliny shrugged off this claim to privileged information. "But no Rhune would forgo the honor of The Gift if it was offered," he informed Zeph.

"There was Eropa's grandmother, Adaya Al'Kandin," Malbuis reminded him. "She was most certainly chosen before she renounced the Rhune path."

Pliny shook his head. "Oh, how my old nan loved telling *that* story; how the Rhunes lost and the old ways won because of Adaya

Al'Kandin. She had Ballatyn blood, but philosophically she was a Keesch through and through, though she would never have admitted it."

"Magic runs through a person's blood?" Zeph asked.

"The tendency, like any other talent," Malbuis explained. "That is why Miratha is so adamant that the position of Matriarch and The Gift should be hers. She believes the cautions about being prepared do not apply to her. Of course, that is complete rubbish. She could not survive it, but Hagriva would also never choose her, so she can pretend she is being wronged and rant about it as much as she wants."

Mithra raised a cautioning hand. "Those who support a change away from Rhune control will not care whether she has The Gift or not. They would prefer she did not."

"Yes, someone with neither magical nor spiritual powers who could not interfere in their plots would suit many of the clans quite well," Pliny agreed.

"So why did this Hagriva acknowledge Miratha at all?" Zeph asked.

The Mirs exchanged looks.

"Only a fool tries to second-guess a Rhune," Mithra quoted the saying. Zeph had heard it before from Eropa's father.

"The sisterhood's strategy plays out over generations, not decades," Pliny cautioned. "Outsiders cannot expect to understand, and in this, we are all outsiders."

"But if you want an educated guess," Malbuis jumped in. "Hagriva recognized Miratha so that Dora would be the treaty bride and Eropa would remain here."

Zeph understood.

"Hagriva is old and wily. For most of three hundred years, she has been guiding, nudging, and influencing Eulon's path. Eropa is young, inexperienced, and not well accepted socially," Mithra elaborated. "If you were Miratha, who would you rather have as an adversary?"

Zeph considered the question. The more he knew about Ebulonian culture and politics, the harder it was to know if what he did was the right thing or not. A month ago, he thought finding Ebulon had solved all his problems.

Now, I have problems I never imagined I could have.

CHAPTER SIXTY-SIX

"For those who must see to believe how to define the invisible?"
(Anonymous; The Book of Rhune).

It had been a long day. They all were, it seemed. Zeph walked out of the suite where he spent his days, frustrated by people he could not control, thinking he could not change.

When he returned to the palace, he returned to his habit of walking the gardens in the long, colored twilight, leaning into the quiet and lush beauty to clear his head. It helped him sleep, which he was finding hard to do these days, his mind constantly churning on the many problems he needed to sort out.

He began to wonder if what he envisioned was even possible?

But you will never know unless you try.

Still, he wished he had someone with whom he could talk out his problems, someone with whom he could share thoughts and confide feelings.

When had he become lonely?

When Eropa left. Whenever she left, which was most of the time.

His security team knew enough to stay back and out of his line of sight during these evening walks. "I'm not asking you to be derelict in your duty, just to allow me the illusion that I'm alone for a few minutes," he instructed them.

It was an odd thing to want to be alone, but also to want to be with someone, not just anyone, but someone who mattered. Someone who he could tell things to and who would help shoulder the burden of what he was trying to do.

"And what are you trying to do?" he asked himself.

Save a world, or two...or three, or four.... As he imagined the worlds that could be helped by this mission, counting them, he began remembering things about Paxlosis and the Thousand Worlds he was beginning to forget: the stale smells of rot and sewage, the aging Plasteel that permeated life under the Dome, the harsh landscape above on the planet surface—all burning sands and bombed out ruins, and poison everywhere, the air they could not breathe. There was no world among The Thousand that did not suffer the after-effects of the Rain of Death.

The path through the garden took a turn, and there was Miratha, sitting with her gray watered silk skirts spread out over a bench, obviously waiting for him. Dressed smartly, the edge of her bodice was trimmed with braided pearls, her youth-enhanced breasts pushed up to her breastbone, long hairpieces filling out her elaborately styled hair, while lace gushed from her sleeves. As usual, her hormone-laden perfume was overpowering. Zeph stepped back from the cloud.

"Ah, Captain Yare, we meet again." She smoothed her dress, her voice controlled and melodious. "I was surprised to learn you did not occupy the Mahal's rooms, and yet you have occupied so much else." Seeing someone near the captain, Zeph's guards came forward. Zeph motioned them to stay, but not come too close.

"I am not occupying anything," Zeph corrected her.

"We'll let history decide," she said primly. "It is not a common practice here for a trade partner to attack their ally."

"That was just a warning shot, Miratha, as one adversary to another." He inclined his head toward her, pretending respect.

Miratha's color rose. "You attacked my home."

"You kidnapped me, conspired to destroy the Taiban District, and had Nikodamus killed. And you may have lied your way through to convincing everyone else of your innocence, but not me."

"I am not responsible for Nikodamus's death," the woman insisted. "I have been truth-read and acquitted of that accusation. My only guilt in that terrible event was listening to fearful neighbors and hiring a scoundrel to command my personal guard." Miratha's mouth pursed into a puckered bud. "But I am not here to discuss the past. I am here to secure the success of your mission and Ebulon's future. I am willing to put what you've done aside in light of all that we have in common, your family and mine. And as a gesture of forgiveness, I offer my hand in friendship." She held out a limp hand. "And my daughter's as your treaty bride."

"We are not friends," Zeph stated, looking at her hand as if it were a viper.

"But our common needs and interests require that we be allies," She changed subjects abruptly before Zeph could address her hypothesis. "I hear you have taken an Ebulonian lover." Zeph's reply was a blank stare. "My maid, Fratianne? Did you think I would not miss my own handmaid? You are not the first to be taken in by that pretty face."

"Fratianne and I are not lovers," Zeph answered brusquely.

"No?" Miratha raised her finely drawn eyebrows. "Then what exactly is her position?"

"She's a guest."

"A guest." The woman mulled this over. "And do you expect her to be your 'guest' until your ship leaves, or have you another plan in mind?"

"Ask Fratianne. Her plans are her own."

"I would like to do that. Perhaps you could arrange a visit? Technically, the girl remains a member of my household, and I feel it incumbent on me to see that she is not taken advantage of."

Zeph snorted. "There's little chance of that."

"I am not unworldly, Captain Yare, but if Fratianne is to be your consort..."

"She's not," Zeph repeated. "Keep your mind and manipulations out of my bed, Miratha."

Miratha's eyes snapped. "Take Fratianne back with you to Paxlosis, bed her--take a dozen like her, but time is passing. Soon you will be leaving, and there are many arrangements to be made. You must announce Dora as the treaty bride."

Zeph stared at her. "Why would I do that?"

"Do you have another option?" Miratha demanded. "You require a marriage of convenience that gives you a strong political alliance—one that will be upheld here on Ebulon in your absence. The Dum'Laiere family can give you that. Dora is dutiful and will give you no trouble. Your personal life can be whatever you want it to be. Dora will never stand in your way. She is too simple. She is not beautiful, but you do have a fondness for her. Even if you and she are not lovers, she will be a good companion. The Dum'Laiere clan has the required lineage. No other family does. We have the support, the will, and the stomach to hold this alliance together even after you are gone."

CHAPTER SIXTY-SIX

"You have no support," Zeph disagreed. "Not after what you've done."

Miratha smiled slyly. "The Dum'Laiere's are a very old clan, Captain Yare, with longstanding allies who owe us many debts. We will have no trouble navigating this hiccup."

"I already have a viper in my family. Why would I let in another?" Zeph demanded.

"As I said, what other choice is there?" Miratha countered. "Surely you do not fantasize that the Pira will go with you? A Rhune sorceress? Poor man, you are the one who is mad," she sneered. "You need a bride like Dora. Someone who will be compliant. A Rhune will give you nothing but trouble."

"We're done here." Zeph turned to leave.

"You have to choose someone, Captain Yare, and soon," Miratha called out after him. "Tell Fratianne I will not hold her position open indefinitely."

Miratha was right. *I have to choose someone soon.* "And it cannot be Eropa."

Zeph felt the hollow well that lived inside him whenever he thought about Eropa and the future they would not have together. The pain in his stomach and chest was dizzying, but leaving Eropa to lead Ebulon was the right thing to do, he knew that.

And that's what matters, he reminded himself. But it did not make him feel better.

Dora would believe that in becoming the Treaty Bride, she had won some grand contest, but she would be wrong. Her future would be sacrificed for the gain of others, himself included. He would provide her with whatever she wanted: beautiful apartments, servants, and any pretty thing her simple, girlish heart desired, but he would not be a good husband. He would not be there when she needed him, and he would not love her. Cut off from her family and trapped in a strange culture, she would come to hate him for bringing her to Pax, and she would have every right, but none of that changed what he had to do. The treaty required an alliance between his family and the premier power on Ebulon.

It was Dora or Eropa.

Dora Dum'Laiere would be collateral damage.

E.F. Winters

CHAPTER SIXTY-SEVEN

"The hubris of sentient beings is in believing their ability to think makes them better than other forms of life." (Hagriva Rhune from The History of the Rhunes compiled in the Third Age).

It did not take long for Terk to weasel himself into Pemitai Bobalo's life. For the daughter of a famous pirate and smuggler, whose family ran the rebellion for years, the girl was very naive. She did not seem to have any friends outside of her family, and all of them were preoccupied with helping the Taiban community survive after the riots and fire and tearing down the remnants of old Little Taiba in preparation for rebuilding a new one.

Certain their little sister was safely doing her part at the infirmary, no one gave her activities another thought.

"I'm meeting Pem later," Terk would confide to Clem, who remained bedridden, bandaged, and unable to speak. The older boy took great pleasure in rubbing in every step forward in the development of his relationship with the Bobalo girl, knowing it ate at Clem that he could do nothing to warn Pem or anyone else.

"You want to warn her, don't you, Clem?" Terk tortured the younger boy. "You want to tell someone. But you can't because you're a mass murderer. You killed hundreds and hundreds of people by starting that fire in Little Taiba. If people knew it was you, it wouldn't matter if Bobalo and his lot tried to treat you fair, the rest of the Taibans would tear down whatever building they kept you in and pull you apart with their bare hands. They're that angry. And you're the reason. You, Clem.

"So don't think to be telling anyone anything, unless you're prepared to die in a terrible way. And here's the thing, because I know you are the self-sacrificing type and you might just decide to try and be a hero, I'm going to make you a promise." Terk leaned into Clem's ear and whispered. "If you do that, I'll kill little nursie girl." He sat

CHAPTER SIXTY-SEVEN

up. "You remember that when you start feeling brave. It's not just your life at stake. It's hers."

Of course, if Clem realized Terk's real plans, he might have tried to tell someone anyway. Terk had no intention of killing Pem Bobalo, at least not until he had gotten what he needed from her, and what he needed was a ship to get himself off Ebulon.

"There are too many rules in this place," he groused to anyone who would listen. "Figured it was run by a pirate and a smuggler, life would be pretty good—lots of rich pickings, but Bobalo and his bunch have gotten old and soft. All they want is a rocking chair on their porch and a soft bed at night. Well, that may be enough for them, they already had their chance to make their fortune, but what about us who ain't yet? We got a right to work the system for our benefit, just like they did in their day, right? But oh no, we aren't allowed to do that here. That's 'bad'. We're all 'good' people here now. The 'bad' ones, Murtevoy's crew, well, they're all run off trying to get away and back to Taiba. Cause as bad as the Warlords are, they're nothing to goody Bobalo and his friends. You can't do this. You can't do that. You can't shit without someone checking to see if it smells right."

Terk had seen what was happening to the Taibans who allied themselves with Murtevoy: "Loosey" Humqualt was dead. Je'anna Peru, too. Tommy Makepeace was still behind the bar at the Hard Pumper Pub, so he must have pulled a fast one and changed sides, or maybe he never was one of them. You couldn't tell about people these days. The mercenaries who stood alongside Saldo Murtevoy were either dead, on the run, or had become pariahs, shunned by the community.

It was unfair, and Terk decided he'd had enough. Only Clem's stupid trick of crashing the Paxlosian ship kept Terk from already being back on Taiba. He had been trying to figure out a new way to get off the damn planet ever since. Paxlosian security was too tight for him to steal another ship from them, and with Clem still incapacitated, he needed something he could fly himself. That meant a Taiban ship. But ever since the desperate escape attempts of the mercenaries after the riots, every ship was locked down and guarded.

E.F. Winters

Terk scouted the situation for weeks, and there was just no way he was getting one of those ships.

Meeting Pemitai Bobalo changed that.

Terk had started off nurturing Pemitai's interest with small things, running into her as she got off her shift at the infirmary and talking as they "happened" to be walking the same way.

After a few sessions walking together, Terk invited Pem to talk more over a chilled tea. A few days later, he walked her all the way to the gate of the Bobalo Compound. From there, it didn't take long to finagle an invitation inside and a tour of the grounds.

The old man who hung out at the Bobalo's gate pretending he was "guarding" it didn't seem to like Terk much, but Terk didn't care. Pem liked him, and that was what mattered. Terk did not need to get "in" with her family. He wasn't trying to marry her. He was trying to manipulate her and take advantage of her family's position. He needed to keep some distance between himself and her family.

"This is really something, your family's place," Terk looked around at the Bobalo compound's grounds, pretending to be properly awed. "There's so much history here, Pem. The Free Men movement was born right here. That's the runway Captain Tai Bobalo and Jayq Jacoby and Menander and all of them used to take off on those early missions. It's amazing."

Pem shrugged her thin shoulders. It was a warm night, as most of them were here in the southern part of the continent, and Bobalo's daughter wore a pale-yellow tunic over wide-legged pants, the short, gathered butterfly sleeves of the tunic fluttering across her sun-kissed arms, the tunic material rippling against her slender waist and hips in the breeze. Terk understood that Pem was pretty. He just didn't care. He had watched the whores on Taiba service their customers lots of times, but he could never figure out what the big deal was, or why they paid good credits to do what they did, or to have someone else do it to them. It seemed pretty uninteresting to him. One of the older whores had offered him to try it once, for free. Afterwards, he still didn't get it. She'd slapped him for saying so.

CHAPTER SIXTY-SEVEN

"The way you see things, Callum, it's so *different*," Pem gushed. "I never think about any of this like that. To me, the old runway is just a good place to play hopscotch or bounce a ball."

"But Pem, it's so much more than that," Terk insisted, laying it on thick. "This stuff should be in a museum."

Pem giggled, embarrassed. "I don't know about that."

"Well, I do. There are things here that are part of the Free Men's history—Taiban history, and someday they're going to be really important. Someone should start gathering them up and taking care of them, so they don't get lost."

"Maybe." Pem sounded unconvinced, but Terk could tell she was thinking about it as her eyes lit on different bits of old machinery lying about the yard.

"What's that building over there?" He pointed to what he knew was the old hangar.

"It's just an old building full of junk, old ship parts, and stuff," Pem dismissed it without a second thought.

Some of the old guys who hung around the landing field told Terk about how, in the early days, everything ran out of Bobalo's compound. Supplies for missions, ships, pods, and weapons were all stored there. Some of the old guys insisted there were still ships stored there, claiming that Bobalo continued to use the hangar and runway.

"Have you ever seen the captain here using the public landing area?" one argued with his friend. "No. Because he just don't. And why would he when he's got a perfectly good ship in a hangar out behind his house and his private place to take off and land? He don't need to come *here*, because there's still stuff *there.*"

"But if it was a ship from the old days, it would be too old to run now," Terk objected. "Captain Bobalo wouldn't use an old, out-of-date ship when he could have a new one. It probably wouldn't be safe anymore."

Both old men frowned and shook their heads. "Just 'cause it's newer, don't make it better, boyo," one of the older men informed him. "Those original ships were handmade by Loosey, Crochin, Menander, and Jayq, and Tai Bobalo himself. They were made strong. Back then, the Founders weren't just friends; they were like family, all of them depending on those ships and pods to stay alive. Taking care of them was job one, and they all took it serious."

His companion nodded. "I remember sitting by a fire one night, and the captain was sitting across from me, and all night his hands was busy working on a sprocket, cleaning it, rasping down any bits he didn't like, then oiling and rubbing in that oil. He worked on it all night as he talked and listened to the other Free Men. If Tai Bobalo has a ship in that hangar, it ain't wantin' for care. That's just not the captain's way."

That conversation got Terk thinking about how he could get hold of a ship.

And now here he was. So close.

"Oh, wouldn't I like to see inside that place?" He laid on the excitement real thick. "Can we, Pem? I mean, can we just look inside? We don't have to go in or anything. We could just look. We won't touch anything."

"Sure." Pem wrinkled her nose. Terk noticed she did that a lot. It was a cute, short sort of shallow bowl affair, but it suited her delicate features and small stature. Terk was glad she wasn't built like her Da, or he might have trouble overpowering her. As it was, he wasn't worried at all. Pem confided that her Mam had not allowed Bobalo to train his daughters, fearing they would want to join the fighting on Taiba.

She led Terk to the hangar's walk-in door, fetched a key from underneath a potted plant, and unlocked it. The door squeaked like a giant mouse whose tail was being pulled, making Terk cringe, sure someone would come out of the house and scold them for getting into stuff they shouldn't. But no one did, and pretty soon Terk's pulse settled down.

Pem pushed the hangar door open enough to slip inside, leading the way. Terk followed.

It was dark, with only faint starlight coming in the crown of high windows that ran around the top of the walls. Pem took a firestick from a low table and lit a lamp, holding it high.

"No glow globes," he teased her.

CHAPTER SIXTY-SEVEN

"I'm only half Ebulonian," Pem replied primly. "I did not inherit those talents."

Good to know. Terk was wondering.

Odd bits of dust-covered machinery, ship, and pod parts were lined up along the walls with later additions thrown on top, all of it swathed in cobwebs; houses for rodents and insects that had moved into the space when the people stopped coming. Terk expected this. What he did not expect but hoped to find was within the meticulously cleared center, where several usable pods and a vintage fighter sat in perfect condition.

It took his breath away.

The clean, beautifully molded lines, the hand rubbed finish, that, despite a few scorch marks and small dents, still retained some shine. The oldsters at the landing field boasted about how the original fighters were handcrafted by the Founders, their eyes going glassy at the memory, but Terk did not realize the level of engineering genius and craftsmanship that was taken. No one made ships like this now. It would take too much time—require too much effort. Terk felt begrudging respect for the men from Bobalo's original crew. They might be old and tired now, but there had been a time when they were inspired.

"We can walk around," Pem offered. "It's okay. Da won't mind."

"We need more light." Terk hurried over to the big hangar doors and unlatched them, swinging them open.

Turning around to face it, the grand old ship drew him. It was the promise of freedom, a new start. He did not know what he would find tonight, cautioning himself not to put too much hope into this first exploratory investigation, but he would not have to spend weeks secretly fixing an old rust bucket. This ship was ready, now. He had his backpack with minimum supplies packed inside; maps stolen from Crochin's, a star-chart filched at the landing field, a gun he wasn't sure worked, and a few knives he knew did. There was also a good, solid rock.

Terk approached the ship's door, grinning broadly when it snicked open like it was brand new.

"Look at that. It still works!" He laughed delightedly.

E.F. Winters

"Of course, it works," Pem chided. "You don't know my Da very well if you think he'd have a ship that didn't work."

He reached out and took Pem's hand, using his awe as a cover for his true intention. She blushed as he pulled her inside with him, and he wanted to slap her for her foolish, girlish misunderstanding, but he needed her to keep it a little bit longer.

Pulling Pem close, but not too close, he playfully spun them so he was in front of the door. He closed it slowly, distracting her with his intense focus on taking in the details of the ship's interior.

"This is so amazing," he spoke in the kind of whisper that said you weren't sure you should talk because the place was so special.

"Yeah, I guess it is pretty great," Pem agreed, shyly, looking around as if seeing the ship with new eyes.

"Have you ever just come in here and sat?" Terk nudged her toward the cockpit.

"Sure. I've been in here lots of times."

"And did your Da show you how to fly it?" Terk's eyes shone brightly.

"Well, I sat on his lap and watched him a lot," she said, shyly.

Terk pressed her into the co-pilot's chair, leaning over her from behind and pointing with one hand while the other fiddled with a pocket on his pack.

"So, like on the new ships, this is the ignition?" he pointed. Pem nodded. "And this is the fuel pump?"

"Yes."

"And electrical is this one?" he pointed.

"No, that one there," she leaned forward, reaching out.

Terk hit her on the head with his rock.

By the time the girl was waking up, they were well out into space on their way to the closest outpost in The String.

Pem groaned. "What happened?" She winced as she touched the spot where the rock struck her head. There was some blood, but it had

CHAPTER SIXTY-SEVEN

stopped bleeding now. Still, it made a mess, sticky and red against Pem's white hair, red brown stripes dripping down her yellow dress.

Terk figured it looked worse than it was.

Pem must have finally been able to focus because she gasped. "Callum, where are we?" Her naivete crumbled quickly. "What have you done?" she demanded, trying to stand. She couldn't. He had tied her to the co-pilot's chair. Her eyes narrowed. "Why am I tied up? And what do you think you're doing, taking my Da' old ship out for a joy ride? Do you have any idea what he's going to do to us? To *you*?"

"We are way beyond joyride status," Terk informed her, all pretense at being polite and starry-eyed gone. "And your Da isn't going to do anything to me because you're with me, and he isn't going to want to do anything that might put you in danger."

Pem went very still. "So, this was your plan all along?"

"More or less. Kind of improvised there at the last. I didn't really expect to find a ship all prepped and ready to fly out."

Pem sat, silent for a bit.

"So, what about Clem? Did he know?"

"Not this time," Terk muttered.

"What did you say?" Pem asked.

"Your precious Clem is not the innocent you think he is," Terk informed her maliciously. "You have no idea what he's done."

"No, I don't. I don't really know what you've done, either, Callum, or what we're doing now. How far do you plan on flying before we go back?"

Terk gave her a look. "I'm not going back."

"Where do you think you're going, then? I mean, do you know?" she demanded.

Terk pushed the star-chart across the control deck toward her. She glanced at it.

"So, you have a star-chart. Great. Can you read it? Do you know how to put in coordinates and navigate out here? We should turn back. I can explain to my father, but what you're doing is dangerous. There are no roads or direction signs out here, Callum."

"I'm not an idiot," he responded. "I know what I'm doing. I've been planning this a long time."

"Have you?" Her eyes flashed, the first indication of real anger. "My Da and the others will come after you. You know that, right? Did you plan for that, too?"

"Yeah. I told you. That's why you're here. You're going to keep me safe, Pem."

She began to bounce in her seat, straining against the ropes that tied her down, shrieking and shouting in primal frustration.

"Stop that!" he yelled over her.

"No!" She continued, a gut-wrenching, teeth-clenching, declaration of anger.

Terk could not believe the quiet, frail Pem could make such a terrible row. She was usually so sweet-natured at the infirmary. Girls made no sense. Terk thought about cutting her throat. That would make her stop, but then he would have lost using her as his shield if Bobalo and his friends caught up with him.

He needed her for a while longer.

"If you don't shut up, Pem, I'm going to have to knock you out again," he threatened. "I can do it. My rock is right over there." He glanced back into the cockpit, where his backpack sat on the floor by the back wall. "I'm trying to concentrate on flying this thing, and I don't think it's asking too much for you to shut the fuck up."

Pem stopped shrieking.

"So, we're headed for The String," she said after a while.

"Where else could we go?" Terk said sarcastically. "There's only one way in or out, and that's The String."

She was silent for an hour before she asked. "Is someone meeting us?"

Terk glanced at her. "Not yet."

"That's problematic, don't you think? The colonists on the outposts aren't just flying out in their ships just in case someone needs help. It has to be arranged ahead of time."

Terk knew that, of course. Everyone did. Making sure that someone was there to "catch you", whether literally in a free-floating pod or to give you additional fuel to make it to the first outpost if you

CHAPTER SIXTY-SEVEN

were in a larger ship, was basic to the experience of travel to and from Ebulon.

"Like I said, some things had to be improvised."

"Not notifying whoever is going to catch you," Pem warned. "Is a detail you don't improvise, because if no one's there, you're dead."

Terk did not have such an arrangement. He did not have a contact. How could he? If he had contacted someone, they would have reported it to someone.

It did not take long for Pem to realize it. "No one knows we're coming, do they?" she demanded. "Do you have a contact?"

"*I* don't, but *you're* a Bobalo." He grinned wickedly.

"I have no intention of helping you kidnap me," the girl declared.

"Don't think of it that way, Pem. Think of it as helping yourself," his tone turned the statement into a threat. "I've had a lot of time to think about how and when I might die, but I'm guessing that a pretty little spoiled girl like you hasn't thought about it at all until now. Do you want to live, Pem? Does life matter to you? Because you need to decide. I know what I'm willing to risk. I don't think you do."

The girl stared out into space at the distant swath of stars known as The String.

E.F. Winters

CHAPTER SIXTY-EIGHT

"Take nothing, seek nothing; that is how to navigate the Void." (A note in the margins of the only known volume of a Book of Secrets. The single existing volume is in the Ballatyn Clan library collection. Attributed to Abrana Ballatyn.)

When Miratha informed Dora that Hagriva had invited her to Alden Baierd for a visit, the girl convinced herself the old woman wanted to begin training her great-great-great niece as a Rhune, teaching her spells or giving her a special charm that would help her fulfill this new role she was being groomed for. She knew about the rumors that she was to be the treaty bride. Despite Yare's perplexing attack on the Dum'Laiere estates, conjecture among the clans was that Dora was set to become the treaty bride, and all that was required was a formal announcement. But there had been no announcement, and after a few weeks, Dora decided perhaps her marriage was not arranged, turning her hopes back to Frevin.

Then Hagriva asked Dora to Alden Baierd.

For Dora, this changed everything.

"But what does it *mean*?" Dora pestered her mother.

"You think the old bitch told me?" Miratha protested.

Maybe she's going to teach me magic!" Dora shared her fantasy before she'd thought out the consequences.

"Don't be ridiculous, Dora." Her mother pulled the dream from Dora's mind and stomped on it. "You have no talent in The Arts. Everyone knows that. She probably wants to make sure you have been brought up well since you will be representing Ebulon in this new world."

"Of course," Dora replied dutifully. But secretly, she still hoped Miratha was wrong, she would play no part in the treaty agreement, and she and Frevin could be together. When she became a Rhune, he would admire her as an equal, and they could become life-partners.

CHAPTER SIXTY-EIGHT

At first, the living conditions and the state of the old capitol were alarming. Dora cringed at the thought of actually having to live in the drab, drafty castle.

She wrinkled her nose.

"It smells like those third-line cousins who live out on the west farm…"

"Poor people smell," Miratha filled in. "Old, damp, sooty, stone and dirt floors. Nothing is ever clean."

Dora wondered how her mother knew that, but she did not want to ruin the day by asking.

"Now you be a good girl for the old witch. Do you hear, Dora? Do not bother her with all your foolish questions and silly thoughts. She does not care what you think about anything. Just listen to her and do what she tells you." Miratha took her leave at the shuttle, not willing to suffer the Matriarch snubbing her in front of her daughter.

Hagriva did not appear that first day, but Eropa and her half-Taiban friend, Corin, welcomed her, though they made no effort to dress up for the occasion-something Miratha would have considered extremely rude.

After she settled in for a few days, Dora found the lack of formality at Alden Baierd freeing. Though she enjoyed the novelties offered her as a young person of wealth in Auhora Whimlan, having no one care if your hair was "done up", your clothes were pressed, or you sat up straight with your hands folded in your lap, was lovely.

Meals were a hit-and-miss affair, gleaned from a pantry stocked from the garden at harvest, the odd gift basket left by supplicants, or occasionally, as a treat, honey from the beehives that they still kept. Sometimes Dora saw one of the Mir Monks who lived at the nearby temple, Inhar Schilla, leave something from their gardens. Staples that could not be grown so close to the North Sea called for the distraction of a day trip to The Crossroads.

At home, Dora enjoyed the ritual of bathing, pampered for hours as someone else kept the water hot, the air scented with oils, a warmed blanket and a bed waiting for her, but having to haul and heat your water and carry wood ruined it for her and she followed the lead of the other girls going with a clean cloth and a bowl of warm water.

Still, days into her stay, Hagriva had done nothing but tell Dora long, boring stories about Ebulon's history and make her read musty old books.

"You have an appalling lack of knowledge about your own people," the Matriarch criticized.

"Why would I need to know any of that?" Dora countered, suddenly as petulant as she was at home with her mother. "If I need to know about something, I will hire a Mir to tell me about it."

"Relying on someone else's interpretations and views is dangerous and lazy, especially for a young woman who will inherit the larger share of her family's fortune." Hagriva dropped a stack of books beside Dora. "Here. Read these." She disappeared back into wherever she spent her time in the maze of the old castle ruins.

Eternally hungry, frequently bored, and increasingly disheveled, Alden Baierd had one thing Dora found no place else: real friends.

"I wish I had come here sooner," Dora pined. "Was it always this fun at Alden Baierd?"

"Never," Eropa answered. "It was always study, study, study. It is having other young people's company that makes it fun now."

"She is very strict, isn't she?" Dora asked. "Hagriva, I mean."

"She has high standards and expectations," Eropa agreed. "She might have been a different sort of teacher when she was younger, but the hand of time weighs heavily on her in these last days of such a long life. She has done so much, and still, there is so much to do. She is a legend, you know. It is an honor to be spending her last days with her."

"Count on you to find a good side." Corin rolled her eyes so only Dora could see. Dora covered her mouth with her hand, stifling a snicker.

Corin was a surprise to Dora, who expected a rough person with whom she would have nothing in common. Equally dreading being in such proximity with the aloof and much disdained Pira, Corin provided a comfortable bridge between the two young women who were potentially both Hagriva's heirs, depending on which camp you subscribed to.

It was Corin who suggested the young women put their books aside each night in favor of lighter pursuits. Neither Eropa nor Dora had any experience with the company of girls their age, but Corin,

CHAPTER SIXTY-EIGHT

having grown up with girl cousins, knew dozens of games that thawed the barriers between them, and in a short time, the three young women found themselves talking, laughing, and sharing.

"Strange that we never knew each other before," Dora commented.

"Not so strange. We were both kept isolated for the purposes of others," Eropa pointed out.

"Was she never mean to you then?" Dora asked.

"I thought she was in the beginning when she took me away from Iredipa and my father. I did not want to go."

"But your mother had just died," Dora commented.

"Yes. So, I could not stay, but Hagriva had so much to teach me, and I was eager to learn. That's all I wanted to do, really, learn about the mysteries of how the world works—well, that and run on the moors and play on the little beach at low tide." Remembering made the Pira smile.

"It is sad to finally have found you both, only to have to leave."

"It has been decided then?" Corin asked, glancing furtively at Eropa. "You will go to Paxlosis?"

Dora twisted the long, loose sleeve of her skirt. "Oh, I have no idea about that. Everyone assumes it, but after what Mother has done, why would Captain Yare want me? I would not." Her attention wandered out the window and to the south, and she sighed.

"He is not bad looking, and though I wouldn't call him nice, he's not cruel to his crew or friends. I can't imagine he would be any different to a wife, and it's a position that will have some influence," Corin tried to encourage Dora. "A lot of young women would be envious of such a match."

"I will still be me." Dora's half smile was an apology. "And I had hoped for..." The girl let her words fall away. "Something else," she finished elusively.

Eropa and Corin shared a silent exchange.

"If you do not want this, you can refuse," Eropa reminded Dora softly.

Dora shook her head. "If I am asked, I must accept. It is an important opportunity for my family. And, it is not like I have other offers."

In the amber light of the fire, they were able to pretend they were three young women facing uncomplicated futures, but a sliver of reality imploded that bubble.

Eropa's eyes took on a glazed look. "Someone is here," she announced.

All three rose and hurried to the tower window.

"Were you expecting anyone?" Dora asked, watching a hired shuttle set down in the open space between the rubble of the old city's ruins and the castle.

"No," Eropa replied. "It is Frevin."

Dora raced from the room, jumping from stair to stair, running across the open ground as the shuttle door opened and Frevin stepped out.

Frevin looked up at the window where Eropa stood, the fire behind her casting a copper sheen to her red hair.

"I need to speak to you," he addressed her mentally. *"Alone."*

Eropa turned and collected her cloak, Corin following her lead.

"Stay." Eropa stopped her friend. "I am in no danger from Frevin." She exited the tower room.

Dora and Frevin were standing together as Eropa came out on the ground level of the tower, Dora eager and nervous, Frevin polite and reserved, perhaps reticent.

"Welcome, Frevin. We were not expecting any visitors." Eropa glanced from one to the other, sensing the quivering energy of intense emotion.

"I need to speak with you, alone," Frevin sent her a private message.

"Dora, could check the garden to see what we have that's fresh for our guest?" Eropa suggested. "I think I saw some late-season berries. They were always his favorite."

"A taste of our youth." Frevin's eyes never left Eropa's face.

Now it was Dora perusing faces, trying to read the unreadable.

"It is all right, Dora. Frevin just has some business from the Capitol he needs to ask me about. I promise I will keep him here until you come back." Eropa gave her a reassuring smile.

CHAPTER SIXTY-EIGHT

"I would love some strawberries," Frevin gave Dora an encouraging smile.

Dora bit her lip, and her face flushed. "Of course." She swept up a basket from beside a gate and headed toward the gardens, but the spring in her step was gone.

"She is very fond of you," Eropa breached the silence.

"She has limited experience of the world, and I was there when she needed a friend, is all."

"I think it is more than that to her, Frevin. You should be careful," Eropa cautioned.

"If she has misinterpreted my friendship, she will soon get over it," the Mir dismissed the young woman's feelings.

"I fear you are going to break her heart."

Frevin snorted. "I think you misjudge the depth of her emotions, Eropa. Dora is a child with a child's attachments." The Mir's placating smile set Eropa's teeth on edge.

"Why are you here?" she asked him.

"I have been sent to officially ask her to become Yare's bride and return to Paxlosis with him." The Mir made no effort to conceal his sense of triumph.

Eropa controlled a gasp, keeping the stab of pain from her face. *So, it has been decided. Dora will marry Zeph, while I will remain here and take Hagriva's place. That is as it should be,* she told herself. At least it was for Ebulon. But what about Dora? The situation surrounding the treaty was too important to change this outcome. The only thing Eropa could hope for was to lessen Dora's pain at how her sacrifice was presented.

"You will ask Dora to marry another?" Eropa's brows knit. "You cannot do that. It will crush her."

"Being chosen as the alien captain's future wife? She will be the envy of every woman at court. I hear he is considered quite a prize. She will be fine, Eropa."

Dora deserves an honorable offer, one that helps her keep her dignity.

"You misunderstand me. What I am saying is, *you* cannot be the one who asks this. Make Yare do it himself. He is the one asking her to give up her life, a life she fantasizes she will have with you. Or just go back and tell them to send someone--anyone else."

E.F. Winters

"You are being oddly emotional, Eropa. This is a brilliant partnership for Dora, far beyond what she could have expected. Her name will be in all the histories. She will be in a position to influence women on multiple worlds. She will be talked about and admired, her success bolstering the hopes of plain girls everywhere. It is what she has always dreamed of."

"This is Miratha's dream, not Dora's," Eropa argued. "History may spin this however it wants, but Dora loves you, Frevin. She will be miserable."

"That is ridiculous." Frevin sniffed. "We barely know each other. You do realize that if Dora refuses to wed Yare, they will look to you?" he said pointedly. "Hagriva made her wishes clear on this matter when she recognized Miratha. Dora is to go to Paxlosis with Yare, and you will remain here, on Ebulon, as has always been the plan. Hagriva cannot lose another apprentice. There is no time to groom someone else to take your place. In a few weeks, Dora and Yare will leave, and things will go back to the way they were before, when it was just the two of us. We will work for Ebulon's future, together, just as we always planned." He took her hands. "There is nothing keeping us now. Let us announce we are Promised."

Eropa's insides cringed, and she stepped back.

"You do not need me to become Mahal, Frevin."

He cringed. "That is not why I am asking."

"Whatever feelings you believe you harbor for me, I do not return them," Eropa declared.

Frevin's expression turned to ice. "And you spoke so convincingly of broken hearts." He spun on his heels and began marching back to the shuttle.

At that moment, Dora came out of the garden. Seeing Frevin leaving, her face pulled together in one massive center pucker of distress as she ran to intercept him.

Eropa did not try to stop her. It would only delay the pain. Better a clean cut than a festering wound. She turned to go back into the tower. Behind her, Dora's wail of despair cut the cool air.

Suddenly, Hagriva was beside Eropa. "I cannot remember ever being that young. I take pleasure in that."

"You expect too much. Dora is not strong enough to do this," Eropa warned her teacher. "She has never been anything but a pawn.

CHAPTER SIXTY-EIGHT

She will be used and manipulated by everyone, without a clue how to stand up for herself or this agreement."

"She will learn."

"Alone there, by herself?" Eropa did not budge.

The Matriarch's black-bird eyes took in her student's rebellion.

"It is either her or you." She walked away.

Dora did not blame Frevin for not loving her. A man like Frevin needed a helpmate whom people would respect, someone who would complement and add to his prestige.

"I have never done anything special," Dora told herself. "I am only important because my family name is Dum'Laiere, and my mother has made that a liability here on Ebulon. In this new world, everyone will not know about our shame, but it will taint everything we try to do here for decades."

But what if she could prove that she was more than her mother made her out to be? What if she could convince Frevin she was someone important—someone who could become the partner he needed? Would he change his mind? After all, she was a blood relative to Hagriva Mac'Reigh, and who knew what she could accomplish now she was free of her mother's manipulations?

Dora pulled a heavy leather book from the bottom shelf in the abandoned solarium. Its spine was broken. The membrane of the leather binding was so thin that only arthritic threads held it together. There was once a design punched and painted onto the cover, but the leather was cracked and spotted, and you could not tell what it had been. Placing the book on the rough wooden table before her, she ran a hand over the magic symbols in the oval at the center. Time and generations of sorceress' hands had removed all but a few flecks of gilt. Of the many books Hagriva had shown Dora and suggested she might benefit from reading, this one she firmly removed from Dora's hands, saying, *"There is nothing for you in these pages.*

But every Ebulonian knew the stories about Faed and Abrana Ballatyne and how, when Faed became trapped across the Void, Abrana refused to accept losing her sister and went to seek her in the worlds across the Void. Everyone said it could not be done, but

Abrana found and rescued her sister's spirit, only to find the Rhunes had burned Faed's body. With only one body available, the sisters joined together, making the double entity which became known as "The Ballantyn."

The Ballatyn's feats were told to every young girl, touted as examples of the greatest magical skill, the challenges of their romantic life as it unfolded in adulthood, becoming the subject of crass jokes as well as a cautionary tale.

Dora returned to look at the book repeatedly, cautiously gathering the items she would need and hiding them in a deserted room in the castle.

She went to the solarium.

Eropa's own mother, Dupira Rhune, like Faed, was lost across the Void, and her Rhune sisters had determined that, not having the strength to return to the physical world of her birth, her body should be burned so as not to cause a drain on her spirit, and she was free to ally herself with a suitable protector. Dora's grandmother told her the tale of how, after Dupira's spirit was lost, it allied with an entity known as Duvrome Dmoledon. Somewhere across the Void, Dupira Rhune's spirit still existed.

"I am tired of being defined by what other people think I cannot do," Dora muttered. "I will not go back to being my mother's pawn." Miratha's propaganda campaign to convince everyone that Dora was mentally deficient had defined the first two decades of Dora's life. Her own actions would define the next two.

"If Dupira Rhune has the chance to return, she will take it," Dora was sure of it. "And if I let her share my body, *I* will become the next Matriarch." A fitting partner for any ambitious Mir.

All she had to do was cross to the other side of the Void and find Dupira. The Rhune would know how to return.

Dora pulled a slip of paper from her bodice and unfolded it so she could see the short line of symbols. Leafing through the book on her lap, she turned pages until she found the page with a portrait of the two separate Ballantynes: Abrana and Faed, before they were merged.

Sitting with the book before her, Dora took a weir seed stolen from Hagriva's herb stores and placed it in her mouth. She nicked the seed's surface with a knife and soaked it in a bowl of water last night. She planned for this.

CHAPTER SIXTY-EIGHT

Daintily, Dora picked the seed from the water, holding it between her forefinger and thumb and carefully placing it on her tongue. Bitterness bloomed in her mouth, quickly leaping to the nearest parts of her, then spreading onto the farther parts.

The directions cautioned the practitioner to keep the seed moving because if left too long in one spot, the chemicals burned the soft, pulpy flesh on the inside of the mouth.

Dora rolled the weir seed around, alternating sides, maneuvering it with her tongue. Then her tongue stopped responding, feeling thick and swollen. Tucked into her right cheek pocket, the fire began to burn the soft tissue. Dora clenched her teeth, the bite releasing the full chemical strength of the powerful hallucinogen into her system all at once.

Sinking to the floor, Dora vomited, but it was too late. A tiny kernel of the weir seed was all that was expelled.

Her tongue swelled, red and white blisters bursting through the green skin at the corners of her mouth, and her pupils became fixed as the chemicals flooded her system.

That was where Eropa and Corin found her.

Hagriva's snow-white hair fell around her tiny, shrunken figure, like a blanket, cascading over her arms and down her back.

"Did you know? Did you know this would happen?" Eropa confronted her old teacher.

Eropa and Corin gently cleaned Dora up and got the temple Mirs from Inhar to help them carry the unconscious girl from the far part of the abandoned castle back to her bedroom, where she lay now, breathing, if just, her face pale, blisters around her lips and eyes, splotchy skin on her right cheek seeping puss from pock-marks worked through from the inside where the skin was burned away.

Hagriva's black eyes looked as Eropa had never seen them before: sad, tired, defeated, and she almost apologized, but she had no other outlet for her anger. Her grandmother, Abrana's questioning of Rhune manipulations kept circling her brain.

"It is not my place to interfere with the decisions of others," the elder sorceress replied calmly.

"Except when it suits you." The pat reply only fed the fire of Eropa's anger at what had happened and frustration that she had not known and stopped it.

"Except when *necessity* requires it," Hagriva clarified.

"Dora was hurt and confused. She was in no place to distinguish between what she wished was true and what really was. She knew nothing about magic except all the romanticized stories everyone told her—including you!"

"You should be embarrassed to speak of her that way. That was exactly the image she was so desperate to escape," the older woman declared. "Dora's life was sheltered, but there was nothing simple about her. She was her mother's daughter. She proved that."

"If that is what you thought of her, then why bring her here and feed these fantasies of her stepping into your legacy?"

"I promised her nothing," Hagriva said stone-faced.

"What purpose could there possibly have been?" The accusation was rife in Eropa's tone.

"She wished to remove herself from her mother's influence and make herself anew. I provided her with the opportunity to do that. The path she chose was of her own devising. Hubris proved that despite her desire to be different from Miratha, she was her mother's creation, with all the same bent notions of her own importance and the same unexamined commitment to ambitious desires."

"There was some of that," Eropa admitted. "But she also had a sweet nature. In time, with guidance, she could have become something more."

"We did not have that much time. I did not, you did not, and she did not. Not in this time in this world. We must do our best in the world we have, Eropa. Wishing and pretending it is something other than what it is has no benefit for anyone." She paused before continuing in a gentler voice. "What has happened here is tragic and painful, and no, I did not know Dora would make such a dangerous choice. I will contact Miratha to come and collect her daughter."

"I will not stand beside her pyre while she is burned," Eropa proclaimed defiantly. "Do not ask me."

"You think of your mother. Dora is dead in every way that counts, Eropa. But you need not worry, Dora is not a Rhune. She has no secrets to be stolen or power to be leveraged. She is the first-line

CHAPTER SIXTY-EIGHT

heiress of the Dum'Laiere clan; however, Miratha's only link to that family. Miratha will not allow that link to be severed. She will plead motherly affection and insist there is a chance that her daughter will wake up and everything will be normal. Miratha will keep Dora's body alive, as it shrivels and sickens until it dies of whatever ailment finally takes it."

Eropa turned away, feeling sick.

E.F. Winters

CHAPTER SIXTY-NINE

"Keeping faith with a dishonorable comrade is like carrying an empty water skin in the desert; it is a weight you cannot afford to bear." (Attributed to the Taiban Leader "Warin the First"; undocumented.)

Pem's wrists ached where the rope Terk tied her to the co-pilot's chair bit into them. She only made it worse, grinding the ropes across her thin skin during her tantrum while struggling against them. It was not so much that she was angry at Callum, although she was, but mostly she was angry with herself. How could she have been so stupid as to fall for Callum's lies? It wasn't that she found him attractive. He just seemed so lonely, and with everyone's lives upended by the riots and the fire, she felt sorry for him, and the least she could do was be a friend, a boy without anyone.

She was surprised when he took her hand in the hangar, and maybe she had blushed, but it didn't mean she liked him *that* way; it was more like embarrassment. Yes, she was embarrassed he thought it was okay—that she wanted that kind of attention from him.

I was just being nice. Too nice. And now look where it got her. Her Da was going to kill her—well, that was not true. Tai Bobalo would be beside himself and jump into action when he figured out what had happened. *If* he figured it out.

He will. Block was at the gate and saw us come in. He would have heard the ship start and seen it take off—that and the hangar doors are open. It would be impossible for her family to miss her exit from the planet and the means of that exit. But would they think she and Callum took the ship out for a short flight—a sort of juvenile adventure, or would they realize something more sinister was at play?

When she and Callum did not return, would her family think she ran away with this boy? If they asked at the infirmary, they would know Callum was a frequent visitor. Did the infirmary staff believe Callum was visiting Clem, or did someone notice the two of them

CHAPTER SIXTY-NINE

walking together after her shift and think there was something more going on?

If they talk to Clem, he'll tell them I would never go with Callum willingly, she decided.

Though Callum pretended he and Clem were friends, Clem never liked Callum. Pem could see it in the only part of Clem's face that she could see: his eyes. She should have paid more attention to those signals and not so much to her guilt for having so much when others had so little. Being nice to Callum was never going to fix anything in the street-boy's life.

You tried to be a friend to Callum to make yourself feel better, not because it would really change anything for him, Pem scolded herself. Her position as a protected daughter of Tai Bobalo, with an Ebulonian mother belonging to a clan with enough influence that she would never be forced to leave Ebulon, gave her security and status few of her fellow Taibans had; Pem struggled with this. If she had been allowed to, she would have trained with her father alongside her brother, Quinn, and Corin, as a way to come to terms with her guilt. But though Pem's mother, Timee, had given in to Corin's desire to follow the revolutionaries' path, she was immovable when it came to the other girls. Being trained put them in the center of the Free Men's culture and would inevitably lead to some mission involving a return to Taiba to work for the cause.

Pem realized, however, that her previous actions and the reasons behind them were not what mattered at this moment. She was being held captive with limited options that did not lead to death, her own or others'. She needed to focus on not being stupid and nice and figure out what to do to get out of the mess she had gotten herself into.

As soon as she reached out to any of the Free Men's contacts in The String, they would contact her father, and he would come. Perhaps her guilt was already morphing into something more mature because Pem felt no remorse for how Callum was treated by her father and his comrades.

But Callum will have realized that too.

So, how did the boy plan on getting around that? Or was this another of the loose details that would have to be improvised in this escape?

E.F. Winters

Callum claimed he had planned to leave Ebulon for some time, and it was only a matter of where he'd get another ship, which made her wonder what happened to the first ship. She needed to work on him a bit and see if she could find out. He did seem susceptible to flattery. But when he realized a friendship with Pem might give him a second chance at a ship, he must have considered what the challenges might be. Of course, Callum admitted he hadn't thought to be presented with the opportunity to escape that first night—hence the improvised solutions he used so far.

Everyone who ever came to Ebulon through The String knew that someone needed to know you were coming. Someone had to have your coordinates and departure time, so they were out there in the Dead Zone to catch you. If not, you would float in cold space, drifting until you lost consciousness, your last thought before you lost consciousness, the hope that someone would stumble on your ship or pod in time to revive you.

"Communication's, right?" Callum's right hand hovered over the communications controls on the ship's control board. Pem nodded absently, and he switched the system on, working the dial. She expected any moment that he would ask her for the digital address of a contact. *Who should I give him? Who?* She racked her brain. Though she did not know many, there were still decisions to be made. She needed a contact who preferably did not have a family. Someone who had enough rough crewmates around them that Callum would not easily cow or threaten, but one who had enough loyalty to the cause and the Bobalo's that they could not be bought by promises of reward. She did not think Callum had much in the way of credits, but he had her father's ship, which was quite valuable, and he had her, which bore the promise of value, either as a hostage or as a reward.

Callum began fine-tuning a signal. Pemitai frowned.

"What are you doing?"

"Setting the distress beacon," Callum answered. "With a beacon, you being a Bobalo doesn't need to come up. No one will know who we are, but they'll still rescue us."

"You can still have only come from one place: Ebulon," Pem pointed out. "And all distress signals and rescues are still reported."

"Maybe," Callum shrugged, then grinned wickedly. "But not as urgently as missing Bobalos."

CHAPTER SIXTY-NINE

It was not hard for Tai Bobalo to procure a Paxlosian vessel. Zeph had given him supervisory powers over several crews for the purpose of hunting down and stopping any Taiban mercenaries attempting to escape. If one of Zeph's men complained to their captain about the Taiban acquisitioning a ship and manning it with his own crew, Bobalo would explain when it happened. Not now.

It took less than two hours to gather his old crew, solicit the longer-distance ship, and get into the air.

"What if I'm wrong, and she went with him because she wanted to?" Block asked his old friend hesitantly. Block never had a family or a long-term relationship, and his confidence that he read Pemitai correctly was fading now that he had time to think.

"You aren't," Bobalo assured the old pirate. "Give yourself some credit, Block. Give Pem some. You've known her all her life. If you say she wasn't trying to sneak off with this boy, I think you're probably right."

Block shook his head. "Didn't seem like the type of boy Pem would be interested in—not in *that* way, you know? Sneaky, he was, with little weaselly eyes and one of them starved faces those Taiban kids get they can't get rid of no matter how much we feed 'em. When he looked at me, I felt like he was sniggering behind those eyes--like he'd just picked my pocket then stuck a knife in my gut, only I didn't know it yet. Pem introduced him as Callum, but the way he smirked when she said it made me think it wasn't his real name. A kid like that ain't goin' to give you a name to pin stuff on when he's out and about making mischief. Does anyone know the boy?"

"It sounds like a boy we brought back on our last mission to Taiba," Ald said, leaning on the back of Block's seat, watching out the front window. "Called himself Terk then." Ald was the last surviving member of Quinn Bobalo's Free Men mission team and had talked his way onto the crew, insisting he should take Pem's brother's place in Quinn's absence.

"I know the boy," Tommy Makepeace spoke up. When he heard what happened, the pub proprietor also insisted on being involved, citing his many business connections in The String. "I've got eyes everywhere, Captain. Not paid spies or informants, you understand, but folk I do business with who rely on that business and have a vested interest in maintaining our relationship," he explained. The explanation had won him a spot.

"I asked at the hospice," Als shared. "An older boy who was visiting a kid burned in the fire was paying a lot of attention to Pem. The description they gave could be this Callum, or Terk, or both."

Block nodded. "He knew what he was doin'. Pem was just being herself, but this kid knew how to get around folk."

"Sounds like he was just being himself, too," Bobalo growled. "You try to do the right thing and help folk, and they just throw it back in your face."

No one felt the betrayal of the mercenaries and the population who supported them more keenly than Tai Bobalo.

"Where's Corin, Captain?" Ald asked. "I can't imagine she'd take to the sidelines on this."

"She doesn't know. She's with the Pira," Bobalo explained without embellishment.

"Right." Ald nodded. Free Men understood some information should not be casually shared, even when you were in what you believed to be trusted company.

Block scratched his neck and pulled at the dirty kerchief wrapped around it.

"I sure wish Timee had let you teach those girls sumptin' practical about protecting themselves, Tai. I'd feel a lot better about all this right now."

"Me too, Block," Bobalo agreed. "Me too, but Pem's smart. We need to have faith in her, faith that she can hold her own against this young man."

I need to have faith in her, he added, silently. He had been fighting off haunted visions of what this disturbed young man might do to his trusting daughter ever since Block found him and Jayq Jacoby at the Hard Pumper Pub and told him what he'd seen.

"If this is Terk, Captain, he came in on that last group of genius kids we rescued from Taiba," Ald said.

"Meaning he's no slouch," Bobalo surmised.

"Smart's good," Jayq agreed, sharing a look with Tommy Makepeace. "And in a civilized world, it might be enough. But that

CHAPTER SIXTY-NINE

world out there is not civilized—not in The String, and certainly not beyond it. Half of these kids coming out of Taiba are broken, and the other half are feral. Pem might need more than brains."

"She's a Bobalo," Block bridled defensively. "Not some fragile flower. She'll be fine."

"Of course, she will. She's a Bobalo." Jacoby put a comforting hand on his friend's shoulder.

"And her pop's friends may have some gray hairs between them, but they're still some of the meanest sum'bitches in the system." Block shared a wide grin that exposed the semi-toothless state of his mouth. "And we're goin' to get that li'l ferrety bastard."

"We are," Bobalo focused on flying.

Pem bit her lip as she watched the outposter ship slide into docking position, and the sheath slipped over, sealing the connection.

"Are they going to recognize you?" Callum asked.

"I don't know. I've never been off Ebulon, and not many of them have ever been to it, so probably not."

Callum's eyes narrowed. "Pemitai Bobalo, why don't I trust you?"

"Why would you?" Pem countered sassily. "I don't trust you either, but apparently we need each other if we're going to stay alive. If we don't get fuel, we'll go into Float, and once we do that, chances are slim we'll ever be found, and if we are, we'll be dead." She did not try to dampen the emotions that welled up inside her. That seemed to satisfy Callum.

"I'm going to untie you. It would be hard to explain why you're tied up, but don't get any ideas about trying to escape." He pulled out a gun. "I can kill this outposter as well as kill you. Then I'll have his ship, his fuel, and no more problems from little Bobalo brats." He looked down at the gun and pointed it at Pem. "Time for you to ask yourself another hard question, Pem. It seems to be a day for them, doesn't it? Do you want to live with the death of this outposter on your conscience? Because if I have to kill them, it will only be because you did something stupid."

E.F. Winters

"I think I'm over my limit for stupid things today, Callum," Pem said sarcastically. "I surpassed my quota sometime last night when I let you in my dad's hangar." The boy chuckled.

"Good girl." He untied her.

The ropes dropped to the floor, and Pem stood unsteadily. Suddenly, she could seriously feel the results of her head injury.

"You okay?" Callum asked, steadying her.

"Just a little dizzy," she admitted, touching the dried blood on her head wound. The outposter ship docked, and Pem could see its doors beginning to open on the far end of the connection. Tension filled her body with anticipation. What would she say? What could she say?

She felt a sharp pain on her head, and her legs gave out.

"Told you. I don't trust you," Callum muttered as she blacked out.

When Pemitai regained consciousness, she was lying on the cockpit floor of her father's ship. There was a folded blanket under her head, slightly cushioning it from the hard metal floor, and another blanket laid out over her. Both smelled like machine oil and dust. Neither looked like something that came out of the Bobalo household.

Must be something the outposters gave Callum, Pem decided.

"Thoughtful of you to make me comfortable after knocking me out again," she said bitterly.

"You were going to do something. I could see it. You're too damned clever for your own good, Pem, or mine," Callum replied.

"What did you tell *them*?" She indicated the outposter ship.

"That you lost your balance when the ships docked trouble and you hit your head."

"Twice?"

"I didn't hit you in two different places," Callum defended himself. "I'm not a monster."

"So, did they fuel us up yet?"

"They don't have enough fuel for that. They're towing us into their outpost."

Towing meant the lead ship had to move slowly and carefully, meaning it was more likely the outposters would report in before they got to their camp. Before the rescue was complete.

CHAPTER SIXTY-NINE

Good for me. Not so good for Callum, Pem figured. At least the outposters were on another ship and out of range of Callum's gun.

"So, once we're down, then what?" she asked. The population levels on most outpost moons were low, but visitors, being a bit of a rarity, got a fair amount of attention. There were unwritten rules about the hospitality you received from an outpost settlement. You paid what you could. You offered to work if you could not pay. If you had skills, you shared freely, and if you had news, you shared that. Stories were as good as currency on some outposts. Everyone had a story. Not sharing yours was just bad manners. Older Free Men often repeated a tale they claimed was true, but was so commonly shared it reached the status of myth. The cautionary tale claimed a group of outposters disliked the ending of one man's story so much they put him back in his pod and threw him back out into space.

Pem wondered what story Callum would tell.

She wondered what story she might tell.

"You said before this was the second time you'd gotten a ship and tried to escape, Callum. What happened the first time?" Pem asked.

It was a long time before he answered. So long that Pem thought he wasn't going to.

"It crashed," Callum said in a guttural snarl. His eyes seemed to see somewhere else, a memory that loomed so large it wiped out the present. Whatever happened to Callum, it still stalked his mind with the malice of an unnatural predator—not a flesh and blood animal that hunted from need, but something twisted that hunted and killed for the pleasure of breathing in the first hints of death and decay that taint a final breath. "That's when the fire started," he barely whispered the words.

Pemitai's heart stopped. *Callum crashed the ship that started the fire in Little Taiba?"* She did not want to believe it, but she knew in her gut and by looking at his face, it was true. He was perverted, cruel, caring for no one but himself. Pem remembered the fear and anguish she had seen in Clemmet's eyes whenever he caught her eye and thought Callum couldn't see. Pem shivered.

What have I done? She thought she knew guilt before, but this guilt sat like a boulder inside her, accusing her of becoming an accomplice to countless atrocities as yet unknown. Callum must have seen the shock and anger on her face.

E.F. Winters

"Oh no, don't think it, Pem," he said, his usual belittling tone back in place. "*I* didn't crash the ship and start the fire. *I'm* not responsible for all that death and destruction. I was just…there. No, it was your innocent little friend Clem. He crashed the ship. He killed all those people and burned down that sad little shanty town you're all so proud of." Callum's eyes glowed yellow and orange like the flames that had consumed Little Taiba, his thin mouth twisted, his body curling over and twisting beneath the clothes she realized had always been too heavy for the weather. "That's how Clem got burned." Callum's fire-bright eyes narrowed to glowing slivers. "He pretends not to remember who he is because he knows that if they find him, he'll have to answer questions he doesn't want to answer, and they'll figure out what he's done."

Pem knew she was on dangerous ground here. Callum had been playing a role, making a pretense of being someone nicer than he really was, and that had moderated his behavior some. But now the monster had unveiled himself, and he was peeking out at her, its dead stare curiosity unbridled by human compassion or norms.

"You were injured," she chose her words carefully, modulating her tone. "He hurt you, didn't he, Callum?" The boy's eyes filled. "Oh, Callum, I am so sorry. I didn't know. Who took care of your wounds? Your burns?"

"No one," the boy muttered, his voice stilted by pain and the weight of his abandonment.

"May I see?" Pem asked, embracing the deep reserves of compassion within her and focusing them on him and only him. Callum slowly slid up his sleeve, exposing the gnarled rootlike ropes of burn scars that vined over the tortured skin of his arm. "Oh, Callum, I wish I had known. If you had only told me, I would have taken care of you."

The boy's tear-filled eyes looked up at her from beneath heavy lids. "Would you? Would you really, Pemitai Bobalo?" His voice was hard and bitter as before; the moment of vulnerability passed. "A dirty street kid like me? When they took us from Taiba, they promised us a new life. They gave Clem a family. He was going to be a real kid with a mom and a dad and a room of his own." Callum snorted in disgust. "What do you think they gave me, Pem?"

Pem shook her head, afraid of where this bitterness would lead.

CHAPTER SIXTY-NINE

"Nothing," Callum answered himself. "I was too old, or too broken for any family to want me, too old to be loved. And the others like me were put in a bunkhouse, all squeezed together like in a prison, and left to find our own way. The others struggled, lying on their bunks all day or begging for drinks in the pubs. Some of the older ones hung out with Murtevoy's bunch and got into that house guard racket. I didn't need someone else to show me my way. I already knew what I needed to do. I managed just fine on Taiba. I just needed to get back, and for that I needed a ship."

"And you found one." Pem smiled. "You actually found two, and now you're on your way back, just like you planned."

Callum's eyes narrowed. "And no little Bobalo brat's going to get in my way."

"I won't, Callum," Pem promised. "I understand now. I'll help you get back to Taiba. You don't need to hurt me."

"I don't *need* to, but I might *like* to," Callum's mouth twisted up on one side, his eyes glittering—not with tears.

"If you try it, you'll pay," she shot back, dropping all pretense of being soft and caring.

Callum grunted. "There you are. Thought for a minute there that I'd hit you too hard that second time and you'd lost it."

"Oh, I'm still here, Callum. Don't you worry about that. I offered to help you, but clearly you'd rather make this a contest." Pem gritted her teeth.

"I like to win," the boy bragged.

Pem did not know what part Callum had played, but there was no way Clemmet was responsible for crashing that ship and starting the fire. Callum had done that.

And he will pay for it, Pem vowed as the outposter ship towed them in to land.

E.F. Winters

CHAPTER SEVENTY

"A smile does not make a friend any more than a sword makes an enemy." (Common Taiban phrase used mostly among the Free Man movement.)

As Pem and Callum opened the door of her father's ship, the pilot of the outposter vessel who towed them in approached. Pem was disappointed to see that their rescuer was a young man, maybe only a few years older than Pem's older sister. Thin, like most outposters, since food was expensive and life in The String required hard, physical labor. An older outposter would have been more likely to have recognized her father's ship and asked questions about why they had it. He also did not land them on the official landing strip, closer to the activity center of the outpost, landing instead on the barren playa north and east of the settlement's cluster of buildings.

"Well, you're here and not floating for what it's worth," the young man said. "I set you down here 'cause it's free, no fees. If we'd come into the main dock, it'd cost. 'Didn't know your plans, or how long you're staying. If you need to store your ship, there's places for that at the docks or private ones, but like everything else, that costs." He was sizing them up as he spoke, noting Pem's new yellow tunic and pants and small pieces of jewelry, Callum's cheaper and less cared-for clothes, their fit shouting that Callum was not the first to wear them. "We're a poor moon, not much in the way of resources," the outposter explained. "Still, everyone chips in as they can to keep things running." It was his way of asking her and Callum to give him something for rescuing them without directly asking.

Pem reached into her pocket, pulled out the few credits she had, and held them out to him.

"Give him whatever you have, Callum," she said. "We owe it to him. He saved our lives."

"We don't have much, sis." Callum reluctantly pulled his bag off his shoulder and rummaged in a side pocket, coming out with a few small credit chips which he begrudgingly handed over to the outposter.

The young man bounced the meager collection of chips in his hand, indicating that it was still a little light.

Pem reached up to the back of her neck and unhooked the necklace she wore, the sudden movement giving her a sharp pain in her head and making her dizzy. She added the necklace to the pile in the young man's hand, using her hand to close his over it. She had seen her father do the same in other negotiations among the Taibans. The gesture said, "This is all you're going to get, or alternatively, it's all we have." Closing the outposter's hand over the cache had another purpose: it kept Callum from studying what she had given the outposter. If the necklace surfaced anywhere in the outpost and Bobalo's crew came across it, they would know it for Pem's. They would know she had been there, and they should easily trace it back to this young man and find out everything he knew.

"Your sister, eh?" The outposter looked Pem over, a quizzical look on his face, as if digging after something in the back of his mind.

Callum put his arm around Pem's shoulders, pulling her close.

The outposter noted the protective gesture, and though it was perfectly explainable as a brotherly action, a question flared behind his eyes.

"You okay?" he asked Pem. For a beat, she thought he was asking if she was in trouble, and she held her breath, desperately trying to figure out how to say "no" without saying the word. Callum must have thought so, too, because his whole body tensed beside her. "Your head, I mean." The outposter indicated Pem's head injury.

It took her a moment to breathe again.

"Yeah, I think so," she replied cautiously, trying to say something entirely different with her eyes as she reached up to gently touch the wound. It was very tender and felt hot, blood dried in the white hair all around it. "I should probably see a doctor or a healer or whoever takes care of medical stuff here, though. You know, just to get the wound cleaned up and get checked out." She smiled at Callum, knowing she put him in a position where he had to agree. His jaw tensed. He could hardly miss the manipulation, but he had to follow through. It would raise questions if he denied her care.

"Definitely." He nodded. "First thing. We need to make it quick, though, because we can't stay. We need to get back to Taiba," he emphasized the words so she would not mistake his meaning. "Our Mother's very sick," he lied. "Where can we catch a ship?"

The outposter squinted, again, sensing something not right, but not experienced enough to know to listen or what to do about it.

"Transport to the Cluster's pretty spendy, depending on what kind of rig you're willing to risk traveling in and who you're willing to ride with. I thought you said you didn't have much?"

"I have a ship," Callum snapped back.

"Then just take it," the outposter suggested, taking in the details of the vessel.

"That would take fuel, and we don't have any credits anymore since we *paid* you to save us," Callum groused.

The outposter pulled the credits they gave him out of his pocket, weighed them in his hand, then handed them back to Callum. The necklace was not among them.

"Never let it be said that outposters in The String aren't hospitable to those in need." The outposter caught and held Pemitai's eyes.

Silently, she tried to convey to him that there was something wrong without letting Callum see her touch her head again, then looking at Callum's hands. They were clenched into fists.

"Where do we find this healer?" Callum demanded rudely, yanking Pem around so she faced away from the outposter.

"Down that side street." The young man pointed. "There's a sign out front. She's not very social, but she knows her business." He strolled off toward the east side of the settlement as Callum marched Pem quickly away.

"Have you no shame, woman?" he muttered under his breath, glancing back at the outposter to make sure the young man kept going. "Damn. The way you do look at men, like you're trying to hypnotize them to do your will or something." He turned them from their original path.

"The healer's place is over there," Pem protested, looking to their left.

"What do you take me for, Pem? A fool? I'm not spending credits to have some desert witch dab at your little scrape so she can try to fleece me for what I can't spare while you drop hints that you need to

CHAPTER SEVENTY

be rescued. Maybe I could sell you as a whore. Might get enough to get off this sand-crater, as long as they don't hear you talk."

He stopped, tracking the young outposter's progress and the growing distance between them.

The "town" was a collection of small shelters made of anything on hand pushed up against anything else that might work, all of it stuck together by strands of hope anchored down by sheer human stubbornness and set up on a sparse grid of intersecting "streets". A dun-colored, wide-open moonscape beneath a putty gray sky surrounded the low-profile, dust-covered buildings. Snatches of color here and there, a sign, a flag, the stripe on a discarded piece of space junk, were all bleached out, encrusted with the same dun-colored dust, as if the moon would morph every transplant into itself through an aggressive uniformity of color.

Outside of the settlement, the broad, flat playa was strewn with an occasional knife-like rock formation or a collection of wind-sculpted boulders. Nothing grew in the shallow dust covering the hardscape rock. It wasn't scenic. It was harsh, dry, and barren.

Callum watched the outposter until he disappeared behind the first row of buildings before returning his attention to Pem.

"What are you going to do with me?" she demanded.

"I'm deciding."

"You don't want to take me with you, Callum. It will cost twice as much for two." She realized too late her mistake in pointing out the urgency of his need to be rid of her.

There was no good reason for anyone to stroll out into the desert. It would be a waste of water and energy. If someone dumped a body out here, it could be years before it was noticed.

"What am I going to do with you?" Callum repeated, reaching out toward her.

Pem flinched.

He yanked the small, decorative comb from her stiff, white curls.

"Give me your earrings," he demanded. "And put this on." He took the filthy scarf from around his neck and tossed it at her. "That damn white hair of yours is a problem.

Pem removed the jeweled studs from her ears. "Take them. Take all of it." She pulled off an arm bracelet, then an ankle bracelet that was covered by her wide-legged pants, handing them to Callum before tying the faded blue scarf around her head, covering her thick platinum curls.

Callum scowled, looking at the jewelry. "It's not enough." He turned his scowl on her as if their lack of funds was somehow her fault. Pem knew what was coming before he raised his arm to strike her. She turned and began to run.

It would not gain her much. Callum was too fast, but every minute she put off the inevitable was a minute in which something might change in her favor, so she kept running, and she began to shout, "Help me! Help!"

"Shut up, bitch," Callum yelled as he chased after her. "You shut up!"

"Or what?'Pem shouted back. "You'll kill me? You're going to do that anyway, but I'm not going to make it easy for you." She ran toward town. "Help, someone! Help me!" She hoped someone would pay attention.

When she didn't hear Callum's feet pounding after her, she took a chance and looked back. Callum had stopped. His pack was at his feet, and his gun was in his hands.

"Stop right there!" he commanded. Pem paused, breathing hard. "One more step and I'll shoot you, Pemitai Bobalo." He smiled cruelly. "Not nearly so brave now, are you? Dying seems very different when it's a certainty that's only seconds away."

Pem looked at the old gun, then at Callum, his narrow face compressed with anger, every feature squeezing together, vying for domination in the center. Though he believed there was only one outcome from here, Pem saw a number of alternatives: his old gun could misfire—or not fire at all. Deep in the grip of uncontrolled anger, Callum was in no condition to make decisions, to aim well, or to notice his surroundings. Several settlement inhabitants were gathering at the side of the street that was several hundred yards behind him.

One of them separated from the others, walking toward Pem and Callum.

"If you kill me, Callum, you'll never see Taiba," Pem warned.

"If I kill you, nobody here will notice or care," Callum disagreed. "They're too busy trying to survive to worry about what's happening to some stranger. That's the way it is in the real world, but I guess your big brother wouldn't want to share that with his little sister. Got to protect that little honey and sunshine heart."

"Walk away, young man." The settlement outposter ordered Callum, raising a long-barreled rifle and pointing it at the boy. It was a woman's voice, vocal chords cracked and splintered by the desert moon's dust. A wide-brimmed hat gleaned from a dustbin was pulled down low, shading a nut-brown, weathered face, dust streaks embedded in the skin oils caking the rivulet wrinkles that time tined across it. The rest of her clothes were equally ill-fitted and utilitarian, with large pockets sagging under the weight of an outposter's necessities, all of it imbued with the moon's colorless dust, bleached of color to harmonize with the space-rock's theme of sparse survival.

Callum spun around, gun in hand, his eyes a pair of muddy moon-puddles in a face suddenly gone pale and bloodless.

"Stay out of this, old woman." He re-pointed his gun at Pem. "This is none of your business."

"Don't know how you can say that, seeing as you don't know what my business is."

Callum licked his dry lips. "Are you here to interfere between me and my property?"

"If you're meaning that girl, The String don't recognize people as property." The woman kept Callum steady in her rifle's sights.

"I'm no one's property," Pemitai protested.

"Keep quiet, girl. The grownups are talkin.'" The woman spared Pemitai a warning glare. A tiny twitch of her head directed Pem's attention toward the settlement.

The figure still standing half in shadow by the building there had a familiar stance.

The outposter who towed us in. He did figure it out. Pem swallowed hard and tried to calm herself.

"Whatever the outposts claim, a lot of bounties are collected from these parts," Callum argued.

"It happens," the woman acknowledged.

"This girl is a runaway. Seeing as how I fund her and that makes her my bounty, she kind of belongs to me now."

"Got papers?" the woman asked.

"Lost 'em," Callum lied.

"It happens." The old woman lowered her rifle a bit. "A bunch of ink scratches on paper doesn't really mean much out here in The String. We're more about who a person is and relationships, you understand?"

"You mean like what we can do for each other? Like a barter system?"

"Something like that."

"I haven't got much, outside my skills."

"Which are?"

"Talking people into seeing things my way and doing what I want them to do, finding my way into so-called secure locations, acquiring items of value, disposing of things people don't want around anymore."

"So, con man, thief, murderer." The old woman almost smiled. "An understandably vague list."

"Your words, not mine." Callum grinned. "I find myself in a bit of a bind here. I'd trade the girl for a full tank of fuel."

"What would I want with a slip of a thing like that? Looks like a good wind would blow her away."

"She's stronger than she looks." Callum shrugged. "Some people say she's kind of a pretty thing. You could rent her out by the hour."

"I'm not a whore," Pem protested.

"You're not old enough to know what you are yet, girl," the old woman shot Pem down. "And you're not in a position to be choosing right now."

"'Can't imagine there's much call for domestic help around here," Callum went on. "No dinner parties or fancy dress balls, but she's young and healthy enough to be taught to do what's needed, and everyone needs a little comfort now and then, whatever their preferences."

"That your ship out on the North Playa?" The old woman tossed her head to her right. Callum nodded. "Nice rig. Custom...distinctive. A ship like that stands out."

Callum threw a worried look at Pemitai. "Maybe out here in The String, but not in The Cluster." Pem could tell he was improvising again. There was a little twitch of his head that gave him away once you knew what to look for. "It's kind of a hobby in the Cluster, fixing up old ships," Callum elaborated on his lie. "There's quite a few of them these days."

"Making them less valuable," the old woman pointed out.

"We're talking about you buying the girl, not the ship," Callum tried to get the focus back where he wanted it.

"Correction, we're talking about how you can walk away today without getting killed," she advised him.

"There's no place to walk to." Callum's frustration was beginning to unravel him. "The only way I can get off this moon is to fly out, and that means I need fuel."

"Or passage on a freighter," the old woman suggested.

"I lose my ship and the girl?"

"And keep your life. Seems fair to me," the rifle-toter replied.

Callum lost it. "You must be out of your mind." He turned his gun away from Pem and toward the old woman. "I could just shoot you and keep them both."

The aging outposter shifted her rifle. A poof of dust exploded beside Callum's feet, the cloud hanging in the dead air as the concussive sound sped away across the open ground. People began coming out of the buildings and into the streets, searching for the source of the shot. The young outposter was no longer among them.

"You're trying my patience and running out of time, young man," the rifle-toting outposter warned Callum.

The boy's eyes seemed to take over his thin face, his nostrils flaring, body twitching, sending micro messages that he was about to run. But what if he didn't? Pem worried. Pressed, with his back to the wall, what if he spun around and took that shot he was bragging about, killing Pem or the old woman?

"Just let him go," Pem pleaded with the old woman, softly. Every fiber in her wanted to shout out that she was Pemitai Bobalo and Callum had kidnapped her, but doubt kept her from trusting the outcome of that. The woman seemed to be interested in helping her, though she had not actually said it. What she had done was negotiate for Pem as a slave. If the Bobalo family name was brought in, would the woman pull out of the deal, seeing it as too dangerous? Pemitai was certain the truth of her identity would change things, but she was not certain in what direction. For now, she needed to leverage the small win she seemed to have.

E.F. Winters

"Give him the fuel and let him go. You'll get every credit back, I promise," Pem declared. "I can work for you. I won't whore, but I can do other things. I used to work in an infirmary. I can take care of people, and I'm a hard worker. I know what I'm asking you to do is a gamble for you, but I'd pay you back and I'd be grateful."

A signal bleeped in one of the old woman's many pockets. Keeping her eyes and rifle on Callum, she pulled out a communication device and glanced at the screen.

"So, you got a deal, boy. You," she tossed her head toward Pem. "Start walking toward town. Someone will meet you. Go with them and don't try to escape or anything stupid. And you," she poked her rifle toward Callum, "go back to that ship you came in and get off my moon. I don't ever want to see your ugly face here again. You understand?"

"The fuel…?"

"It's all ready to go. All you have to do is get on board and leave."

Callum licked his lips, grabbed his pack, and took off running north.

The crop-haired, dusty, military style overcoated person who collected Pem gave her the once over, then muttered, "This way," the brevity and tone maintaining the mystery of their gender. They led her to the main street without looking back to see if Pem followed, something that would not normally have bothered Pem, but she was finding the heat intolerable and desperately needed a drink of water. The excitement and lack of food were beginning to tell on her, making her dizzy and weak-kneed.

At the main street, they turned right and walked about a hundred feet, then turned right again on the next road heading toward a metal building that looked like the underside of a spaceship cut in half and flipped over.

Pemitai quickly recognized it from the rusted metal sign out front. Wired to a fencepost, the word "healer" was scratched in scribbled crosshatch, gouged into the metal by knife or nail.

Drawing closer, Pem noted an odd sort of fin created by two short metal walls that ran down the center of the building's rounded roof. The sides of the makeshift structure were long and straight, unaltered by any additions that would have undermined the original seamless dust-proof engineering of its half-circle design. Additional walls were

CHAPTER SEVENTY

soldered onto the front and back of the tubular half-circle to close off the ends.

Crates and heavy boxes, metal and wood, were stacked all around the building with no attempt at order, and moon-sand was piled high against the metal sides, partially burying the structure.

Opening the door, the mysterious overcoat indicated that Pem should go inside.

"Don't touch anything," they mumbled. "She don't like anybody touching stuff." They stood just inside the door, leaving Pemitai standing at the edge of the room, hot, directionless, and dizzy, awkwardly, awaiting the next turn in her life. Was she here to get her head wound cared for before she was taken to her new place of employment? Was she being cared for as an investment so that she could be sold again? She hoped her father found her soon, before it was too late.

The inside of the metal structure was surprisingly well-lit by a strip of daylight coming through the flat plastic inset in the roof. The short walls on each side were what formed what looked like a fin on the outside.

Though the jumble of boxes and crates scattered around the building gave Pem the impression its occupant was less than tidy, the inside was exactly the opposite, with orderly shelves assiduously labeled as to what supplies or tools resided where. The furnishings were rough; two wooden benches edged a crate table. Over another two crates pushed together, a pad and a pillow were added. A step stool, made of boxes pushed together, sat at its side to help patients climb onto the makeshift "table".

Like the world outside, the only color was brightly patterned curtains hung on wires that closed off the back half of the otherwise empty space: presumably the healer's living space.

The rifle-toter entered, accompanied by a gust of air-blown dust and the piercing sounds of a ship taking off not too far away. Removing her hat revealed long gray and white hair messily gathered into a single braid that snaked down the woman's back between suspenders that held up bulky, oversized pants. She stuck her wide-brimmed hat on a peg on the wall by the door and announced, "He's off," as she turned. Pale blue eyes made placid pools among the strong features of her weather-tanned face.

"Thank you," Pemitai replied, trying to hide the fact that she was steadying herself on the crate table.

The mystery overcoat nodded to the rifle-toter and left, their secrets still held close and private.

The rifle-toter gathered clean cotton squares and something in a bottle that smelled very alcoholic, a curved needle, and some thread.

"Sit," she directed Pemitai.

"You're the healer?" Pem realized her question was both stupid and rude, as it revealed she made assumptions about the woman that were at best inaccurate and at worst prejudicial.

"It's not my first choice, but yes," she admitted flatly. "Do you want me to look at that?" She nodded at Pemitai's head wound. Pem's face must have registered some surprise at the mention of her head injury. "There's blood coming through that scarf," the woman added. "Or were you thinking to keep that filthy piece of cloth over it until it gets infected?"

"No," Pem muttered, embarrassed. "I'd be grateful if you'd look at it and do…whatever you think needs to be done." She hoped she had shown a polite amount of confidence to remedy her earlier faux pas towards the woman, who was, what, her new employer? Her mistress? Pem did not know what label might apply, if any of them. It hardly mattered, she reminded herself, because her father would be here soon, and he would soon find her. He would, of course, be disappointed that his ship was gone, but he would never say so as long as Pem was safe. Bobalo would pay back the healer for the cost of the services and the fuel, or whoever was responsible for that, then Pem would be on her way home.

The healer untied the scarf, dabbing with a clean, wet cloth to loosen the dried blood before carefully peeling the material away where it had stuck to the wound.

Pem winced and bit her lip, but she did not cry out.

"It's a lot of hair." The healer scowled, gently pulling a few of the tangled, now brown and pink-stained strands apart, trying to clear a space around the wound. "The blood's caked and the hair's been mashed down into the wound."

"He hit me in the same place more than once," Pem explained. "It was easier to cover up that way."

CHAPTER SEVENTY

"Hurt like shit though, didn't it?" The healer stopped her exploration and stepped back. "I'm going to have to shave your head, kid."

For a moment, Pemitai thought the woman was testing to see if she really meant what she said about doing whatever she thought was necessary, but that thought was short-lived as the healer went to a shelf, turning around with a razor and a cup with a bar of soap, and a round brush in it.

"I can just take off the part that absolutely has to come off so that I can clean and work around the injury and then try to even out the rest of your hair afterward so it looks like you meant to cut it that way. Or I can just shave the whole thing now."

Pemitai bit her lip. Her hair was a sore spot her whole life, something that never fit into anyone's definition of acceptable. It had always been too messy, too curly, too stiff, too white. But she was not on Ebulon now. No one knew or cared if she stood up to the standards of propriety and hygiene her cautious mother demanded from one of Captain Bobalo's daughters, every action watched, judged, and commented on. But Pem no longer had to think about the expectations of Little Taiba's small-minded, gossipy women.

"Shave it all," she said.

The healer eyed her suspiciously. "You sure?"

"I am."

And in this moment, Pemitai Bobalo realized that in becoming an indentured servant, she had become freer than she had ever been.

CHAPTER SEVENTY-ONE

"There is no wrath like a Rhune's." (Common Ebulonian saying.)

A woman's shrill keening shattered the quiet of the Dum'Laiere country estate, where the family had taken up residence until the manor in Iredipa could be repaired. Rumors flew that Kirk had reinstated the tortures of old, also that the clan's scion, Dora Dum'Laiere, was dead.

The second proved to be close to the truth.

"Hagriva has destroyed my child, our family legacy—our future, Kirk." Miratha's anger burned bright and dark.

"Dora's own foolishness was responsible for what happened to her, Miratha, not Hagriva," Kirk argued. "What were you thinking, sending her to the old woman--a girl you claim could not boil an egg?"

Miratha looked petulant. "Hagriva asked to spend time with Dora before she left. It was part of our agreement."

Kirk did not believe her, and her wording made him doubly suspicious.

"What 'agreement'?" Miratha pressed her lips together and did not answer. "Dora went to Alden Baierd as part of Hagriva's agreement to recognize you? And nothing about that gave you pause?" Kirk pressed.

"She said nothing about teaching Dora magic." Miratha paced the floor. "This was deliberate, Kirk. She pretended to support us while plotting against us. But I promise you, we will not be stopped."

Kirk Dum'Laiere's mouth twisted in disgust. "Your daughter is in a coma, and all you can think about is how it has affected your schemes? Have you one true motherly feeling?"

"Do not presume to lecture me about parenthood. You have no idea how I feel, so do not pretend to," Miratha snapped.

"I am sorry," he apologized. "That was thoughtless. Look, we are both upset and liable to say things we do not mean. Let us talk about this after Dora's funeral."

"Funeral?" Miratha looked horrified. "There will be no funeral. Dora is not dead. She is in a coma, and as long as she is alive, there is hope that she will recover."

"You know there is no such hope," Kirk said, not unkindly.

"I do not," she flashed. "Dora will be brought home and given every care."

"So that you can remain a Dum'Laiere," Kirk muttered. She ignored him.

"Dora's condition changes nothing, except that at this time she cannot accompany Yare to Paxlosis. He will have to wait for her to recover or go without her and return."

Kirk smirked. "Very clever."

"I have invested twenty years in that girl. She has been the center of my life," Miratha huffed. "Everything I have done has been for her and this family--so the Dum'Laiere clan can regain their position here."

"And yet you have only succeeded in making us pariahs. Don't try an deny it, Yare targeted our properties because of your scheming," Kirk accused. "None of this would have happened if it were not for your infernal ambitions, Miratha."

"Do not pretend that you played no part." Miratha's thin lips twisted into a snarl. "You agreed with the hiring of the army, Kirk. You had them trained here on the farm under your watch," she reminded him of his complicity.

"I did not know you planned on assassinating the Mahal and starting a riot," Kirk Dum'Laiere countered.

Miratha looked shocked. *"You* accuse me? I did neither of those things. I was truth read and acquitted."

"I heard about that," Kirk raised one eyebrow. "How did you manage it?"

"I had no idea that rogue, Murtevoy, was involved in such subversive activities. If I had, I would never have hired him."

Kirk guffawed.

"You condemn me over a lack of feeling, but have you no feelings about our clan's future? Yare's attack on our estates was unjust and unlawful, but no one will do anything about it because as long as his starship is circling us, they are terrified to speak against him."

"You did kidnap the man," Kirk reminded her.

E.F. Winters

"I certainly did not." Miratha absently fluffed her satin skirts. "I rescued him and hid him to keep him safe."

"Sadly, he misunderstood your unselfish motives." Kirk's lips snarled.

"In our own way, we both try to do what is best for the family," Miratha tried to make peace.

"And the family will survive," Kirk said. "We always do."

"Surviving is not good enough. If Dora does not recover, you are all that is left of the First-Line Dum'Laieres, Kirk," Miratha challenged.

"The notion of First-line and Second-line and all is out of date. It is as irrelevant as a glister sword. A Dum'Laiere is a Dum'Laiere."

"You could still father a child," Miratha suggested.

Kirk shook his head. "I am too old and do not have the right... instincts."

"You are mature, not 'old'. You are strong, as am I." Miratha stepped closer, stroking his arm. "We could make another heir, you and I. Combining our lines would make our child important on so many levels. We would be unstoppable."

Kirk looked down at her with pity. "You and I do not even like each other."

"But we *understand* each other. That is more important."

"No." He pulled away from her.

"You would rather have some sniveling, pert-nosed bitch that your mother chooses for you, who imagines she can make you happy, and from whom you must hide your indifference?"

"I will hide from no one. My sexual preferences are well-known. It is only Mother who refuses to accept them."

"Please, Kirk, tragedy has stolen the destiny of our clan, but we could still save it. I am the Matriarch's recognized descendant. I have powerful friends, influence. There is more here than the treaty and trade contracts. Much more."

"What are you plotting now?"

"If Yare refuses to honor our agreement for Dora to be the treaty bride..."

"Which he will," Kirk interrupted.

"Then someone else must be chosen, and there is only one other option."

"You are too old, glamour spell or not," Kirk cautioned her.

"Not me, you idiot." Miratha slapped his arm. "The Pira. She is the only other female who fits the requirements this Consortium of Yare's set down. And if she leaves…"

"You think you can step into her place," Kirk completed her thought.

"I am Hagriva's descendant."

"Hagriva will never accept it."

"Hagriva will be dead." Kirk looked alarmed. "I only mean that she cannot live forever," Miratha added. She walked to the window and looked out at the fine estate. "Those who did this to our girl will pay. This is not over. I promise you."

"By the Mother, you make me feel tired, Miratha." Kirk groaned.

CHAPTER SEVENTY-TWO

"A cluttered life keeps the traveler close to home." (Documented in The Book of Simple Truths by Emman'eve Keesch but predates her work. Anonymous.)

The String outpost, referred to as Colla's after the original couple who settled it, was a community of tightly woven, interdependent, radically independent individuals. Its inhabitants freely followed their own paths, keeping to themselves or interacting as they chose to, except where it came to the welfare of the outpost. In that, everyone was expected to contribute fully with whatever they were able.

Shortly after the healer, Skillhands, began to work on Pemitai's head, Pem lost consciousness. For ten days, while she lingered near death, Captain Tai Bobalo and his friends searched for the Taiban Captain's daughter and Bobalo's missing ship, unaware that Pemitai was right there, on Colla.

Pem did not know how much the healer heard about this search, or if she heard about it at all while Bobalo's crew were at the outpost, circling questions. Skillhands was required to stay beside Pemitai, actively nursing her, and by the time Pem woke and the fog cleared from her brain, Bobalo's people were gone.

No one said anything to Pem about the search. There was no reason to. Colla's residents were close-mouthed about business that wasn't theirs to share. If Skillhands heard anything about the search, she never said. Her focus was on keeping Pem alive.

Once Pem began to heal and was able to take on small tasks, she realized she had been purchased by the outposter not for any selfish motive but to see if she was suitable to be trained as the healer's apprentice. Outposts without access to skilled healing had high death rates, highly transient populations, and did not thrive.

Skillhands was often called on to travel to other moon outposts after an accident or illness, but that took time. Often, too much time.

CHAPTER SEVENTY-TWO

The average life-term of an outposter was low. Merle Skillhands had already beaten the odds, but she knew that her luck would not last forever. She needed to train her replacement.

"Mac and May Colla gave Skill a safe place when she needed it. Like they did for most of the folk who ended up staying," Budge, the young outposter who towed Pem and Callum's ship into Colla, explained as he helped Pem carry supplies back to the healer's hut. It was Budge who told her about Bobalo's search—Budge who helped her understand what Skillhands wanted from her and why. Budge was well known and liked among Colla settlers. Pem found reading the hermit-ish outposters with their mastery of expressionless masks difficult, but Budge, who was younger than most of the settlers, except for the sparse few children who were born on the outpost, was always ready to help out, never asking questions or requiring conversation, but eager to share if encouraged.

He seemed to hang around Skillhand's hut a lot.

"Grandma and Grandpa Colla helped Skill find a purpose and make a home here," Budge shared, an unusual breach of the silence that blanketed most outposts' pasts. "Skill's done the same for those who came after her."

There were a hundred questions Pem wanted to ask about her benefactor, Skill's friend Doil, and a dozen outposters she met since starting to help the healer. Her natural gregariousness faced a challenge in the closed-mouth settlers, but she saw the advantage. No one asked her where she'd come from, or how, and Pem was grateful for it. On Colla, a person's past was theirs to share, alter, or sever as they chose.

They did not even ask her name, waiting for her to offer whatever moniker she chose. If she waited too long, though, the community would give her a name and she'd be stuck with it. Reluctant for her connection to the Bobalo family to be revealed, and conflicted about purposely hiding her identity, Pem offered nothing. The settlers began to call her "Skill's girl", which quickly morphed into something that sounded like "skullgirl".

The longer Pemitai lived in this strange anonymity, slowly re-inventing herself as the person she wished to be, the more reluctant she was to go back to her old life on Ebulon with its many expectations and boundaries. She knew her family was worried and would still be hunting for her, but she could not bring herself to tell Skill who she was, knowing it would mean she had to leave the healer.

I made a promise, Pem justified her silence.

She mulled over and discarded plan after plan as she worked for Skillhands, cleaning, preparing, doing basic home care for those who were unable to do for themselves during their convalescence, and shadowing the outpost healer.

The questions she would have to answer on her return seemed more daunting and more uncomfortable with every day that passed, a deep sense of guilt embedding itself within her at the consequences to the Free Man's movement with Callum's return to Taiba.

It's my fault. I did this. In her mind, there was nothing she could say to excuse the damage she caused, and she alone was responsible.

The day she opened Skillhand's hut door to find her cousin, Corin, there, Pemitai felt her new self shatter.

She realized she should not have been surprised. After Quinn's death, Corin took on the role of protector to his sisters, a situation complicated by Corin's loyalty to the Pira Eropa—a commitment Corin and Quinn had shared.

"I have a few questions, Pemitai," Corin stated bluntly, her eyes changing quickly from relief at seeing Pem to hard judgment. Pem had been here all along, and she did not reach out to let the family know she was safe. "First, are you alright?" Pem nodded. Corin made a face. "What happened to your hair?"

Pem reached up and rubbed the soft stubble on her head. It was easy to forget how changed she must look to someone who knew her before the head injury. Not only were her stiff white curls gone, but with all the weight loss, she must have looked like a skeleton. Her clothes were plain, sensible cast-offs produced by the mysterious Doil. Pem realized she must look a lot like Corin now, except for the hair. Corin always dressed for interacting actively with her environment. She was never the kind of girl like Pem who chose clothes because they were pretty.

Corin seemed to be taking in the differences in Pemitai as well.

"Whatever you've been through, we understand it could not have been easy," Pem's cousin said. "But they're over now. I'm here to take you home."

CHAPTER SEVENTY-TWO

"I can't leave, Corin. I'm bonded to Skillhands, the healer here on Colla. When Callum, the guy who kidnapped me, would have killed me, Skill bought me from him at some expense. She saved me--twice, really. She operated on my head, where Callum hurt me. Then she nursed me through the healing. It was a lot. I owe her, and I made a promise to repay her."

Corin's body was tense with anger, ready to spring and fight something--anything. "She *bought* you, Pem?"

"It's not like that. She paid for the fuel so Callum would leave without me--so I'd be safe," Pem explained.

"She bought you and helped your kidnapper escape." Corin's brows wrinkled, her face skeptical of Pemitai's summation. "Terk— the boy you call Callum, was responsible for the fire. The kid with the burns in the infirmary told us."

"Clem?" Pem brightened. "How is he?"

"Worried about you, but other than that, no worse off than before, I guess. You can ask him yourself when you get home." Corin started to turn, expecting to lead Pem away, but paused. "You know, Uncle searched here. You were here all along? How's that possible?"

Pem felt a terrible weight in her stomach, like she had swallowed a stone. How could she explain? In the beginning, she was afraid Skill would react badly to the truth about who she was, but in time, she realized that though Skill would be disappointed, she would never hurt Pem. And then there were the complications of worrying about her guilt and the decidedly selfish piece of liking this new life and the person she could be here on Colla.

Pemitai's eyes welled with tears.

"No one hid me, Corin. I was unconscious when they were looking for me. No one knew who I was. Only a few people knew the girl who travelled with Callum—or Terk, as you call him, didn't leave when he did. Skill made sure of that. And there was no reason they should know."

"Except your family was here asking about you--looking for you," her cousin reminded her unnecessarily.

"Callum--Terk didn't exactly parade me through the settlement," Pem defended her situation.

E.F. Winters

"But why not tell them once you were better, at least let the family know you were safe? They've been through enough. They shouldn't have to worry like this."

Just then, Skillhands walked in. Corin spun around, pulling her sidearm out, ready to fight. Skill's was out as well, and the two women faced off, weapons in hand.

"You okay, girl?" Skillhands asked, without taking her eyes off Corin.

"This is Pemitai Bobalo," Corin said, her jaw tight. "Yes, *that* Bobalo," she confirmed when recognition struck Skill like a blast from afterburn. "And her family is looking for her. Maybe you hadn't heard, or maybe you had." Corin's eyes narrowed.

"Is that true, kid?" the healer asked.

"It is," Corin answered for Pem.

"I'll hear it from her, not you." The healer turned her attention back to Pem. "Is this true?" Pem nodded. "We made an agreement, you and I. I invested in you. Did you have any intention of following through?"

"I did. I do." Pem pulled her shoulders back and stood as straight and tall as she could. "My father will pay back everything you're owed and more."

"I don't want your damn metal tokens," the healer spat back. "They're no good to me here. There's nothing to spend it on. What we need is someone to learn how to heal folk so when I'm gone, they're okay."

"You don't even like them, Skill," Pem said, petulantly, speaking from guilt more than conviction.

Skill nodded. "Most of the time they're asses or idiots who're lucky to still be alive with their stupidity intact and all the things they don't know about how to live on this space-rock. But there's honor in being there beside them to catch the newborns and witness their last breath. They're none of them bright or shiny, but what they're trying to do out here on the edge of all worlds is brave. I thought you saw that. I thought you understood."

"I do." Pem looked at her cousin. If there was anyone in the Bobalo family who could understand the changes she had gone through in the past month, it was Corin. "Please, give me a moment to

CHAPTER SEVENTY-TWO

talk to my cousin." Pemitai walked past the healer and out the door. Scowling, Corin lowered her weapon and followed.

"I can't go back, Corin. You see how it is. I owe them, mostly Skill, but all of them. They've been kind to me when they didn't need to, and they need me. No one needs me at home." Pem turned away, looking down the main road, so her cousin could not see the effort it was taking her not to cry. "Part of me would like nothing more than to leave and put this whole terrible thing with Callum behind me, but I can't go back to the Pem I was. I'm not her anymore. Maybe I never was that Pem, but I kept trying to be because that was what Mum expected. It was different for you. Da talked her into letting you train with Quinn and the others. He might have accepted a different version of me, but not Mum. I don't want to go back to being someone whose life is defined by other people's disappointment, always wondering who I might have become."

"You can be whoever you want to be," Corin assured Pem. "They'll just be happy to know you're safe."

"Then tell them that," Pem said. "But I'm staying here."

"Pem…"

"No, Corin. If I go back to Ebulon, even for a little while, I'll never get back here. The work--the expectations, they'll just eat me up. Like you, I want my life to matter, but I wasn't allowed to decide my own path. Now I can. I have." Pem's chin went up. "Tell the family that I gave my word and I'm a Bobalo. I won't break my promise. I have a lot to atone for in helping Terk escape."

"You're not responsible for that asshole's actions," Corin growled.

"Aren't I?" Pem argued. "He got off Ebulon because I was stupid and naive. He got the fuel to get back to Taiba because I was afraid to die. Now he's headed back to the Cluster, ready to tell his story to who knows who. My foolishness has put everyone in jeopardy. How can I face the Free Men and Women who have risked their lives trying to keep this secret all these years? They're going to think of me as the spoiled little Bobalo girl who ruined everything.

"I need to become someone else, Corin--someone better. I have a responsibility to fix what I've done."

"Terk's a monster. You'll get no argument from me on that, but you've got no business going into The Cluster."

E.F. Winters

"And you can't stop me."

"I'm not trying to, but you need training—a lot of it. Come back with me, Pem. We can talk to Timee. We'll let Uncle know about everything. He can teach you. He's the best—You know he is."

"I'm not going back on my word, Corin. Go home. Tell the family I'm fine, but I'm staying here. Whatever I need to learn in order to do what's right, I'll learn it here."

Merle Skillhands squinted past the rust-colored rain marks that stained the ragged curtains in the front window, trying to see the two young women outside her door.

Bobalos. Both of 'em. She harrumphed. They didn't know it, but the two were arguing over Skill's future—Colla's, too, maybe. Their faces were serious, their words full of passion, both trying to convince the other that their way was the right one. Skill noted with some pride that the younger one with the stubbly, white, pinfeather hair was holding her own. Skill had come to believe that the girl would stay…she would be the one who sat beside Skill when she passed, easing her pain as she crossed at the end of the illness that was slowly killing her.

"Hell, I *bought* her." Skill muttered angrily. If the healer pressed the issue, Pemitai Bobalo wouldn't be going anywhere. The healer paid a whole tank of fuel for the puny little thing. She *owned* the boney butt. But Skill didn't want the girl, Pem, to stay because she *had* to. A resentful healer was no good to anyone.

But Pemitai Bobalo, Skill's girl, didn't want to go back to her old life. Skill grunted.

"Stupid kid." What was she thinking? Why would anyone choose to stay on this burned-out rock when they could live an easy, cushy life among all that green?

But Skill knew why. It was the people. They grew on you—clung to you like the gritty, dusty dirt that coated everything on this crappy little desert moon. Colla folk weren't rich—most struggled to eat enough to maintain their weight above starvation and buy potable water, and they sure weren't educated. Most couldn't read and used an X to sign their name if they had anything official enough to need signing, which most tried really hard not to have. If the truth were known about their past, folk who weren't outposters would probably say these people weren't halfway good. But whatever they'd come from, by the time they got to Colla, they felt like they mattered just by the fact that they were alive and on Colla.

Colla needed every single one of them.

On Colla, Skill wasn't just another old person, invisible and dismissed. After a glance at her rough, dusty clothes, greasy, gray hair, and sun-marked skin, she was of no worth. On Colla, Skill was *their* healer, the only person who could stand between them and their loved ones, being maimed for life or just being plain dead.

Merle Skillhands had no illusions. She knew she had never been easy to get along with. She had never been cheerful, or soft, or dread on dread: "motherly," and the years only made her more prickly. But from Skill's first sight of this girl, the healer recognized not only a sweetness, but a strength. There was a comfort that hugged the girl's thin shoulders, bunching up over her heart like a shawl clutched to her skinny, flat chest. When people were close to Pem, they felt like she was sharing the comfort of that shawl with them, placing it gentle around their sorry, stooped shoulders. Skill needed to save this girl because she was sure--she hoped--Pem was the one who would be there through the final breaths of her final day, listening with all her attention to Skill's last breath, as if it were a sacred thing—just like Skill did. And knowing this girl would stay on Colla and take care of its people, Skill knew she could leave this world without guilt because her people were in good hands.

The two voices outside the hut stopped. They said their words and were now all talked out. The girl's cousin was turning away from the door, walking across the hard-packed clay, dust blowing around her legs so it looked like she was floating or didn't exist below her knees.

The front door creaked open, then closed, the whine of the wind and the percussion of grit smacking against it increasing and decreasing like a loud yawn. The latch snicked into place, and the girl, Pemitai Bobalo, stepped forward. Her body language was hesitant, even penitent, her expression anxious, apologetic, and hopeful. She longed for Skillhand's approval. Skill didn't quite know how to handle that.

E.F. Winters

"Well?" The healer's jaw was pushed out, strengthening her underbite, but deep down, she was proud of this wayward bit of humanity with the chopped, pin-feather hair that she'd taken a chance on.

"This is my decision. Corin understands, and she'll explain it to the family."

It seemed Merle Skillhands would be getting a visit from Tai Bobalo. She was not looking forward to the reunion.

"Gonna cause a lot of trouble around here," she grumbled.

"I'm sorry for that," Pem apologized. "My family is very close."

Skill snorted, thinking, *always were.* Things were going to get more complicated with high-visibility players in the rebellion against the warlords, like the Bobalos, making regular visits to Colla. The little moon had been trying to avoid that sort of attention for a long while. They weren't ready for it, but there was no undoing what was done. They were going to be noticed, whether they liked it or not.

The girl was working up the courage to say more, and Skill braced herself, not knowing what was to come. Always expect the worst, was her motto. There were fewer disappointments and no harm if it turned out better than disastrous.

"Skill," Pemitai said, "You're not much for sharing or explaining what you're thinking, but I don't think you've ever lied to me. The only way I know to make this right is to be totally honest with you about what I'm thinking and feeling. I'm sorry if that makes you uncomfortable." Skill shrugged, indicating it was no big deal. "When we first met and you...*saved* me, I was grateful, but I was also worried. I didn't know you or what your plans were, so I questioned your intentions. But though I can't say you were kind exactly, you stood by your commitment to save my life and pulled me through, and once I was better, I began to find something in myself through the work you had me do and what you taught me. I could have told someone who I was. They would have come and got me and paid you for your efforts on my behalf, but I couldn't do that. I didn't want to do that. The longer I was here, the harder it was to face going back."

"You don't need to tell me all this," Skill said. "I've seen who you are." The girl kind of smiled. It was as close as Skill had come to complimenting her efforts.

CHAPTER SEVENTY-TWO

"So, the boy, Callum? His real name is Terk. He was brought to Ebulon as part of a mission to save the bright young minds the warlords have been scooping up to train into their next generation of weapons engineers."

"Didn't seem so smart to me," Skill harumphed.

"I don't know if he just didn't fit in or maybe it was always his plan to leave, but he tried to steal a shuttle to get back to the Cluster. That shuttle crashed, starting a fire that burned most of Little Taiba." Skill tried not to let the girl see how hard it was for her to hear this. The girl went on, "He didn't make it that time, but after he met me, he tried again, stealing my Da's old ship, and you know what happened after that, except for this part; Terk isn't just going back to the Cluster to blend in. He's going to try and find someone who'll listen to him and who'll get him to one of the warlords. He's going to tell them everything he knows about Ebulon, the Free Men and Women, and The String." Pemitai paused to let the consequences of what she was saying land. "Someone has to go after him, Skill. Someone has to stop him. And I'm responsible. It has to be me."

The healer broke into a laughter too high-pitched to be natural.

"Oh, dread of dread, that's a good one." She wiped her eyes. "I admire your pluck, kid, and it's a good thing you wanting to fix what's been broke, that's why I knew you'd be a good healer. But you are one hundred percent the wrong person for this job. You'll be dead before you're in the Cluster a week. You're too young, too soft, and too clueless. You've got no skills—not the kind you'd need anyway."

"You can teach me," Pem said. "You know how to handle yourself--you've done things. You've been involved with the Free Men in the movement. I can tell."

Skill gave the girl a tired look. "That was another life. I'm a healer now, not a fighter. I fix folks. I don't break 'em." Pem crossed her arms, looking like a three-year-old about to have a tantrum.

"You've been trying to teach me that taking care of people isn't just standing on the sidelines then patching them up after they're hurt, that it's also protecting them before they get hurt. See, I was listening. Well, that's what I'm trying to do. Someone needs to stop Terk, or a lot of people are going to get hurt." Skill held her hands up, as if blocking Pemitai's words flying through the air toward her.

"Stop. Just stop. You can't play me. I'm not being handled by some skinny little girl still smelling like her mother's clean laundry."

"I'm not trying to 'handle' you. I'm telling you the truth," Pem protested.

"Kind of late for that, isn't it?"

"I said I was sorry. I was scared, then I was sick, and then I just got confused and didn't know what I wanted or to fix what I'd done, so I was silent," Pem admitted.

"If silence is a lie, we've all lied, Pem." Skill's eyesight got a little blurry, and she had to toss her head back and sniff up the snot before it dripped out to clear it. "They're not bad people as people go," she muttered.

"No, they're not," Pem agreed. "Look, I'm not abandoning you or the settlement. I'll work here, with you, and we can train when it's not busy, and when this is all over, and I've stopped Terk, I'll come back. I promise."

"Huh." Skill grunted. It was as much of an acknowledgment as she was going to give.

"One more thing." Skill looked at Pem dubiously. "There's someone else who needs to be part of this," the girl pressed on as if she needed to get it all out before she lost her nerve or Skill cut her off. "There's a boy, he's just a kid, but he's a genius or something, and he's brave--braver than any kid his age should ever have to be. It was him, Clemmet, who actually crashed the first ship that Terk tried to steal when he realized what Terk was trying to do."

"I thought you said Terk was responsible." Skill's ice blue eyes were piercing, cutting through any extra shit to find the core.

"He was," Pem insisted. "But Clem saw what Terk was going to do. He was just trying to stop Terk."

"And he ended up causing more problems. Maybe you can see the lesson in this?" Skill suggested.

"Clem had a choice to either go back to Taiba and keep quiet, or try and stop Terk, knowing it would probably kill him. He didn't know the crash would start a fire. He couldn't have seen that. I met Clemmet in the infirmary on Ebulon. He was burned bad. Everyone thought he might die, but he didn't, and then Terk showed up. That's where we met. I'd never seen anyone so terrified as Clem was of Terk. But I didn't realize what it was until much later—after I was here." Skill

CHAPTER SEVENTY-TWO

could feel Pem watching her, trying to gauge her reaction. "No one on Ebulon knows about this, not about Terk, not about Clem." Pemitai paused. "I think we should bring Clem here."

"I'm not running an orphanage," Skill's throaty voice cracked like Colla's hardpan.

"You're going to love him." Pemitai beamed, undiscouraged.

"I doubt it," the healer grumped. But she did not say no.

E.F. Winters

CHAPTER SEVENTY-THREE

"When 'magic' collides with 'science', no one knows what will thrive and what will vanish." (From the Book of Simple Truths, Emman'eve Keesch.)

"So, have you spoken to the Pira about your plans? With Dora Dum'Laiere out of the picture, it changes things, doesn't it?" Pliny mused.

"There is only one way forward," Zeph speculated. "And everyone knows what that is."

"I doubt Eropa or the Matriarch sees it that way. Surely you have been cautioned about Rhune unpredictability?" Pliny suggested.

"Several times. I have also been told they have a strong commitment to protecting their people. Eropa will accept her position as the treaty bride because it protects Ebulon. There is no other way through this now."

"Only a fool tries to second-guess a Rhune," Pliny recited the cautionary phrase. "By recognizing Miratha as her kin, Hagriva has shown that she's willing to go to great lengths to guarantee Eropa remains here. That cannot be discounted. You believe Eropa's cooperation is inevitable because you do not understand the Rhunes. They don't see the world the way we do. We don't know what they know or have the resources they have. This whole treaty could vanish like smoke in water. Your only option is to convince Eropa herself."

"Do you think that's possible?" Zeph wondered out loud.

The Mir chuckled. "The two of you are so stubborn and proud, I'm not sure you could agree on how to cross a road, but there are many types of partnerships we enter into as adults, Captain Yare. Some are based on friendship or loyalty, others on common need. The fortunate ones find something that is all those things and more, where mutual respect, admiration, friendship, and love all exist together."

"This is a political partnership, not a romance," Zeph said quietly. "Eropa knows that."

CHAPTER SEVENTY-THREE

"Well, I suppose you would know. The Pira is unquestionably a strong person. For many, she is too strong. You must have noticed how Ebulonians are all half in awe and half terrified of her. So, suitors have not exactly lined up with proposals to partner with her.

"Except Frevin," Zeph muttered.

"Yes," Pliny agreed. "The question always remains if someone seeks her as a partner because they have feelings for her or if it is because they are interested in the shadow of power she will throw someday?"

The two men sat watching the first moon rise over the ruins of Little Taiba.

"Nikodamus didn't tell me Eropa was his daughter," Zeph mused.

"And yet he sent the two of you to Auhora Whimlan together and arranged to keep Frevin away—an interesting action, do you not think? I think our late Mahal saw something between you and Eropa that gave him hope," Pliny added.

"Hope for what?"

"His daughter's happiness. He was a wise man, Nikodamus. After he lost his wife, he decided he wanted other options for his daughter. When you showed up, he thought he might have found one. Of course, he is no longer here to advocate on your behalf, so it is only Hagriva and Eropa's decisions that matter. If this treaty hangs now on Eropa's agreement, you should speak with her, because until you do, I guarantee she and Hagriva are exploring other options."

"There are no other options," Zeph repeated his belief grimly.

Pliny frowned. "That kind of thinking is naïve and dangerous."

Do you even know what you want? He asked himself.

Zeph thought of Eropa as he had seen her in the courtyard, stars and planets sweeping along in her wake. The image and the sense of awe that had given him remained sharp in his mind.

The honest answer made his bowels feel weak.

"I need to go." Zeph stood.

"Yes, you probably do." Pliny stood and saw him to the door.

E.F. Winters

CHAPTER SEVENTY-FOUR

"The past is one breath before the now. The future is the breath not yet taken. " (Wei Tai from the Book of the Rhune compiled in the First Age.)

Following the directions he was given, Zeph flew the Paxlosian shuttle north and west, chasing daylight over fertile farm and grasslands. Golden heads heavy with grain bowed to the planet, row upon row shot from the ground, standing shoulder to shoulder, covering acres of gently undulated land.

After months of living on Ebulon, Zeph still found himself awed by the planet's huge tracts of land left solely to food and forest. He saw few houses and fewer beings who would live there.

The Paxlosian felt his mind rolling with the changing terrain below, grain fields becoming the serpentine rows of vineyards, which gave way to long avenues that ribboned across the flatlands defined on either side by strung-up hop vines triple the height of a person. These vine-lined avenues ended in geometric patterns made of rectangular orchards interspersed with rectangles of waving green pastureland.

As the sun lowered in the blue, moon-tinted sky, the last remnants of civilization fell behind. The land swelled like hungry yeast-dough, bread like mounds of gray-green speckled by rare islands of white-barked copse rising from a carpet of close scrub. The isolated landscape made the young captain feel pensive; the savage monotony freeing his mind of thoughts about yields and trade and how many could be fed on such abundance.

As Ebulon's purple moon, Rampal pushed blue Teagra across the sky, the terrain changed again, plucked, pocked, and wind-blasted, but always steadfastly inclining toward a distant northern vanishing point. The home of the Rhunes, where he would find the Matriarch, Hagriva.

When the sun fully set, Rampal's purple twilight lengthened. Zeph flew the shuttle above the stippled purple and gray shadows,

CHAPTER SEVENTY-FOUR

their gradations giving shape to the undulating moor.

And then, with only Rampal's purple moonlight shining over it, the continent narrowed, sharpening to a scythe-pointed peninsula.

From his seat in the shuttle's cockpit, Zeph could see glistening stretches of water on either side, a silver ocean, reflecting the purple moon, rolling to the horizon.

Before him, the gnarled, broken fingers of an abandoned castle's turrets pierced the sky.

Alden Baierd.

Dread sat like a stone in Zeph's gut.

"I am here. Come to me," Zeph felt the Matriarch's touch in his mind, its strength and intensity intimidating. Every gut-wrenching, mind-twisting doubt he experienced after Eropa disappeared reasserted itself. The helpless rage and terror he felt as the mysterious Dum'Laiere witch crept around inside his head, working to change his memories.

His body began to shake, waves of pain, like molten rock sliding beneath the thin sheath of his skin, popping and fizzing through the marrow of his bones. He could not think. He could not move; his brain was caught in a closing vise from which he could not free it. He felt like he would vomit, the contents of his bowels threatening to turn to water, and he was certain he would simply explode.

At least that would make an end to this.

Zeph rooted his feet on the shuttle's floor and shook himself violently.

I will not give in to this. I did not give in to it then, and I will not do it now. He set his jaw. Whatever manipulations were tried on him, Zeph was determined. *I will control my mind, my thoughts, and my decisions.*

The Paxlxosian landed his shuttle in an open space near a pile of tumbled stones that looked like a giant child's blocks, ran out the shuttle's ramp, and took a deep breath.

Tendrils of fog approached the shuttle, swirling inside, spreading out to surround it, like raiding ghosts seeking hidden contraband. *Don't let her play with your head, Zeph,* he cautioned himself. *You were raised by Morladja Yare. How much worse can this old woman be?*

Zeph walked down the ship's ramp, and the door shut behind him.

E.F. Winters

Beyond the cliff's edge, the North Sea rolled and swelled, pushing its tattered, froth-limed waves against the cliff's rocky foot, the waves' low, rhythmic snore providing a humming base to the silence that hovered over the bluff.

Zeph took a deep breath of the moist air. It tasted of salt and sage, windblown grass with a rancid tang of seaweed and the squelchy, ripe flesh of unknown marine creatures. He knew nothing of the sea and what it held.

He licked the salt from his lips and walked on.

Swirling and folding, the fog rolled into a cloud surrounding the base of one ruined tower. A sliver of light winked from a single high window. The shadow of a person moved within its frame.

I am being watched.

Zeph steeled himself, cautiously picking his way through the scattered piles of broken stone walls, using the light in the tower as his compass.

Bleak and unwelcoming on the outside, the tower with its arthritic stone walls was doubly so within its hollow core. Decaying timbers, fallen from their supports, propped each other up in the center of the circular structure. The rotted wooden stairs leading to the tower's top story stuck out from the wall like broken teeth with wide gaps now more common than regular intervals.

Zeph stepped cautiously onto the first tread, testing his weight. The worm-eaten wood creaked and moaned as if it were dying, but it held. The next two steps were missing, and Zeph had to stretch his legs across the broad gap. It would not be the last time. He began to climb.

Above, the old door hinges of a heavy door slowly squeaked open, spilling a warm amber glow riding on a wide beam of steam out onto the landing, splintering the tower's gloom. Like the breath of a great beast, the warmed air frothed over the landing and fell down the tower's hollow center.

"Come up," a gravelly, female voice urged Zeph.

His hand felt for his weapon. It wasn't there.

The unseen woman grunted. *"If I wanted to harm you, I would have done it long before you were climbing up my stairs, Zeph Yare."*

"Get out of my head," Zeph growled, feeling not a little violated and possessive of his internal space. A cold sweat stuck his hair to his

CHAPTER SEVENTY-FOUR

forehead, making his clothes stick to his skin uncomfortably.

Where is Eropa? he wondered.

"You may see Eropa after we talk. We will see," the voice addressed Zeph's fleeting, private thought.

So much for not reading someone's mind without permission, he reminded himself how little privacy he had been allowed in his interactions with practitioners of magic.

Climbing from one tread to another, stretching or leaping across the many gaps, he finally reached the landing on the top floor.

A grizzled, white head poked out from behind the curtain of steam bubbling from a large cast-iron pot on an old stove inside the tower room, her long, white hair floating around her head like curling ribbons of moonlight.

"Captain Yare, we finally meet." The crone's lipless mouth stretched back into a toothless grin.

"I've seen you before." Zeph's brow creased deeply as he struggled to stay standing, dizzy and disoriented.

"The day after you arrived at the Iredipa market, yes. It seemed a poor way to start, allowing those Taiban ruffians to accost you since you were our guests."

The details of the lost memory returned, striking Zeph like an electric shock. "I remember."

"So, we know each other already. At least *I* know *you*," the Matriarch declared.

Zeph watched the Rhune's features morph from a child through the many stages of her 300 years and back again. At every age, the Rhune's face was angular, with high cheekbones and an arrow-point chin reinforcing a razor-edged manner that made Zeph feel uncomfortable when her face finally settled back into old age. Furrowed mounds of parchment-thin yellow-green skin half hid the intense black eyes burning with intelligence and power, two dark bonfires scrying a moonless midnight.

Zeph began to wobble, and his legs were weakening; the skin was burned, now becoming prickly, as if bugs were nibbling their way out from the underside.

He tried, but could not step forward, and he would not go back down the empty throat of the crumbling tower either—not without settling what he came to do. He looked toward the ground far below, envisioning falling to the puddle-pocked floor.

I would break my leg at the least, maybe my back, or my head.

"Be careful," the old woman cautioned him.

Yes. I should be careful, Zeph thought.

"Step forward," she commanded him. Zeph did as he was told, not because he chose to, but because he was unable to complete a decision-making thought of his own.

"Step again. And again," the Rhune walked him off the landing and into the warmth of the room, Zeph's anger rising with each step.

The door slammed shut behind him. The Rhune had not moved.

Zeph scowled at her. Clinging to his anger seemed the only thing he could do.

"It is natural to resent being manipulated," the Rhune acknowledged his frustration. "But having you fall and injure yourself would cause many problems between our two worlds."

"I'm not afraid of you," Zeph warned between gritted teeth.

Hagriva's eyebrows raised quizzically. "Did you think I meant you to be?" she scoffed. "No, I am merely an old woman trading on the superstitious fears of a primitive people," she repeated his words from early in his time on Ebullon, her black eyes dancing with humor.

"People tell me you are a sorceress of some skill," Zeph commented.

"But you did not believe them," Hagriva stated. "You do not believe in such foolishness. That is good. Neither do I."

"So, you're not a sorceress?"

"I am a Rhune," Hagriva corrected him. "Only the ignorant call what we do 'magic'. Our practices are based on an understanding of the natural laws of the multiverse. It requires training, however, and a serious commitment. Few possess the patience and discipline to reach an adept's skills."

"And yet you claim you have an army of warriors skilled in these practices."

"And you claim to have an unstoppable starship. I do not know if this is true. I have not seen it. And of course, technology is reliant on the physical beings who command it," she pointed out.

"As your warriors are if they're dead," Zeph countered.

"In my experience, making threats you cannot achieve is a tactical error commonly made by those who are either naïve or arrogant."

CHAPTER SEVENTY-FOUR

"The Taiban warlords are coming. Do you plan on fighting them with sorcery?" Zeph baited the Rhune. "No. Because there is only one way to protect Ebulon, accept this treaty between our worlds."

"And surrender Eropa to you?" The old woman's face was suddenly so close that Zeph could feel the fuzz of her cheeks tickle his. "You know nothing of Rhunes." Her voice was the low, throaty growl of a predator. "I command the hearts and minds of millions of souls on a hundred worlds, Captain Yare. Do not think to bully me." The cold fires of her dark eyes blazed, reflecting nothing.

Zeph felt like he had swallowed a glass of dust. But he would not back down.

"Whatever you imagine you might do, it will be no match for the Lamdra," he announced confidently.

"Really? So, you can explain how Eropa passed through your shields to stand on the bridge of your ship?" she taunted him. "Certainly, you have not forgotten that moment? You were so certain nothing could penetrate your ship's shields, and yet something did. Hold on to these naive beliefs in your technological superiority if it helps you sleep at night, Captain Yare, but I would advise against betting your people's lives on it."

The air in the room began to press against Zeph, the intense pressure inching him toward her against his will, every cell being sucked forward despite his desire; they do the opposite. His body began to tremble and spasm with the effort of resisting.

"Give in," Hagriva's crackling contralto whispered.

"No." A force gripped his head and began to peel it open at the crown.

"I am not here to harm you, but I need to know who you are, Zeph Yare, and I need to know it now."

Zeph sank to his knees before the diminutive woman. She raised her pointer and middle fingers, and as before, she pulled down the lower lids of his eyes, looking deep inside his psyche.

Teeth bared like a trapped animal, adrenaline raced through Zeph as he felt the layers of his mind being peeled back.

"Let go," Hagriva's words held no command, and they trickled over Zeph's senses with the promise of relief.

"What will happen to me?" he begged.

"You will meet your true self," she answered into his mind.

Zeph's knees buckled, and he lost consciousness.

Zeph opened his eyes. Nothing looked familiar. He flashed back to the night he passed out drunk on the docks of Auhora Whimlan before realizing he was not outdoors on a floating dock, but weeks had passed, and he was now indoors, lying on the wooden floor of a tower room.

Alden Baierd... he remembered where his mission had taken him.

A folded wool blanket was tucked beneath his head. Papery fingertips lightly touched his fingers, a serene peace flowing through him from the connection. He turned his head. The Rhune Matriarch sat beside him.

"You will feel better shortly," she said as their eyes met.

"Will I?" Zeph pushed himself up to sit, moving his head from side to side to test his stability. It did not feel as if he had been drinking. He did not remember drinking, but his head told him he had done something that he did not want to do again. "It feels like someone just kicked their way through my brain."

Hagriva chuckled. "It will pass. Are you able to stand?" Zeph tentatively found his balance, and the old woman helped him cross the room to a willow rocker. "I have no ver'coute these days, but I can offer you tea." She disappeared behind the curtain of steam rising from the boiling pot.

A wave of nausea swept through Zeph. Hanging his head to breathe through it, Zeph saw glowing ribbons of light issuing from his belly. They stretched out, reaching toward the Rhune. Alarmed, the Paxlosian tried to gather the glowing strands in his hands and press them back into his belly, but his hands passed through them.

"What you are seeing is your vital energy," Hagriva explained, hidden within the cloud of steam. "Rhunes attract it like bees to pollen. Place your hands over your abdomen and close your eyes," she directed him. "Now take a few deep breaths and focus on bringing your energy back into yourself."

He followed the Rhune's instructions, and the ribbons settled back into place.

Hagriva hummed as she brewed the tea, a timeless peace settling

CHAPTER SEVENTY-FOUR

over the room.

Zeph opened his eyes again.

The beams supporting the tower room's ceiling, arrayed from a center point, like the spokes of a wheel. Bundled herbs were suspended from them, and bird's nests occupied the crooks of the supports. Birds large and small, perched along the beams, cooing softly, the gentle fluttering of their wings a soothing accompaniment.

The fire in the fireplace popped and crackled, the warmth pushing back at the steam rising from the bubbling pot on the stove on the opposite wall, the air tasting of spices and applewood, spring grass, and fresh bread.

Everything about the room looked different from what it did when he first arrived, and yet there was a comforting familiarity--like someone returning home after being away a long time.

Hagriva shuffled across the floor in her worn leather slippers and placed a rustic clay cup in his hands.

"Try this. It should help." Zeph hesitated. "There is nothing in it that will hurt you, or make you say things you do not want to say," she reassured him. "You do not need to take my word for it. Check in with yourself, and you will feel the truth."

Zeph wrapped his hands around the clay cup. There was such simplicity to the warmth radiating from it, the satisfying feel of his fingers sitting in the shallow troughs left by the potter's fingers. Without embellishment, it spoke of an honest humility that a more intricate piece could not have matched.

"Eropa grew up here," Zeph said, looking around as if being here helped him understand the Pira better.

"Yes," the old Rhune acknowledged, once again retreated to the steaming pot.

What must it have been like for Eropa growing up here as a child, knowing she was safe and loved? Unexpected emotions engraved on his soul rose unbidden, startling Zeph.

"Were things always like this?" he asked in a whisper. "The colors, the sounds, the scents?"

"Yes. You were simply unable to see it."

"Why?" She did not answer, and Zeph understood it was because she could not—only he could. "Will I always see it as I do now?" he whispered, his face aglow with wonder.

E.F. Winters

The old woman cocked her head to one side, examining him. "It depends on the choices you make. The construct of our worlds is held together by our concepts of reality and functions according to the rules our culture has taught us to define them by. The mind craves certainty and seeks to maintain its grip over the life it considers its own. You will see more clearly for a time, then slowly it will fade. How your mind will decide to explain what you have experienced here is uncertain, but most likely it will label our encounter as a hallucination resulting from my manipulating you. There is no room for 'magic' beneath the Dome."

Zeph watched the old Rhune putter about her stove, adding powders and herbs into the boiling pot, then stirring absentmindedly as she casually relayed the secrets of the multiverse. He smiled, feeling a surge of fondness for the old woman.

"You're not what I expected."

"You are not what I expected, either, Captain Yare." Hagriva returned his smile. "But you are what I hoped for."

"That sounds out of character for one of us," he quipped, uncomfortable with the compliment.

"There are no certainties," Hagriva informed him. "But there are events that can seem almost certain because of who we are and the predictability of our choices. We can predict with a high degree of success whether someone will let a bee linger on their finger, unharassed, or slap it, based on who they have shown themselves to be by their previous actions."

Zeph stood and walked to the high window cut into the stone wall that looked north toward the jutting arrow-point of the cliff below, smudged to a gray-scale pastel by the heavy fog.

"I no longer know what to do," he said. "Dora Dum'Laiere is alive in name only. She can't fulfill the requirements of a treaty bride to seal this agreement, but I am not ignorant of what the alternative would mean. Miratha will press hard to become the next Matriarch if Eropa is not here."

"And in all likelihood, she would prevail," Hagriva agreed. "Perhaps even if Eropa is here."

"Do you think so?"

"It seems possible considering who she is and how she has acted in the past," the Rhune explained.

CHAPTER SEVENTY-FOUR

What will happen when you die, Hagriva?"

The old Rhune stepped away from the stove. "Things will change. The same as it is everywhere."

"You've seen something?" Zeph prodded. "You've had a vision of the future?"

Hagriva flittered a tiny hand like a bird in the air. "Probabilities, like air, are the most changeable energies in the multiverse. Even trying to express what we have seen alters the vision. How do you bring something as formless as a possible future into the world of matter? In the struggle to translate it into language, it morphs. Like the use of magic in an attempt to control events, there will never be a guaranteed outcome. Unnatural manipulation used to solve one problem creates a dozen more. No single will can, or should, command the future, Zeph."

"Even a Rhune's?"

"Even a Rhune's. And politics is very like magic; rife with possibilities that cannot be controlled."

"But you said some outcomes were more predictable because of people's character," Zeph argued.

"So many characters, so many choices, all interacting." Hagriva shook her head. "Take my choice, in holding on to life longer than was 'acceptable' in the judgment of others, I have put Ebulon in this position. Now the dynamics of leadership here must change."

"But they don't have to," Zeph said quietly. "I could still…"

Hagriva stopped him. "Recognize the Mahal and not the Matriarch as Ebulon's leader, leaving Frevin Mir or Kirk Dum'Laiere in charge?"

Zeph's brows knit. "I'm sorry. When I said I didn't understand anything…" he tried to explain.

"Do not bother. It is not the worst option we have," Hagriva dismissed his embarrassment. "The title of Matriarch is not what makes me who I am, Zeph. My knowledge and skills are not diminished because of a title someone adds to or takes away from my name."

"And Eropa?" Zeph asked. He could not reconcile the needs of the treaty with the cost for the Pira and her people.

Hagriva's eyes twinkled, a most unsettling and secretive smile playing at the edges of her thin, alluvial plain-wrinkled lips.

E.F. Winters

"I lingered in this body for one reason: to direct Eropa's education. That task is done. I have three hundred years of experience on her, but two hundred years ago, I was not her equal in skill. Let the Council of Elders and the Mahal be named the decision-makers in your treaty. Eropa will still be Eropa."

"Even if she leaves?" Zeph demanded.

Hagriva studied him. "Absolutely. Do not ask me what to do, Zeph. That is for you and Eropa to decide. Follow the path beyond the stone gate. It will take you to the bluff above the north cliffs. You will find Eropa there." The sky outside the tower's window had lightened to a false dawn.

"What would I say?"

"Tell her why you came here and what it is you truly want. You will not be disappointed."

"How do you know?" despair thinned Zeph's words to a whisper.

"Because it is what she wants as well. Zeph turned to go, but she stopped him. "Zeph, the promises you make here tonight, you must uphold beyond your last breath," Hagriva cautioned him. "Promise me."

"I'm only one man," Zeph tried to sidestep the weight of the Rhune's expectations.

"Not with a Rhune beside you, you are not," she corrected him.

Eropa traveled the path that wends its way North and South along the cliff's edge north of the castle ruins. The pitched moan of the wind's passing through the standing stones on the bluff fluctuated between harmony and dissonance with its fluting through the pockets of caves in the cliff face below, where the first Rhunes made their home.

Great waves crashed against the cliff, shattering into droplets that sparkled on the slick, sharp rocks, bearding them with white sea foam.

The young Pira sensed the alien captain before she saw him, feeling his spirit calling to hers.

As it was before we met, when he was on the Lamdra. The feeling had always disturbed her, for such compelling attractions were often the harbingers of danger for an adept, their outcomes resulting in

CHAPTER SEVENTY-FOUR

destruction more often than good. She avoided him, hid from him, and tried to ignore the connection to no avail. He remained a challenge, representing a pivotal point in her life that she must deal with.

She did not shield herself from the mysterious link, acknowledging it without giving in to its premise of inevitability. If there was ever a time for truth between them, it was now. Whom they were in some life or lives before was irrelevant to the present. Who they might be was unclear, but whatever path they decided to take forward required a foundation—an agreement between them from which they would start.

The crucible of Hagriva's presence burned clean Yare's spirit; the conflict between his soul's commitment and his ego washed away like footprints in beach sand cleared by the rising tide. The man who remained, who approached her now, was not the cocky captain first met at the reception or the charming one she began to fall in love with at Auhora Whimlan. This Zeph Yare was the man who ran into a burning city to fight at her side, carrying her to safety when she became frozen by grief over another man. He rescued her from imprisonment across the Void by sheer determination, all strength and potential, passion, and longing.

Whether he remained this person or not-- whether he would ever find it within himself to be this man again, she could not know, but a piece of him would always exist within whatever version he chose to embrace, taunting her with the possibility from behind those mocking gray eyes.

Whatever I decide, it will be a gamble.

Zeph's gait was purposeful as he strode over the moisture-rich turf along the bluff's edge. When he reached her side, he stood there for some time without speaking, just breathing in the moor and mist.

Eropa waited in silence.

"It's cold here," Zeph commented finally.

"Most of the time," Eropa agreed. Even when he was not looking at her, she felt him focused on her—felt the connection between them, the way their breaths found unison, their hearts quickening together.

If she turned to him now, would he try to kiss her again? They were close enough. Her face flushed, remembering her foolish reaction to his romantic overtures on the beach at Auhora Whimlan. It had not been an opening to stealing her power. It had not been a declaration of love. It was merely a kiss, and she rejected it in the most severe way.

The only thing that could have been worse was to have killed him for it. She was not sure she might still have to do that, but not today.

"I was sorry to hear about Dora," the captain said unexpectedly.

"It was unexpected," Eropa agreed, forcing her thoughts to subjects apart from her feelings.

"I've been thinking a lot about our situation, Eropa," he stumbled, searching for words. "The treaty; Paxlosis… Ebulon. Without Dora, there are few choices left to preserve the treaty, and without it…. Well, the options are not good. One would be for me to withdraw the thing entirely." Eropa turned her head, staring at him in disbelief. "You'd be free to stay here with your people, and in time, you would take Hagriva's place as the Matriarch. I wouldn't have a new planet-partner, but I'd still have a hold full of imports to placate the Consortium."

"There are a thousand men aboard the Lamdra," Eropa reminded him. "And the coordinates to Ebulon are in its computers. How is this a reasonable option?"

"I don't know, Eropa. I'm just trying to find something—some way to get us out of this without killing a lot of our friends."

"And if the Taiban Warlords do not get here first, what happens when that next Paxlosian ship arrives? Who will be the captain? You?"

"Probably not," Zeph admitted.

"So, a new captain, with new orders. Tell me they will not simply take what you did not," she challenged him.

"I can't."

"Then what is the purpose of this gesture?"

"It would give you more time to prepare to defend yourselves."

Eropa bristled. "You still believe we cannot do that now."

"I don't doubt your people's commitment or skill, but they cannot stand against a starship's weapons, Eropa, and insisting otherwise is a fantasy that will get them killed. I am trying to stop that. Why won't you help me?"

Eropa watched the waves crashing below, the fog creeping back up the bluff.

"How much time do you think this would buy us?" she asked after

CHAPTER SEVENTY-FOUR

some time.

"Maybe as much as six years," he replied. "Now that the Navigator knows where she's going, it won't take as long."

"And then the drama starts all over again, with new characters and no treaty to protect us."

"Did you ever plan to keep your part and protect Ebulon?" she demanded. "Can you keep that promise?" She truly wanted to know the answer from *this* man—*this* Zeph, who would not lie to her.

"Absolutely. I still do," he declared. "All the reasons I gave your father are still there, and many more besides." The sincerity and unspoken desire scrawled across his face was embarrassing and intoxicating. Emotion spilled from his gray eyes with the riotous abandon of water leaping over the edge of a waterfall, beautiful to look at, treacherous to experience. All Eropa's training warned her that tumbling over the falls with this man represented a terrible risk, but her heart still longed to take that leap with him.

"My father believed in this treaty—in you. I will not dishonor his memory by supporting actions that make it fail," she declared, knowing her choice limited their options.

Zeph's expression became more hopeful. "I came here to find a way to save my world, Eropa." He took her hands. "But I found so much more, and I don't believe that is an accident."

His body stood like a shield between Eropa and the cold ocean wind, creating a calm harbor of protection.

"Come with me," he said.

Their eyes caught and held each other—uncertainty and possibilities crowding the space between them. Their people walked the razor edge of war. Mistrust had always separated them—other people's agendas pushing aside any possibility of them discovering what they themselves wanted.

If I were not a Rhune and he was not so proud.... But that was not how things were for them in this life.

If there could be something lasting between them, it would have to grow between the people they were.

She could go with him. All she had to do was trust him and this connection that whispered of some hidden purpose was dependent on this decision. There was no such thing as destiny. Sentient beings had free will, and free will introduced the variable of chaos.

E.F. Winters

"Hagriva did not try to stop this," Adaya's voice slipped into Eropa's ear as if transported from the heart of the Hidling to Alden Baierd.

The young Pira stood once again beside the Ombrah's nest cradled within the roots of the Great Tree, smelling the musky scent emanating from the sun-warmed eggs and their mother. The Ombrah raised her scaled snout, her eyes closed in bliss at the feel of the sun on her back, contentedly thumping her long tail, flattening long lines in the tall grass.

If I leave, I will not be here when they hatch, Eropa thought, aggrieved. *I will never see them grow or see them again.*

"There is a contrivance of import being played out here, Granddaughter," Adaya's voice said. *"In turning away from one path and taking another, the future of worlds beyond our own will be changed. All energy is connected,"* Adaya quoted the Rhune saying.

"Then which shall I choose?" Eropa asked.

"I do not know, but consider the outcomes you have witnessed in your life when a decision is based solely on duty."

Eropa thought of her grandmother's refusal to remain on a Rhune's path but instead returned to Ebulon's oldest ways, remaining with the man she loved. Adaya was reviled by Rhunes and the Ebulonian court, becoming an outcast, and yet she was happy, aware of events in the world as none of those who judged her were. Eropa's mother, Dupira, chose duty over her family, unleashing a version of their lives that none had anticipated or would have chosen—thrusting Eropa into a world of power before most children her age could count beyond their own fingers. Her father did not want that future for her. Her father put his faith in this man, believing there was something more important than duty.

Eropa studied Zeph, weighing her concerns against her hopes, watching the scales tilt back and forth.

Zeph's storm-sky eyes watched her as well. Loneliness and longing, misery and hope wound through him, his strengths snagging on all the broken bits left littering his psyche.

He stepped closer to her.

"I know I will never be good enough for you, Eropa, but I promise I will give everything I have to keep my promise to keep Ebulon safe, and someday I will bring you back. I can make you happy, Eropa. At least I can try," he added.

"I will not hold you to that." The Pira looked away. "One person cannot be responsible for another person's happiness. Happiness is not something we give to others. It is something we each must choose."

He said nothing of love, though she could see he struggled to say more than he had. Did he love her? Did it matter? Being loved was not integral to her path as a Rhune. She had two primary duties: to protect her people and bring the Truths to Paxlosis. But were these truly why she would go with him to Paxlosis?

No.

Eropa slipped into the protective circle of Zeph's arms, breathing the mingled scents of the moor; already thinking of it as something in her past, and Zeph, whom she was choosing to make her future.

Raising her face to his, their breath mingling.

"I will go with you," the wind swept the words from Eropa's mouth to his as their lips met.

"Hold on, Bibi," Hagriva sent a message to the little albino Cumin. *"Help is on its way."*